HOMININE

It's time to choose

BY
LEWIS EVANS

*Stay in bed!
Read the whole book
before you go back
to work -
Be well!
Lewis*

For Olga

PRAISE FOR *HOMININE—IT'S TIME TO CHOOSE*

I am a big Tom Clancy fan and love thrillers. Lewis has created a masterpiece here. It is amazing to think that it is a first foray into thrillers for the author. I found this book a compulsive page-turner that drew me in deeper and deeper. A must for your book shelf, ipad or reader!

—*Brendan Foley, author of* The Yin Yang Complex and The Five States of Success

I had the privilege of reading a pre-release first draft of *Hominine*. At about the halfway point, I noted that it felt like a master work the caliber of Grisham, Clancy and Brown. This is clearly no entry-level work, but the craft of a masterful storyteller. In retrospect, the Hominine Project represents the Sword of Damocles for the information age.

Hominine weaves a tale of intrigue and espionage tightly coupled with political greed and a global power grab. Like any good power struggle, the roots of the story lead us back to an effort to better mankind through noble efforts. Purpose coupled with power tends to corrupt. In the world today, political corruption frequently lead to weapons of aggression, and Evans surpasses our worst fears, turning an effort to better mankind into a possibly indefensible weapon.

Yet *Hominine* goes far beyond simple entertainment. It provides clarity and a path for mankind that can alter our course and lead us all to an understanding that will alter even outcomes already set in motion. It should be required reading for anyone in politics, technology and business who's looking for new ideas in doing something extraordinary.

—*Ken Camp*

Is this really a novel? A very timely book with a plot so plausible yet so scarily close to the bone that you pray it's not real. *Hominine* is a masterful mix of political spin, human frailty, high-tech corruption and love on the rocks.

From the White House to the Somali desert, from Bali to Afghanistan, its characters are by turns dysfunctional, bumbling, gut-wrenchingly naive and refreshingly sane.

A compelling read and an exceptional debut that leaves you hungry for more ...and hoping that the world takes note.

—*Olga Sheean, author of* Fit for Love—find your self and your perfect mate

Hominine is an interesting and timely piece of work—*Zeitgeist* meets Dan Brown meets *24*. Modern geopolitics and terrorism, as seen through the eyes of an aging, disillusioned hippie who's now very much a part of the establishment he once railed against.

It is a tale about deadly next-gen weapon technology developed through 'new age' discoveries—but implemented without the corresponding 'new age' wisdom. It's Einstein, Oppenheimer and the Atomic bomb all over again.

Can mankind's 'higher awakening' empower him to exist beyond the confines of modern consumerism—before the powers (both governmental and corporate) behind the status quo eliminate critical thought and the dissent it leads to?

—*Randy Paré, Editor, RYKV Online E-Zine*

Hominine is so spot on and moves further away from fiction with each passing day's headlines.

—*Paul Biedermann*

Hominine is a great modern-day thriller that brings you on a page-turning rollercoaster, with occasional philosophical interludes that make you ponder where we are going as the human race. This fast-slow-fast pace is a very appealing characteristic of the book. It weaves together several plots, leaving subtle clues as to how they might come together in the end, but keep you guessing all the way. I got as much of a kick out of reading this book as I would from other masters of the art—Lee Child, Kathy Reichs, Stieg Larsson. Looking forward to the next one, Lewis!

—*Stephen Cullen*

A great novel illustrates our personal connections to questions of humanity. *Hominine*, a new novel by Lewis Evans, is therefore fittingly titled. It poses essential questions we all face, weaving them from beginning to end through a nail-biting thriller that takes you around the world, across cultures and through the eyes of intimate lives.

—*Linda Stringer*

ACKNOWLEDGEMENTS

Writing my first novel has taken me on a journey that has been as surprising in its twists and turns as it was heartwarming in the many interactions I had along the way. During the months I was ensconced in research and development of the story, many people befriended me online, and generously gave support, help and advice, without which this book would have been left wanting in many ways.

For their invaluable assistance in helping me to get facts right in the early stages, I am grateful to Wais Barakzai Nimruzi, Philip D'Afflisio and Patience Mason of the *Post-traumatic Gazette*.

I found the whole process of writing very enjoyable but, as a newbie, I was concerned to maintain a realistic perspective on what I was producing. So I broadcast a request for reviewers. I was humbled that so many responded, so enthusiastically, with suggestions, advice, help and reviews. They came from a wide variety of backgrounds and professions—journalists, publishing professionals, computer experts, doctors, students, healers, housewives and more. I am particularly grateful to Paul Biedermann, Marcella Caldwell-Gadson, Ken Camp, Bernie Corbett, Stephen Cullen, Drs Andrew and David Evans, Ziona Etzion, Brendan Foley, Pranay Gupte, Adam Huber, Randy Paré, Aline Perrette, Eoin Purcell, Vanessa O'Loughlin, Barbara O'Shea, Gerald Sheean, Linda Stringer and Anthony Uhlemann.

With the world of publishing in a state of turmoil and change as it adjusts to the digital era, I am particularly grateful to Zorba Publishers in Delhi, India, who have enthusiastically taken me on board as a first-time author, and I am especially thankful to Geetu Goel for her encouragement and support.

I discovered that being an author meant that I needed extended periods of solitude and concentration, and a fairly anti-social lifestyle. I also needed help when *I* wanted it, in terms of editorial skills, constructive criticism, food and sleep. All of this was facilitated by my wonderful wife and partner, Olga, to whom this book is wholeheartedly dedicated. I am eternally grateful that our paths crossed and fortune conspired to join our lives together on a wonderful journey through a passionate, rich and wonderful life.

HOMININE – IT'S TIME TO CHOOSE

Prologue

He can't be more than 17 years old. Laughing, talking, enjoying the attention. The evening sun casts an orange hue over the massive hood of the gleaming white Cadillac Escalade EXT truck. He stands on the gold-chromed bumper, eyes glinting, teeth sharply white against his deeply tanned face, and sprawls across the hood to caress the bulbous, gaping supercharger inlet that bursts like an unwieldy phallus from the smooth surface. He is shouting, excited. He slides down to stand on the dusty earth, a glimpse of Nikes as his long white robe snags on the elaborate trim. He is bending down, showing us the huge wheels—impossibly thin tires on vast, spidery gold-chromed rims. His fingers follow the outlines of the high-tech spokes. The throaty roar of engines revving all around him at the desert drag race obscures everything he says. He jumps into the cockpit and the monster truck twitches violently as he pumps the accelerator. Twice, three times, ten times. Dust swirls. But for the array of lights mounted on the roll bar, the Escalade is all but lost from view. Happiness.

It probably took half a second, maybe less. A change of focus a second before may have been long enough to register the BMW careening across the desert road, wildly fishtailing from out of left field. But we are not designed to alter fate, to change what is to happen. We are passive observers of our own madness. A second ago, there was curiosity, a fascination for the other-worldliness of a young man with his dream machine, and disbelief that such a youth could possibly own such a toy. Assaf thought that even if he worked 24 hours a day for the next 30 years, he would never own such a thing. Such outrageously conspicuous consumption would not go down well in his world.

Real death is so blunt, so final. No Hollywood slo-mo, no extras diving dramatically for cover as the explosion hits, no admirer watching in horror as the impending disaster snuffs out the life of their loved one. No realization, no revenge, no justice. Just death. Stop.

Yet somehow the cameraman had the presence of mind—or was it the total lack of sensitivity, morbid curiosity, or just a shock reaction—to carry on filming. After a second or two of jerky grit, sky, smoke, screaming and blurred sand, a black finger wipes the lens. The camera swings to and fro, the cameraman's hands shudder as if emphasizing his hoarse cries. He is crying, but still filming. What *is* he thinking? Had he become so inured to media shock, so used to violence, that even the death of his friend becomes an online video event? Was he excited?

There's something curiously interesting about the underside of the new car. It is still shiny. All the car's intestines, the silver panels and pipes, deftly arranged to efficiently form a flat, aerodynamic under-belly. The necessary made practical and conveniently stored out of sight below the sleek and sexy. But now it is displayed to the viewer—a perfect fit in the open driver's doorway of the Escalade. It doesn't look as if the big truck has sustained much damage. Just shifted a few feet sideways and there is an arch in the driver's doorway where the BMW tried to get into the driver's seat.

The upper door of the BMW is being lifted slowly, erratically, as the camera moves round to the far side of the Escalade. The heavy passenger door of the gleaming white monster, with its sophisticated side-impact protection, looks as good as the day it left the showroom, except that the triple glazed window is almost completely red, but for some black hair, teeth and part of a jaw.

Cut.

'Happiness is a white Escalade'. 1m 47sec. Star rating three out of five.
Editor's comment: 'Hey, now daddy can pimp his coffin!'
Viewers' comments.
Erghx3812: ROFL!
ARABHTR: Fuckin Arab rich kids. Yur all gonna get whats cummin to ya!!!!
JIBBAJABBA: Eat that Beemer, kid!
Juiceman: Waste of a fuckin rockin truck if you ask me. Dam!

"Assaf! Are you coming down for dinner?" He remembered to breathe again. That video hadn't helped at all.

"Give me ten minutes, mother." He wasn't satisfied yet.

Chapter 1

Bob Marley's 'Redemption Song' drifted from the radio alarm clock, through the bedroom to the en suite where Griffin Kirkland was enjoying a few precious moments of solitude. On this bright Sunday morning at the carefully chosen house in Westchester County, he was shaving.

Air guitar.

Rolling his head from side to side just didn't have the same effect without the dreadlocks. He toweled off his face, smoothed back his tightly cropped silver-grey hair, and chose a shirt and a neutral tie.

He figured it was a ten-minute hop from La Guardia to Westchester County in the Citation, and then another 15 from plane to limo, up the 684 and along the winding road to his door. But they'd be traveling in separate planes and in separate limos, so they wouldn't arrive together. That had been thought through as well.

Everything was in place. Controlled. Organized. Nothing could go wrong, so he could give his undivided attention to the job in hand.

He knew the routine. As the President's Special Negotiator for Middle East Affairs, he had unparalleled access to information, resources and the President himself, to put a speedy end to the age-old problems surrounding Israel. But the history of conflict was just too long and too complicated for anyone to completely understand, let alone resolve in a way that would be acceptable to even just two of the parties involved. No organization, political party, individual or national figure could broker a lasting deal without being accused of selling out in some way. Despite all that he'd learned in the past five years, all the time he'd spent wrestling with this problem and month after month of meetings with as many of the factions as would meet him, progress was painfully slow. Privately, Griffin Kirkland didn't think anything had changed at all, except that more people had died or been misplaced, and hatreds had become even more entrenched. Publicly, the spin was meant to give the impression that he was making huge strides toward a deep and lasting peace. A few setbacks along the way were perfectly understandable, given the complex issues and processes involved. It was all under control.

The truth was that the last two years had taken a toll on him, politically and personally. There had been some particularly vicious suicide attacks aimed at middle-class Israeli communities in supposedly safe areas. Predictably, these had been followed by high-tech retaliations fueled by reactionary politicians backed by a well-equipped and impassioned army, laying waste to the previous three years of negotiations. Sleepless nights, shuttle diplomacy and endless 'off the record' conversations had led to nothing that would quell the tide of negativity toward him in the press, and the growing perception that the peace process was doomed. The extreme weight of public opinion that he felt now, along with his own private misgivings about the entire peace process, made him question his own effectiveness and abilities, and tempted him to seek some form of escape. Redemption.

Griffin Kirkland had always proclaimed himself a peacenik. Back in the 1960s, he was respected and admired for it by his friends, and his boyish good looks earned him a gaggle of female followers. He was the epitome of cool, which gave his parents another reason to disapprove of him—along with his shoulder-length hair, tie-dyed shirt and his dreadful taste in music. Worse still was the second-hand Fender guitar in his bedroom, attached to a Marshall amp complete with fuzz box and wah-wah pedal. Like his hero, Jimi Hendrix, he knew that one could only truly appreciate the finer points of *Purple Haze* when the walls were buzzing and plaster was falling from the ceiling. Their neighbors, who used to love 'little Griff' in years gone by, now avoided eye contact with his parents. They whisked their groceries from the Volvo station wagon to the front door, which they slammed shut behind them, leaving Jack and Mary isolated and tense and praying for the day when the little shit got himself into college or found a proper job—anything that would take him far away so they could restore the bland equilibrium of their lives.

He went to college. It wasn't that he had a particular interest in studying anything and, in those days, nobody seemed to care, as long as you enrolled in some classes and showed up occasionally. Here, his easy affability and knack of making friends flourished. Social discourse moved on to impassioned discussion and debate. He started to find his political voice. Because of his predilection for standing out front and shouting louder, and because people listened to him, he began to feel that his opinion was important. Privately, though, he knew that he had absolutely no experience of the stuff he was spouting. But he started to build a political image of himself. He became skilled at parrying arguments from more experienced and better informed opponents, with a mix of heavy emotion and a masterly dexterity in word play that appealed to a grass-roots audience. He learned how to manipulate emotions. Most people, he discovered, were 'grass-roots' fans at heart, because that seemed to represent family values and the basis of the Christian ethic that pervaded US society. So, even when he was arguing something that was sophisticated, intellectual or a bit obscure, he made sure he couched his argument in popular terminology. He distilled everything into simple language delivered with extreme economy. He understood sound bites before they'd even invented the term. The admiration he received, his growing popularity, his deep anti-establishment, anti-war, anti-anything-representing-the-middle-class-generation-before-his   commitment, led him to become an activist for political reform in his early twenties. As he started treading a political path, he met the love of his life.

For Griffin, the young man from middle-income nowheresville in Utah, Sheryl represented the ultimate in radical sophistication. She had fascinating bohemian parents. Her father wrote novels that were considered somewhat avant-garde, and her mother was a freelance journalist. Sheryl had what seemed to be a very healthy, friendly relationship with them that contrasted sharply with his lack of relationship with his own boring parents. Sheryl's parents made a great impression on Griffin. They had traveled a lot, had African masks in the kitchen, wore ethnic clothes from India, burned incense and had big messy abstract paintings leaning against the walls in their hallway. Her father kept his Ducati in the living room because "hell, it's so much more beautiful to look at than a TV". They actually used the 'f' word in arguments with their daughter—but not in a trailer-trash sort of way. Sheryl introduced Griffin to them one sunny Sunday morning in their SoHo apartment, after she and Griffin had enjoyed a sleepless night of sweaty sex. Her parents were in bed, apparently naked under burgundy silk sheets, surrounded by a wasteland of books, newspapers, a couple of empty wine glasses and two comatose cats, when Sheryl, wearing only his T-shirt, casually dragged him into their room. At the time, he was scratching his scrotum through his underpants.

"Oh, hi. You must be John. Nice to meet you. Sheryl, are you making coffee?" Her father glanced up from a book he was thumbing through.

"Griffin," Sheryl corrected him. "I told you last week." Her mum was still asleep. Before Griffin had a chance to reply—or, rather, before he'd gathered his groggy senses and recovered from the unexpected nature of what seemed like a pivotal moment in a blooming relationship—Sheryl snorted at her dad and pulled Griffin out of their bedroom and into the kitchen, where she made some strong coffee using a real Italian coffee machine from Italy.

There was nothing boring about Sheryl. She was the first truly free spirit that Griffin had met who actually walked the talk of their generation. They'd originally bumped into each other in 1969 at Woodstock—literally. They were in their underwear then as well, in a group that was laughing hysterically in the rain as they ran and then slid on their backsides in the mud, in a lull between listening to music and smoking weed. Sitting at the bottom of the slide after a particularly exhilarating run, his first sight of Sheryl was a pair of wildly splayed brown legs spattering mud in all directions as they ploughed down the hill directly at him. Scrambling to get out of her way, his legs cartwheeling in slo-mo, gaining zero traction before her hips slammed into his chest and she planted her face in his crotch.

"Oops." Lifting her congealed head, Sheryl wiped caked mud from her face and opened two clear, clean, smiling eyes. "Should I apologize?"

"You've got to be kidding me!" It was love at first sight.

But where had the popularity drug led him? His ideals and passions were shaped by his ability to woo public opinion, rather than being the inspiration that drove them. His popularity had yielded in him a seductive vision of how his life could unfold. He went on to do what he seemed best qualified to do and, as far as most people were concerned, he deserved all the success and praise he attracted along the way. In his own mind, he had not seen his progress up through the political ranks for what it truly was—ruthless ambition. He saw it as his natural evolution. Nor had he seen the insidious change in his own radical values and ideals as anything more than a growing maturity—a logical progression fed by information, myriad experiences and acquired wisdom. Now he knew things that only the privileged elite could know, and it was better that way for everyone. A little knowledge was dangerous, especially in the wrong hands.

His one remaining link with his former self was his wife, Sheryl. She was the rock he turned to in his dark moments, at times like this when none of the knowledge, wisdom, intelligence or learning seemed to count for anything—when his world disintegrated into a kind of madness that he felt he wasn't equipped for. Five intense years. No answers. How much longer could he spin the illusion?

His career had taken a toll on Sheryl as well. After Woodstock, she'd become something of an icon for the event when a photo of her muddy body being hoisted aloft on a sea of hands had been published in *Rolling Stone*. Articles followed in minor celebrity gossip mags when the press discovered that not only was she a rock party animal but, once the mud had been washed off, she was also extremely good-looking and elegant. They also uncovered the fact that she'd had a short involvement with a prominent rock star, so they were on her case from then on. The early years of her increasingly public marriage to White House potential—Griffin—were a frantic climb up the party political ladder that precluded any discussions about starting a family, and that absorbed Sheryl's life into his. She became more his PA than his wife, which had advantages as well as disadvantages for her. On the one hand, she worked so closely with him that any opportunities he may have had to stray from the path with occasional extra-marital affairs were snuffed out long before they amounted to anything. She kept a close check on everything in his life—and that meant everything. She'd never been particularly keen to have a career of her own, and living her life through her husband gave her the perfect opportunity to justify not striding out on her own journey, while still enjoying huge success by proxy. On the other hand, she felt a growing resentment—both in the way she had to distort herself and suppress her creative side in order to play the political wife, as well as the control that she found herself increasingly exercising over her husband. She felt conflicted, because although it was clear they were a great team, she had lost respect for him. Added to that was her suppressed and largely unspoken desire to have children in the early days of their marriage. She'd reluctantly accepted some time ago that a family would be impossible due to their advancing years and heavy workload. Her wild child now straight-jacketed, her manner tight and precise, she was prone to barbed and thoughtless remarks, but only in private with Griffin. And whenever she sensed she had cut too deep, she tended to over-compensate with exuberant displays of public affection that were cut dead by the time they reached the bedroom. To the rest of the world, she was a perfect wife on the cover of *Hello!* magazine.

Griffin stood at the window, motionless. He had seven minutes before Sheryl called him. The whole event was pure theatre, out of which he knew he had to produce a real result. The rambling lakeside mansion had been carefully chosen and rented for two days at an exorbitant rate, which gave his people the freedom to reorganize, re-furbish and re-equip the relevant rooms for the occasion. The owner was probably quietly chuckling to himself that these government people not only paid big bucks for the weekend but threw in a free make-over as well. Across the fields, he occasionally caught sight of a dark-suited agent talking into his wrist, or a slow-moving Suburban watching for… what? Nobody could possibly know about this meeting. Security was just too tight. If anything, these goons were advertising the fact that something important was going down here. *Idiots,* he thought. *Why do they always put on this kind of show?*

Seven minutes. He blanked his mind and drank in the warm morning air. He let his eyes turn a little skyward, just enough to take all human forms out of his field of vision. The trees looked especially beautiful against the deep blue, perfectly cloudless sky. Birdsong.

From where he stood at a window at the rear of the mansion, he couldn't see the arrival of one and then a second black limo, three minutes apart. The Israeli arrived first, and was shown into an ante room where he was offered tea. The representative of Hamas arrived second, but only after the first limo had been parked discreetly at the side of the house. He was shown into a second room, and offered sparkling water. Griffin felt a knot in his stomach and a dull anxiousness as his programming kicked in and his briefing replayed in his mind. *I hope Sheryl got the right colored napkins.*

"Griffin." He was startled back into the room. "They're ready for you."

CHAPTER 2

It was hard for Assaf Barak to reconcile his deep disgust for violence, war and the siege of Gaza with his magnetic attraction to videos depicting violent acts and graphic sex. He had stumbled upon websites that displayed such things two years ago when he was 17 and, since then, his voyeuristic appetite had grown, pushing him to seek out greater and increasingly graphic extremes. He often spent the late hours surfing for a fix, getting aroused and, later still, after he had relieved the pressure, falling into a guilt-ridden sleep. Outwardly, he was an intelligent and caring Jewish student of political sciences, spending his time between his home in Modiin and his rooms in Oxford. In his school years, he'd been an active 'Community in Action' member of Sadaka Reut—an organization dedicated to building a better understanding between Israeli and Palestinian youth. He'd taken part in many of their summer programs aimed at challenging and dissolving the segregation and alienation between Arabs and Israelis. He was the son of proud parents who'd guided him with strong values and encouragement to apply himself to his studies, and driven him to achieve a scholarship that could launch him into the kind of respectable professional career that had been denied to them.

However, for someone with his sensitivity, life had been a series of difficult challenges. He wasn't the world's most handsome boy, and he knew it. He had a large, hooked nose, bulbous eyes that required heavy glasses, a receding small chin and a pale complexion topped by a mop of hair that he pulled forward into a heavy fringe in an effort to hide himself. These features combined to give him the appearance of a cartoon nerd, earning him merciless ribbing at school. Maybe it had been his unrequited desire to be accepted by his own community that had led him to be so active in Sadaka Reut in his later school years. It had worked, to some extent; his own experience of isolation and rejection enabling him to make a valuable contribution to the organization's work in healing the Arab/Israeli divide. But these days he tended to keep to himself and only communicated with a few trusted friends at Oxford, who seemed to be more accepting of him than his peers in Israel. He had not been successful in attracting girlfriends, apart from one.

It was difficult to have a relationship with Salma, but somehow Assaf managed to keep her attention for two years. They had grown emotionally close, despite the geographical distance between them, and the political barriers that made a physical meeting almost impossible. Recently, their communications had become quite intense, though it was hard for Assaf to figure out if she felt as much for him as he did for her. He guessed not, but he was hopeful.

They had met online in the Israel–Palestine Forum. She lived in a small, lackluster town called Nuseirat, south of Gaza City. She had a clerical job in her father's small business, but in her spare time she helped organize local theatre productions, based largely on political themes. Email had been a surprisingly effective way to build their relationship in the early days. Each had the opportunity to speak their mind about their likes, dislikes, concerns and interests, without the added complications and chemistry of physical presence. They started talking on Skype after about six months, but this had its own frustrations as Salma only had a dial-up connection, and the calls were prone to failing. Then she managed to convince her father to get his business hooked up on broadband. They were both very excited about this, especially as Salma also planned to get a webcam. Assaf was also filled with dread at the thought that if he also used his for their video conversations, Salma would soon be able to see his face.

And so, one summer night, Assaf and Salma virtually breached the siege of Gaza and 'met' face to face, webcam to webcam. Assaf had arranged a late call so he could make sure his face was badly lit, and he also blurred the image a little. He had apologized for its quality, saying that his camera was old and he couldn't afford a new one. She, on the other hand, appeared to him crystal clear. They'd both giggled nervously, even though they'd known each other for two years and had already shared intimate details about their lives. They'd spoken carefully and politely as if they had just met. She'd searched the small video window to see if the image she had held in her mind reflected the boy she now saw. It hadn't been clear enough to see him properly; even so, it was evident that it didn't. But on the inside, they were like old friends, so the outward appearance was more easily forgiven. He'd marveled at her bright, mischievous eyes, her long, dark wavy hair, which would surely have been covered up had he met her for real, and her mouth that smiled just for him. He'd studied the shape of her shoulders and the suggestion of an ample bosom under her black T-shirt.

This evening, Salma's father had left the office early, and they had taken the opportunity to talk as soon as he'd gone. They had talked about Salma's latest production, which had been inspired by two recent suicide bombings in Tel Aviv. Two women had detonated themselves—one in a shopping centre in Ramat Aviv to the north of the city, and the other outside a hotel in the Beach Zone. The fallout was horrific, and Salma was devastated that after all the efforts for peace, these two events could blow the whole peace process apart, yet again. Assaf admired her guts for being part of something that so publicly condemned such actions at a time and in a place where everyone involved in the production was at great risk. He also felt impotent. He had no stomach for such radicalism, such exposure, and couldn't help her if she needed help.

Part of him wanted to be with her in Gaza, yet part of him wanted no more of Israel and Gaza and all the hatred and violence, pain and anger that constantly lurked beneath everyday life.

He was happiest now in Oxford, where he was discovering and enjoying a new life with new friends, and he limited his time in Modiin to holidays. His family had moved there so his father could take up a teaching post in nearby Ramla. His father had chosen a somewhat featureless house in Modiin—a new town nestled defiantly up against the border with the West Bank that the government was keen to see nicely populated. While it was neat and clean and every effort had been made to give it the air of an established leafy, green and pleasant community, Assaf thought it was bland and boring, and he hated some of the more prominent architecture. 'A people factory', he called it.

But there was Salma. Between her concerns and her passion to do whatever she could for peace, she was bursting with humor and gossip and flashing smiles and light-hearted surprises. And then a pause, and a nervous smile and Assaf felt the warmth of her through the screen. She was infectious in these intense moments. She rested her elbows on the desk in front of her, leaned forward and blew him a kiss. Leaning back again, her hand drifted across her breast. *Was that a sign? A signal?* Then she glanced sideways. "I have to go."

She disappeared. Damn. Why was it always like this? Shit, shit, shit.

He logged in and opened up his latest find, which had come to him via a circuitous route through Ayan—a trusted friend in Oxford. He'd paid a fee for this one and it was clear that they knew who he was, but he felt the risk was worth it. Actually, he wasn't sure what risk there was, if any, but such low-grade material surely carried some. 'ShocknWhore' was a nasty hangover from the Iraqi invasion. A collection of extreme violence and tacky porn made for, and with some content supplied by, the American forces, for precisely the same reason that Assaf was viewing it now. It also had an extra dimension of high-adrenalin, jingoistic, ignorant prejudice against anything that wasn't American Pie. The owners of the site took great delight in trashing anything Arabic and especially Muslim, and loved to see them suffer. To Assaf, it was like the Bush administration-induced fear-of-terrorism-emanating-from-Muslim-backed-organizations on speed, with a massive dose of depravity thrown in for good measure. It was very popular with a lot of the lower ranks who faced life or death uncertainty every day in Iraq, and it was quietly tolerated as an unfortunate but acceptable 'relief valve' by the few that knew about it in the upper ranks.

Assaf didn't really enjoy clips like 'Happiness is a white Escalade'. He felt bad that he was transfixed by the shock that they induced and that he seemed to have become addicted to. But as long as nobody but Ayan knew what he was doing, he really didn't see any need to change his habits. So he scrolled down the page to find something else. Still a virgin at 19, Assaf was obsessed with the idea of having sex with a real woman, but it was such a remote possibility that he blanked it from his mind during the day, obsessively applying himself to his studies. The night hours hurt most, when he was alone and confused—about everything, it seemed. He knew that he was being sucked into these websites filled with impossible promises and pop-up temptations. He felt used and abused by their exploitation of his desires and weaknesses, but loved the physical intensity that they engendered in him, and the rampant orgasms they released. But then, in his exhaustion, he felt an insufferable weight of betrayal. He betrayed himself, he betrayed Salma, his family, his body and heart. This cheap transient pleasure betrayed his ethics and dishonored his values. Night after night after night.

He paused at a thumbnail of a woman with smiling eyes looking at the camera, her cheek distorted, wide open mouth engulfing a massive black penis. His was nothing like that. Is that what women enjoyed? Would he be man enough when, one day, God willing, he eventually took her into his bed? He thought of Salma and imagined her in the same position as he looked down at her. Her cheek was flat. Oh, no.

He quickly scrolled on. The violent clips were less painful for him. The more violent, the greater the distraction from his own feelings of inadequacy. Nothing on that page. He clicked 'next' and a whole new set appeared. The third one down caught his eye.

The thumbnail was a close-up of a man's face. Just half of it was in shot. Assaf could just make out a tear falling from the inner corner of the eye. The white of the eye was crisscrossed with veins, and the lower lid was pulled down by his hand covering his nose and face. He was an old man, heavily wrinkled with bushy grey-black eyebrows and a darkly tanned, ruddy complexion. Assaf could just make out some form of cloth head covering. The image was unusual because if wasn't typical of the thumbnails that usually introduced brutal acts, severed heads, dismembered corpses, executions, cat fights, gang warfare, vehicle crashes or 'collateral damage'.

He clicked on the thumbnail.

There was no title or heavy metal rock music overlaying the mayhem, as with so many of the clips. It went straight to the action. Blurred and jerky with several wild movements where nothing was visible. Assaf figured it was a mobile phone upload, which was unusual because the military usually used compact video cameras. They liked to show off detail. But that wasn't the only thing that was unusual about this clip. From what he could make out, this clip was set in a small, primitive village in a mountainous area. Crudely built single-storey buildings, with rough wooden rafters supporting flat stone tiles, looked onto a dirt square that sloped steeply. He saw no trees.

The man he had seen on the thumbnail was holding the phone away from him, pointing the camera at his own face, screaming at it. Tears streamed from his eyes, which he periodically wiped from his cheeks and beard. At times, he seemed to be covering his nose as if to avoid breathing in a smell. Assaf couldn't understand a word he was shouting, and a buffeting wind made much of the sound inaudible. The shouting stopped as the man appeared to climb down some steps. Dropping the phone to his side as he went, Assaf could see that he was wearing long robes that must once have been white, but were now stained and dirty with the color of the earth that surrounded him. He was walking quickly now, past a goat, an old jeep, two or three other men in white turbans and long white robes. They stood motionless, some weeping. Then the phone passed by someone dressed in a loose white shirt and a long, dark-colored waistcoat—only the torso was in view. He came to an abrupt halt and turned the camera on the scene in front of him. The phone shook as he showed a body directly below him. It was a woman, probably in her fifties, wearing an ornately patterned long dress, her hair covered. A necklace of beads, elaborate rings on her fingers. Her mouth had fallen open; her eyes gazed lifelessly upwards and away. The camera scanned down her body to reveal a clear, black hole about two inches across, in her solar plexus. The man let out a deep groan. His hand caressed her cheek as he collapsed onto her. The phone was taken from him. Assaf momentarily saw the dark waistcoat again as the camera was lifted to reveal several more bodies, twisted and lifeless as the phone-bearer moved slowly among them. Men, women and children. Assaf couldn't figure out where this clip had been made. They looked like a simple peasant community living in the hills. Some had similar holes in the lower part of their chests; others had been hit in the throat or the head. Many still had items in their hands—baskets, tools, a skipping rope, a toy. There were no signs of any violence, no fear registered in their faces. It was as if they had been going about their business and suddenly dropped dead. Assaf thought of Pompeii, and how so many of the population seemed to have been caught unawares, or of Hiroshima and a photo he had seen of the silhouette of a man on a charred wall—a ghostly outline of his last living moment. But this was bizarre.

He ran the clip again, suddenly focused and awake. It didn't make sense. He had seen, on TV, the devastation wrought by the Americans on the road to Basra when they obliterated an Iraqi convoy. But there, the people had all been burned up in the intense heat and nothing remained of them. He'd seen plenty of clips of people who had been shot or blown up, or maimed by landmines. But never this. There was something odd about the consistent positions of the wounds on their bodies, and he could only wonder at the surprise element. What could they have possibly done to deserve this? Had they not seen or even suspected anything at all? There was no easy explanation. This looked like a massacre of innocents.

Assaf wracked his brain. He checked other clips and searched online to try to find out about the types of injuries inflicted by modern warfare, but soon realized that it was ridiculous to imagine that such data were freely available, and gave up. He wanted to find out more, but he also realized that anyone he asked would naturally want to know where he found the clip, and he didn't want to take that risk. But there was one person he trusted. He didn't want to send a link because his friend would then have to subscribe to the site to get access to it, so he found some freeware, downloaded the clip and emailed it to him.

Hi Madoowbe! I got this just now. It's a bit strange. See what you think. Have you got any idea what's going on here? Could it be something to do with Afghanistan? It doesn't look like Middle East material. I am back Tuesday 14th. I hope you managed to finish that tedious book on macro-politics. Took me two weeks! Khuda Hafiz. Assaf.

Chapter 3

"Hey, David, take a look at this one." Ken Fellows made a quick call as he read the email he'd just pulled up a screen.

"Will this take long? I have to be out of here by five. Barbara's got an evening class so I'm on baby-sitting duty—" The voice was tight with a weary impatience.

"Up to you," Ken cut in, "but there's something strange here and I think the old man will want to be informed today if you think there's anything in it."

"Give me five and I'll come to your booth." So far, the day had gone according to plan for David Arbuthnot, but things seemed to go off the rails every time he arranged something after work. He was contracted to finish at five every day and hand over to the night watch, but it rarely happened. Recently, he'd been wondering if it had been such a good idea to uproot his young family from England for this 'opportunity' to further his career in the US. It had been a unique offer, and the money was good, but he hadn't bargained on the American work ethic. He missed free evenings with his wife, Barbara, and their friends in the local pub. But then, since the birth of their son, nothing would be the same again—not just because of the addition of this tiny bundle of joy to his new family, but because Josh was a Down Syndrome baby.

Just a few months after they'd started to come to terms with it, he was head-hunted by an employment agency in the US. At only 22, he'd already earned himself a minor celebrity status as a prolific blogger on all matters concerning new media, and that's what had caught their attention. The first interview had been in London, followed by a head-spinning trip to Washington where he was picked up at the airport in a stretch limo and treated like a movie star for three days—apart from two pretty rigorous interviews where it became clear that his potential employer knew more about him than was comfortable. But that really didn't surprise him, knowing what he himself was capable of finding out via the Internet. In fact, that's just what they wanted him for. Once he had satisfied his interviewers that he really could deliver the goods, they fast-tracked a two-year contract to him back in the UK and gave him a short window to accept and move to a Washington burb where they had already found him a three-bedroomed house and a Mexican maid to help Barbara. They had even used Josh to lure him there, by introducing David and Barbara to the ominously named American Association on Intellectual and Developmental Disabilities, which had an impressive reputation for research into, and treatment of, those with an extra Chromosome 21. He was now an employee of Arlington Online Data Systems Inc., located in an anonymous suite of offices above a bank on New York Avenue, and living in a neat little house in Alcova Heights that made Barbara feel she was rapidly becoming a Stepford wife. It was only a month after he started the job that he discovered who his paymasters really were.

They'd had their first big argument just three days after they'd arrived. Still jet-lagged, overwhelmed by the speed at which their life had been turned upside down, and grappling with a completely alien environment, they were both a bit edgy. After the winding streets and compact size of Tunbridge Wells, Washington was just *so vast*. Endless grids of houses surrounded them. Journeys to shops involved major planning, especially when it came to figuring out how to negotiate the spaghetti of highways around the Pentagon City shopping mall—the best place for major purchases when setting up their new home. David's journey to work seemed to take a lifetime each morning and even longer coming home. His preferred route took him over the Theodore Roosevelt Memorial Bridge and around the White House, rather than going south round the Arlington Cemetery and along the 'race track' past the Pentagon, as he called it.

Their big tiff was over the choice of car. David was allocated a modest amount to put toward a vehicle. He wanted an economical, eco-friendly compact hybrid but Barbara insisted that, with a new baby, they should get something bigger "to hold everything they would need".

"I was looking online while you were at work, and I think we should get one of these" she said, opening a newly bookmarked page on the laptop they kept on a packing crate in the kitchen. 'One of these' was a Chevy Tahoe—to David, a massive dinosaur of a vehicle that he wouldn't be seen dead driving. And it was way beyond their budget. A lot of emotion, but not a lot of reasoned argument, followed. Eventually, they settled on a Chevy Traverse—$20,000 cheaper and 'ever so fuel-efficient', according to Barbara. The only other hybrids that came close in size were way out of their league on price or, like the Ford Escape, just "too clunky".

To David, family life was starting to feel like a heavy weight rather than an exciting joint venture. It was only the following morning that he discovered the real reason they were committing to a piece of real estate on wheels. Barbara was frightened. She felt intimidated by the huge vehicles all around them when they were out driving. Articulated trucks, big vans, refuse trucks, even school buses all seemed somehow more crude and dangerous than the equivalent vehicles back in England. And with a baby on board, Barbara wanted to feel protected and safe in this strange and violent land.

David logged out of a Twitter account, scanned his email one last time and made his way over to Ken's booth.

"What've you got?"

"Doesn't look like much, but hang on..." Ken brought the email back onto his screen and David leaned over to read it.

"It's nothing! What's the big deal?"

"I'll show you. But first, there's a bit of background you should know." Ken swung round in his chair to face David. "It's a real oddball message, out of somewhere called Modiin in Israel..."

"I know that place from my portfolio. It's by the West Bank. A sort of hilly Milton Keynes."

"A what?"

"It's a 'new town' in England... Never mind. We've never had much out of Modiin. It's all been pretty conservative stuff. Tell me."

"It flagged because of a couple of standard keys that we always check out. Nothing new there," Ken continued, "and the guy who sent it is a lightweight—a student who spent some time at school as a peace activist of some sort. But the recipient is interesting. You see he's used a nickname here—Madoowbe—which just means 'very black', and is quite common in that country..."

"Which country?"

"Somalia." Ken looked up to see if David showed any sign of interest. He didn't, so he carried on.

"But his actual name is Ayan." He looked down at a note he'd scribbled on a pad. "Ayan Korfa Nadif." He looked up again. "Mean anything to you?"

David knew he was being tested. He'd only been on the job a couple of months and the volume of data and knowledge that he needed to absorb, just to cover off his allotted portfolio of Israel, Gaza and Lebanon, was going to take him at least another three months. That was mainly because the idea that you could specialize on a tight area was a bit of a fantasy dreamed up by their boss, Troy King, who had extensive military experience but pretty much no Internet knowledge. David quickly realized that he needed to get a thorough understanding of the complex international terrorist network if he wanted to impress the upper echelons of Arlington Online Data Systems—or move beyond this office warren once his two years were up. That's if he made it to the end of his contract, which was looking less likely every day, despite his best efforts. Ken, on the other hand, had been in this job covering the same area for three years already, had gone through the continuous learning pain barrier, and was a mine of fascinating information that was cross-linked better than any database in the entire organization. So he was playing with the new boy—the 'blue head', as Troy King called him, harking back to the freshly-shaved heads of new white army recruits whose blood vessels made their heads look blue. Ken was also just a little resentful at this kid coming in on the same salary as him when he seemed to know so little.

"Somali names go like this: first name, Ayan, is the name his parents gave him; second name, Korfa, is his daddy's name; third name, Nadif, is his granddaddy's name. So we got the whole family history in one."

"That's handy." David didn't know where this was going.

"It's more than that, when you dig around a bit, and that's what I done." He clicked on a database icon and waited for it to load.

"There he is." Ken pointed at a name.

"No, that's—"

"Korfa Nadif Samakab. Bingo!" He looked pleased with himself and sat back, clasping his hands across his stomach, challenging David to take the bait.

"Are you suggesting they're related?"

"I'm damn sure they are!" Ken was leaning forward now, talking loudly for the benefit of the ranks of translators, cryptographers, techies, secretaries and others in the office, who were sure to be listening in on his little initiation ceremony.

"Korfa Nadif Samakab is a 'name'. We have him tagged. He's a big noise in Somalia, but kinda shrouded in mystery. He moves around a lot, does a lot of business, seems to stay out of trouble but we have our suspicions that he's not entirely clean. He's been Stateside three times this year already. He sent his son to study in Oxford, England, paid for four years, the whole shebang— upfront, according to the DIA who got some friends over there." He paused for theatrical effect. David couldn't see why a rich person paying for his son's education in Oxford was anything to write home about, but the connections and some of the words in the email started to tick boxes in his mind. He peered at the email again, searching for a deeper meaning.

>*Hi Madoowbe! I got this just now. It's a bit strange. See what you think. Have you got any idea what is going on here? Could it be something to do with* **Afghanistan**? *It doesn't look like* **Middle East material**. *I am back Tuesday 14th. I hope you managed to finish that tedious book on* **macro-politics**. *Took me two weeks!* **Khuda Hafiz**. *Assaf.*

It was possible that there was something else hidden in here, but his gut said it was just a casual email with no encrypted alternative meanings. No, this was just too luke-warm for the performance that Ken was putting on. Ken was onto something and was just dangling a carrot, confounding him. Reading David like a book, and enjoying every moment of it, Ken continued "I know what you're gonna say. That's not all that interesting either—until, that is, you look at the attachment." Ken clicked his mouse with a flourish and a small, blurry video started up. David moved in closer to the screen, and frowned as the video progressed to the point where the bodies were shown.

"What the heck…?" David had no idea where to start on this. "You're right. King had better see this. Shit. I'll call Barbara."

So far, David hadn't had much to do with Troy King. Mr King was a tall black man, about sixty years old, David guessed. He'd been a lifer in the military, and had a broad scar across the top of his head where his short cropped graying hair no longer grew. He sat in a glass-walled office, which everyone called the Fishtank, at one end of the warren of booths. He made it clear that he didn't want to be disturbed there, unless something of real importance came up. This was his haven of peace and sanity, and no one dared to disturb him unless they could include the words 'national security' in the first sentence they uttered as they walked in the door. He was tired of low-grade wet-behind-the-ears cadidiots swanning into his office with dumbass stories that meant squat, trying to convince him that some towelhead was going to blow up this or that before they had really CHECKED OUT THE FACTS. The Internet was full of crackheads, as far as he was concerned, and the kids they gave him to filter out the dumb shit that was going down there were just titless college shower-shoes on a big ego trip.

That's probably why Ken suggested that David go and break the news to Troy King, rather than him.

"It'll be a feather in your cap, old chap," he smirked as he patted David on the back and sent him on his way.

"Gee, thanks," he mocked, mimicking Ken's accent. *Why do Americans think that all English people talk like Roger Moore?*

Whenever someone approached the Fishtank, Troy King made sure he was concentrating on something on his computer screen, hoping they were just on their way to the washroom. David knocked.

"Come."

"Mr King, I think we've found something…"

"Is this important? What's your name?" Troy King peered over the top of his glasses.

"David Arbuthnot….sir." As an Englishman, he wasn't accustomed to adding the 'sir' at the end of every sentence, but when addressing this particular ex-military man, it seemed to be a wise precaution.

"Are But What!?" His look of incredulity almost turned to a smile, which he quickly suppressed.

"Arbuthnot, sir. It's a name derived from a small town in Scotland where—"

"Okay, okay. You're new here, yes?" David hardly had time to catch his breath before each question was fired at him.

"I've been here about a—"

"Good, good. So, what's so important that you've decided to take up my valuable time?"

"Well, sir, we've intercepted—well, actually, Ken Fellows who works with me in sector—"

"Get to the point R. Butt, or not, in which case get the hell outta my office!"

"It's a video attached to an email I think you should—"

"This had better not be one of them YouTube pieces of crap." He looked back at his screen. David realized he only had seconds to get his point across before he was dismissed from Mr King's company.

"We think it's a matter of national security—"

"Congratulations!" King looked up, a thin smile on his lips. "What took you so long?"

"I'm sorry, sir. It's on K3 for you to see right now." David breathed again, as King navigated to the email and the video.

"Nothin'... nothin'... nothin'..." King mumbled as he scanned the email. Standing there, David was reminded of his school headmaster reading a report of one of his many pranks that had always cost him dearly. He'd been hauled into the headmaster's office many times and made to stand in silence as the lurid details of his complex practical jokes were assessed and a suitable punishment decided. In those days, his parents were worried that he had some form of multiple personality disorder. They'd had various experts look at him to see if he needed medication. It turned out that he was fully in control of his thoughts and actions, was unusually intelligent and had a unique quality that brought him great acclaim in school plays. His ability to portray different characters, to mimic accents and mannerisms, and to play more than one part at a time was legend in his school. It had been hard for him to make the choice to drop the arts in favor of sciences but it was "the more practical option for getting a good job", as his parents had said.

"You've checked these guys out—Madoowbe, Kooda Hayfiz, Assaf?"

"Yes, sir. Actually Madoowbe is a nickname. This is his real name," David pointed to Ken's attached note on the screen, "and that is his father. He's someone we tagged a while ago, according to Ken. You can find out about him on the link."

"And this guy? Kooda Hayfiz? Why have two of them signed it?" David paused. He wanted to avoid embarrassing his boss, but he felt under pressure, and frankly couldn't see why he should spare King's feelings.

"Khuda Hafiz isn't a name, actually, sir. It's a way to say 'goodbye' or 'yours sincerely'. Literally, it means 'God go with you'."

"Uh huh. Why'd he say that? This guy is Israeli and this one's Somali. Is there some significance?"

"No, I don't think so. They're studying Political Science at Oxford....in England... together..."

"Uh huh. Pinkos. Okay." David guessed that King used 'pinkos' as a blanket derogatory term for anyone in higher education, although he couldn't quite understand what Communism had to do with it.

"Lemme aks you a queshion, R Butt." King gestured to David to sit on a plastic chair on the other side of his desk.

"Sorry?"

"I said, lemme aks you a queshion." He glowered over his glasses.

"Oh, sure. You want to ask me a question?" David sat.

"Well, I'm glad your hearing is good and I don't have to SHOUT." A bead of sweat was forming at the end of the scar at the top of King's forehead.

"What the fuck are you doin' in my office?" He was straining to keep his control with this English idiot. "Is there actually anything at all in this email that is of any interest to me or my mother or my pizza delivery service or anyone else, or do you just have a particularly bad case of Cranial Rectosis!?"

"Look... at... the... video... sir." David calmly and carefully mouthed the words. This guy was really beginning to get under his skin.

"This'd better be good." He clicked on the video and the blurry images sprang to life. King sat back in his chair and drew a heavy breath of weary resignation. He had to follow procedure just in case his ass was on the line later for missing something important. The first few seconds were of some guy crying into the lens.

"Anyone translated this yet?"

"No, we thought you'd like to see it first. You'll see why in a minute." David was feeling more comfortably in control of the situation now. King continued to look bored. He stroked his chin, and then froze. Lurching forward he stabbed at the mouse to pause the video. He slid it back a fraction and clicked play again.

"What the fu...?" the word trailed off. He moved closer to the screen, squinting.

"I gotta get this enhanced." He punched a number on his telephone.

"Dick? Troy. Look, I got somethin' here that needs clarifying. I'm sending it over now. Looks like a cellphone job. Do what you can with it and get it back to me PDQ, okay?" he put the phone down and went to work on his computer.

"You got no plans this evening? Good. Get Ken in here."

Back at his desk, a post-it note stuck to David's screen read 'call Barbara'. He knew he didn't have time to do that right now, so he left it there to remind himself later. He also knew that Barbara would be really disappointed. Although David referred to her evening appointment as a class, it was not just some indulgent extra-curricular study she was doing, but important learning that would help Josh lead a happy life. He also knew that she wouldn't have time to arrange for Alicia, their Mexican maid, to stand in for him. And his iPhone was locked away in reception. Regulations didn't allow cellphones in the office, and he didn't have time right now to dash down there and send her a text. This job had already demanded a lot of trust on Barbara's part and put some strain on their relationship. He didn't want that to sully things between them, but what could he do?

"How did it go with the old man?" Ken asked cheerily. David clenched his fist and put his middle finger up.

"He wants us both in there—right now."

"Damn. I guess that's a result, but I was hoping the nighthawks would be pickin' it up from here." They each grabbed a notepad and headed for the Fishtank. One of the female translators waved them happily by as she cleared her desk to leave for the night.

David motioned for Ken to slow down as they walked.

"Ken, just so I know, is there some particular reason the old man is a prime candidate for anger-management classes?"

"Nobody told you?" Ken looked surprised, came to a halt and feigned checking something in his notebook in case they were being watched from the other end of the room.

"No. And that—thanks very much by the way—was the first time I've had a chance to have an intimate chat with the b—"

"It was the Gulf that did that to him."

"Oh. He saw a lot of action?" David's anger turned quickly to concern. "I saw the scar. Well, you can hardly miss it."

"No, exactly the opposite. He didn't see any action at all, and that's what's eatin' him up."

"How so?"

"Well, he comes from a military family. His father was a general or something. So their golden boy was destined for great things, as far as they were concerned. Problem was, King didn't make the grade at West Point. He ended up duckin' out, getting married and moving to Walla Walla—"

"He moved to Australia?"

"No. Walla Walla's in Washington State. They ended up running an orchard there. Anyway," Ken continued, "this military thing was bugging him, so when the Gulf War started in 1990, he got himself enlisted for whatever they'd let him do. By then, he was forty, so they found him a desk job in VII Corps. At that time, they weren't turning anyone away. So he was real glad when he got sent to Kuwait. One day, he hitched a ride in a Bradley. There was a truck in front, kicking up a shitload of dust, and the driver didn't see the mother of a pothole that sent them tits up and put the old man's head damn near through the roof. That's how he ended up with the zipperhead."

"Ouch!" David winced.

"Hurt his pride more than anything else. He had to sit out the rest of the war in the orchard. It made his brain a bit fuzzy for a while—kept forgetting things, slurring his speech and stuff." Ken motioned to David to start walking again.

"Anyways, 2003 comes along, and he seems to be okay, so he jumped at the opportunity to get a ride to Iraq. Same thing happened. The Humvee he was ridin' in hit a rock and, being a tall fucker, he hit the roof again. This time, it screwed up the base of his spine when he landed badly on an M16 rifle that was flying around in the cab. That's why he walks funny now."

"I haven't even seen him standing up, actually. He's always been sitting whenever I've passed by him."

"Well, that's a pleasure you got coming to you." Ken pushed the door of the Fishtank open and they each pulled up a chair.

Troy King had calmed down by the time they sat and leaned their elbows on his desk. He was looking pensively at his computer monitor. Slowly and deliberately, he took hold of the edges of the screen and turned it so they could all see the freeze frame that was flickering there. The image was of the middle section of the woman—the closest the camera had got to any of the bodies, and the clearest view of the wound that had caused her death. It appeared to be a clean circular hole, about two inches in diameter. How deep the wound extended into her body was not possible to see, as its sides were dull black and somewhat blurred.

"I wanna know what in hell did this." King turned to look at them both. "And I wanna know where it happened and why. I wanna know who did it and I wanna know who these people are. Clear?"

"But surely that's not part of our remit, sir." David felt uneasy about where this might be leading, but he was also concerned about getting home that night. The phone on King's desk rang. While King took the call, Ken leaned nonchalantly over, close to David, and said quietly, "For God's sake, David. Sierra – tango – foxtrot – uniform. Right?" NATO phonetic for 'Shut The Fuck Up'.

"Roger." Perhaps, David thought, this was not the time to assert his rights. It wouldn't take much for King to blow a fuse and send him packing, back to the UK. King replaced the handset.

"What?"

"Nothing, sir. What's the MO here?" David thought he might be impressed by a military-sounding acronym.

"MO?" King was starting to have serious doubts about this English guy. "The enhanced video won't be ready till tomorrow morning, for some goddamn reason. Staff shortages or somethin'. So, what we gonna do...?" He trailed off and looked at the screen again. David resisted the temptation to help out with an answer. A quick glance from Ken confirmed that staying shtum was the preferred option. "What we gonna do," King continued, "is take the rest of the day off and reconvene at 0900 tomorrow. I don't see why I should bust my ass if those pussies can't get their dickbeaters outta theirs."

David breathed a sigh of relief and reached to pick up his notepad from the desk, but King waved him back.

"I'm gettin' a ballistics guy over here to check out that hole." David went to pick up his notepad again, but the old man still hadn't finished.

"And tomorrow, we're gonna find out everything—and I mean everything—about this evolution, and that means the both of yous doing whatever it takes." He challenged them with a glare but neither said anything and he dismissed them with a wave of his hand. "Tomorrow morning, 9am sharp," he said, as they backed out the door, "an' I don't want any of that 911-type bullshit we was fed back then. I want the real facts!"

Despite his impatience, David was starting to think he understood this man whose derailed dreams had left him hurting from his head to his butt. He was still in there, fighting for his dignity. "You know, Ken, I think I 'misunderestimated' our Mr King. That was a speech worthy of your previous president."

Chapter 4

"Ladies and gentlemen, thank you for coming." The President smiled and buttoned his jacket against the light breeze on the White House South Lawn. It was the usual set piece press call, with the usual carefully selected and invited press pack held in place by the gaze of the security detail, carefully positioned just off-camera, either side of the lectern bearing the Presidential Seal. Only two mikes on long booms, covered with huge wind muffs carefully maneuvered by sound engineers with cans on their ears, bridged the gap between the lectern and the assembled journalists. The President preferred a clean top to the lectern rather than a jumble of branded microphones obscuring his chest. He also preferred to use the lawn rather than the claustrophobic Press Briefing Room, whenever the weather allowed. He waited until everyone was paying attention, glancing back momentarily to check that Griffin Kirkland was in position two feet behind him and slightly to his right so he would be neatly framed in shot on one side. His Chief of Staff would complete the picture on the other, with the White House Press Secretary lurking in the wings.

"Today, I am pleased to announce that there has been a major breakthrough in the Middle East Peace Process. Before I go on, I would like it to be known that I am particularly grateful to our Middle East Negotiating Team led by Senator Griffin Kirkland," he said, turning slightly to his right, "for their unwavering dedication and commitment, which has resulted in this landmark achievement." He smiled and raised his hand to his chest as cameras buzzed and clicked. "And it is only fair to add that I myself played little part in this. I want to be sure that you give proper credit where credit is due, when you report this." He looked down at his notes, then continued. "The past five years have been beset by problems, as you well know. Every hard-earned step forward has been accompanied by events and complications that have taken us a step backward at each stage in the peace process. Recent events have been particularly damaging. However…" Griffin Kirkland could scarcely hear the words—partly due to the breeze, but mainly because he had drifted into a euphoric state. The secret Westchester talks had gone surprisingly well, thanks to the unprecedented cooperation he'd skillfully engendered in the two other participants, despite a distinctly frosty start to the proceedings. He knew he had achieved what no other politician ever had or could have done, and he had done it at a time when it seemed that all hope of a settlement was lost. Now, he was receiving the recognition he had been working so desperately for, all his political life, from the President himself and in public. As the President spoke, all he could think of was how he was going to deal with the onslaught of acclaim, the interviews, the chat shows and the intense press focus that would follow. Sheryl had shown the now-familiar mix of intense excitement and jealous depression when Griffin had called her the previous day at their home in New Jersey, to tell her about the press call. He'd been excited about sharing the news with her, but had no illusions about how she would react. She was probably sitting in their home cinema right now, watching him on CNN with a half-finished bottle of bourbon next to her recliner. Either that or she was taking out her frustrations on their new interior designer. Oh, boy, could she decimate sensitive souls! But she wasn't going to stop him celebrating his personal victory with his team this evening. He was so pumped, he felt he could explode.

"…And so, ladies and gentlemen, thank you for your time, and I'll leave you in the very capable hands of Senator Kirkland, who can answer your questions." Kirkland brought himself rapidly back to the present. There was a smattering of applause and the press were already calling out their questions. The President turned and made a show of shaking Griffin's hand—smiling for the press yet not making eye contact with him. Then he turned and walked quickly back into the White House, leaving Griffin to step up to the lectern.

He had prepared well for the scripted questions and added little embellishment to the answers he trotted out in the smooth manner of the experienced sound-bite politician he had become. Something in the back of his mind was bugging him, though, and he wanted to get away from the lectern as soon as he could, and back into the White House. While he knew full well that the stage-managed handshake was just that—a presidential photo op—the speed of it, the averted eyes, the lack of *personal* engagement at such a historical moment, unsettled him. He tried to convince himself that he was being over-sensitive, but the feeling wouldn't go away. The Press Secretary must have sensed his uneasiness and he interjected with his usual closure. "Thank you, ladies and gentlemen, that's all we have time for right now. Senator Kirkland has another appointment, so, it's a wrap. Thank you all again." A mad flurry of questions ensued as Griffin turned and headed briskly into the White House, followed by the Secretary. His three minutes in the spotlight had somehow felt depressingly anti-climactic.

He hurried into the West Wing and found a friendly young face. Dan Zielinski had done some very competent organizing for him the previous year, so Griffin had put in a good word for him. Today, he was running the briefings schedule at the press event.

"Hey Dan!"

"Griffin! Good to see you. You did well out there!" They shook hands vigorously, Dan seeming even more preoccupied and wired than usual.

"When does he want to see me?"

Dan checked his organizer. "Um, well, you're not actually on the list. That's odd…" He checked again, then his face brightened. "Oh, I remember—he told me that you were going on vacation right after the press call. Lucky you. But, hey, you deserve it, after pulling off the big one!" He slapped Griffin on the back and beetled off down the corridor.

Vacation? *Vacation?* Something was very, very wrong. His stomach churning, Griffin strode from the White House Complex toward his car, dodging the few remaining journalists. He dialed his office on his cell phone as he walked.

"Hi, Judy. Any calls?"

"*Any calls?* Are you kidding? It's going ballistic here! We've got press from all over—"

"Well, that's great. To be expected, I guess." He kept his voice calm. "Anything from the President's office?"

"No, nothing, sir. Hey, we saw you on CNN—that was awesome! We're all really looking forward to—" He cancelled the call. What was going on? *Something* had happened. What wasn't he being told? He quickly dialed the number of the one person he could trust with his life. The call was answered almost immediately.

"Larry! Thank God you're there! Have you heard anything?"

"Hey, Griffin, long time no hear. How's Sheryl?"

"Fine, thanks, Larry. Look, something's come up. Can we talk?"

"Listen, that was a brilliant maneuver you pulled off with those guys in the Middle East. Fantastic! Now I hear you're heading off for a vacation. Excellent idea. Where are you headed? I hear there are some great deals to Bali, right now. You deserve a break after what you've done."

"Larry, didn't you hear a word I said?" *What the fuck… why did everyone think he was going on vacation?*

"Oh, sorry, Griffin. Terrible line. Call me at the office. We can talk then." The line went dead.

Griffin punched in Larry's office number.

"Hi, Myrtle, can you put me through to Larry?"

"Oh, is that you, Senator Kirkland? Hold the line, please." The line clicked and spun dead air for about half a nerve-wracking minute. As Griffin approached his car, his driver smiled and opened the door for him. He slipped into the tinted quiet of the back seat. A window separated him from the driver's seat, which he immediately slid shut. The line clicked again.

"Myrtle?"

"Senator Kirkland, are you still there?"

"Yes, of course, I'm still here. What's happening?" There was a short pause. He could hear her rustling some paper before she spoke again. "I am authorized

34

to inform you that Lawrence Davidson is no longer employed at this address. Should you wish to…" Griffin was stunned.

"Myrtle, it's me, for chrissakes! Griffin!"

"I am authorized—" He shut his cell phone and sat rigid in his seat. His mind was racing.

"Where to, sir?" The voice came over the car's intercom. Griffin leaned forward and slid the window open wide.

"3865 Little Creek Drive."

"Would that be out Galesville or Shady Side—somewhere east? I don't know it."

"Bel Aire." Griffin was thinking fast, and this conversation wasn't helping.

"Bel Aire?" The driver blurted out the words as if Griffin were asking him to drive to Mars. "Is that LA, Miami Beach…?"

"Yes, that's what I said. Bel Aire. It's just before Virginia Beach. Now, can we go, please?"

Their eyes met as the driver peered into the rear-view mirror. "Sir, I reckon that's over 200 miles away, and I wasn't planning on being way for the night—"

"Well, you are now. Get going."

CHAPTER 5

David had been relieved to get home at a reasonable time. Barbara had gone to her evening class on establishing an 'early intervention' program for Josh with the Down Syndrome Society up near Fort Reno. She'd been very glad to feel safe in the SUV on the 12-mile trip from Alcova Heights, and the sat nav had been an absolute necessity once she crossed the Chain Bridge. Now that she was getting more confident with driving, they agreed that it was much more useful (and cheaper) to keep the car at home during the day, and she would ferry him to and from nearby Virginia Square, where he could catch the Orange line Metro to and from work. They'd talked about the program over dinner until Barbara, tired after sleepless nights with Josh, went to bed. David stayed up, working on some ideas.

At 8.30 the following morning, Troy King was already at his desk when David arrived. He raised his head in acknowledgment as David passed the Fishtank, then continued making notes. Ken arrived ten minutes later.

"Coffee?" Ken's habitual greeting was followed by David's already habitual response.

"I'll come with you." They marched off to the coffee machine, which was in a tiny kitchen at the far end of the warren.

"I've been meaning to ask you," David said, "why so many empty booths? I reckon about half of them haven't been occupied since I started working here."

"Ah. I wondered when you'd ask." Ken selected his coffee fix almost as automatically as the machine made it. "You're thinking that, with this government's widely proclaimed 'war on terror', the place that's contracted to listen for any signs of anti-American activity from all over the world would be teeming with hundreds or even thousands of clones in identical uniforms and dark glasses riding round the office on a monorail. Yes?"

"Something like that, Dr Blofeld." David laughed, looking around and imagining the Bond scenario.

"Are you disappointed?"

"No, not really. It doesn't really matter to me; it just seems a bit strange."

"Cutbacks." Ken gave a dismissive wave of the hand. "At least, that's the official line, and I have no reason to doubt that. I mean, look at you."

"What are you suggesting? I'm cheap?"

"Of course you are. Lemme aks you a queshion." It was pure Troy King.

"What?"

"Do you have a college degree?" David was having trouble positioning the paper cup to catch the brown liquid that passed for coffee in this machine.

"No. I do have a college cert, though. What are you getting at? They chose me because I'm brilliant at what I do. What did they choose *you* for?"

"No, seriously. How hard was it for you to get this job? I bet it was dead easy."

"Well, actually, it was. I didn't have to try to get the job at all. They head-hunted me."

"Wow! Classic! And how old are you?" Ken made a theatrical gesture of surprise.

"Twenty-two and a half. What has all this got to do with it?"

"*And* a half! Jeez. And—don't tell me—they got you over here, did the 'limo from the airport' thing, gave you a couple of easy interviews…"

"Not easy, I can assure you!" This wasn't fun anymore. He'd actually found the interviews quite tough but, on reflection, maybe that was because he'd been so damned nervous at the time.

"And, lemme guess—now I could be wrong on this one—but I'd say, knowing that you're already married and all, they gave you the Alcova Heights house! Am I right or am I right?"

"Spot on." David was beginning to feel uncomfortable. Ken was looking more and more smug.

"Welcome to the first stage of the Empty Booth Syndrome and, by the way, you didn't hear this from me, okay?"

"Okay. But you can't leave me hanging now. What's going on here?"

"You've been suckered and you're gonna be exploited to hell while you work here. But it's not all bad. It just helps to know the score here, that's all." He checked his watch, then gestured to the small table and chairs in the corner. "Take five and I'll give you the scoop."

Ken leaned forward and, in a hushed conspiratorial tone, painted a picture that turned David's initial discomfort into a sinking sense of entrapment. Since the new administration had taken over, Ken explained, everything was being done as cheaply as possible at Arlington Online. The rights of employees had been stripped down to the minimum, and employer liability for staff was being effectively removed by shipping in foreign workers who had no rights as citizens beyond any contract that was in force. Contracts were short, mostly six months, so Ken had been impressed that David had been given a two-year run. However, he didn't think that there was any real possibility of David completing two years as they were working in an extremely volatile environment, where technology was changing almost daily and no one employee could be trusted with too much information. That made them vulnerable to 'unhealthy interference' so, in order to reduce that risk, they made sure that there were reasons to fire people at will, and it was much easier to fire and remove an alien from the workplace and the country than it was to fire a national. If anyone wanted to make an unfair dismissal claim, they'd most likely be broke before they passed the first of many expensive legal hurdles and, anyway, most of the people they hired were young, one-trick-ponies who were wet behind the ears.

"How's your coffee?" Ken asked. David seemed transfixed by his mug.

"Bitter."

Ken went on to explain that everyone was thoroughly checked out before they were approached, and assessments were made as to whether there'd be any resistance to the kind of manipulation they intended to exercise on them. They only considered employing tech heads like David, for instance, when they were satisfied that their political interests and knowledge didn't extend beyond being bored by TV news. So, yes, David was cheap for Arlington Online, and they could be sure that he would earn every penny he made for as long as he was needed. For a start, he was renting a house that they owned, so he was paying a portion of his wages back to them. They also had his full attention and commitment for the time he was employed there because, before he entered the country, his vulnerability was made clear to him by Immigration and Homeland Security. Additionally, Arlington Online's ace-in-the-hole to ensure that he wouldn't give them any trouble was, unfortunately, his son, Josh. It was clear to them that the availability of cutting-edge expertise for Josh in Washington, as opposed to the less-than-superb help he and Barbara could get in the UK, gave David yet another very clear reason for not rocking the boat.

Shit! David was furious but he decided not to mention any of this to Barbara; he'd handle it himself. "Why are you telling me all this now?"

"Well, I liked the way you handled the old man yesterday. You didn't let him get to you, which kinda earned you a few respect points, I guess."

"I suppose I should be flattered, but somehow I don't feel like celebrating." He thought for a minute. "How come *you're* still here, after three years?"

"That's simple. I got a better contract before the rot set in, I'm an American national and, well, I know too much now, and they know that."

The old digital clock by the coffee machine flapped over to 08.59.

"We'd better get in there," Ken said.

"Okay. Here we go."

As they walked toward the Fishtank, Ken quietly sang 'do not forsake me, oh my darling' from *High Noon*.

"Notepads at dawn," David mumbled, in an effort to lighten his mood.

✳✳✳

"Good mornin', genlmen. Siddown. Take a look at this." King had got the enhanced video back and had already picked out several frames that he'd copied and cascaded onto his desktop.

"I got good news and I got bad news. Good news is we can now see a hell

38

of a lot more detail than we could yesterday. Bad news is they ain't gonna send us a ballistics guy. I don't know how they expect us to do our job without the proper information but that's just the way it is. Anyways, they're sending some other so-called experts down from Fort Fumble—that's The Pentagon," he explained, nodding to David, "later this mornin'." He looked at his notepad, and then at the screen. "Look, this don't really add up to a whole lot of sense, at the moment, with the clothes and all, and that hole… but I reckon this is Afghanistan, all the same. Ken, get Gulnaz in here and we'll see if she can figure out what this guy at the beginnin' of the clip is whinin' about."

As Ken left the office, King turned to David. "R Butt, I want to know everything we can know about that student in Israel, where he found this clip, why he sent it to his friend in Oxford, and I wanna know if he is any sort of terrorist under his milk-n-honey exterior." He paused. "And then I wanna know everything there is to know about this Madoowbe character or whatever he's called, his daddy and any known associates he may have in the UK, Somalia and here."

"Got that, sir," said David.

"Well, just get on with it then. I'll see you this afternoon."

"No, what I meant was, I've got that. I've done it already."

King sat up straight. "What the hell d'you mean, you've done it? When? You only just got here and you've been pissing around that damn coffee machine gassin' with that faggot like some old fishwife." He peered at David suspiciously. "Have you got a terminal down there? Or have you fixed up the coffee machine with a pipe to The Beast?" The Beast was a highly sophisticated heavy-duty mainframe computer linked to everything the Pentagon and the government were prepared to let Arlington see—as well as a whole bunch of their own purpose-built snooping software and databases. It was generally considered to be a far-fetched rumor because it was supposed to be able to do things that were, as far as leading computer experts were concerned, beyond the physical capabilities of the available technology. Rumor also had it that the CIA funded its development with cash diverted from some secret ops in South America, to further embarrass the FBI who were smarting from the uselessness of their own expensive version of the same thing, called Carnivore. As far as they knew, nothing as powerful or invasive as The Beast existed anywhere in the world outside of that office block—and they did seem to know a hell of a lot.

"No, I did it last night, at home."

"You're shittin' me. Now look here, R Butt, if you've figured out some fancy way to hack into The Beast from outside, and I very much doubt that you're that smart, you'd better tell me right now or you're gonna be well and truly fried. I'm waitin', boy." King re-arranged himself on his chair and eyeballed David.

"Er, I actually did it on my iPhone… sir." *Always good to add 'sir' in a tight situation.*

"You did it on *what!?*"

"My iPhone, sir." David felt a surge of unstoppable satisfaction welling up inside him. He couldn't help smiling. He knew he'd worked out everything that King needed to know while he was lying on his couch watching a late-night movie.

"Is there something funny here, R Butt? Because, if there is, I sure could do with a laugh right now." David stifled an urge to laugh, quickly disguising a snort as a sneeze.

"Pardon me." He took a handkerchief out of his pocket and blew his nose. "Sir, this is why they hired me. I can do this stuff. It was simple. I just used some of my Twitter and Facebook identities, a few apps I developed, some advanced Google searches linked to Twitter and other Twitter-related free facilities, LinkedIn and a couple more academic and industry search facilities, downloaded it, processed it with my own cross-referencing software on my laptop, printed it out and… Bingo. Here it all is." He produced a few sheets of paper he'd folded into his notepad and placed them on King's desk.

Ignoring the sheets of paper, King looked hard at David. "Show me."

"It's all here, sir."

"No, I mean, show me what you did."

"I can't. Sorry."

"Show me how you did it." The scar seemed to be pulsating.

"I really wish I could sir." *This is wonderful*, he thought.

"That's an order, R Butt, and you'd better comply with it right now or you're gonna be seriously X Butt. You clear on that?"

"Yes, sir. That's clear, but unfortunately, I can't show you. It's out of my control."

"Don't… " Mr King squirmed in his seat, "Don't you dare fuck with me R Butt. I've killed for less than this. You don't want me to—"

"Regulations." David interjected before his guts were virtually scrambled.

"What?" King couldn't believe that this little jumped-up college kid was trying to run rings around him.

"My iPhone is locked away in reception because the regulations of this company don't allow me to bring it into the office."

With perfect timing, Ken arrived back at the office, followed by a middle-aged woman. To David, she had a sophisticated air. She had dark eyes, deep red lipstick, olive skin and dark brown, almost black, hair. Despite appearing a little overweight, she was very attractive. She was smartly dressed in a well-cut suit that he thought looked expensive. She and Ken waited expectantly as King pushed the folded sheets of paper back to David. "Hold on to those for now."

David put them back inside his notebook.

"David, meet Gulnaz. Gulnaz, David." David stood, they shook hands and exchanged smiles. King's tone transformed immediately to one of polite consideration.

"Gulnaz, we got a bit of a situation here and I'm kinda hoping you can help us out."

"Of course, sir. How can I help?" Her Afghan accent was muted and her words clear in a way that suggested she'd been educated in the West.

"I'm firing a video over to you right now." King tapped some keys. "I want you to take a look at it. I gotta hunch that it's Afghan. If that's in the affirmative, I want a translation of everything voice-wise." He turned to face her. "It's not pretty, but do your thing…" She nodded and headed back to her booth. Taking a deep breath, King brought his attention back to David and Ken.

"R Butt, I want to know everything we can know about that student in Israel, where he found this clip, why he sent it to his friend in Oxford, and I wanna know if he is any sort of terrorist under his milk-n-honey exterior. And then, I wanna know everything there is to know about this Madoowbe character or whatever he is called, his daddy and any known associates he may have in the UK, Somalia and here." David did a double-take. *Have I got a bad case of déjà-vu, or did he say those exact same words to me less than five minutes ago?* He could only guess that King didn't want to explain to Ken what he had just told him about his iPhone while Ken was out of the office. He searched King's face for a sign, some clue as to whether he was doing this intentionally or if he had temporarily lost it. King gave nothing away, so he played along.

"Yes, sir. I'll get onto it right away."

"Show me what you got at the end of play today." Then, turning to Ken, he said, "Just hold off and see if Gulnaz gives us the nod on Afghanistan. As soon as we know, I want you to identify the location where that clip was shot. If necessary, talk to our guys on the ground over there but do not—and I repeat, do not—send them the video or show them anything on those people we seen there. The only things they can see are the enhanced frames with buildings and mountains. No people. You got that?"

"Got it, sir."

"Okay, genlmen, let's do this. Reconvene 1645 hours, Meeting Room Four." Ken and David glanced at each other, stood up simultaneously and left the Fishtank, almost colliding at the door. The walk back to their booths was becoming a regular opportunity for some friendly banter.

"I think that was a 'high-five moment', wasn't it, Ken?"

"I guess, but you're English."

"Maybe I should have just saluted."

"You're gonna get yourself in some deep shit, man."

David spent the rest of the morning checking his emails, cruising the Internet, reading a novel and taking a long lunch break. Since this video clip was obviously a priority, he didn't want to log any activity on the system that would suggest that he was working on something else, so he kept it simple, and even re-did some of the more obvious parts of his previous night's work.

Gulnaz confirmed that the language in most of the clip was Pashto—the official language of Afghanistan, spoken by about 35% of the population. Because of that, she had initially thought that the incident was more likely to have occurred in south or central Afghanistan, where Pashto is most widely spoken, although it could have been in the north because many families from the south had relocated there in recent years. Gulnaz also detected what she thought was Uzbek being spoken, at one point, when the dark waistcoat was visible, although it was virtually incomprehensible, muffled as it was by a gust of wind. That small piece of information was useful for Ken, though; if it was indeed Uzbek, it almost definitely placed the incident in northern Afghanistan, since the small percentage of Afghans who spoke Uzbek were all around the border with Uzbekistan. Ken had also noticed that the waistcoat had a small badge with an image of a face clipped onto it. There was some writing that was blurred by the movement, around the face. It looked more as if it came from the US than from the local market, suggesting the close proximity of a US military base. As part of a program to 'win hearts and minds', young people living near bases were often given small items and sweets that were regarded as a big status symbol among their peers, though they were often deeply disapproved of by their elders.

By early afternoon, they had gathered most of the information King had asked for. Gulnaz had translated and typed up a complete account of the voice, and even identified the type of jeep that was fleetingly seen, based on the wheel arch and front-wing detail. It was a UAZ Hunter model that Russia had shipped by the thousand from the town of Ulyanovsk in 2004. But she was confused by the man at the beginning of the clip, and the others standing and looking at the bodies. They weren't wearing the typical Afghan *kurta*—a long tunic often covered by a sleeveless jacket—or baggy trousers. She hadn't seen the long robes and cloth headgear before but, as she explained, Afghanistan was a big country with many cultures and religions, and she only really knew the south of the country where she'd been brought up.

While David and Ken were comparing notes, David glanced up and noticed two men in suits going into the Fishtank. "Must be those 'experts' the old man mentioned," he said, watching them as they stood talking to King from the other side of his desk.

He turned back to Ken. "You having any luck pinpointing that mountain?" Ken muttered something in response but David was distracted by what was happening in the Fishtank. One of the men was leaning forward on King's desk, while King was jabbing his finger at the air between them.

"Hey, Ken. Look at this." Ken raised his head over the partition and they watched as a blazing row played out silently at the other end of the warren. At one point, both of the visitors looked straight at them. Ken ducked down and David lowered his head in mock concentration. It was only when they heard the door of the Fishtank slam shut that they dared to steal another furtive look. King was sitting in his usual place, looking as if nothing had happened.

"That mountain, yes..." Ken said. "Could be anywhere in this region, if we're right about it being in the north of the country." He had drawn a line around an area on a map of the region.

"How many square miles would that cover, do you think?" asked David.

"Oh, about 80,000."

"Brilliant, but I don't think we'll be able to narrow it down to anything useful by 'end of play'." David glanced at his notes. "I have a suggestion," he said, returning to the map.

"Okay, maestro, hit me with it."

"The American bases. Check around those."

"Doooh." Ken winced dramatically and slapped his forehead. "You're one clever cookie. Even Homer Simpson couldn't have figured that out!"

"I'm worth every penny they pay me, right?"

Ken switched on another screen—one of six that he'd set up for viewing and analyzing vast ranges of data. Over the three years he's been there, he'd developed an intricate system that no one else would have been able to figure out.

"We've just got one ISAF base—a small one, in the RCN, apparently. Okay, so that's the International Security Assistance Force, but what the fuck does that second acronym stand for?" Ken was feeling under pressure as their deadline came closer. He checked the acronym on Google. "Oh, simple— Regional Command North. Do you think that's enough information to keep the old man's blood pressure down, or should we contact them and see if they can get us some visuals? That's if ISAF can find the damn mountain..."

"It's probably enough for now and, anyway, we don't know what those two suits gave him. Did you recognize either of them?"

"No, never seen 'em before." He copied down the name of the base. "Mazar-e-Sharif. I've heard of that place. Around there, and especially over in Kunduz, they've had a shitload of action."

David checked his watch. "It's 4.40. We'd better show him what we've got. Do you think we can risk doing that, or do you think we can risk not doing that?" Ken shrugged.

"We've all got to die at some point." They called Gulnaz over and made their way to the meeting room.

CHAPTER 6

It was only as the car was speeding over the Potomac that Griffin finally managed to calm down and start thinking. *Am I getting paranoid? I could end up looking really stupid if I don't handle this right. Am I jumping to crazy conclusions?* He was beginning to realize that his fear of being wrong was getting in the way of any logic that might explain this bizarre situation. He *had* to think clearly. He'd just delivered a ground-breaking speech on the greatest achievement of his life, in the presence of, and with the seeming endorsement and support of, the President. Within seconds of delivering it, it seemed as if he'd been cut adrift, isolated. The press was all over the story, digesting every detail and spewing it out to every news channel, newspaper and website worldwide at this very moment. Yet here he was, sitting alone in his car heading for Bel Aire. *No, no, no!*

"Hey!" He rapped hard on the interconnecting window. They were passing the Pentagon. "Hang a right here!"

"But, sir—" They were virtually at the junction.

"*HERE,* God dammit!" The car lurched violently as the driver quickly switched lanes off the Shirley Memorial Highway and onto the slip road down onto the South Washington Boulevard. Griffin banged his head on the side window.

"Sorry, sir." The driver glanced nervously in the rear view mirror. Griffin waved him off, rubbing his head, lost in thought.

"It's okay. Look, forget it. Take me back to the office, and step on it."

"You got it, sir." Keen to compensate for possibly injuring a very popular senator—and very conscious of the fact that this one had just shaken hands with the President—the driver floored the Lincoln Sedan. The car shot down the ramp, weaving erratically through the late afternoon traffic. The driver swung alarmingly to the right to join the Columbia Pike, so he could get on to Washington Boulevard back toward the Arlington Memorial Bridge. As he barreled through the junction, the car under-steered. He pulled hard at the wheel—too hard. The rear end swung out and slammed into the rear wing of an SUV coming from the opposite direction. The SUV swung wildly and screeched to a halt, as did Griffin's car.

This isn't happening! Griffin Kirkland was sweating profusely now. "Deal with it!" he shouted at the driver, who was already scrambling out of the car. He sprinted across the road toward the driver of the SUV—a young woman who was screaming at him as she ran round to open the back door, and struggled with the straps securing her baby in its car seat. From where he sat, Griffin observed the ensuing argument, the angry exchange of details, with insurance dockets held down on the hood of the SUV and licenses compared, but his mind was elsewhere.

He figured that whatever was going on at the White House, only a few people knew about it and, for now, it was best that he kept to the schedule that his secretary had arranged. Bel Aire would have to wait. He was under the press spotlight and anything he did now that was out of character would only attract unwanted attention. He had to go back to the office, celebrate with his team and, no doubt, provide a few more 'insider details' to his close press contacts there, hoping for a scoop. He'd been dreaming of this event for weeks. The last thing he'd expected was the gut-wrenching nausea he felt now.

The driver closed his door carefully and turned in his seat toward Griffin.

"Sir, I must apologize for—"

"The office," Griffin cut in, "in silence, and in one piece." Griffin watched from the privacy of his tinted world as the young mother closed the rear door of the SUV, glanced at the crumpled rear wing, returned to the driver's seat and slammed the door.

"And one more thing." He looked preoccupied, his mind still processing. "That address I gave you earlier—you didn't log it, did you?"

"No, sir."

"Forget you ever heard it. That's if you want to keep your job. Clear?"

"Yes, sir."

Griffin spent the early evening on auto-pilot. He pressed the flesh with his staff, his 'inner circle' of journalists and some colleagues and their wives— all of whom were gushing with pleasure to be present at such an auspicious gathering. He gave a well-received short speech, thanking everyone who had 'made this day possible'. He smiled, he laughed, he felt nothing.

As soon as he'd done what he felt was necessary, he made his excuses and headed back to the apartment on tenth that he and Sheryl had bought when he first starting making extended visits to the Capitol. He needed to disappear off the radar for a while, so the Sedan and driver weren't an option. He decided to walk. It would help clear his head. He stopped at an ATM on the way, and drew out as much cash as the machine would give him in one go. At the apartment, he changed into casual clothes, micro-waved half a pizza, sliced it and ate as he checked his mail, caught up with the news on TV and packed an overnight bag. Everything was normal, which he found strangely unnerving. His gut had been telling him that everything was far from normal, and he'd feel a lot better once he'd figured out what the fuck was going on. So far, though, he had absolutely nothing to go on.

He made sure that no one saw him leave the apartment and took the elevator down to the garage, where he slid the dust sheet off his pride and joy. His 1995 Aston Martin V8 Vantage V550 was one of only 80 hand-built specimens with a manual shift six-speed gearbox and left-hand drive ever produced. It was magnificent—finished in Buckinghamshire green, with magnolia piped dark-green leather upholstery. It was also a brute of a car to drive; its twin-supercharged 550 bhp engine blasted it from 0 to 60mph in just over four seconds, and it had a top speed in excess of 180mph. He'd bought it from a banker friend who'd run unto some trouble as the worldwide recession kicked in, and he'd hardly ever driven it. It only had 12,000 miles on the clock and was still in showroom condition. The parking lights flashed as he clicked the remote and he slung his bag into the trunk. In the confined concrete space of the garage, the engine sounded like a bomb going off when he started it, and even though he kept the revs as low as possible as the car rumbled throatily toward the exit, he imagined he could be heard ten blocks away. *Hardly inconspicuous*, he thought, *but at least it's off the system.*

Throughout his lifetime, Griffin hadn't expended a lot of energy trying not to be noticed. Now that he wanted to be invisible, he could see that it wasn't that easy to do. His official sedan had a tracking device, the driver logged all journeys, his secretary knew where he was most of the time, and his cell phone, credit cards and any computer access he had all revealed his location, purchases and conversations. What else could be traced? He wasn't sure. Up to now, he'd never been interested. Although he was now a world-renowned public figure, he was an amateur when it came to his own privacy.

The Aston Martin throbbed impatiently along the streets. Its angry growl echoed back at him off glass-clad office blocks, as he worked his way self-consciously through the business area toward the George Mason Memorial Bridge. It was nearly 11pm when he passed the Pentagon for the second time that day, on the Interstate heading toward Springfield. Only then could he allow both himself and the V8 to start breathing normally again.

He flicked through some radio stations looking for classical music. Despite his bourgeoning concerns, it felt good to be on the road, on his own. He found some peace in the rhythmic strobing of the streetlights across the car as he traveled. As he left the city behind, he welcomed the enveloping darkness. He switched the radio off, preferring to hear the steady hum of the engine as he concentrated on the patch of road illuminated by his headlights and tried to avoid looking into the glare of oncoming vehicles. By 12.30, the stresses of the day were catching up with him. He was tired and this wasn't a car he wanted to make any mistakes with, so he pulled in to the car park of an all-night family restaurant, just off the highway at Mechanicsville, north-east of Richmond. He drove slowly past it to check it out. The place was virtually empty. All the same, he parked a good distance away from the building—as much to avoid being heard as being seen. The late-night staff made a valiant effort in serving him their 'special' grilled chicken baby spinach salad 'with hard-boiled egg wedges and a special warm bacon dressing on the side'. The plump, friendly server assured him that "the food here is always well-cooked" and that he was especially fortunate because this was a 'menu test store for the company', which meant they offered entrees that he wouldn't find at their other outlets. Griffin was quietly pleased to hear all this detail—not for the information she was giving him, but because her flat delivery and obvious disinterest in him made it clear that she had no idea who he was.

"Would you like a coffee with that?" Suddenly, Griffin felt like laying his head on the table and falling asleep.

"Yes, thanks."

"Latte, americano, cappuccino, espresso, mocha, macchiato—?"

"Coffee." The server seemed about to protest but settled for a "thank you, sir" as she ticked a box on her menu slip, sighed and waddled back to the counter where she barked the order to the lethargic kitchen staff three feet behind her.

Maybe it was the stress of the day, or it could have been the warm bacon dressing, but as soon as he'd finished his meal, Griffin felt his intestines heave alarmingly. He made a quick exit with his coffee in a paper cup, and farted all the way back to his car. He sat there for a while, waiting for his coffee to cool and debating whether or not he should visit the washroom.

"Excuse me, sir." He was startled by someone knocking on the window. Opening his eyes, he checked his watch: 2.30am. Damn. He'd fallen asleep.

"Excuse me, sir." The voice came again, insistent. A State Trooper was bending down, peering at him with great interest. Griffin lowered the window. "It's kinda late to be sittin' out here, ain't it, sir?" He casually checked out the car's lush interior, and the cold cup of coffee nestling in Griffin's crotch.

"I beg your pardon, officer, I must've fallen asleep."

"That would appear to be the case, sir." He paused as Griffin wiped the grogginess from his eyes and sat up. "Sir, is this your car?"

Here we go. Having reached such an elevated position in society, Griffin had a particular dislike for petty officialdom, and didn't really think that any of its tedious procedures should apply to him. He hadn't dealt with any basic paperwork for years, he'd never taken his driver's license out of his wallet before, and he didn't even know what his insurance certificate looked like. Luckily, Sheryl was thorough and everything was as it should be and in its correct place, so he was able to show the officer everything he asked for, and he managed to stay calm.

"Says here that this car is insured by one Griffin Kirkland. Is that you, sir?"

"Yes it is, officer."

The officer chuckled. "Hey, ain't that the same name as that guy who just done that deal in the Middle East?"

"The very same."

"Well, you're in good company, sir. I gotta take my hat off to that guy." He handed the paperwork back through the window. "You goin' far tonight, sir?"

"Not much further. I just have to get to my hotel at Virginia Beach."

"Well, you drive carefully, sir, and make sure you stay alert. I'd sure hate to have to make an insurance claim if this beauty was mine. Good night to you, sir." Griffin gave a weary sigh of relief as the trooper sauntered back to his cruiser. He had not been recognized, thanks to the media's portrayal of him as a cosseted senator who never had to drive himself anywhere.

He waited for the cruiser to disappear from sight before starting his engine and heading back toward the highway.

The following morning, he woke early, ate a light breakfast, paid cash for his room and headed for Little Creek Drive. The house at 3865 was a modest home of early 1900s vintage, set in a lightly wooded area next to a creek that wound its way lazily to the private moorings at Port Virginia and then out to sea. Larry Davidson had bought it over 30 years ago as a haven to escape to when things got too hectic in Washington. Back then, it had been left to rot by an old couple who had relocated to a nursing home. Larry had spent ten years lovingly restoring its original colonial character, and now it was resplendent in its sculptured gardens and it had its own little jetty where Larry kept a small boat for shopping trips or for visiting neighbors.

"Evelyn? Are you in?" Larry and his wife had been close friends of his for longer than Griffin could remember and he'd worked with Larry on numerous projects since entering politics. Griffin could always rely on his strength, vision, character, integrity and, above all, his connections, to get things done and to help him along in his career. He was never quite sure what, exactly, Larry did. His job description seemed to change on a regular basis but, in Griffin's experience, he was a rare and valuable find. He was the best White House fixer he'd ever found, and a solid friend, with an exceptionally strong and loving wife. On their frequent visits to this place, Evelyn had always been there for Sheryl, whose life as a politician's wife was fraught with unfamiliar demands, frustrations and, for Sheryl, a crushing loss of personal identity that regularly jeopardized their relationship. Larry and Evelyn had always been the port they'd sought out in every storm.

"Come in, Griff, the door's open." That wasn't unusual. He'd never known it to be locked. What was unusual was that Evelyn hadn't come to the door to welcome him, as soon as she heard him arrive. Her voice sounded weak and distant. He walked through to the kitchen, then out to the porch at the back, where he found her sitting on a bench, cradling a cup in her hands, her elbows resting on the rough wooden table that had been the site of so many wonderful evening meals.

"Hi, Ev. I see you're wasting no time taking in this beautiful morning." He looked toward the creek, where a green heron stood motionless in the shallows, head cocked slightly to one side. It made Griffin suddenly aware that he was no longer in the city, with its crude buildings and brutish pace. Here, there was silence that awoke a different awareness in all but the most insensitive. Somehow, in its stillness, it spoke to him so much louder than the city. This felt right, balanced and beautifully natural, whereas the city was just a glaring symptom of man's insanity. *Everyone needs this.* It was only after this reflective pause, this tiny but powerful adjustment that created an almost physical change in him, that he could really see her.

She looked wrecked. Her eyes were red, her grey hair wild. She didn't turn to look at him, but gazed blankly toward the creek. His heart surged.

"Evelyn? What's happened? Where's Larry?" She turned to face him. He was shocked to see that her face was creased up with pain. She went to speak, her mouth quivered but no sound came. All she could do was slowly turn her head from side to side, and try to hold back the storm of grief welling up inside. He sat down beside her and wrapped his arms around her. She collapsed into his embrace and stayed silent and still. This wasn't the time to ask her what awful thing had happened. This was a time to simply hold her, and just be there for her, for a change.

They sat there for what seemed like an eternity. Time stopped. Griffin's brain was paralyzed. He couldn't process this and everything else that had happened in the past 24 hours. He stopped trying. For a while, Griffin wasn't there. For a while, there were just two souls, lost on a bench overlooking a creek, beyond the churning madness and noise called life.

But life came back, unstoppable with all its demands, its confusion, its pain. And unanswered questions.

"He's gone, Griff. Where did he go?"

"I didn't know… I don't know, Ev."

"Will I ever see him again? He doesn't answer."

"What?" Griffin was struggling now, to find words that were of any use at all. "I'm sorry, Ev."

"Is he alive? Have they done something to him?" Griffin's chest hurt. He searched the sky and the porch, the bench, the jetty, the creek—*anything* that would give him any answer at all. None came.

Gradually, he started to come around. He had no answers, but at last the fight was beginning to return as the shock was beginning to wane. He looked around the porch. *Am I paranoid, or should I be?* He wasn't about to take any chances.

"Ev, come with me." He coaxed her gently from the bench, and she let him support her as they walked together to the jetty. Having helped her climb into the boat with him, he pushed off, yanking the outboard into life as soon as they were clear. They cruised in silence down the creek, Evelyn gazing dully at the water as they passed the comfortable homes that cosseted their neighbors in tranquility. One of them was fishing. He waved them by. Another was mowing his lawn. The creek eventually flowed into a lagoon, about a quarter of a mile wide, where Griffin steered the boat to the centre and cut the motor.

"Ev, I spoke to Larry yesterday on a restricted cell phone number he gave me." She looked at him with pleading eyes. "He sounded fine, just the same as always. The same Larry."

"But he's gone, Griff. Gone." The word fell from her mouth like a lead weight. "He's never been *Gone* before. He's always been here, even when he was somewhere else." He knew exactly what she meant. Larry always left strong traces, permanent marks, deep feelings, unavoidable evidence of his intelligent, compassionate and humorous presence. Sheryl and he had often laughed about his *Pure Larryness*—his unique character that, once it had visited your life, you would never quite be able to define and yet you'd definitely never forget. It made him smile, just thinking about it. But that phone call the day before— he realized now that it had lacked that Pure Larryness. It was the first time he could ever recall not having a proper conversation with him. They hadn't connected. Something inside him had told him that at the time, but he'd been so preoccupied with the day's events that he hadn't let that small realization surface in his conscious mind. What was that banal chat about? He gradually recalled the conversation. And then there was that nonsense call to his office...

"What was Larry working on when you last saw him?" Evelyn regarded him with something bordering on suspicion.

"You know he would never tell me, Griff. He couldn't, and I knew that. I never asked him." She looked at him quizzically. "Why are you asking me this? You know better than that."

"Straws… just clutching at straws." He turned to face her. "I'm sorry, Ev. All of a sudden I have absolutely no idea what's going on—and now I'm wondering if I ever did, because if I had known, I'd surely have seen something coming. Wouldn't I?" She turned her head away to the horizon. He followed her gaze, then scanned the shoreline in the distance. The houses, boats at their moorings, the sky itself—all seemed to be watching, disguised as a tranquil idyll, as they drifted without power in the middle of the lagoon.

"He needs my help." The words came from Griffin's mouth involuntarily, before he had a chance to completely formulate the thoughts that prompted them. Evelyn glanced at him but said nothing. She dropped her head into her hands and stared at her feet. The boat swayed gently as the waves slapped against the hull with a dull, hollow rhythm. Evelyn's silence made Griffin self-conscious. He knew what she was thinking, and he knew that she was right. How preposterous of him to think that Larry could possibly need his help. Needy, ambitious Griffin, weak Griffin, social-climbing Griffin, shallow and grabby Griffin. Did she even think of him as 'friend Griffin'? Larry had always been the rock, the advisor, the helper. Griffin didn't fit that role, in her eyes, however much she liked him. No, she was alone. Larry was Gone.

"I know. I know." Griffin sighed. He knew that saying such things carried no credibility for Evelyn, and she didn't need platitudes and crass, unfounded assurances. She deserved so much more than that. He was a hollow shell, searching in a void. *Giving* was foreign territory for him, and it hit him like a slap at that moment. All his life he'd been taking, bleeding every last drop out of everything that was good, attractive and nurturing—just for himself. He had drawn in only those who would satisfy his insatiable appetite for popularity, his star career, his massive ego. He had used those closest to him in the most heartless and ruthless ways simply to further his own path to glory. Even the successful peace talks for which he'd just received international acclaim had been manipulated and engineered with their main focus on him. Did he really, honestly give a damn about those bickering, vicious, argumentative, conniving, slippery, inflexible, self-serving politicians and armed groups that he had so skillfully steered to a delicate stalemate with all its suppressed suspicion and aggression? Clearly, the answer was in the question.

Loss is a cruel and hard space; he could see that in Evelyn's downcast eyes. There was agony there, but there was also anger, and a kind of cold understanding that only she could know. It enveloped an arid loneliness that could never be completely taken from her, even if Larry were to walk back into their home right now, simply because she had come to know it, and now it was permanently etched deep inside her. That was the second thing that Griffin realized at that moment: he had never *experienced* loss. Yes, he had lost his parents, he had lost battles in his political career, he had lost some money recently in a commercial deal that went bad, but he had never *experienced* loss. Loss, to him, had always been like figures on a balance sheet. It was something he understood, and that just happened now and then. You expect your parents to die when they get old. Political battles are won and lost, just like money. But real loss? That was different. This was different. Evelyn was showing him that right now.

Had he always been like this? He searched his mind and was, for the first time, ashamed at what he saw. His life had been a seamless progression of indulgences dressed up to please and impress. Thinking of his early campaigning days, he could only remember debate being an intellectual battle to be won. The real human values, passions, feelings and needs that sprang from the lives of others, and that underpinned his arguments, were simply factors to consider, but they'd never touched him emotionally. He'd used ideals that seemed popular, in order to gain support, but he'd never felt impassioned about those ideals. Had he ever actually believed them? None of the ideals he preached at a young age were based on anything more than theory and the popularity he gained from subverting middle-class values—the easy targets of naïve adolescent revolt. Not knowing any better at the beginning, and not choosing to learn from real-life challenges, he had solidified his belief in his own image as the years passed. His image had become fact; it *was* him. Building, massaging and adjusting his 'ideals of convenience' with age, events and an ever deeper knowledge of government, along with his deft handling of people, had stood him in good stead. Yet now he felt empty and, worse still, completely inadequate. This one event made it very clear that he had much to learn, and he felt a deep weariness seep through his limbs. It would be a daunting task to become truly worthy of Evelyn's respect and friendship, let alone Sheryl's—not to mention his constituents' and the countless other people who admired and believed in Senator Griffin Kirkland.

"Ev." He was struggling. "Let me try." He knew it didn't make a lot of sense. He felt like a child.

Evelyn watched him struggle, and although she felt some pity for him, she could not be concerned with his feelings now, when a much greater man—her husband—was missing. She needed all the strength she could muster, and she needed extraordinary strength from others to help her through this. In her mind, Griffin was not sophisticated enough to figure out the machinations of the powerful, focused and extremely clever men who were passionately driven by a political vision that they fought to realize, whatever the cost. Griffin was just a clumsy front man, a clown for the media, blindfolded and easily manipulated by such men. And Griffin *had* no passion beyond himself. The sad thing was that Griffin also seemed incapable of seeing any of this. Maybe it was just as well. She didn't think he could survive—politically or emotionally—if he discovered the reality of his life.

Griffin drew a deep breath and re-started the outboard. A single gannet flew low over them as he steered the boat toward the creek.

"That's a good sign," remarked Evelyn, "I haven't seen one of those for ages. Larry thought they must have moved further south for better fishing."

Chapter 7

"Okay genlmen—and lady. It's showtime. What have we got?" Troy King had gathered everyone in a meeting room with a large table, projection screen and assorted computers around its perimcter. As usual, King had got there first. David, Ken and Gulnaz took their places around the table, arranging files, photographs and printouts in neat piles in front of them. Ken started.

"Sir, you were right about Afghanistan. We've been able to place the video in the RCN—that's Regional Command North—"

"I know where that is." King interjected impatiently. Ken looked at his notes and stumbled on.

"...the RCN. There's an ISAF base in the region."

"I know that too, Ken. Where was the video shot?"

"We can't pinpoint it exactly, but—"

"Ken, lemme aks you. What have you been doing all day?"

"If you'll permit me, sir, I have more."

"Well, I'm glad. Please continue." King rolled a pencil between his fingers and watched Ken pull up a map on the projection screen.

"We are sure that the video was shot in this mountainous region." He circled a small area with his hand.

"What makes you so sure?"

"The buildings, sir. From what we can ascertain from the little detail shown on the clip, we have identified the style of building and the building materials as being from one of 25 villages. However," he went on quickly before King could interject, "the presence of the vehicle suggests that we're looking at one of these five villages only."

"Oh?" King was starting to look interested.

"Yes, sir. The vehicle is a UAZ Hunter of Russian manufacture," he nodded his acknowledgment toward Gulnaz, "and we know that, as far as the locals are concerned, fuel availability is limited to here and here." He pointed to two towns, one called Balkh, the other, Mazar-e-Sharif. "As you can see from the topographic detail, sir, Balkh is on a wide plain. Most of the area around it is cultivated and farmed by the locals. Only Mazar is close to the mountains."

"It don't look like more than twenty clicks from Balkh to the mountains," King commented.

"That's true, sir, but the only serviceable roads into the mountains go up from Mazar. To get into the mountains from Balkh is a much longer journey than it looks on this map. It's not definitive, but it's our best guess that the UAZ drove up from Mazar." Ken paused and looked down at his notes again to give King the opportunity to comment. He didn't. "I was able to further narrow down the location, sir, because of some additional factors. The absence of trees in any of the clip was significant. You can see…" he zoomed the image in to a smaller area and overlaid a satellite photograph, "that most of the villages are built in or next to areas of greenery. Obviously, that's where the water is most likely to be and these guys sure ain't on a main supply." He grinned but then caught King's expression. Clearing his throat, he continued. "As you can see, there is only one village that has no greenery surrounding it, and it has a big mountain behind it. We reckon that's where it happened."

"Does the village have a name?" King asked.

"None that we can ascertain at this point in time, sir. It looks like more of a settlement than a village. It's a real dump. Half the buildings are falling down."

"So, what were these people doin' there? Were they living there, working… what? They sure didn't look like insurgents, with kids there an' all. And they sure weren't tourists. Did the guys at that ISAF base know anything?" King glanced at Ken over his glasses.

"We, er, didn't make contact with them, sir, after what you said in the briefing and—"

"Good. That's fine." Ken couldn't hide his surprise at King's offhand comment, but decided to wait and see what developed, rather than asking about it. He carried on.

"You will see, sir, that this mountain, here, is characterized by this kinda craggy bit stickin' out. The satellite image shows just such a feature… here." He stabbed his finger into the screen.

"Okay, so we think we know where the clip was shot. Thank you, Ken." Ken sat down, visibly relieved at having got through his part without sustaining any serious damage. King pressed on. "What do we know about what this guy was saying on the clip? Gulnaz?" Gulnaz rose from her seat and passed sheets of paper around the table.

"This is a translation of everything we could pick up from the clip, sir. Some of it was inaudible due to wind noise, some was obscured when clothing brushed against the cell phone, and some of the audio from the other people at the scene was just too far away to be heard in its entirety. All those points are marked and, in some cases, I have given my best guess as to how the gaps could be filled in. Those are the parts in red. Most of the dialogue is in Pashto. One person said just a few words in Uzbek. Because of the timing and proximity of the voice, I'm almost certain that the Uzbek was spoken by the person wearing the waistcoat, near the jeep." They scanned through the jumble of words with assorted edit points, alternative meanings and 'inaudible' notations. King placed his pages side by side on the table and looked up at Gulnaz.

"So, what it comes down to," he said, "is that this guy is upset, naturally. He's cursing the people who did this, and he says it was the Taliban who did it. He's saying his countrymen and women who died were all innocent and he expects that God will have mercy on… everyone, he seems to be saying. Well, apart from the last bit, what else would you expect? It looks like some red-on-red to me. Some sort of internal squabble that the Taliban wasn't puttin' up with."

"That's what it looks like at first, I agree," Gulnaz said, "but there are several things in this clip that don't make sense to me, and when I look at the words, I feel in my heart that something else may have happened here." She dipped her head momentarily, self-conscious at using the word 'heart'. "Excuse me sir, but I feel sure that what we see and hear in this clip is not telling us everything we need to know about what happened to these poor people. However, I think there are some clues in the words."

King leaned forward and spoke reassuringly. "It's okay, Gulnaz. Sometimes all we got is hunches. We'd like to hear yours, if you please."

"Thank you, sir." She brushed a strand of hair off her face and secured it behind her ear. "These words on line 25, for instance, are not normal. The translation was difficult because I was trying to interpret the sense of what was being said within the context of the situation. Whatever way I did it, I could not make it sound as if it was a natural expression." She read the words. "'*The star falling whisper*.' What is that? I don't know. Maybe it could read '*the whispering falling star*', but I don't know. Does that mean anything to you, sir?" They all focused on line 25.

"That is strange, I admit. It's nothin' to do with Islam, is it? Some sort of religious expression or somethin'? That's what I assumed, when I read it." King looked around the table for feedback. No one replied, so Gulnaz continued.

"He also seems to be saying on lines 34 to 39 that they had given them—and referring back to lines nine and 14, I think we can assume he was talking about the Taliban—everything they had asked for. It seems that he is saying that even though this group had met the demands of the Taliban, whatever they were, they had then gone ahead and executed them anyway. I don't understand. These are just simple peasants. They have nothing! They are peaceful people! Why do they—"

"Okay, Gulnaz." King could see that Gulnaz was getting upset. "That's what we gotta find out." David glanced questioningly at Ken who gestured subtly with his hand in an 'I'll explain later' sort of way. "Is there anything else that don't add up here, Gulnaz?"

She took a deep breath and went on. "The Uzbek. I don't talk much Uzbek because I'm from the south but, from what I can tell, and from what The Beast came up with, he is saying something like 'picture story the world'. That's what this word, *fotoxronika*, means—story in pictures. It's actually Russian, but this Uzbek seems to be using it, which doesn't surprise me if the location is just two hours south of Friendship Bridge, where the Russian army entered and left my country. *Jahonnamo*, the only other word I can identify, means, literally, 'looking-glass that can show anything in the whole world'. Whether it is the clip itself he is referring to, the cell phone, or what he is going to do with it, I am not sure, but the inflexion suggests intention. He seems to be saying that he's going to put this clip on the Internet. But that doesn't make any sense either—not to me, anyway."

"Why so? If this guy has seen some sort of atrocity in the region, and he wants some support to get these Taliban characters nailed, surely the Internet is a good way to go, so far as he's concerned?" King was circling words on the sheets in front of him as he spoke.

"It doesn't make sense to me either," Ken interjected. "First off, any local in that area putting stuff like this on the Internet wouldn't be able to do it without someone else knowing. That could potentially put his whole family at risk, should the boys in black figure out who he was—and you can bet they would. Secondly, there ain't no good broadband in that area anyways. The local service supplied by AWCC is patchy, at best. Whenever any of my contacts try to reach me through it, the best they can do is instant messaging. Skype, and anything that requires more than just a little broadband width, fails every time. Our man in the UAZ would've had to travel halfway across the country for a good connection. Afghanistan is only just entering the Internet age, and the RCN isn't exactly the centre of Afghan commercial or educational activity. They've got the 'Virtual Silk Highway', but that's mainly for the academic community further south, and we've got a handle on everything that goes through it, because it's mainly funded by Norway and run out of Kabul."

"And I am guessing that we didn't pick anything up from the Virtual Silk Highway?"

"Correct," said Ken.

"So, what the hell is goin' on here? Middle East Man, what you got on the guys sendin' emails with Afghan clips attached?" All eyes turned to David as he pulled his folded sheets of paper from his notepad.

"I can confirm that the clip that Assaf Barak sent to Ayan Korfa Nadif was not the original clip that was recorded on the cell phone. The reason I know that is simply because the file format was FLV. The type of cell phone that the person who recorded this clip would have been using would have recorded it in 3GP format, which is like a stripped-down version of MPEG-4. I know that because The Beast told me what phones had been imported and sold in that region over the past five years. It really is a remarkable computer." He glanced over at King, who was not amused. "Conversion of such files for display on the

Internet can easily be done with downloadable freeware. Whoever did that would have been an English speaker, since no freeware site—to my knowledge, at least—is written in Pashto, Uzbek or any of the other languages that could be involved here."

"So the guy with the phone converted it to FLV and sent it to Barak, who then sent it to the other guy in England?" King continued to make notes.

"Possibly, but I don't think so," David continued. "There would have been little point in converting it just to email it. For a start, it would have increased the file size, thereby demanding a good connection to transmit it and, as we've just heard, the driver of that UAZ was hardly likely to have access to, or be conversant with, such software or Internet access. No, my guess is that our man with the cell phone had access to someone else who could get onto the Internet, and it was uploaded onto a site from a different location. It could have been converted to one of several formats on the upload, but to download it from a website, FLV would have been the normal option. This is useful information, because it tells us that the person who made the clip didn't email it directly to Assaf Barak, and that it was much more likely that Barak downloaded it from a website where it had been uploaded by a third party."

"But didn't we just establish that it would have been nearly impossible for anyone in that area to do that?" asked King.

"Exactly. So we must look to the people who are around that area, who can get Internet access."

"God damn." King stroked his chin.

"Would you like me to put in a call to the ISAF base, sir?" Ken was already getting ready to head for his phone.

"No." He paused and reflected. "No, not yet." Sitting up straight, he asked David, "So, what else have you got on Barak and the other guy?"

"Ayan Korfa Nadif, sir?"

"Yes, him."

"Assaf Barak, 19, is a student studying Political Science at Oxford, as is Nadif. He lives with his parents in one of the newly-built houses close to the West Bank in a town called Modiin. He has a record of political activism and he regularly talks via the Internet to a female Arab of a similar age in Gaza who is also involved in political activism in the Gaza Strip, where she lives. Neither has a criminal record and neither appears to be attached to any paramilitary organization or cell in either area. To me, they look like a couple of young innocents with peace on their minds."

"And you are not a young innocent, I guess?" King smiled.

David thought it best to ignore the jibe and carried on. "I have a list of all their known associates," he said, placing his hand on a file in front of him, "and I've spoken to both of them on a number of occasions via the Internet over the past month. I'm personally convinced that they are innocent parties in whatever's going on here."

"Whoa, wait a minute. Let's backtrack for a second, here!" King was astounded at this last comment. "Are you telling me that you *know* these two!?"

"Well, yes, sort of."

"*Sort of?* What the hell do you mean, sort of?"

"Well, I know them, and they *think* they know me. We're just friends, in a way. Well, actually, thinking about it, they think they know three people who just happen to be me."

"R Butt, R Butt. Hold it right there." King raised his hand. "Let's have it, from the top, R Butt. Leave nothin' out, please."

"Well, sir, you might want me to leave part of it out." He paused, waiting for the penny to drop. Would King remember their earlier conversation, and was there definitely some part he wanted to keep from the others—such as using his iPhone, rather than The Beast, to figure things out?

"Fine, but give us the gist of it. I think we'd appreciate that." King fixed his gaze on David. Out of the corner of his eye, David could see Ken shrugging at Gulnaz, who appeared to be preoccupied with her computer.

"As part of my general surveillance of my target area in the Middle East, I have developed several identities—"

"How many, exactly, and why don't I have them on my system?"

"Um, at the last count, I had 187 on LinkedIn, 426 on Facebook—oh, I just added another three yesterday, so that's 429 on Facebook—plus 1,345 on Twitter and—" King dropped his pencil and gazed at David, open-mouthed.

"Okay, forget the technical explanations, for now," King interjected. All this Internet stuff just made his head ache. "I'll aks queshions instead." He paused and stared at David while he gathered his thoughts. "As I understand it from our little conversation yesterday, you have a laptop at your home that has a ton of classified information on it that belongs to Arlington Online. That is a major security risk and you damned well know it and you're gonna get your ass fired if you keep goin' down this road." He dialed a number. "Is that you, Alicia? Good. There's a laptop there, you know it? Okay. Bring it in, right now." He slammed the phone down. David couldn't believe his ears.

"Was that—?"

"Alicia, your Mexican maid, yes. Who the hell did you think I was talking to?" He fixed David with a cold stare. "What the hell kinda game do you think we're playin' here, R Butt? Do you really think this is just a bit of fun? A chance to show off how damn' clever you are? We are not in the business of social fuckin' media here. This ain't no get-rich-quick-personal-development-live-your-dreams shit. This is life and death we're talkin' about, and how to make this world a safer place where people ain't turnin' up video clips of dead communities and sendin' them to their friends for some kinda sick entertainment value. If you want that kinda entertainment, you can get it much closer to home. Just ask Gulnaz how she came to be here." He turned to Gulnaz, suddenly contrite. "Pardon me for saying that Gulnaz…" His voice trailed off as Gulnaz bowed her head again and studied her pen. Turning his attention back to David, he continued. "My job is to sort out this little clusterfuck, and your job is to help me do that *and* keep me informed at all times as to what you are doing, *and* to follow proper procedure. Proper procedure, as you well know, involves only using the very expensive and capable equipment that we have in this building and never—I repeat, *never*—taking any of it, or sourcing anything else, and especially not *keeping* anything else, outside!" He paused for breath, and to wipe his mouth where froth had gathered at the edges.

"I don't keep classified information on that computer." David was more shocked to find out just how much of his life with Barbara and Josh was under Arlington's spotlight, especially after his *tête-à-tête* with Ken earlier, than he was about his laptop. It didn't hold anything of importance. The programs he'd developed were straightforward and the few data they generated went straight to his private storage on the Internet, although he had enjoyed discovering a way to hide that fact when he developed them. His programs simply generated and executed procedures that worked with a variety of social tools to execute multiple actions across multiple identities. They saved him time.

"Well, we'll see about that real soon. I'll talk to you later." King looked at him pointedly. "In the meantime, can we please get back on track? What do you know about Barak and his friend in Gaza—is she a girlfriend, as such, or just a 'friend' friend?"

David tried to re-focus. It had been quite a day for surprising revelations. "Her name is Salma. She does some clerical work at her father's company, and the rest of the time she helps out with a radical theatre group that puts on edgy political plays. She seems like a really nice, genuine girl, to me. Assaf is totally besotted with her, but I think that their relationship doesn't go beyond the Internet because of the siege. I think she's hoping it will lead to a way out of Gaza for her, whereas he thinks it's a bit of a 'liaison dangeureuse' with the hope of some sexual engagement, albeit virtual. He met her online when he was doing some work with an outfit called Sadaka Reut—one of those organizations that tried to get Palestinian and Israeli youth talking and understanding each other in the hope that aggression and prejudice could be alleviated over time. Unfortunately, most of these organizations don't really get very far with that."

"How did Barak get hold of that damn' clip? Seeing as you seem to know so much about him already, perhaps you can give us some insights on that."

David paused. He was skating on thin ice, and didn't have the answer he needed. He decided to take an explanatory route around this question that would at least get him off the hook for now and give him time to investigate further.

"We know that he didn't have the original clip, and we know that it wasn't posted on the Virtual Silk Highway. We also know that it wasn't on an 'A' or 'B' listed website on The Beast. Furthermore, having checked his provider through IP Hunter, I know that his other emails don't include this or anything remotely like it. Luckily, he's using a web-based service, so I was able to check that, and he hasn't accessed the server to wipe anything off it in the last three days. And there was nothing on his ftp server either. All I can suggest at this time is that he found it on a 'C', or lower category, website, so I can run a scan on that as soon as we finish here." David wished he could get to his iPhone right now. All he had to do was fire off a quick message under one of his favorite identities that was a close friend of Assaf Barak, and he'd probably get an answer overnight. *So much easier that figuring out the intricacies of The Beast!*

"Okay, do that. Anything on, what's his name….?" King seemed to have a problem pronouncing Ayan Korfa Nadif.

"He's an interesting one. He's never been involved in anything remotely political, other than choosing Political Science for his degree course at Oxford. He's a year older than Barak, but they're both in the same year at Oxford. Both he and Barak seem to be loners. By that, I mean they don't mix socially, which is probably why they get on with each other. They don't mix much in their respective homelands either. In Nadif's, it seems that he's up in the stratosphere of society, whereas all his peers are struggling to even eat, at times. It's not so much Nadif who's interesting here, though, as his father. Through getting to know Barak, a 'loner' identity I developed has got to know Nadif as well, so we have our own little 'lonely hearts club', you might say. Most of what I hear from him is that, as a family, they are pretty much split up all over the place. His father appears to have a couple of mistresses in different countries, and we know that he's extremely wealthy. He comes to New York a few times a year, and Nadif says he mixes with some pretty powerful people. He doesn't know who they are, but I'm working on that as well."

"That's… interesting." King looked pensive. "Any thoughts on why Barak would send him the clip?"

"None at all, at this point. I'm checking out Nadif's associates to see if he's developing any kind of radical political interest but, so far, that line of enquiry has turned up bugger all."

"Bugger all?"

"Diddly-squat, zilch," volunteered Ken. King grunted.

"Is that it?" King asked. David tried to measure the meaning of the question.

"For now, sir, yes. Unless there's something you think I've missed."

King either didn't think so or wasn't saying. He rearranged the papers on his desk and clicked a mouse to reveal the enhanced close-up still image of the wound in the solar plexus of the woman. Gulnaz drew a sharp breath. The technical guys had done a good job clarifying the wound. It was the first time King had shown them the gory detail. They all peered at it. It was a perfectly round hole, about two inches across. There appeared to be a thin black edge to the hole, although the hole itself was also black, so it was difficult to see it clearly. Surrounding the hole, the flesh appeared to have swelled and small bubbles could clearly be seen, forming a rough whitened ring.

"As you know," King turned to face them, "the authorities, in their wisdom or because of 'cutbacks' or some such thing, have decided not to send us anyone from ballistics to identify the cause of this unusual wound. But I'm working on a plan to resolve that problem." He sounded frustrated. "Fact is, though, by the time we find out what caused this mess, these bodies will be long gone and no autopsy will be possible."

"Why's that?" David asked.

"Islam. That's the problem. When a Muslim dies, they gotta bury them quick. We can be pretty sure that this clip is at least a few days old. Right now, this poor woman will be wrapped in five layers of clothing and buried under several feet of Afghan dust, and I don't think that asking the local Imam to dig her up to check out this hole is an option."

"No, that's wrong, sir." They all turned to Gulnaz who had moved to sit at a computer terminal and was studying the monitor intensely.

"I beg your pardon?"

"She's not a Muslim. None of them are." She was still studying the screen.

"But everyone's a Muslim over there. What else could they possibly be?" King waited for her answer as she scrolled down a page.

"I knew there was something strange about the clothes," she muttered to herself. "It makes sense now." She peered at the screen again before turning back to face them. "Zoroastrians," she said. "They're Zoroastrians and the men are Zoroastrian priests." She breathed a sigh of relief and smiled for the first time since entering the room. David, Ken and King looked at her as if she'd just gone mad.

Ken made a gesture of surrender. "Tell us."

"I'd learned a little about them before, when I lived in Afghanistan, but I've never met any of them." Gulnaz started to explain, glancing at the screen every now and then. "Zoroastrianism is a religion and philosophy based on the teachings of the prophet Zoroaster. It pre-dates Islam in Iran where it really had influence around the 5th century. It was the State religion of Iran for some time, back then. They worship a deity called Ahura Mazda that they regard as the supreme divine authority. It seems it spread to the wider region, through Afghanistan to Pakistan and India, but started to get marginalized because of the uptake of Islam." She continued reading from the screen. "In Zoroastrianism, Mazda is all good, and no evil originates from Him. Good and evil have distinct sources, with evil trying to destroy the creation of Mazda and good trying to sustain it. For Zoroastrians, active participation in life through good thoughts, good words and good deeds is necessary to ensure happiness and to keep the chaos at bay. This *active* participation is a central element in Zoroaster's concept of free will, and Zoroastrianism rejects all forms of monasticism." Gulnaz raised her eyes from the screen to face them. "What I also know is that, because of this, their peaceful nature and the fact that they don't preach or impose their ways on others, they've been ostracized, bullied and marginalized to the point where only a few small communities remain. There are even a few communities here in the United States but, in Afghanistan, they've pretty much retreated to the area in and around Balkh."

"So, this town is kinda their last stronghold in Afghanistan?" asked King.

"Yes, sir, you could say that. But there's one more thing I don't fully understand, although I do have a theory that could be very significant in this case."

"I'm all ears," King, was already beginning to tire of religious education.

"Well, if Zoroastrians are still accepted in Balkh, why has this community chosen to live in an almost derelict settlement in the mountains, far away from their main community and in extremely inhospitable conditions?" Gulnaz looked around the table, but was met with blank stares.

"And your theory is...?"

"I think they may be what you might call 'fundamentalist Zoroastrians'. Over the centuries, evolving influences have impacted on their beliefs, practices and values. While they've sometimes complemented and enriched their traditions, more often they've displaced them. As with many centuries-old religious groups, there are those who want to keep the sacred essence of those traditions. Such people sometimes separate themselves from those they believe are not 'true believers', preferring to live according to what they consider to be the correct rules, in isolation. I think we have, or had, such a group here."

"And how does that help us now?"

"Sir, your concern about not being able to do an autopsy on the bodies made me think. I'm sad to say I believe those bodies will not have been buried yet."

"Why not? This video clip could be more than a week old now. The stench of all those bodies lying around would be—" King grimaced, "horrific!"

"I agree, sir, and it's only a theory, but if this is a fundamentalist community…" Gulnaz seemed to be having difficulty forming the words. "They have this ritual, sir. It's not generally accepted any more, and may even be illegal in Balkh."

"Go on, Gulnaz."

"Well, as I understand it, traditional Zoroastrians believe that a corpse is a 'host for decay'—a repository of the bad and the negative that Mazda is constantly battling. So, in order to ensure 'safe' disposal of the dead in a way that a corpse does not pollute the 'good' creation, they have what they call 'ritual exposure'. They kind of put the body out to dry on what they call a 'tower of silence' where scavenger birds will eat the flesh. I've heard that a few Zoroastrian communities still do this in parts of India, but they're trying to get it stopped because scavenger birds are virtually extinct due to diclofenac poisoning they get from feeding on dead dogs that have been treated with the drug."

"You're telling me they actually *want* the vultures to eat the flesh?" King couldn't quite take this in.

"Yes, sir. It takes… the bad… away."

"Thank you, Gulnaz." King glanced up at the image of the wound that was still on the screen, clicked the mouse again and it was gone. Then, without any change of tone, he announced, "Thank you, everyone, for your contributions. I'll call you when there's more." They sat in stunned silence for a few seconds, then slowly gathered their things.

"R Butt. A word." King scribbled something on a pad as he called David over. *Shit,* David thought, *what now?*

"Come with me."

Chapter 8

Ruku was running as fast as his skinny legs would carry him. He had been battling his way through thick undergrowth for nearly an hour now, avoiding the path so he wouldn't be seen. The light was fading and he knew he had to get home before nightfall. It was too dangerous to be outside after dark. His heart was banging in his little chest. It was a potent mixture of fear and excitement that spurred him on, giving him extra strength on the final stretch down the muddy track and around the corner where the lights of distant Bukavu assured him that he was nearly there. He needed all the strength he could muster as he scrambled barefoot over roots and stones that caused him to check his pace every few steps. He couldn't wait to show his father his new prize, and tell him the incredible news that was bursting to be released from him. But it was heavy, this AK-47, and awkward to carry. His shoulders were too narrow for him to sling it across his back, the way he had seen the men do, so he was holding the end of the barrel in one hand and the shoulder strap in the other as he dragged it, banging and clattering, through the forest. It never occurred to him that it might be loaded or, worse still, that it could go off and put a bullet clear through his chest. He had no idea how it operated. All he knew was that now they'd both be safe.

He stumbled and fell as he reached the clearing where his home stood—a simple wooden structure with a rough thatched roof and assorted sheets of plastic to keep the wind and rain out.

"*Ruku*, is that you?" His heart lifted when he heard his father's voice. He never knew what he was going to come home to.

"Yes, papa. I am here. I have something for you. Look!" He felt so proud. His father hobbled out of the house to find him. He hadn't been able to walk so well since the troubles with Rwanda, when he'd received a terrible beating simply because he was in the wrong place at the wrong time, trying to help the wrong refugees.

"What is this!?" He picked up the weapon and studied it, then looked sternly down at his son. "Where in God's name did you find such a thing?" He replaced the gun on the ground, bent down and shook Ruku by the shoulders. "Did you steal it? Ruku? Did you steal it off a man? Tell me!" *What kind of hell has my son unleashed upon us?*

"He was dead, papa. He was dead!" Ruku was shocked and confused by his father's uncharacteristically aggressive reaction. His eyes filled with tears. His father calmed himself and sat down beside him.

"What? You found a dead man with a gun? What happened to him?"

"I don't know. I don't know. He was just dead, so I took his gun for you. Aren't you pleased? Now when the men come, you can kill them." He smiled as he held an imaginary gun and fired it. "Bang, bang!" Ruku's face creased up in laughter, and his father couldn't resist sharing this happy moment with him, so he did the same, making the rat-tat-tat sound of a machine gun before he fell by Ruku's side and tickled him into hysterics.

"Ruku, come and tell me all about it. I'll take that." He shouldered the gun as Ruku watched proudly, and they went into the house. "I wish I'd been able to use this earlier today." He was subdued now, and spoke quietly.

"Why, papa?"

"The men came through the village with their guns. They took Lora and raped her. Six of them." He stared at the wall. "Poor, poor girl. When will the government stop all this?" He spat the words out, angrily shaking his head. "It's getting worse all the time. How will she ever find a husband now? She was such a nice girl, but I guess she will end up in Bukavu like all the rest. There is nothing for her here now." Ruku cast his eyes down. He didn't really understand what rape was, but he'd often heard men talk of it. He though it must be a disease that men gave to women. He'd seen the darkness and bruises come over girls who had caught it. Nobody seemed to be able to cure it.

"So, Ruku, tell me the whole story. I can't wait to hear it." They sat together at the doorway as they did every evening, but it was usually Ruku's father who was telling him some marvelous story as they watched the lights of Bukavu twinkle in the far distance from their hillside. Tonight, Ruku felt like a film star. Well, he guessed that film stars would feel like this all the time, although it was only his father's wonderful story-telling that had instilled in his imagination what a film was, and he'd never really understood the idea. The story came out in an excited, unstoppable torrent.

"I was in the pit today, working hard for the master, when suddenly there was a lot of shouting and everyone ran into the forest. I thought I should keep working because if I stopped I thought he would beat me or he wouldn't pay me, but everyone was shouting and saying 'Look, look, come here, come here!' So I went into the forest with them, and the master was very excited. There was a man lying on the ground and he still had his gun. No one had taken it. So we crouched down in case it was a trap and the men were coming to kill us or take the master's coltran again. But there was no sound except for some birds, so we went very slowly further into the forest. And then we saw four more men—all dead, just lying there. Their faces were angry but they were dead so it didn't matter, and they had black on their chests—all of them. So the master took their guns and money from their pockets and their bullets and he gave me a pen that one of them had in his jacket." Without pausing for breath, Ruku pulled an old biro from a pocket in his shorts and showed it to his father. "The master was so happy, he was laughing and dancing around and saying 'thank you, thank you', and looking up at the sky and thanking God. And then he said he had to go and tell his friends in Kisangani on the radio, but we had to go back to work now. So I went back to work in the pit, and I worked really hard so we could have money and the master would be more happy again. When we finished, I walked through the forest past all the dead men and there were lots of flies and a bad smell so I didn't go to them to find any more things to bring home because I was afraid to catch their rape. So I ran and then I saw another man and he was dead as well, and his gun was away from him, so I picked it up and brought it home for you and why are all the men dead, papa?"

It took a minute or two for his father to register that Ruku had asked him a question at the end of that story. This was very, very confusing. Congo was a violent place, of that there was no doubt. The problems with Rwanda, the exploitation of the land, the warring factions trying to gain control of different parts of the country, the poaching of gorillas for 'bush meat' and the people who came after the poachers, the increasing violence toward women by gangs of armed youths and men—there seemed to be no end to it. For Ruku, his father and everyone else in the area, violence and death were just everyday events and, every day, his father feared that Ruku might not come home as the sun went down. He constantly worried about him going into the pit. It wasn't safe. They paid no attention to anyone's safety. All they wanted was the coltran, and they seemed to want more and more of it all the time. But this was strange. If a man killed another man in the forest, he always took his gun, without exception. He also recognized the formation that these thugs had used to protect themselves as they made their way through the forest. One went in front as a scout to warn the main group of any impending danger, and one picked up the rear to alert them to anyone following. So how come the middle group weren't warned by either the scout or the man at the back? Which of them had been killed first? Surely, if they had heard a shot as one was killed, the others would have taken cover. Unless there was a large group of men lying in wait for them, how would they all have been killed at the same time? Was there a large group of men in the area? No one had told him, and he would surely have heard. These things could not happen without anyone knowing. The pathways were all known and there was nowhere for a helicopter to land around here.

"Well done, Ruku. That was a wonderful story." He patted his son on his head, but Ruku could sense his reticence.

"Was it really, Papa? Am I a good story-teller like you?"

"Yes, you are, and I'm very proud of you." He smiled down at him, and told him he was tired and wanted to sleep now.

Chapter 9

Troy King stood up. David had so far only ever seen him sitting down. Now he understood what Ken meant about King's posture. King was a tall man; David reckoned he must have been six foot five, had he been standing straight. But he didn't seem to be able to do that. He had broad muscular shoulders that suggested an athletic past, but he also had an alarming pot belly that looked as if it had somehow been grafted on to his torso by a bad surgeon who had no idea that he would need to wear pants most of the time. Consequently, his belt had the delicate yet essential job of catching some grip on his hip bones before it dived down under this strange aberration in such a way that the buckle couldn't be seen. His back was straight and stiff, but bent forward. When he walked, his arms hung loosely forward so he moved like an aggressive baboon. Whenever he paused, it was all David could do to resist putting a hand up to stop him falling forward. That was the moment that David's attitude to Troy King shifted. He suddenly felt that he wanted to stand up *for* him.

They passed by the Fishtank, where King picked up a large padded envelope and handed it to David. He looked inside.

"I, er, don't understand…" It was his laptop. King waved his hand dismissively.

"That little show was just for Ken. Don't worry about it." They walked in silence to the elevator, and didn't speak all the way down to reception, where David checked his iPhone out, and King gestured for him to follow as he headed for the revolving doors. The evening traffic noise hit David like a wall as the revolving doors spilled them out from the silence of the lobby. It all seemed completely mad, out of control—all this urgent activity, this mess. They crossed the road and King led them round a corner and into a bar.

"Evenin' Troy. What'll it be?" The barman was on the case.

"A couple of beers. R Butt, what can I get you?" David was slightly confused by this, so he made like he was considering his choice while the barman placed two beers in front of King, who was awkwardly maneuvering his buttocks onto a barstool.

"A beer would be fine, thanks." The barman slammed a third beer in front of David, while King threw his first one down his throat in one go. David switched his iPhone on and was immediately alerted to the fact that he had three emails and a message from Barbara—'call me, urgent!'

King was already into his second beer as David took his first sip.

"Gimme a couple more. R Butt, want a re-fill?"

"Maybe in a minute, thanks."

King seemed lost in thought, so David didn't disturb him. He was still confused about the way that King had made a great show of embarrassing him in front of Ken and Gulnaz about his laptop, and then given it straight back to him so nonchalantly—without, it would seem, having even looked at its contents.

The bar was virtually empty. The office workers hadn't got there yet. The TV mounted in one corner was showing a re-run of the CNN report of Griffin Kirkland answering press questions following the President's announcement of the Middle East peace deal.

"There's a man with an election erection, if ever I seen one," King mumbled. "So, R Butt..." he considered this for a second, "actually, do you mind if I call you David?"

"That would be nice. No, no problem with that."

"Well, good." He paused again, as if giving this transition to informality some deep thought. "You can call me Troy. But just here, not in the office. Understand?"

"Sure, I understand... Troy." *What the hell is going on here?*

"Okay, R Butt, I guess Ken used that time down by the coffee machine to help you understand your situation here?"

"How did you know that!?" *This is getting too weird.*

"I aksed him to. And I want to let you know a little bit more, if that's okay with you."

"I think so, but I can't work out why, after I've only been here just over a month, I'm being entrusted with information that our bosses probably wouldn't want me to hear. I'm also finding it a little weird, to be frank, that I'm sitting here with you talking about it in a bar over some beers rather than in the office. Maybe I am a bit young and naïve, but..."

King took another drink, just a sip this time. "Yeah, I know. It's all a bit strange, but there's stuff going on here, and you seem to be a smart cookie, so I wanna tell you about it before you catch up with me and figure it out for yourself."

David felt flattered. He took a gulp of beer and turned to face the back of the bar where Troy King's face was reflected in the mirror. He looked tired. "There are several parts to this, so bear with me. First off, your contract is with Arlington Online Data Systems Inc., an independent company contracted to the United Stated Government to do some sophisticated snooping on their behalf, correct?"

"Correct."

"Not correct." He turned to look David in the eye.

"Not correct?"

"No. Arlington is fully owned and funded by the CIA and the DIA as part of the National Security Agency setup that works closely with Homeland Security and the President's office."

David exhaled loudly and King waited for him to absorb this information.

"And I thought Arlington was just a cemetery for American heroes that I drive around to get to work."

"In a sense, that's correct," mused King, "but it's a cemetery for information, and we drive around it every day—in circles, going nowhere." He paused and studied the contents of his glass. "And I'm a dead man walking."

A flash of anger welled up in David, and spewed out. "What the hell am I getting into here, Troy? I'm English, for God's sake. I'm just a computer geek they employed to figure out some stuff on the Internet and now you're telling me that I've got my family into some sort of fucking American political psycho-drama!? Please tell me that this is just some big fucking sick joke you've dreamt up and that Dan Brown is going to walk through that door and tell me you're working out a plot together for his next novel."

King gestured to him to keep his voice down. "Aks yourself a queshion, R Butt... sorry, David. Do you seriously think that the Pentagon and all these other agencies here, with all their fancy equipment and experienced and very smart people, really need you or me to help them find out what's goin' down out there? Don't you think they could do it all themselves, with a lot less fuss and security risk? Of course they can!" He fixed David with a glare. "For God sakes, David, pay attention." He turned back to face the mirror behind the bar. "Think about this as well, 'cause I got to thinkin' about it when I been in this job a couple of months, and it made me sit up." He started his third beer. "All my life—and I mean all my life—I wanted to be a good military man. Started out wantin' to please my old man and make him proud of me. Then, after a while, I found I wanted it 'cause I really believed in what all this stood for—country, honor and all that shit. So, all my life, I willingly trained myself to take orders and *not* think and *not* aks queshions. That's what you do, if you're a good military man, so I did it. I bought the whole story they spun me without queshion, and without thinkin'. Then what happens? I have a coupla accidents that cripple me up so I can't no longer be a good military man and I can't even haul a sack of apples, and they decide to gimme this job. And this job is *all* about aksing queshions and thinkin'. Now why would they do that, smart guy?"

"I have no idea." David really had no idea.

King turned to face him again. "Because all they want is someone to watch over this information cemetery to make sure no corpses get out, that's why. We're just here to snoop on the snoopers, and show them what any old fool can find out about what they are doin', so they can make the necessary adjustments to make sure those damn' zombies get back in their coffins. The last thing they want at Arlington Online is heroes."

"So you're saying that we are just one big joke in the American intelligence system?"

"That's just about it, yeah." King waved to the barman to get David another beer. "So, how does that make you feel?"

David didn't reply. King watched him seethe for a minute before responding.

"Well, I guess we feel much the same." A couple came in and sat down beside them. King motioned for David to move. They searched out a table in the corner, out of the way, taking their beers with them. King continued, "I wasn't going to mention this, not yet, anyways, but when you started doin' stuff outside on your iPhone and such, I could see things getting' a bit complicated. You see, Ken's not that smart. He just does his job like most of the others, and he likes to think he's got a handle on the situation. It suits him that way 'cause he's not going any place special in life. But if he starts spreadin' it around that The Beast can easily be by-passed by somethin' like an iPhone and a few simple apps and clever programs, then the powers-that-be would get real jumpy and shut down the whole operation. As I said, Ken's not that smart and his big mouth would put him and the rest of us out of a job. That's why I made all that fuss about your laptop as a sorta decoy to keep the iPhone out of the conversation. And, by the way, I really appreciated you keeping your mouth shut when you needed to." He paused again, collecting his thoughts. "But this ain't just about job security." King looked decidedly uneasy. "There's somethin' else going down here, and now that, for the first time in my life, I've gotten around to thinkin', I can't seem to stop."

"What's giving you cause for concern, Troy?"

"We're off this case."

"What?" David was really feeling out of his depth now. Nothing was making any sense at all. "You mean the one we just spent the whole day researching? I thought it was a big priority."

"Those two guys that came to see me just after lunch were CIA. They told me, in no uncertain terms, to drop the whole thing. Forget it."

"Just like that? What reason did they give?"

"These guys don't give reasons. They'd have to be *reasonable* to do that, and that's a word they don't seem to have in their somewhat limited vocabulary."

"But we were still working on it, and we did the briefing, after they left."

"Yes, that's right. They usually put it down to lack of funds, cutbacks and other excuses, but this time they were a little more blunt than usual." He casually checked around to see if they were being overheard. "I smell a bad case of BO."

"BO? Is it me, I'm sorry, it's been a long day—"

"No, no." King put his hand up and laughed. "It's not you. Look, the story goes something like this. Our previous great leader, GFWB—"

"FW?"

"Fuck Wit. Our previous leader took us into a few 'unwise' wars. As a result of them and a few other stupid decisions, the country got a mother of a pain in the ass in its financial situation. The new guy was elected as a reaction to the ways of the Texas cowboy, because he looks all squeaky clean and much smarter. He knows he's in a deep financial shit-hole but he also knows he's gotta keep his suit pressed for the country to keep believin' that we're gonna get outta this mess. Now that is pretty near impossible to do, so some people are saying the country's gettin' a bad case of BO, if you get my drift. Just those who are close to him can smell it, he ain't aware that they can and he probably don't even know he's got it."

"Thank you for that enlightening take on the American political situation." David was warming to King again, and keen to hear more. His iPhone beeped, but he ignored it.

"Welcome to the land of freedom and democracy, kid. Like I said, I smell a bad case of BO here. The message I got today came via those two goons in a manner that told me it came from the White House itself. So, I got to thinkin' about what we seen on that clip, which they would've seen when it got enhanced and before it got back to us."

"Why on earth would they want to suppress anything that we might come up with on that? It looked nasty but seemed pretty innocuous to me—until you start digging, that is. Even so, you'd think they'd want it explained just to clarify any terrorist threat in the area."

"Exactly, and why would the White House get so jumpy about it anyway? Why would it even have gotten onto their radar?" He leaned in toward David. "Look, there's somethin' else here that don't sit right with me, and I want to find out what's goin' on. Another beer?"

"I think so, yes…" David was too preoccupied to think about beer and yes seemed like the easiest answer. King waved at the barman again, and pointed at their glasses.

"It's that hole—you know, the one you can see clearly in the woman on the ground."

"What about it? Somebody shot her and it made a hole, surely?" The barman delivered two more bottles to their table.

"I ain't never seen a hole like that before. It ain't natural."

"They never are…"

"And it was when I aksed for a ballistics guy to look at it, that's when they clammed up and started sayin' things weren't possible. Well, I ain't been sittin' in offices all my military life, and I did learn some about ballistics, and I seen plenty of bullet wounds too."

"So, you know enough to analyze the ballistics yourself?"

"Theoretically, yes. Look, when a bullet goes in, it makes a small hole. The kinda weapon the Taliban use makes a hole about yea big"—he held his fingers about five millimeters apart—"and it ain't usually perfectly round. You see, the way a bullet hits a body—and it may not even be traveling straight on its axis, so the hole may not even be round—it penetrates the skin and makes what they call a chamber inside where the bullet breaks into splinters. If it penetrates on an angle, the skin tear can be about three times the length of the bullet, but it definitely won't be round. That's how it works with a military bullet, the full metal jacket type. And it probably wouldn't have killed them outright. Even if they were using civilian bullets, which would almost certainly have killed them at close range, it wouldn't look like that. They're hollow and mushroom on impact and make more of a mess, but not perfectly round and clean like we saw on that clip."

"Am I understanding this right? A civilian bullet would be more likely to kill than a military bullet?"

"In certain circumstances, yes. They design 'em that way 'cause it takes a lot more enemy energy and resources to look after a wounded soldier than a dead one."

"Charming."

"Yes, and it can be a real problem when a military rifle is fired and the bullet is going at a much higher velocity than a civilian bullet, so they can cover bigger distances with more accuracy. The bullet can go straight through and not cause enough damage. That's why some fighters are changing from, for instance, the AK-47 to the AK-74, 'cause the bullets they use in the AK-74 are smaller and lighter, and instead of creating the optimum chamber at, say, nine inches—which for many areas of the body can be straight out the other side—they create it at about four-and-a-half inches. So, even if it don't hit bone and fracture, it still causes maximum wounding in soft tissue, or a more messy exit wound. There ain't no exit wound apparent on any of those bodies."

"How can you tell? You can't see the other side of their bodies."

"Ain't no blood spreadin' out on the ground beneath them."

"I see." David considered the ramifications of what King had just told him. "So, what you're thinking is that the Taliban and, by extension, other terrorist groups, have some new kind of weapon that we either don't know about or the White House is trying to hide because it could cause a loss of confidence in, or within, the military?"

"Somethin' like that, but I don't know enough yet. Whatever is going on, though, I think the White House may be putting our guys at risk in order to save face."

David's iPhone rang again. "It's Barbara. Do you mind if I…?"

"Sure, go ahead."

David took the call, excusing himself as he moved toward the open door of the bar and listened.

"Wow," David said, as he sat back down again. "It never rains but it pours around here. She was really upset. Apparently, she was just driving home from the Pentagon Centre shopping mall and some guy in a black sedan side-swiped her at a junction. Josh is okay but the rear wing is trashed. That was quite a shock for her."

"Did she get the driver's details?"

"Yes, she's just emailed them to me from an Internet café. She was also pretty pissed because she thought I'd taken the laptop." He glanced at King, who shrugged apologetically. David pulled up the email. "Shit, that's the last thing I need right now—to have to sort out an insurance claim."

"Here, let me help you with that," King invited, and David showed him the screen.

"Hmm, that's interesting. That's a government plate. Why don't you send that on to me and I'll see if I can fast-track it through the system."

"Thanks, Troy. That would be great."

King was playing with the iPhone now, which made David a little uneasy.

"You know, I really would like to get the hang of one of these. Maybe you could show me how it works—and how you do that stuff with it…"

"Sure, I'd be happy to."

"And I'd really like to know how you got to know that guy Barak and his friends."

"Okay, well, to me, everything we're doing at Arlington Online is all about relationships. As soon as I knew I'd got the job, I made a point of developing as many online relationships in my assigned areas, under different aliases, as I could. See, my theory is that whereas computer systems like The Beast look at instances, keywords, tags, metrics and so on—to establish what relationships are happening out there—I just go straight to the relationships themselves, and then work out the structures and relevance. I turn the process around. It's more natural, a lot quicker, and I get better information that way. And it often includes a lot of additional and very useful stuff that I wouldn't expect to find. In the same way that people are alarmingly open with, say, their hairdresser, they tend to talk openly about just about anything when they feel they've got to know you online. And, of course, the seeds of any revolution germinate among trusted friends exchanging confidences in coffee bars, homes and, nowadays, online. Look at what we're doing right now."

David spent the next hour running through the basic features of his iPhone and the not-so-basic procedures he had developed for it. King thanked him and said, "You know, David, I've said a lot of stuff, and I know it won't go any further..." He paused for David to acknowledge this. David nodded. "... and, given your situation, I guess you might be thinkin' of sending Barbara and Josh home for a little visit to grandma or somethin'?"

"The thought had crossed my mind." David was feeling nervous again.

"Well, my advice is, don't. Any move like that would bring the wrong kind of attention into your life right now. No harm will come to her here, especially with Alicia there. She may look like she's harmless, but I can tell you she packs quite a punch!" He smiled and checked David's mood. "They're not interested in Barbara or Josh. They just want to keep Arlington employees in line, and you ain't been there long enough to be of any real concern—just so long as they don't find out too much about your 'alternative' methods. Okay?"

"I don't think I have much of a choice, do I?"

"No, you don't." King looked lost in thought as he downed the last of his beer. "David, this has been real helpful, and I'm sorry to have to drop this on you right now, but with everything we talked about, and everything you now know, I think I have no choice."

"What is it, Troy?" *Surely it can't get any worse...*

"David..." This was obviously difficult for him. "...you've gotta go."

The bottom dropped out of David's world right there and then. He felt crushed, betrayed, angry, hurt and desperate. He could hardly speak.

"Why? Troy, what more could I have done? What about Barbara and Josh and all the promises Arlington made when I came—?"

"No, no, no!" King cut him off. "I'm not firing you!" He smiled, broadly.

"So... where have I got to go?"

"Afghanistan."

CHAPTER 10

British Airways flight 175, London (LHR) – New York (JFK)

Assaf Barak smiled as he looked out through the window. The British landscape became obscured by cloud as the Jumbo climbed steeply out of Heathrow. He was very impressed—and very excited.

"I never expected to be doing this when I got back to Oxford last week!" He turned and grinned at Ayan. "And I can't wait to meet your father."

"I think you'll find it an interesting experience." Ayan winked at him and returned to his novel. He'd made this trip several times since he'd been in England. It was the best way to get to see his father, who seemed to be making longer and longer visits to the US. He even wondered if his parents were thinking of moving there, but he couldn't see that happening anytime soon, knowing how involved his father was in the politics of Somalia, as well as his considerable business interests there. For now, though, he put all such concerns out of his mind. New York was such a great place to visit and, this time, his father had made sure it would be even better than usual. On previous visits, his father had felt bad that he'd had to attend so many meetings, leaving Ayan to spend hours and hours on his own, most days. They sometimes didn't even get together for dinner, as that seemed to be the best time to for his father to meet with some of the politicians and civil servants. All he could do was snatch the odd half-hour in between appointments. He would tell Ayan where to take a taxi to, so they could rendezvous over a coffee or a late breakfast. That had its advantages for Ayan, though. It meant he got to know Manhattan—where the good restaurants and diners were, the cinemas and theatres, the art galleries and the sights worth seeing. He'd be able to put that knowledge to good use on this trip, as his father had suggested that Ayan bring a friend this time. Ayan suggested Barak, and he'd happily footed the bill for both of them.

Korean Air flight 94, Washington (IAD) – Denpasar (DPS)

"Sheryl, I still can't believe you managed to get us on this flight. You never cease to amaze me." Even as he spoke, Griffin Kirkland was sadly aware of his tendency to take Sheryl's organization of his affairs for granted. New feelings were arising out of these days of turmoil and uncertainty and it was good to be aware of his own discomfort. He was reminded of past times with Sheryl— good times, when he made more of an effort to pay attention to her feelings.

Throughout their relationship, though, she had always been his confidante. He trusted her completely and, despite her recent prickliness and the distance she kept from him, he'd been happy to confide in her about the press conference, his confusion at being left hanging and, of course, his meeting with Evelyn. Sheryl had been shocked by his revelations, and was particularly concerned about Larry. But at the same time, he'd seen in her a steely determination to get to the bottom of whatever was going on. That had given him new strength. As soon as they'd finished that conversation, she'd taken the bait that Larry had dangled in his call with Griffin. "Okay, as far as everyone's concerned, we're on holiday. I hear there are some great deals to Bali." The following day, they were checking in at Dulles Airport for a direct flight to the island.

633d Air Base Wing, Langley Airforce Base, VA – Ramstein Air Base, Germany, Connect to German ISAF supplies flight by C-160 to Termez, Uzbekistan

They weren't in the mood for talking. David was worried sick, not so much for himself and for what could be lying in wait for him, but for Barbara and Josh, whom he'd left in the hands of 'kung-fu Alice', as he now thought of their Mexican maid. He hadn't dared tell Barbara where he was going and he'd worked hard the previous evening to project an air of happy domestic normality. He and Troy King had dreamt up a story about David having to go to a five-day secret training session in Los Angeles where he would not be contactable 'for security reasons'.

Gulnaz sat in silence next to David while, all around them, young marines, fresh from training, engaged in boisterous conversation. She'd hardly said a word since King had told her that she would have to accompany David on the trip to act as his interpreter. It was clear to David, from her near-hysterical reaction to this instruction, that she had her own very clear reasons why Afghanistan was the last place on earth that she wanted to go. King had given her no choice, saying that from what they had seen on the clip, many more lives could be at risk if she didn't cooperate. David wondered what compromises, apart from this dreadful trip, she was having to make to either keep her job or stay in the US—or both. He also felt sick, trapped and angry that within days he could be in danger of getting shot or blown up—without the protection of his employers, the US Government or the military, who they would be avoiding once they reached Termez.

King had explained to him that since their investigation was no longer official, he didn't want them turning up on any civilian airline passenger lists and, anyway, there were no commercial flights that would get them to the settlement in Afghanistan quickly enough. So, he'd called in some favors with friends at Langley Airforce Base to arrange their covert arrival in Afghanistan as soon as possible. In the matter-of-fact manner of a cheerful mortician, King had emphasized the need to get to the bodies during what is known as the 'putrefaction stage' of decomposition, and before the 'black putrefaction' stage. Because the bodies were located at quite a high altitude, the process of decomposition would have been slowed somewhat, and the absence of scavenger birds meant that they would probably be reasonably intact by the time they got to them.

Acela Express R2150, Washington DC – New York

Taking the 5am express train from Washington, King expected to arrive in Manhattan just before 8am. That would give him enough time to have a good breakfast and check out the lay of the land on his new toy—an iPhone—which he'd been busy getting to know over the past 24 hours. Despite David's resistance, King had also persuaded him to explain some of the unique capabilities David had developed, that linked with his online space. However, the mutual respect that was growing between them had made the whole situation a little less painful. Behind the disgust and fear that David had expressed about the nature of his mission to Afghanistan, King had also detected some excitement. That didn't detract, though, from the deep uneasiness that King now felt. He was not only putting his own career and pension at risk, but he could end up doing time for a whole string of offences he was committing, as well as being responsible for illegally putting two of his colleagues in great danger that neither of them were equipped or trained to deal with.

Perhaps it was because he felt guilty, but in the little time he had to organize all the logistics that were now being played out, King made a point of looking into the insurance claim on the collision that had shaken Barbara up. He'd had a copy of the sedan driver's report faxed over to him the day before. At first sight, there was nothing unusual about it. As she was merging with Columbia Pike just west of the Pentagon, taking Senator Griffin Kirkland to his downtown office, a Mrs B. Arbuthnot, with an address in Alcova Heights, appeared to lose control of her vehicle—a 2010 silver Chevy Traverse SUV— as she traveled in the opposite direction, toward the sedan. The Chevy Traverse SUV crossed over the centre of the Columbia Pike, causing him to swerve. He had been unable to avoid a collision. He had stopped and parked his vehicle in a safe manner, ensuring that the vehicle was locked and that his passenger was in no imminent danger. He had then proceeded to inquire as to the condition of Mrs B. Arbuthnot and her passenger—a child properly secured in an approved model baby seat. Neither Mrs B. Arbuthnot nor the child had received any injury, and Mrs B. Arbuthnot had insisted that there was no need to call for medical assistance or a recovery vehicle. The driver had exchanged insurance details with Mrs B. Arbuthnot, who was in a state of agitation but was not exhibiting any signs of shock, and continued to Senator Kirkland's downtown office.

"Bullshit." King filed the report, for the time being.

The train journey gave King an opportunity to reflect on the events of the past two days. Despite his concerns, he was growing ever more confident that he was onto something big. If his hunches were right, all he had to do was mind his head and he'd make his dead father proud. By the time he'd checked in at Day's Inn on West 94th and found his way to a diner for breakfast, Troy King was looking forward to a few relaxing days in the Big Apple.

American Airlines flight 1247, Washington (DCA) – Springfield, Illinois (SPI)
Avis car rental at Capital Airport Drive – Lincoln Illinois

Ken Fellows was particularly pleased with himself as he drove along Route 66 on his way from the Abraham Lincoln Capital Airport at Springfield to the small town of Lincoln, Illinois. He slid the window down and switched the radio on, loud. Talking Heads accompanied him on the road to nowhere as he cruised along the legendary highway, slapping his hand on the door frame in time to the beat, as the breeze buffeted his shirt sleeve.

He had not only pulled off some very smart investigative work very quickly, but he also felt he'd done something to eclipse the star quality that was showing up in the new boy, and was obviously impressing Troy King.

They had all overlooked one small thing on that video clip. The guy in the waistcoat, speaking Uzbek, was wearing a small badge. When Ken had seen the enhanced digital image of the badge, he'd been able to make out the illustration and the wording around it, but only after some further manipulation on the individual frames of the clip. It had been difficult, because there was no single frame that had shown either the wording or the illustration without a considerable amount of blur, but he found that by tweaking some image settings and overlaying several of them, it became clearer. The image was that of a face, but not just any face. Peering closer at the screen, he's been able to see that there were two small horns sticking out of the top of the head. The Devil!

The wording around the image spelled out the words 'Give 'em 'L!" His first thoughts had been that in a war zone, you'd expect to see such imagery, but clipped to a US military uniform, not being worn by a local. Wearing such a badge could be taken the wrong way, if it looked as if one of their own was openly supporting the American troops. No, there had to be another explanation. So, he'd done a search on images of the Devil and that phrase, Give 'em 'L', and it had come up with a college football team based in the small town of Lincoln, Illinois. On checking the yearbook for the college against military personnel who had served in Afghanistan, he came up with just one match: Dwayne Waldron.

CHAPTER 11

The pungent, heady aroma of a thousand tropical flowers greeted Griffin and Sheryl as they walked out of the air-conditioned arrivals area and into the airless heat. They each donned sunglasses and slung their jackets over their baggage. Then they stood and waited. Unusually for Sheryl, she hadn't planned anything about this trip beyond the flights. When they passed through immigration control, they had filled in the forms, giving the name of a hotel that she'd found on the Internet, length of stay and purpose of visit. 'Holiday'. Their passport had been shown to someone behind a glass window, a short conversation had ensued between two officials, and then they had been waved on their way with a smile and a "Welcome to Bali, Mr and Mrs Senator Kirkland. Enjoy your stay." *It's so damned difficult to disappear*, thought Griffin.

After half an hour in the sweltering heat, fending off offers of taxis, hotels, various tourist trinkets and visits to 'the best restaurants', the jetlag started to set in.

"Do you think he knows?" Sheryl wiped her forehead with a tissue.

"Of course he does." Griffin was beginning to have his doubts.

"But... he's always so punctual. What if no one—"

"He'll be here, Sheryl. For God's sake…" But all they could see were taxis, minibuses and motorbikes swarming in endless chaos, dropping off passengers, picking people up, waiting aimlessly, talking. A crowd of people focused in on each new group emerging from the terminal building, each one of them intent on extracting some small amount of income, using charm or, failing that, just plain persistence.

"Mr Kirklan?" A short, slim Balinese man in a white shirt and black trousers suddenly appeared at Griffin's side, smiling broadly.

"That's me." He turned to Sheryl with a look of relief.

"I am Yan. Mr Davidson ask me to pick you up. You come with me, please. Mrs Kirklan, I carry your bag." For a small, almost frail-looking man, he had a reassuring manner and the ease with which he picked up Sheryl's heavy suitcase suggested he was strong and fit. Griffin nodded at Sheryl, and they followed Yan to a tiny minibus parked nearby.

"So, where are we off to?" Griffin sat in the front passenger seat, his legs bent to the side around the bulge of the engine cover. He held on tightly to the strap over the door. Sheryl found it easier to sit across the back seat, rather than negotiate various plastic bags, newspapers and other junk that littered the floor. Griffin glanced back at her. She wasn't amused. Nowadays, anything less than a stretch limo to greet them on arrival was unacceptable.

"Nusa Dua, Mr Kirklan." Another toothy grin.

"Oh, that's great." He smiled back at Sheryl, but wasn't sure if she was acknowledging his efforts to placate her, as her eyes were hidden behind reflections in her sunglasses. "My wife and I stayed there… it must have been ten years ago, wasn't it, honey?" No reply. "At the Grand Hyatt, I think. Great hotel. Nice people. We had a great time."

"Yes, yes, lovely hotel." Yan negotiated his way around a small motorbike that was laboring under the weight of an entire family, its driver meandering aimlessly around potholes and drain covers. A small child was perched in front of him, another child was sitting sideways on his mother's lap, and the mother herself held two bulging plastic bags of shopping. "You like Bali? You come here often?" They continued to make light conversation as they passed shops, several temples and eventually came to the peninsula where many of the popular tourist hotels were situated. Sheryl sat glumly in the back, her mood sinking lower the further they went. Past the Grand Hyatt, the Melia, the Westin—where on earth were they heading? It obviously wasn't to one of the hotels she'd seen online when she was browsing the day before. But they'd agreed that it wasn't worth booking anywhere as, if their hunch was correct, their accommodation would have been arranged for them. That was clearly what had happened, and Griffin, at least, was happy to go along for the ride.

Eventually the minibus lurched to a stop. To the right, they could see a hotel with its own driveway where porters were hanging around, chatting.

"Are we going in?" Griffin asked.

"No need." Yan jumped out and opened the back door to take out the baggage. "Follow me, please." Pulling both their sets of baggage behind him, he walked briskly through a small doorway to their left, and onto a wooden walkway that was covered by a thatched roof. "Already checked in," he said, over his shoulder as he walked. They followed him as the path gave way to stepping stones across a beautiful pond, alive with multi-colored fish and surrounded by traditional Balinese carvings of sensuous goddesses, then through into a corridor to an accommodation block. Their room was up a flight of stairs. It was simple, yet elegantly traditional. The king-sized bed faced a single window that ran the full length of one wall and looked out over a plush tropical garden, a pool and a Jacuzzi with a bar. Beside the bed, a narrow doorway led to a windowless bathroom. Yan handed the key card to Griffin and left a spare on a table by the door. "Mr Davidson call you later. Five o'clock." Then he was gone.

"Thank you," said Griffin, to the door, just after it closed.

"Well, this is freakin' plush, isn't it?" Sheryl said sarcastically.

"Well, it looks comfortable to me." He was tired and he didn't have the energy to argue. "Sheryl, can you just bear with things for a while? You know this isn't exactly a normal holiday."

"When did we last have one of those?" She ripped the zip open on her case and started pushing clothes onto shelves in the closet, grimacing at the musty smell of the wood, and running fingers over the shelves to check for dust. "Is there even a beach here?"

"I'm going to have a shower, freshen up, and then let's go and explore. Okay?" Griffin hadn't expected Sheryl to be on top form after the long flight, and he was trying hard to keep things civil. She gestured a resentful apology and continued unpacking.

They each felt crowded by the other. Being confined in small spaces was no longer easy for Griffin and Sheryl. Over the years, they'd grown accustomed to just 'touching base' with each other. It had become a lot easier to organize dinners, meetings, events and Griffin's political schedule than it was to sit together in a room and talk to each other, simply because they wanted to express how they felt or pass the time of day with idle chat. They only did busy chat. Typically, it took the form of a series of staccato observations, instructions, requests, arrangements or opinions, spoken quickly and sometimes harshly. It didn't usually involve eye contact, and it certainly didn't involve intimate feelings or real connection. Quick replies were required to show that each was on the case, alert and dealing with things efficiently and intelligently. There was no room for wasting time with contemplation, absorption or consideration. Answers had to be immediate, fast and correct. Conversation was little more than a battlefield. Shots were fired—some hit home, some missed their target, and only the fittest survived.

For both of them, the notion of a holiday had become a somewhat foreign concept. It represented more stress than relaxation, with personal and relationship challenges that neither of them were prepared to address. So it gave Griffin some relief to know that this *was* no ordinary holiday, and that there was something important for him to do that would divert him from paying too much attention to his wife.

Sheryl felt as if she was suspended, emotionally and physically, as if motionless in a parachute, high above the earth, unable to chart her course, but knowing that one wrong move could cause her to plunge to her death. Somewhere deep inside her, she wanted Griffin to know that, but she'd lost the language to speak it. The cold, routine façade was all she could do now.

The call came at 5pm, as promised. They were flaked out on the bed. The journey had finally exhausted the last of their energies. Griffin extended an arm to where the sound of the phone was coming from.

"Hello?" He rubbed his eyes.

"Is that you, Griffin?" Griffin sat up, suddenly alert.

"Larry, where are you?" It was *so good* to hear Larry's voice!

"Meet me at the Bumbu Bali at 7pm. It's a restaurant just down the road.

You can get a hotel car to bring you. Just ask one of the porters. Give them my name."

"Should I bring—?" Griffin was uncertain as to what was required. It was all so cloak-and-dagger that he didn't want to risk assuming anything.

"Yes, of course. Bring Sheryl. It'll be great to see you both." There was a click as Larry hung up. Sheryl snorted and woke up.

"That was Larry. We're going to see him this evening."

"That's great." She turned over, away from him.

"Swim before dinner?" She grunted and went back to sleep, so he got into his trunks and headed for the pool.

* * *

As they entered the restaurant, a loud chorus greeted them.

"Good evening lady and gentleman!" The smiling Balinese welcome came from the open kitchen where six men in white, with traditional Balinese black-and-white-checked sashes around their waists, were engaged in a frenzy of culinary preparation. They were led to a table in a back corner by a warmly smiling hostess. As they approached the table, Larry stood and came to meet them. They embraced warmly before they sat down, and Larry wiped a tear from his eye. He looked a little thin. He'd always been a keen athlete, right through to his sixties, so he'd never put on the weight of a thousand political lunches like so many did. He'd always been careful and looked after himself— as well as everyone else he cared about—but he looked drawn and older than when Griffin had last seen him.

"How's Evelyn?" asked Larry. Griffin detected a slight quiver in his voice. Sheryl placed her hand on Larry's and bit her lip.

"She sure is strong, Larry," Griffin had to force himself to sound upbeat. "But, you know..." He was still struggling to find ways to express matters of the heart in helpful and constructive ways. Larry bowed his head, and then, with a sad smile, said, "Thank you both so much for coming. It is *so great* to have you here. Can we just talk about nothing important this evening? There's a lot we have to get through in the next few days, Griffin, but this evening I need a little time out with two of my dearest friends." Griffin and Sheryl agreed willingly and they turned their attention to the menu. The food, the wine, the conversation, the warm Balinese air, the ever-smiling staff and the sheer relief of being able to talk to Larry again helped Griffin relax a little, for the first time in months. Sheryl seemed to be infected with the convivial mood, and started to show some of the fast wit and warm wisdom that she kept locked away so much of the time. Halfway through a delicious desert of warm black rice pudding and coconut cream, Larry turned to Sheryl and asked, "Have you read *Eat, Pray, Love*? It's a book about... I think the author, an American girl called Elizabeth Gilbert, describes it as 'One woman's search for everything'."

"No, I haven't. Why do you ask?"

"Part of it is based on her experiences here on this island."

"Which part is that?"

"The part about love." Larry smiled at her. "You should read it. It's a great book."

"Well, maybe I should." Sheryl kept her eyes fixed on Larry's.

"What are you up to, Larry?" Griffin chuckled.

"Oh, it's just a little treat I've arranged for Sheryl while we are putting the world to rights tomorrow. I've arranged for Yan to take Sheryl on a 'Liz Gilbert tour' to Ubud for the day." Sheryl perked up at this news.

"Larry, thank you so much! But why did you go to all that trouble? You know I can find my way around, and you have a lot on your mind right now."

Larry looked a little embarrassed. He turned to Sheryl. "Well, I thought you'd enjoy it, and I thought it was important."

"How so?" Sheryl asked, perplexed by his concerned look.

"Unfortunately, I got the sequence reversed in my own life, and I don't want that to happen to you two."

"What do you mean?"

Larry put down his spoon and said, with careful deliberation, "I had the love, but it got taken away from me. Now, all I can do is pray, and most of the time I don't want to eat. You two, on the other hand… Your life has fed you well, but now I feel that you both spend a lot of time praying and not admitting to it. And where is love?"

They sat in silence as the waitress brought them coffees, and the first few drops of rain drumming on the roof signaled an imminent spring downpour.

CHAPTER 12

"More coffee, sir?" Troy King waved the waitress away. He was up to his eyeballs in coffee, having sat in an Upper West Side diner for the past three hours, waiting. He'd finished his breakfast two hours ago and he'd been chain-drinking coffee ever since, so the staff would tolerate his presence. Every now and then, he'd squirm his way out of the booth to the washroom and back. He'd slowly read the *New York Times* from cover to cover. These days, he had little interest in the news. He'd seen and read all he needed to in his life—the way the economies of the world waxed and waned, the conflicts that came and went, the sports teams that won and lost. He felt remote from it all. And, having seen man at his worst in Iraq, with all the brutal suffering that it entailed, all the rest of it seemed like superficial nonsense to him now. He wished he could have retired. That had been the plan, though he'd been bitterly disappointed at having had to end his military career without any great achievement—some personal contribution to mankind and peace. He felt flat. His life, which had begun as an exciting adventure, had become a slide into cynicism, devoid of any belief in the ideals instilled in him in his youth. Even his retirement plans had gone awry. Having bought the orchard, thinking that at least he'd be doing something wholesome, natural and beneficial to the local community, the bottom had immediately dropped out of the market for Granny Smiths. His orchard had become a casualty of superstore buying policies and the power of the fast food culture. Granny Smiths had become boring.

He would have loved to explore New York, but walking was painful for him. After just a few blocks, his lower back had seized up, as it did most days. He checked his watch: 12.30. He paid, left the diner and hailed a cab. Just as he was about to get in, his iPhone pinged.

"Ah. Good." He smiled as he read the message, then put the iPhone back in his jacket pocket. "West 57th," he told the driver. The plastic seat was collapsing under him and he tried to hold himself upright to minimize the pain in his back.

"57th and what?" the cab driver asked, in a thickly accented voice. King leaned forward and peered through the scratched plexiglas divider to check the driver's ID attached on the dashboard. He guessed he must be Ukrainian. He'd heard that most New York cab drivers were Ukrainian these days.

"5th," he said loudly.

"You got it," the driver replied, like a native New Yorker. He gunned the cab, throwing King painfully back into his seat. It lurched through the intersections as the driver raced the lights toward the junction with 5th. King kept his head down and braced, pressing one hand into the seat and grasping the strap over the door with the other. As they crossed the Avenue of the Americas, his cell phone rang. There was no way he could release a hand to get the call, so he shouted at the driver to stop. As soon as it was safe, he pulled the phone from his pocket.

"Ken. What you got?" The driver turned to him, pointing at the meter. "Hang on, Ken." He paid and slowly extracted himself from the cab. It was getting hard to stand. "Ken, lemme call you back. Just gimme five, okay?" He was breathing heavily now. The pain in his back was excruciating. He searched around for somewhere to sit. There was nothing nearby, but he spotted a big red sculpture over the road that he could park his butt against for a few minutes. Once in position, he waited for the pain to subside, then called Ken.

"Okay, Ken. Fill me in."

"It was a piece of cake, sir." Ken was upbeat. "The guy—Dwayne Waldron— he was a real redneck. Lived just outside of Lincoln in a small apartment over a store. He didn't want to talk, at first, and kinda threatened me—'git, or you'll be eatin' floor, mister'. But as soon as I mentioned NSA, he caved. Sweet as honey after that. Showed me round his place; and showed me his computer gear. He's running his own server and provides what he refers to as his 'support service for our boys over there'." He paused. "Sir, this guy is a real asshole. He's put up this site called 'ShocknWhore', and you never seen such perverted junk in all your life. That's where the clip was."

"When did he upload it?"

"Six days ago, sir. And here's the interesting bit. He did it as soon as he got back from his last stint in Afghanistan."

"And where did he get it?"

"That's the thing, sir. Before he left, he was on patrol someplace near Mazar, and this local kid comes up to him and starts hassling him. He says he knew this kid and he was alright. He'd already given him some stuff including his Lincoln College Football badge—that's the one on the clip— that the kid seemed real proud of. So as far as this kid was concerned, he was his friend. Anyways, this time he had no idea what the kid wanted, and he said he told him he hadn't got any sweets or cigarettes or anything. But it turned out the kid was actually trying to give *him* something—wrapped up in some cloth. Well, he tells me that he didn't want to take it in case it was a bomb or some such, so the kid unwrapped it for him, and it was this cell phone. Well, he makes a sign at the kid to say 'no thanks, I already got one', but the kid insists he take it. So, he thinks he wants some money. So he goes to get some out, but the kid gestures 'no, no'. He didn't want any money, and he ran off shouting at him something that he couldn't understand. That was all he knew about it till he got home and checked the phone out. And that's when he found the clip. When he saw it, he just thought, 'shit, this is good stuff,' and added it to all the other junk he got up there."

"And he never thought to report the clip?"

"I guess not. No, sir."

"And he never thought there was anything strange about it?"

"Sir, I don't think that thinking is one of this guy's fortés."

"Hmm. Well, I guess that's why it didn't come up on our radar just yet. I don't think porn sites are high on the list of security threats—though maybe they should be…" He thanked Ken and said he expected him back in the office ASAP, *without* running up unnecessary expenses. "Oh, and before you go…" King wanted to catch as much detail as possible, "…were Waldron's clients in the habit of downloading clips like this?"

"Yeah, loads of them got downloaded, although he did say that he was thinking of taking this one down as it wasn't that popular."

"Popular?"

"Yeah… hardly seems to be the right word, I guess."

"And could he tell you if Barak had downloaded other clips?"

"No."

"No, he hadn't, or no, he couldn't tell you?"

"Probably both, sir, but I don't think this guy bothered with much web traffic analysis. He just analyzed revenues and spent it on Buds, judging by the empties lyin' around his place."

As King was replacing his cell phone in one pocket, the iPhone pinged again in the other.

"Damn." King felt slightly embarrassed at having two mobile devices. He hoped he wasn't turning into one of those techno-gadget-happy people. He checked the screen and smiled. "Better and better. They must be high on daddy's money." This was a follow-up message to the one he'd received as he was getting into the cab. According to one of David's online identities, Assaf Barak had just let him know, via Foursquare, that he was really excited to have checked into the Atelier restaurant at the Four Seasons on West 57th for lunch. King couldn't imagine why anyone would want to advertise their every move over the Internet, but he was glad that some did. He wondered if he was near the hotel.

"Excuse me, sir." He caught the attention of a businessman walking quickly by. "Can you tell me what number on 57th this is?" The man laughed and said, "You're sitting on it!" and walked briskly on.

"Thanks for nothing," King muttered to himself as he stood up as straight as his back would allow and walked a few paces. He wasn't even sure which direction he was meant to be heading. He scanned the street and burst out laughing. Pain shot through his back, but at least he'd got the joke. He'd been supporting himself against a sculpture of an eight-foot-high number—nine.

He was relieved that the cab he took for the two-block trip was a more recent model, with a seat that hadn't suffered years of abuse from obese passengers. However, he felt he had to apologize to the driver for the short distance. He needn't have. The driver overcharged him and also took the apologetic tip that King offered him.

The sight of the Four Seasons building was something of a shock. From his bent standing position, King had to turn his head sideways to look up at its 54-story tower, soaring high above him. I.M.Pei's fantastic *art moderne* construction was not only the tallest hotel in New York, but also one of the most expensive. When the doorman looked disparagingly down at him from the steps leading to reception, King realized that he must have looked like the Hunchback of Notre Dame eyeing up the bell tower. Nevertheless, the doorman held the door open for him.

Well, that was a first, thought King. And it was—the first time a doorman had ever opened a door for him at a fancy hotel, and the first time he'd set foot in such opulent surroundings. He felt distinctly uneasy. He didn't belong here. He also felt a little angry as he cast his mind back to Iraq and the young men fighting and dying there. Was this the lifestyle of people they ultimately took their orders from? He had to put such thoughts aside for now.

The Atelier restaurant was an oasis of calm. Sumptuous comfort and quality oozed out of every inch of its elegant, discreet design. The restrained clinking of cutlery and hushed conversations gave it more the air of a church than the sort of eateries King was used to. He wished he could stand up straight.

"Do you have a reservation, sir?"

"No... I'm here to meet someone."

"And who would that be, sir?"

"A Mr Barak." A list was checked.

"I have no one of that name here, sir. Perhaps—"

"It could be under the name of Nadif." Another cursory glance at the list.

"No, nothing under that either. I really don't think I can help you, sir." The maître d' was trying to edge him out of the restaurant.

"Look, I know he's in here somewhere, and I'm going to find him myself if you don't feel like doing it for me." King quickly flashed his identification. Fortunately, it included the NSA logo but, actually, as Arlington Online was officially a private contractor to the Agency, it carried no official weight whatsoever. But it seemed to do the trick. He indicated that he was looking for two young men who answered to those names. One was black, the other was white, but he couldn't describe them in detail. The maître d' frowned and gave a terse nod.

"Let me make some inquiries." He strutted back into the restaurant. King looked around for some support for his back, and saw an elegant plinth with a tall, very expensive-looking vase perched on top of it. *It's okay, I'm not accident-prone*, he told himself as he breathlessly wiped some sweat from the scar on his brow with a tissue. But he decided not to risk it.

"We do have a Mr Samakab, in a party of three. The two young men who are with him would seem to fit your description." It took a moment for King to realize the significance of the name, but when it dawned on him how unexpectedly fortunate he had been, he blurted out, "That's them!" and had to restrain himself from punching the air with excitement. King was thinking quickly now. How was he going to handle this situation? He had anticipated easily handling two young and possibly frightened students, but now he knew that they were backed up by a powerful businessman who was used to mixing with plutocrats and politicians. He would just have to wing it and see what happened. He did have surprise on his side, and some information that would certainly grab Samakab's attention and could potentially embarrass him if it was connected to his son, Ayan. Even so, given these foreign surroundings, his feelings of social inadequacy, his lack of preparation and his deteriorating physical state, he felt nauseous.

"Sir, if you need to talk with Mr Barak alone, can I suggest—"

"No, you can't." King smiled and gestured to the maître d' to show him to the table. "Thank you." He didn't want anyone slipping out of this room before he got to them.

Samakab and his son were sitting with Barak at a corner table that had been hidden from view by a screen. Samakab was chewing on a bread roll, chatting cheerfully while they waited for their first course. The two students sat facing him. Samakab looked up as the maître d' introduced King to them, then promptly left, making an exaggerated gesture to the barman as he did so.

"Mr Samakab, Mr Nadif, Mr Barak... good to meet you." King was still trying to process a possible approach to this conversation. He'd never played the investigating officer before, other than in virtual.

"What's this about and how do you know our names?" Samakab barked. He was extremely annoyed at being disturbed at a rare private lunch with his son, and he was appalled that this man not only knew who they all were, but also that they would be there at this precise time.

"It's my job to know," King said as he leaned on the table. It was the only explanation that came to mind quickly enough. He instinctively felt bad about showing his ID, but he needed to quickly establish some credibility with Samakab, and it was all he had. Samakab took a pair of reading glasses from his breast pocket and peered at the laminated card, which King held onto as Samakab grasped it and pulled it closer.

"Arlington Online Data Systems... who are they? I don't know this company. What have they to do with me and my son... and his friend?"

Samakab had a calm confidence about him. His accent suggested that he'd spent a lot of time in England, mixing with the upper classes. There were just a few inflexions and pronunciations originating from his Somali origins. The two students watched the exchange, transfixed.

"Arlington Online is contracted to the NSA and deals with matters of national security." *This is getting worse and worse*, King thought.

"National security!?" Samakab's tone changed abruptly. He turned in his seat, waving to try and get the attention of the maître d'.

"I wouldn't do that, if I were you, sir." King knew he'd almost lost it. If the maître d' called security and had him thrown out, he'd have a lot of explaining to do to keep his job.

"I have no business with you." Samakab waved to the maître d' again, who was busy seating a party of six on the other side of the restaurant. However, sensing the urgency of the situation at the corner table, the barman caught his attention and he quickly came to see what was going on.

"Sir?"

"This man is harassing us. Have him removed from here immediately. I do not expect this kind of intrusion in this hotel, and I want to see the manager as soon as I have eaten. Now, make sure we are left in peace so I can enjoy my meal with my son." With that, Samakab turned back to his guests, and they resumed their conversation.

"Sir, you'd better come with me." The maître d' took King by the arm.

King cursed himself for such a clumsy performance. Not only had he burst in completely ill-prepared, but he'd also shown his ID to Samakab, and he knew he was now in deep, deep trouble. In a last, pathetic attempt to reduce the fallout from this disaster, as the maître d' pulled subtly on his arm, he mumbled, "Apologies for the intrusion, genlmen. I hope you all have a great stay in New York. According to the weatherman, you got some nice sunny days to look forward to."

Samakab suddenly stopped in mid-sentence and stared up at King, who held his gaze.

"Well, I think it is I who should apologize. I'm sorry, Mr King. Please, would you join us for some lunch?"

"Wha…? Sure. Thank you." King unhitched himself from the grasp of the maître d' and steered himself into the seat beside Samakab. Nadif and Barak looked as confused as King felt.

Samakab handed a menu to King, who was admiring the magnificent silver table setting and unfolding a stiffly starched, whiter-than-white napkin to place on his lap.

"You might like to try the free-range caramelized quail stuffed with foie gras, potato purée and summer truffle. It's really very good. Or perhaps the steak tartare with hand-cut French fries is more what you are used to." King forced a smile. He scanned the menu for anything that looked as if it might be edible.

"Steak and fries is good for me, I guess." King handed the menu to the maître d' who had waited to see that the storm was over before returning to his other customers.

"Thank you, sir," he remarked stiffly, then marched off.

Samakab continued, "So, this is very interesting. Tell me, Mr King, how are we three of interest to Arlington Online Data Systems? Have you identified us as a terrorist cell, based in the Four Seasons Hotel? I must say, it's a far cry from the Al Qaeda camps in the mountains of Pakistan!" They all laughed at the joke.

"Yes, I have, absolutely." King watched their faces drop before he gave a broad smile. "Only kiddin' you!" King continued, "But I do have something we're concerned about," he turned to Barak, "and you seem to be the one to start with." Assaf Barak laughed nervously, as King's confidence began to return.

"Me? I haven't done anything." His already pale face now looked as white as the napkins. Having received the information about the website from Ken, and now having met this weak-looking, nervous boy, King felt there was no more useful additional information that he could gain from him. Barak certainly didn't have the defiant, confident air of someone who might be involved in terrorism. However, although outward appearances could be deceiving, it was the company he was keeping that was of interest to him now. If there was some connection between Barak, Ayan and Samakab that was more than just friends and family, he wanted to know about it. He'd found it strange that he'd been able to turn up virtually nothing on Samakab at the office, which was odd for such a high-profile business figure and regular visitor to the USA. Even if there was no connection to the video, his curiosity about this man was growing. For now, though, he had to be careful how he played the few cards he had. If he could generate some uncertainty in their minds, he might be able to extract other nuggets of information, that could lead to… something—but he'd no idea what.

"It's okay. Don't worry. You're not gonna end up in Guantanamo or nothin'," he reassured Assaf with a smile. The boy looked somewhat relieved, but King immediately regretted the choice of words. "Do you mind if I talk about this in front of your friends, or would you prefer to step out to the lobby?"

"No, it's fine. I have nothing to hide from anyone." He looked nervously at Ayan and his father.

"Okay." King thought for a moment, trying to compose a line of questioning that would yield something useful while at the same time not isolating these three. "You used to be involved in the peace movement in Israel… Sadaka Reut, I believe, when you was at school, yes?" Assaf drew a sharp breath. *What is going on here?*

"That was a peace movement. It had nothing to do with terrorism. We were trying to create dialogue—"

"Yes, yes, I know. And now you have a girlfriend in the Gaza Strip, correct?" The poor kid was squirming in his seat now.

"How do you know that!? What has she got to do with this? I am sorry, Mr Samakab. I swear I don't know what this is about. Please believe me!"

"I'm sure you don't, Assaf." Samakab patted his hand. "Are you going to get to the point of this soon?" He glared at King.

"Yes, I am." He brought his attention back to Assaf, who was looking down at the table, kneading his napkin between clenched fists. "Now, we all know how difficult things are over there right now, for you and especially for Salma—" Assaf shot King a frightened look. He knew her name! "—and I was just wondering, if, because of all that strife, the failings of the peace process, the siege and all…" King leaned forward on the table "…if some of those peaceful thoughts might have turned to, well, angry thoughts."

"No, of course they haven't! How can peace ever, ever come from anger!?" Assaf shouted at King with tearful eyes. The maître d' glanced over, as did most of the other guests. The restaurant was filling up, and people were being seated close to them now. Samakab was getting very edgy with this line of conversation and, leaning in, he said in a low voice, "What on earth are you suggesting, Mr King? Can't you see that this young man is scared out of his wits at what you are saying, and what you know about him? You had better explain yourself, and quickly."

King turned to Samakab. "I intend to do that, sir, right now." Turning back to Assaf, he again asked, "Are you sure you wouldn't rather do this in private?" Assaf was paralyzed with fear, and still had no idea where this line of questioning could be leading, but he indicated that he'd prefer to stay and at least have the support of his friends around him, rather than risk being alone with this nightmare of a man who seemed to think he was some sort of terrorist.

"Okay, then." King searched in his inside pocket as he spoke. "Why are you sending videos of terrorist activity to your friend in the UK?"

"That is ridiculous! I have never done such a thing!" Assaf replied urgently, but now in a quieter voice. King pulled a piece of paper out of his pocket and, without a word, showed it to Assaf. "Oh, my God! What… where did you—? I don't understand. That was just a bit of fun!"

"Well, I know it was the first 'bit of fun' you downloaded from that website, but my queshion is, why'd you do it? And why send it to your friend here." He glanced across at Ayan who was leaning over to read the email. Before Assaf could reply, Samakab snatched the email from Assaf's hand.

"What is this?" He angrily scanned the email. "This is a perfectly innocent email. Assaf is just curious about what is going on in a video, and he's asking my son if he has read a book. What harm is there in that? What is wrong with the American Intelligence services? Have they nothing better to do than harass perfectly innocent students?" King sat in silence, watching Assaf. Assaf said nothing, so King pressed on in a hushed tone.

Turning to Samakab, he said, "Sir, you haven't seen the video." Samakab didn't respond, but turned to Assaf, concerned. King continued. "What I want to know is, how you knew to find that video on that particular website, and why, immediately following a conversation with a girl whose father has known Hamas connections, you downloaded just this video, and attached it to an email to Ayan Korfa Nadif." King knew this line of questioning was unfair, as he was fairly sure that Assaf was only looking for porn at the time, and the clip he downloaded had simply attracted his attention because it was unusual for that website. Also, as a student of political science, he most likely had a healthy interest in what was going on in Afghanistan. All King wanted now was to get Samakab's confidence and find out why he'd suddenly had a change of heart about talking to him.

"What website are you talking about? Is it a terrorist website?" Samakab asked.

"No, sir," King volunteered as he kept his eye on Assaf, "it's just a general video entertainment website… Assaf?" Assaf was quietly grateful, as was Ayan, that King had not revealed the nature of the website. He tried to pull himself together to answer the question.

"It had nothing to do with my conversation with Salma. She knew nothing of it." He wiped a tear from his eye. "Hamas is not a terrorist organization. It's a political party. Many, many good people in Gaza support Hamas, as I'm sure you know. In fact, I don't know why you say such things."

"And the video?" King pressed him to answer.

"I found it interesting—and strange."

"Why was that?"

"It didn't make sense to me. Many poor people lying dead. The wounds looked… odd. And there was nothing about it in the press or anywhere online, that I could find."

"What did you find odd about the wounds, Assaf?" King held his gaze now, urging him on, giving him confidence.

"They all looked as if they were in the chest, throat or head… all in identical places." As he spoke, King noticed through the corner of his eye that Samakab was sitting back, composing an SMS on his cell phone. *That must be urgent*, he thought. Assaf was still speaking. "How could that happen?"

"Thank you, Assaf." King said, without answering Assaf's question. He glanced over at Samakab who was pressing 'send'.

"Sorry about that," said Samakab, leaning forward to re-engage in the conversation.

"So, Ayan, when you received the video, what did you think of it, and did you send it on to anyone else?" King asked.

"I thought it was odd as well, but I didn't really get into it and study it—and I didn't send it to anyone else. What's so important about it that got your attention?" Ayan asked.

"I can't tell you that, but thank you both for your help on this."

"Shall we eat?" asked Samakab, signaling an end to King's questioning as the waiters brought their meals to the table. King studied the dish as it was placed in front of him.

"Goddam! What's this—a raw burger? I aksed for a steak." Turning to Samakab he said, "In a fancy place like this, you think they'd at least know how to cook a steak." He fired a glance at the waiter. "Take this back and gimme a proper steak—well done."

"Sir, it's steak tartare. It's—" the waiter quickly realized the futility of explaining the finer points of haute cuisine to this guy. "Very well, sir." Samakab smiled at Ayan, and the three of them started their meals. King shook his head and took a sip of water. Turning to Samakab, he said, "You come over here quite a lot, I gather. You got a lot of business goin' on here?"

"Yes, I do some trading—various products from Somalia and other places."

"Oh… what kind of stuff are you trading?"

"This and that. Clothing, raw materials, that sort of *stuff*." He emphasized the word 'stuff' as if to let King know that he didn't appreciate such a disparaging term for the considerable and important business he was doing.

"Well, it seems to do you pretty good." He scanned in the room, with its high ceiling, elegant bar and expensive furnishings.

"It works for me." Samakab was all but ignoring him as he savored his scallop cooked in its shell, with spicy chive oil. He was wishing he could have the meal he'd planned—a relaxed lunch chatting about Oxford and family matters with his son and his friend. He had tired of King and was annoyed at being trapped in a rambling conversation while King's meal was being cooked.

"I was reading the *New York Times* earlier," King continued, oblivious to the subdued mood around him. "They reckon there's an increase in the number of ships bein' hijacked around your way these days. Just yesterday, another one got taken. They reckon it had a whole bunch of T-32 tanks, guns, ammo—enough to kit a small army, they were sayin'—on their way to Kenya. You hear about that?"

"No, I haven't read today's papers yet." Samakab sighed, laid his cutlery on his plate and folded his arms. He'd been hoping that if he didn't engage in conversation, King would shut up and he could continue his conversation with Ayan and Assaf. The subject that King was drifting toward was one he did not want to discuss with him, of all people.

"I think you'd find it interesting, being from that country. What's the government doin' about all this piracy? It looks like things have gotten really out of hand over there."

"It's a difficult situation, I agree, but I really don't get involved… Ah, here's your steak."

"Now, that's what I call a proper steak!" King smiled, and tucked in enthusiastically. It was the best steak he'd ever tasted. The chef had cooked it under sufferance, compelled by a tense maître d', who'd had to defuse the tantrum that erupted when the steak tartare had been returned. Samakab, Ayan and Assaf were at last able to talk uninterrupted. Every now and then, they glanced at King, regarding his unsophisticated eating habits with some amusement. The minute he'd finished, Samakab took the opportunity to drop a heavy hint that it was time for him to leave.

"Mr King, have you got a number I can reach you on?" King gladly obliged, writing his cell phone number on the back of a receipt he found in his wallet.

"Maybe you could give me yours, too?"

Samakab paused for thought, then wrote a US mobile number on one of his business cards, being careful to obliterate his landline number in Somalia.

"Enjoy your stay in New York, Mr King. We'll talk later."

You betcha! thought King, as he flashed a triumphant smile at the maître d' on the way out.

CHAPTER 13

"Griff, I know you want me to explain what happened, why I had to leave the States, and why Evelyn isn't with me. I've been thinking about this meeting for the past week, and the longer I think about it, the more I feel I have to tell you. There are no simple, quick or, I suspect, acceptable answers I can give you, no matter how I try to gift-wrap them." Larry had invited Griffin to walk with him on one of Bali's endless, beautiful beaches. The previous night's downpour had given way to a fresh, bright, breezy morning. They had started early. Larry had a lot to get through and he wanted to make the most of the few days Sheryl and Griffin were there.

"Okay. Where would you like to start?" Larry kicked his sandals off and let the surf wash over his feet as he walked.

"With you, Griff… if that's okay with you. I need to know where you're coming from, and then I need *you* to know where you could be going, if you choose to." Larry's tone and the ambiguity of his comment made Griffin uneasy. Larry had always been so direct and clear—something he'd always admired in him. This was a new Larry. The Larry he'd known had been a sharp-suited, ball-busting intellectual politician, super-fit in body and mind. It was definitely the old Larry they'd been with at the restaurant the evening before, with *Pure Larryness* flooding over them as humor, wit and great story-telling. This Larry was a little older, with wild grey hair blowing in the breeze, open-shirted with baggy khaki trousers dragging in the surf. He was contemplative, softer, with a hint of bohemian lifestyle.

"Shoot. I'll do all I can to help." Griffin smiled, but felt a lump in his throat as he turned to face his friend. Larry was gazing out toward the horizon. Then he smiled and brought his attention back to Griffin.

"Okay, but bear with me if I seem to be rambling on." He picked up a shell and cleaned the sand off it as he walked. "Griff, have you any idea what happened to you back there, after the press conference?"

"Not a clue, Larry. I guess it was what you'd call a 'defining moment', although, till then, I thought those only happened on the podium, not afterwards—especially when you'd just delivered a historical peace deal. This one completely threw me." He stopped and looked at Larry. "It made me question everything—and I mean *everything*, Larry—even my own sanity. After all these years, I thought I meant something, stood for something in this whole political machine. But this… I can't even process it *now*. The finality, the crazy stuff about a holiday... Yet everyone had a story—an angle that seemed really normal to them. And the President said nothing. *Nothing*. No confidential chat, no 'Dear John' letter." Griffin raised his hands in exasperation and let them fall heavily by his sides.

"Have you read the papers today?" Larry asked. *My God!* Griffin realized that it was the first time in years that he hadn't scanned the headlines. "I think you'll find," Larry checked to see that no one was within earshot, "that your Israeli negotiator has been killed by a car bomb on his way home from the airport at Tel Aviv."

"What!?" He couldn't believe what Larry was telling him. *All that work! Not again, please…*

"I'm afraid so. It was the easy option, and the most effective way to counter your agreement. They're all back at each other's throats again, just like old times." Larry spoke matter-of-factly. He almost sounded bored. "Keep walking, Griff." They strolled on. A young family was staking out their patch of beach with bags, toys and a sunshade.

"What do you mean—'counter my agreement'?"

"They didn't want it, Griff. Nobody wanted it."

"Come on, Larry, that's ridiculous! I've been working on that agreement for years, overcoming huge obstacles, impossible odds. I had the full backing of the President and the cooperation of the Israelis and the Arabs. Who else is there? Who are 'they'? Everybody wanted this!"

Larry threw the shell into the surf and turned to Griff as he walked. "If you remember, when I started this conversation, I said that some of this stuff would probably not be acceptable to you. This is just one of those 'unacceptable' things—and there are plenty more. You'd better decide, right now, if you want to continue this conversation, or just go and have a nice holiday in Bali with your face in a beer trying to figure things out without me. Your choice, Griff, but you're right about one thing: this is a 'defining moment' for you, and the only reason I'm talking to you right now is because you might choose the wrong definition and, if you do, it'll be all over. Everything."

"What the hell does that mean? For God's sake, Larry, stop talking in riddles and give it to me straight."

"Like I said, Griff, it's not that simple and I need you to bear with me. You may think I've gone nuts for a while, but I know I have, at last, gone sane."

"Okay, okay. Sorry." They walked in silence as an elderly couple passed by with a cheerful 'good morning'.

"So, what was I doing wrong all that time, and why didn't anyone tell me?" asked Griffin, once the coast was clear again.

"You weren't doing anything wrong. You were doing what you were told and what you thought was right. That was your job and, for a while, it was important that you were seen to be doing it well. It made the White House look good, it kept the international press and public opinion on our side, and it kept them happy in the Middle East—albeit reluctantly for most of the time. You did a great job."

"So, I say again, what *did* I do wrong?"

"You succeeded." Larry slowed to a halt and looked out to sea again. "And now the whole agreement has been blown out of the water and no one can get hold of you. Nice and neat, right?"

"Larry, what the fuck are you saying?"

"What I'm saying, Griff, is that nothing is the way it seems. Well, that's pretty obvious now, isn't it? But before you have your 'defining moment', maybe you'd better wake up to a few more unpalatable truths. How about a nice strong coffee to help with that?" He pointed to a restaurant further up the beach, and they headed toward it. The sun was well and truly up, now, and the sound of speedboats—towing excited tourists over the waves on huge inflatables—filled the air. They sat at a table that was listing at a precarious angle in the sand and ordered coffees as the waiter jostled the table to a roughly level position. Griffin looked at his old friend, suddenly aware that he'd become totally absorbed by his own troubles and knew nothing of Larry's. What had caused him to leave so abruptly? Why on earth had he left Evelyn behind? Had there been some deep, unspoken rift in their marriage that Griffin and Sheryl had not been sensitive to, simply because they were only ever interested in themselves? That was unthinkable, so what was the reason? Why the secrecy at his office about him no longer working there? So many questions. The only thing he was beginning to understand was that the answers would take some time to emerge.

"Why didn't the President just fire me, or is that a stupid question?" Griffin asked, then thought about it and added, "I'm sorry Larry, but I feel any question I ask may seem stupid right now. I feel as if all logic and order have been stripped away."

"Oh, he doesn't want you gone. You're a great public figure, a popular front man, a dedicated grafter with good, solid American values. He doesn't want to get rid of you. You're a protector of the image and a spinner of the spin. Let's face it, Griff, that's what you've been doing all your life. And you're really good at it."

"Am I really that transparent?"

"Only to someone who knows you as well as I do—and to your paymasters, of course. Everyone else is seduced by your skill. Even if they don't like what you're saying—and some of them may even feel in their gut that what you say is just plain wrong—they *like* you, so they want to believe in you. And you have status and power, as far as they're concerned, and people like that too. You do, on their behalf, what they could never do themselves and would never want to take responsibility for. For your part, you love the adoration, the power and the glory, and you're happy to go along with the idea that you're in control. On the outside, that will not change when you go back to Washington. On the inside, they just want you to know you've been dumped on from a great height, and if you decide to change course, they can change your situation any way they want. They just opened the door to that. Don't worry, though; you can bet that your office has managed your absence flawlessly, because they'll have seen to that, as well."

"Is that what happened to you, Larry? You got dumped on, and decided to change course, despite knowing what the consequences would be?"

"Something like that." Larry looked weary, all of a sudden. "But I didn't know the consequences were going to be so huge. Without Ev, my life is…" the words wouldn't come. He sat up, took a deep breath, and said, "Griffin, this is why I wanted to speak completely openly to you. I have nothing to lose now. If, for some reason, I don't wake up tomorrow—and without being melodramatic, that's a distinct possibility—I don't want to go down with this whole bag of worms inside me." He smiled mischievously. "So I thought I'd give it to you and you can figure out if there's anything you want to do about it."

"Well, I'm flattered, I think… but why me, of all people? If you see me as a shallow spin doctor and social climber, shouldn't you be offering this distinguished prize to someone with a more deserving character?"

Larry considered this. "I admit I did think about it. But look, it's like this: I spent all my political life behind the scenes, working relationships and making deep connections. I still have a few good ones, who keep me up to date with what's going on. Because I wasn't public, it was easy to make me disappear. You, on the other hand, being very public and an attractive power-monger—if you'll excuse the expression—have other advantages. As we've just seen, they don't want you to disappear because, if you did, there'd be a big public hole to fill. That's not impossible to do, but these days anyone can get on the Internet and our own agencies are keeping tabs on everything like we're kids in a nursery, so it would take more time and energy than they want to expend.

"Secondly, I've known you for longer than most people in this game. I know you and Sheryl have become strangers to each other, but that's not irretrievable, and I know that, despite that, you're still rock solid in your relationship. That speaks volumes to me about the parts of your character that are buried, most of the time, but are also not irretrievable. All you've got to do is to stop the asshole in you dominating the loving, powerful part of you that is full of integrity and many other wonderful qualities the world has yet to see." Griffin went to speak, but Larry held up his hand and carried on. "Griff, there's stuff going down in our country… in the world, that could take us all down the pan." Griffin raised an eyebrow. "I know, I know. It's always been that way and that's why people like you and me keep doing what we do. But this is different, sort of." Larry knew that he wasn't being the least bit convincing. He needed more time to put some structure and order around the myriad thoughts that were running amok in his mind. He needed Griffin to stick with him, so he could plant a seed of new understanding in his mind. There was simply too much to elucidate, too much that would challenge and upset his friend's deeply-held beliefs if he didn't explain things properly. He knew he had to take it one step at a time. He had to wait and watch for the signs of recognition that he hoped would emerge from beneath years of conditioning and success, before he could get to the real reason why he'd summoned Griffin to Bali. "If you think I'm being a little dramatic… and extremely vague, at the same time, I can understand that, but I can't think of a nicer way to put it. I'm all out of spin. Fortunately, or unfortunately, for you," he said, putting on his best Bogart voice, "of all the bars in all the towns in all the world, you had to walk into this one."

"I don't get you." Griffin was puzzled.

"When we make friends, we don't know where those friendships are going to take us, or what we will be required to do. You are the only, and the best, person I could think of to talk to about what I know. You're also the only person I can think of who may be in a position to do something about it." He paused, looked out to sea again, then turned to Griffin and said, "Neither of us is getting any younger, Griff. I'm 65 and you're… what, 60?" Griffin nodded. "When we started out in this politics game, I guess neither of us really knew what it was about. For us, as kids, it was a career with glossy benefits if we succeeded. And that's one of the big problems with civilization. Each generation—each and every one of us—starts off from zero. Unlike the rest of the animal kingdom, we don't even instinctively know our place in the world. We appear to be the clever ones, but we're complete amateurs at relationships with each other and, as a race, our knowledge isn't cumulative. If we could be born with the knowledge of all our ancestors already programmed in, maybe we'd have a chance of taking civilization to a much higher level. But all we do is go round in the same old cycles with more and more sophisticated trinkets. Government by self-interest, driven by dysfunction, is all we can seem to manage—generation after generation. So the scrapping, wanting, bullying, winning and losing goes on. But eventually there's a tipping point, Griff, where it won't work anymore, and we're almost there. It doesn't look like it, I know, but that's the danger. We've got to start doing things differently, at the deepest level. And I'm not talking about peace deals, or environment, or better schools or economic reform or electric cars or any of the millions of ways that good people around the world are genuinely trying to address the symptoms of our failure. We've got to get down to the root cause or we're done." He paused as the waiter brought their coffees. "Should I continue?"

"Well, you asked me to bear with you, and I'm doing my best." Griffin fiddled with a sugar sachet, avoiding eye contact with Larry. "But really, what you seem to be saying is that we need some sort of political revolution in the US. If you're looking to me to be involved in some way or other, you'd better stop talking right now because I'm not your man." He glanced up at Larry and looked him straight in the eye. "To be honest, Larry, I'm a little surprised that you're talking to me like this. This is kids' stuff. You're talking like we're back at college, smoking weed in the dorm." Larry stared back at him, expressionless. He went on, "I've been in this game for 40 years now, and I think I know how things work. I know it isn't perfect, but we just have to work with that. That's the journey, and it always has been, in civilized society. As you say, we're all on a learning path." Griffin paused, searching his mind for a reason for Larry's rambling homily, and all he could think was that Larry had been so devastated by his forced separation from Evelyn—which must have been precipitated by a serious security breach or something that Larry had been doing that he should not have been doing—that his mind was going. He'd seen that happen to other colleagues as they aged, when they became less sharp or the pressures of politics eventually got to them. Some of them blew fuses, others suddenly suffered some sort of rapid deterioration, and yet others just stopped thinking and spent their final years prattling on about nothing in gated retirement communities. Griffin was starting to think that all this talking, the secret meeting, were all just symptoms of the onset of a sadly demented mind. All the same, he wanted to be kind to Larry.

"Look, Larry…" Griffin continued, "I know you must have gone through some sort of hell—"

"You know nothing. *Nothing!*" Larry snapped back at him.

"…and I know that the circumstances surrounding my peace deal were a little strange…"

"A little strange—is that what you *really think*? Griff…" Larry was trying to control his exasperation. "Don't you think that's just a little delusional?"

"I accept that even I don't necessarily know every detail of what's being done at the highest levels of government, and of course I know that everyone's expendable. I'm sure there were good reasons that I'll know about very soon—"

"Griff—*wake up!* Denial is not the way to deal with this. Have you so little trust in your own feelings—in yourself? Just remember what they've put you through in the last few days, never mind what you think may or may not have happened to me."

"Okay, Larry, help me out here a bit, here." Griffin spat his words out. "Who the hell are 'they'? You're talking about 'them' all the time. Let's flesh this out. Give me some names. You know who 'they' are, don't you? Go ahead. Hit me with some real people." Larry shook his head, sat back in his chair and let out a deep sigh.

"Boy, this is difficult. Let's backtrack a few steps. There are things you need to understand before we get into specifics. Now, I know you think I must be going down some loony tunes roads here, and maybe you're figuring I have Alzheimer's or something, but I'm going to ask you to keep trusting that I'm still completely sane and have all my ducks in a row. Can you do that for me, even if it's just for old time's sake? If nothing else, it will be a nice way to pass the time before you fly back. If you want to write me off then, well, that's up to you." He dipped his head toward Griffin, offering him a peace-negotiator's smile. Griffin glanced at him, then turned his attention to the gently rolling surf as he tried to make sense of the situation. Tourists were strolling along the sea shore, soaking up the sun and the peace. Simple pleasures on a paradise island that hardly registered in the turmoil of Griffin's mind. He felt weary, but for all the years that this man had supported Sheryl and him, he more than deserved just a few days of his time now.

He turned back to Larry and smiled. "You've got my full attention, my friend. Please, tell me what I need to know."

CHAPTER 14

Lush, verdant rice fields stretched away into the hazy distance, punctuated by brazen bursts of brilliant orange blossoms and the rhythmic bowing of a rice farmer, threading his way through the tender shoots like the lazy needle of a sewing machine. The sky was a flawless blue, interrupted only by two swooping lily-white egrets. It was an idyllic vista to behold. But that would have meant lifting her head out of the face cradle and she just couldn't be bothered.

Sheryl lay completely naked, face down on the massage table. Merpati, the tiny Balinese woman who'd been massaging her for some timeless eternity, had the face of an angel and fingers of steel. But her touch was also surprisingly gentle. She had caressed Sheryl's knotted shoulders with the softness of hot baby's breath, traveling down the tightness of her spine and—oh my God— even caressing the inside of her thighs. Her touch was as soothing as it was sensuous and Sheryl had never felt so profoundly relaxed. She lay in a state of rubber-jointed ease and mellow mindfulness yet her body had an awareness that she'd never felt before. It was as if every pore were an active receptor for touch, yearning toward Merpati's magical hands before they even landed on her skin. That author Larry had mentioned had got it all wrong; she'd left out a crucial part of the process: Eat, Pray, *Relax*, Love. She couldn't imagine how anyone could experience love, feel love or even *make* love without this kind of sensory induction. Had she ever really done any of those things? Certainly not with Griffin.

This kind of soporific bliss was so far removed from their crazy, *crazy* life in Washington and New Jersey that she wondered if she'd truly lost her mind somewhere along the way. A wave of hot sadness washed over her. That life was empty and brittle, superficial and meaningless—like an expensive porcelain vase that did nothing more than decorate a space. Right now, she wanted to fling that vase at the wall and smash it to smithereens. She never wanted to see it again. Her body tensed and Merpati's hands moved over her shoulders again, returning her to softness. Was this like a holiday romance—something that felt amazing while it was happening but then seemed utterly ridiculous as soon as you got back home? Yet she felt different at some intangible level. It was as if she'd been abducted by aliens and returned to earth profoundly changed, yet with no memory of what it was that had so changed her.

If Griffin were here... but, no. Even if he were here, she'd never be able to explain to him in words what she was feeling. She couldn't even articulate it to herself. This was something you had to experience yourself—like a nugget of exquisitely sublime dark chocolate ...or the delicious build toward orgasm. Her eyes shot open. What was she *thinking*? Where was all this coming from? "Lady no think, feel only," Merpati said softly, as she kneaded the back of Sheryl's neck. If only it were that simple, Sheryl thought, staring at the two tiny brown feet on the bamboo mat beneath her. Maybe it was. Those feet—so unhurried, so calm and steady in their purpose—seemed like a metaphor for a peaceful life. She closed her eyes again, lulled back to languidness and happy to escape all images and thoughts of her frantic life back home.

It took a minute for her to realize that Merpati's caresses had ceased. Then she felt a hot hand on her right shoulder. *No!* Her whole body rebelled. *Please don't ask me to get up.* "Lady stay. I bring jasmine tea." Merpati laid a cool sheet over Sheryl's back and gently closed the door behind her.

Sheryl relaxed back onto the table, blissfully relieved to let gravity reign again. How could she possibly go back to her life in New Jersey after this? How could she even bring herself to stand up, for God's sake? Her biggest fear right now was that this blissful tranquility would evaporate as soon as she walked out the door—and she would never get it back. That was simply too depressing to consider. There had to be a way to cultivate this. It all resided inside her, after all—this deep well of emotion and sensuality that had been locked away for far too long. How *had* she kept the lid on it all this time? How had it gone so far underground in the first place—without her even missing it?

Merpati padded back into the room, her bare feet whispering on the bamboo mat. Sheryl slowly rolled onto her back and watched as Merpati placed a small rattan tray on the floor beside her. Easing herself into a sitting position, Sheryl felt like a wobbly geriatric after major heart surgery. Merpati passed her a steaming earthenware mug and Sheryl reached for it gratefully, smiling her thanks. Did this woman have any idea what she'd done to her? Did this happen to every uptight, neurotic, coarse, self-important American who came here? She sipped the hot fragrant tea and inhaled its heady vapors. Her body was slowly coming back to mobility. But the thought of being upwardly mobile—as in 'walking upright'—still seemed a thought too far. She had no idea how long she'd been here but she knew it would never be long enough. And there was still the rest of her tour to complete. The guide who'd brought her here, at Larry's instruction, was waiting for her outside in his jeep. She didn't feel ready but she finally eased back the sheet and gingerly lowered her feet to the ground to get dressed.

CHAPTER 15

'Call in' read the message on Samakab's cell phone. It was five hours since he'd sent his query during lunch at the Four Seasons, and he couldn't help wondering why it had taken so long to get a reply. Ayan had noticed that his father looked unusually preoccupied following King's departure, but Samakab had assured him it was just 'pressure of work' and Ayan had thought no more about it. They'd talked about life at Oxford, the challenges of the Political Science course and Ayan had gone to great pains to reassure his father that he was spending his time responsibly. It was 3.30pm by the time they finished and Samakab had suggested they spend the rest of the day at an exhibition of recent works by Wangechi Mutu, a Kenyan artist, nearby at the Guggenheim.

"I think you will both find it interesting," he said, feeling a slight resistance from them; it was clear they wanted a few days of unstructured freedom. "Mutu seems to be emerging as a leading voice in African art when it comes to representation of the African female figure". That seemed to get their attention, although he deliberately left out the fact that Mutu also strongly objected to what she saw as the portrayal of black women as either tribal aborigines or sexy pin-ups. *Maybe this will help to drag them out of the gutter of Internet porn— although I doubt it.* "I went to a show of hers in Ontario a while back, called 'This you call civilization?' It's powerful work that you could say has a strong relevance to political science, from a social point of view. She explores female and cultural identity, in the context of beauty, consumerism, colonialism, race and gender. I was actually thinking of starting a collection of her work, and I'd be interested to hear what you both think." Samakab was pleased that he was not only giving the two young men something constructive to do, but also inviting their feedback on the artist's work.

Once Assaf and Ayan had left, he'd gone back to his suite. What had happened during lunchtime had caught him off guard. Pacing his room, he tried to piece together a rational scenario in his mind, but he was unable to come up with anything that made sense. Who the hell was King and what did he know? What was he doing turning up at the Atelier Restaurant like that, and who did he *really* work for? He also found it hard to believe that King was as stupid as he appeared to be, if he really was with the NSA. But it was the video that intrigued him. He hadn't wanted to be too inquiring of Assaf, who genuinely seemed to have accidentally stumbled upon it, but the way Assaf described its contents had given him a very bad feeling. Altogether, there were too many coincidences for him to let this go, and too many unknowns.

He punched a series of numbers into his cell phone, pressed 'send' and waited for the response. It came a few seconds later, when a short series of letters and numbers appeared on the display. Samakab took a small calculator-sized code generator from his pocket. He copied the series into it, pressed enter, copied the generated code back into his cell phone and pressed 'send'. It rang almost immediately. Samakab checked his watch.

"What is going on?"

"Nothing. It's being dealt with." The voice at the other end of the line was unemotional.

"If it's nothing, why do you need to deal with it?"

"It's nothing. Don't concern yourself."

"Nothing doesn't take five hours to deal with. You'd better tell me, or I'm going to have to make my own arrangements."

"Nothing changes our arrangement."

"I want some details or 'nothing' will definitely change our arrangement. Meet me."

"You know we can't meet."

"Well, that's the first change to our arrangement."

"We'll send you a weather report. Wait." The line went dead. *A weather report?* So he was finally to meet The Weatherman. Samakab checked his watch again: *23 seconds. Damn. Too short for a trace.* He thought he'd check, just in case. He punched in: 'anything?' The answer came back in an instant: 'need min 35'. *I'll get you next time*, he thought.

Half an hour later, the hotel phone rang at his bedside. He picked up, listened and waited.

"Mr Samakab? This is the concierge downstairs."

"Yes?"

"You have a visitor, sir. A Mr Gerald Shanning. Shall I send him up?" He didn't know anyone called Shanning, but he had no other appointments that day. This had to be him. Knowing the Guggenheim closed at 5.45pm, Ayan and Assaf could turn up at any minute. They might have found something else to do once it had closed, but he didn't want to risk them bursting in and, anyway, he wanted to meet this particular person in a public place.

"Tell him I'll meet him in the Garden Wine Bar."

"I'll do that, sir."

Samakab felt distinctly uncomfortable as he made his way downstairs and through the wine bar. His guest was sitting beside one of the fully grown trees that had been arranged so incongruously in this concrete tower. It was the last thing he wanted—to show himself to the man he'd only known up to now as 'The Weatherman'. But here he was—Gerald Shanning—if that was his real name. Samakab was angry at being compromised and exposed after all the precautions he'd taken when negotiating the deal—a deal, he reminded himself, that was making him a very rich man indeed. However, he also knew that having done the deal, he now had something in his possession that The Weatherman would not want to compromise, under any circumstances.

"Good evening, Mr Samakab. I'm so pleased to meet you." The man who rose from his chair and extended his hand in greeting was not the man Samakab had envisioned. Gerald Shanning was a slight, silver-haired man in his 70s, wearing a tweed jacket and corduroy pants. He had the air of a retired university professor. He spoke softly with a hint of a Southern accent and his handshake, though firm, was friendly and warm. "You are very fortunate to be in New York right now, with your son and his friend." They sat. A waiter approached and Samakab waved him away.

"And why do you say that, Mr Shanning?"

"We're having some very fine days here, this spring. Historically, in March, we have an average precipitation of four inches. Well, it's already late in the month, and it looks as if we're well below that this year. I suppose it's all part of the global weather changes we're seeing now; but, for you, it's a marvelous opportunity. Coupled with the benefits of a slow-moving anticyclone, you can be sure of pleasant weather for the remainder of your stay. I hope you're able to take good advantage of these unseasonably warm days." He spoke slowly and deliberately, enunciating each word very carefully and clearly, as if talking to someone who was hard of hearing.

"You seem to know a lot about the weather, but I suppose you would, given your nickname," Samakab remarked.

"Ah, yes, it was always my passion. I wanted to be a meteorologist in my youth, but life takes you on its own journey, and sometimes you end up in places you never dreamed you would. However, I'm lucky. I continue to be able to include my interest in the weather in the work that I do, albeit in a much broader sense, these days."

"Mr Shanning, you know my time is limited. Cut the niceties, and let's get down to why we're here."

"Certainly." Shanning's tone remained convivial. "Troy King. I hear you had a visit from him today." He crossed his legs and laid his clasped hands casually on his lap. "Arlington Online has received clear instructions not to pursue the line of inquiry that resulted in him being here. He won't bother you again."

"Not good enough, Mr Shanning," Samakab said, dispassionately. "How come he found his way directly to me? And when was that instruction given?"

Shanning raised a quizzical eyebrow and smiled apologetically. "You know I can't tell you that." Samakab sensed the man was enjoying himself.

"Then what are you doing here? You know I can't accept that as a reassurance.

It would seem that your security is leaking like a sieve." He checked around him. Even a place as public as this provided no guarantee of safety. And five hours was a long time—plenty of time for this man to set up listening devices and a whole host of other surprises, if he wanted to. Samakab was starting to doubt the wisdom of calling this meeting at all, given the way the conversation was going.

"You need not be concerned," Shanning said, reading his mind, "we have a clean situation here."

"It's anything but, and you know it. And what about the other matter? How do you plan to explain that?" Everything in Samakab's gut was telling him that nothing was as it should be. He didn't want to be playing conversational ping-pong and guessing games with this man; he wanted real answers and concrete reassurances. But he didn't trust this situation, with this old man. He was getting decidedly twitchy and a little paranoid. He imagined agents crawling all over his suite as he spoke with Shanning, and where was Ayan? He took a deep breath and calmed himself. After all, the deal was done. Which of them had the most to lose? It seemed to him that the balance was even. He needed to stay alert, not concerned.

"I have no intention of explaining anything, Mr Samakab." Shanning gave Samakab a concerned look. "You seem a little nervous. Please, don't give me cause to think we have made a... mistake?" *Someone has surely made a mistake and you know it, Mr Shanning. You're firefighting. Bluffing. It's all in the balance because someone didn't perform.* "You insisted on meeting me, Mr Samakab, and I am here. Now, how can I help you? Or are you having second thoughts?" Samakab sat rigid in his chair and said nothing.

"You see, meeting solves nothing. It only creates more problems—if only in the mind. Are we done?" Samakab was churning inside. Shanning was right, and both of them knew it. There was nothing more to be gained from this meeting. The stakes were too high and Samakab calculated that the risks of continuing this discussion far outweighed the potential fallout from King's visit. He had to trust. He had no choice now. But he berated himself for revealing his insecurities and fears around the events of the day. He had displayed his weakness under pressure, like a huge banner, to this irksome little man, and he was used to being in control. After all the struggle—fighting, building his businesses and rising to the height of eminence in his own country—was this all it took? The frightened, angry child was still in there, running barefoot, searching for his home and family in the fire that raged through his village and took them all from him. No one had ever been able to explain that to him, either. Without a word, he stood up, turned his back on Shanning, and walked out of the bar.

CHAPTER 16

The silence was deafening. David's ears were bursting from his skull, following their rapid and steep descent to the runway at Termez. He ached all over. All he could think about was where he could get some sleep. As the engines wound down to a stop, he and Gulnaz were surrounded by frenzied activity. German voices, incomprehensible and dreamily distant in his soporific state, were organizing the offloading of pallets of military equipment, ammunition, generators and food. Fresh air blew onto their faces as the huge rear ramp was lowered onto the tarmac, and they squinted at the brightness of the world they had just landed in. The first leg of their journey had been relatively comfortable, strapped into the sidewall seating of a C-17 Globemaster 3, configured to carry them and 80 members of the 42nd Infantry Division over 4,000 miles to Ramstein Air Force Base in Germany. The second leg also involved being strapped into sidewall seating, but this time in the hold of a German C-160 Transall. Gulnaz had been relatively lucky in that she could stretch her legs out and rest her feet on top of a generator. David had to be content with jamming his knees into the side of a large metal container that completely blocked his view of the rest of the compartment. Luckily, he did have a window close by, with a view of one of the turbo props spinning endlessly as the plane groaned its way at 304 miles per hour, all the way from Germany to Uzbekistan. Since there were no other passengers on board, the crew had enjoyed watching them being subjected to their pilot's sadistic sense of humor as he made steep turns or sudden drops, particularly whenever they needed to use the toilet. This part of the journey had been about 1,000 miles shorter than the transatlantic leg, but it had felt much, much longer.

Knowing that David would only have a few days to get to the bodies before decomposition made it impossible to examine the wounds, King had worked fast. In late March, the temperatures in the region were still relatively low, which would have slowed putrefaction. Even so, the bodies could have been subjected to rain and possibly frost so, on top of all the risks he was taking, there was also a great degree of uncertainty as to whether this mission could succeed. Once King had made the decision, though, he had put aside his doubts and fears—for himself as well as David and Gulnaz—and pushed the arrangements through with sheer, bloody-minded determination. By calling in favors, cajoling and bribing some of his military acquaintances, King had arranged for them to be kitted out with military uniforms, false ranks and identities for the journey to Termez. He'd also managed to find 200,000 Afghani in cash—just under $5,000—for their three-day stay in Afghanistan.

He had wanted to fly them straight to Mazar-e-Sharif, but there were no US military flights into that airport, which was controlled by Germany. However, he'd been able to connect the flight from Langley to a supplies shipment from Ramstein to Termez. And he'd gained some comfort from knowing they'd be going nowhere near Kunduz, where it would have been extremely dangerous to travel along roads where hijacking, bombings and indiscriminate attacks were common. Before they'd left Washington, he'd stressed the absolute importance of sticking to the schedule. Once they'd finished their work, they were to catch a scheduled commercial flight from Mazar to Dubai, where they could easily get a connection back to the US.

"Come this way, please." The German officer waved to David and Gulnaz from the bottom of the ramp. They gathered their bags and staggered toward him. The pilot had radioed ahead and arranged for them to be picked up and taken the few miles to Friendship Bridge. Before they climbed on board the Eagle 4 armored vehicle, they visited a washroom where they washed and changed out of their military uniforms, which they disposed of in a bin.

"They will probably think you're gay," Gulnaz remarked with a tired smile, when David emerged wearing a pair of shapeless baggy trousers, an old pair of boots and a heavy padded jacket over his T-shirt. He regarded his outfit quizzically.

"How come? I thought we agreed I'd blend in like this."

"No beard. You will have to hurry that along." Gulnaz laughed as David stroked his two days' worth of soft stubble. "And it's the wrong color. If it's brown, they will probably think you are German." The smile was leaving her face now. Her eyes went cold. "This is the very last place I want to be. Let's get going and get it over with." They both knew that there was no way that David was going to 'blend in', and that resentment of all Westerners was on the rise. Despite the efforts being made to rebuild the country and create some sort of order, the situation in Afghanistan wasn't improving. Coordination of a coalition of forces was no easy task in a country ravaged by centuries of tribal hostilities, religious divisions and a reputation for repelling invaders in one of the world's most inhospitable environments. Mistakes were being made every day and insurgents were piling on injuries, deaths and disruption everywhere they could. There was a growing feeling among Afghans that the foreigners were to blame for all of it, so while the area around Mazar-e-Sharif was thought to be one of the safest in the country, everyone knew that this state of relative peace was as fragile as an eggshell. Gulnaz had given her take on the situation before they'd set out.

"We should be fine, as long as we are careful," she'd said, as they drove to Langley Air Force Base. "All around that area, the Taliban have set up a logistics network to supply their friends in Kunduz and the south. They don't want to disturb that, so they keep a low profile. Also, when they're comfortable and they're making money, they don't worry too much about making others stick to the letter of their law. There are even reports of some of the Eastern European Coalition units doing deals with them so they don't have to fight and they can just get drunk every day. I guess human nature is the same the world over."

"Funny we don't hear about that on the news..." mused David. Gulnaz gave him a wry smile.

"What you hear in the West about the problems in Afghanistan bears little relation to what's happening on the ground. And much of it has little to do with the conflicts that are reported. You must understand that Afghanistan is and always has been a relatively lawless country. You don't have nice British Bobbies strolling happily round village communities, greeting housewives as they do their shopping."

Gulnaz had also briefed David on basic phrases he needed to know to enable them to their job. She'd explained some of the Afghan traditions and social niceties, and what to do—and not do—when they were in company. David just hoped he could remember enough of it to avoid making any serious gaffes. It was much more complex than he'd imagined it would be. He kept repeating to himself: *assalaam alaikum (peace be upon you), respond with waalaikum assalaam (and peace also upon you). When meeting someone, shake their hand, then place your hands over your heart and nod slightly. Always enquire about things like health, business and family. Women and men never shake hands let alone speak directly to one another. Avoid eye contact with women. Between men, eye contact is acceptable as long as it is not prolonged. Only look a man in the eyes occasionally. Point with your whole hand rather than one finger. Don't forget to belch after a good meal, to show appreciation. Don't drink alcohol in front of Afghans, give the 'thumbs up', wink, blow your nose in public, eat with your left hand or sit with the soles of your feet facing anyone.* The list went on and on.

He was beginning to realize how heavily he'd have to rely on Gulnaz and her knowledge to perform even the simplest of tasks. Even those were going to be complicated. First of all, what was a young Englishman doing, roaming around the country with an Afghan woman nearly twice his age who was clearly not his wife? As a man, how could he perform any transactions with anyone at all, if he couldn't even speak the most basic Pashto or Dari—the two most commonly used languages? As a woman and, specifically an Afghan woman, how was she going to initiate a conversation with any stranger and particularly a priest, should that be necessary? In their culture, this was just not done, and it would be regarded as strange, at best, or a crime, at worst. But Gulnaz was also pleased to inform David that they had at least one factor on their side. She was a Pushtun. That was better than if she'd been, for instance a Hazara, who were hated by the Taliban and regarded by many Afghans as being people with loose morals.

They'd worked out a plan in an effort to get around all these potential problems. Gulnaz prayed that it would work. David saw it as interesting, challenging and fun.

For the trip from Termez to Mazar, they'd agreed to be 'backpacking tourists'. Gulnaz wore a khaki jacket over generously-cut jeans, sunglasses and a headscarf that covered her head and chest. They each carried a rucksack, and Gulnaz had an additional holdall containing what she referred to as her 'survival clothing' for the next part of the mission.

It was only when he watched the vehicle drive away from them, back toward Termez, that David started to get a deep, sinking feeling. *What the hell am I doing here?* Tunbridge Wells seemed like another planet. Barbara and Josh flashed though his mind, and then they were gone. The Friendship Bridge, spanning the Panj River, extended into the distance in front of them and, beyond, they could see the town of Hairatan, a desolate place with a motley collection of anonymous offices, portable buildings, railway sidings, trucks—and the Afghan border.

"Whose great idea was it, to call it 'Friendship Bridge'?" David asked. Gulnaz ignored the question and turned her eyes back to the road to watch for traffic heading to the other side. Neither of them had the energy to walk the length of the bridge, so they sat by the roadside. It wasn't long before a truck stopped and asked them if they wanted a lift. Well, David assumed it was a truck, but he'd never seen anything like it before. Gulnaz noticed his startled expression.

"It's a jingle truck," she explained.

"It's a freakin' work of art, more like!" And it was. The cab was a mass of elaborate imagery—birds, scenery, sunrises, strange, god-like, winged creatures and flowery graphics. As the truck wheezed to a halt, a skirt of chains with bells hanging from the fender swayed and chimed happily. The door of the cab was a specially made and intricately carved wooden panel with brass hinges. When David opened it, he was greeted by a toothless smile.

"*Assalaam alaikum*," David said, hoping that he got the words right. *Hey*, he thought, *my first Pashtu words... or were they Dari?* They seemed to work, as the driver gestured enthusiastically while saying something that David didn't understand at all, invited them on board and proceeded to drive extremely slowly across the bridge. When he saw the border guard lazily get up from his metal chair and step up to the side of the road, he stopped and motioned to them to get out, before he carried on to the barrier without them. He'd driven on before they reached the border guard, who eyed them with officious contempt as they approached.

Gulnaz quietly briefed David as they approached him. "Okay, even though we are tourists, and for this part I don't speak Afghan, you need to convince him to let us through. He won't like it if I say anything, so I'll keep quiet. Border guards make less than 1,000 Afghani per month, so if it looks as if he wants to make it difficult for us, let him see you pull 500 from your pocket. Say nothing. Just smile and give it to him when he waves us on.

David was impressed. After a few minutes of play-acting, gesturing and repeating 'tourist' and 'Mazar' while pointing to the south *with all his fingers*, the guard let them through and David slipped him the 500 as they moved on.

"Well, that was easy." He was beginning to think this was going to be a piece of cake. Gulnaz stayed quiet. They had identified the route to Mazar from maps before they set out, so they found their way to a road that ran parallel to the riverbank, and started walking. "You reckon we'll get a lift okay?"

"Anyone with any vehicle here is a taxi driver, so don't worry about it," Gulnaz assured him. "Buses, trucks, cars, donkeys and carts—even taxis." David offered to carry her bag. "No, it's better that I do. Walk in front of me, please."

Sure enough, within minutes of them setting out, an old Toyota hatchback, with two men in it, stopped just ahead of them. David swung into action again, smiling, gesturing and using all the Pashtu words he'd learned. He bargained with the driver for a good rate to take them to Mazar, showing him notes and coins according to occasional briefings from Gulnaz from where she was standing two paces behind him.

The car was falling apart on the inside, with ripped headlining and seats. Rusty nuts, bolts and bits of chain littered the floor under their feet. David stacked the bags between them on the back seat rather than risk losing sight of them in the trunk. The two men, who chatted continuously to each other as they drove, were middle-aged and quite bulky. They had ruddy faces, short black beards and gnarled hands. Gulnaz guessed that they were railway workers, on their way home to Mazar.

Within minutes, they'd left Hairatan behind them. After five miles of featureless surroundings, the road took a long, sweeping left turn into what appeared to be endless desert. David and Gulnaz knew that it was only 30 miles to the junction for Mazar, which was then another 15 miles further on, but they were both struck by the absolute emptiness of this place. No features, hardly any vegetation—nothing to break the monotony of the landscape; the road pierced the sand as straight as an arrow till it disappeared into a pinprick on the horizon. David was glad of the breeze from the open window. It helped keep him awake.

As they cruised lazily along the ribbon of tarmac, throwing up a plume of dust behind them, David became aware that Gulnaz had started to breathe more heavily. He looked across at her, trying to signal his concern. She avoided his stare and looked out of the window. A few minutes later, she slammed a fist into the door. Beneath her sunglasses, David could see that tears were falling down her cheeks. The two men in the front seats continued talking happily.

"Gulnaz! What's going on?" She was clearly suffering terribly. She shook her head, and held her arms around her. "Gulnaz, are you ill? What is it?" David hadn't figured on having to deal with a sudden illness, and certainly not in this situation.

Then out of nowhere came a scream. She screamed and screamed, louder and louder. The driver started shouting and his friend turned and started shouting at Gulnaz. David was afraid the man was going to hit her, so he brought his arm around in front of her to offer some protection. She continued to cry out, her face contorted in pain as the driver slammed on the brakes and started to shout at the top of his voice. David grabbed their bags and pushed the door hard. The bags tumbled out onto the road as the car skidded to a halt. David, falling after them, grazed his elbow on the tarmac. He rolled over and looked up to see the passenger was out of the car, pulling Gulnaz roughly out through the door. He lunged at the man but only made contact after the man had swung Gulnaz away from him and sent her sprawling onto the sand by the side of the road. The man was strong. He brushed David off with little effort and a string of curses, and got back into the car, which sped off.

David retrieved the bags from the road and rushed to comfort Gulnaz.

"Gulnaz, what happened?" She was sitting, head bowed, sobbing and shaking. She shook her head. David sat close beside her, shielding her from the sand whipped up by the breeze. He hoped that whatever had upset her would subside enough so they could talk. Gradually, Gulnaz calmed down. She removed her sunglasses and wiped her eyes.

"Bacha Baazi. They were talking about Bacha Baazi." She looked at him, her eyes red-rimmed.

"I'm sorry, Gulnaz, I don't know what that is. Tell me."

"They do it a lot up here. They find young boys from all over the country, and bring them here and…" Her lips were trembling. She was finding it hard to talk.

"Gulnaz…?"

"Sometimes they never find them again." She wiped her nose with her hand.

"What is this, some sort of pedophile ring or something?"

"Some men, they go out and find young, young boys. They get them to dance for them. And sometimes…"

"What Gulnaz? Look, if you don't want to discuss it—"

"No, you should know. We have to work together, and it's only fair you understand."

"Okay." David wasn't sure why Gulnaz felt she had to explain this, but if it would help, he wanted to listen.

"These men in the car were saying they were at a party, and everyone was drunk. And this boy was dancing. They were saying how good looking this boy was, and how well he danced."

"Yes?"

"And afterwards, they got the boy drunk and laid him in the car, and then they all… committed sodomy with this little boy. It was lots of fun, apparently." Gulnaz stared at him with empty eyes.

"Oh, God." David felt as if the wind had been kicked out of him. "Does this happen a lot? What kind of age are these boys?"

"They range from very young to adolescent. Mine was only seven." She closed her eyes. David's chest tightened with shock. He couldn't speak.

"And, no, this is not the evil doings of the Taliban," Gulnaz continued, as if in a dream. "These men in the car mentioned an army commander and a policeman were among the party guests. I don't know if the Taliban do this sort of thing. All I know is that the same year I lost my son, the Taliban burned down my house and shot my husband dead. He was a professor of journalism at Kabul University. I was teaching there when they visited our home in 1996."

CHAPTER 17

It was a new experience for Griffin—to be feeling that he was merely tolerating the company and conversation of his best and oldest friend. When he was the old Larry—it already seemed as if it was such a long time ago, yet it was only a matter of days—his company had been something he'd valued and sought at every opportunity. Now, he seemed to be such a different person—indecisive, rambling, pensive...

"'Them'. You asked me about 'them' and who 'they' are." Larry's comment brought him back to the present. Griffin took a sip of coffee and waited for Larry to continue. "They actually don't exist, as such." Griffin sighed an impatient sigh, then caught himself and apologized,

"Sorry, Larry. I did promise to listen."

"I understand." Larry paused again, gauging Griffin's mood before he continued. "The fact is that 'they' come and go. It's like an amoeba, constantly forming, splitting, re-forming, dispersing. Parts appear and disappear, grow and diminish without any apparent rhyme or reason. You and I have been there longer than most, watching this process—as an integral part of it. As we've grown, others have joined the game and picked bits off us or added bits to us and then moved on. And we've done exactly the same to others. So, to look for a 'them' that we think may be responsible for something is unlikely to take us very far. By the time we focus on a 'them', it's moved, changed or is no longer there. Or what we thought was there was just something we imagined. Or someone else has a new theory—an interpretation that's validated once it gains enough support—whether or not there's the tiniest grain of truth in it. We both know that's the way it works." He leaned toward Griffin, holding his attention, not giving him a dismissive inch. "So, here we are now," he gave a wide sweep with his hand, "searching for some real, meaningful answers, to neatly explain what happened to us both, what our place in the world is, and what we should do about it now. Yes?" He raised a questioning eyebrow at Griffin, who nodded slowly. "It's a bit like looking for a diamond in a mudslide. And it's funny, if you think about it. We've spent our whole lives looking for answers, filling in bits of the jigsaw as the random chaos of world politics shifts from one crisis to another. And how do we do it? We surround ourselves with experts, we build increasingly sophisticated computers, we negotiate, we build power bases, do deals, make compromises, we ask focus groups and the electorate—but only when we feel we have to, because actually we think we know better than them. And, anyway, the electorate is paying us to do the job, so we dare not lose their confidence because, if we do, our whole world goes 'pop', and we're gone. So we create a façade of control and competence." He shook his head. "But I digress... There is no 'they'. There is only us. Whatever happened to you and me is just as much to do with our part in all of this as anyone else's. We took part, wholeheartedly. We were fully committed to the merry-go-round, and we enjoyed the ride, most of the time. It fed our bank accounts and our egos. But you must understand that it was only possible because we chose—*we chose*—to be blind to what we were doing and what was going on around us. *We chose* to believe in it all to the extent that it served us. *We chose* to ignore or justify the parts of it that were unpalatable, disgusting, unjust, cruel or damaging. Of course we did. And we don't need to get on some useless guilt trip about it. We couldn't have coped with the magnitude and the multitude any other way. I don't believe that, as humans, we're capable of that degree of sheer processing, let alone utilizing it to deliver solutions in a humane and balanced way. But we can't get away from the fact that whatever happened to us is a direct result of what we did. The amoeba changed. That's all."

"And you're happy with that? Larry, you have a fantastic wife back there in Bel Aire, and you're happy to explain away your life with her as the result of a shift in a fucking—excuse my language—amoeba? And what about *my* life? Sheryl and I have just been pushed off a cliff, and you're telling me that I just go back to Washington and carry on as if nothing has happened?"

"That's exactly the point, Griffin. No, *of course* I don't expect you to do that. And, just so you're clear on this, if there is any way I can get back with Evelyn again, that will be my first priority when we've finished here." He leaned back in his chair. "Bali is a wonderful place, Griff. Wonderful if you want to live in denial and wonderful if you want to find yourself."

"Larry, I think you know I'm willing to face up to hard realities, as the evidence of the past few years surely proves. What I don't buy into is all this 'finding yourself' new age stuff and I don't think it's the corollary to living in denial. If there's something you think I should be doing to fix things back in Washington, now that you can't, I'd like to hear about it. And I'd like to understand how this situation came about." Larry took a long look at Griffin. He'd known that it would be an uphill struggle to open Griffin's eyes. He just hoped he had time to get through to him, and to say what he needed to say, before Griffin left the island.

"We'll get to it, I promise. We have to. We could be sitting on a time bomb."

"What kind of time bomb?"

"It's just a theory, but the chances of lightning striking twice in the same place are what, trillions to one?"

"I guess so… what are you getting at?"

"It's the chair you're sitting on." Larry was smiling now. Griffin looked down at his chair, firmly rooted in the sand, but couldn't see the joke. "By my calculations, your chair is directly above the spot where, on 1 October 2005, one of the Jimbaran bombs went off."

"That's not funny." Griffin quickly stood up.

"No, it's not. But think about this, Griff. Now that you know your life can be taken from you at any time—by political maneuvering or by some nut blowing your brains out while you think you're safe on a paradise island—are you going to spend the time you have left on this earth trying to find ways to insure against such events? It's a thankless task, and you never can predict or control the threat. That's what you've been doing all your life and, to put it bluntly, you've failed. Surely, if ever anyone was living in denial on a grand scale, it's you."

"That's not fair, Larry!"

"*Fair?*" Larry stared up at him. Griffin immediately realized how stupid that must have sounded.

"Bad choice of words…" Griffin was all churned up inside. An unwanted truth was banging on his chest, demanding to come in and be accepted. This truth had been beckoning, haranguing him for the past five years, particularly, and it was hurting him. He didn't know what to do with his hands or where to look. He held on to the back of the chair, bowed his head and mumbled, "I suppose if you want to see it like that, yes, you're right."

Larry got up and put his hand on Griffin's shoulder. "I'm not trying to score points. You know that, don't you, Griff?" Griffin nodded. "Let's take a drive. I'll show you my place."

They made their way up to the road, where Larry pointed out an old Suzuki Jeep. It was a 1980s open-top model, white with pink 'features'—a roll bar and tubular fenders—and a surf board graphic on the hood. Its big dumpy tires were cracked and bald, rust lined every welded seam and the floor pan had sand wedged in every corner.

"Well, this takes me back." Griffin smiled as he climbed into the passenger seat. "Have you got a tie-dye shirt I could borrow, and a headband?"

"No, but I found some Ray Ban Wayfarer sunglasses in the glove box if you want to make like Tom Cruise."

"Kewl." Griffin gladly took on the role, and the two aging hippies headed for the main road, merging with the sea of motorbikes and cars that, out of great skill or pure luck, somehow managed to avoid colliding with each other.

"Nice statue," Griffin nodded at a dramatic work of art that adorned a roundabout along the way.

"Oh, that's Dewa Rutji," he said, as if Griffin would know who he was talking about. "Some of these statues are a mystery to me, but there's a well-known story about that one. It's often performed as a play. In it, the hero asks his teacher how to learn the secret of life. His teacher tells him to go to the bottom of the sea, where he has a fight with a serpent. Once our hero has dispensed with the serpent, a god—this guy, Dewa Rutji—appears before him in miniature, and tells our hero to enter his ear. He obeys this impossible command and, in passing through Dewa Rutji's ear, reaches the unattainable."

"Sounds like an everyday tale of life on Capitol Hill," remarked Griffin.

"You're absolutely right, of course, although I guess you're joking." He glanced across at Griffin. "What they say is that the serpent represents human passions that distract us, and the fight is the struggle to master our base impulses. We can only experience our divine inner essence once we've overcome our serpent. It's a universal story that I'm sure you'll recognize. In the Bible, it's the apple in the Garden of Eden—I suppose most religions have them."

"Yes. I wonder why that is… all these commonalities between religions," Griffin mused.

"I guess it's because they're true, at some level." Larry made a right turn toward Denpasar. "I'm living up here, in town, for now. There's my local supermarket." He pointed to a Carrefour store as they passed it.

"Why not the beach? Aren't you missing a golden opportunity here? You've already bought into the surfer image!" Griffin cast a admiring eye over the car.

Larry laughed. "No. I want to see how things develop. For now, I can get better Internet in town, and I don't spend much time hanging around beach bars these days. Anyway, I'm happy to keep a low profile."

"But it's easy to find you, if anyone really wants to."

"Yes, I know. I'm 'hidden in plain sight', you might say. Everyone's happy with that, and as long as I don't create any problems sleeping dogs will lie. Those that need to know where I am can find me; those that don't have a pressing need are unlikely to go to much trouble once they find I'm out of circulation. Once someone like me has been gone for a few weeks, people adjust and find other ways to get their business done."

Griffin glanced at Larry as they drove—one hand on the wheel, grey hair blowing in the breeze, leather open-toed sandals. When he'd been in the US, Larry had lived in considerable style. He'd never been showy but had elegant taste. As a young man, he typically took his dates to an opera, or out for a meal at an ethnic restaurant. No rock concerts and burgers for him. He had taken Evelyn to Prague and Vienna for their honeymoon, rather than St Lucia or Cancun—the preferred choices of Griffin's crowd. His town house had been a temple of discreet European design. He'd imported his glassware from Finland and many of his furnishings were modern classics from Germany and Sweden. Griffin could remember only one American piece—the bed that Larry and Evelyn slept in for most of their married life. It was hand-built to contain a high-tech mattress from California that was scientifically constructed with multiple layers, including one of latex. Griffin had never understood how Larry could possibly justify the cost of it, and he'd always wondered if it had made that much difference to the quality of their sleep. To Griffin, on his manic climb through the political system, sleep was just an inconvenient pause in the day's work that he'd always kept as brief as possible.

After traveling for several minutes up a pleasant, tree-lined road, with a mixture of houses, shops and small workshops, Larry turned left. The sign read 'Jalan Gunung Lawu'.

"Welcome to Volcano Road," Larry said, cheerfully. It was more like a wide alleyway than a road, lined with high walls that hid single-story homes behind them. He stopped the car, opened a high gate, drove through and parked. He closed the gate and led Griffin down a long, narrow walkway between two buildings to a door.

"How on earth did you find this?" Griff lifted his sunglasses to see his way in the shadows of overhanging roofs.

"Yan. He's a great guy, and he's been a great help to me since I arrived. In fact, he was the first person I met when I landed here. I came out of the terminal building and there he was, offering me a ride to my hotel. I told him I actually hadn't booked a hotel, and I needed to find somewhere to live for a while. After a couple of hours driving round, talking to his contacts on his cell phone, he came up with this." Larry unlocked the door but it was stuck. He put his shoulder into it and it gave way. "It's perfect for me. Come in." The first room was dark. The only light available was through a small window in the front door that was covered by a blind, which Larry was rolling up. It was about ten feet square, with a low bed, a desk with a laptop, telephone and assorted papers on it, a folding chair and a small closet. A rough rattan mat covered part of the concrete floor, and a screen of hanging beads separated this room from the next. Larry led Griffin through it to the adjoining kitchen, which had a small gas cooker, a gas bottle, a refrigerator, a sink and some warped wooden shelving for food and utensils, two chairs and a tiny circular wooden table. "Like it? It's cozy, isn't it." Larry smiled at Griffin's shocked expression.

"Er, yes. It's kind of compact. Where's the rest of it?"

"You've just had a guided tour of the entire estate."

"That's it?" Griffin stood in the doorway and looked from one room to the other in quiet amazement. "I guess you have a washroom? I could do with one right now. That coffee…"

"Sure. Follow me." Larry led Griffin out of the kitchen into a small courtyard that was surrounded by other doors and windows that Griffin guessed belonged to other homes. In the centre of the courtyard was a stone structure with an assortment of traditional Balinese carvings on it. "We share this." He opened a door that lead into a small shower room with a toilet in one corner.

"Well, at least it's clean…" Griffin walked in and closed the door. When he re-emerged, Larry had arranged the two chairs and the wooden kitchen table in the courtyard, and was busy in the kitchen preparing something.

"Make yourself at home," he called out, "I'll be with you in a minute." As soon as Griffin sat down, he was startled by a cat that jumped soundlessly onto his lap, then started purring loudly. He wasn't sure if it was a kitten or just a very malnourished adult, but it seemed friendly enough, so he let it stay there as he took in the details of the courtyard. The sky was clouding over again. There was a distant rumble of thunder. The courtyard was neat and clean; no rubbish anywhere. The eaves of the surrounding houses were carefully carved with delicate patterns and symbols. Each doorway had a canang sari— a small offering tray containing minute amounts of rice and other food, flowers and money all carefully arranged on a bed of leaves—placed beside it, to appease the gods and bring good fortune and health to the household. The soft fragrance of jasmine filled the air. To Griffin, this tiny, enclosed space was a haven of peace. He felt cosseted; his fears and concerns were beginning to melt away. He was isolated and insulated from everything. He let his shoulders relax and breathed into his stomach in an effort to relieve the knots that had plagued him these past few days. He was dozing off when Larry came out to join him, with two tall glasses on a tray.

"Ah, I see you've met Entahlah," he said, cheerfully.

Griffin opened his eyes and smiled sleepily. "Entahlah? That's a nice name. Does it have a meaning?"

"I don't know. I cleaned her up a bit, gave her some food, and now it seems we're inseparable."

"Does it belong to someone here?"

Larry sat down. "She adopted me as soon as I arrived. I asked the lady who lives opposite if 'she'—I was able to figure that much out—had a name, and she told me 'Entahlah'. It was only later that Yan told me what that means."

"And what was that?"

"I don't know."

"But I… oh, I see. Well, it's probably very appropriate!" Griffin laughed and stroked Entahlah's head.

"Don't be fooled by the angelic looks. I think she knows more than she's giving away." Larry handed Griffin one of the glasses.

"What's this?" Griffin studied the glass. "And don't tell me it's *entahlah*."

"No, I know what that is," Larry grinned, "it's *Arak Madu*. I thought you could do with some. It's got a nice little kick to it." Griffin took a sip and gave an expression of satisfaction.

"Wow, that's good. What's in it?"

"*Arak*, water, honey and lime. I buy the *arak* off a *warung* down the—"

"Whoa!! Slow down. One new word at a time, please." Griffin took another sip. *This is good stuff!*

"Sorry. *Arak* is a Balinese liquor distilled from *tuak*, a sweet wine made from the coconut palm flower. A *warung* is one of those roadside stands you see all over the place here. The guy who has the *warung* probably makes the *arak* himself, at home. You buy it in a knotted plastic bag. They are refreshingly unconcerned about branding here when it comes to *arak*. In fact, if it's in a bottle with a label, local people don't reckon it's up to much."

"Frankly," Griffin drained his glass, "I don't give a damn, but if you've got another one of those…" Larry went back into the kitchen for a refill.

"Just go a bit easy, Griff," said Larry, handing him the glass, "you don't want to meet Rangda. She's the witch demon who's likely to meet you in your dreams if you drink too much of this."

"Dreams." Griffin looked pensive. "Here's to dreams," he said and downed his drink in one. He felt relaxed, warm and comfortable. It was safe here.

"Unfortunately, we've been dreaming too long." Griffin's brief moment of euphoria was cut short.

"Larry, give me a break, will you? For just a minute there, I was… happy."

"Okay. Look, you sit here while I check my emails, and we'll get back to it in half an hour." Larry stood up to go back into the house. "I'm sorry, Griff, but we don't have any time to waste, and we can't afford the luxury of falling apart." Griffin nodded, closed his eyes, and continued to savor each minute. Although the *arak madu* didn't seem to be making him drunk, it was definitely working its wonder. He put it down to the fact that he was still a bit jet-lagged and hadn't eaten since he and Sheryl had an early breakfast at the hotel. He felt light-headed yet alert to every sound and smell. He drifted in a state of heightened awareness, super-conscious of everything around him—the chair, Entahlah on his lap, every movement she made and every breath she took. Even the very stones of the courtyard, the shrine at its centre, the houses leading off it and especially the aroma of the jasmine—they were all somehow *present* and alive to him. *Is this what peace is like?* He just wanted to stay there, be in it. He wanted to be trapped forever in this seductive limbo. There was nothing else…

The half hour passed in an instant. For Griffin, it didn't register as time passing. He just moved out of a timeless space, back into the courtyard. With Larry, the cat, two chairs and a table, two empty glasses, spots of rain on his forehead.

"We'd better get under cover." Larry was moving the furniture back into the kitchen. Griffin couldn't move for a few seconds. Then he gently placed Entahlah on the floor, picked up his chair and followed Larry into the kitchen. Entahlah tucked into some of the food in a *canang sari* next to Larry's door.

"I see she has no compunction about eating the offerings to the gods,"

Griffin remarked as the rain started drumming on the wooden roof, forming a screen of rivulets as it fell to the courtyard. Larry smiled down at Entahlah.

"Typical feline behavior," he said. "They know what they want and make no apologies for it. Comfort, food, warmth, affection, sleep. When they want it, they just go for it. If another cat is in the way, they'll do whatever they can do to win it. When they're done, or just bored, they move on, till the next time. Typical hominine behavior as well, I guess."

"You're getting a bit philosophical, Larry. Must be all the *arak madu*." He smirked at Larry. "But 'hominine'? What's that? It's not a word I've come across before."

"Characteristic of humankind. That's the dictionary definition, anyway. That's what I want to talk to you about first. Human characteristics… and the state of the world."

"So you *are* getting philosophical. Be careful though, Larry, politicians can't afford to do too much of that sort of thinking."

"Ah, but remember, I'm no longer a politician." Entahlah finished her meal and returned to Griffin's lap, where she promptly fell asleep.

"I thought you said that you two were inseparable," Griffin commented as he stroked her back.

"Oh, she just likes a bit of novelty. That's another hominine trait."

The rain protected them in their discussion, encasing the small kitchen in a thrumming liquid cage deep in the sprawling suburbs of Denpasar. Away from everything that was familiar—his support systems, people, technology, diaries, telephones, busy-ness and noise—all Griffin had to concentrate on was this man and what he had to say to him. It was beginning to feel as if it was the only important thing he had left to do.

Griffin looked around the room. "So, what's with the frugal lifestyle? Surely you could have done better than this *and* kept a low profile?"

"I suppose I could have, but somehow this just felt right for me at the moment. As soon as I stepped into the place, I felt comfortably cocooned and very much at peace."

"I have to admit, I felt the same. It's infectious."

"And I'm living within my means, Balinese-style."

"Come on, Larry. Surely they didn't take all your money off you before you left. Don't tell me you're broke."

"No, nothing like that. But it's a good point. If most people back home were truly living within their means, they probably couldn't even afford a place like this. Their grandchildren certainly won't be able to, the way things are going."

"I'm guessing you're talking about our famous deficit."

"That's right. The good ole USA is broke."

"Well, that's arguable."

"In fact, it's not. But if you'd rather get the financial institutions to dress it up and give you some convincing arguments, I'm sure you can continue to buy into the illusion that everything is under control or, at least, fixable."

"Oh, come on, Larry, you can't just go making sweeping, alarmist statements like that! The fiscal situation is complex. I know things got pretty close to the wire in 2008 and the Euro has had its problems, but a hell of a lot's been done to get things back on track, and arguments like that insult the intelligence. They're just too simplistic."

"Too simplistic? You think so?" Larry sighed and turned his chair to face Griffin's. "Do you seriously believe that anyone has a practical, workable plan that will get everything working properly and on course for health, wealth and happiness in the US? Is anyone saying that even the most basic standard of living is guaranteed in our country—which, by the way, is the model we arrogantly expect all other nations to aspire to? Sure, we've got lots of new ideas, new policies, fancy laws and all kinds of technological breakthroughs, but what difference do they make? Every month, financial practices are discredited and replaced with increasingly complicated ones, and nobody really sees the full picture—no, not even you, Griffin. But let's be simplistic for a minute, for the sake of argument. Let's not go the route we've always been told to go, and see if we can get down to some simple truths about what we're dealing with." Larry poured them each a glass of water. "You and I know that with every day that passes our nation's children and grandchildren are being lumbered with a debt that's already heading for $15 trillion, is rising faster than the analysts can crunch the numbers and will soon be bigger than our total GDP. While that deficit is growing, our ability to deal with it is diminishing, in real terms… and I don't want to get into all the whys and wherefores right now. You can look them up for yourself when you get back, if you want to. But just take energy as a simple example."

Larry leaned forward and rested his elbows on his knees. "It's a relevant one, because, as you'll see, it neatly leads on to my next point. Currently, the US has 2% of the world's oil stocks and, of course, it consumes a disproportionate amount of the world's oil. Oil is going to disappear within 30 years—maybe even sooner, depending on whose figures you look at. Our renewable energy sources are only predicted to be able to produce 13% of our needs by that time. It's a big gap, isn't it?" Griffin nodded. *Where is this going?* "And why is that gap so big? Simple. Short-sighted economic thinking, short-term business greed, and the pressure of business *and* consumers to keep things as they are for the sake of a wage packet, as well as the suppliers maintaining as much profit as possible for themselves and their shareholders. It's simply not sustainable. Everybody pays lip-service to that fact and environmentalists make a lot of green noise, but the government is elected by the people and business interests shape economic policy. So everyone makes a big show of making an effort, but most people either have their heads in the sand or are busy focusing on some other problem, so nothing much actually changes. Even when the facts present themselves, the processes of realization, discussion, lobbying, acceptance by government, changing public opinion and eventually taking action are simply not keeping pace with the rot that's set in. However much you think is being done, you can be certain that nothing is changing quickly enough."

"A lot of people would argue that the expected lifespan of the world's oil supply is not just dependent on the current demand," Griffin said. "Technology is developing all the time, and the way we use oil is changing and becoming much more efficient. Add to that the growth in alternative technologies that will reduce demand in the coming years, as well as protecting the environment—" Larry held up his hand.

"Griff, yes, yes, yes, yes, yes! I know, I know. I know all that, and that's why I said I don't want to get into all the whys and wherefores of each element of the problem. Don't you see? That's the game that keeps the whole mechanism lumbering on. Argument and counter-argument, the hope that new technologies and knowledge will come along to fix it all in the future. They call it 'balance' and 'being reasonable' and 'serving the interests of all groups fairly' and all that bull. And the manic drive for solutions in the future to solve the problems we have created now and in the past is called progress. It's just a smokescreen. And I know you'll disagree with this, but the environmental arguments, to my mind, are much the same."

"I certainly do. But why do you say that?"

"Well, I suppose, at heart, I have what you might call a Carlinite philosophy on the environment."

"I'm not familiar with that one."

"I went to one of George Carlin's shows, some years back. You can see the video on YouTube. It's called 'Saving the planet'. It's a real hoot."

"Ah, now I see you're following one of our greatest philosophers," Griffin mocked with a smile.

"Yeah, he reckoned we're being just a tad self-important about our effect on this planet. His argument was that man is actually making very little impact at all; 90% of all the species that ever existed have gone, and we're still losing about 25 species a day. Nothing to do with anything man has done or is doing. Furthermore, the planet has been around for about 4.5 billion years. Man has been here for 100,000–200,000 years, and industry for only 200 years. The planet has had to deal with volcanoes, earthquakes, moving tectonic plates and a whole lot more than a few aluminum cans, oil spills and plastic bottles sloshing around the oceans. Basically, he said that the planet is fine, it will adjust and cope—we're the ones who are fucked! And, whether or not you think his arguments are funny or are just plain crazy, he's got a point. We are fucked, but not just for environmental reasons. Unless I can find someone to help put things right, as I said when we first started, we're done." Griffin was struggling to decide where the humor started and ended in Larry's remarks, but there was an unmistakable gravitas in that last statement.

"What's going on behind these words, Larry? Maybe now's the time to tell me."

"Griff. I hope you'll be able to forgive me for what I'm about to tell you. You probably won't understand it, at first, but I'm hoping that you will, in time, understand that I did what I did with the best of intentions." Larry took a deep breath and kept his eyes fixed on Griffin's. "The three superpowers know full well that we're on a knife edge, in terms of our existence on this planet. Behind the scenes, Russia, China and the US have each agreed that this is not the time to fight over what's left in the world. I was looking for solutions, and all three of the governments were paying me to do it. They believed that, with my track record, I was the man with the knowledge and experience best placed to head up the team they selected to get things back on track. I had vast technical resources at my disposal, some of the best minds and radical thinkers on the planet—from all around the world—and a huge budget. That is what I've been working on for the past seven years. I'm sorry I couldn't confide in you about it, but I knew you would understand.

"What we came up with was an incredible new technology, a vast database and a major report. We had solutions. Real solutions. As you might expect, they were extremely radical. After all, we're not going to fix the world's problems by using the same thinking that generated them. What it came down to was relatively simple, yet extremely difficult to implement, given the complex and self-serving nature of mankind that we've just been talking about. However, we made suggestions and recommendations that, with the concerted will of the major powers, could have brought the situation under control within ten years and into some sort of balance within 15.

"What I didn't know was how our findings would be interpreted by certain people. It seems that when you shed light on the human mind, however pure and positive your intention, much of it just gets absorbed into the darkness that is there, and feeds that darkness with additional energy, extinguishing all that is good.

"Griff. We had the solution in our hands. It was real and good, and I foolishly let my ego think that I'd found a way to save mankind from itself. But it was a trick, and I was well and truly suckered. They had no intention of saving anyone but themselves, which they now can do. I just gave them the means to do it, and they're using my findings in a way that leaves me reeling in disgust, shame and ...fear for all of us."

CHAPTER 18

Within an hour of being dumped so unceremoniously by the roadside, David and Gulnaz had arrived in Mazar-e-Sharif. David had been careful to accept a ride in a vehicle with just one occupant. The driver of the jingle truck who brought them into town was a softly-spoken older man, who barely spoke as he drove. Nevertheless, David hadn't taken his eyes off Gulnaz for the whole journey, keenly watching for signs of the slightest distress.

"Thank you, David," Gulnaz said as they walked along dusty roads, in search of a hotel.

"For what?"

" For being so kind back there."

David smiled and gestured that it was nothing. "This place is humming. Are towns like this always so busy?"

"No. I asked about that at the last hotel we tried. On Fridays, they have Buzkashi games, and today they've had one of the last of the season."

"Buzkashi? I've a hell of a lot to learn about this place, don't I? Maybe we should stay longer. I'd love to find out so much more about your country." David stopped dead in his tracks. *You stupid, stupid idiot! What are you saying? How short is your memory?* "I'm sorry, Gulnaz. I—"

"Don't apologize. It's better to try to understand… although even I don't, sometimes, and I was born here. This is an ancient and complex country, inhabited by many tribes following different versions of different religions with different customs. Throughout our history, there has been movement to and from our neighboring countries, and that makes for huge diversity in the culture here. It would really help if, next time some stupid country wants to invade us, they get to understand a little about us first, rather than trying to do it while they're picking up the pieces from the rubble they create. To me, it's crazy to see all these foreigners coming here with their sophisticated technology and self-righteous ideas about peace and helping to re-build this place, when they don't even understand the first thing about it. But what do they care? Their politicians are only interested in what they can get out of Afghanistan."

"And what do *you* care, after what happened to you and your family?"

"I don't care. I don't care at all."

"Then why are you here?"

"One way or the other, I was going to have to come here, and I preferred to come for just three days, rather than the rest of my life." Gulnaz took her pack off her back and laid it on the ground. She looked wrecked.

"But you would never have to come back here for good, now you've got into the US, would you?" David picked up her bag and her backpack, and they continued walking. The light was beginning to fade and they were keen to be off the streets before dark.

"My place in the US isn't guaranteed. They took me because I was educated and useful at the time the Taliban took Kabul, but my status there has never been assured. King knows that and 'asked' me to do this trip, to help out."

"The bastard! The more I get to know about that man, the worse it gets."

"Oh, don't be too hard on him. He's a good man at heart. He just feels he has a lot to prove, and I suppose he feels that time is running out for him. He's desperate. Why else would he have risked everything to send us here?" David remembered his conversation with King in the bar: *and I'm a dead man walking.* Were all his colleagues walking dead people? Gulnaz certainly had that look about her now. She had no interest in being part of this political game. It seemed so cruel, to David, that someone could be manipulated and compromised in such a terrible way for the very reason that she had lost everything that was dear to her, in the most horrific way. Is this how a civilized society treats the weak and vulnerable? Would a simple bullet to the head have been more humane than the blatant exploitation of the walking wounded, year after year? Physical wounding, it was clear, used up more of your enemy's resources and energy, but psychological wounding of one of your own also provides a useful weapon against your enemy. *What am I thinking!? It would be better to have killed Gulnaz as well?* David caught himself. He'd only touched the virtual surface of this world of violence and death through one short video clip, and already he was thinking such thoughts? He was appalled at how easily and quickly his mind wandered into such dark places.

"Buzkashi." Gulnaz brought him back from his thoughts.

"What?"

"You were asking what Buzkashi was."

"Oh, yes. What is it?"

"You could say it is the Afghan equivalent of your polo."

"Ah, upper class twits on horseback, batting a little ball around a field while their friends sip G and Ts?"

"Not quite." Gulnaz gave the slightest of smiles. David's heart lifted a little.

"I confess, I had my suspicions…" David said.

"In this version, twenty Afghan horsemen try to gain control of the decapitated carcass of a calf that's also been disembowelled and had its legs chopped off at the knees. The winner is the one who, using any means at his disposal—like whipping or kicking his opponents—throws the carcass into the 'Circle of Justice' at the other end of the playing field."

"Charming. And then, I suppose, they all pop into the marquee for tea and scones…" No response.

The Barat Hotel was one of the more modern-looking hotels they found on their search, and it had two rooms available, much to their relief. It was in the centre of town next to the impressive Shrine of Hazrat Ali—the Blue Mosque. The only other place with available space was the UN guest house, which was a 15-minute walk from the mosque. It was a beautiful country house with huge rooms, a lovely garden, a well-stocked bar and good food. If they had stayed there, they would have been in the company of other English-speaking guests, as well as, no doubt, some UN staff. David would have welcomed that, after the journey they'd just endured. Since they wanted to keep a low profile, though, they went for the Barat. Unfortunately, it didn't have a restaurant, so they agreed that once they had showered, the receptionist would order meals for them from a local *chaikhana*—a teashop—and have it sent up to their rooms. They agreed to eat separately, as neither had the energy or the desire to risk the disapproval of other guests who might see one of them going into the other's room.

From his position seated cross-legged on the floor, practicing eating Afghan-style, David could see the Blue Mosque through his window. It was an incredibly ornate architectural masterpiece and, to David's mind, extremely beautiful. He couldn't help admiring its intricate design and the incredibly fine detail in the tiling that covered every inch of its surface. Yet, as he watched the sun finally go down, he was overcome by a feeling of deep depression as its majestic dome and minarets turned to silhouettes against the darkening sky. *All that love, devotion and energy put into a building, and what does it give them? Was it even love that built this huge edifice, or just fear? Did it just amount to a place of solace, of refuge, to escape from the brutal realities of those who order their lives in the name of the deity it represents? How crazy is that?* Then he thought of the religions he was familiar with in the West, and had to admit that they were all the same.

The meal was excellent and, as he ate, his mood lightened again. The man who brought it to his room had explained in English that it was *mantu*. It was delicious—ground beef mixed with spices, mint and garlic, wrapped in parcels like wantons and covered with yoghurt. Suddenly ravenously hungry, he wolfed it down. But he was also dead tired and intent on getting horizontal as soon as he could. As he finished his meal, the mullah was calling the faithful to *namaza esha*—late night prayer. That night, despite his growing apprehension concerning the work he had to do, he slept deeply. At some time in the early hours, Barbara came into his dreams, playing with Josh in the living room in Alcova Heights, laughing and encouraging him to join them.

The following morning, with Gulnaz in her tourist outfit, they went out of the hotel for breakfast. They found a nearby *chaikhana* where there didn't appear to be any tourists who might overhear their conversation and where it would be acceptable for David to be talking to an apparently Western woman. Here, David was introduced to *chaikhana* etiquette. The proprietor greeted them at the doorway as they arrived, and they entered a dark, whitewashed room with a tamped dirt floor. In a far corner, a wood-fired oven, or *bukhari*, was heating water for tea. The walls were decorated with a few old posters of Indian film stars. Just inside the door, a man was strumming a two-stringed *dambour*. Several men sat cross-legged on blankets arranged around a cloth laid out with various dishes that were being shared. David and Gulnaz found a space to sit. The proprietor brought them an enamel pot of hot tea and some glasses. David couldn't help noticing that the glasses weren't clean.

"In the *chaikhana*," Gulnaz caught his eye, "the customer's first duty is to rinse the glasses out with hot tea."

"No problem," said David, "as long as we don't have to cook the food as well."

"Please, be respectful," Gulnaz replied in a hushed tone, looking uncomfortable. "This is a tourist town. Many people here may understand some English."

"Sorry. I don't think I've fully recovered from our journey."

"And I know you are left-handed, but you'll remember, won't you...?"

"Yes, yes. Right hand. Got it."

"Good. First things first. When we've finished here, I think we should go and buy a car for the journey to the mountains."

David looked startled. "Why on earth would we do that? Taxis round here are as cheap as anything, and we're only here for two more days."

"Just think about it. Who are you going to trust to keep their mouth shut about what we're doing up there? The driver would have to hang around all day in the settlement, and he'll no doubt talk to people there. It's a strange thing we're doing, to say the least. Anyway, the taxi driver will most likely be a Muslim, and would find the Zoroastrian tradition of the Tower of Silence completely abhorrent. As far as Muslims are concerned, death is the pinnacle of one's religious journey to Allah, so the body must be treated with utmost respect, prayers offered and very strict procedures observed. As King mentioned, the body should also be buried within 24 hours of death, and no autopsy should be carried out unless absolutely necessary. If our taxi driver thinks we're poking around some ten-day old bodies that have been left for scavenger birds to pick at, I don't think we need think about coming back to our hotel afterwards."

"Well, I guess that settles that. Do we have enough money to buy a car?"

"Yes, plenty, and we won't have to look far. As soon as I mention it to the hotel manager, we'll be approached by a vehicle bargainer."

"A what?"

"Here in Afghanistan, the vehicle trading centre—car showroom, in your country—doesn't do the selling. Independent vehicle bargainers sell on their behalf. There are often many of them for each trading centre, so if you want to do a good deal, it's best if one of them hears about you and comes to you." Gulnaz smiled. "I don't think a nice Englishman like you would enjoy haggling with a crowd of vehicle bargainers. Most of them work just on commission, without a wage, so it can get a bit frenetic. Because of that, I thought it would be better to get one on his own first, so you can, at least, have just one point of contact and you won't get overwhelmed by a group of them. You have to be the one doing the deal. They won't deal with me. It wouldn't be polite or acceptable."

"Blimey. It's hard enough to deal with car salesmen in Clapham. This should be fun." He cautiously took a sip of tea. "Actually, I quite like that. It's not exactly Twinings, but it's nice." He swilled the tea around his mouth. "A bit too sweet for me, but spicy. Yes, I like it." No sooner had he taken the glass from his mouth than it was re-filled by the proprietor who had been watching him appreciating his concoction. "*Ma-na-na.*" he expressed his thanks and turned back to Gulnaz, "And what type of car do you think we can get?" Gulnaz rolled her eyes at what was, to her, a completely pointless question. *He's young, and I guess he's into cars...*

"If I am guessing correctly, it will be a yellow-and-white 2002 Toyota Corolla. Is that specific enough?"

David laughed. "I guess that's what it will be, then. How can you be so sure about that?"

"Because they're the most common family cars in Afghanistan, and they imported lots of them immediately after the Taliban were removed from power. The Taliban themselves imported many in 1999, but only to re-export them to Pakistan. Therefore, the 2002 models are the best we can get at a cheap price."

"I'm impressed! But how do you even know the color combination? I thought only taxis were yellow and white."

"They're all taxis here, as I said before. Having a yellow-and-white car just creates more opportunities for the owner to make some money with it."

"But doesn't that mean we'll have to stop and give lifts on the way?"

"Not with me sitting in the back."

"I suppose not. And I'm right in thinking we're not going to find a local, friendly insurance agent to cover us in the event of us breaking the sump on a rock or anything?"

Gulnaz sighed. "Ah, here's something else you can do with that over-active mouth of yours." A large plate of *palaw* was placed in front of them. "Tuck in.

It's lamb shank and saffron rice with carrots and raisins—a typical Afghan party dish. You seem to be in a party mood, and I thought it might help keep your spirits up when you get down to work later."

"Thank you." David was suddenly sober again. He had managed to put the nature of their mission out of his mind for a while, and he was beginning to enjoy Gulnaz's company. He also felt a deep respect for her. That she could be so level-headed and caring of him in such thoughtful ways after what she'd gone through was hard for him to comprehend. That she had survived with her sanity, and carved out a life for herself in the US that was, to everyone who knew her there, quite normal, beggared belief. It made him feel completely shallow, and somehow idiotic with his cynical British humor, to be in her presence. Part of him wanted to let others know—her local shopkeepers in Washington, her hairdresser, the local MacDonald's… did they have any idea what a powerhouse of strength and character they were dealing with when they sold her a burger, or gave her a wash and blow dry? It all seemed so ridiculous, somehow. The emptiness and facile futility of everyday life in a civilized country. Petty concerns, pointless arguments, meaningless comforts.

David felt a bit clumsy, trying to ball up the *palaw* in his right hand, but he wanted to impress Gulnaz, and he knew he stuck out like a sore thumb in the *chaikhana*.

"I did some reading on the flight," he said between mouthfuls. "It was about the Zoroastrians. A bit of research."

"Oh, yes. What did you find out?"

"They claim it's the world's oldest known religion and, interestingly, it's also, arguably, the world's first proponent of ecology. They're the original tree-huggers. Followers of the Zoroastrian faith care for the physical world, and not just for the sake of ensuring their own spiritual salvation. They say that human beings, as God's creation, are the natural overseers of the Seven Creations—sky, water, earth, plant, animal, human and fire. As the only conscious being, every human's ultimate task is to care for the universe. So, the Seven Creations are sacred, and Zoroastrians try to develop great clarity and awareness of them, because at the end of time, humanity must give to Ahura Mazda, the supreme divine authority, a world in its original perfect state. The fundamentalists among them take this thinking to great lengths. For instance, they never enter a river to wash in it or pollute it in any way. Purity of nature is seen as the greatest good." He paused to reflect on what he'd just said. "It's interesting, if you think about it. Just imagine if this, the self-proclaimed oldest religion, had prevailed as the majority religion in the world. There would be none of this 'my god is better than your god' nonsense, and we'd have looked after the planet because we knew it was the right thing to do all along."

"And these are the people who got persecuted and driven out by so-called

'God-fearing' people." Gulnaz glanced at David as she took another handful of *palaw*.

"Therein lies the problem, I suppose."

"How do you mean?"

"God-*fearing* doesn't seem to equate to God-*loving* in so many religions. All the others I've ever come across have somehow lost that simple connection along the way, as people manipulate the memories of what their founding master said and did, for their own purposes."

"You're very cynical, for someone so young."

"Well, maybe I'm being a bit judgmental making generalized comments about motives, but I do wonder about some of the weird and wonderful interpretations of God that people have arrived at over the ages. I mean, do you think that there is just one God, or have we got a selection of carefully branded entities that only have jurisdiction within certain areas of the world? If so, we really do have a problem!"

Gulnaz took a last mouthful and sat looking down at the ground in front of her. "I don't know about any God."

"Well, if there is one, I hope God's with us when we buy this car," said David, unsuccessfully trying to lighten the mood. "Shall we?" He gestured for them to leave.

They decided to make their way back to the hotel, where they could put the word out. "What's the MO for this type of op, Gulnaz?" David started psyching himself up for the novel experience of haggling over the price of an old Toyota, through an interpreter, while appearing to be in charge of the situation.

"First of all, they're going to think you're a pushover. You're a foreigner who doesn't speak a word of Pashtu, and I'm a woman. As far as they're concerned, I know nothing about cars. Unfortunately for them, I know a lot about cars as I've had to look after my own in the US for the past 14 years. The first car I bought when I got to the Washington was a Toyota Corolla, because I was familiar with them, and American cars were too flashy for me. When 2003 came around, I was in the market for another car as my first Toyota had died. That's when I started finding out what all the problems were with this model, by checking carcomplaints.com. There are plenty of problems, but nothing that we can't handle as long as we can get a test drive."

"Well, that's good news. What kind of problems?"

"Oh, just excessive oil consumption, engines failing, transmissions breaking… things like that."

"You're joking, right?"

"No, I'm not. But if you think about it, we only need the car for a day and a half, to carry us about 100 miles total. I think we can make a safe enough decision on the basis of a test drive, don't you? And, let's face it; they do keep them running well here. No one wants to waste their time going to Dubai for spares, because that's what they have to do."

"But that's obviously when they sell them—when they need spare parts!" Gulnaz dismissed that comment with a wave of the hand. "It doesn't exactly fill me with confidence—"

"Stop worrying, David. Once it's got us into the mountains, it's all downhill back to the airport."

"You're enjoying this, aren't you?" David felt a bit silly. Gulnaz burst out laughing.

Within minutes of them arriving back at the Barat Hotel, a phone call had been made and a car slid to a halt at the front door, kicking up a cloud of dust that drifted into the reception area.

"I think Clint Eastwood's just arrived," David said, as a short man in his 30s, wearing a long coat, a turban and a broad smile emerged from the dust.

"*As-salam aleikum*," he said, extending a hand to David. "*Zem-ma num Wais dai.*" Good morning, my name is Wais. David responded by trying to say the same words back to him, inserting his own name at the appropriate place. He even remembered to put his hand on his heart and bow slightly. Wais looked confused until Gulnaz repeated the words to him. David thought it sounded exactly the same as when he'd said it, but this time the sparkle of recognition in the man's eyes confirmed that David needed to work on his accent. *Plan B. Take command, be the man*, he thought. Turning to Gulnaz, he said, "Tell him you are my translator and that I want to buy a car."

"I'd figured that part out already." Gulnaz translated, keeping her eyes averted from Wais all the time. It seemed to David to be a lot of words being exchanged between them, and he didn't want to lose track of the conversation.

"What did you say?"

"I introduced you and told him that you wanted to know how his health was, whether his business was going well, and how his family was doing. He explained that he is in good health, thanks be to Allah, business could be better and that he is proud that he can be of service to a fine young Westerner, and his family is prospering and he thanked Allah for that too."

"Great... Well, are all the formalities out of the way? I don't want to appear rushed, but we don't have a lot of time." David maintained a smile and eye contact with Wais as she continued talking to him. "But don't translate that!"

"I'm not." She carried on talking to Wais, who suddenly became quite animated. David feigned understanding and played along with his enthusiastic gestures. After a minute or two, Wais appeared to finish what he was saying and looked at him with expectation in his eyes.

"What was that about? Where exactly are we with the car purchase?" David asked behind a clenched-teeth smile.

"I was asking him if he had enjoyed the Buzkashi games. It seems he is quite a fan of the sport. David, you have to give a little to gain some trust."

"Of course. Is there anything else I should ask him?"

"No, we can move on now, I think."

"Can we find out, then, what he has got in the way of cars that will take us at least 100 miles without a major overhaul?" Gulnaz launched into another seemingly endless dialogue with Wais. Eventually, it stopped. Wais looked up at him and beckoned to him to follow.

"You'll be amazed to hear that he has a 2002 Toyota Corolla. By his description, it's done just a few miles and it's in showroom condition."

"Oh, good. I suppose it also has a full breakdown warranty, only one careful lady owner, a service record since new, blah, blah, blah. Did he train in Clapham?"

"Is that a college for car dealers?"

"You could say that…" They arrived at Wais's car, where he opened the passenger door for David, leaving Gulnaz to open the back door for herself.

Wais drove through the town to the outskirts, talking constantly as he wove his way through a network of narrow streets. For David, Wais drove a bit too fast for comfort, and he would have felt more relaxed if he'd spent more time looking at the road ahead, rather than at him. The roads were busy—market stalls, people cooking food to sell on makeshift cookers, gypsies sitting on the ground displaying vast selections of jewelry, children playing, trucks maneuvering and barbers meticulously trimming beards. They eventually came to an open area where about fifty cars were parked and a cargo container served as an office. A group of men made their way toward them as they entered the compound.

"It doesn't look as if they have much business today," David remarked.

"The market is flooded at the moment. Some of these men probably haven't sold a car in days—possibly weeks. It's not easy for them and even when they do sell they usually make either a small flat rate—around here that would be about $20 for a sale—or they get 1% of the deal." When they got out of the car, the other bargainers jostled for David's attention. It was all good-natured, but David found it difficult to avoid their entreaties. He it best tactic to simply smile and shake hands as he walked. Gulnaz stayed behind the crowd, preferring to wait until she was needed for the negotiations.

"Hey, it's silver!" David waved Gulnaz over to take a look. She walked toward the car, but stayed a short distance away from it, while the men went about inspecting it. David walked slowly around it. One of the headlamps was badly chipped and was half-full of brown water. The laminated windscreen had a crack that meandered across its entire width. Wais continued talking as

David studied the car in detail. Gulnaz contributed the occasional translation. "It's a very good car… very reliable… it belonged to a friend of mine… he is a gentle man…"

David stroked his chin, apparently in deep thought. "It's very nice. It has a nice selection of three different hubcaps, the paintwork on the roof has developed a nice matt patina—I hope that isn't extra. The end of the exhaust pipe is surrounded by an attractive black soot effect. Let's look at the engine." He gestured to Wais to open the hood, then leaned into the engine compartment, fiddled with a few connections and squeezed some hoses. He had no idea what to look for, but it was clear that the engine hadn't exploded or sprayed rusty water all over the place, so he was reasonably confident that even though it probably burned a lot of oil, at least the head wasn't warped or the head gasket broken. He held his hands in the 'steering wheel' position and moved them up and down. Wais handed him the keys and climbed into the passenger seat, talking continuously. David wondered if this man ever stopped for breath. He could feel springs through his seat. David checked the odometer. It registered 195,047 miles, but he assumed that meant very little. The engine was smooth, suggesting it may have been a reconditioned unit. A quick look at the well-worn pedals confirmed that this car had been heavily used. Having done two circuits of the compound in second gear, David thought he'd like to take it on the road for a short spin but, judging by Wais's expression, that wasn't an option. Instead, he went through the entire gearbox at 15mph, virtually stalling it, but he was happy to find that all the gears worked to some degree. Stopping the car next to where Gulnaz was standing, he got out and made a great display of checking to see that the tires had enough tread to withstand a beating on the mountain roads. Then he popped the hood again and scrutinized the dipstick for traces of water—as well as the existence of at least some oil. *This should last one and a half days*, he thought to himself. "How much does he want for it?"

Gulnaz asked Wais. "He says he'll do a very special rate for you: 175,000 Afghani." Then she added, "It's far too much, but don't act surprised—you could embarrass him in front of his friends. Doing business here is all about maintaining a sense of honor."

"Yes, that's over $4,000. Suggest to him that, because it burns oil, has done many, many miles and it only has one headlight, a fairer price would be 100,000."

"He says the engine is new and the headlight will dry out now that spring is here. It worked fine last year. He cannot really afford to lower the price because it was an expensive car. If he sells it to you for 150,000, he will make nothing on it."

"Tell him that I can see that he is an honorable man, and I thank him for his time but 150,000 is too much for me as I am not a rich man."

"I'll tell him that," said Gulnaz, "but I just noticed something else that brings the price down. Wait a minute." She continued talking to Wais. "He'll do 120,000, if that works for you. I suggested that it would."

"I think we have a deal." David smiled at Wais who looked surprised to have done a deal so quickly and easily, shook his hand again and walked with him to the office to pay the owner of the business.

"Pure luxury," David smirked as they drove out of the compound. "What did you say to him to get him under 150,000?"

"The car is right-hand drive. They banned imports of right-hand drive vehicles in 2004 because in Afghanistan we drive on the left. That also stopped them exporting cars to Pakistan where they drive on the right. He was never going to sell this car to anyone if we didn't buy it. Once I made that point—in a way that didn't offend his sense of honor—he also threw in a gallon of oil so we wouldn't beat him down further. One of his friends put it in the trunk while you were in the office."

"Nice one, Gulnaz. You're one sharp cookie."

CHAPTER 19

Troy King's head was buzzing pleasantly as he downed his second beer. It was 10pm, and he was perched on a barstool, wedged between two rowdy groups of party-goers in a bar just off Times Square. He'd just enjoyed his first night out at a Broadway show in 25 years. *That was somethin' else!* The choice had been vast—almost too much. Should he go to a family show? Maybe something off-Broadway, a little risqué? In the end, he decided that the former would be too bland—a missed opportunity—and the latter too dry and intellectual for him. He wanted some *fun!* Green Day's 'American Idiot' seemed to fit the bill. Checking out the write-up, he could relate to the story. The rock musical, he'd read, 'follows working-class characters from the suburbs to the Middle East, as they seek redemption in a world filled with frustration'. After a head-pounding, hyper-energized hour-and-a-half, he couldn't quite see how his journey related to those of the characters in the musical, but he'd had a hell of a good time.

His cell phone rang.

"Heeey, who's this?" He signaled to the barman for another beer.

"This is Samakab, Mr King." King stiffened and held the phone away from his mouth as he stifled a belch. He was feeling a little too merry for a conversation with this man, however much he wanted to talk to him.

"And to what do I owe this pleasure, sir?"

"I think you know what I want to talk about, Mr King, and I'd appreciate it if we could do so without another of your little charades this time. Are you alone? I hear people...?"

"Mr Samakab, I don't know what you're talking about and, yes, there are lots of people here. What can I do for you?"

"Can you go somewhere quieter so we can talk?"

"Sir, this is Times Square on a Friday night. What do you suggest?" The barman placed another beer in front of him. This conversation was taking the glow off his evening, and he wanted to end it as quickly as possible.

"How about a drink at the Michelangelo? It's just a few blocks from where you are."

"You know where I am?"

"You just told me you're at Times Square."

"Oh, yes." It had been a long and eventful day. The beers were already going to his head, and King knew it. But he was still awake enough to realize that he wasn't awake enough to have a conversation with someone as sober and sharp as Samakab, without running the risk of saying things he shouldn't. "I think it's kinda late, and I'd like to head off for some shut-eye after I've finished this beer.

It's been a long one."

"That's a shame. We may not get another chance to talk, and I have some information that I think you would find useful." *Damn*, thought King, *damn!* He put his beer down and tried to clear his thoughts. Samakab obviously wanted to take advantage of the fact that King was tired and had been drinking. King wasn't sure why, and he couldn't imagine what information Samakab could possibly have that would be useful to him. King had assumed that *he'd* be prodding Samakab for information to fill in some gaps for Arlington Online.

"I'll meet you in the lobby in a halfhour," King said.

"Fine, I'll look forward to it."

King closed his cell phone and called to the barman. "Coffee, please. Make it a strong one." He cast his mind back to lunchtime, trying to remember the sequence of events. He was still puzzled by Samakab's sudden change of heart when he was about to be shown the door, his guarded comments about his business interests, and the way he showed complete disinterest in the piracy situation that was causing so much mayhem for shipping off the Somali coast. Surely it would be affecting him as well, if he was importing and exporting? He wondered if Barak or his son had shown him the video clip. *I'm just gettin' too old for all this.* What he really wanted to do was enjoy another couple of beers, have a nice, relaxing night in a comfortable bed, then hop on a plane to Seattle and make his way down to his orchard. He'd be really happy to while away the rest of his life, sitting on the verandah doing nothin' much at all.

He was jolted out of his reverie by a sharp, stabbing pain at the base of his ribcage, just near his right kidney. He froze. It felt like metal. It moved very slightly. He couldn't turn to see what it was, partly because of the problems in his lower back, and partly because everyone around him was pressing against him. He waited to see what happened next. *Is this it? Have I crossed one too many lines?* Even though his mind was racing to find an explanation—*why would anyone want to take me out?*—he remained calm. An all-enveloping tiredness came over him—an acceptance of defeat that somehow seemed justified and preordained. He just sat, and waited, and let his mind go blank.

It was only a few minutes later, when the group to his right moved away from the bar, that he dared to slowly turn his head to try to engage with his assailant. The perceived threat turned out to be a very attractive girl in a tight red dress, sitting on a high stool with a steel back that she'd unwittingly pushed into his back she sat down. She was talking happily to three friends—totally unaware of the killer status that King had suspected her of. He smiled at his own paranoia. *Maybe I've been watching too many violent movies.* He paid and pushed his way through the crowded bar to the door. He was happy to be alive, but all the conviviality exacerbated his feeling of loneliness, and he was relieved to be out on the sidewalk, with something to do. He hailed a cab. In the relative quiet of its enclosed passenger space, he tried to remember good times in bars with girls, and with his wife, Dolores. It was all so long ago. He ran his hand over the scar on his head, and thought about the last time he'd had sex. That was when he was fit and strong—a basketball hero at West Point, before the war. They'd been celebrating with friends after he'd just led his team to victory in the championship semi-finals. It was a warm night and there was a white-hot connection between him and Dolores as they eyeballed each other across the dinner table. So much so that, when she excused herself to go to the washroom, he couldn't resist the urge to follow her a minute later. He'd pinned her against the washroom door in a breathless, fumbling embrace, slid her dress up over her hips and pushed himself into her. They'd barely been able to hide their secret when they returned to the table, blushing, giggling and happily guilty. *Wow, she was hot!* And that thought made him sad—for her, for him, for the physical passion that got taken away, and the shift in his mind that disconnected him from ever being with her in the same way again.

"Sir? You asked for the Michelangelo?" the cab driver asked.

"That's right."

"Well, is this close enough for you?" They were sitting directly in front of the hotel's main entrance.

"Oh, sure. Thanks."

To Troy King, the lobby of the Michelangelo looked like some upper-class bordello, with its lavish marbled walls and pillars, red velvet-covered soft furnishings and gold fittings. As soon as he walked into the lobby, Samakab strode over to him and shook his hand. King was all too aware that he was still wearing the same blue checked shirt and tie, coat and badly creased pants that he'd been wearing since 4am that morning. Samakab, on the other hand, looked as King wanted to look. Tall and elegant, with an easy, athletic walk, he looked immaculate in an expensive suit. As they shook hands, King caught sight of a very fancy-looking watch. Samakab noticed.

"You like it?"

"I never seen one like that before. Kinda antique-lookin'. Does it keep good time?"

Samakab took it off and handed it to King as they walked to the lounge bar. "Please, be my guest. Keep it. I have plenty of others, and they're becoming a bit redundant these days." They found a table in a corner where they could talk privately.

"What type is it?" inquired King, who was fascinated by the delicately detailed design, numerous dials, and gently oscillating gold moving parts.

"It's a Blancpain Carrousel Volant Une Minute."

"I never heard of them. Looks nice."

"Yes, I like it. It doesn't surprise me that you haven't heard of them, though.

You don't see many for sale. Its movement is based on one they first made in 1892, so I guess they knew how to keep good time even then."

"Very nice," King said, and handed the watch back to Samakab.

"I meant what I said," Samakab said.

"I know and I appreciate it. It's just that I don't have much use for a timepiece like this either. None of us have enough time, but you say it keeps good time. That's the kind of time you wanna keep." Samakab acknowledged the gesture with a smile, and returned the watch to his wrist.

"I've ordered something for us. I hope you don't mind," Samakab said as a waiter arrived with a tray with a bottle of wine, two glasses and a plate with a variety of beautiful-looking morsels arranged on it. As Samakab tasted and approved the wine, King was aware that he felt a bit woozy. He'd never had much success mixing drinks, and he knew he needed to stay on top of this meeting. But his tiredness was becoming a real problem.

"I'll have some water with that," he said to the waiter, who nodded and poured them each a glass. Turning to Samakab he said, "So, tell me, why did you aks me to come here this evening?"

"You're very direct. I like that." Samakab took a sip from his glass.

"I speak my mind, and I'd appreciate it if you would do the same. Do you think you can do that?"

"I will tell you what I can, and what I feel comfortable telling you. If I don't want to discuss anything or tell you something in particular, I'll let you know as plainly as possible. How does that sound?"

"Sounds good to me," King said and, against his better judgment, lifted his wine glass and smelled the bouquet. It was excellent, as he knew it would be. He managed to resist the temptation to taste the wine, and returned his glass carefully to the table.

He turned back to Samakab. "What exactly is the nature of your business in New York?"

"Fuck off. Is that plain enough?" Samakab smiled as he watched King suppress a shocked reaction.

"Touché," King smiled. He decided to take a drink of wine after all.

"Mr King, you know I don't have to tell you anything. I know you are in the intelligence business—the operative word being 'business'. You're not even part of NSA, CIA or any other government agency. You work for a company that is contracted to provide services to the government. You have no jurisdiction over me or anyone else. You're just a manager in a small company in Washington. Those are the facts, as far as I am concerned, unless you can tell me otherwise—although if they were 'otherwise', you wouldn't be telling me anyway. So, while I can appreciate your directness, I cannot trust you, because I don't trust the 'facts' that I have just outlined about you, given the nature and content of our discussion earlier today, at lunch."

"If that's the way you feel, Mr Samakab, is there any point in us talking?" *If you're in a hole, stop digging, thought King. I want out of here. Big mistake. I should have gone to bed.*

"I think we both have something to gain from talking to each other, but if you'd rather not, we can leave it here." Samakab sat back in his chair. "Please, help yourself," he said, gesturing to the food. King felt a shift in the conversation. Behind the words, he felt there was some concern in Samakab's voice.

"What could possibly concern you about our conversation at lunch, Mr Samakab? As I recall, I quizzed your son's friend about a video that you hadn't seen, and the only other topics of conversation were—and tell me if I'm wrong—Somali piracy, the nature of your business again... oh, and I mentioned the weather."

"Exactly."

"Which parts of that have given you cause for concern?" King leaned forward. Samakab turned his head to the side, thinking.

"I do not want my son to be seen to be connected to any of this, Mr King." He turned to look at King.

"You'll have to do better than that," King responded. "And what do you mean? Connected to any of what?"

"Pornographic websites—"

"No, no, Mr Samakab. I'm not buyin' any of that," King cut in. "I work for intelligence, as you so rightly pointed out, not the *National Enquirer.* And anyway, who cares if some kid likes to look at a few titties on the Net. No, it's one of them other subjects that got you all upset. Now we just got to figure out which one it was." King tried a miniature quiche. "Mmm... very good. You should try one of these." It was his turn to feel a bit of confidence.

"You're right, of course, Mr King. I should have known better than to try and spoof a spook!" They both chuckled at the expression. "Look, between you and me," Samakab leaned toward King, who took another mouthful of food, "I don't work in clothing. I am currently negotiating some really nice contracts for communications systems that we plan to install in several African regions. It's all very hush-hush. You know how competitive things are these days and, to be honest, some of the dealings aren't—how shall I put it—completely straight."

So it's not that, either, thought King. "Sure, I understand. Well, how the wheels of industry turn ain't no concern of mine."

"I'm so glad we understand each other," said Samakab. *Like heck we do,* thought King.

"When you called, you said you had something for me. What is it?" King wanted to get the conversation back on track. He tried one of the fancy-looking miniature pastries. The waiter brought his water.

"It's about that video," Samakab replied.

"Oh? What about it? You seen it yet?" King feigned disinterest and continued eating and sipping his wine, watching Samakab's body language in his peripheral vision.

"Yes. Ayan sent me the email with the video attached, and I watched it a few times."

"What did you think?"

"Before I say, would you tell me why it interested you enough to come all this way to ask Assaf about it?"

"It seemed like a massacre of innocent people. Usually we get reports on that kind of stuff, but not this one, so it was kinda odd. It was real odd to see it traveling from Israel, when it had nothin' to do with Israelis or Arabs and, at the time, we had no idea where it came from. Did Ayan tell you about the website?"

"Yes, he did, eventually." Samakab sighed. "Raging hormones, I suppose..."

"I guess so, but ain't that a *good thing* in a young man?" King smiled at Samakab, then continued with a serious expression. "The point is that this website, ShocknWhore, is one of ours, run by one of our less savory examples in our own military. So, I'm employed to check out all the angles, and since I knew young Barak was goin' to be in town—"

"And how, exactly, *did* you know that—down to the exact time and place?"

"Sorry, sir, that's classified information," King lied, feeling the iPhone against his chest in his jacket pocket.

"That's impressive... or extremely worrying for all us people innocently going about our everyday business."

"It's usually not the innocent ones that need to be worried. What did you think?"

"About what?" Samakab asked as he refilled their wine glasses.

"The video clip."

"When I looked at it, I could understand what Assaf said he felt about it. There was something strange, but I couldn't put my finger on it, if you know what I mean."

"No, I don't know what you mean." King detected a half-truth in what Samakab was saying. He was normally so precise and efficient with his words.

"Well, of course, you must understand that I am not used to seeing such things... You say it was an American military website. Was it uploaded by a soldier who shot the clip, do you think?" King was becoming more alert by the minute. Something in him was getting excited by this conversation. He could feel he was onto something. He didn't know what it was, but there was something in the way that Samakab was talking, and fishing for information.

"Did I say an American military website? Apologies if I did. No, it was uploaded to a site run by an unsavory military person. I don't think the military would run a website like that, and call it ShocknWhore. Do you?"

"Of course not. I apologize, I misunderstood. But if soldiers are knowingly shooting and uploading clips of military incidents to that sort of website rather than reporting them, surely something is very wrong."

"I don't think a soldier shot the video," King said. He was clear now, and watching carefully for Samakab's reaction to that statement.

"Oh," Samakab said, and sat back in his chair again. He looked thoughtful.

"So, you were going to tell me what you found strange about it." King was keen to keep him talking.

"It was those wounds..." Samakab began.

"Yes?"

"I have a theory as to what caused them."

"I'd love to hear that." King turned to face Samakab again.

"I think they were caused by a caltrop, or some variation on that weapon."

"What on earth is a caltrop?" King asked, completely confused all of a sudden.

"It's an ancient weapon that is still in use to this day. It's made up of four prongs arranged in a way that three of them create a stable base and the fourth one points vertically upwards. They made them with iron in ancient times and scattered them in the path of oncoming soldiers or horses. I know of them because they have been used in some of the conflicts that have unfortunately beset Africa in more recent times. After I saw your video, I looked them up on the Internet, and found that the US Office of Strategic Services uses them to puncture vehicle tires. The interesting thing about the type they use is that it is made of hollow section tubular steel with sharpened ends. If you held one in your hand, clasping it at the base, you could feasibly use it as a weapon that would cause the kind of punctures we saw in those people in the video."

"Well, that's very interesting. Thank you. I'll check that one out. I'm checking out all the angles right now, as I said, and this could have some merit." King took another sip of wine. He couldn't believe his ears. Surely Samakab wasn't expecting him to buy this story? Either he was spinning him a line, or he knew as much about weaponry and hand-to-hand combat as King knew about expensive watches. As far as King was concerned, all of those people died at almost exactly the same time. None of them knew it was coming— whatever it was—and it certainly wasn't delivered by hand. To orchestrate such a simultaneous attack would have meant choreographing all the moves with tighter precision than Riverdance. He would have burst out laughing at any other time, but he still hadn't got to the bottom of things here. *What's the next subject? There's just the matter of piracy we haven't covered.* "I was just curious to know— Damn, who could that be?" A feint buzzing in his pocket announced the start of his cell phone ringing. He looked at his watch: 11.30. "Hmm... must be important. Excuse me." He opened his cell phone, and sat back in his chair. "Hello, who's this? ...yes, this is King... no... yes... uhuh... mmm... sure, that would be fine... yes, I was planning to stay here another day but if this is important... mmm... I see... yes, I'm with someone right now... no, I won't... don't worry, I won't say a thing, why would I?... no, that's fine... oh good... really... that's good... fine weather all the way... great... a what?... oh, anticyclone... okay... tomorrow then." As he slipped the phone back into his pocket, he said, "Seems like I been called back to the office for something. Gotta go tomorrow. Pity. I was hoping to get just one more show in before I headed back."

"So, it's going to be a fine day for traveling tomorrow, from what I overheard—sorry, I couldn't help but—"

"No problem." King brushed the apology aside. "Yeah. Strange thing, that. He gave me a detailed weather report—as if I care at 11.30 at night. Anyway, where were we? Ah, yes, I was aksing—"

"I think we've finished, Mr King," Samakab snapped, getting up from his seat. He was fuming. "And you can give him a message from me. As far as I'm concerned, the deal is off."

"Excuse me?"

"And you can charge him for this little tête-à-tête as well." With that, he stormed out of the bar.

King stared after him. *This guy's moods are as unpredictable as the weather!*

CHAPTER 20

Back at the Barat Hotel, David collected his bag and went downstairs to the lobby to wait for Gulnaz. As he caught glimpses of life in Mazar-e-Sharif passing by the open doorway, it occurred to him that this was the first time he'd actually stopped and had a chance to reflect on his situation since King had said that word in the bar: Afghanistan. *This is absolutely ridiculous*, was his first thought. *If only my friends back home could see me now*, was the second. For the next five minutes, his mind played games with him, swinging wildly back and forth from deep uncertainty and fear, to heady excitement, a feeling that he was on some great adventure. *I'm a complete idiot! How could I have possibly allowed myself to get into this situation?* And the next instant, *hey, I'm Indiana Jones, Raider of the Lost Zoroastrian Settlement.*

"Are you ready?" Gulnaz's voice interrupted his rollercoaster mind game.

"Ready and waiting," he replied, turning to find not Gulnaz, but a carbon copy of just about every other woman he'd seen since they'd arrived in Mazar. She was wearing a traditional light-blue full-length *burqa* over a long dress of the same color. Together, they completely neutralized her identity. "You look, er... well, I haven't a clue, actually."

"Good. It's doing its job then."

"Do any Afghan men ever find they've taken the wrong wife home after a trip to the supermarket?"

"Funny man."

"Just stay close by me today. I can't afford to lose sight of you, and I definitely don't want to be accused of trying to pick someone up if I talk to the wrong *burqa*." David peered into the veil, searching for her eyes, but they were well hidden and he certainly couldn't see her expression. It was a remarkably effective way to remove any kind of connection between two people. Suddenly, he didn't know this person. She was remote. He had little feedback on anything that he said other than the words and the inflexions in her voice. Before, he would have thought that would have been enough, but now he could see how incomplete words were, particularly in a situation like the one they were about to enter, where body language and facial signals could be crucial to their success.

David was glad of a clear sky as they drove south. It not only meant that his work would be a little less messy than if it had been raining, but it also meant that the temperature would have been low the previous night, especially in the Zoroastrian settlement, which was at about 2,000 feet up in the mountains. He glanced at Gulnaz in the mirror. Sitting in the back seat, she was a featureless blue lump, framed in the mirror with the Blue Mosque beside her receding into the distance.

They had discussed her outfit and their approach to the Zoroastrians at length the night before. It had been difficult to predict how they would react to the two of them. Should she remain as the tourist, with her face showing? As fundamentalists, would they have been uncomfortable with that, even though they weren't Muslims? Given the local social norms of women not talking to strangers and men not addressing women directly, how would the conversation be conducted? Even though Zoroastrians were not traditionally as moralistic and strict as Muslims and, in particular, the Taliban, how would they view a young man traveling with an older woman? There were so many questions that even Gulnaz had no answers for. In the end, they chose to take a traditional approach, with Gulnaz in the *burqa*, acting as an interpreter for a foreigner. They felt that her anonymity would raise less suspicion, and the familiarity of seeing an Afghan woman in a *burqa* might also help put them at ease when David started asking some very odd questions. They knew they only had one chance for David to do his work, so they wanted as little resistance as possible from the community. But no matter how well they tried to prepare, this was going to be a delicate mission.

The outskirts of Mazar-e-Sharif gradually gave way to a flat plain. Small houses dotted the sides of the road, the inhabitants surviving on crops grown in the dusty soil. In the distance, rugged mountains rose sharply from the barren landscape. Closer to the mountains, the road became a dirt track, which merged with a dried-up riverbed as they headed uphill toward a gap in the mountain range. As the road got steeper, it also became more uneven. David shifted down to coax the car through the ruts and stones. Black smoke started to billow out behind them, and the smell of burning oil filled the car. He was already having doubts about its ability to even get them to the settlement, but he kept his concerns to himself. It was with some relief that he passed through the rocky archway that marked the entrance to the Ali Baba Pass. But his heart sank when he saw that there was still another 1,000 feet of steep and winding track to climb before the road dropped away into the valley beyond. The engine revved and the car juddered as he slid over loose stones, spinning the wheels, fighting to get it to the top of the hill. Once there, he cut the engine and came to a halt. He felt it would be better to give it a rest before they carried on and he took the opportunity to check the map.

"I guess this isn't a commuter route into Mazar every morning," he said. The car hissed as the engine cooled down. Taking one of the plastic bottles of water they'd packed, he got out and splashed some of it over the dusty windscreen. He turned the wiper switch. Nothing happened. He glanced over at Gulnaz. She was sitting silently. He felt slightly irked that he couldn't read her expression. He resisted the temptation to make a characteristic quip about secondhand car dealers, and quietly cleaned the water off the screen with his sleeve.

"Look," Gulnaz said, lifting a hand to point at the view before them. After the track dipped slightly, it meandered along a broad, dry riverbed, virtually flat, for about a mile. The mountains rose steeply on either side of them at the pass and, beyond the valley that lay before them, they were progressively higher and more impressive. The entire vista was a vast terrain of dust and jagged rocks, broken occasionally by a thin coating of green from the last remnants of winter rain. "Perhaps now you understand a little more about my country, why so many have tried and failed to conquer it, and why our people are so resilient." Turning toward David, she asked, "How long could you survive in these mountains, do you think, even in the summer?" David shook his head and got back into the car.

The track split at the end of the valley. The broad, more comfortable route continued to the right; David took the left turn, and immediately wished they'd been able to buy a 4x4. This track didn't appear to have been used by vehicles at all. In fact, as far as David could see, he was driving up the dried-up bed of a mountain stream. The only way to negotiate the first half-mile of it was by keeping one side of the car on the bank, with it leaning over at an alarming angle. Holding onto the doorframe to keep himself in the driver's seat, he carefully nursed it around any rocks that he thought might foul the sump. Occasionally there was a piece of smoother track that provided some relief, followed by more bone-shaking rubble a few yards further on. After 20 minutes, they'd traveled one mile to a junction that David recognized from the map.

"Oh, good, we're nearly there. Just one-and-a-half miles to go," he said, as he turned to face a steeper and rockier track, between two hills, which had no discernable flat surface at all. "Oh, shit. What now?" He stopped the car and got out to see if he could find a way around the problem. It hadn't shown up on the satellite image as being this rough, and he could only imagine that there had been a rock fall since the image was produced. He scrambled up the hill, tripping over loose boulders. From a point 20 feet further up the rock slide, he could see that a track emerged from it a few yards further on, but there was no way he could get the car to it. *Damn! I hope I haven't screwed up.*

As he opened the door to give Gulnaz the news, she said, "I think we can get around this." She had lifted her *burqa* and was looking at the satellite image of the area. "All we have to do is drive another quarter of a mile up the riverbed, then we can take this path here…" she pointed to a path that looked as if it was no more than a foot wide, "around the side of the hill, and re-join the main track here. Would that work?"

"We don't seem to have any other options. Let's give it a shot. Thanks, Gulnaz." David winked at her and smiled. "Nice to see you again."

"Come on, let's get going." Gulnaz said gruffly. *Was she blushing?*

When they reached the path, it was indeed little more than a foot wide. The hill sloped at about 30 degrees to the right at the shallowest parts—more, in some places. David considered the possibilities and couldn't see any. "I don't feel confident about this," he said, "maybe we should have bought a couple of donkeys. What do you think?"

"We can do it," Gulnaz said. "All you have to do is set the right-hand wheels in the rut of the path and drive along it."

"But Gulnaz, this is a right-hand-drive car, remember? If I do that, all the weight will be on that side, and it'll tip over as soon as we hit one of the steep bits, if not before."

"No, it won't. Where's your sense of adventure? Of course it will work!" David still looked skeptical. "Look, I'll stand in the doorway and lean out as you drive. You know, like a yachtsman?"

"Are you serious?"

"Yes, of course I am. Come on!" She laughed as she took up her position as an outrigger on the side of the car. David shook his head in disbelief.

"But don't blame me if this thing rolls and you're catapulted over the car into the stream!"

"Oh, David, try to be positive, at least a little bit! Come on, let's go!" David put the car in first gear, and carefully inched forward. He felt certain it was going to roll, but somehow it stayed where it was meant to. When they came to the steepest part of the slope, he could feel the car start to teeter, but Gulnaz leaned out further, pulling it back to the ground.

David called out, "Gulnaz! Are you okay?"

"Don't worry about me. I'm fine. Just look where you are going!"

"Gulnaz!" David shouted again. He couldn't resist this.

"What?"

"You're the sexiest piece of ballast I've ever met!"

"Shut up and drive!"

They eventually managed to re-join the track, and Gulnaz was able to return to her seat. The last half-mile of track took them up a gentle slope to clearer ground. Gulnaz replaced her *burqa* as the car chugged and spluttered past a farm. Children waved to them.

"Okay, it should be just a few hundred yards up here that we turn left to the settlement." David exhaled with relief that they had conquered the worst part of the journey. "We'll have to find another way back, though. It'll be getting dark by the time we're done here."

As they drove on, the countryside became ever bleaker. Devoid of trees and greenery, it was the most inhospitable place David had ever seen. To him, it had no redeeming features.

"Why on earth would anyone choose to live in a place like this?" he said, as they passed the burned-out wreck of an old Russian troop carrier. Gulnaz had become quiet again. David was, at last, becoming more sensitive to her private melancholy and no longer expected her to respond to every comment.

Within five minutes, the road took them up a steep slope and into a small village. David recognized it immediately.

"We're here," he said. He stopped the car and stepped out. Silence. Nothing moved. He couldn't see anyone. Gulnaz got out of the car, and cast her eyes around. The buildings looked deserted and in bad repair. Many of the roofs looked as if they had caved in long ago.

"David." David turned to Gulnaz, and then followed her gaze—or where he guessed she was looking, behind her *burqa*, and there he was—the man they'd seen in the video, standing in a doorway just across the road from them.

"*Assalaam alaikum,*" David called across the road. The man disappeared into the darkness behind the doorway. David instinctively checked his watch: 3pm. He had about four hours of daylight to get the job done. He quickly walked over the road, with Gulnaz following a few paces behind. "Where did he go?" As his eyes got accustomed to the darkness in the room, he saw the man's white robes and his turban. He was sitting in a far corner with three other, similarly dressed, older men. There was no furniture apart from a rug in the corner that served as seating, and a low table. A wood-burning stove— a *bukhari*—with a metal flue that vented through the wall, stood behind them. Glasses were laid out on the table. "*Assalaam alaikum,*" David said again as he cautiously took a few steps forward, bowing slightly and carefully extending his hand to the man he had seen in the video. The four men regarded him without expression and in silence. "*Zem-ma num David dai.*" My name is David. They didn't respond, but kept staring at them both. David turned to Gulnaz, who was standing in the doorway. "What do you suggest, Gulnaz? They look as if they are in shock or something. Can you tell them who we are? Maybe it's best not to mention why we're here just yet." Gulnaz stepped forward, but before she could say anything, the man from the video spoke.

"*Assalaam alaikum,*" he said, "*Zem-ma num Vaspan dai. Ta la cherta ragh-ley?*" Hello, my name is Vaspan. Where do you come from?

David breathed a sigh of relief, and smiled at Vaspan, who took his hand and shook it warmly with his other hand placed on his heart. Vaspan invited them to sit, and the six of them drank tea together. With Gulnaz acting as interpreter, David began talking to Vaspan. He felt it would be particularly insensitive to ask how his family was, so he first explained that he had seen the video clip, that he was very saddened by what he saw, and that his government in America immediately dispatched him and Gulnaz to investigate the massacre. This news immediately caused a clamor of animated discussion between the four of them, and David asked Gulnaz to interject so they could make some quick progress.

"What, exactly, happened here? Why were all your families killed?" David asked.

Vaspan explained. "We came here many years ago, to be close to *Azar-i-Asp*, which is the sacred fire temple in Balkh. It is a very holy place—the first place where Zoroaster first preached and where he died. We are peaceful people, and we have lived in peace for many years. Even when the Taliban took Mazar-e-Sharif and killed many people there, and when the Hazaras were being persecuted, killed and driven out, we were left in peace. We thought that there was going to be no more killing, and the Taliban left us alone to farm our land and raise our children. We are not wealthy people. We have no use for riches. We just want to be good people, serve Ahura Mazda, and keep the earth and all of creation pure for Him. Then they started to visit us here."

"Who started to visit?" asked David.

"The Taliban. They came in their trucks with their guns. At first, there were just a few of them, and then more and they came more often. Now they come nearly every day."

"What do they want? Do they threaten you?"

"They demand food. At first, we were happy to help them. We shared whatever we had with them. That is only correct. When a visitor arrives at our house, of course we invite him in and share with them what we have. I am sure that is the same in a great country like America." David said nothing. He gestured to Vaspan to continue. "One day, they came and took a goat, and the next day they came back and demanded two more goats. They accused us of hiding food from them, and they cursed us and said we would pay for our deception."

"What time of day do they come?" David asked. He didn't want to run into any hungry, gun-toting, bad-tempered Taliban fighters.

"It's a different time every day. We never know when they will come." *Terrific*, thought David.

"And have they been here today?"

Vaspan checked with the other men. "No, not today."

"Excuse me," David said to the four men, and turned to Gulnaz. "What's going on here, do you think? Our intelligence says that this is a quiet, relatively safe area. There's no fighting in the Mazar region and, as you told me, the Taliban are supposed to be managing their logistics network and keeping a low profile. From what I've seen in Mazar, that seems to be the case. There are tourists all over the place and everyone's happily going about their business. Why would they suddenly be turning up here, in the middle of nowhere, hassling these people?"

"I don't know," said Gulnaz. "I can only guess that the Taliban are hiding out up here, preparing an offensive or something." That made sense to David.

He knew the airport at Termez had only recently been opened up to American military traffic again, after the Uzbekistan and US governments fell out over the massacre of citizens in Andijan by the Uzbek National Security Service in 2005. After that, the US only had access via the new Freedom Bridge from Tajikistan to bring supplies into the country, but now they could also use the Friendship Bridge from Uzbekistan again. The route from the Freedom Bridge through Kunduz was now really dangerous for the Americans, so the Taliban were probably watching to see if there was an increase in military traffic around Mazar. If so, they would be keeping an eye on the airport and the ISAF base, and these mountains were the ideal place to base themselves.

"Yes, but I still don't understand why these people would be under threat when they were supporting the local Taliban with everything they had." David turned back to Vaspan. "Ask him what happened on the day of the massacre… as delicately as you can."

Vaspan's eyes softened with tears as Gulnaz put the question to him.

"We had given them everything. Everything we had to eat. Everything. We told them that we had no more food to give them, and we showed them that there was nothing left. We thought they would leave us alone. They laughed at us and got into their truck. The Muslims like to torment us." He paused and looked at Gulnaz in her *burqa*. "They have done this for a thousand years, so we were not surprised, just unhappy as we had no food left to eat. When they had left, all the families got together in the square. Everyone was angry, but we four are priests, so we said to them 'anger will not feed your stomachs, it will only consume you and make you more unhappy'. We left them in the square and returned here to pray to Ahura Mazda to give us understanding and the wisdom to find a way to return to our harmonious way of life. But they were angry and blinded by hatred of these people who had taken everything from them. And then…" He stopped dead. Gulnaz urged him to carry on. "Then it happened. The whispering from heaven, falling like stars into all the hearts of our families." All four men sat staring blankly into space.

David was confused. "I don't understand, Gulnaz, can you translate that last bit again? What are they talking about?"

"That's exactly what they said," said Gulnaz. "It's the best I can do."

"But it doesn't make any sense. Come on. We need more than that. Ask them again. I mean, were shots fired? Where did these falling stars come from? Please…"

"I'll try." Gulnaz turned back to Vaspan and tried to extract a clearer explanation from him. "No, he says it was very quiet. There were no explosions, just a rushing noise, and a hiss, and a smell of burning, and screams… And then they were all dead. All dead…"

They all sat in silence for some minutes. David was trying, with very little knowledge of ballistics and modern weaponry, to figure out what kind of weapon could do what had just been described to them. Nothing came to mind. None of it made any more sense to him now than when he'd first seen the video clip. And he was beginning to feel very nervous about the possibility of a Taliban visit. Not only were he and Gulnaz at risk, but so were these four men. He needed to get moving as quickly as possible.

"Gulnaz, can you find out if the bodies are still here somewhere, and if I can inspect them? Tell them it is very important that I see the bodies, because we may be able to stop more people being attacked this way if we know a little more about the weapons they used."

"The bodies are on the *dakhma*—that's the Tower of Silence—but you cannot go and see them," Gulnaz said.

"Bullshit, Gulnaz. I'm going to see those bodies. Get permission." David was feeling the stress of the situation now, and getting very tense.

"Only the *nasellar* can do that. A *nasellar*, roughly translated, is a pallbearer or caretaker who oversees the putrefaction process and deals with potential pollutants from the bodies to prevent them going into the earth."

"Well, tell them I am a *nasellar*, then—fully qualified, from Harvard. Anything. Just make it work." Gulnaz kept calm and entered into a long discussion with the four men as David sat and tried to prepare himself for his next task. He'd read up a little on forensic science in the short time he had before boarding the flight at Langley, but he'd never actually seen a dead body before, and he had no idea what a ten-day-old dead body was like. He glanced toward the doorway, hoping that no unwelcome visitors would disturb them. *Why do they take so damned long to make a simple decision?*

"They don't like it one little bit, but they have agreed," said Gulnaz eventually. "There's just one condition. Their *nasellar* must accompany you. His name is Taronish. This man here." She nodded in the direction of one of the men. He looked as if he was the oldest of the four. With a deeply lined face and few teeth, he had the cloudy eyes of fading sight.

"Thank you, Gulnaz," he said as he bowed in acknowledgement toward Taronish, who nodded back at him and smiled. He wanted to squeeze Gulnaz's arm in gratitude and to appease his feeling of guilt for snapping at her, but he remembered just in time that making any such gesture could risk sabotaging the delicate agreement that Gulnaz had just won. "Can you ask them to show us where we can hide the car while we are here, just in case...?"

David had to try several times to get the car to start and, when it finally did, it only fired on three cylinders and smoked badly. He swore under his breath, feeling a flutter of panic as he thought of the trip back down to Mazar. There was a building across the steeply sloping square with a doorway that was wide enough for him to drive in. He parked the car as far inside as possible.

As he opened the trunk to get a small shoulder bag containing equipment he needed from his backpack, one of the men was already sweeping the square behind with his foot, removing all traces of tire marks. As soon as David had closed the trunk, an old door was placed across the back of the car and, looking back as he walked across the square, he could see that it was well-hidden.

"*Dakhma*," Taronish was standing beside him and pointing up the hill, away from the settlement. David took a deep breath.

"Here we go, then," David said, and gestured to Gulnaz to follow.

"I cannot go with you," she said, much to David's surprise.

"Why not?" As soon as he said it he could have kicked himself. Of course she couldn't. First, she was a woman. Secondly, she was clearly a Muslim, as far as the Zoroastrians could tell, which meant that she would regard the traditions they had around death as extremely distasteful. Thirdly, she had seen death in her own family, and it was incredibly insensitive of him to even contemplate asking her to witness this gory scene. "I'm so sorry, Gulnaz." He stared at her silent, anonymous visage and then turned to walk up the hill. Looking back, he said to her, "Lie low and keep out of sight. I'll be back in half an hour or so." He invited Taronish to walk in front of him, and he and the old man slowly made their way up the hill.

Once they had passed the last of the buildings in the settlement, David could see the Tower of Silence. It was about 200 yards directly up the hill from them, a gentle slope with patchy grass sprouting from its rocky surface. The circular stone structure was much larger than he'd expected. It must have been 20 feet high and 30 feet across, tapering slightly toward its top, which appeared to be flat as he looked up at it. He'd read that the top, in fact, is not quite flat. The perimeter is slightly higher than the center and the surface is divided into three concentric rings. The bodies of men are arranged around the outer ring, women in the middle ring, and children in the innermost ring. Traditionally, scavenger birds assisted the process of cleaning the bones, but that happened rarely these days and David saw no birds flying around this tower. After a period that can be as long as a year, and the bones are bleached by the sun and wind, they are collected in an 'ossuary pit' at the center of the tower where lime is added and they gradually disintegrate. Rain then washes away any remaining material through coal and sand filters.

When they reached the top of the hill, David saw a crude wooden ladder resting against the far side of the tower. Taronish looked tired after the walk, and he sat down with his back against the tower. He gestured to David to climb the ladder, and closed his eyes. *So, what was all that fuss about letting me come up here, then?* David adjusted the bag on his shoulder, and placed both hands on the ladder. He couldn't tell how solid it was, so he simply resolved to test each step as he ascended. He checked his watch again: 4.45. The sun was already starting to sink lower in the sky. He took some satisfaction from the thought that, despite all the hold-ups, the difficulties with language and culture, the car purchase, its poor performance and the dreadful roads, he was here, about to get the job done—on schedule. This part would be simple. All King wanted to know was what had made the wounds, so he was keen to get hold of some metal fragments, and he wanted to know the dimensions of the cavities that had been made. David was to take a few photos, gather some samples of the congealed blood in the wounds and put them in sample containers, and then they would be on their way back to the US.

Despite its crude construction, the ladder seemed to be solid, and he was able to climb with some confidence. Two feet from the top of the tower, he stopped to check on Taronish. Looking directly below him, he could see that the man hadn't moved and appeared to be happy to sit and wait for David to finish whatever he needed to do. David looked up. The sky was a perfect clear blue. At the top of the tower, he could see something dark blowing in the wind. He realized it must be hair. That was when the theoretical image of this trip that he'd so hastily developed in his mind—his meticulous plans, the sense of adventure that he'd started out with, the confidence and even arrogance with which he'd approached this mission—all started to dissolve into a deep, visceral pain in his gut. It was a pain that would stay with him for a very long time to come.

He continued up the ladder, but slower now. He stopped again. In the blustery wind, he was now picking up a smell unlike anything he'd ever smelled before. It was dreadful. Each time the wind blew it in his direction, the air he breathed was filled with it, and it invaded his lungs and body with its heavy pungency. It felt almost physical, as if it would enter his very skin if he exposed himself to it any more. He clutched the ladder and looked down again. Taronish had lain down on the ground and appeared to be sleeping. David dropped down two rungs and, wrapping his arm around the ladder, he opened his bag and took out a face mask, which he quickly donned before continuing. He found himself grasping each rung tighter than the one before. His heart was pounding in his chest, his palms were sweating. His head was buzzing. He felt he was no longer in control of his own actions and could lose his grip and fall at any moment. *Hold on!* He didn't know what he was going to see when he reached the top, but it was as if his body was involuntarily preparing him for something terrible.

Taronish was jolted out of his slumbers by David's scream. The old man looked up, squinting at the bright sky above him. He could just make David out, at the top of the tower. But the ladder had moved. He got up as quickly as he could. The ladder had slid sideways and David was holding on to the top of the tower with one hand and his face with the other. He seemed to be shaking.

One of his feet was still on the ladder, the other hung in mid-air. Taronish shouted to get David's attention, before pulling the ladder with all his might, trying and get it back into the upright position. Once David realized what was happening, he grabbed it with his free hand and pulled it straight. The ladder was stable again.

David stayed still, trying to breathe deeply to stop the shaking. He kept his eyes closed, waiting for it to subside, trying to control the muscles in his hands, hoping his legs wouldn't collapse from under him and send him headlong onto the rock-strewn dust below. Slowly, he opened his eyes, but turned his head sideways. The distant mountains looked like a picture postcard as the fading afternoon sun cast deep shadows across their rugged features.

Nothing had prepared him for what was in front of him now. Nothing could express the physical effect of the scene. It was way beyond anything he could have imagined and it invaded every part of him with its nightmarish presence.

Eventually the shaking abated, and he could feel himself regaining control. *Okay, David. Eyes front. You can do it.*

There were far more bodies lying there than he had seen in the video. They were lying two and even three deep, in places. He couldn't even think about counting them. Not just yet. There was nothing of the neat order of concentric circles that he'd read about. They weren't lying peacefully with their arms gently crossed over their stomachs or on their chests, eyes closed in tranquil surrender to death. This was hell on earth. This was grotesque. They were distorted, gesturing, open-mouthed, twisted—a macabre jumble that was devoid of dignity. Men, women and children of all ages were simply piled on top of each other. David could only guess that the priests had been so completely overwhelmed with the task of getting them all up there, as well as with their own grief, that rigor mortis had set in before they could even carry them here. And they'd had no one to help them in their gruesome task.

After ten days, some of the bodies were in the advanced stages of putrefaction. Many were bloated with gases that were forcing liquids and feces out of them. Their necks and faces were swollen—mouths, lips and tongues ballooned into terrifying grimaces. Bacterial activity had turned the lower parts of their abdomens dull shades of green or brown. The blood in their veins had 'marbleized', showing up as red and green streaks though their shoulders, chests and thighs. Many were covered with blisters filled with a pale yellow fluid. Some had reached the stage known as 'black putrefaction' already. Their body cavities had ruptured, and the gases escaped. They had turned a darker color. And as dead as these people were, there was life on the top of that tower. It was seething with it. A shimmering multitude of insects crawling over and flying around every one of them, and thousands of larvae wriggled and squirmed from broken flesh and every orifice. And there was that deep, physical, haunting smell that David would never forget for the rest of his life.

His mind couldn't comprehend this macabre vista. It couldn't rationalize or assess it in any normal way. The shaking slowly transformed to a numbness, an other-worldly dream state in which he was present and yet detached at the same time. It was as if something in him had irreparably broken. He could feel it. But then another part of him seemed to kick in—something almost mechanical, resilient, impervious to all that was around him, taking over his functions, moving his body and distancing his emotions. He slowly climbed onto the top of the tower. He stood on the edge and looked down to where Taronish was still looking up at him. He waved at Taronish, who nodded and sat down again.

Searching around the apocalyptic scene, he tried to identify a suitable subject to start work on. They all had remarkably similar wounds, from what he could see. He decided it would be best to work with bodies that had been hit in the solar plexus, rather than the base of the throat or the top of the head. Those wounds presented an easier area to work with, as there was no interference from hair, and he could avoid looking at their faces as he worked. He found a young man, although it was hard to tell if he had been young. He was so bloated that his skin was pulled tight in every direction. However, he was close to the outer edge of the tower, and he was facing upwards, so the wound in his solar plexus could be seen clearly. He removed the camera from his bag and hung it around his neck. He took a series of photos that would form an overall picture of the scene once they were combined. Then he focused in on the wound and took several more close-up shots. He checked the digital images through the viewfinder, and zoomed in on one of the photos to check the definition. He could see the white edge of the wound quite clearly. It looked as if the skin had melted, rather than simply being punctured. He took out some calipers and measured the hole. One-and-three-quarter inches diameter. He fixed the caliper at this measurement so that he could check for consistency on other victims, and put it back in his bag. Snapping on a pair of surgical gloves, he then removed a plastic sample container and a knife from the bag. Removing the lid of the container and wedging it carefully between his subject's arm and a woman's leg, he crouched down to look more closely at the wound. It looked as if the congealed blood that had seeped into the end of wound was helping to keep the skin around it from popping open. He cautiously prodded at the edge of the wound with the knife, his hand shaking, keeping his head to one side just in case it burst. It held firm, so he cut around the edge of the blood, to see if he could take the whole 'plug' of congealed blood, and put it in the container. Once he had cut around the circumference, holding the knife in one side of the wound and carefully pushing his gloved hand into the other side, he started to edge the blood out of the body.

"Oh, God!" A blast of putrid gas sent him reeling backwards. He lost his balance and dropped the knife, which spun toward the center of the tower, landing and sticking into a dark, collapsed cheek about six feet away from him. David sat down hard on the edge of the tower, managing to brace himself just in time and avoiding a perilous fall to the ground below. The dry lump of blood broke apart when it landed on the man's ribcage, now visible as his flesh deflated and collapsed onto his skeleton. Where the base of the plug of dried blood had been, inside the body, there were a mass of writhing larvae. The hole it had left was black-edged and slimy with rotting flesh. He instinctively wiped some sweat off his forehead with his sleeve, only to feel a cold dampness on his brow. It was more than his system could cope with. He retched violently. Vomit spurted through the edges of his face mask. Tearing the gloves from his hands, he yanked the mask from his face—spitting and blowing his nose to clear it. The mask fell away, down the tower. *No water! I didn't bring any water with me! Damn!* He remained seated and calmed himself by looking out toward the mountains again, gathering his thoughts. The stench was suffocating him and he felt absolutely wretched. He checked his other sleeve, which was clean, so he used that to wipe his mouth, then he wiped his hands on his trousers before pulling his T-shirt up to cover his nose and replacing the gloves on his hands. Looking back into the wound, it was impossible to know how deep it had been when it had been made, but judging by the amount of dry blood that was now sitting on the man's ribcage, he estimated it must have been about three to four inches deep. Taking a spatula from his bag, he scraped the blood off the ribcage and put it in the sample container, being careful not to drag any of the larvae with it. Prodding around inside the container, he couldn't detect any metal fragments at all, so he used the spatula to search inside the wound itself. Nothing. Maybe any fragments would have sunk further into the body before the blood congealed. He put the container in his bag and discarded the spatula.

Searching around the top of the tower, he looked for another body with a wound in the solar plexus. The body of a woman lay about eight feet away. She had long, dark hair. Her features and body were so distorted by the bloating that David couldn't see whether she was young or old. He could see an earring. One of her arms was raised, with a hand pointing upwards as if to heaven. A ring was cutting deeply into one swollen finger. He paused to consider how he could get to her and, in his mind, he plotted a course whereby he could reach out and retrieve the knife along the way. The first step he took was the hardest. He chose to walk on bodies that were in the more advanced stages of putrefaction so there was less risk of puncturing skin and releasing more gases. His strategy seemed to be working so far, but he could hear bones shifting and giving way beneath his foot as he brought his weight to bear on them, and he winced at the images that came to mind. To retrieve the knife, which was standing just four feet away from him to his right, he had to make a one-step detour. There was a space between two bodies where he calculated he had enough room to insert his foot. He carefully maneuvered it down into the space and started to put his weight on it so he could reach for the knife. As he transferred his weight, it suddenly felt as though he were skating on ice. His foot slithered sideways and he fell forward.

As he grabbed the knife with his right hand, his left hand flew out instinctively to try to break his fall, but slid, offering no resistance at all, as he collapsed into the pile. The shaking returned, and tears blurred his vision as he quietly wept. He lifted his head, spitting a foul liquid and maggots out of his mouth. He still had the knife. He looked across at his other hand. It was covered with hair and sticky flesh. Underneath it, the flesh on the woman's lower body was bizarrely rucked up over her stomach. He looked at this strange apparition, dazed and confused, before he realized that, as he fell, his hand had caught her pubic bone and simply pushed the skin off. Shaking uncontrollably, he somehow managed to stand. The light was getting lower. He looked at the knife and wished he had fallen on that. But he hadn't. He was still here, somewhere. All he could do was tilt his head back and stare straight up into the blue, hoping all the time that his legs wouldn't give way.

Somewhere in the silent scream in his mind he became aware of movement in the settlement, down the hill. He lowered his head to where the sound was coming from, and tried to focus. There was the sound of a vehicle. The settlement was in shadow now, but as his eyes adjusted to the darkening view, he could make out a pick-up truck leaving the settlement and heading up the hill, bouncing over the rocky terrain, directly toward him. Three men stood in the back, holding onto the roll bar. Shit! He didn't need to ask himself who they were. They must have seen him, standing there, silhouetted against the sky. Hyper-alert now, he crouched down and watched. There was shouting and the truck stopped. He saw Taronish making his way down the hill to meet them, waving to them as he went. Then there was another figure in the shadows, running up from the settlement. It was Gulnaz. She was shouting at the men in the truck and they shouted back at her. David had no idea what was going on but, from what he knew of the Taliban, this looked very, very bad. Taronish was running now, further into the shadow. The truck stopped and the men in the back dismounted as Gulnaz caught up with them. David could see she'd removed her *burqa*. He was astonished. *What is she doing!? She's crazy! Gulnaz!* Taronish arrived on the scene and joined in the shouting match. One man pushed him aside, another one grabbed Gulnaz and forced her to kneel on the ground. The shouting stopped as the driver got out and walked over to where Gulnaz was kneeling. David watched, paralyzed with fear and powerless to do anything. The driver walked casually round behind Gulnaz. There was a flash, followed by a loud *crack*, and Gulnaz fell forward.

✷✷✷

What else could he do? What else? Was there anything more he could do for her right now? David placed a few more rocks on the mound that he'd made to cover her body.

The Taliban had left, but only after they had emptied their weapons, firing up at the tower in a vain attempt to dispense with him as well. Despite their inhumanity and cold-blooded cruelty, they didn't have the stomach to climb the tower. And the four priests were still alive. Vaspan had sat with him as he cried and cried—a cry from deep within his soul, from depths in him he never knew existed. They'd helped him wash and brought him a change of clothes from his backpack. They'd helped him to lift her onto the back seat of the car, and pointed out an easier route back to Mazar, which he could follow in the dark.

It was only when he had got the car started again and it was coughing and spluttering along the track toward the road to Mazar, that he was able to gather his thoughts. What was he going to do with Gulnaz? He couldn't have left her with the Zoroastrians, knowing where she would have been laid to rest, so he had been right to take her with him. But where to? Even though she was a lapsed Muslim, he felt duty-bound to see her buried quickly. But he couldn't take her back to Mazar, and hand her over to anyone else to bury her. With his scant Pashto, he could never have made them understand what had happened to her. They would have stuck him in jail, or lynched him or something. He didn't know. Nor could he take her to the ISAF base. He couldn't be sure that he could convince them to repatriate her body to the US, given her unconfirmed status there and the fact that she was clearly an Afghan. They would probably have put both of them in the hands of the Afghan authorities. And anyway, why take her to the US? She had no family there. She had gone there on a promise of freedom and a new life. She had kept her promise to the US and she had earned her freedom more than most, as far as David was concerned. But all it had done was use and betray her and bring her life to a brutal end. And David knew that she had died in a valiant and selfless effort to save him.

The light was fading rapidly now, but he knew he had to find somewhere… somewhere nice and somehow appropriate. Turning a corner, he found himself looking out over the barren landscape to the dark outlines of distant mountains. There were no lights in the valley. It appeared to be a view free of civilization. He stopped the car at the top of a rise so he could bump-start it down the hill if necessary and, with his eyes welling up with tears again, he pulled Gulnaz's body onto the ground. Using the light from the headlamps, he started to gather rocks, which he gently laid over her body until nothing more of her could be seen.

David wasn't a religious person. He'd been brought up as an agnostic in a Church of England community. As a child, he'd gone along with the rituals of Christmas for the presents and of Easter for the eggs. He'd repeated the Lord's Prayer at school, parrot-fashion, ad infinitum, without ever giving any thought to what the words might have meant. In his later school years, he'd come to regard Christianity as a guilt trip imposed by the education system as a way to keep people in line.

So, now, with the body of a dead colleague laid out in front of him on an Afghan hillside, covered with stones, he had no idea what to do or say. He'd heard people talk about 'closure' but he wasn't sure what that meant or how to achieve it. Was it even relevant? What could he possibly 'close' right now? How do you 'respect the dead'—another phrase that came into his confused mind. Everyone in the world, it seemed, had a different idea of how to do that, and what he had seen that day seemed entirely devoid of respect. And would a dead body appreciate being respected? He doubted it. If those bodies on the tower had wanted anything at all, perhaps it would have been dignity. *Maybe we should spend more time respecting the living.* He tried to think of a ritual. Why do people have rituals? Is it just a measure of our inadequacy as human beings to deal with the incomprehensible? We get so attached to things being normal, to people being alive, that we forget... He placed her sunglasses under a stone, approximately where her eyes would be, and said, "You'll need these where you're going." He immediately felt stupid. *That's the kind of thing the cowboy would say in some dreadful B-movie. Pathetic.* He searched his thoughts for something meaningful. *Say a prayer.* Maybe he should do that. What language? What religion? What prayer? *I don't know how to do this.*

"Gulnaz." He spoke her name. "Gulnaz." Perhaps by saying her name, he could connect with her soul, if such a thing existed. There was no reply, so he just sat and waited until it felt appropriate to leave. He would know when that was, he thought. But he didn't really.

It was a very dark night.

CHAPTER 21

Things were getting out of control. What started out with some low-life soldier in Illinois uploading a video onto his website was developing into something that was taking over Troy King's life in ways that he could never have imagined and didn't welcome. Someone had once told him that a little knowledge was very dangerous. He was really beginning to understand what that meant. The moment he'd seen that wound, the video clip had become an obsession—an obsession that had awakened a curiosity in him that was taking him into situations where he was totally out of his depth. He'd only made things worse by blatantly ignoring a direct order to drop the investigation. As soon as he got back to the office today, he'd received his final warning after an hour-long dressing-down from his boss. He could see his pension slipping away forever if he didn't stop, so he had agreed to tow the line from now on.

But he couldn't stop thinking about it. What was the connection with this man, Gerald Shanning, who had been so keen to meet him that he called him at 11.30 the previous night and insisted on having him picked up outside Starbucks at 58th and Columbus at the ungodly hour of 5.30am? It was clear, on his arrival back at the Fishtank, that even though he'd been instructed to get back to the office PDQ, there was no desperately urgent business for him to attend to. They'd just wanted him out of New York. Was it the video clip that had caused all the fuss, or was it the fact that he was bothering Samakab? He couldn't tell, but he knew there was much more to all this than he understood, and that was eating him up. He'd made some connections in his mind, but none of them made sense to him. Obviously, Samakab had some sort of deal with Shanning that was not going well. And, judging by the way Shanning rambled on about the weather all the way back to Washington, King understood how he got his nickname: The Weatherman. That could also explain Samakab's sensitivity to the word. Who he was, how he'd been able to get hold of his cell phone number and what relationship he had to Arlington Online were all a mystery to him. And how come he had a Gulfstream, for his own personal use, standing by at Teterboro Airport in New Jersey? He must be a powerful man and was most likely in, or connected with, the upper echelons of the government. Why the urgency to meet King? He appeared to have nothing important to say to him, and King was confused by the tone and content of their conversation on the flight. He suspected that Shanning was fishing for information. Whatever the real purpose of that flight, he doubted that Shanning's intention was simply to give him a fancy ride back to Washington.

King aimlessly pondered these things as he sat in his office studying a pot of yoghurt that he was slowly eating with a plastic spoon. He'd decided to go on a health kick, just for a while. He suspected that his mind wasn't as sharp as it should be. He must be missing some obvious connections. He knew he was drinking too much beer, and combining it with wine and rich food had given him indigestion that he couldn't seem to shift. His doctor had also told him a while ago that the increasing size of his stomach wasn't helping his back injury. His cholesterol was through the roof, so he had to cut down on red meat and a whole bunch of other things as well. He had to slim down, or end up in a wheelchair. His choice. "Healthy body, healthy mind," the doctor had said, so instead of picking up doughnuts and his favorite bagels on his way to the office, he'd dropped into the 'healthy lifestyle' section of his local deli. He'd picked up several products with photos of smiling, fit-looking people, and bizarre lists of ingredients that he'd never heard of. Buying all this healthy junk depressed him, and he wondered when he'd be able to get back to real food. He'd then popped into the pharmacy for some Pepto-Bismol and some maximum-strength painkillers for his stomach.

"Low in kcal, high in calcium, trans fat free and Vitamin D fortified," he read, between mouthfuls, "…contains at least 18% DV (Daily Value) of calcium per 4oz serving." Guess I'd better read up on this stuff. He turned the pot around. "*Cultured pasteurized Grade A low fat milk, sugar, strawberries, modified corn starch, high fructose corn syrup, kosher gelatin, citric acid, tricalcium phosphate, natural flavor, pectin, colored with carmine, vitamin A acetate, vitamin D3.* Hmm… it don't mention yoghurt in the ingredients…" He frowned at the pot before scraping the last spoonful from the bottom and throwing it in the bin. It had done nothing to ease his hunger or stomach pain. *Food used to be simple*, he thought. *You fry it, you eat it, you feel good—end of story.* He popped a painkiller and got to work.

"Okay, so what are we doing today…" He booted up his computer and opened his email inbox. As the emails were downloading, he opened his desk drawer to get some paper and take notes. The first thing he saw was the file containing the details of David and Barbara's insurance claim against the driver of the government sedan. King decided he should deal with it before David got back, so he scanned through it to refresh his memory. He remembered that he'd smelled a rat when he'd first read the sedan driver's accident report, and it still didn't make sense to him now. He hoped to save some time by calling the garage where the driver worked and seeing if he could get him to answer the questions that were going around in his head. He asked reception to locate the number and put him through.

"Williams. How can I help?" The man at the other end of the line sounded efficient, but tense.

"Hello. Are you in charge of the garage there?" King asked.

"For my sins. Twenty-four hours a day, seven days a week. At least, that's what my boss thinks."

"Do you have an Albert Lindemann as one of your drivers?"

"Depends who's asking."

"I beg your pardon. Troy King. I work within the NSA network, and your Mr Lindemann unfortunately collided with a car belonging to one of my colleagues here. I'm helping him process the insurance claim."

"Sorry, can't help."

"Well, can I talk to him?"

"No, we fired him when he smashed up the car. No second chances here, not with the kind of collateral we carry."

"Damn. Well, can I just aks you one queshion?"

"Look, friend, I'd really like to help but I've got five cars to get ready for some feckin' motorcade, and I've only got half an hour—"

"Okay, okay. Just one thing. Was the senator in the car when Mr Lindemann had the collision?"

"What are you talking about? Of course he was in the car. It was on the log and his office signed for the car."

"Are you sure Lindemann wasn't on some sort of joy ride, a shopping trip of his own or something?"

"Look …Mr King, is it? I run a tight operation here, and I feckin' know where my drivers go and who is on board every second of every trip. All the cars are tracked and it's more than my life's worth to lose a senator. Now, will you get outta my face so I can make sure this next bunch of our high and mighty leaders are happy and safe on their journey? Thank you." The phone went dead.

"A tight operation?" King said to the mouthpiece. "So, why was your driver swerving onto the Columbia Pike, south of the Potomac, when he was meant to be taking the senator on the short journey from a White House press call to his downtown office for an important reception?" That, calculated King, was about an eight-mile detour. He decided to leave it there, for now. He was sure that Lindemann had fabricated the accident report to try and keep his job. He'd deal with that later, with a stiffly worded letter. He also appreciated that getting Williams to cooperate on changing the report might be difficult, and he wanted to keep his promise to David to fast-track the process. He called the senator's office to see if they could help, but the senator was not available for the next few days. His assistant said she would 'do what she could', which didn't give him much hope either. But what was really bugging him was the fact that the car was not where it should have been when the collision happened.

He picked up the phone to reception. "Jane, could you get me a skinny latte?"

"Sure, Mr King, one cappuccino coming up."

"Jane. Listen. Skinny latte."

"Oh. Yes, sir."

"Much obliged." He heard Jane stifle a giggle.

"Oh, Mr King, are you still there?"

"I'm here."

"I just had a call come in. It's international, I think the caller said it was Afghanistan."

"Put it through." King checked to see that his office door was closed. "Hello? ...Hello?" The line crackled and then cleared. "Hey, David! I was just thinkin' about you, doin' your insurance claim and all. How's it goin'? All done? You two checked in for the Dubai flight okay?"

CHAPTER 22

"Do you ever wish we'd had kids, Sheryl?" Griffin was sitting on the bed in the hotel, trying to decide between the conservative blue shirt that he'd brought with him, and the yellow, short-sleeved shirt with exotic birds printed all over it that Sheryl had just bought for him in Ubud.

"What made you think of that?" said Sheryl. She was relaxing in a rattan chair, her feet propped up on the balcony rail as she watched the birds flitting in and out of the lush foliage outside. The air was cool from the downpour that had just abated. Water sat on leaves like glass beads, catching the early evening light, some rolling downwards, forming rivulets and hanging for a moment before dropping out of view. The thought of walking to the hotel restaurant for an evening meal just seemed like too much effort. The idea that she would ever have to move from that chair seemed like a huge imposition. She didn't want anyone disturbing her feeling of deep tranquility.

"Oh, I don't know. I was just thinking." Griffin felt heavy, stalled. The sudden release from the pressures of political life and the strange conversation he'd had with Larry had left him unhinged from all his familiar points of reference. Cold turkey. He berated himself for thinking that it was a good idea to leave the cell phone at home—*Let's have a complete break, for once. It will be good for us, and no one seems to want to be in touch, so they can all go to hell!* He was already planning to find some way of accessing the Internet. He'd seen a place down the road with some ancient-looking computers arranged in a line against the wall. There was no TV in the room. In fact, he couldn't remember seeing a TV anywhere in the hotel. He wondered where he could find a newspaper stand nearby. Yellow or blue? Why is it so damned difficult to make a decision, all of a sudden?

"What were you thinking?" She wished he wasn't thinking at all. He was invading her space with his words, and disturbing her mind with the thoughts they generated. Sheryl wanted quiet, right now. Just quiet.

"Nothing… nothing, really." The decision had already been made, so there was no point in asking. Sheryl had just bought the yellow shirt for him, so gratitude demanded that he wore it, at least once. The only decision he wanted to make was whether he liked it or not. That's what was frustrating him. He didn't seem to have the mental capacity to even decide *that*. Was it a nice shirt or just a dreadful, garish piece of tacky design? He tried to imagine what his colleagues would say if they saw him in it. Whenever he'd seen any politician of a certain age wearing something other than a suit, especially something that either his wife had bought to 'show his creative side' or, worse still, she had made for him, he'd been deeply embarrassed for them. No, to be seen in this shirt would be like watching his accountant break-dancing. It was just too awful to contemplate.

"I can't wait to see it on you." Sheryl had given up on the idea of peaceful solitude, and had walked back into the room. It was a conscious decision. For once in her life, she didn't want to give way to feelings of anger and frustration that would result in the usual bitchy spat with her husband. *Well, it's great to say that now, isn't it? You were the one who said we couldn't afford to have kids when we got married, and then your bloody career took over and apparently we didn't have time to have kids. For God's sake, Griffin, how many times did I say that I'd love to start a family? And you ask me that now? Well, it's too fucking late, isn't it!* Instead, she looked down at him, sitting there on the edge of the bed, Buddha-like, with his stomach spreading over his underpants, hands resting at his sides, each holding a shirt. She stood in front of him, arms folded, and contemplated him afresh. The warm glow had stayed with her since her massage and the visit to a tea shop in Ubud, and she wanted to savor it for as long as she could. He looked wrecked—old and a child at the same time. He had the sophisticated demeanor of a man who had won all his battles, the advanced ageing of a man who had lost the war, and the fear of a child who didn't know how to fight.

"You're the only man I've ever loved." The words tumbled from her mouth without her permission. "And I still do." She kissed him gently on the forehead, and eased the blue shirt from his hand.

"Sheryl—"

"Don't worry. You'll look great." She undid the buttons and helped him into the yellow shirt. He stood up.

"How do I look?" he asked, with an uncharacteristically sheepish grin.

"Wonderful. But I think you need some pants. I don't think the world is quite ready for that." A triumphant rush ran through her body, and she laughed. Griffin felt a powerful warmth from her that he hadn't felt for a long time.

He got away with wearing a pair of neat dark-blue pants with the excuse that they contrasted well with the shirt, but Sheryl won on the footwear. She wouldn't let him near his sock drawer, and insisted on open sandals rather than lace-up shoes. As they walked arm in arm to the restaurant, Sheryl said, "In answer to your original question, yes and no."

"What do you mean?"

"I mean that it's all hypothetical, isn't it? We made a conscious decision to build your career at the expense of family life. Sometimes, I've even wondered why we got married, if there was never going to be a family. You could argue that we'd both have made stronger individual choices if we'd stayed single. But we got married. I can't pretend that I haven't resented you sometimes, and been very frustrated with my life, but that was my choice. Nobody made me do what I did… and I'm sorry you've had to bear the brunt of my failings and weaknesses in dealing with my own choices." Griffin wanted to speak, but she carried on. "So, that's the hypothetical 'no'. *If* we'd had children and *if* we'd continued to live the life we did in exactly the same way, I'm sure I'd have been a dreadful mother and you'd have been an absent father. But from what I've seen with my friends over the years—the ones who had kids and really loved them, gave them time and guided them with their best interests in mind rather than projecting their own ideas onto them—they've had fantastic lives and reaped wonderful rewards. They say having kids changes everything. I'm sure that when you hold your own baby in your arms—a little miraculous part of you that's been released into the world for you to protect and guide—your career takes on a new purpose. Had that been the scenario, that's my hypothetical 'yes'." She smiled at Griffin, but couldn't hide her sadness. "What's done is done, Griff. Let's make it a good thing."

Griffin stopped walking. He turned to face her and took both her hands in his. "Sheryl, I never thanked you properly for this shirt. It's magnificent. I feel like a whole new man. Thank you." He kissed her full on the lips. Before they continued on across the stepping stones over the pond to the restaurant, he added, "I'd really like to have a talk. Can we do that?"

"You mean talk?"

"Yes, talk."

"A real *talk* talk? Not just a talk?"

"A real *talk* talk."

"Wow. I'm not sure I can remember how to do that with you. I'll have to dig out some notes or something."

"Oh, I don't think you'll need those. They'll be out of date by now, but if you're game, maybe we can figure it out together."

"I'd like that very much." Sheryl squeezed his hands.

"Well, let's start at dinner."

"And carry on afterwards?"

"We'll see, but I have a feeling—"

"So do I."

✳✳✳

"Sergeant, we have the Dubai flight going out in one hour, can you give me a weather report?" Sergeant Connelly looked out at the clear blue sky. The air was still.

"Yes, sir." He got on the radio. "Gimme a weather report west out of Mazar airport for a 1300 hours takeoff, over." He turned the volume down when a blast of static preceded the reply.

"Roger that. We have…" there was a short pause. "Okay, Mazar, we have a warm front heading in from the south. Heavy showers imminent. Hold the flight. Wait for the all-clear."

"Hooah." He put down the radio and signaled with a low sweep of his hand to his colleague, who nodded back in acknowledgement.

An American contingent had set up a base at the airport, adding considerable numbers to the German military presence there. Some troops were standing guard, others sitting, passing the time of day. David looked out of the window to the west. Clear blue sky. The other dozen or so passengers waiting for this infrequent flight were taking no notice. Terminal boredom had set in, following several delays. No planes had landed or taken off for at least three hours. David didn't care. He was numb. He could hardly keep his eyes open.

After he'd left Gulnaz, he'd driven slowly down the mountain toward the Ali Baba Pass. The car was running intermittently on two and three cylinders, and he was finding it increasingly difficult to keep the engine going. Once he reached the broad, dry riverbed that led directly to the archway of the pass and then down onto the plain to Mazar, he'd decided to abandon the car. Having removed his backpack from the trunk, he took one last look at Gulnaz's belongings before slamming it shut and torching the car. It was simpler that way. The light from the blaze illuminated the road sufficiently for him to find his way to the archway. As he walked through it, the first rays of morning light were glancing across the rocky landscape. He'd walked down the road and hitched a ride to the airport, made a short call to Troy King to brief him on what had happened, then gone immediately to a check-in desk that was being handled by military personnel.

"Open the bag for me, please, sir." David showed his business card to the young female officer. "NSA? What are you guys doing out here?" He really wasn't in the mood for officialdom. He looked at her blankly.

"NSA work."

"You don't sound American."

"Is that a problem? Look, just do your job and let me catch my flight."

"This is my job, sir. Open the bag for me, please." She remained expressionless, almost mechanical.

"Oh, this is your job, is it? They actually train you to become a brick wall, do they?" She shot him a cold look as he opened the bag and pushed it across the counter to her. She proceeded to delve inside it.

The bag had very little in it. He'd destroyed most of his clothes. The officer pulled out the shoulder bag and placed it on the counter.

"I'll need you to open this, sir." *For fuck's sake, what is her problem!?* David opened it, very slowly. The officer was starting to feel a bit uncertain about this rather aggressive man.

"Step away from the bag, please, sir." David made a theatrical step backwards, treading on the feet of a man waiting in line behind him.

"Sorry." David realized he was being unreasonable. "Sorry," he said, turning to the officer again.

"Is this your bag, sir?"

"Yes." *Give me strength!*

"What is this substance?" She pulled out the sample container.

"Blood." David was past caring who knew what he was doing there, who he worked for or what his cover was meant to be. The man behind was glancing over his shoulder.

"And what have you been taking photos of?" She held up the camera.

"Nude fucking sunbathers! Take a look, if you like! What do you think?" David was beginning to lose it. *No, don't do it like this!* The officer switched the camera on and immediately recoiled at the first photo, stifling a cry with a hand over her mouth. "Look, it's been a bad day for me," David said. *Just let me get on that plane!*

"Can I have a word?" The officer gestured toward a door behind her. She picked up his bags and he followed her into a small office. She closed the door behind them.

David felt his anger subsiding. "Are you okay?" He went to put his hand on her shoulder, but she pulled away from him.

"Do not touch me, sir." But then she nodded, so he continued. "I'm on a covert mission—well, I guess it's not that covert any more—to investigate some suspicious deaths. We believe that American lives may be at risk, but for reasons that I can't talk about, this mission was not to come to the attention of ISAF. I'd appreciate your discretion, and I'm sorry I've been rude to you. I meant no offence, I'm just very, very tired, and pretty shaken up, right now."

"I think I can see why you'd be feeling like that. Those photos… no one should have to do that kind of work."

"I couldn't agree more. Thanks for your understanding." David managed a weak smile. "Can you tell me what the delay is on the flight? I heard someone talking about weather problems, but it looks really fine to me."

"Oh, that's the new standard we're working to these days. The new regulations say we have to get what they call 'Weatherman' clearance before any flight movements. We don't know what it means and we don't ask. I reckon it's some fancy new security measure, but as far as I'm concerned, it's just part of the routine these days."

"But there's not a cloud in the sky and only the slightest of breezes."

"It sure looks like that, doesn't it? We always get the clearance, though, so don't concern yourself. I'm sure you'll be on your way shortly."

CHAPTER 23

By 8am the next morning, Griffin was in a cab to Larry's place. He felt as if a great weight had been lifted from his shoulders, although he suspected that another one was going to be placed there before he went back to Washington. For now, though, he was cautiously enjoying an unfamiliar lightness. He hadn't realized just how much he'd been struggling in his relationship with Sheryl. He'd got used to the pain and had been accepting it for far too long. Grit and determination were no substitute for tenderness, communication and understanding. If only he'd found that out sooner, he could have done things so much better, and they could have enjoyed so much more of their lives with each other. Since their conversation over dinner, he knew they'd been given a second chance, an opportunity to build a fresh, exciting, creative and loving life together. When they'd made love later that night, he'd experienced a new power, a sacred communion and a depth of connection that extended far beyond the physical act. He'd slept deeply, supremely relaxed and content, and dreamed beautiful dreams.

He wasn't laboring under any false illusions, though. When the new day arrived, he knew there were demons to fight and hard, negative thought patterns and habits to break. Somehow, though, a tiny spark of hope had flown miraculously into his life. He knew, in his heart, that it was something real, good and dependable—if he could only nurture it and allow it to grow.

It was that fresh certainty that inspired him to get back to Larry as soon as he could. He knew Larry had a lot more to share with him and, this time, rather than merely tolerating what sounded like the ramblings of a hopeless idealist, he really wanted to listen. Any weight that he took on now would be of his own choosing. He was beginning to feel that he could carry anything, but he cautioned himself as he got out of the cab and made his way through the gate to Larry's front door; he had no idea what Larry was going to ask of him. Larry wasn't simply bemoaning the state of the world; there was a purpose to all this that was going to become clear to Griffin very soon—possibly today.

They arranged the kitchen table and chairs in the courtyard again. Larry made coffee, and Entahlah made herself at home on Griffin's lap as soon as he sat down.

"I've got to hand it to you, Larry," he said, as Entahlah gently padded her paws on his knee, purring loudly, "giving Sheryl that trip to Ubud was a wonderful idea."

"Did she enjoy it?"

"Very much. And so did I." Griffin smiled as Larry put the pot of coffee on the table. "Thank you. From the bottom of my heart. Thank you."

"You're welcome, Griff." Larry poured the coffee. "You both needed it. Everyone needs it, and I don't just mean a trip to Ubud."

"You're so right." Griffin looked around the courtyard. It was still in shadow; the sun was still low in the sky. A deep stillness pervaded the whole space. Griffin could almost touch it. "I love this place," he mused.

"I love your shirt," Larry said. Griffin laughed. He'd forgotten that he'd put it on again that morning.

"Sheryl reckons it's the new me."

"I think she could be right."

Still. The courtyard was just *so* still. Yet it was also very much alive.

"You know, Larry... You're going to think this sounds crazy, but wouldn't it be amazing if we had all our political debates somewhere like this? Can you imagine the outcomes we'd achieve if every discussion started from this kind of peaceful place?"

"It doesn't sound crazy to me. Not a bit. Why do you think I like it here? It's the first place I've found where I can think clearly."

"But I thought you'd spent the last seven years thinking clearly—about how to put the world to rights."

"When I started, I thought I was clear. As we progressed—setting up the teams, finding experts, deciding on the schedule, planning and all the other things that you would normally do to put a project together—I was fine. All the organizing was second nature to me and I did it very well."

"So what changed? When did things become less clear?"

"When we started finding out what needed to be done. The rationale we originally followed supported our feelings about what the world needed, but then conditioning started to drive the rationale. That started to mix the feelings up, and things became muddy, unclear. That's when the problems started."

"You'd better take me through that one step at a time."

"It's the age-old problem. We go through it collectively and individually, and we've been going through it since time began. Heart versus head, good versus evil, darkness versus light and so on."

"I thought we were talking about a political process here, an international working group of experts, not religion." Griffin was puzzled.

"We are talking about that and, no, we're not talking about religion." Larry paused for thought. "We *are* talking about the *causes* of religions, though."

"How so?"

"Let's backtrack a little. Just remember, though, that we're talking about an international working group, as you rightly said, tasked to find a way to get the world back into some sort of balance." Larry took a deep breath and searched for the best way to explain what he was getting at. "The key word in that statement is 'world'. We're talking about creating balance in the whole world. That's a hell of a big job, and while it gives me some hope that the superpowers have at last come to the realization that the system is broken, they're the ones largely responsible for making and sustaining the mess that we were tasked to clean up. And there was an added complication. Every one of the parties contributing money and people to the project wanted to keep their vested interests intact. So I guess we should have expected exactly what we got—a lot of lip-service and very little real commitment. You could say that with such overriding insincerity and self-interest, we had a hopeless task from day one. So, I suppose I shouldn't have been surprised when the cracks started to appear. Whatever." Larry shrugged. "I took on the task and I started to make good progress.

"I was talking about what *causes* religions. The way I see it is this. We all start making wrong choices very early on in life. We don't do it deliberately. When we're kids, we're totally influenced by what our parents say and do. As we grow, the influence widens. Our parents, teachers and others around us pass on their dysfunction, ideas, prejudices and beliefs that they think are true and factual—as well as a lot of good stuff, of course. We soak it all up passively, like sponges, and store it. That's how we build our belief systems. In the first seven years of our lives, a deep imprint is made in us, that we relate to completely, and we end up thinking of it as who we are."

"'Give me a child for his first seven years and I'll give you the man.' Standard Jesuit thinking," mused Griffin.

"Exactly. The perfect setup to make sure the child fits the desired mould. What it *actually* represents is indoctrination with a whole bunch of second-hand ideas, thoughts and beliefs that may or may not be true. We certainly didn't actively choose them for ourselves, but because they get buried deep in our subconscious, we have no reason to question them. For many of us, they become 'facts' about 'the way things are'. However, because they've been introduced to us, and we didn't originate them ourselves, we tend to get confused. When we have to make a choice about anything, this programming kicks in and tells us what's 'right' and 'wrong' and we base our decisions on, effectively, someone else's thoughts. We often override our feelings, which we suppress and fail to develop as we go through life. We eventually end up distrusting our intuition because it doesn't necessarily fit with what people around us are saying, although, of course, they're also being guided by their programming. So, it stands to reason that, in this confused state, we're open to all sorts of influences. We actually *want* to find something that we can believe in, since we feel we can't believe in ourselves, we don't really know how much we can believe in others and we're uncomfortable about being alone in that confusion. We become disempowered and feel much safer when we find something that lots of other people also believe in.

"Now, when someone has a fantastic experience or some sort of realization, and they tell you about it, your authentic, natural feelings and intuition are triggered *before* the conditioning kicks and you start intellectualizing and, perhaps, judging. As a result of this, two things happen. First, you want to have that experience yourself. But unfortunately, experience isn't directly transferable between people."

"How do you mean?" Griffin was having a hard time keeping up and absorbing all this.

"Well, think about it. I have my coffee and you have yours. Tell me what your coffee tastes like."

"It just tastes like coffee, you know, kind of bitter, rich… I don't know how to describe it."

"Exactly. And you don't know how mine tastes to me, either. For all you know, the taste I experience when I drink coffee could be like oranges. You can't tell. So we communicate in stories—parables, if you like—to try to express something that will approximate to the actual experience. That's religion."

"No, it's a cup of coffee." Griffin was starting to get frustrated.

"Religion is the packaging that people put around an experience in order to communicate that experience. They desperately want to be able to share the actual experience but that's the best they can do. Religion is just the story, it's not the experience. And look how elaborate that story can become. I don't need to expand on that, do I?"

"No …and the second thing?"

"Manipulation. It's much easier to manage and control a lot of confused souls if you give them fixed rules to live by, and it's a lot easier for them to follow rules than it is to figure out their own direction. If you have enough people who genuinely want the same experience, you can easily manipulate them for your own purposes. Feelings—they're so much more powerful than intellect and reason, however much we try to override them. People gladly suppress rational thought, or find ways to rationalize the incomprehensible, in order to justify beliefs that will give them even the faintest hope of achieving salvation. It's incredible, when you think about it, because all they're actually trying to do is to find themselves. The clues are in all the scriptures—the stories written, through the ages, about the ultimate experience. The problem is that people end up believing in the stories and the stories become horribly distorted by those who use them." Larry could see Griffin's eyes starting to glaze over. "And here endeth the lesson. Sorry, Griff. It's one of my pet peeves—religion and what it has done to mankind. Let's move on."

"Please do!" Griffin shifted in his chair.

"Politics and commerce exploit our sense of disempowerment all the time, of course. Having left the US, I'm acutely aware, for instance, of how I was brought up to 'need' stuff and to live in fear, and how that need and fear is preyed upon in so many ways that we all accept without thinking."

"I accept that we all buy a lot of stuff we don't need, because it's presented to us in seductive ways, but I wasn't aware of living in fear. Life seemed pretty good to me, until last week…"

"Insurance is just one example. An entire industry built on fear. Fear of being ill or destitute, fear of losing your possessions, fear of being attacked, mugged or nuked, fear of death. So many things to fear."

"That's just taking sensible precautions and protecting yourself and your loved ones," said Griff. Larry shook his head and continued.

"Naturally, that's what you're conditioned to think, but let's not get too far off track. We don't have a lot of time for intellectual banter. The key point about all this is that when we started to do our work, we quickly realized that there's no point in gathering a ton of data on different religions, cultures, beliefs, ways of life, politics and philosophies."

"But, surely, everything about the way the world works is dependent on those things. You can only change things if you take all of those things into account and work with them to find solutions."

"No. All those things are merely symptoms that point to the source of the problems. They're the coping mechanisms that provide some sort of structure to people's lives, precisely because they're not empowered. If people were empowered, balanced and whole, they wouldn't need political or religious leaders to tell them what to do. Politicians would be servants and managers, and religious leaders would become irrelevant. People would be making their own decisions for themselves, from a strong and wholesome perspective."

"That sounds a bit utopian, and completely impossible," Griffin scoffed. "I can't imagine the Church or Islam agreeing to shut down operations, or the political and economic systems of the world all just stopping one day because you present an idea like that. It's a nice theory, though."

"Of course, none of that will happen anytime soon. But try to put your conditioned thinking aside for a minute. That's what it is, after all. If you could truly start from zero, without all the pre-conceived ideas about what society is and what you are, and if you believed what I was saying about how we develop those pre-conceived ideas, would you come to the same conclusion? Probably not, because the current situation doesn't make any intuitive or rational sense." Griffin looked puzzled, and extremely doubtful. "I know, it's almost impossible to even go there. Our minds are so 'made up' and full of stuff, that it's actually very difficult for us to think from a truly fresh perspective or even have a single creative thought that isn't prompted by past experience."

"That's what I mean," said Griffin, "it's utopian, impossible. We have to live in the real world. Are you suggesting that we ditch all the leaders who guide and influence millions of people throughout the world, send everyone on alternative therapy courses and have housewives deciding national economic policy? No offence to housewives…"

"Please, give me some credit, Griff. Remember, I spent seven years on this, along with some of the best brains on the planet."

"And the fact that we're sitting here, hidden away in Bali, talking about it— is that meant to reassure me that those seven years were somehow worth it?"

"We've some way to go but, I assure you, we'll get there before you leave." Larry got up from his chair and brought a tray of cat food for Entahlah, who immediately woke up and sprang from Griffin's lap.

"Larry," Griffin said, deep in thought, "bear with me, will you?"

"I thought that was my line." Larry smiled.

"It's just that I know I can be a bit dismissive, but all this is kinda strange for me, right now. If I didn't know you so well, I think I'd be long gone."

"Of course, I understand, and thanks. It's difficult for me, too."

"Really?"

"Sure it is. I have the same resistances in me that anyone would have. Thinking things through on this level and then trying to find brand-new solutions is the hardest thing I've ever done—especially when there's so much getting in the way in my own head. Communicating it is even harder, because I have just a few days to pull you through the processes I took several years to go through."

"Okay, then." Griffin felt as if they'd been dancing around the subject for too long. "Let's cut out the amateur psychology—I was never any good at it anyway—and get down to what you were actually doing, and what you had hoped to achieve."

"Good. Let's do that. More coffee?"

"Thanks." He was keenly aware that he and Sheryl only had a few days left on the island, and he was feeling increasingly nervous about being out of touch with his office. Things changed quickly in Washington, especially if you were absent. Knowing that his office would have to field questions about the death of the Israeli negotiator, without his input, was weighing heavily on his mind. And although Larry seemed to understand why he'd been cut off, they hadn't really covered that subject to his satisfaction and he felt sure he'd face a firestorm of abuse and criticism when he got back.

Larry returned with the coffee, a jug of iced water and two glasses with slices of lemon.

"When we put the team together, I originally had about a hundred people in it. We had all sorts of experts from a vast range of disciplines. But we realized we were getting too much extraneous information. It was confusing things, and we really needed to focus on fundamental human characteristics. So we started to pare the team down. Eventually, we ended up with a solid, tight team of twenty, and we contracted out some of the grunt work to private consultants who knew nothing about the project as a whole. The two main players were me and an old friend of mine—a guy called Gerald Shanning. I think you met him once at a drinks party at my place. Do you remember?"

"I can't say I recall—"

"Older man, talked about the weather a lot…"

"God, yes, I was bored to tears. What was *he* doing on the team?"

Larry smiled. "We had a few weirdos, believe me. The thing is, we were tasked with breaking new ground and looking at things in new ways. We couldn't afford to discount anything just because it sounded oddball. Gerald was—is—the world's leading expert on what he loosely terms 'human climate-related psychometrics'."

Griffin snorted into his coffee. "Am I right in thinking that he's not only the world's leading expert, but also the only one in that field?"

"You'd be surprised. I once met some of his fellow 'climate psychometricologists' or whatever they're called, at one of their conventions in Costa Rica. It was like train-spotters anonymous. But Gerald is very, very smart, and he brought a lot to the project, initially."

"I already have an ominous feeling about Gerald. What does he do—what's this psychometric stuff about?"

"Well, it's fascinating—all to do with psychological variables around intelligence, personality and other characteristics. We already know that environment is the biggest factor in how anything develops—simply because everything is connected and affects everything else, one way or another. There's the external environment but also our internal, bodily and neurological environments, and there are many different ways of observing and investigating how these environments interact. Astrologers, for instance, look at how even the farthest planets exert gravitational pulls that affect us and our individual paths in life. We also know that our moods and emotions can be affected by both external emotional stimuli and homeostatic factors—like thirst or hunger. Gerald's particular specialization was everything that is affected by the weather—and everything is, if you think about it. It affects our moods, the crops we grow, the things we do—even our physical make-up. Where we live in the world affects our character, psyche and mental make-up in a multitude of ways. So, if we work in a factory, we're affected in different ways than if we live in the same climate but work as a fisherman or on a market stall. Obvious stuff. But Gerald was the first to create a comprehensive, quantitative rationale and database on this subject, with cross-related metrics that reveal a plethora of fascinating things about the human race in relation to the weather, worldwide.

He'd already made significant contributions to various studies on climate change by the time he joined us, but was finding that most of the leading psychological associations found his work a bit too off-the-wall for them. They preferred theoretical approaches to the subject and an empirical approach to research, based on events as they occurred. He was far too dogmatic and purist for them but, for us, his work was ideal because it was founded on fundamental factors. He went to the source of things for his data—which is where we were concentrating our efforts—not the outcomes caused by events."

"What other kind of data did you gather? What did you plan to do with it all?"

"I won't bore you with all the details, right now. It would take too long. Let's just say that we achieved something that no one else has ever done before. We built a comprehensive hominine database—"

"There's that word again..."

"A worldwide database of all human characteristics—traits, feelings, desires, thought processes, beliefs—you name it. We even managed to quantify intention."

"That's impossible. It can't be done. That's all ethereal, theoretical. You can't put that lot in a box and measure it. Whatever you have there, Larry—"

"You can, and we did."

"Forgive me for saying so, but that has got to be the biggest load of bull I've heard since we invaded Iraq on the premise that they had WMDs."

"I did say it was radical." Larry calmly poured himself a glass of water and continued in a flat tone. "I also said we had a bunch of weirdos on the team. Let me define 'weirdo' for you. 'Weirdo', in this context, is a derogatory term for a specialist who works in a field that isn't generally accepted by those in the community who subscribe to methods that *have* become generally accepted. In their times, Leonardo da Vinci, Galileo and many others were 'weirdos' in their time. They tend to be ostracized, ridiculed and even feared, simply because they're different. Original thought challenges the status quo. But, if you want new answers, sometimes they're the most able to provide them. Understanding them and accepting them can be difficult, but if their arguments stack up and what they say works, who are we to question them? We would do well to be more accepting of them when we've got ourselves into such a mess and they can contribute to finding a way out of it."

"Point taken." Griffin sighed. "Can you give me an example of how any part of this works?"

"Gladly. Raise your arm."

"What?"

"You heard me. Raise your arm." Griffin dutifully raised his arm.

"What did you just do?" Larry asked. Griffin frowned and felt like a kid in school with his arm in the air, so he lowered it again.

"I engaged my arm muscles and it went up."

"That's part of it. But you first had a thought and an emotion. You were puzzled and a bit angry."

"No, I—"

"Yes, you were," Larry interrupted, smiling again. "Then electrical impulses from your brain went to your arm and activated another electrical process to raise the arm. I'd say the arm movement generated about two volts, the thought and the emotion preceding it, a few millivolts. The characteristic wave forms of both the emotion and the thought are distinct, and we now have equipment that can identify which is which, how much thought energy is used, and the depth and nature of the emotion."

"I heard that this kind of work was being done in Russia—"

"It's been around for years and, in itself, isn't that remarkable. A lot of the specializations we used are not new, but have largely been discredited and marginalized by the scientific community. Take 'neurological rewiring', for instance. That uses a combination of several of the brain's electrical functions that create our 'reality', in conjunction with quantum physics. It works something like this. In order to change our results, we must change our behavior, as we've already discussed. A behavior or habit is just an actualized neural network in the brain. Neurological rewiring is a process of creating new neurological pathways so we develop different behaviors and arrive at new conclusions. First, it discovers how each behavior is wired in the mind, then it develops new neurological patterns that create better outcomes.

"Aside from less scientific and esoteric methodologies, there have also been great leaps forward in human-computer interaction, which also helped us a lot. Science is moving from simply giving computers instructions, to allowing them to understand feelings and emotions. When neurons interact in the brain, they create electrical impulses that can be mapped to a computer. Again, that's relatively old technology, but till recently these impulses could only be measured using cumbersome 'hairnet'-type sensor arrangements, which weren't very accurate. The reason for that is that most of the brain's activity happens on its surface. In order to increase its capacity, the surface is folded. This 'cortical folding' was a problem because every single brain is folded in a different way. Eventually, an algorithm was developed to effectively unfold it, allowing access to the source of the signals, but still the problem was harvesting and cross-relating that information. On a mass population level, the hairnet was impractical, of course, and the existing technologies all involved time-consuming machine-learning processes. That's where we made the big breakthroughs with the Hominine Project.

"Thankfully, the proponents of all these marginalized sciences are, mostly, extremely dedicated people. We were the first to welcome them on a grand scale and 'join all the dots' of what some of them were doing. What resulted was something that went far beyond the mechanics of the human body and measuring electrical characteristics of thought patterns."

"Yes, but people are being born and are dying every second, so this database can't relate to everyone."

"You're right, of course, but we're not concerned with analyzing every single person in real time. Do you remember all the fuss about DNA and the Genome Project some time ago?"

"I heard about it, but didn't pay much attention…"

"Back then, the popular—and not very scientific—belief was that DNA defines the individual. Well, it doesn't. It's just a blueprint. It doesn't actually *do* anything, it just is. You need to go one step back from the physical to find the key to the human. The active part of the identity is in the micro and macro *environment* of the person. It's the relationships and interactions that define us. We already know that everything is made—ultimately—of pure energy. What we see is an illusion. The boundaries of the physical world we experience are also an illusion. Energy connects everything—within us and around us. We've now learned enough about it to define and differentiate everything about us at a very specific energetic level."

"So, the Hominine Project was looking to rebalance the human energetic environment in order to facilitate a positive and sustainable development of the race? That sounds incredible and frightening at the same time."

"It is. Look, Griff, we're not talking about creating some sort of high-tech mind-altering brainwashing system. Human beings are far more sophisticated and innately smarter than anything they can create. We know in our hearts what's good and bad, what's right and wrong. And our hearts are much bigger and stronger than our heads. We've just forgotten how to access that part of ourselves, even though we've always known it. Our race couldn't have survived this long if we hadn't got that essential knowledge deep inside us."

"But, for God's sake Larry, we've come a long way, as a race," protested Griffin, "and we clearly haven't forgotten that part of us, as you suggest we have. We have the Declaration of Human Rights—I saw a Charter for Compassion on the web the other day—we have countless initiatives working to make things right wherever there are wrongs. I can't see what makes the Hominine Project so different and valuable."

"Do you know how long the concept of human rights has been around?" Griffin shook his head. "Thousands of years. People have been struggling since the beginning of civilization to find a basic set of rules that we can adhere to, that will provide the guidance we need to live together on this planet. The problem is that it doesn't work like that. It's not an intellectual process. We can't rely on

Eleanor Roosevelt and a bunch of well-intentioned people on a committee to fix this problem for us. You can't apply those rules from the outside, through the brain with all its limitations and failings. They have to come from inside. And they can. They're at the very core of every human being. They naturally reside there, in each and every one of us. *That's* what we've been working on—a means of re-establishing a *real* connection with *ourselves*."

"Sounds pretty far-fetched to me, but I'm open to hearing more." There was a chink of light developing in Griffin's mind. He was beginning to understand. The implications of what Larry was saying were finally starting to make some kind of sense.

"In time." Larry paused for thought then turned to Griffin again. "What we have is something that's as close as we can get to understanding the fundamental nature of mankind. I'm talking about the soul, Griff, if that's a term you're comfortable with. Maybe you'd call it consciousness. You see, we're essentially spiritual beings living in an electro-mechanical body—an infinitely subtle molecular machine, for want of a better description. Although mankind has always been aware of the existence of his own 'higher self', it's something that he has never been able to rationalize, quantify or see. And the connection between the spiritual and the 'electro-mechanical'—the physical—has never been clear. What we have produced, although it has none of the elegance or refinement that Mother Nature exhibits so brilliantly, is a crude connection—something that can help us to rectify the imbalances, take away the fear, remove the anger and reveal the true—the best—nature of mankind. Once you start that process and, yes, it will take years and a concerted effort on the part of many people, we can naturally replace the philosophies, practices and processes that have held us captive and are driving us to our own destruction. It could bring us back off the knife-edge, and we could genuinely start afresh—from the inside out."

"Well, if all of that is really possible, that's fantastic. So… what's the next move?" Griffin was cautiously excited. It still sounded to him like a utopian dream, but something was nagging at him to trust.

"Unfortunately, I don't think it will ever happen."

"What? I thought you said all the work was done."

"Yes, but there's just one problem."

"What's that?"

"Gerald Shanning."

"Ah, back to our friend, Gerald the weatherman."

"Actually, you've hit the nail on the head. What started out as the Hominine Balance Regeneration Project has now become the Weatherman Project."

"So, Gerald Shanning continued with the work and dumped you? I can't imagine anyone unseating you from your own project."

"No, I left of my own accord. I still stay in touch, just in case I can influence him in any way, but it really looks as if our relationship is over. And anyway, once I'd gone I was considered to be a massive security risk, so they found ways to keep me quiet and make sure I wouldn't disrupt things in the future."

"What happened?"

"Power is seductive. Poor Gerald has never been properly recognized for his contribution to the scientific world, and I know he resented the way he was regarded by his peers as being obsessive and a bit crazy. His extreme passion for what he did made him an outcast in his own community. That's been eating away at him for years." Larry rested his elbows on the table, shoulders hunched, frowing at his clasped hands. "But I'm not trying to excuse what he did. It was just weakness that took him there."

He took a sip of water as he pondered his explanation.

"The closer we got to realizing the implications of what we were developing, and the more the pieces starting falling into place, the higher the energy got, among the team. I can't think of a better way of putting it, but it was as if the deepening focus and realization of what we were achieving was accompanied by an equally progressive 'spacing out' by some of the team members. The closer we got to the source, the bigger the craziness that manifested. It was as if the magnitude and power of what we were discovering somehow blew fuses in their minds and sucked them into a black hole. We had one very eminent Ukrainian scientist who completely lost his memory, and an English medical researcher who started inflicting injuries on herself—deep cuts in her arms and abdomen, things like that—every night when she went home. It was very frightening."

He leaned back on his chair and gazed into the courtyard as he remembered.

"After about three-and-a-half years, I was so busy that I didn't notice that Gerald was doing things that didn't quite fit with the project goals. I didn't ask him about it at the time. You have to give people space to get on with what they do best. Anyway, after a while, he'd gone so far down another route that he couldn't hide it from me anymore. One rainy September day, he admitted to me that he'd been approached by the central committee that was overseeing our work and organizing the funding. Apparently, they were getting very twitchy about the amount of money the project was eating up, and the length of time it was taking. The wanted quick results and tangible benefits. He introduced them to the idea he'd been working on, which shocked the hell out of me when I found out about it."

"What had he been doing?"

Larry's expression darkened, his jaw tightening as he forced himself to explain.

"He was developing a military application using the knowledge and the database we were developing."

"A what?"

"A military application. A weapon." He brushed the air with his arm, as if to dispel these unwelcome words from their haven of peace.

"I don't get it. I mean, I can see he had some personal stuff to get over, but this…"

"I know. The problem was that while we'd reached a very high level of understanding of humanity at the individual level, the central committee who facilitated the whole project—and who keep their identities secret—hadn't. And although they had initially worked out in their minds that this work needed to be done, they didn't really appreciate the wonderful implications of what we were achieving. They were also under increasing pressure to get a result and, so, ironically, the very knife-edge situation that gave birth to the Hominine Project also became its undoing."

"But how did he develop a weapon with information about everything good that we aspire to as human beings? Or am I not understanding this properly?"

"This is where it gets really scary." Larry cast his eyes around the courtyard. "Look, I don't want to talk about that here. I like to sleep at night. Do you mind if we take a drive? Let's find a beach to sit on for a while."

"Sure. Let's get a beer at the same time." Griffin thought for a moment. "Larry, I like to sleep at night as well. Maybe not that beach we visited yesterday?" Larry smiled and they made their way to the jeep. "Don't worry. We'll find somewhere quiet and peaceful. And I'll steer clear of the tourists in Kuta."

They took the back roads through the outskirts of Denpasar and headed toward Canggu, eventually finding their way to a secluded beach with an empty car park next to it. There was a stall where Griffin bought two beers from an old lady who was sitting under a tree beside it, watching her cherubic little grandchildren trying to fly exotically-colored kites. The surf was strong and Griffin soaked up the energy of the sea. They walked a little way and sat on some steps that led from the beach to an ancient, deserted temple. It was guarded by fierce-looking statues, open-mouthed with teeth bared and tongues extended, brandishing swords as they overlooked a paved area where fully grown trees had broken through the masonry to claim their space.

"I'm beginning to wonder why I would ever want to go back to Washington," Griffin mused. Compared to the absolute tranquility of Larry's courtyard, this felt like a rock concert—waves crashing, wind in the trees and children shouting and laughing. But there was still peace there. He'd started to become very attached to it. Like Larry, he was beginning to find he could think more clearly and things felt more… well… just *right*. "It seems a shame to be talking about the world's problems in a place like this."

"Yes, I know. Somehow, we have to try and clear up the mess we've made, though, or we won't be able to enjoy it anymore," Larry said.

"Okay, let's hear it." Griffin took a swig of his beer.

"Rewind to where we were talking about America being broke."

"I'm there. What about it?"

"It's really broke. In fact, it always has been, in a way. Ever since that shady deal on Jekyll Island that gave birth to the Fed in 1910, we've been promising to pay for things, starting with money that didn't exist in the first place. To my mind, the dollar is just a fancy confidence trick. Once confidence is lost, it's lost and it'll no longer be accepted as the world's reserve currency. Once that happens, inflation will rocket and the American Dream will be consigned to history. That confidence is being eroded daily, especially since it became known that China has been bankrolling our indulgences and our idiotic financial practices. But a whole host of factors have combined to put the dollar in an extremely precarious position. Talk of oil being priced in Euros didn't help either, and now there are murmurings of a new, unified currency being developed by the nations in the Gulf Co-operation Council to set oil prices. Worse than that, as we discussed earlier, oil is running out, and the US now has to import what it needs at ever-increasing prices. And when I say 'ever-increasing prices', I mean that in absolute terms. The law of conservation of energy still applies."

"How do you mean?"

"Energy can neither be created nor destroyed. Even though the financial health of the country may look better at some times than at others, in absolute terms, it's going down the pan. As we print more money, or create the illusion of more money being available, the real value of each dollar is reducing. The planet is a finite place with finite resources. I sometimes think that the only people who are putting anything into it are small-scale organic farmers. The rest of our activities simply rape the earth of resources, screw up the natural balance and distribute ownership. It's not just the US doing this, of course. Most countries are playing a version of the same game. And, of course, we're all too aware of how interdependent economies are now, and however cleverly it all has to be managed, but there's a point at which we can no longer keep all the balls in the air. Once they start falling..." Larry knocked back the rest of his beer.

"What's this got to do with the weapon that Shanning developed?"

"Simple. As I said, initially, the superpowers got together with the intention of finding a long-term solution. They'd at last put the idea of nuclear arsenals aside, realizing that Mutual Assured Destruction is, as its acronym suggests, MAD. The obvious alternative to that is mutually assured survival. As the squeeze got tighter, they became more and more susceptible to the suggestion of a short-term solution that would ensure that. Gerald Shanning's weapon seemed to be the most attractive option."

"Go on."

"He calls it HAPISAD. Ain't that a joke? He used to enjoy talking about how 'one minute you're happy, and then, poof!'" Larry threw his arms in the air, "the next minute, you're sad'. Gone."

"What the hell is it, Larry? Is it some sort of nuclear bomb, a WMD? What?"

"No, it's far worse than that. It targets individuals," said Larry, wearily. Griffin was confused.

"You mean, it's just a gun? I'm sorry, Larry, but much as I hate guns and I've never owned one myself, this doesn't sound like an apocalyptic scenario that we're facing."

"Let me explain. I'll give you an over-simplified, incomplete potted version, but you'll get my drift. As I said, we're talking about the three main superpowers. America is broke. We've covered that. China has money but it's hyper-inflating—growing far too fast for its own good and facing shrinking export markets. Russia is getting a little stronger in its economy, but it's still recovering from the low of 2008, when it had to spend a huge amount of its reserves propping up the Rouble. Most of the money in the private sector is concentrated in a few hands, and the government interferes when it feels like it, to keep control. Both Russia and China have a lot of hungry mouths to feed, and Russia has a shrinking workforce. All three have populations that are used to, or are demanding, a higher standard of living. None of the governments want to introduce any draconian austerity measures for fear of being toppled and creating an anarchic situation. They saw what had been happening in Europe, and the thought of having that kind of trouble at home, with their large populations, wasn't one they wanted to entertain.

"Europe is the 'spanner in the works' in all this. They have a big, complex structure and lots of people. They don't have the natural resources they need, so they are big net consumers of raw materials that the big three would prefer to keep to themselves as things get tighter. Also, Europe has, for instance, been talking to China about some really hefty military equipment deals. The US doesn't like that because it owes China big time, and they'd much rather keep Europe out of the picture and have China buy their hardware from them. So, what do these three powers do about protecting their interests? How do they ensure their survival?"

"I have a feeling you're going to tell me."

"Traditionally, the approach by the US has been, in its self-appointed role as the world's policeman, to engineer a problem, blame it on a less-developed country that also happens to be resource-rich, bomb the hell out of it in the name of national and world security, and then take over the business.

Unfortunately, that's hellishly expensive and gets the US embroiled in too many problems and extended, expensive commitments. It can't do that anymore—at least, not on the same scale. But it is still doing it—on a smaller scale. For instance, now they've discovered oil on the Congo/Uganda border, the US is already establishing a military base there and conjuring up terrorists to fight. Anyway, with the help of our Mr Shanning, the three big powers get together. America says to China, 'in lieu of repayments to your people for all the money we borrowed off them without their permission, we'll ensure you can get your hands on good mineral resources so every Chinese person can buy a nice electric car in the future. And, into the bargain, we can help you deal with some of those terribly annoying dissidents that you're finding such a nuisance. Oh, and by the way, to do that, we'll need some more cash off you, just for a while.' The Chinese think, 'We know these guys are broke, so what choice do we have? Anyway, it sounds like a good deal.' Then they say to Russia, 'Hey, your guys should get together with our guys, and we can use your steel and oil to build some nice fancy new technology and a whole bunch of other things. And, into the bargain, we can help you sort out some of the problems you seem to be having with some of your more troublesome neighbors.' The Russians think, 'Da, okay. This could be a great way to get into the US market. Our labor is cheaper than American labor and we can take advantage of American know-how. We can also lend them some of our wacky scientists that they seem to be interested in. Good deal!' So, financed by Chinese money, and with the help of some cheap materials, wacky scientists and other resources from Russia, they start working on a solution. Gerald Shanning then introduces them to the idea that, while controlling and managing all their troublesome neighbors and dissenters, they can also protect their lines of supply, very cheaply. That's what HAPISAD does."

"And HAPISAD is an acronym, I guess, for…?"

"Hominine Aggregation: Personnel Identify Seek And Destroy."

"I see. Shanning was proposing using the data from the Hominine Project to—"

"To wage an internationally coordinated covert war against anyone who stood in the way of anything that the three of them wanted to do, by eliminating individuals who could be acting against them. This war could be carried out using one invisible weapon, without the costs or risks associated with deploying any soldiers. Modern warfare is not like it used to be. Terrorist cells, lightweight, mobile units moving about and hiding are what modern armies are faced with, so conventional methods of engagement have become outmoded. The concept of HAPISAD was perfect for dealing with the modern enemy. But it's worse than that. Remember that the Hominine Project had identified ways of determining and pinpointing all human characteristics. By adapting the data, adding in geo-positioning, infra-red and a bunch of other technology, they can now identify the position, thoughts, moods and intentions of anyone on the planet. They can then program individual HAPISAD missiles—tiny missiles, just over an inch in diameter—to take out individuals and groups, based entirely on where they are, what they may be thinking, how angry they are or even what their intentions are at the time. No one has to declare war, or worry about international concern or condemnation. It's all done quietly and most of the people that are being taken out are regarded as a nuisance by most of the interested parties. Usually they're troublesome key individuals, terrorist groups, private militia—those sorts of people. Who's going to miss them? Lines of supply are protected and deals can be done to shut out other potential customers."

"That's horrific, Larry. The wider implications of that don't bear thinking about. When will this be deployed, and how do they plan to deliver it? Surely any delivery mechanism would be traceable before the weapon could be activated?"

"I'm afraid there's no good news to counter-balance the bad. They're testing it already. When that started, I knew that there was no more I could do to stop them. I'd fought them all the way, up to that point but, as you can imagine, I was given some stark choices to consider, and these guys weren't taking any prisoners. Disappearing to the other side of the world was the only way I could protect Evelyn."

"I'm so sorry, Larry." Griffin saw again the tower of strength and integrity that this man was. How could anyone carry such a burden? He felt guilty for treating him with such suspicion and disdain over the past two days.

"Don't be sorry for me, Griff," Larry said, "be sorry for all the poor people who will live and die under the world's ultimate blackmailing scheme. Be sorry for those who will, unfortunately, be in the wrong place at the wrong time thinking the wrong thoughts, or even just having misguided intentions. They may not even do anything, and yet they will receive the ultimate judgment. Think of all the passionate young people who will want to protest at some injustice, or the communities that may justly resist the dominance of a greater power. The list is endless."

"But surely there must be some way to stop this—some way to defend against it?"

"As far as I know—and you will appreciate that I have not been privy to the latest details on this—they haven't built in an Achilles' heel. They deliver HAPISAD with a new stealth aircraft that's all but untraceable. It doesn't even need an airport to take off from. They call it AVTOL—Advanced Vertical Take-Off and Landing. It's like a bigger version of the B2 Spirit—the original stealth bomber they introduced in the 1990s. It was already in the design stages when this application came along, and they fast-tracked its manufacture. Each one costs over $2.5 billion, and they're planning to build six of them. It sounds like a lot of money, but when you consider that they have spent over $3 trillion so far in Iraq alone, when you take everything into account, it's a very cheap alternative. And whereas the $929 million price tag for the B2 raised a lot of eyebrows back then, the Chinese Government doesn't exactly worry about public opinion on this sort of thing, so the cost wasn't flagged by anyone, and the project remained secret.

"Since the days of the B2, they've made vast improvements to the stealth aspect of the aircraft, they've been able to reduce the maintenance duration and frequency, and they no longer need air-conditioned hangars to protect their stealth properties. The vertical take-off feature also means that you can put this baby anywhere you like, as long as you can get fuel to it—and that can easily be done with a mobile tanker or two. Its range is about 7,000 miles, when they use the vertical take-off, and 8,000 when they don't, but since you won't see any of these at airbases, the 7,000 miles is probably more accurate. And it's a high flyer. It operates higher than most other aircraft and, once it's got sufficient forward momentum, they can shut off the jet vents on the underside and remove the possibility of heat detection."

"Holy shit! And what about HAPISAD itself? Surely that could be taken out from the ground after it's launched."

"That would be difficult. Remember, this is a very small anti-personnel weapon, just over an inch in diameter and about five inches long. I've never held one in my hand; I've only seen drawings, but from the little I've been able to find out, they use them in clusters of up to 200 per drop. The cluster is loaded into the AVTOL in a stealth container, and each HAPISAD is programmed before take-off, from a unit on the ground or in AVTOL, while the aircraft is in flight. Using the information we developed on the Hominine Project, they can program them for a whole range of physical attributes, emotions, intentions and thought patterns, as well as defining the location, down to very specifically measured areas. Using JDAM technology—that's joint direct attack munition that's been used in Iraq and other places—they can attach them to cruise missiles so they don't even have to go anywhere near the actual target when they release them. But if they know they have no opposition in an area, they don't even need to go to the additional expense of a cruise missile. When they get near the target area, they simply drop the container, which free-falls, adjusting its position as it goes with a GPS-aided smart guidance tail kit. When it gets to a pre-defined altitude, it peels open and releases the HAPISADS, before veering off and self-destructing. Once the HAPISADS are within 500 feet of their targets, they activate tiny rockets and seek out their quarry using a combination of infra-red and a new technology that recognizes the particular electrical signature of the body that it's been programmed to target. Once they hit the body, they burn up at a very high temperature, creating a hole a couple of inches in diameter and about four inches deep. There's very little mess as the high temperature of the small explosion immediately cauterizes the wound. They're terrifyingly accurate, they're so small they're virtually impossible to intercept and there's no heat signature until they're very close to their target. By that time, it's too late to stop them. So, for instance, if you want to kill a group of terrorists in a room in Baghdad, but not their wives who are serving them tea, you can pop the HAPISADs through a window and the job is done."

"Jeez…!"

"A HAPISAD attack is easy to identify but, of course, you can't do that unless you know it exists. It leaves a clean black hole with nothing in it. It burns at such a high temperature that it vaporizes, leaving no evidence of its existence. Also, the positions of the wounds are always the same."

"How come?" Griffin was stunned, not wanting to interrupt, but feeling greater and greater despair at every revelation.

"Do you remember the Falklands war that the UK had with Argentina?"

"Yes, of course."

"The Argentineans sank a British warship, the Sheffield, with an Exocet missile. Remember?"

"Sure, I remember."

"Effectively, HAPISAD performs a similar function to the Exocet, but on humans instead of machines. The Exocet was designed to seek and find the control center of the ship. That's where it hit. HAPISAD seeks out control centers on the human body. It effectively goes to specific energy centers located at major branchings of the nervous system—depending on the programming. It always hits either the solar plexus, the base of the throat, or the top of the head. And it's fatal, every time.

CHAPTER 24

"Here?" John Pollard shifted a little to the left.

"Just take one more step to your left… and you, if you would, Captain… that's perfect." The two of them were framed just clear of the white bulk of the superstructure, against a clear blue sky. Pollard adjusted the zipper on his marine jacket over his pronounced paunch and pressed his windswept flap of hair onto his glistening scalp.

"Thanks. I think we can go." Cameraman Jim Short focused in on Pollard, signaled three—two—one with his fingers and—

"I'm on board the *Norfolk Defender*, one of our very latest merchant ships, its design based on the New Panamax class of bulk carriers, on its maiden voyage, which has taken it here, to the notorious Gulf of Aden. The past three months have seen a vast increase in the number of pirate attacks in the Gulf and in the Indian Ocean. So much so, that ship owners have gotten together with designers and the military to build in sophisticated anti-piracy measures." CTV reporter John Pollard was standing at the center of one of the vast covers designed to protect over 8,000 metric tons of cargo beneath his feet.

"I have with me Captain Philippe Baptiste, who has the dubious pleasure of being in charge of this vessel in such dangerous waters." Pollard turned to Baptiste as Jim Short zoomed out to frame them both in shot. The captain cut a stark contrast with Pollard, being somewhat taller, athletic and tanned. "Captain Baptiste, thank you for coming on the program. First, tell me about the name of this ship. I understand it has some special significance."

"Yes, indeed," Baptiste replied smoothly, his words accented by his French-Canadian origins. "This vessel was actually built in Japan, but fitted out by the US Navy in Norfolk, Virginia, with some special equipment and features that make her very difficult to hijack."

"That's very interesting. Is the design of this ship likely to start a trend in bulk carrier design, in your opinion?"

"I very much doubt it. You see, this particular vessel is shorter than the average cargo ship, and I also think the cost considerations would put a lot of companies off. This ship is designed to carry, um, sensitive, high-value cargo and so, for most companies, the cost would probably outweigh the benefits."

"And how much did the *Norfolk Defender* cost?"

"I cannot tell you that. You would have to ask the owners."

"But I guess it was a lot of money, wasn't it, Captain?" The Captain had lost his smile.

"I cannot say."

"What valuable cargo do you have on board today, Captain? What is lurking in the hold beneath our feet that pirates would just love to get their hands on?"

"I cannot discuss the cargo."

"But this ship is on its regular route from the US Navy base in Norfolk. Of course you have military equipment on board for our troops in the Gulf, right?" Pollard didn't want to let this line of questioning go, but Baptiste put his hand up to cover the camera lens. He looked very annoyed.

"You will please cut that from your report," he said, tersely. "When we agreed to do this interview, it was made very clear to you that the contents of this ship are off-limits. Now, I want to see that those questions have been deleted from your camera, or we finish this now." Pollard turned to Jim.

"Okay, Jim. You'd better do it." Jim dutifully ran the tape back, pressed buttons and checked the viewfinder as Baptiste watched his every move. They got back in position and Pollard continued.

"So, Captain, tell me a little bit about the anti-piracy defenses on this very expensive-looking ship."

"Well, I can tell you about some obvious features but, of course, much of it is classified. Those are the features the pirates will find out about if they try to attack us."

"Indeed, yes." Pollard gave an ingratiating smile. "And what *are* we allowed to know?"

"If you look at the stern of the ship, you will see that it has a very high transom. Also, the gunwales are smooth and designed to be hard to grab hold of, so it is very difficult for pirates to approach us and climb aboard."

"Well, that's certainly something you want to avoid, I guess. Tell me, Captain, do you know what it's like to have some of these guys board your ship?"

"Fortunately, I have never had to deal with that situation, and I hope I never do. These pirates are well equipped with RPGs, AK47s—even the big knives some of them carry are pretty frightening. One thing merchant ship crews do have in their favor, though, is that these pirates aren't really interested in killing anyone. They want the ship intact so they can extract a ransom from the owners. The crew are often used as hostages and for bargaining. Sometimes they even use the crew of a previously hijacked ship, to add weight to negotiations on another. They are well-organized."

"But people do get hurt, don't they?"

"Sometimes, yes."

"What kind of injuries have you heard about? Has anyone you know been killed?" Baptiste stayed silent. Pollard glanced over at Jim, who motioned for him to continue. "Captain, can you tell me a little more about the design features of this ship that help you resist attempts by pirates to hijack it?"

"Certainly. We have a much higher top speed than any other bulk carrier in this class, due to our advanced hydrodynamics and extremely powerful engines. Also, everything has been done to reduce weight and increase maneuverability. You will notice, for instance, that this vessel only has one crane on deck. This reduces wind resistance, makes the ship lighter and helps increase its maximum speed. Most ships in this class have four fixed cranes to access all sections of the hold. This crane has a specially designed extending gantry mechanism that runs up and down the length of the hold. It is computer programmed to adjust ballast around the hold during loading and offloading. That is the most dangerous operation we have to deal with."

"You mean, pirates are actually hitting the ports, now, as well as hijacking ships on the high seas?"

"No. Loading and off-loading has always been dangerous for bulk carriers. The ship can become unbalanced and can even capsize or break in two if the transfer of cargo isn't managed with great care."

"That's very, um, very interesting." He glanced at Jim again. "Jim, can we just do a quick link, and then I'll get back to the Captain here. Excuse me, Captain."

"Sure." Philippe Baptiste was gaining in confidence as he successfully dodged sensitive questions. Pollard needed some time to think. He continued to camera.

"In case you've just joined us, this is John Pollard and I am here in the notoriously dangerous Gulf of Aden, aboard the very latest pirate-busting merchant ship, the *Norfolk Defender*. Now, our boys at the Norfolk navy base in Virginia have kitted this ship out with some very special features—features that will certainly shiver the timbers of any pirate who wants to get his hands on this high-tech treasure chest. With me is Captain Philippe Baptiste, the man the pirates would love to keel-haul, and he's going to tell us about some of the surprises that would-be hijackers have in store for them. Captain?"

"Yes, John. We have many ways to keep the pirates away. For instance, if we are approached, we have the capability to bombard the pirates with powerful sound waves."

"What, you mean heavy metal, like Iron Maiden?" Pollard smiled to camera.

"No. These are extremely powerful sound waves. They disorient the pirates, prevent them from communicating and cause them considerable pain, but without causing any permanent injury."

"Well, that's very considerate, bearing in mind their intentions."

"It's humane. We only want to protect the crew and the ship. We are not the aggressors."

"Of course not, and it's the right way to go. But if they do manage to get on board—say they have climbing equipment and ear plugs," Pollard glanced toward the camera, "what then?"

"Should anyone get on board, we can lock down all hatches and armorplate all windows and portholes in seconds, so the pirates would be faced with a big ship they can do nothing with."

"That's very impressive, Captain." *I need better than this*, thought Pollard. "And did the Navy incorporate any weaponry to fend these people off?"

"That is not our job. If we need assistance of that nature, we are in constant touch with the naval vessels from many countries that patrol these waters. As I just said, my responsibility is first the safety of my crew, and then the ship. If there is any fighting to be done, we call in the experts. If we get involved in fighting pirates, not only do we put ourselves at risk, but every other cargo ship in the region would be at increased risk of violent attack. Not only that, but any violent act that we performed could be in contravention of international law." Baptiste gave Pollard a warning look.

"Well, that may be, Captain, but are the coalition forces doing enough to protect vessels like yours? After all, there has been a significant increase in attacks on merchant shipping. We've seen as many attacks in these past three months as there were in nine months last year. I mean, to have to go to these measures just to deliver some... expensive... cargo, doesn't that mean that stronger military measures are necessary? Do you feel let down by the international community?"

"We are just dealing with the situation in the best way we can. I have a job to do, and I am doing it with the best equipment available at this time, so I am satisfied with that. In the long term, I am sure the international community will find a solution." *This guy is just one big brick wall*, thought Pollard, getting more and more frustrated.

"And what do you put this increase in attacks down to?"

"I am a captain of a ship, not a military intelligence expert."

"But today, Captain, you are steering your crew through pirate-infested waters. Are you happy that you're fulfilling your responsibility of care for your crew?"

"Yes, of course I am, and each crew member on board knows the risks before they embark. And they are minimal, thanks to the design of this ship. Now, if you'll excuse me, I have work to do."

"Thank you, Captain." Baptiste walked briskly away. *Jeez, we came all this way, just for that?* Pollard turned to the camera and said, "So, there you have it. There appears to be no end in sight to the dangers that mariners are forced to face every day, delivering essential cargos to keep the wheels of industry turning and to ensure that our soldiers get the equipment they need to do their jobs and keep us safe, as they fight terror in the far-flung corners of the world. I can tell you that standing here on the deck of this high-tech ship, I feel very exposed and alone." Jim zoomed out to wide view, panned to the sea, then slowly back to zoom in to Pollard for a sincere sign-off. "We all owe a debt of gratitude to men like Captain Philippe Baptiste and his brave crew, who are doing a great job that not many of us would have the stomach for. This is John Pollard, for CTV, in the Gulf of Aden."

"Okay, that looked good. Let me just check it," Jim said as he lifted his camera from the tripod onto the deck.

"It was shit and you know it," said Pollard.

Jim shook his head. "Don't worry, I'll just do some fillers. Then we can do some more from the chopper when it comes back, and you can re-do whatever you like on VO later. And don't forget, we have some footage from that professor at the US Army War College that we can cut in to make the story worth telling. Baptiste was never going to give you what you wanted." Jim checked the playback on the video monitor. "This looks fine to me."

"Do you think they'll allow us onto the bridge till the chopper arrives? I don't feel comfortable out here."

"Feeling a little nervous, John?" Jim smiled as he heaved the camera back onto his shoulder and walked off to do some more filming. Turning back to John, he said, "After the roasting you just gave him, he's probably battened down the hatches and radioed the nearest pirate ship to come and get you."

"Fuck you, Jim." Pollard headed as quickly as he could for the doorway through which Baptiste had just disappeared.

CHAPTER 25

Troy King knew the house well. He'd been allocated the same house when he'd taken up his post at Arlington Online. This place had allowed him to immerse himself in his new job while he looked for an apartment closer to the office. He'd hated the long drive to work every day, the traffic jams and the daily tussle for parking, especially if he'd been a little late leaving the house. After a few weeks of this tedious routine, he'd worked out that every five minutes of lateness cost him ten minutes of painful walking at the other end, as the cheaper city center car parks filled up, and he hated spending good beer money on a parking space. So, for the sake of keeping the pain in his aching back to a minimum, he'd chosen to rise early every day and find breakfast close to the office after he'd parked his car. This arrangement had additional advantages, as it meant he had little need of trips to the shopping mall for groceries which, to him, were tedious and time-wasting. He'd have a coffee and a bagel or two at a diner for breakfast, pick up a lunch-to-go from the deli, and have a few beers and a bar meal at the end of the working day—whenever that happened to be. So he'd been relieved to find a studio apartment just five minutes' walk from the office. Troy King liked routines, and this one seemed to work nicely for him. He could now get up later and leave his car in the garage.

All of a sudden, though, routine had disappeared from his life. But this time it was of his own doing. It wasn't something he could blame on an act of God. It wasn't a pothole, a rock or even a roadside bomb that had turned his world upside down. It was his own stupid curiosity, his own arrogance, his own desperate need to prove to himself, his father and the world that he, Troy King, was worth *something*. He was wallowing in a nightmare of his own making, and he had no plan. No plan whatsoever. All he could think to do was to firefight and hope that somehow, somewhere, something would happen that would miraculously get him off the hook—even just a little bit, just enough to let him disappear with at least his pension intact. In the meantime, he had to keep up the appearance of competence and confidence while managing the knots in his stomach with large doses of assorted pharmaceuticals. He suspected that his change in diet was also adding to the new pains in his gut, but he was desperate to find a way to relieve the greater pain in his back, so he'd resolved to stick to it for now.

The house looked the same. Maybe the paintwork was more flaky, and the weeds had eaten a little more into the surface of the driveway that led up the side of the house. It had the look of a lonely, unloved place. It was, after all, a company house—temporary accommodation for new employees. The yard was basic and practical. No potted plants greeted visitors, no carefully-cut hedgerows or lovingly-tended flowerbeds. The lawn was patchy and dry. An old ladder lay along one side of the house, the neighbor's garbage bins were wedged up against the other. Standing in the driveway was a brand new Chevy Traverse. King ran his hands along the crumpled back wing. Black paint mixed with the silver of its bodywork in deep scratches. A neighbor from the house opposite, whom he'd never once spoken to during the time he'd lived there, smiled and gave him a limp wave as he backed his car onto the road.

King had been dreading this moment every since he'd called Alicia two days previously, and she'd explained why David hadn't been into the office since he'd returned from Afghanistan. King walked up to the front door, pressed the doorbell, and braced himself.

"Hello?" Barbara opened the door. She was holding Josh in her arms, wrapped in a blanket. Josh looked sleepy, Barbara looked tired. Red-rimmed eyes betrayed tears she'd been shedding. She had the disheveled look of someone who was past caring.

"Mrs Arbuthnot. My name is Troy—"

"I know who you are."

"Mrs Arbuthnot, I—"

"Wait here." Barbara disappeared and returned without Josh. "What the hell do you want, Mr King?" she hissed, "Don't you think you've done enough damage?"

"Mrs Arbuthnot, I cannot express how much I regret—"

"Well, that's nice, isn't it?" Barbara could barely contain her anger. "At least you can express *that*, can't you, Mr King? My husband—well, I think he's my husband, but it's getting harder and harder to know if he *is* the man I married—can't seem to express anything at all, let alone make up some neat little scripted fucking apology."

"Mrs Arbuthnot, I—"

"What!? What, Mister bloody King? What are you going to say? What? How is this all going to go away? Eh? Tell me. I'd really like to know." Barbara folded her arms and glared at King. He struggled to find any words that would work. His head was spinning with random panicky thoughts that wouldn't stop long enough for him to form a sentence.

"There were some unforeseen circumstances…" King said, weakly, cursing himself for his inability to rein in the turmoil in his mind and come up with something strong and reassuring for Barbara.

"Oh, wow! You mean you didn't plan this, then? This wasn't part of the training, after all? Well, that really surprises me, Mr King. I thought this must be some very clever process, some sort of character-building, mind-altering procedure designed to launch David into the stratosphere of US intelligence and make him an all-American superhero. And now you're telling me that this wasn't the way it was meant to go? Unforeseen circumstances? Oh, well, I suppose that's good enough. That's fine, then. You people call it collateral damage, friendly fire or something, don't you? That's okay, then. Thanks for the explanation. I understand now." Barbara slammed the door with such force that the glass cracked and King instinctively raised his arm to protect himself in case it flew out at him. He looked around to see if Barbara's outburst had attracted any attention from the neighbors. All was quiet, apart from her sobbing on the other side of the closed door. He stood, looking at the door, hoping that Barbara would calm down, waiting for an opportune moment to ring the doorbell again. But she continued sobbing. He walked slowly back down the driveway and got into his car. *I can't leave.* He sat in the car with the window down, his hand covering his eyes, trying to think. Alicia had said that David appeared to be deeply traumatized. Since he'd spoken to David before David took the flight to Dubai, he appeared to have sunk into a deep depression. He wouldn't talk to Barbara, and he'd locked himself in one of the bedrooms, only emerging late at night when Barbara and Josh were both quiet and he thought they were asleep. From the way Barbara looked, King guessed that she hadn't slept at all since David returned. He also guessed that what had happened to Gulnaz was still something that only he and David knew about. That was far too heavy a burden for any person to carry alone, especially someone so young, just starting out in a new career—a cheerful, intelligent young man full of hopes and dreams of building a happy life with his wife and new family.

King got out of his car again and walked to the front door. He could hear Josh crying. Barbara was comforting him, talking softly. He rang the doorbell. Barbara opened it slowly, stroking Josh's head with her cheek as she undid the latch and pulled the door with her spare hand. She looked up and stared blankly at him.

"Mrs Arbuthnot. Somethin' terrible happened when David was away. It was my fault, and I swear that I'm goin' to do everything in my power to put things right for the both of you, if you'll allow me to try, ma'am," King said.

"And what power do you have, Mr King? Is it the same power that sent my husband on some hare-brained mission to train for a complete mental breakdown? I don't think he needs any more of that kind of power, right now." King forced himself to keep eye contact, although Barbara's look of despair was tearing him apart.

"No, ma'am, this ain't nothin' to do with that sorta power. This is me, Troy King, talkin'. Not David's boss. For what that's worth..." Barbara took a deep breath and opened the door wider. Taking a step back, she said, "You'd better come in." The next-door neighbor was watching them from a window.

"Thank you, ma'am." Barbara showed King into the living room and motioned to an easy chair. He lowered himself carefully into it, sighing heavily when he got comfortable. "You all settled in here, okay?" he asked without thinking. It seemed to be the polite thing to ask, but he was immediately appalled by his insensitivity. He shook his head. Barbara didn't answer.

"What happened to him in Los Angeles? I want to know what happened to him," Barbara looked down at Josh as she stroked his hair. King did a double-take. He'd completely forgotten that he and David had agreed to use the story of a training session in LA as a cover for his mission. David hadn't told her what he had really been doing. Now wasn't the time to let her know about Afghanistan—if ever there was one. The trouble with starting the conversation with a lie, as King well knew, was that keeping it intact and convincing got more and more complicated. If David decided to tell Barbara, or if his mind was so messed up that he couldn't stop himself talking about it, King also knew that he could forget any hope of a happy retirement, and would almost certainly be facing jail time.

"There was an accident, and David saw it."

"What kind of accident?"

"Someone died."

"Mr King. Am I going to have to drag every single detail out of you, or are you going to show me at least some decency and tell me what you know about what happened?"

"Ma'am, this kind of evolution is classified, so I am not at liberty to discuss details with you, ma'am." King was playing for time while he thought up a scenario that he felt could be credible, without telling Barbara outright lies, just in case the truth came out later.

"Mr King, my husband has been sitting in the spare bedroom for two days. He doesn't speak, he isn't eating, he won't open the door if he knows I am around. The only way I can get him to eat anything or even give him space to go for a crap, is to wait until the middle of the night, keep Josh quiet and pretend that I am asleep. Now, you know David, a little bit, yes?"

"Yes, I do ma'am. He's a fine boy—a fine man."

"He was. Yes. He was a fine man. He'd actually only just stopped being a boy, and he had retained many of the attractive traits of boyhood. He also had a wonderful sense of humor, he was witty and charming, and a wonderful lover, husband and father to Josh."

"I am sure he was—is, ma'am." King lowered his head and looked at his hands. Where to take it from here? "Ma'am, I spoke to David just before he got back the flight back here. He sounded real shocked, but he seemed to be coping with it real good at the time. How was he when he arrived back home? Did he go straight into the bedroom and lock himself in as soon as he got back? Did he talk to you at all, see Josh, anything?"

Barbara thought for a moment and then said, "He talked. He held Josh. He told me that you were supposed to be sorting out the insurance on the car for us. He didn't seem to be that upset, just a little distant. I put it down to flights and work. I thought he was just tired."

"Was there anything that happened that seemed to precipitate this deterioration in his state of mind?" King was relieved to be having a conversation at last. Maybe this could lead somewhere.

"Nothing. No, nothing that I could put my finger on. But when it happened, it was completely out of the blue and especially hurtful."

"Tell me," King said. Barbara turned her eyes away.

"It was when we were getting ready for bed. I'd got undressed and was waiting on the bed for him. I thought he'd like to…"

"I'm sorry, I didn't mean to pry or nothin'."

"He came into the bedroom, took one look at me lying there, screamed the place down and I haven't seen him since." She turned back to King. "Any thoughts on that, Mr Intelligence Man? Have I turned into some sort of terrifying monster or something?"

"No, ma'am. Nobody could say that. I'm going to get to the bottom of this, and get David—and you—the best expert help available to get your lives back on track again, so David can get back to work and you and Josh can build a happy life together with him."

Barbara shook her head. "In your 'expert' opinion, as a man whose job is 'intelligence', do you think that David will come back to us, or do you think that Josh and I are condemned to live with a frightened, mute troglodyte for the rest of our lives?"

"Ma'am, I am sure that he will get over this shock situation that you have here right now, sooner than you think. In my military experience, I have seen hardened men react worse than this to the death of a comrade. They always recover within a relatively short space of time. I can't say that there won't be emotional scars—"

"A comrade? Did you say a comrade?"

"Yes, ma'am."

"You mean that this was someone who was on the training exercise with him?"

"In a manner of speaking, yes, ma'am."

"What do you mean by 'in a manner of speaking'? Was it a comrade or was it not a comrade who was on the training exercise with him?"

"Yes, she was—"

"*She?*" Barbara was staring fiercely at King.

"We employ both men and women in the service, ma'am."

"I thought it was a company that David worked for, not 'the service'."

"I'm sorry, I meant to say that, but—" King was getting more confused as Barbara increased the pressure.

"Is there something here I should know, Mr King? Are we just talking about state secrets, or are we talking about buddies sticking together to protect each other from each others' misdemeanors?"

"Now, look here, ma'am—"

"Will you stop bloody calling me ma'am? I have a name. It's Barbara."

"I'm sorry... Barbara. Look, David wasn't up to anything he shouldn't have been, if that's where you're goin' with this and, frankly, I'm surprised at you for thinking that he'd do that sort of stuff." King took a deep breath before carrying on. "David was doing some specialist trainin' and his female colleague, who, by the way, was twice David's age and one hell of a professional, did somethin'... and she didn't survive."

"Well, I can tell you right now, Mr King, that you can forget about David ever coming back to work at Arlington Online, or whatever it's called. *I'm* going to get David some help as soon as I can figure out how to do that in this goddamn country, and if and when he is fit to take a flight, we're out of here. There's no way that he's going to spend his time working for a company that routinely puts their staff at risk of death. You'll have to find yourself a fundamentalist jihadist, or something, to take his place."

"Barbara, if you think that we routinely put staff at risk, you'd be very wrong. This has never happened before, and likely will never happen again. Nobody at the company *did* anything to cause Gulnaz to be killed—"

"*You* did, Mr King. You did! You sent them both on this training mission."

"Yes, I did, and I take full responsibility for that."

"You take full responsibility? How do you do that, Mr King? How do you take responsibility for what happened to my husband... my beautiful, happy, wonderful husband?" Barbara's face softened. Tears filled her eyes.

"Barbara, I—"

"Gulnaz. That was her name? This very professional woman who got herself killed—doing 'something'?"

"Yes, that was her name."

"That's an unusual name. Where was she from?"

"She was... of ethnic extraction."

"Jesus bloody Christ, My King! Why, exactly, are you here? Why? What do you want? You obviously haven't come here to help me understand, or explain anything... or help us. What do you want?"

"He wants this." They were both startled to see that David had come into the room. He was wearing just his underpants and a vomit-stained T-shirt.

His hair was matted and wild, and he held a dirty shoulder bag in one hand. Barbara wanted to rush to him with Josh in her arms, but he signaled to her to stay seated. He threw the bag at King, who caught it and held it to his chest. "You'd better go now."

"David, it's good to—"

"Go." David pointed to the door. Barbara and David watched as King struggled to his feet. He looked at each of them in turn, walked silently to the door, and left. Once in his car, he drove two blocks before stopping again. He grabbed the shoulder bag, opened it and rummaged around inside. Among the various medical instruments and assorted junk, he found a sample container with a black substance inside. He set it down on the seat beside him. And then he saw the camera.

"You did it, David. Well done," he said. Switching the camera on, he scanned the photos. The images hit him, hard. "Oh, God… oh, David… oh, no."

CHAPTER 26

Life felt good. Not just good—it felt *really* good. Griffin Kirkland felt energized yet deeply peaceful at the same time.

"Are you ready yet?" he'd called out to Sheryl who was still in the bathroom minutes before their airport taxi was due. As he packed the last of his clothes into his suitcase and clicked it shut, he couldn't help smiling to himself. Since Ubud and their heart-to-heart over dinner, they'd rediscovered sex. Every night since. Raw, passionate and without boundaries, the fire had returned with explosive force, transporting them beyond anything either of them had experienced in their youth.

"Just about."

The bathroom door clicked.

"Good. Let's—" Griffin turned to face her. He caught his breath as his heart skipped a beat. She stood, framed by the doorway, breathing deeply, magnificent. The years hadn't diminished her athletic beauty. The sun cast bright patches over her naked breasts, stomach…. He walked slowly towards her and cupped her face in his hands. He went to speak, but instead, found her mouth with his, and they kissed. At first gently, then with rising intensity until he coaxed her over to the bed, laid her gently down and started urgently pulling at his clothes. He stumbled out of his pants, treading on discarded shoes, throwing his shirt in a crumpled heap on the floor. She lay back, arms outstretched, as she bent her knees and parted her legs.

He could still taste her now. He'd chosen First Class 'Kosmo Suite' on the Korean Air flight back to Washington so that Sheryl could be right there with him. The extra-wide seat afforded just enough room for them to snuggle up together as the airliner winged its way through the night, across the Pacific. So, there they were, cocooned under a blanket, window shades down, in the softly muted light of a luxury 500mph dormitory.

Their trip to Bali had indeed been an unusual holiday. Meetings with Larry every day, followed by evenings and nights talking with Sheryl—but *really* talking. Being out of touch on the island had put them very solidly in touch with their feelings and each other. He had re-discovered her and she had re-discovered him, and they each both really liked what they found. The stresses of all the years of pushing and shoving their way through life, grabbing at everything they could get for themselves had, somehow, miraculously, been lifted off them. What had been dangerous, no-go areas in their lives had been exposed for the pointless and unimportant blockages that they truly were. Once they had each worked up the courage to talk about those things, they'd usually ended up in fits of laughter at the importance and gravity they had given them. It was unbelievably simple, when Griffin thought about it—the way his ambition had pulled them apart. Once that had happened, the wall that established itself between them had seemed impenetrable. His ego had put it firmly in place and Sheryl's despair and frustration had held it there for both of them. And it was so gratifying to discover how a few simple acts of kindness could make that wall crumble so quickly. Griffin was also extremely grateful to Larry for his persistence, in the face of Griffin's initial stubborn resistance, in starting that wonderful demolition process and nurturing in him his own realizations. He knew he'd gone through a deep, fundamental shift in himself, and that the bad old days of his marriage were behind him. Holding Sheryl in his arms as they traveled, he felt a fresh, new commitment to her that had sprung from a new understanding and commitment to himself. He'd learned to accept who he was and what he had been. Bali had been one huge sigh of relief and a transformational rebuilding process for both of them. He felt powerful now, but not as he had experienced power before. This felt good—it felt *really* good.

And now he had a job to do. But even the thought of the work that lay ahead of him didn't diminish this feeling. For the first time in his life, he was looking forward to the challenge of doing something that he felt was absolutely right. No reservations, doubts, compromises or uneasiness clouded his mind. Nor did he carry his new intentions as a burden, surrounded by fears of failure and dire consequences.

Griffin never slept well on long-haul flights, so he used the time to think, reflect and prepare. At least now he understood why he had been treated the way he had, after the press conference at the White House. He knew the President wasn't to blame for that, and he doubted that he had anything other than respect for Griffin's work. The President had been embarrassed. He wasn't in control of that situation any more than any other single person could have been. True political power resided behind the presidency—the very power that got him there in the first place. Larry had given Griffin a very simplified explanation of the President's dilemma and why he had to distance himself from taking the credit for a peace initiative that was bound to fail. The political power that had got him elected also knew that the billions that had been invested in Israel, in recent years, had served the US well. However, those investment channels were drying up as the world recession bit deeper, and Israel had very little to offer in the way of its own natural resources. Pacifying Israel's argumentative neighbors offered little benefit to the US economy, so it was better to keep the conflicts going, keep Israel under pressure to keep prices of Israeli goods keen, and enjoy profitable sales of defense equipment. Creating the illusion of an active peace process kept the Israeli lobby in the US happy, and helped keep well-educated Israelis, knowledge and high-tech products flowing into America to further support the economy. What Griffin had done was to disrupt this process by negotiating a settlement. It had to backfire, and it only took a quick phone call to arrange for an impassioned anti-Zionist to eliminate the Israeli negotiator and re-ignite the conflict. The President would not necessarily have known what was going on. It may simply have been strongly suggested to him that although he should endorse the settlement, no one expected the peace to last. It was so fragile. Hatreds ran deep and Israel was not doing a very good PR job for itself, much of the time. The President, knowing that he had to protect his image as the living symbol of everything that the US was supposed to stand for, had no choice but to do what he did. Whatever the circumstances of this event, though, the entire situation was just a side show—a publicity event to keep minds occupied while the three superpowers concentrated on what was really important to them. Larry had also shared with Griffin some more chilling thoughts about wars.

"In the past," he had said, "it could be argued that wars created a net benefit to the victors and even to the whole world. They propped up economies and kept populations in check. Imagine how much closer we would be to the tipping point now, if the 50–70 million people who were killed in the last world war had lived and brought up two or three more generations. At current rates, the world's population is growing at over 50 million *each year*—a growth rate of about 7.3%. Economies are shrinking in absolute terms, the world ain't getting any bigger and the world's ability to generate natural resources cannot keep pace with the way we're using them up. The problem with waging big wars now is that national economies can't support them and the interconnected nature of the world economy would cause them all to collapse under the strain."

But their discussions hadn't all been doom and gloom. They were a rare opportunity for Griffin to find out how Larry ticked and what he knew. To break through Griffin's conventional thinking and get him engaged in finding new solutions for old problems, Larry had deliberately been pushing Griffin's buttons. Griffin had learned a lot, and had come to see things very differently. He'd realized that he'd spent his life looking through the tunnel vision of received information, nicely packaged and prepared for him, usually to support the national interest. Any doubts or arguments that he may have had about political ideas or even purported facts, had all been wrapped up in convincing explanations that he'd accepted without question, and used to support his own ambitions. He'd become aware, on this trip, that there *were* no neat answers. The Presidency and the whole system of government, the UN and the international community, the world of commerce, philosophies, religions and beliefs all had fundamental flaws. It was this system of ill-founded collective beliefs and living practices, established over generations, which had brought the world to the edge. Like lemmings, oblivious to impending disaster, we were all following each other over the cliff. The whole rotten mechanism needed to be stopped, taken apart. Only then would people have a chance to make new, real and empowered choices. All the signs had always been there, but he'd chosen not to notice them.

"Whatever happened to the notion of government of the people, by the people, for the people?" he'd asked Larry when they were sitting on the beach one day.

"Well, in a sense, we do have that," Larry had said. "We always get what we deserve—and what we truly want."

"That hasn't been my experience."

"Well, think about it. Maybe it has. Take this President, for instance. He started out as a real fighter, campaigning in rough areas, paying his dues, learning the ropes. Eventually, he had some success. He started working his way up through the system and finding ways to use new media and the press to get the grassroots of society to give him a leg up. He knew he was a bit of an oddball to most people, but he had lots of really good ideas, a lot of integrity and he was smart. He managed to overcome a lot of the disadvantages he had and became the hot ticket for high office. But he didn't have quite enough, and he knew it.

"Now, let me digress a little here before I continue with him. The road to the White House is long and winding, as you and I know only too well. If you want to be the darling of the country when you're campaigning, you have to become the person who represents the conscience of the people. Conscience, as we know, is the awareness of a moral or ethical aspect to one's conduct together with the urge to prefer right over wrong. Okay so far?"

"Yup."

"Once you do that, you give yourself a problem."

"Why's that?"

"Because although the people want to satisfy themselves that they have a good conscience—which is why they like politicians who campaign conscientiously—when the elections are over, they actually want a leader with a strong will, not a conscience. He had this problem when he was campaigning, and people were pleading with him not to change if and when he got elected. But the fact is that people want to survive and to prosper more than look after their conscience. So, on the way up, he increasingly meets with all sorts of pressures that conflict with his declared conscience. They are pressures from the forces that underpin the economy and national security that are actually supported, either passively or actively, by just about every American citizen. It's a fine balance to strike, because those forces are very powerful and you don't get elected unless you work with them.

"So, getting back to my original point, what could he do to tip the scales in his favor? How could he keep his conscience intact, as far as people are concerned, while also satisfying their desire for a strong-willed leader who wouldn't just have nice ideas that are costly to them?" Larry had asked.

"He developed a better PR strategy?"

"Well, you could say that, but no. He joined a popular club that much of the population belongs to, making them feel that he was one of them, while demonstrating conscience in a way that they would find acceptable."

"And the club is…?"

"Christianity. As soon as he 'saw God', I knew he was on the road to the White House. Whether or not he was completely sincere about it, it was bound to be a big plus point for him, as it has always been in our country, which is odd, if you think about it in a historical sense."

"Really?"

"Yes. The Founding Fathers hoped to escape the oppression of the established religions of Europe, not simply get embroiled in the same game over here. Well, at least Franklin and Jefferson felt that way, and there's no mention of this being a Christian nation in the Declaration of Independence." Larry chuckled.

"What?"

"I was just thinking. Imagine if his religious epiphany had led the President to become a Muslim. It could have happened. After all, he spent many of his formative years in a predominantly Muslim country." Griffin had taken a sharp breath at that thought. "But I'll tell you something funny," Larry had said.

"Please do."

"I have a theory about religion and its relationship to pornography."

"I hope this isn't going to be too distasteful."

"It depends what you're attached to and whether you react from prejudice and conditioning, or you're open to seeing things from a fresh perspective, and letting them in."

"Try me."

"They're very similar in some respects."

"Really?"

"They're both huge distortions that serve powerful desires for ultimate love. The only differences are that religion is spiritual and porn is physical—and, of course, their treatment and image are worlds apart. Religion tends to get the upper hand when it comes to open acceptance—as opposed to hidden acceptance—simply because when it gained political power it was in a position to lay down the law, in terms of morals. But it wasn't always that way. For instance, before most of the mainstream religions decided that nudity and sex were bad, there was none of the paranoia that we have around them now. There are still tribes who haven't been touched by religious indoctrination, who manage perfectly well with nudity and sex between consenting adults as a normal and accepted part of everyday life with no guilt agenda attached."

"Interesting theory, but what's this got to do with anything we've been talking about?"

"Not much, but it does demonstrate the power of symbolism in society, and how our entire perception of the most powerful, natural and procreative human function can be distorted and confused in our minds by those with a desire to control us or profit from it."

"But many people need guidance—"

"Do they? Or do they need to be empowered to think it through for themselves? You know the saying; 'give a man a fish and he'll eat for a day; teach a man to fish and he'll eat for the rest of his life'. The same thing happens in politics, of course. Service and power get very confused. I question the motives of anyone who claims they want to serve, and then uses every devious trick in the book to gain the power to do so."

Larry had shaken him up—challenging him with alternative ways to view the familiar. It wasn't comfortable, but it was starting to make sense. That day, Griffin had even come to the conclusion that HAPISAD, terrifying as it was, was something that could even appear to be attractive to 'the people', even though they knew nothing of it. The potential to eliminate opposition in business and politics, efficiently and cheaply, would surely be beneficial in the race to survive. And wasn't the right to survival ingrained in the American culture, born out of the efforts of struggling pioneers, whose descendants still retained the right to bear arms?

In the quiet of their luxurious pod in the sky, Griffin's mind expanded these thoughts beyond his discussions with Larry, as minds do when they find freedom to roam on the verge of sleep. He even came to see his own recent career as a bit of a joke. *Peace negotiator. How on earth can you negotiate peace? All you can do is broker an agreement, and all agreements can be broken. Peace is an internal state, not an intellectual bargaining process. It can only be realized, not imposed or arranged by a third party. So what is peace, in political terms? Maybe it's an alignment of conscience and will, the ethereal with the physical. That's the constant battle in politics—trying to get that alignment, or hiding the disparity between the two, in what the government is doing.*

He drifted in and out of sleep, but this theme of the relationship between conscience and will kept taunting him to find answers that made sense. Had America succumbed to the corrupting influences of will over conscience when the government ran out of money way back, at the beginning of the twentieth century? Was the world about to see a new manifestation of that now, with the superpowers turning to HAPISAD as they faced economic crisis? Had the ideals of the hard-won Declaration of Independence been compromised by fear, greed and the relinquishment of ideals when survival was at stake? Was America just a country led by the powerful and willful, with weak consciences? Were they simply imposing self-interested leadership, rather than serving the nation?

And he looked at his own life. Hadn't he fallen into exactly that mould? His own career had been fueled by blind ambition and an obsessive determination, certainly not by conscience. He hadn't really had any values of his own, other than a belief in the right to his own success—built on a deception that he delivered with increasing skill. He pretended he had a conscience, when he actually didn't. That quality had served him well as a negotiator—juggling facts, balancing the wants and needs of the parties, balancing the books on their economic demands. For the government, it was ideal. And there was another advantage that made Griffin perfect for the job: he would never succeed in achieving peace because he lacked the fundamental qualities to deliver it. As far as the government was concerned, his recent success had been an unfortunate aberration.

Despite all this, he'd climbed almost to the top of the political tree, with the most important part of him, he now realized, missing. But it was there, buried deep inside him, and Larry had recognized that. Larry had also realized that if Griffin could get that far with such a large part of himself absent and unused, he would be incredibly powerful once he engaged his full self in any task he had to perform. Once he engaged his conscience and his heart, Griffin could do anything.

CHAPTER 27

Captain Baptiste had been particularly pleased to see John Pollard and his cameraman climb aboard the Sea King helicopter after he had aborted the TV interview. Pollard was a pain in the neck, but however much he despised him and his reporting style, he was pleased that a TV report would be airing in the next few days. It would lead people to believe that the *Norfolk Defender* was heading toward the Persian Gulf. He strongly suspected that Jim Short had only pretended to delete the part of the recording where the Gulf had been mentioned, and he knew that if his suspicions turned out to be well-founded, a hack like Pollard would certainly include it in the report. Once the chopper was out of sight, the *Norfolk Defender* made a 90-degree turn, and headed due south at a brisk 35 knots.

We'll make Berbera by 1600 hours, as scheduled. He scanned the radar screen for other vessels that might inadvertently cross their path and spot them. Thankfully, the route was clear. The approach to the port of Berbera was marked by a spit of sand almost two miles long, containing a spacious and deep natural harbor equipped with a dock. Being strategically placed on the oil route to the Suez Canal, and the only harbor on the north coast of Somalia, it was the main commercial seaport for the country. Nevertheless, it was relatively quiet and easy to negotiate, without drawing too much attention. Once he'd docked, no questions would be asked, and they could go about their business of unloading equipment undisturbed by customs officials or the military at the small garrison based near the dockside. The Weatherman had made precise arrangements, so he also wanted to make sure everything would be ready belowdecks for their arrival. He handed over to the chief mate and walked down the four flights of steps to the deck level, then punched in a code to open the door to a lift that lowered him into the hold. As it descended, the hum of the four nuclear-powered gas turbines grew louder.

The lift opened onto the vast hold—400 feet long by 100 feet wide. An array of powerful halogen lamps, mounted high on the side walls, lit the space with a cold white light. Above him, two vast sliding hatch covers formed the roof. Captain Baptiste stepped up onto one of two platforms, each positioned below a hatch cover. Beneath the platforms were powerful hydraulic ram mechanisms. To get to the other end of the aft platform, Baptiste had to squeeze between several vehicles sitting in lifting frames, their wheels strapped in place and the frames bolted to the platform. The biggest of these was the Oshkosh 15,000-liter tactical aircraft refueler. Its massive six-wheel tractor unit, equipped with a 445-horsepower engine and all-wheel drive, was designed to haul the jet fuel it carried in its trailer over any terrain it encountered. Next to this were two ominous-looking eight-wheel HEMTT A4 Heavy Expanded Mobility Tactical Trucks, each powered by a 500-horsepower Caterpillar engine mounted behind an armor-plated cab. A 20-foot container was clamped to the load area of one of them, its rear doors open, with a multitude of wires spewing out and trailing along the platform. The other carried a sealed container. Just beyond these two massive vehicles were two M-ATV all-terrain vehicles, a SandCat protected multi-role vehicle with a gun mount on the roof, and three Prowler light tactical all-terrain vehicles that looked like military-style dune buggies. All the vehicles were filled with metal boxes and equipment. Fuel cans and spare wheels were strapped and bolted to every flat surface.

Once past the Prowlers, Baptiste jumped down off the aft platform and up onto the forward platform. It was empty except for four metal foldable tables supporting several pieces of computer hardware poking out of their protective boxes. Six faces, all deep in concentration, glowed in the light from monitors. Keyboards clattered. An assortment of cables and wires wove their way across the platform, back to the open container.

"Ralph, how's it going? We'll be docking at 1600 hours. You'll be finished and cleared away by then?" Baptiste addressed a young man who seemed to be in charge. His hair was gelled into a peak from the back to the front of his head. He wore jeans and a *Dry County* country rock band T-shirt.

"Coolie doolies. No prob," Ralph replied, "we just gotta make sure this thing plays the right tune this time. We're still ironin' out the bumps in this crazy software, and them digilliterates back home don't want no more mistakes now."

"I'm sure you'll do an expert job." Baptiste tried to smile. *How on earth could they entrust this sub-human geek with such a crucial responsibility and all this expensive equipment?* He looked around at the mess—equipment covers, bits of notepaper and dirty plates were strewn across the platform, empty coffee cups lay on their sides—spilling dregs onto the tables, dripping onto the cables. *Thank God they're not allowed to smoke*, he thought. The floor was sticky, in places, with ketchup footprints punctuating the space between two of the tables. Amy, a young girl with blue streaks in her asymmetrically-cut hair and a stud in her nose, had a cold, so her workspace was littered with used tissues. *Is this really the best they could come up with?* He shook his head, yet he knew this was a brilliant young team, hand-picked by the Weatherman, to develop and operate the software. He had chosen them for their fresh, creative approach to the challenges they'd been facing—analyzing and programming data from minute currents and delicate wave forms—and for their dedication and passion for programming that was not complicated by other concerns. They asked no questions, made no judgments, were excited and flattered to be involved in a project that was highly confidential, weren't concerned about unsociable working hours, loved the money they were being paid and simply got on with the job. They had no idea what their programming would ultimately bring about.

As Baptiste turned to go, Ralph said, "Hey, Captain, got any more of that there sushi in the galley? We're climbin' the stick down here." He smiled warmly.

Baptiste rolled his eyes.

"I'll arrange it." He sighed, tripping over a wire on the way back to the lift.

"How long have we got, Ralph?" asked a skinny young man in brown cords and an open-necked cream shirt.

"Two hours max, Bobby. Can you swing it?" Ralph cracked a ring-pull on a can of Coke.

"Hell, I don't know. Never done it like this before…" Bobby peered at his monitor and punched some keys. "I just hope they don't make any more last-minute changes." He unconsciously stuffed the last piece of nigiri sushi into his mouth from a plate beside his keyboard.

"Yeah, right." Ralph was still a little uneasy about the changes. The Weatherman had made it crystal clear to him at the outset that instructions would follow a strict pattern but, in fact, they never did. There had been so many changes along the way, as they'd been developing systems and procedures—particularly since that one big mistake the previous month—that he had not queried it. In fact, questioning instructions was something that he was staying well away from since he'd asked what he thought was a completely innocent and reasonable question: *What does it actually do?* He'd never had such a paranoid client before.

They were still working two hours later when they heard the engines change pitch, slow, rev and grind with a different tone. A gentle bump shook the monitors and announced their arrival at the dock. The engines slowed to a quieter hum.

"Okay, team, whaddawegot?" Ralph asked as he furiously punched his keyboard. Silence from the others. "Team! I mean you guys! Speak to me, we're outta time here!" Then, just as the ship finally came to a dead halt, a cry went up.

"Yes, yes, yesssss!" Amy was breathing heavily.

"What's up with her?" Bobby turned to look at her.

"Oh, Amy," said Ralph, a smile forming on his lips, "tell me it's another of your multiple nerdgasms comin' on!"

"Yessss!" Amy pushed herself away from the table on her wheeled office chair, punching the air with her fist.

"There is a god!" Ralph got up from his chair and ran over to hug her. They all laughed. "Koolioawesome! That's total awesomeage, team! We done it!" A chink of daylight blasted through from the top of the hold as the cover above the vehicles started to slide open. Ralph clapped his hands, suddenly all action. "Okay, guys, get those wires out of that can over there and wrap it up." Two of the programmers leaped across to the other platform, climbed onto the truck and disappeared into the container. They emerged a few minutes later, heaving cables and bunches of wires over their shoulders, all of which they dropped onto the floor of the hold before closing the container ready for it to be offloaded.

As the hatch cover slid open, they were drenched in an oppressive, humid heat. Storm clouds were gathering overhead.

"Where are we?" one of the programmers asked as he removed his T-shirt.

"No clue, bro," said Ralph. "I thought you guys were the brainbags around here. Anyways, no time for idle cluelessness right now. We gotta stash the kit—and *fast!* Reckon we're in for a mother of a rain dump any second now!" Within half a minute, computers had been shut down, power cables disconnected, carry case lids clicked into place and tables folded. Everyone in the team knew what to do, and even Ralph was impressed at the way his intensive training in 'how to program on the run' had turned this bunch of *dorcus ficus* wimperialists into a fast and efficient team that operated with military precision—albeit with its own unique character and flair. He regarded the resulting patch of unseemly, sticky detritus they left in their wake as they stored the gear under cover at the other end of the hold. *Oh, well, one step at a time. I guess they have cleaners around here who can fix the alcohollateral damage...* The rain was now pouring into the open part of the hold, drumming loudly on the vehicles. Steel lifting cables were being winched down to cargo handlers who, squinting up at them, extended arms to catch them as they whipped and swayed toward them.

"Ralph, can I call my mom now?" Bobby shouted above the noise of the rain, electric motors and metal clanging against metal as he passed Ralph on the way to the lift.

"Sure... and thanks, Bobby. You did a great job today. I think we have a few days off now. Shoot some pool later?"

"Yo." Bobby grinned delightedly as he pulled his shirt up over his head and made a dash for the lift with the others. The lift wouldn't move for ten minutes—'for operational reasons', they were told over the lift intercom—so they had to wait before they could return to their cabins to freshen up for the evening's entertainment.

High above them on the bridge, Captain Baptiste was orchestrating the removal of the cargo. He'd already made sure that all the starboard portholes and accesses were closed, covered and secured, so the only view that anyone on the lower levels had was out to sea. The Weatherman was determined to keep his programming team from knowing anything about the ship's location, so they were never allowed to see the ports they visited, let alone disembark. Nor did he want the programmers coming into contact with the maintenance team who had been disembarking, accompanied by a protective detail of six marines in civilian clothing, while they were stuck in the lift. Although the *Norfolk Defender* had been kitted out with substantial accommodation facilities, including a cinema, two restaurants, a gym, a sauna and a bar, it was quite a logistical challenge to monitor these two groups and keep them apart.

Once he had unloaded the cargo, Baptiste was looking forward to some downtime, although Berbera was not exactly his idea of an exotic destination for relaxation and enjoyment. Right now, though, he had to carefully monitor the unloading procedure from the aft hold. He wanted to do it as quickly as possible to avoid attracting unnecessary attention. As each vehicle was placed on the dock and unstrapped from its lifting frame, it was immediately driven out of the port to a pre-arranged rendezvous in the desert a few miles to the south. The SandCat was the first to go, followed by the Prowlers, with their drivers grumbling about the unusually wet weather, knowing that they were about to get covered in mud and soaked to the skin. The M-ATVs followed and were sitting on the quayside within an hour of docking. The larger vehicles took longer, as Baptiste chose to offload the containers first and replace them on the trucks once they were on terra firma. The last, and riskiest, maneuver was lifting the tanker, which was full of jet fuel. He went down to the hold to personally check the fixings on the lifting frame, cursing the Weatherman all the way. It would have been easy enough, he'd told the Weatherman, to fill the tanker in Berbera, where there was an airport with jet fuel readily available. But the Weatherman had not wanted to have such a noticeable vehicle driving into the airport, and then have to explain why it was driving out again once it was fully loaded with fuel. There was no other airport in the area, so that would have raised suspicions and it could possibly have been followed. It had been placed into the hold using a dockside gantry crane, which was a relatively simple task. Unfortunately, there were no such facilities at Berbera. With the truck, its load and the lifting frame weighing just over 90 tons, it was going to test the ingenuity of the computerized ballast system. Not only that, but the weight itself was a potential problem. Most ships' cranes were rated at 60 tons. The crane on the *Norfolk Defender* was rated at 80 tons, so Baptiste was working way above its maximum load. The safest option was to lower the truck onto the quayside, as close as possible to the ship. That was risky because if any part of the crane failed or broke, he risked damaging the hull. He would have preferred to separate the tractor from its trailer, and remove each separately, but that would have delayed the rest of the team and could have jeopardized the whole operation. No, he just had to bite the bullet and pray that everything worked as it should. Fortunately, he could control the crane from the starboard side of the bridge, where there was a vantage point that gave a clear view straight down over the side of the ship.

The first, vertical, part of the lift was relatively simple and allowed Baptiste to see if the crane was under undue strain. Once the truck was clear of the deck, Baptiste stopped the crane and made another visual inspection. All looked good, so far, although it was difficult to tell in the pouring rain. He went back to the bridge and flicked the switch to start the traverse to the dock, on the slowest setting possible. As the gantry extended toward the dock, massive pumps kicked in, transferring water ballast to the port side of the ship, keeping it on an even keel and balancing the stresses in the infrastructure. The truck swayed very slowly in its cradle. The cables held. Baptiste resisted the temptation to pause the movement to reduce the sway, which was putting more strain on the system, because he wasn't sure that, with the crane operating over maximum capacity, it would be possible to make the correction at all. The truck inched slowly over the gunwale. Handlers on the dock edged away. Once it was clear of the ship, Baptiste stopped the movement. Unfortunately, with the sudden halt, the truck increased its swing to within inches of the hull. Baptiste had to act quickly. He started to lower the truck—faster than he would normally. If there were a breakage, the nearer the truck was to the dock, the less damage there would be, and there would be less chance of sparks that could ignite the jet fuel. Standing where he was, an explosion like that would almost certainly kill him and possibly sink the ship. The truck continued to swing as it approached the dock. Once Baptiste judged it to be within four feet of the concrete surface, he slowed the descent. There was a loud, metallic bang on the port side of the ship, and the truck dropped two feet. *What the hell was that?* Baptiste couldn't see where the noise had come from, but he knew his only option now was to release the load as quickly as possible, so he let the truck fall the last two feet to the ground. It crashed onto the concrete, sliding toward the hull and stopping just inches short of it.

The handlers quickly checked for damage as they released the truck from its lifting frame. The ship lurched to port before the computer recognized that the crane was no longer under load and activated the pumps, quickly returning water ballast back to starboard. A thumbs-up to Baptiste assured him there was no damage, and the truck drove off in a cloud of spray, along the quay and out of the port. Baptiste ran down the steps and across to the port side, where he found that the crane had been pulled out of its fixings. Its huge steel wheels were suspended two feet above the rail that they normally traveled along. He rubbed his sweating face. That was just a bit too close for comfort.

***

He had pondered long and hard on how to get to the bottom of this. How should the conversation go? How could he lead in to the ultimate question without appearing to be needy or, God forbid, fearful? He'd already dropped one card. He wasn't sure if his opponent had seen it, but he wanted to make damned sure that he held the rest of the pack tightly to his chest. In the end, he chose the simple way, but asked the question with confidence.

"What exactly do you want, Mr Samakab?" Gerald Shanning was pacing his office in Hackensack. This was their first telephone conversation since Samakab had dramatically announced to him that the deal was off. Shanning knew that he'd made a few, very dangerous mistakes. He had to resolve them quickly, and he couldn't afford to upset Samakab. The Weatherman Project had hit a few unforeseen snags during the development of HAPISAD, and now, thanks to that bumbling idiot, Troy King, he suspected that Samakab may have discovered more about the project than he wanted him to. Although he couldn't be sure that he had, he couldn't risk its integrity and he certainly couldn't afford to have any more security leaks. He believed he'd managed to plug the leak as far as King was concerned. On the journey to Washington, in the Gulfstream he'd hired for the day, he'd come to the conclusion that King actually knew nothing and could be easily managed through the NSA. He'd also convinced his Chinese paymasters that King's line of inquiry had been stopped. However, he still had the Russians on his back. They were very concerned that the research they'd carried out into remote human energy field measurement didn't fall into the wrong hands. The Americans, strangely, were oblivious to what was going on with the Weatherman Project, probably because they were concentrating their attention on the more immediate concerns of their over-burdened economy and the various interminable wars they were fighting. So, although he was juggling some pressing concerns, Shanning took some comfort in the fact that he'd managed to re-open communications with Samakab, following their falling-out in New York. While Shanning was the world's leading expert in his chosen field and a skilled and manipulative negotiator, he was beginning to understand that his brilliance didn't extend to security planning. That weakness had laid him open to bribery by this clever and unsavory man, in whose hands his fate now rested. He was just hoping that Samakab wasn't aware of that.

"I think we should make some further adjustments to our arrangement," Samakab replied. He was calculating that if Shanning had been so willing to enter into such an expensive deal with him—a deal that also effectively endorsed criminal activity by the American Government—maybe he had pitched his price too low. Whatever Shanning was up to, it must be worth a lot more than what he was getting. He recalled their recent conversations and that embarrassing first meeting with Shanning, searching for clues. He thought back to the initial approach that was made to him several months previously, when he had first been introduced to the Weatherman Project by a man who had remained anonymous. He'd been sitting in his office in Mogadishu when the call came through.

"*Ma nabad baa?*" Hello—the traditional Somali greeting, meaning 'is it peace?'

"*Waa nabad,*" he'd replied: hello, it is peace.

"Mr Samakab?"

"Yes. Who's this?"

"Ah, good. Mr Samakab, I have a client who is very interested in talking to you about some land."

"What land?"

"Some land in the north, in Somaliland, near the coast."

"But I am not a land agent, and I don't own land in that part of the country. I didn't get your name."

"I didn't give one. Mr Samakab, my client is very influential and I am sure that you would find it worthwhile, in terms of your main business, to accommodate him."

"And what do you understand my main business to be?"

"How shall I put it…? Maritime acquisitions?"

"Goodbye." Samakab slammed the phone down. *What the hell is this? Who knows about my business?* The telephone rang again. He picked it up.

"Before you put the phone down again, Mr Samakab, please hear me out. It will be worth it for you."

"You will have to be quick."

"Mr Samakab, you're a man of influence in your country, and I have a proposal for you that will undoubtedly increase that influence. I also know that you are a patriot, and that you are striving to improve the lot of your fellow countrymen. After all, why else would you be sending your son, Ayan, to Oxford? If you accept our proposal, you would be in a better position to do much more for your country."

"Why are you not talking through the proper channels—the government? Why me?"

"Why would anyone not talk to your government? I thought that would be obvious. They cannot deliver what you can deliver for us."

"Who is 'us'? You sound American."

"I am."

"And what can I deliver that my government cannot?"

"As I mentioned, a piece of land in the north."

"As *I* mentioned, I don't own land in the north, so—"

"We know that. We just want to acquire it for a while."

"So, why don't you find the owner and buy it from him?" Samakab was getting impatient now.

"Because the owner is the government, and the land isn't for sale… Don't hang up."

"Give me a good reason not to."

"Money, information and power."

"Go on."

"There's a piece of land just south of the Sheikh mountain range near Berbera that we would like to secure for a while, and use without being disturbed."

"I can think of more attractive locations. That land is just scrub and desert. Nothing grows there, it's arid and inhospitable and I imagine there aren't even any roads. Wouldn't you rather do what you plan to do in Florida or somewhere like that?"

"No, it's actually ideal for us. The only other thing we will need is unmonitored and free access via the port at Berbera, which, of course, you do control."

Samakab laughed. And then, in a more serious tone, replied, "Look, I don't know who you are and what this is about, but I can't help you. If you do your homework, you will find that the port is controlled by the port authority. It is the only port the country has on the north coast and it's our primary link to important export markets in Aden and through the Suez Canal. Do you seriously think that I could control Berbera?"

"Of course, it has the port authority, and they have some soldiers billeted nearby as well, but you control the hearts and minds of Berbera. People there know who took those three foreign factory trawlers out of action and then pocketed a few million by ransoming them. The reason the fishing communities in that area are doing so well now is thanks to you, Mr Samakab. You're a hero up there. And you know what a small community it is. The men who run the port authority are local men…"

"So, I may have a bit of influence, but what makes you think I have control?" Samakab was amused by the man's obvious attempt at flattery. He'd also enjoyed the fact that he'd made himself a little richer by organizing the hijacking and then ransoming the trawlers, while at the same time stimulating business in the local fishing communities.

"From what I hear, the authorities up there, such as they are, also live in fear of a powerful man like you turning up on their doorstep one day."

"Why on earth would they fear me?"

"You are from the Raxanweyn clan, a Sab from the south, yes?"

"Yes, that's who I come from originally."

"As you know, around Berbera they are mainly Samaale, but particularly Isaaq."

"So?"

"Well, a long time ago—way before the Battle of Beledweyn in 2007 and the recent takeover by the Islamic fighters—many Isaaq herdsmen were involved in fighting north of the city. Some of them were accused of burning villages. You would only have been a young boy at the time, I'm sure you wouldn't remember…"

"I remember well. Carry on." Samakab was fully alert now, remembering that terrible day as if it was yesterday.

"As I understand it, many of them gave up the life of a herdsman after that, and went to live up north on the coast. They swallowed their pride and became fishermen. Now their sons are fisherman as well. I don't suppose there's much else for them to do up there."

"So what you are saying is they burned my village, killed my family and now I help their children prosper?"

"Something like that, yes. Perhaps you can understand now—"

"Perfectly, thank you. And what are you offering me?"

"As I said, money, information and power. Are you interested?"

"I might be."

"You've visited New York, Mr Samakab?"

"Many times."

"Maybe we could meet at your hotel. It's the Four Seasons, isn't it? Shall we say next Wednesday?"

Samakab had taken a flight to New York and had a meeting with a middle-aged American man who didn't give his name or any means of contacting him. The man had offered him a very attractive financial package involving staged payments amounting to several million dollars, along with an agreement to supply detailed information on high-value shipping—commercial and military—in the Gulf of Aden and beyond. The suggestion was that he, unlike most of his competitors in Somalia, could invest in better equipment for his business and improve efficiency and profitability. He would also be able to extend his operations deep into the Indian Ocean, where there was much less competition and it was much more difficult for the authorities to disrupt his operations. All he had to do was keep secret any visits to the port of Berbera by a certain vessel, and keep any wandering herdsmen out of a fixed area of desert scrubland just beyond the mountains south of the port. When he had asked what they needed the land for, he'd simply been told that they were running a highly secret project there, called the Weatherman Project, and that in the interests of national security he could know no more about it. He had also been assured that no one in the area would be affected in any way at all by the project, and the last thing the man did was to give him a code and a handset for contacting the project should he need to do so. The following morning, he checked one of his Swiss bank accounts and discovered a deposit of $5 million had just been made. It had seemed too good to be true, at the time, but when intelligence agents like Troy King started turning up unannounced and asking strange questions, he'd immediately jumped to the conclusion that he'd been set up. He still wasn't sure if the email and video clip were just some sort of decoy mechanism, but the fact that Ayan had become involved, if only as a completely innocent party, sent shivers down his spine. The way that Gerald Shanning had agreed to meet him, and had then dismissed King's visit in such a matter-of-fact way, also disturbed him. As soon as Ayan and Assaf had returned from the Guggenheim, he'd made a surprise announcement that he was packing them both off on an 'eco-adventure' holiday to Costa Rica, where they would be completely out of touch and difficult to trace as they canoed and hiked and climbed their way through two weeks of fun.

But Samakab hadn't been idle, these past few months. He'd used a considerable amount of the money he was being paid to carry out his own investigations into what he might be involved in. Most of his inquiries had ended up blind alleys. However, some interesting information had come to light, and he was beginning to feel that Gerald Shanning wasn't the confident, smooth operator he liked to portray himself as. This call from him right now, unsolicited and from Shanning, rather than the other way around, suggested that Shanning had concerns. The fact that he was prepared to change the arrangement and increase his offer confirmed it. He also knew that the *Norfolk Defender*—the vessel that he'd been asked to keep secret—was a commercial cargo ship that never seemed to come up on marine tracking services or even on radar. It had just docked at Berbera, where vehicles and equipment had been offloaded and driven south. They had traveled through the Sheikh Mountains and through the town of Sheikh itself, before turning off the road some ten miles short of the next town, Burco, and disappearing into the desert. There'd also been mention in Burco of distant rumbles, like rockets or aircraft taking off, but no one had seen anything. No one had risked getting close to the vehicles or attempted to follow them into the desert for fear of being shot at, either by their occupants or by armed men that Samakab had stationed at various intervals along the way.

He was also keeping an eye on the US Navy base at Norfolk. Private investigators had been hired through trusted Somali friends in Toronto to keep a watch on the *Norfolk Defender* every time it docked and to trace anyone who disembarked. Their instructions were simply to befriend anyone they could and send any information on them, however irrelevant it might seem, as an encrypted message to an email address. He'd had Troy King followed for a while, but was drawing a blank there. The man seemed to be a loner without a life other than going to the office every day via the deli, boozing in a bar after work and then returning home to a small apartment and watching TV all evening. There was just the rare call to an address in Walla Walla, where his wife lived, but other than that, he was another dead end. He'd never been able to trace Gerald Shanning or the location of the Weatherman Project. He'd tried and failed to have his phone calls traced, and this was a continuing source of frustration.

He knew he didn't have enough information to play hard-ball with Shanning on this call, but maybe he didn't have to. After all, Shanning was asking him what he wanted. It was clear that Shanning could not afford to disrupt the Weatherman Project, for whatever reason, and Samakab's cooperation had become crucial to either Shanning's position or the success of the project. Which was it? Both, maybe? He needed to find out what the Weatherman Project was. He needed a little time to think about that, and to work out a plan.

"Let me call you back on that. I have a lot on my plate right now, and I have a charity gala to attend this evening." *Play it cool.*

"Tomorrow, then?" Shanning didn't sound so confident now.

"Certainly. Oh, and how are you enjoying this ridge of high pressure we seem to be experiencing these days?"

"I'll call again tomorrow." The line went dead. Samakab sent an SMS. The reply came back: still too short. *Never mind, I think I'll have you tomorrow.* Samakab smiled and called his office in Somalia.

CHAPTER 28

David checked the window again—for the tenth time that night. The driveway was clear, but he'd heard a sound an hour or so earlier. Maybe it was just a cat, but he couldn't be sure. He checked the neighbor's tree—a laburnum in full bloom. It was hard to see the house beyond, and he wasn't sure if he was being watched. He closed the blind, ensuring that it fitted as close to the window frame as possible, all the way round. He couldn't see much in the darkness, but he didn't dare put the light on. He knocked his hand on the edge of the bedside table. *Damn!* There was a small flashlight on it for exactly this kind of situation. Grabbing the flashlight, he got into bed and pulled the bedclothes over himself, being careful to lay them gently on top of his body, rather than letting the sheets slide over any exposed skin. Knees, knuckles and elbows were particularly vulnerable. Switching the flashlight on, he located the part of his hand that had hit the table. No damage. The skin was still intact. He switched the flashlight off and carefully returned it to the bedside table. His head itched. He hadn't washed since he'd left—where was it?—he couldn't remember. He knew he couldn't scratch his head, so he let it itch. He'd forced himself to put up with the constant irritation. His whole body stank, and so did his clothes, but he couldn't risk pulling the T-shirt off, or sliding his underpants down, so he'd found cumbersome but safe ways to work around problems like going to the toilet. His stench was okay. At least it wasn't *that* stench, and the stronger he smelled, the more it prevented the possibility of that other smell re-surfacing. He knew the smell was still inside him, in his lungs, his stomach—it had invaded his whole body and there was nothing he could do to expel it from his system. He felt so tired, but sleep wasn't an option. He'd tried that and regretted it. Sleep brought pictures and sounds and nightmare video loops into his mind, repeating over and over again. He wasn't sure if he was alone. Was there someone in the room? If he stood up, would he slip on something slimy? Would the floor be silent when he put his weight on his feet, or would it crunch and burst and emit suffocating fumes? He preferred the hardwood floor. He had started to trust it, but had pushed the woolen bedside mats up against the wall using a lamp stand, so he wouldn't have to touch them. He couldn't stand their texture, and the fine hairs that could so easily become detached and get under his fingernails. He picked up a small mirror he kept on the bedside table and very carefully leaned over the edge of the bed, holding it down near the floor. Shining the flashlight into the mirror so that as he moved it from side to side, he was able to safely check underneath. *All clear, good.*

Somewhere in his mind he knew this was all wrong, but he seemed to have lost the capacity to section that part off—the part that was running amok—in order to create some perspective. On the other hand, it seemed perfectly natural to be cautious. He had to protect himself, after all, and take precautions. Surely he was just being sensible, responsible. Barbara was taking so many risks out there, and what about Josh? If he didn't go and check on him every now and then, who knows what danger he could be in? Really, Barbara was so irresponsible with her cavalier attitude to safety. *Better check on Josh.*

He carefully extracted himself from under the bedclothes, arranging the sheets in a position that would allow him to slip back into bed with minimum disruption. Positioning himself lower down the bed so as to avoid the sharp corners of the bedside table—he wasn't going to take *that* risk again—he tentatively lowered his feet to the floor. It felt alright, so he stood up. He'd also discovered that if he lifted each foot up vertically in order to take each step, he reduced the risk of abrasion or worse. The thought of touching the wooden floor with the bones of his feet exposed made him feel nauseous, but it was so important to check on Josh that he'd repeated this risky action several times that night already. He walked to the door and grasped the handle, checking, as he turned it, that his joints were holding up to the strain and not flying apart. The first time he'd done this, he'd felt sure that the bones in his fingers and wrist would dislocate, leaving his hand limp and helpless. He'd worked out that, if that happened, he could use his elbow to push the handle down. But everything seemed to be working okay so far. The door opened, his hand was still working. This was the most strenuous action he had tried, other than throwing the shoulder bag at that man—was it Troy?—when he'd experienced a strange surge of energy and anger. But it had passed and, afterwards, he'd felt so panic-stricken that he'd retreated as quickly as he could, back to his room, where he could think clearly again.

"Josh." He was so glad to see him lying there in his crib. "It's okay, you're safe." David smiled and leaned over his son, peering at his little sleeping face, trying to make out his features in the light of the dimly lit room. He looked at the position of the blanket. *She's been in here! She's moved the blanket! How could she? Doesn't she know what that can do?* He took a tissue from a box by the crib to cover his hand as he carefully lifted the blanket off Josh and checked underneath. There was no blood and Josh seemed to be peaceful. David breathed a sigh of relief and laid the blanket back down. "My little ace in the hole," he said. *Where did that come from?* He wasn't sure how long he'd been in this place, or even why he was here, but he knew Barbara and Josh—or, at least, he was learning to know them. Barbara seemed to know him fairly well, and on the odd occasion that their paths crossed, she asked him if he remembered things, such as where he'd left his car keys. Did they have a car? Had he driven one? He couldn't remember. Some things she said made sense, and he was convinced that he did remember them, but he just couldn't piece them all together. They were isolated memories that inhabited separated parts of his brain. "My little ace in the hole." He said it again and a distant connection was made in his mind. He tried to grasp it but, like a dream, it evaporated like a morning mist. This was happening more frequently now, and it made him angry with frustration. "My little ace in the hole." This time he said it with more deliberation, slowly, as if to delay the flight of its hidden meaning back into the ethers. Still no result. "My little ace in the hole!" he shouted, and suddenly realized that he was still standing over Josh. He put his hand over his mouth.

"David?" Barbara was standing in the doorway, wrapped in her robe. David swung round and stared at her, wide-eyed.

"My little ace in the hole," he said again, and then again, before he burst out crying and collapsed onto the floor. He was frightened and helpless, and Barbara was rushing toward him. "No!" He put his hand up to stop her touching his skin, but she grabbed his arm, fell onto him and held him tightly. "Oh, God, help me, help me!" he wept, and struggled, all the time looking at his arms and hands, trying to limit the damage Barbara must be doing, trying to keep his body intact. But there was no damage, and that made him even more confused and frightened. Eventually, weak and exhausted, he gave way. Barbara held him in her arms till the first shafts of sunlight made their way through the bedroom window. David dreamed peaceful dreams for the first time in an eternity, and slowly—ever so slowly—his crippled mind started to mend.

✳✳✳

"PTSD," said Dr Ruben, when Barbara called him, having tried and failed to get David to leave the house and go with her to the clinic just half a mile away. "David is suffering from Post-traumatic Stress Disorder," he said. "It could require years of therapy, an extensive program of drugs and a lot of patience." He adopted a conciliatory tone and said, "You may have to consider the possibility that David might be intellectually and emotionally scarred forever."

The longer he talked, the less reassured Barbara felt, and she was suspicious of the doctor's negative attitude. She hated the idea of David taking mind-altering drugs that could have unknown side effects, on top of all his other symptoms—violent moods, persistent re-experiencing, paranoia and emotional numbing-out. The symptoms themselves seemed to be evolving, in heart-breaking, disturbing ways. The day before, she'd found him minutely examining the leaves on their rubber plant, talking to them as if they were part of some vast social media network. *What had happened to her sane, loving husband?* She wanted him back and she needed a positive, lasting solution—not just a coping mechanism to help David get through the day. But this was a whole new subject for her and she had to learn about it fast.

She scoured the Internet, searching for natural therapies and treatments. Most sufferers of the disorder seemed to be children and adolescents who had been subjected to prolonged abuse—some of them in foster care—and war veterans. There was a publication, *The Post-Traumatic Gazette*, which was very informative, although it brought home to her just how horrific David's suffering was:

'As a person is traumatized, at least for the first time, the sense of personal safety is shattered. Two things start to happen immediately. The person will strive to survive using three available systems: fight, flight or freeze. What they called the reptile brain in highschool biology seems to take over and choose. Military training is designed to get soldiers to always choose fight, but they wouldn't have to train us to do that if we were natural born killers. Culture and religion often train women to freeze, to take it and endure. In nature, flight is most common. Simultaneously, while survival is at stake, feelings will shut down and information taken in and processed will become focused so the person can do **whatever it takes to survive.***'*

She found several forums for vets who talked about Vietnam and Iraq but they all sounded like pharmaceutical horror stories. Alpha-adrenergic agonists, anti-convulsants, mood stabilizers, heterocyclic and tricyclic anti-depressants, glucocorticoids, monoamine-oxidase inhibitors—even the names sounded frightening and wrong to Barbara. And they just managed the symptoms; they didn't cure anything. There was even a suggestion that monoamine-oxidase, more commonly known as ecstasy, could be used in conjunction with psychotherapy. Psychotherapeutic interventions seemed to be a more constructive approach to treatment, although many seemed to be open-ended, rather vague in their methodologies and varied in the results they achieved. One of them—exposure therapy—which involved the patient being stimulated to re-experience the traumatic memories, seemed brutal and potentially damaging, although it had apparently worked for some.

But what she feared the most was the psychological effects on David—and Josh's safety, should David turn against him. She wondered if she was capable of recognizing all the possible symptoms and working with him through the flashes of extreme anger sparked by the simplest of communications. Earlier that day, she'd asked him if he knew where the garlic press was.

"How would I fucking know where the sodding garlic press is? Haven't you got anything more important to think about than a bloody garlic press?" Then, turning his attention to the back door, he shouted, "Did you lock the door when you came in? You didn't, did you? And Josh is sitting on the floor in there. Anything could happen!" Rushing over to the door, he'd bolted and locked it.

"David, Josh is fine. I checked on him just two minutes ago," she gently reassured him, praying that he could hear her and would calm down. David held onto the door bolt, breathing raggedly, confused and disoriented by the emotion surging inside him. Then he disappeared back into the spare bedroom and didn't come out again for two hours. Barbara's heart sank as she heard the door shut behind him. She had to keep her emotions in check and her mind clear, despite the pressures. She was acutely aware of her own feelings and how they could—and had already started to—change toward him. Would she remember, in the months or years ahead, that his deep depressions and withdrawal were all part of the PTSD and not just a bad mood she might react to with anger? Even in these early days, she was thinking of his periods of withdrawal as opportunities to look after Josh or do some housework. *How appalling! No, I most definitely do not look forward to his silent suffering!* And how would she cope with the abrupt changes of mood that took her by surprise every time? How would she reassure him, over and over again, in his moments of hypervigilance, that they were safe and secure and there was no danger lurking? If he re-experienced the trauma, due to some simple incident in a shopping mall, or on a beach holiday somewhere, how would she look after him and Josh at the same time? How long would it be before they were able to re-connect with each other, in loving, meaningful ways? Could she handle it?

To Barbara, it was hard to tell which was worse—the condition or the treatment. What also confused her was the fact that, before this, David had suffered no profoundly traumatic events in his life—as far as she knew. He had only been away for five days in Los Angeles on a training course where someone had had an accident and died. Even though it must have been extremely distressing, the effect on David seemed to be out of all proportion. Maybe there was something in his mental makeup that made him particularly susceptible to this kind of shock, but her gut feeling told her that he was a normal, healthy man with a young and robust constitution. Or maybe there was more to Troy King's story than he would have her believe. Whatever had happened to David, it was now dawning on her that his road to recovery was going to be a long one, and the chances of a full recovery appeared to be slim. She would have to brace herself for a different life than the one she'd envisaged, if she chose to stay with him. As soon as that thought came into her mind, she was shocked to see that she'd already introduced an 'if' into the mix. 'If' had never ever entered her wildest dreams or most difficult moments before, and her recognition of it engendered a new resolve in her: to fight this and win. She was determined to keep her family together. She thought she'd been ready 'for better or for worse', but who really thinks, on their wedding day, how 'worse' could manifest? She knew that if she succumbed to self-pity, their lives would fall apart.

Returning to the UK was the easiest option. There, at least, she would have the support of family and close friends. She had two dependents now, and she was going to need help. The impact of moving would be significant—at least in the short term. Now that David's career was indefinitely on hold, although it would probably be financially easier to remain in the US to avail of the compensation that she could claim, everything in her said go. Leave this country and don't get embroiled in dealing with insurance claims or taking action against Arlington Online. Don't get absorbed by the medical machine and risk losing the David she knew and loved, forever. She could see herself years down the road, fuming in isolation, frustrated by professional responsibility-avoidance tactics, tortured by long, drawn-out legal proceedings and drowning in paperwork. This wasn't a country where powerful organizations willingly and generously faced their responsibilities and would make things easy for her. Saving face and saving money were much more important to them. And she wasn't going be fooled into taking part in that process through some stage-managed PR event followed by a mean-minded and limited settlement with conditions. No, she was more interested in re-building her life with David and Josh, if that was possible, and that would take all her energy and more. Better to accept a drop in living standards and take back control.

If she moved back to the UK, though, she would be turning her back on some of the best help that Josh could get, especially during his crucial, early development, here in Washington. But she told herself that she was underestimating the power of her own love for her child, and that was, after all, what would help him more than anything. And there was something that David had said that same day, during one of his more lucid moments, as he stood in his favorite place next to Josh's crib: "At least he's safe. He's fine." Barbara could see, in David's watery eyes, a sad envy of this tiny little person. For all the disadvantages that he would face in the world with his Down syndrome, for all his susceptibility to different illnesses, for all the learning difficulties he was destined to have, Josh would never go through whatever David was going through. Josh would be loved, and would love everyone around him in equal measure. An innocent, gentle light in a diseased world.

CHAPTER 29

Samakab was in a more sober mood when he returned to his hotel. His conversation with Shanning, as he was about to leave for the gala, had sparked distant memories—disturbing memories that he thought he had resolved long ago. The charity gala he'd attended that evening had re-awakened a deep-seated anger in him, adding to his discomfort. He'd been invited to attend to help raise funds to combat the recruitment of child soldiers in Somalia and neighboring Kenya.

The technical term for the condition of his homeland was a 'failed State'. To him, the words sounded sterile, a convenient phrase that masked the devastation with terms that were almost 'reasonable' and acceptable. It said nothing of the brutal reality of Somalia. Who better to talk about that than the young people who had spoken that evening, much to the discomfort of the rich and self-satisfied who showered them with praise, applause and the odd tear before writing a check and returning home in their limos? Plucked from the madness and delivered, wide-eyed, confused and emotionally numbed to the glitzy hotel on Fifth Avenue, these three children offered a snapshot of a life that few in that room could comprehend. The last of the three children to speak was a gangly young boy, freshly turned out in a Gap outfit.

"Hello, my name is Liibaan." The presenter translated for him and held his arm as he squinted in the glare of the stage lighting.

"And how old are you, Liibaan?" she continued, translating to Liibaan as she went.

"Fourteen." Another young boy and a girl stood nervously next to him, holding hands.

"Fourteen? Well, you're a fine young man, Liibaan. And where are you from?"

"Wajir." Liibaan covered his eyes against the light. A rather rotund man sitting at the same table as Samakab ordered another bottle of wine from a passing waiter. Samakab gestured to him to pay attention to what was happening on the stage.

"Wajir. Thank you, Liibaan." Turning to the audience, she explained, "Wajir, ladies and gentlemen, is in Kenya, not Somalia." Turning back to Liibaan, she asked, "So tell me, Liibaan, why were you in Somalia, near Mogadishu, when our staff found you by the roadside?"

"I was fighting, but I was shot so I couldn't fight any more."

"You were shot?" the presenter, turned to the audience. "Who shot you?"

"I don't know. Some soldiers…" his words trailed off to a mumble. Liibaan shuffled his feet and turned his head away from the audience. The presenter decided the audience had heard enough horror stories from the other two children and didn't need to add to this young boy's distress by insisting that he continue his story.

"Thank you, Liibaan. Now just sit down over there, will you?" An assistant shepherded the three children to chairs at the back of the stage. Turning to the audience again, the presenter continued, "It's hard to believe, ladies and gentlemen, that these three beautiful young children are death machines, trained to kill by al-Shabaab, which has been linked to the world's most wanted terrorist—Osama bin Laden. Many poor Kenyans have been lured to enlist with al-Shabaab by the promise of riches that none of them ever see. None of them are interested in their ideology. None of them understand why they are fighting. Al-Shabaab trains them in guerrilla tactics, the use of deadly weapons, assassination, intelligence collection and the use of improvised explosive devices. Some have spent up to three years fighting in the jungles of Somalia. Many Kenyan children, just like these three, have joined the violent movement, which has imposed a form of Sharia law in parts of Somalia, where it rules ruthlessly. The militants like to use children because they are easy to brainwash and don't ask questions." She paused and turned toward the three children. "Ladies and gentlemen, it deeply saddens me to tell you that the recruitment of children like these three is on the increase. Some are as young as nine. And, of course, they are not just from Kenya. Many are from central and southern Somalia. Some join because they have been orphaned by the war, separated from their families, abandoned or left to roam the streets—easy targets for the recruiters. But they are not even safe in their family homes. Recruiters have even been known to kill parents who try to prevent their child from being taken. The number of bases and camps used to train these children is large and constantly growing. Once in these camps, the children are brainwashed with radical ideas by evil men with a violent agenda."

The presenter went on to explain how too little was being done to protect the children. Heads nodded sagely, hands covered mouths as horrific examples of abuse, violence and death were described. The wealthy, well-meaning audience listened or chatted quietly, sipped their wine or passed the petit-fours. To Samakab, of course, this was old news, as it was for many present. The subject had been reported for several years in the press and on TV, all over the world. As he looked around the tables, all Samakab could see was the 'charity fatigue' that had set in. Demands for charity were ever-present in the lives of people in New York—from the bum on the street and the NGO at the supermarket exit, to the endless letters falling into the mailboxes of homes in the 'right' areas. Efforts like this gala seemed, to him, increasingly futile. Money and soldiers were all most governments seemed capable of offering. Lengthy reports and technical support programs were churned out by the UN, leaving NGOs to deal with some of the worst and most risky aspects of conflict on the ground. All the individual efforts were laudable in their own ways, yet cumulatively they did little to stop the pain, and many had withdrawn from Somalia when it became too dangerous for foreigners—especially whites. Something much more fundamental had to change before the shattered ruins of his country could be pieced together again.

Despite his raw upbringing and warlike-conditioning, and despite the fact that he gained his considerable wealth by illegal and often violent means, now that the pressure to survive had been lifted from him, Samakab's aggressive, devious nature was being infiltrated by new feelings, new desires, new thoughts and ideas.

The telephone rang at his bedside as he arrived back at his suite.

"Samakab?"

"Yes."

"Did you think about my offer?"

"Yes, I did." Samakab sat down on the bed. "Mr Shanning, what exactly do you think you can offer that will be of any interest to me?" His previous conversation with Shanning had made it clear that there was more at stake for Shanning than mere money, and the intelligence he was getting from his various contacts suggested that something big was going on. He had a growing feeling that his cooperation was pivotal to its success. All he had to do now was tease some more information out of Shanning, and then decide what he really wanted to do.

Shanning was quiet for a minute, then said, "Am I right in thinking, Mr Samakab, that this isn't about money?"

"As you know, I have plenty, and with the help you have already given me, I can get as much of that as any man could possibly want. And now that I have it, I am less interested in having more. I'm beginning to think that quality of life is more important to me now, and I doubt that you can deliver that for me."

"Are you asking for US citizenship?" Shanning was fishing. He had no idea where Samakab was going with this conversation, and that made him feel uncomfortable.

"Ha, that's funny!" Samakab retorted, sarcastically. "Empty status, Mr Shanning. What would I want that for? To waste my days in a California mansion while Homeland Security keep tabs on everything I do and the IRS recover most of the money you gave me? Really, Mr Shanning, you insult me. But then, I suppose that, in your arrogance, you thought I could be easily bought. After all, I'm just a stupid African—a black man who wants to join a white man's yacht club. Is that what you thought?"

"Well, you seemed happy with the arrangement—"

"Until you turned it into a dangerous farce," Samakab cut in, "with your stupid intelligence man and his dumb stories about videos on the Internet. Maybe we can start there. You want to know what I want? An explanation that checks out and makes sense. That would be a good start. And then, perhaps, you can tell me of any other security leaks you have caused, or are we going to see the whole story on TV someday soon?"

"You know I can't do that. I cannot discuss matters of national security with—"

"National security?" Samakab laughed. "This isn't about national security, Mr Shanning. It's about *your* security. Now, tell me about King. What was that really about? And remember, Mr Shanning, that *you* broke the agreement, not me. As of this moment, I have instructed my people to end the protection of that area of land and remove your personnel and equipment back to Berbera. I only hope that your ship is still capable of loading the equipment, as I understand that there was an accident when the last consignment was unloaded, and the crane was damaged."

"You cannot do that." Shanning's tone shifted. Samakab sensed his bluff had worked. Shanning had to think quickly. He could easily repel an attack on the base by Somali fighters, but he'd have to deploy AVTOL to do the job. The last thing he wanted was to attract attention to the base in that way. The arrangement he'd originally made with Samakab had required minimal security on the ground. By minimizing the number of personnel who had direct contact with AVTOL, he'd hoped to avoid any security leaks. Because AVTOL was miles from any habitation, behind the Sheikh Mountains, and there were no flight paths over it, there'd been no need for a secured area, which would have meant constructing something and attracting unwanted attention. It was also the perfect location for test flights, with many of the trouble spots to be targeted—including the Democratic Republic of Congo and Afghanistan—within AVTOL's range. And it was a location that, by agreement with Russia and China, would not be photographed by satellites while AVTOL was there. So it was well-hidden for very little effort and cost.

"Why not?"

"Your men would be in grave danger. They would all be killed."

"None of my men expect to live very long and, while I am paying them, they are not starving to death. They know that's the choice they have. You see, unlike you, while we are not experts at saving face, we are experts in survival. When survival in this world isn't an option, we prefer to die with honor and be welcomed into the next."

"I'm not interested in your religious philosophy. I'm only interested in protecting the Weatherman Project and I will do everything in my considerable power to do so. Don't believe for a minute that I do not mean what I say."

Shanning spat out his words.

"In that case, once you had done your dirty work, I would invite the world's press to come and take a look."

"Oh, this is ridiculous!" Shanning let out a tense laugh. "Here we are, fighting like kids in a schoolyard, when we both have so much more to gain if we cooperate. Look, I understand that the incident with King gave you cause for concern, but short of giving you his head on a plate, I'm not sure what more I can do to reassure you that I have dealt with him. Time will show that this is true, so I suggest we leave that incident behind, we honor our agreement and we reap the rewards that it will bring us both. There's no point in killing the goose that lays the golden egg, is there?"

"Not good enough, Mr Shanning." Samakab felt a surge of excitement. "The only way I will continue with this is as a full partner. That is the only way I can be certain that security is dealt with properly. You must understand that without that confidence, I cannot continue."

"Let me suggest something that I think you will find acceptable. Call your men off, and I will agree to have one of your representatives stationed at the site and one on the ship—as long as they agree to abide by certain conditions and I can remove either or both of them at my sole discretion. Any person present on the project is, naturally, subject to minute scrutiny, so we can begin this process immediately on receipt of the names of the two you recommend." To Samakab, this sounded like a prepared speech.

"Very well. Let's do that, for the time being. We can talk about the conditions of partnership later. My men will arrive at the base tomorrow, first thing, and at the port the following day."

"But I said—"

"These men have my complete confidence. I would trust them with my life. That's good enough for me."

"Very well." Shanning knew that he had been outmaneuvered and had no choice but to acquiesce to Samakab's demands. He also knew that his position in the project had just become very tenuous, partly because he assumed that Samakab's men would have had time to trace the call this time.

"I'll call my men."

"Yes, please do." The line went dead. Shanning sat in the silence of his office, blankly looking at the wall. Minutes later, he lurched into action again and contacted Captain Baptiste and the AVTOL base commander on the secure system to give them strict instructions on dealing with the new arrivals they were about to receive.

We have an address, the message read on Samakab's cell phone. *Good*, thought Samakab, *and we have a lot more than that now, as well.*

He had two calls to make.

"Raage, *subax wanaagsan*." *Raage, good morning*. "My friend, I need you to do something. You're in Burco, yes? Good. I want you to go to the base you are guarding. Take the SUV and get the men based in Sheikh to follow you in the truck. It's okay, they won't shoot at you. Trust me. I just want them to see the truck full of armed men, but there must be no fighting. Understand? Only take your most trusted men. No slip-ups. You will be staying at the base on your own, as my representative, so pack a bag. Once you are in, send the men away again and tell them to get on with their usual patrol schedule. Find out what's going on at the base and call me on my cell every day with whatever you discover. I will be available around the clock. If they don't cooperate or treat you well, just call me. And Raage, the SUV has a false floor, doesn't it? Okay, there's something else I need you to take with you." Samakab had finished giving his instructions within five minutes. Then he dialed another number.

"Kaahin, *subax wanaagsan*. How is your family? Good. And your son, is he still studying as I told him he should? Good, that's wonderful. Yes, Ayan is well. He and a friend are taking a short holiday together. Kaahin, I have something I want you to do. Have you ever been to Berbera, on the north coast? I need you to be there in two days. Pack a bag. You'll be away for a while. Take the HiLux 4x4 at my house. I'll explain when you get under way. And, Kaahin, stay safe."

Chapter 30

David felt strangely out of place in Tunbridge Wells. To be sitting on the sofa in the living room of the home where he grew up, with Josh on his knee, felt really odd. Better to not think about it. Zone out. He'd learned to do that well in the past few days. It seemed to be the only way to cope with all the sudden activity. Barbara had gone manic once she'd decided to leave Alcova Heights. She'd become obsessed with organizing things—canceling the electricity, turning off the gas, getting the mail re-directed, shopping, booking flights, getting the car fixed, selling stuff by the roadside, clearing cupboards, packing boxes. He thought it would never end. And then some guys came around to the house, took all the boxes away and all they were left with was the tatty old furniture that had been there when they arrived, and a few suitcases. Thank goodness he'd been there to look after Josh! Who knows what would have happened if he'd left her to look after him. He'd held him close every day as people came and went and moved things all over the house. Once, both the back door and the front door were not only unlocked but wide open. It was terrifying! He'd rushed into the bathroom with Josh, bolted the door from the inside, put Josh carefully in the bath and closed the shower curtain while he listened at the door. He was ready. Just let them try anything!

Luckily, his skin was alright and so was Josh's. Maybe they were both getting stronger. He was glad to be rid of the itching, but it had been really stressful when Barbara had bullied him into getting undressed and into the bath. That was really frightening, but he had to do it or Barbara wouldn't let him hold Josh anymore, so he'd steeled himself and found that he could let her wash him as long as she didn't use anything abrasive on his skin. She'd shown him each part of his body in the mirror, as she'd washed it, so he could see there was no damage.

"More tea, David?" Margaret, his mother, was leaning over him. *Damn, I wish she wouldn't wear that perfume. It stinks! Why does she want to choke everyone within six feet of her?* "David?"

"No. No thanks, Mum." David leaned away from her, holding Josh close to his chest to prevent the noxious fumes from reaching his tender nose.

"What on earth are you watching, David?" His mother looked disapprovingly at the large TV in the corner.

"Nothing." It was QVC, turned up loud. She had listened from the kitchen for three hours as advertorials trumpeted the benefits of a slew of products that she couldn't imagine anyone actually buying. David watched each one, expressionless, only looking away when Josh moved or woke up. Whenever

Josh cried, David didn't seem to know what to do with him.

"Here, David, let me take him," she said, cautiously trying to gauge his mood. She was never sure how he would react to her approach. He could be completely passive and hardly notice her or he could flare up and shout foul abuse. Luckily, this time, he was more interested in a laser-powered fishing device that was sure to be the next big thing in course fishing and wasn't on sale in the shops but could be bought via QVC at a super-knock-down price with some very tempting extras thrown in, but just for a limited period—so you'd better hurry and order now. "I'll just take him into the garden for some fresh air," she said, as she lifted Josh onto her hip.

"No, not the garden," David said, without taking his eyes off the fisherman who swore that this was the only way to fish and every other product out there was just a waste of time and not worth the postage.

"I'll just take him into the kitchen, then. Is that alright, dear?"

"Don't open the window."

"I won't." Margaret smiled down at Josh, who landed a gentle punch on her cheek. "Are you interested in fishing, David? Maybe you and Dad could go down to the river together. I'm sure you'd like that, and it would be a nice for you to have a chat with Dad."

"Jesus, Mum, you know I have absolutely no interest in fishing. It's fucking moronic."

Margaret fled to the kitchen. She was tight with pain—anger and hurt swelling up, hurling themselves around her head, sometimes breaking out, but only when she was alone or with Roger. Barbara had briefed her and Roger on David's condition, but although they knew when to react and when to keep quiet, it didn't make things any easier for them. Roger was determined to "get to the bottom of this" and "make those responsible do something about it", in his usual aggressively protective paternalistic way, but he had no idea where to start. Barbara urged him not to get involved. She didn't want him shouting down the phone at Troy King, frothing at the mouth on a rant that would get him nowhere. She'd already explained that she'd chosen not to take legal action, and pleaded with Roger to restrain himself and to help David and Josh by providing a safe and happy environment. Roger had agreed, reluctantly, but he still seethed at the injustice done to his son, and the complete lack of a satisfactory explanation for it. Thank God he had a demanding job in the City to distract him during the week. This weekend, though, his peaceful home in leafy Culverden Down had become a battlefield of wits and self-control. He tried to dance around David's fragile emotions, but sometimes he thought he might blow a fuse, so he'd decided to do some gardening. He jabbed the trowel into the roots of a peony. *Damn!* Looking up at the kitchen window, he saw Margaret gently swaying Josh back to sleep as she filled the kettle with her free hand. She saw him and waved to him to come into the kitchen.

"What now?" he mumbled to himself. In the past, a wave from the kitchen had always been the signal for lunch, a tea break, a glass of wine or some freshly-baked morsel. Now it rang alarm bells. Approach with caution. He's done something, he's upset someone, Josh is screaming the place down and David's falling apart. Before, he'd approach the kitchen with flowers or a freshly-picked vegetable, now he marched with resolve and a serious demeanor, primed for a problem.

"What's up, Mags?" he said, as he pushed his boots off at the door.

"Nothing at all. I was just making some tea and I thought you might like some." Roger relaxed his shoulders and sat down at the breakfast bar overlooking the lawn.

"I'm going to have to cut that vine back on the pergola. At the rate it's going, we won't be able to get into it to sit there in the summer."

"Do you think we will?"

"What?"

"Be able to sit out there in the summer?" Margaret poured the tea and handed Roger a mug. Josh dribbled over her shoulder as she sat down.

"Of course we will… Of course we will," Roger insisted. "Is he still watching that bloody shopping channel?" Margaret nodded. Roger turned toward the door. "Hey, David, come and get Josh, will you? Mum's having a cuppa with me." Margaret shot him a look of concern. "He's got to come back into the real world sometime, dear." There was no response from the living room. "David!"

"Shh! You'll wake Josh," Margaret protested.

"Darling, this isn't going to be easy whatever way we do it, but if we keep avoiding the problems, it will take a darn sight longer to get to the solutions." He tried again. "David! Come in here, please." He took a sip of tea and glanced at Margaret over his mug as David appeared in the doorway.

"Where's Barbara?" David asked.

"She's out shopping. Back soon, dear," Margaret replied.

"But she never told me…" Neither of his parents was sure, at times like this, whether to reassure him or to just tell the truth. Barbara always let David know what she was doing, even though David often argued endlessly over some small, scary detail. He simply couldn't remember things or rationalize the simplest of situations, so the tendency was to make every effort to reassure him, even tell white lies occasionally. But no one was sure if this was just putting off his recovery and adding more confusion to his mind. Margaret preferred to 'keep everyone happy', at any cost. She couldn't bear confrontations. Roger had been her protector ever since they'd got married. He'd risen through the ranks of his firm using a mixture of bullishness and straight-talking, arriving at the top by way of a seamless path that would appear as a 45-degree line if it were plotted on a graph. He never questioned the way he did things, and he applied his business philosophy at home as well. To him, a soft and sensitive approach to David's recovery would just keep him stuck. At the same time, he realized he was dealing with an unbalanced mind and he wasn't sure how to tackle that kind of weakness—especially in his son. Aware of his dilemma, Margaret usually tried to handle things. While Roger hid behind his mug of tea, gulping it down with focused attention, she spoke soothingly to David.

"That's my fault, dear. She went early and told me to mention it to you when you got up. I forgot. I'm sorry."

"That's okay. Thanks, anyway," David replied, much to his parents' relief. Roger jumped at the opportunity to keep a dialogue going.

"David, could you give me a hand in the garden for a few minutes? Mum will look after Josh, and you'll be able to see him through the window."

David stood in the doorway, looking at his feet, saying nothing.

"Look, it's no problem. I just thought you might like to get out into the fresh air for a bit, and we could have a chat." David was churning inside. What could he possibly talk about with his father? What did he want to know? Was it some sort of trap? Why did he want to get him away from Josh? A memory flashed through his head—his father, pushing him on the swing when he was about seven years old. He'd lost his balance and fallen, breaking his arm. It was his fault! It was all too much. He drifted back into the living room, sat down again on the sofa and picked up the TV remote. He aimlessly flicked through the channels and stopped at the coverage of a House of Commons debate. He liked the neat green rows of leather-covered benches and the random movements of people as they walked in and out, or stood up to speak.

The Speaker was bringing the House to order for question time as David studied the layout of the chamber. *"Order, order. Questions to the Secretary of State for Foreign and Commonwealth Affairs."* The Secretary of State stood and laid an open file on the dispatch box.

"I regularly discuss piracy off the coast of Somalia in both bilateral and multilateral meetings. Recent discussions took place in the Yemen conference in February and the EU Foreign Ministers' Meeting in January of this year." He sat down again, awaiting the first question. Frank Boyle, a silver-haired barrel-chested opposition back-bencher from the industrial north of England was the first in line. Speaking without notes in a strong Yorkshire accent, he barked his question in the manner of someone expecting an inadequate answer.

"Is the Minister aware that attacks on merchant vessels in the Gulf of Aden have quadrupled in recent months and that the level of successful attacks and hijackings of merchant ships in the Indian Ocean, in the region of the Minicoy Islands, in particular, has also increased to epidemic levels? Can he assure us that

the government is doing everything in its power to prevent these attacks, and will the Minister please inform the House what measures are being taken?" Boyle sat down amid shouts of approval from the opposition benches. The Secretary of State rose to his feet.

"The Honorable Member makes a very good point. The government is fully aware of the urgency of the situation as regards piracy off the Somali coast and has paid great attention to the recent escalation of this activity in the Indian Ocean. At the Yemen conference, we agreed far-reaching measures to ensure that attempts to launder money though Dubai, in particular, are stopped. Money gained through piracy and other illegal means, and transferred through the informal hawala system, shall be vigorously investigated and stopped, where possible.

"The Honorable Member will also be aware that our government is providing a frigate to support Operation ATALANTA, the EU Naval Force Somalia operation that is already having great success in its mission to protect World Food Program vessels in the region. This operation was launched in 2008 in support of United Nations Security Council resolutions 1814, 1816, 1838 and 1846. Those who have registered to avail of the protection it offers have seen a significant decrease in pirate attacks, loss of capital equipment and cargo, and human distress. Furthermore, Mr Speaker, we are working tirelessly with our counterparts in Kenya and the Seychelles, in particular, to help bolster their judicial systems to ensure that the attraction that piracy currently has, for many, is effectively and permanently removed."

Boyle couldn't wait to get to his feet.

"Thank you, Mr Speaker. Surely this is yet another example of an issue of grave international concern that has been dealt with by this government in its usual lackadaisical manner. I put it to the Secretary of State that this government has done far too little, far too late. It dragged its feet in committing to playing a responsible part in support of operation ATALANTA. Since 2008, our intelligence services at Northwood have indeed provided an excellent service—but much of it has been to support naval vessels belonging to The Netherlands, France, Spain, Norway, Belgium, Germany and even Greece, as well as aircraft supplied by Portugal, Spain, Germany and France. Why, Mr Speaker, does it take this country three years to decide to send one single frigate to the area when our own national interests are as much at stake as those of the other participating countries?" Members on the Government front bench smiled and muttered comments among themselves at Boyle's performance, as those behind them waved order papers and shouted at Boyle to sit down. Boyle remained standing.

"Furthermore, this government's efforts to deal with the legal position have been ad hoc and completely uncoordinated, leaving the Kenyan and Seychelles judicial systems reeling under the weight of dealing with the problem. In rejecting the idea of forming an international tribunal to put these pirates on trial, they have

passed the responsibility for developing a regional prosecution centre to the Seychelles, who are hard pressed to find the resources to do so. In practical terms, the pirates are protected in their racketeering in a number of ways. For instance, in demanding and being paid ransoms, they are not breaking any laws. It is only when they spend the money that it can be regarded as the proceeds of a crime. Also, in using fishing boats to carry out their hijackings, they are within their rights to roam the seas at will, looking for targets miles out in the ocean, whether or not they have any ice on board to ensure that any fish they may catch isn't high before they get back to port."

Cries of *"hear, hear"* echoed around him as the government benches quietened down and paid more attention.

"And how can the government have the audacity to boast about successes when it is clear that piracy that was once limited to two uncoordinated gangs of criminals—one in the north and one in the south of Somalia—who just used the proceeds to buy 4x4s and houses in Kenya, has now escalated to a whole new level. The huge increase in attacks would appear to be coordinated, efficient and well-equipped, extending far into the Indian Ocean. In case the Minister doesn't realize this, you can't take a small outboard fishing boat all the way to Minicoy from Puntland to pound a cargo ship or tanker with RPGs and AK47s. You need something a bit bigger and better equipped."

Boyle sat down.

"Can we move on—" The Speaker interjected. The Secretary of State jumped to his feet and caught The Speaker's eye.

"If I may, I would like to respond to the Honorable Member's question—if that's what it was. Our government is well aware of the concerns surrounding Somali piracy. We are, as I mentioned, working tirelessly with many of the stakeholders to put the strongest measures possible in place to address it."

"Rubbish!" someone shouted.

"Order, order!" The Speaker interjected again. The Secretary of State referred to his notes and waited for the jeers to subside before continuing.

"There is much debate around Europe as to how to deal with it, given the precarious position of the Transitional Federal Government of Somalia. The security issues have to be addressed alongside the needs for a more inclusive and representative government. The situation is also complicated by general instability in the wider region. Insurgency is rife and, as we speak, our presence in Somalia is limited to Mogadishu. I will be attending an extraordinary meeting, in two days' time, of foreign ministers from the EU as well as from the region in question, where we will be proposing far-reaching measures that will extend the capacity of the EU, in conjunction with NATO and the African Union, to deal with the situation beyond the confines of the Mogadishu area."

Guffaws of disbelief erupted from the opposition benches. It was only as he sat down that the Secretary of State realized the implications of what he had just said. He had spoken off the cuff and without proper forethought, and knew he was going to pay for it. Boyle pounced.

"Is the Secretary of State suggesting a military invasion? Are you planning to take us into a military commitment along the lines of the bungled US invasion of Iraq? Mr Speaker, I think this is the first any of us in this place have heard of this government's intention to make such a decision on behalf of the British people."

Pandemonium broke out on the benches.

"My, oh my…" David's attention was brought back into the room at the sound of his father, standing behind him with his mug of tea in his hand. "I don't believe it! This government…"

"What's up, Dad? I thought you, of all people, would want to put the Somali pirates in their place." David was suddenly lucid again.

"Yes, but there are two problems here, as I see it," Roger replied. "You have the pirates and then you have the Muslim insurgents who are keeping the country on its knees. I saw a report the other day that showed the prime minister of the country holed up in his fortified house, with people having to run the gauntlet of machine-gun fire to get to meetings with him. Unless they can address the political instability, they'll never stop the piracy—unless, God help us—we go in and police the country with tanks and aircraft. Either way, I fear we're going to see a lot of dead bodies littering the country."

Too much information. David's eyes glazed over and Roger knew he was gone again. "Where's Josh?"

"Your mother has him." David got up and went into the kitchen.

"Thanks for looking after him, Mum. I'll take him." He reached out and pulled Josh away from Margaret, returning to the sofa, where he sat and rocked him gently.

Roger went into the kitchen, where Margaret was fighting back tears. "He's using Josh like his own personal security blanket," he said, frowning as he looked back at David.

"That's alright, though, isn't it?" asked Margaret. "He's the only security he has, right now, and Josh is too young to understand what's going on."

"But for how long?" said Roger. "Does Barbara have any idea?"

"Not yet. She's doing all she can, and she still has things to sort out in the US. Once that's all settled, she plans to take him for therapy in London."

"Poor girl. She didn't bargain for this, did she?"

Chapter 31

Samakab drove across the Hudson River on the George Washington Bridge, through the New Jersey Turnpike, and followed the Interstate 80 Express to Hackensack. He made his way up Hudson Street, passing mile upon mile of small industrial units, DIY stores, shops and restaurants, eventually finding his way round the one-way system into State Street. This was a soulless street with anonymous office units and large, half-empty concrete parking lots. He passed various depressing buildings—the New Jersey Department of Labor, Vocational Rehabilitation Services and Unemployment Service Claims—before he reached a grey, three-story office block on a junction. If his tracking service was right, this was the one.

He parked his black BMW X6 in a parking bay. No company name was on display and no brass plaque was fixed to the pillar by the entrance. Glass doors led into a dingy reception area with beige, hessian-covered walls and old easy chairs. Cartons of printer paper were stacked next to the chairs and an old print of Andrew Wyeth's *Christina's World*, faded blue and pink by years of sunlight, hung pointlessly over a heavy, 1960s reception desk. A middle-aged woman, who looked Mexican, glanced up at Samakab as he entered.

"I'm here to see Mr Shanning," he said, handing her his business card.

"Is no Mr Shanning here, sorry," she replied, a little too quickly and without looking at his card.

"He's expecting me."

"Is no Mr Shanning here, sorry." She looked up at Samakab, who stared back at her, expressionless. "I will ask. Please sit." Samakab went and stood at the other end of the room. She picked up the telephone and mumbled something into the mouthpiece, glancing occasionally at him. She replaced the handset. Samakab stood and waited as she studiously avoided eye contact. After a few minutes, a door opened and a young man invited him to follow him. Neither man spoke as they took the lift to the third floor, where the doors opened into an open space. The entire floor area was covered with computer monitors on desks. Wires trailed across the floor or were loosely looped through straps supported by the struts that held the false ceiling in place. Many of the wires disappeared into a smoked glass-encased cubicle in the centre of the room, containing yet more computer equipment—a large black eight-foot-high unit. Arrays of tiny flashing LEDs inside it cast colored patches on the glass. Throughout the room, paint marks on the walls and ceiling and long, narrow gaps in the carpeting indicated that this was a hurriedly converted office suite, where little regard had been paid to aesthetics or design. Walls must have been ripped out and furniture and equipment moved in immediately. There was just one small office at the far end of the room, which looked more like a packing crate. It was roughly constructed in plywood held together with batons. A small window overlooked the main work area. The young man showed Samakab into the office and closed the door behind him.

"Welcome. I'm so glad you found us." Shanning was sitting behind a desk, in the only comfortable-looking chair Samakab had seen since his arrival. The office was a mess, piles of paper, reports and books covering every flat surface. A TV monitor was mounted on one wall with bolts that were angled down under its weight, looking as if it might topple at any moment. There was a small round table next to a water dispenser in one corner, with three office chairs placed around it.

"I wasn't expecting an invitation, so I thought I'd take the initiative," Samakab replied, dryly.

"Coffee? Water? That's all I can offer you, I'm afraid."

"No thanks," said Samakab as he wiped some specks off the chair and sat down. He looked around him. "This isn't quite what I expected."

"Ah, I suppose you were thinking more along the lines of the film, *Minority Report*. High-tech holographic touch-screens, transportation pods going up and down the sides of the building—that kind of thing?"

"Not exactly, but something a little more salubrious, perhaps…" Samakab surveyed the office with a look of distain. "I thought that such an important project would be organized with at least a modicum of efficiency and tidiness."

"We're dealing with something that isn't tidy and certainly isn't efficient. The human mind, in all its chaotic color and diversity, is as complex and fluid as the weather patterns that rule our actions and our lives. It's when we stop and try to tidy things up that we truly get stuck."

"If we don't stop and tidy up occasionally, we get lost in the chaos."

"That's the fear, yes. The trick is to master ourselves, so we can work with the fluid nature of things intuitively, rather than trying to dream up and work with fixed rules that can never perfectly integrate with it." Shanning reflected on his own words for a moment. "We don't learn that, do we? We laughed at King Canute for attempting to hold back the tide while we all continue to build pathetic defenses against life's inevitable twists and turns." He filled a glass with water and sat opposite Samakab.

"That's a bit rich, coming from someone who wants to control everything."

"That's where you're wrong, Mr Samakab. I can no more control the weather than you or anyone else can. I just report it. I'm just a humble weatherman. The world controls the weather, but doesn't know it and doesn't take responsibility for it. It's the actions of man that have brought about changes in the climate, as we well know. It's the condition of man that created the imbalances that we see on an ever-increasing scale. So when you see one of the ever-increasing numbers of cyclones ripping through the homes of good citizens, you don't blame the weatherman, do you?"

Samakab sat back in his chair. Something inside him wanted to keep as much distance from this self-satisfied amateur philosopher as he could. Despite the insipid nature of the conversation, he was wary of this man's apparent ability to manipulate and control people. From what Samakab had discovered about the Weatherman Project from his people in Norfolk, Toronto and Somalia, this man was the kingpin in an operation of unprecedented scale. He had considerable influence over the US Government, the intelligence agencies and the military. But although Shanning was outwardly calm, Samakab could now see the insecurity and egocentricity in the complex mix of his character. He appeared to have made mistakes and left himself open to manipulation in the most alarming ways, which left Samakab wondering how on earth someone like Shanning could have gained such influence. Even that thought came to him with doubts attached. Was Shanning playing him? Was he drawing him into his confidence by playing a game, pretending to be inept? Maybe the answers were hidden in the seemingly banal statements he made. He decided he should take notice of Shanning's every comment, in case he was missing hidden truths in his deceptively simple and unsophisticated language. Perhaps it was this simplicity that had enabled him to cut through the intellectual and the complicated, get to the core of human motivation and desires, to reach such a powerful position. Yet it was hard for him to take this man seriously. Samakab didn't respect him. He disliked his smarmy smugness intensely and his values appeared to represent the epitome of corruption and everything reprehensible in mankind. To Samakab, Shanning appeared to be low-grade, low-key—*ordinary,* in so many ways. The untidy state of the office supported this opinion. It was the office of a small businessman with his sleeves rolled up, a startup going through the throes of a funding battle, proving itself to its investors or in the first stages of getting traction in a market. The image didn't fit. He didn't appear to be a man of sufficient character or ability to deliver what the Weatherman Project appeared to be. Having at last made the connection between the video that Assaf had sent to Ayan and the Weatherman Project, thanks to Raage's rooting around at the base in Somalia, he now realized the significance of this project. All of this left Samakab feeling uncertain. While he thought he had some power over Shanning because of the way he'd been able to seemingly compromise him, he also felt vulnerable—confused by these contradictions. He was standing in a minefield.

"I didn't say you *could* control everything," Samakab continued, "I said you wanted to."

"No, I don't want to control," Shanning replied, "I just want to influence the weather a little, for the good of our country. I am fortunate in that I have been blessed with the opportunity to do that, and I intend to carry out my duty to the best of my ability. What more could a man ask for in this life, Mr Samakab?" Shanning pointed to a framed text on the wall of his office. "I am not the first to ask for this privilege."

Samakab turned to the text and read:

> General Patton's prayer at Bastogne, 1944.
> Almighty and most merciful Father,
> we humbly beseech Thee, of Thy great goodness,
> to restrain these immoderate rains with which we have had to contend.
> Grant us fair weather for Battle.
> Graciously hearken to us as soldiers who call upon Thee that,
> armed with Thy power, we may advance from victory to victory,
> and crush the oppression and wickedness of our enemies
> and establish Thy justice among men and nations.

Samakab turned back to Shanning. "That's sick bullshit, Mr Shanning, and you know it. And, frankly, I'm tired of playing around."

"Is it really, Mr Samakab? Is it any more sick than what's happening in this world—to its people, to the planet itself? Do you really think that the problems of the world will be solved by fighting among the weak-minded and the ill-informed? Or is it better to control the blood-bath and ensure that good comes of what little resources we have left, for our survival?"

"What good? Whose survival?"

"We now have the opportunity to protect our own, Mr Samakab," Shanning replied, dodging the wider question. "Isn't that something you would like to have had in your childhood? Isn't that something you value above all else when it comes to your son, Ayan, whom you have hidden away while you survey the battlefield?"

"That was a cheap shot."

"I like to call a spade a spade."

Samakab shot him a steely glare. Shanning held up his hand, possibly in apology, or possibly just to end an argument that was threatening to get too personal.

"Mr Samakab. You've obviously come here for a reason. You've found out where we are, just as I would expect a man of your undoubted capabilities—"

"Just as you expected or as you planned?"

Shanning laughed. "Oh, Mr Samakab, you give me far too much credit. Don't you think I would have preferred to keep this under my full *control?*"

"I'm sure you would have preferred that, but control doesn't seem to be one of your strong points, does it?" *Whether that's by design or by accident, only time will tell*, thought Samakab. "But then, for you, it's not about control, if your claims are to be believed."

"So, how can I help you today? Would you like a tour of the facilities?" Samakab glanced through the small window to the computer and cable chaos.

"I don't think so. There's something I want you to do for me, if you want to retain any control over this project at all."

"Hmm... fighting talk, Mr Samakab. Your man—what's his name... Raage—at the base?"

"That's right."

"He's a loyal, lifelong friend of yours, yes?"

"Right again."

"Very well. What do you want me to do for you?"

"I want you to exert your influence. As that's your stated mission in life."

"Tell me."

"The successes that I am having in the Gulf and in the Indian Ocean threaten to be undermined by actions that are being proposed in the EU, particularly by the United Kingdom. As you know, in their efforts to prop up our transitional government, they and the African Union have installed troops in Mogadishu. However, because the government is, as you well know, almost entirely powerless in my country, and the pressure to find a solution to their shipping problems has been increased, there is talk of extending the foreign military presence to the whole country. That would be inconvenient for me. I'm guessing that it could also cause you some problems, since you clearly parked your aircraft in Somaliland to hide it—even from your allies."

"I still don't understand what you want me to do."

"I want you to influence the EU to take the heat off Somalia."

Shanning held up his hands in mock defeat. "I'm afraid I can't help you there," he said, smiling at Samakab as if it was the most naive thing he'd ever heard. "I have absolutely no influence in Europe. They are not a player in this."

"Not a player?" Samakab didn't know who the main players were.

"No." Shanning sat still, waiting for Samakab's response.

"Is that all you have to say?"

"Yes, I think so." Shanning fixed Samakab with a stare. "I have given you a dream deal, Mr Samakab. The fallout you create is no concern of mine."

"Actually, it is your concern. And so is the safety of my good friend Raage."

Samakab stared back at Shanning. Shanning looked away as he thought of a suitable reply. The hole that he was in as a result of that damned test going wrong in Afghanistan was getting deeper and deeper with every contact he had with this wretched man. If only all the tests had gone as well as they had in the Congo, where they were protecting the supply of coltran for western technology. Then there was the test they'd used to demonstrate HAPISAD's effectiveness to the Chinese when they 'disappeared' 150 Uighurs from various locations near the city of Urumqi in the Xinjiang region—a successful operation designed to prevent further ethnic riots. He was particularly pleased about the way that had worked and had received a lot of praise from the head of their army. It had tested AVTOL beyond the calculated limits of its range. They had discovered that they could use much less fuel at very high altitudes by allowing it to glide for short periods, virtually unpowered. And HAPISAD had been faultless in targeting men and women in the mountainous region around the city. That operation alone had saved the Chinese millions in terms of troop mobilization, as well as avoiding the unwelcome publicity it would have attracted via the international press. As it turned out, only one human rights monitoring organization had publicized it, to little effect, because several of the bodies were never found and it was difficult to make a case for those that were discovered. The authorities innocently put their hands up and said that they could not possibly know of the intentions of that many unconnected people in different locations. It was relatively easy for them to put the deaths down to other causes. That was another unexpected advantage of the weapon.

This problem with Samakab, though, was turning out to be a real nuisance. Shanning had only been partially responsible for choosing Samakab as the way to get AVTOL established in Somalia; the intelligence services had concurred with his suggestion following several months of intelligence gathering and surveillance. They had all agreed that Samakab had the right profile and could be bought. However, the unfortunate events that led to King meeting Samakab, inadvertently brought about by the failed test in Afghanistan, had put the whole testing phase in jeopardy and, with it, his own credibility. He'd seriously misjudged Samakab and cursed the random act of fate that had created this fucking mess. He couldn't admit to Samakab that his influence only extended to limited operational matters, and that the superpowers were shortly to take control of AVTOL, now that the testing phase was coming to a close. His continuing agreement with the superpowers only extended to software support, and it was only a matter of weeks before the US military would be sending their own personnel to oversee operations and move the office out of Hackensack to one of their own bases. He had to tidy things up before that happened. If he didn't, he'd lose all the respect he'd earned and all his hard work would be wasted. He had already unwittingly compromised the security of the project and he couldn't face being dismissed for ineptitude, should his paymasters find out about the situation with Samakab. He was under pressure from all sides now, although Samakab was the only person who might have an inkling as to why that was so. He had to somehow regain control, but was fast running out of ideas.

"Is Raage getting all the cooperation he wants at the base?"

"You know damned well he isn't. He's kept away from all the equipment and only one person is authorized to talk to him—and that man's conversation hardly extends further than passing the time of day."

"Well, I'm sure I can arrange for the men at the base to extend a hand of friendship to him," said Shanning. *And then they can take him out before I hand over control.*

"That would be a start," said Samakab as his cell phone beeped. The message read: '*All on board accounted for*'. *Good*, thought Samakab. *Now Raage can get to work.* "But you must also do something about Europe, otherwise I could end up with a net loss and my people could lose everything they have gained." He made the demand, but he already knew that within days he would have no need of Shanning's help to sort that problem out. However, if Shanning had anything to offer, it could possibly save him some effort.

"I will certainly talk to some people, but I can't promise anything." Shanning sighed. The pressure of dodging and weaving around problems with Samakab as well as the demands of the project were too much for one man to deal with. The past few months had been his most intensive work period ever, and he was no spring chicken. His fitness schedule had been severely disrupted and his concentration was slipping. Pressures from above and below were forming a vice-like grip on his life. He was all too aware that the tests had been rushed and the programming team had taken shortcuts to meet his tight deadlines. They had done it, but the product was substandard. His superiors were growing increasingly impatient. They'd refused to increase the budget to cover the unforeseen developments, and he'd even had to start plowing some of his own money back into the project to ensure it got finished. He'd been frustrated by the trip to Washington in the Gulfstream—that had been expensive and yielded absolutely nothing, other than an assurance that King was the bumbling idiot that he'd suspected he was.

Deep inside, though, he had to admit that things started to go wrong the moment he decided to oust Larry Davidson as project leader, and make sure that he disappeared forever. But that was perfectly justified, he had told himself. No way were Larry and the team ever going to achieve their lofty goals, and it was pointless to pretend that they would. It was human nature, Shanning assured himself, not to strive to save the whole planet but, as history consistently attested, to strive to save oneself. Surely 'survival of the fittest' is the only way that a species survives and gets stronger. The weak perish. Every part of the natural world confirms it. That's just the way things are. And if you try to disturb the natural order, you perish in the process—eventually, if not immediately. That was the mistake man had made. Being humane bucked the natural trend and upset nature's delicate balance. There was always a cost for supporting weaker or non-productive members of society. They ended up weakening the supporters.

Likewise, whenever one nation protected another, there was a bigger cost. So it was up to each individual person to support that balance. However, due to karma, luck, destiny—whatever you wanted to call it—none of us could decide where to be born and what our family circumstances would be, what religious beliefs we'd be told to follow, what education we received as youngsters, how our belief systems would evolve. It was all random, an accident. Among the accidents, there were configurations that simply didn't work and that made no useful contribution. And, ultimately, how important was it to protect a weak, dysfunctional, probably troublesome and disruptive individual in a world of seven billion? Could the world afford to keep such people? As the world approached the tipping point, it made much more sense to support the strong in surviving and make the process more efficient by removing anyone who got in the way. It wasn't just good economics, it was good sense. Once the weak had gone or were under control, the world would survive for longer. If Larry had succeeded in starting the transformation process, with all his airy-fairy ideas of enlightenment, education and self-empowerment, there would have been total anarchy and everyone's survival would have been put at risk. Shanning couldn't let that happen. He'd done the right thing. And those in power agreed that it was the right thing, when they realized what was at stake.

In that case, he thought as he looked across the table at Samakab and pondered his next move, *if I am to protect the planet, I must do something about this man, and quickly.*

Chapter 32

Alexei Sidorov clicked the remote to unlock his Mercedes SLS AMG. The car responded with a short flash of the indicators and a satisfyingly solid clunk. Not a speck of dust broke the smooth reflections that glided across its paintwork as he approached it.

"*Bonjour madame.*" He waved to Mme Jeanneret as she busily arranged a duvet over the windowsill of an upstairs room. She acknowledged him with the quickest of glances, diligently continuing to make sure that the duvet lay smooth and flat, and the corners lined up while displayed in public. She'd done the same thing, at precisely the same time, every fine day since Alexei had taken up residence in the house opposite hers three years ago. They had never once had a conversation, but that was fine with Alexei. Like the Swiss, he liked his privacy. In fact, he liked everything about the order, the predictability and even the distant politeness of the Swiss.

He'd done very well for himself, and he'd felt particularly proud when he bought the house in the aptly named Rue de la Jalousie—road of jealousy. *If my friends back home could see me now!* Actually, the last thing he wanted was to meet up with old friends from his home town. He didn't have friends any more, save one. He had 'colleagues' and contacts that occasionally called him but whom he rarely met. He spent his days alone, but that was fine with him too. Relationships had always proved to be too complicated. He'd made his choices in life and he was grateful for the peace of isolation.

Life hadn't always been so organized. The contrast between the chaotic city of Khasavyurt, his home town in Dagestan, and the quiet village of Denens could not have been greater. He had always detested Khasavyurt, and had cursed his parents for moving from the civilization of Volgograd to the tenement blocks of this crude city, with its ugly river, filthy marketplace, terrible school and dead-end prospects for an ambitious boy like him. He'd left home just as soon as he could and, aged 15, had moved to nearby Grosny, only to end up living on the streets, unable to find work. That's where he'd got the education that had ultimately led to his current lifestyle. In late 1994, in the early stages of the first Chechen war, he'd been holed up in a derelict building near the city center. It was late afternoon, freezing cold, grey and overcast. The sky, the street, even the people he occasionally saw walking by, all blended into a colorless monochrome. The building had suffered several direct hits. Rubble and burned wood littered the floor. Dusty, broken furniture was all that remained to show it had once been an office. Everything useful had been looted. He didn't dare light a fire in case it was spotted by one of the Russian soldiers prowling through the city, searching out and killing all the Chechen guerillas they could find. He also feared being found by a Chechen guerilla, since his accent was clearly Russian. But he knew that he'd have to deal with some human contact at some point. He couldn't survive on his own in the middle of a war zone. But a sharp wit, an intelligent mind, and his life on the street had already taught him how to deal with unexpected dangers.

He heard footsteps running toward the building. There were people shouting further down the street. The footsteps approached the doorway close to where he sat on the floor, covered by an old blanket he always carried with him. Heavy breathing released plumes of mist that drifted through the doorway. Alexei peered round the door pillar. A man stood, panting, rifle held close to his heaving chest, his face pressed hard against the wall next to a window through which he anxiously monitored the advance of his pursuers.

"Psst!" The man looked round, alarmed. "It's okay. Come here." The voices were getting closer and Alexei could hear the familiar sound of Russian boots on the road outside. He motioned to the man to get down on the floor next to him. Dislodging the end of a charred plank from a pile of rubble next to him, he pulled it over them. As they ducked under the blanket, more rubble and dust fell over them to complete the deception. The soldiers raced past, one of them briefly checking the window. Their footsteps faded into the distance, eventually disappearing out of earshot.

That evening, the Chechen had taken him to a better hideout, introduced Alexei to some of his friends, and then introduced him to guns. In the weeks that followed, Alexei earned his meals shooting Russian soldiers. He quickly got a reputation for accuracy, which was important as ammunition was valuable. By the time the Russians threw in the towel with the troublesome Chechens in 1996, after tens of thousands had died, he had come to see killing humans purely as sport. His primary concerns were to make a clean kill, to be thorough and professional in his preparation and to rigorously maintain his weapon. His ambition was to find and own the best rifle in the world, perfect his art and become known as the best hit man on the planet.

He was given that opportunity during the second Chechen war in 1999. Things had got messy in Grosny. Money meant for rebuilding the shattered city and the country's economy was being distributed among warlords favored by the new government, so for those who were used to violence but had no money, kidnapping became a lucrative way to earn a living. Alexei didn't consider himself a gangster and resisted invitations to join in these activities. He returned to live in Volgograd, before offering to help the Russians regain control of the country using his services as a sniper. Again, his talents brought him great notoriety, and his knowledge of the Chechen environment served him well. Toward the end of the war, he was paid considerable sums to take out several high-ranking Chechen military and political personnel, thus playing a significant role in bringing about a speedy conclusion to the brutal Russian military campaign. Since then, he'd built up an international business, and he'd bought some impressive equipment. As he'd become more proficient at his trade, he'd discovered that he needed different rifles for different jobs in different conditions. No single weapon could be considered the best in the world. His personal favorite was his recently acquired $34,000 Accuracy International L115A3, with Schmidt & Bender day sights that magnified up to 25 times. With a muzzle velocity of 936 meters per second firing a heavy 8.59mm bullet, it was accurate up to 1400 meters. However, when he had the opportunity to use it, he also liked the surprise element that his McMillan TAC-50 tactical rifle offered. It was regularly in use in Afghanistan, with Canadian forces successfully hitting targets as far away as 2430 meters—one-and-a-half miles. The victims didn't even hear the rifle go off.

He loved living in Denens. The house he'd chosen was at the top of a gentle rise. There were fields all around and he was able to survey the flat terrain around him for several miles. He loved the mountains too, but only to look at from a distance. Close up, they were just too untidy, too disorganized and dangerous. He didn't like surprises and a trip to the mountains was full of them. There was one around every hairpin bend, and many of the roads leading to them were heavily wooded. There was simply too much to think about, too many possibilities for events that he had no control over. But Denens was nice. He could enjoy a level of anonymity here that would be difficult to find elsewhere, and his standard of living was beyond his wildest childhood dreams. It was also the first Swiss village he'd found where the residents exhibited a sense of humor. Nowhere else he'd looked had suggested that this quality was something the Swiss recognized—let alone possessed. Even when they made an effort to enjoy themselves, sitting in neat lines at tables, drinking and singing at some commune celebration, they seemed somehow awkward and unfamiliar with the process of letting their hair down. Generations of excessive attention to orderliness seemed to have drained any notion of wild abandon or reckless passion out of them entirely. However, he'd immediately warmed to this place. Approaches to the village were marked by strange sculptures in fields and gardens. A scarecrow made of bottles around a lamp stand so the head lit up at night, strange smiling totem poles constructed from flower pots and scrap metal, a delicate sculpture of bicycle parts.

So, it was a little annoying for him to find that, having achieved a good living and a pleasant home, it looked as if the circumstances of his life were about to change once again. *Why can't I just keep doing what I enjoy doing and not have to keep adapting to change?* He opened the gull-wing door and lowered himself into the driver's seat. A warm glow came over him as he watched the dashboard lights and LED display come to life as he fired up the V8. This was heaven, and the funny thing about living in Denens was that even though this monster of a car was obviously very expensive, no one took the least bit of notice of it. He often suspected, though, that natural curiosity was carefully masked behind the Swiss ultra-politeness.

He made his way out of the village, toward the lakeside town of Morges, parking in his usual spot behind the Club Nautique, where he'd made a habit of spending his lunchtimes, which often extended into the early evenings.

"Monsieur Sidorov, welcome." The waiter went through the routine of showing him to the table they kept ready for him. It was outside, under a sun shade, close to the pier. Alexei liked to watch as customers came and went, as boats were launched at the jetty next to the club, and as the Lac Léman ferry plied its way up and down the lake from Geneva to Lausanne.

"I have a guest today, so please set an extra place." He sat down. The lake was calm. Fluffy clouds punctuated the clear blue spring sky. The air was so clear that he could almost see the buildings in Évian, on the opposite shore.

"Your usual while you wait for your guest, Monsieur?"

"Yes, thank you." The waiter returned with a blue bottle containing his favorite sparkling mineral water. He used to drink, but not anymore. The greater high was squeezing the trigger, full control and absolute accuracy— from a seemingly impossible distance. Alcohol highs didn't come close, and their effect in slowing his reactions, blurring his concentration, were simply not worth the bother. He'd given up sex for the same reason. Whether solo or with a woman, the cost was too high.

It was lunchtime on a Thursday. Alexei didn't expect to see too many other customers, but he had taken the precaution of also reserving the table next to him, so they wouldn't be overheard. The proprietor was happy to accept this arrangement. He would recoup the lost revenue from Alexei within days, simply by overcharging him for his meals. Alexei never looked at the bill.

Alexei's lunchtime entertainment arrived in the form of a Swiss couple, backing their speedboat trailer into the lake. There was always a fine balance to be struck. Do you reverse the Land Cruiser far enough into the water to float the boat, getting it wet and dirty, or do you keep it clean and dry and push the boat off the trailer, risking damage if it hit the bottom? He'd seen many an impatient husband shouting at his wife as he made such a crucial decision. They were usually dressed in smart pants, designer pullover draped over the shoulders and expensive sunglasses, whatever the weather. They'd never hidden from Russian soldiers knee-deep in mud, starved in the freezing, bombed-out remains of their home, or been given the choice of kill or be killed.

"Alexei! *Bom dia*, good to see you!" He turned away from the comedy to greet his guest—the only friend he'd ever known.

251

"Luis! *Dabro pazhalavat*. Welcome. Thank you for coming." Alexei stood and shook hands warmly. Luis de Granja was a stocky, short Portuguese man with a very pleasant manner—as long as you stayed on the right side of him. Today, as always, he was wearing his trademark brown bomber jacket over a blue striped shirt with a paisley cravat tucked into the open collar. His thinning hair, kind eyes and soft, carefully manicured hands completed the picture of a friendly local council clerk, rather than the deadly marksman he actually was. Alexei had got to know him as a colleague in the second Chechen war. They had worked together on a number of occasions when a two-man team was required. This happened quite often. In a country where everyone felt vulnerable to attack and those who were targeted often knew that they were, sophisticated backup plans were often required

"So, what is happening, Alexei? How is life treating you?" Luis slammed a rolled-up copy of the *New York Times* on the table.

"*Harasho*—so-so. I can still eat, but I am not sure for how long."

"Why you say that?" Luis was thrown by this remark. Alexei was the best in the business, as far as he knew.

"Let's order." Alexei beckoned the waiter over to their table. "*Je voudrais le rôti de veau au jus de thym et les légumes grillés, s'il vous plaît.*" Turning to Luis he asked, "And you?"

Luis, who didn't speak a word of French, asked, "What you order?"

"Roast veal with thyme and grilled vegetables."

"I have same, thank you." It was the easy option.

"Thank you, sir," the waiter said, in perfect English.

"And bottle of your finest red wine," Luis added. Once the waiter was out of earshot, Luis asked again, "Alexei, what is going on?"

"I don't know, but the work seems to be drying up."

"That is crazy. If that is happening for you, I think we all better be on lookout. What is matter? Are they going for more cheap deals?"

"Not that I can see. How is it for you?"

"Well, I not getting the government work I used to get. Is mainly commercial, and even some private jobs..."

"So, it is affecting you as well?"

"What?"

"The worldwide recession."

"It cannot be that." Luis sat back in his chair. He looked confused. He had thought that he must be losing his grip, but if it was the same for Alexei, something else was going on. "Whenever there is recession," he said, "things usually pick up. Is *so* confusing. I trying to figure out where government jobs are going. It is not like peace has suddenly come to planet."

"It certainly hasn't, and I don't think it ever will."

"Me, I am offered private work now. You know, husbands, wives, small business. Otherwise, there is always work in Italy—"

"Tell me about it! But I wouldn't touch that bunch of thugs whatever they offered."

"Yes, well. I have my family to feed back in Porto…"

"And I have expenses here. Have you any idea how much it costs to keep your nose clean in this country? This chocolate-box lifestyle isn't cheap." Alexei chuckled as the man with the Toyota cleaned mud off the rear wheels with a towel. "The problem is the commercial world doesn't have the resources any more, and polarization of interests is removing the opposition simply by squeezing them out. That's another reason they have less need for us."

"Is possible, yes, I suppose." Luis looked dejected and picked up his newspaper. "I read maybe ten of these every day, just to look for clues…"

"But what I don't understand is the sudden reduction in the political contracts. They were my bread and butter—and caviar." Alexei took a drink of water as the waiter poured a glass of wine for Luis. "And I really don't want to get involved in the messy stuff that I get offered from Moldova, Lithuania, Belarus—you know, all the usual Eastern European countries the Russians are working, let alone the rubbish that comes out of Africa. My friend, it's getting really hard to make an honest living."

"You are right. It is a killer."

"So, who do you think is getting all the work? Somebody out there must be picking up a lot of contracts."

"Well, it is not me, I can tell you." Luis felt the slightest twinge of nervousness at this line of questioning from Alexei. Knowing how good this man was, he didn't want to detect even a whisper of suspicion that Alexei thought he might be taking his jobs.

"I did get offered a nice one in New York, yesterday, but it's the first one in a long time," Alexei continued, "and I'm not sure I trust it, either. It's a private individual going for an African commercial target. I'm not sure of the security, just yet, so I'm waiting for him to get back to me on that. If it happens, I just hope it's in New York. At least I can take in a show or two while I'm there. I cannot stand the food in most African countries."

"I even tried to go east, even to China." Luis mused. "With their quick expansion, there should be something to pick up, no? But nada. Of course, they have strong system with triads, so this does not surprise me so much. Only tinpot regimes have work, but such bad management and high risk. I get many, many bullshit requests from politicians I cannot trust. I not want to go there. I hate to think my wife and kids they end up without an income because I make bad decision."

Alexei sighed deeply. "Ah, here comes our food."

LEWIS EVANS

CHAPTER 33

Raage had found it particularly difficult to do his job at the AVTOL base. He had been kept isolated in an office and had no contact with anyone—other than Samakab, via his satellite phone, and a very unhelpful American who stood guard outside his door. He'd even had to argue with the guard to get the phone batteries charged so that he could make his daily reports. He'd managed to keep an eye on the SUV, though; it was parked a few yards away and he was confident that no one had tampered with it.

Even today, after he had been let out, he couldn't make much headway. However, Samakab must have been exerting his influence in New York, as he'd received an apology from someone he only knew as Eric, for being kept prisoner in an empty office for so long. It wasn't a heartfelt apology, and it came with its own conditions. But at least he was free to roam the base and talk to people, albeit about unimportant things he had no interest in discussing. However, he knew he'd make some headway with some of them soon.

His arrival at the base had been orchestrated at night. He'd rendezvoused with Eric in the desert. Raage had waited—with a truckload of armed men, as Samakab had instructed—at an agreed location. Within ten minutes, the SandCat and one of the M-ATVs had arrived. The SandCat had parked a short distance away. A man in the roof turret trained a machinegun on the truck. The M-ATV had swung round from behind the SandCat and parked directly in front of his SUV, blinding Raage with its headlights and kicking up a cloud of dust that obscured his view of the the SandCat. Raage stayed seated in the SUV. Eric stepped down from the M-ATV and walked over to him.

"Come with us." Eric opened the door to let Raage out.

"I'm driving myself," Raage protested.

"No way. You're coming in the M-ATV."

"I must keep my vehicle. It was agreed." Raage picked up his satellite phone, indicating to Eric that he would call to confirm this, if necessary.

"Shit." Eric turned impatiently to the M-ATV and beckoned. Another man climbed down from the vehicle. "He'll drive this. You come with us." Raage had weighed up the situation and decided that he'd have to trust Eric to keep his word. Eric would not have wanted to upset his superiors in the US, but he had to take all sensible precautions. He frisked Raage once he was out of his vehicle, then led him into the dark interior of the M-ATV. Raage handed his keys to the other man on the way. As soon as they'd climbed into the vehicle, Eric switched on a light, closed bullet-proof metal shields on all the windows in the rear compartment and banged on the wall to let the driver know he could head off.

254

Raage had estimated that they traveled about ten miles, although the M-ATV gave a surprisingly smooth ride, so it was difficult to tell what speed they were traveling at. When they arrived at the base, he'd been firmly guided by the arm straight into the isolation of the office with a bed and basic washing and toilet facilities, where he'd spent all his daylight hours until now.

First things first, he thought. He headed toward the canteen to order a hamburger and fries. On the way, a glint of sunlight on metal caught his eye. Looking over to his left, beyond the portable buildings, equipment, pallets and vehicles that littered the base, he could see something in the distance. An ominous dark mass cast a deep shadow on the sand. Wires and pipes trailed across the desert to vehicles that surrounded it like drones attending a queen bee. It was the first time he'd seen the AVTOL. Men were checking under its low belly and working on machinery that stood in the dust beside it. Tarpaulins, laid over the wings and engine air intakes, flapped lazily in the breeze. An M-ATV stood nearby, its driver leaning against it as he talked into a radio. The Prowlers darted between the AVTOL and the offices. Resisting the urge for a closer look, he continued walking toward the canteen. Inside, several men were chatting over coffee or watching TV. It looked like the best place to make friends. The men seemed to have nothing to do, and Raage planned to use this opportunity to escape the oppressive heat of the day in an air-conditioned environment and gather information. He knew that many of them were military personnel—some from the CIA's Special Ops Group, some from the Marines—but none of them wore name tags or displayed their rank. They just used first names, and he didn't even know if those were real. But Samakab had said he needn't concern himself with names when he'd phoned in his recent report. That would be handled from New York. Raage had other things to do right now.

"Hi, guys!" he said cheerfully as he entered the canteen. Several faces looked up from what they were doing, but no one replied. "Nice to meet you too," he said, cheerfully, and ordered his meal from a stony-faced chef. There was a NASCAR race on TV. "Hey, is that Adams County Speedway? Fantastic! Any of you guys been there?" No reply. Not even a turn of a head. "No matter. I was just curious. Anyone think Morris can do it again at the Motor Mile?"

"Fuck it, man," one of the men looked up at him, aggressively. "What the fuck do you know about NASCAR? Who d'you think you're kiddin?"

"I have always followed the NASCAR Sprint Cup. It's one of my favorite American sports."

"Sure you have. It's only natural out here in the middle of the desert, ain't it?" The man smirked at his friend; then, turning back to Raage, he said, "Okay, give me the name of another driver. Just one will do." The two men laughed and returned to watching the race. What they didn't know was that

Raage, like many Somalis, had traveled extensively. He'd spent some time in the US as well, where he'd not only trained as a pilot, but also worked as a mechanic for a NASCAR team.

"Well, let me think," he stroked his chin, smiling. "How about Jamie McMurray, Greg Biffle, Todd Bodine, Carl Edwards, Jeff Burton, Kurt and Kyle Busch, Dale Earnhardt Jr, Denny Hamlin, Ricky Craven, Kevin Harvick, Bobby Labonte, Elliott Sadler—"

"Okay, okay!" They held up their hands in defeat. "Man, we've gotta NASCAR aficionado here! Give the guy some room!" Inviting him to join them, they introduced themselves as Ben and Charlie—*and, no, don't call me Jerry unless you want a knuckle sandwich*—then the questions started. "What's a guy like you doing on our base?"

"I'm with the Weatherman Project. We provide security for you here."

"From the looks of things, we've been providing you with security! What was all that about?" Ben said.

"There was a miscommunication, that's all. It's all been sorted out now."

"So let me get this straight," said Charlie. "That truckload of swinging dicks that showed up when you arrived— they're the ones providing the security? Hey, I feel real safe!" They both laughed.

"Ah, so you were both there? I didn't get a chance to introduce them to you, but I wouldn't underestimate them, if I were you." Raage smiled at their naïve joviality. "You are just a few. Out there, we are thousands."

"Ha! You lookin' for a big dick contest, yeah? Well, how d'ya think a bunch of starving herdsmen are gonna babysit that high-tech motherfucker, huh?" Charlie pointed out of the window toward the AVTOL's menacing shape in the distance.

"In much the same way they protected General Aideed from your high-tech Blackhawks before Clinton was forced to withdraw his troops from our country." Raage winked and stood up to get his burger and fries from the kitchen hatch. "We all need each other. That is how we will succeed. *Ilko wada jir bey wax ku gooyaan!*" He threw a fist into the air.

"And what does that mean?"

"Unity is power."

"True enough," said Charlie, and continued watching the race in a more subdued mood.

"And what are you two doing here?" Raage thought he'd chance a question or two.

"We were kinda volun-told to come and help out—do some driving, technical work, that kinda thing." Ben glanced at Charlie conspiratorially. They both knew that conversations with this man had to be limited to broad generalizations.

"So, you're not here of your own volition?"

"Volition?"

"You didn't choose to come?"

"Like I said," replied Charlie, "we were volun-told. We had a choice, but didn't, okay?"

"I see. Are you glad to be involved with the project? Is it interesting?"

"Look, man," Ben cut in, "we're just doin' our job. Now we have far more important things to do than gas with you about this bag of dicks we got suckered into, so can we get back to concentratin' on the race?"

"Sure. Sorry. Can I get you guys a coffee, Coke or anything?" Ben and Charlie shook their heads, continued to diligently ignore him and fixed their eyes on the screen in front of them. Minutes later, Eric arrived at the canteen. Everyone visibly stiffened when he came in the door.

"Coffee, please, Walt," he barked through the hatch.

"Comin' up, sir." Walt shuffled his overweight frame around the kitchen.

"Mr Raage. I see you're enjoying a bit of American culture. We must get you a baseball cap to complete the picture." Eric gave a thin smile and sat down at an empty table.

"Ben, you and Charlie had better get over to the ops room. They need to refill the tanker and there's some problem with the ship. Go and find out what it's all about."

"Sir!" Both men shot to their feet and dashed out of the canteen. Eric grabbed the remote and changed the channel to CTV. "What the—" John Pollard was smiling at the camera. The shot widened to include the captain of the *Norfolk Defender*. Raage, Eric and the others in the canteen all watched as Pollard bumbled through his report on Somali piracy in the Gulf. At one point, the captain held his hand up to the camera after a question about the cargo he was carrying. Then there was a short clip showing a US Army War College professor pontificating about the possible ramifications of the design improvements in terms of vulnerability of cargo ships to hijackings. The report finished off with Pollard giving an impassioned eulogy for all those who had died in the Gulf, an emotional tribute to those non-military personnel who risk their lives to support them and, no doubt, a sizeable boost to the program's ratings for bringing such a daring report to viewers around the world.

"That was quite an endorsement of the fight against terror, yes?" said Raage, with an innocent smile. Eric glanced sideways at him.

"Sure it was," he replied, sardonically.

"Well, enjoy your coffee," Raage said, swallowing the last mouthful of burger. While Eric was watching TV, he wanted to check out the base, unchallenged. He donned his sunglasses and nonchalantly sauntered out of the canteen.

This was no ordinary military base. It was more like a temporary encampment. For a start, it had no perimeter fence. Anyone could wander in or out. There was no munitions dump in a remote corner, because most of the personnel here weren't armed. There was no watch tower. All that protected this place was its isolation and the fact that, apart from a small circle of trusted people, no one knew it was there. The accommodation block was simply three 40-foot units joined together along their length, with partitions inside. There was a washroom with showers next to it and, 50 yards away, the canteen. Behind the canteen was a refrigerated container used to store food. A water tower stood between the washroom and the canteen, with pipes feeding both from its base. A suite of three office units joined end to end formed the third side of a 'U' shape. The two HEMMT tactical trucks, complete with containers, were parked at the end of the offices, and the accommodation that Raage had been allocated was in the end office nearest to them. Raage's SUV was conveniently parked outside his room. The aircraft refueler was parked behind the refrigerated container. Other vehicles were parked randomly around an equipment storage area, beyond which, 100 yards away, stood the AVTOL in the center of its own blast area of blackened sand, cut through with weaving tire tracks. A makeshift wooden blast deflector had been constructed to protect the portable buildings and the equipment store. Raage wandered round to the back of the offices and made his way to the rear end of the truck he was interested in. Its container was bolted shut but the bolts looked a little rusty. He looked toward the AVTOL and checked his watch, noting the positions of the different personnel, what they were doing, how many were involved. The SandCat, with its roof-mounted machinegun, was the only vehicle standing on the far side of the AVTOL. It was the only defense against intrusion into the camp from the plain beyond. Behind him, the Sheikh mountain range rose up, shimmering in the heat haze, about a mile away. The terrain between them and the base was rough and difficult to navigate on anything other than a camel. Not that Raage had to worry about intrusion. There wasn't even going to be a fight, if all went according to plan. Once he received the call from Samakab, in the next day or so, he was sure he'd have their full cooperation. He just had one more job to do before that happened.

Walking back around the offices, he was surprised by Eric, who had followed him out.

"Anything I can help you with?" Eric asked, looking over Raage's shoulder to see if anything had been disturbed on the truck.

"I was just looking for a piece of rag or something. I want to check the oil in the SUV. I have a feeling it's going to need some and, well, I've nothing else to do, so…"

"I'll get you something." Eric barged past him and opened a metal box behind the engine on the truck. He pulled out a grubby oil-stained rag and tossed it to Raage. "Here. This okay?"

"Perfect. Thanks." They walked together back to the SUV, and Raage popped the hood. He lowered his head under it and searched around for the dipstick. "It's a great vehicle, but I don't look after it well. You know, this sand and the long journeys I do, they're not good for…" He glanced round and noticed that Eric had walked away. He was almost back at the canteen. Raage pulled the dipstick several times, wiping a generous amount of oil onto the rag. He closed the hood with an exaggerated bang and wiped his hands on the rag, which he then placed on the front tire, hidden from view.

✱✱✱

There can't have been more than thirty personnel at the base, Raage estimated. Most of them were in the canteen from 6pm till the food service was finished at 10pm. By then, some had started to drift back to the accommodation block. Everyone seemed relaxed, apart from Eric, who always had an edge to him—a tense alertness and a slight impatience that everyone seemed wary of. The food varied in quality from junk to edible. No alcohol was allowed on the base. During the day, some of the men relieved the boredom playing soccer or going through their own fitness routines. While identities were hidden, it was easy to differentiate between the intellectual techies and fitness-obsessed marines. In the evening, they all mingled together in the canteen like long-time buddies. As a precaution, window blinds were closed when lights went on, and there was no external lighting at all. This made it quite difficult to move between buildings at night and when the weather was overcast, as it was this evening. Raage had seen two men using night-vision goggles to find their way to the washroom after their meal, so he knew that he had to be careful, but he guessed that the goggles were mainly used for looking beyond the base, in case some wandering herdsman had to be encouraged to find a different patch of desert to graze his animals.

At 2am, there was complete silence. Raage slipped quietly out of his room and retrieved the oily rag from the top of the front tire. Outside, it was as if the desert and the rest of the world had simply disappeared. Without sound or light, he felt alone on the planet, his senses acutely attuned to any sign of life that might disturb him as he worked. He knew he only had one chance to complete his task, and this was it.

Crouching down, he walked round to the back of the office and climbed up onto the truck to inspect the shipping container. It had two vertical locking bars on each door. A handle on each bar was slotted into a keeper. Fortunately, no padlock secured the locking bars in place as the contents of the container always had to be accessible. The doors were opened by turning the rods, which

259

in turn released hook-like cams from brackets welded into the end frame of the container. Raage only had to open one door, but the container acted like a huge sound-box, amplifying the slightest noise of any movement on the handle. He used the rag to smear oil onto the locking mechanisms, where rusted surfaces rubbed against each other. Using the handles as steps, he climbed up and oiled the top hinges and cams, stepping down again to do the same at the bottom. He climbed down off the truck to check that he hadn't attracted any attention, then returned to the container. He tested the handle on the first locking bar. It was stuck. He applied more pressure, increasing it until he was using all his strength, praying that it wouldn't suddenly give and send him flying to the ground. It flinched and let out a muffled, hollow groan. Raage released the pressure and dropped to the ground again, squinting through the darkness to check for any movement. All was still. He applied more oil to the mechanism and carefully eased the handle back and forth to work the oil into it. Gradually, the movement became easier and he was able to turn the handle far enough to disengage the cams from the frame. The second bar was easier to move, and within minutes the door was open.

Leaving the door ajar, he returned to the SUV. He'd left its tailgate open, earlier in the day, so he was able to lift it without a sound. Running his fingers around the edge of the carpeting in the trunk, he found a hidden latch that released the floor panel. He lifted it up and, using a canvas strap, tied it open. Raage then lifted a large metal case from the enclosure beneath the panel. It was heavy and difficult to maneuver over the tailgate without banging or scraping it. Straining under its weight, he placed it carefully on the ground. He was breathing more heavily now, and wondered how he was going to lift such a heavy item up into the container. He hadn't taken into account the height of the container above the ground, and the fact that he'd only have one free hand to lift it. Fortunately, the case had strap hooks and he had the canvas strap. That would get over the problem... although he had nothing to cut the strap with. He probably had something in his toolbox that would do the job. It was on the floor behind the driver's seat. The lock clicked loudly as he opened the rear passenger door. Somewhere in the wall of blackness over in the direction of the AVTOL, he heard a distant voice. He froze and waited. There was a dim flash of light and another voice, but they were so far away he couldn't make out what they were saying. He slowly lowered himself to the ground, where he would be hidden if they had night vision. Even so, the open tailgate of the SUV would probably be visible to them. He lay on the ground and peered between the wheels into the darkness. There was a short laugh, followed by the glow of a cigarette momentarily lighting up a face. Raage breathed again, stood up, opened the door, crouched down on the seat inside and pulled the door almost closed behind him. The toolbox contained no knife—just spanners, screwdrivers, pliers and assorted spares. He tried to visualize the way the strap was attached to the floor panel. He wasn't sure if it was a bolt or a screw that held it in place. If it was a bolt, he couldn't be sure what size it was, and he couldn't lift the whole box out or rummage through it to find the right one. He didn't have an adjustable wrench either, so he took a screwdriver and a pair of pliers, carefully putting them in separate pockets. If it was a screw, it would be easy. Or would it? Was it most likely to be a straight screw, a Phillips, a star, a hexagon or a square? Damn it! He had no idea, so he removed the screwdriver from his pocket and resolved to chew through the canvas strap using the pliers.

Carefully opening the door again, he slid down from the seat onto the ground, and back to the rear of the vehicle. Feeling his way in the darkness, he untied the strap supporting the floor panel, traced it back to where it was fixed, and started working with the pliers to cut through it. It took five nerve-wracking minutes, and he was sweating profusely, despite the chilly night air. Knotting the ends into the strap hooks on the case, he shouldered the strap and tested it for strength. It held, so he carefully lowered the rear door of the SUV and lifted the case. Standing absolutely still for a good half-minute, he listened. If anyone had been approaching, he would surely have heard them, but there was no sound. He proceeded cautiously around the office, back to the truck.

The floor of the container was level with his head. It had been relatively easy to climb up, using the truck's mudguard support brackets as steps and the container's locking bars to grip onto with his hands. But with the case weighing him down and the strap cutting into his shoulder, he had to figure out something else. He was frustrated and angry with himself for not thinking this through properly beforehand. But he had to stay calm. Samakab had stressed how important the job was and he would not let him down.

He pulled the container door open wide, untied one end of the strap from the case and tied it round his ankle. He stood the case on its side with the attached end of the strap uppermost. Climbing up onto the truck, he found that the strap wasn't long enough for him to stand on the floor of the container and haul the case up. Instead, he had to sit, his legs dangling, and hold on to the closed door while he struggled to lift the case by bending his leg and grabbing it by the handle with his free hand. It was his worst nightmare, and he was sure the case would slam against the truck before it reached the safety of the container floor. Once there, he had planned to close the door behind him and, with a small penlight held in his mouth, he'd re-arrange the contents of the container and hide the case. That wasn't to be. As he pulled the case up, it banged on the truck's chassis. He immediately heard voices, and he knew he only had one choice. He quickly hauled the case the last few inches onto the floor, opened the lid and felt inside for the switch he knew was there. He flicked it on, closed the case, locked it with a key he wore on a cord around his neck, and shoved it as far back into the container as it would go. It hit a storage case with another metallic thud. He dived for the door, climbed out and closed it as fast as he could, making sure both handles were back in their keepers. As he dropped to the ground, the headlights of the SandCat swept across the base in his direction. He lay flat on the ground as they spread across the office block and into the desert beyond the truck. *They're looking for intruders!* The SandCat blasted past him in the direction of the mountains. As it passed, the gunner was silhouetted in the turret as he switched on the searchlight and wildly sprayed the desert with light. More voices. Eric was shouting. Raage made a dash for the office, head down, using the SUV for cover, and just made it inside before flashlights started to play in all directions around the base. He ripped off his shirt and flung himself into his bed. His door burst open.

"What is happening?" Raage squinted in the glare of the flashlight.

The marine slammed the door behind him and rushed to the next door shouting into his helmet mike, "Raage, office six clear… office five clear… office four clear….," until Raage could no longer hear him. His heart was beating fast as he tried to regain his composure. After about ten minutes, he heard the SandCat return and silence reigned once again.

The following morning was anything but quiet. Eric was throwing his weight around, intimidating the techies and whipping the marines into shape. The only two who didn't seem to be involved were Brian and Frank, who turned out to be the AVTOL pilots. In all the pandemonium, no one ever bothered them. It was as if they were royalty—privileged and protected from the mundanity of security alerts. All around the base, there were tense, urgent discussions as Eric barked orders and made impossible demands. He had them all running around, taking the place apart, trying to find out what, if anything, had happened. Had anything gone missing, what was out of place, were there any loose camels on the horizon that might have wandered into the base? Eric was bristling. He wanted answers. He wanted blood. All morning the SandCat's engine was kept running and the gunner sat in its turret, machinegun loaded, scanning the horizon with powerful binoculars. The M-ATVs were sent out in different directions to look for fresh tracks in the desert. The Prowlers bounced over the rough ground toward the Sheikh Mountains, popping up every now and then like meerkats fleeing a predator. It looked as if the drivers were having great fun. Four gum-chewing marines were stationed around the AVTOL, M16s at the ready. To Raage, it looked like a very inadequate security capability—which, of course, it was.

The moment came, though, when Raage thought all was lost. Two men opened the container and went inside. Raage casually walked over, concerned to see what they were doing but, to his relief, saw that there was little to be worried about. In the daylight, he could see that his case was in full view, but so were several others that looked very similar. They were stacked untidily on the floor next to what looked like a wall of metal packing crates that filled over half the length of the container, from floor to ceiling. Different-colored cables were draped over some of them and an electrical racking system containing several pieces of equipment stood to one side. He nearly laughed out loud when he noticed a step ladder leaning against the stack of crates. If only he'd known about that last night!

By the end of the morning, Eric wasn't getting any closer to figuring out what had happened the previous night, so he turned his attention to the obvious suspect: Raage. He cornered him in the office, ordered him to sit down on the bed and questioned him aggressively as he paced the room. It quickly became clear to Raage, however, that Eric was bankrupt of ideas. The lack of any evidence of a misdemeanor had done little to allay his suspicion that Raage was very possibly responsible for the commotion the previous night, especially as it was the first night that Raage had been free to roam the base. This was just too frustrating for Eric, whose every instinct was to lock this man away, but whose orders were to treat him as one of the team. But why the hell should he do that? What purpose did this man serve on the base? No one was telling him, beyond the fact that he had something to do with their security. If last night was anything to go by, he should be forcibly removed immediately, but he'd already checked with the Weatherman and met with a brick wall of silence about his purpose and a confirmation that Raage was to remain there, be treated well and not be unduly restricted in his movements.

"Okay," Eric said, when he'd exhausted all possible avenues of questioning, "I will continue to allow you free access to all but the most sensitive areas of the base, but if I find out that you were behind this, you're fucked, Raage, and I mean well and truly fucked. I'll personally make sure you end up confined somewhere where your ass will break every record set by Letitia Roxxx, and with the same kind of guys that helped her reach such a position of notoriety." With that, he marched out of the office and slammed the door. Raage smiled to himself and took out his satellite phone. He gave Samakab a quick progress report. Samakab responded with the news Raage had been looking forward to hearing all morning.

Lunchtime, he thought to himself, *and then I think I'll catch some afternoon TV.*

CHAPTER 34

Word had reached Shanning that the Russian wasn't happy with the terms of the contract and the security arrangements for the hit. The man was on the verge of pulling out. That left him with a dilemma. Time was running out. He was soon to relinquish control of the Weatherman Project and Samakab was closing in on him. There was only one person in the world he could turn to now, despite everything that had happened between them. Shanning wondered if he would be online, wherever he was in the world. He tried it.

@laurelcrown246 how are you weathering the storms?

He sat and waited. He was feeling woozy. Samakab's second visit to his office the previous day had sucked the last remnants of wind from his sails. His life was in freefall and he felt utterly alone. Even after all the years of being sidelined and marginalized for his ideas and theories, he had never felt loneliness like this. Then, he had at least gained some recognition among a small circle of scientists. Now, he was cast adrift and out of touch with his peers, on a secret project that he himself had inadvertently sabotaged.

Shanning hoped that Larry hadn't deleted this Twitter account. When they were working on the Hominine project together, they had both set up accounts. They had wanted quirky names that they could remember but that would keep their identities private. In the end, they had simply looked up the original meanings of their names and used them. *Lawrence*, apparently, meant 'crown of laurels'. So Larry was the victor—in battle and in athletics. It kind of suited him, and he had enjoyed the association. In order to individualize the name, Larry had added '246'.

"Numbers have their own mystical meanings," Larry had told him, in a surprise burst of esoteric knowledge. "I'll take three numbers and you can take three different ones, according to your character. Let's see," he pondered, "I think I'll have 2, 4 and 6. 2 represents balance, tact and a kind of quiet discernment."

"Ha. So modest."

"It also represents the need for planning, which I believe is important, and it's about relationships and communication, the need for unity and clear decisions. It urges us out of duality, to do the best thing for ourselves and our fellow man."

"Very fitting," Shanning had said at the time.

Larry smiled and continued. "4 is about stability and being grounded. It represents solidity, calmness and 'home', as well as persistence and endurance. And 6 is about harmony, balance, sincerity, love and truth. We invoke the 6 when we need delicate diplomacy or when we want to deal with sensitive matters, compassionately and with forgiveness."

"Very laudable, I'm sure. Do you think you can live up to all of that?"

"They're what I aim for." Larry looked pensive. Then, smiling at his friend, he said, "And you, what numbers are you?"

"I have no idea," Shanning laughed. "I know nothing about this numerology, or whatever you call it."

"Well, let me think." He logged into a website, tap-danced over the keys and said, "I think you are spearuler359."

Shanning looked mildly confused and amused.

"Yes," Larry continued. "That's what Gerald originally meant—'spear ruler'. It doesn't sound much like the genteel intellectual that I know, but maybe you have hidden aggressive tendencies that I'm not aware of."

"Damn it, Larry, you've seen right through me! And the numbers—359?"

"You're not a 1. That's about pure energy and purity. I think I've known you too long and know too much about you to give you that honor. Besides, if you are a spear ruler, you can't be all that pure. But 3 works. It's about intuition, versatility, expression and the pure joy of creativity. And—you'll like this—it symbolizes reward and success in whatever you do. 5 is a bit of a wild card. It's unstable and unpredictable and represents radical change. Maybe it's the weather number, for you. It draws our attention to the wonders of life and the need to appreciate what looks like chaos all around us. From what I know of you, that would seem to be your life's work. And then the 9 represents attainment, satisfaction and accomplishment. It's about intellectual power, inventiveness and influence over situations and things."

"I'm liking this more and more! Yes! I shall rule the world, control the climate, bring man out of his confusion and the world will recognize me for the creative genius that I am!"

Thinking of those words made him feel quite nauseous now, as he sat and refreshed his computer screen, waiting for a reply. *Many a true word...* He refreshed the screen again.

@spearuler359 these storms I can cope with. And you?

Shanning's excitement flared then nosedived at the thought of the conversation he knew he had to have with his old friend.

@laurelcrown246 changeable, poss. cyclone imminent

There were strict limits to how much Shanning could say in this conversation. He just wished that there were some way Larry could come back.

@spearuler359 poss. or prob.?

@laurelcrown246 imminent

Shanning knew that was enough to give his friend a clear indication that something had gone terribly wrong. He was out of options and although he didn't even know if Larry could do anything from where he was, he didn't underestimate his ingenuity. If anything could be done, Larry was the man to do it. He refreshed the screen again.

@spearuler359 need storm defenses?

@laurelcrown246 need Zeus to control his son. Shanning hoped that Larry would be aware that he was talking about Ares, Zeus's unpopular and troubled son of war.

@spearuler359 that is what we started to do

@laurelcrown246 affirmative - my mistake

@spearuler359 your biggest

@laurelcrown246 and last

@spearuler 359 how long?

@laurelcrown246 no time left

There was a long pause before the reply came back. Shanning felt the nausea roll through him again and a flare of panic puckered his insides. He had developed a nasty cough that morning and now he could taste blood in his mouth.

When Samakab had returned to Shanning's office earlier that day, he had appeared to be more confident and relaxed than before.

"I have been making some inquiries and, from what I have discovered, I am protecting a weapon for you that can see into the minds of people and decide if they are fit to live or not," Samakab had posited, as Shanning poured himself a glass of water from the dispenser and sat down at the table.

"Something like that, but the weapon is programmed. It cannot think for itself."

"Who, then, is the judge, jury and executioner?"

"As it has always been: the strong."

"Strong in what—spirit, mind, arrogance, economy, brute strength?"

"It's always been a complex combination of those things. They all swirl around our existence in ever-changing patterns. Fluid systems forming and dissipating, building and dying off, organizing our lives, just like the weather. Luckily for mankind, we can now capture all the elements of the human condition—those parts of us that we have previously seen as intangible. We've learned how to predict, and we can exert our influence in order to avoid the problems of the past that have led us to the precipice."

"In your God-like opinion, which of those are the most important?"

"In my humble opinion, it doesn't matter. If we are strong, we have choice. If we want to survive, we can make that choice now." *What does he want now?*

Samakab appeared to be deep in thought. "You know, Mr Shanning," he said, after a short silence, "in my culture, people first greet each other by saying '*ma nabad ba*', which means 'is it peace?' Peace is the first thing on the mind of a Somali. We have had a particularly turbulent history, as you probably know, so the concept of peace among us is a bigger priority than the health of the individual. After all, when there is peace, health can be attended to more effectively. In your culture, you say 'how are you?' You inquire about the health of the other, although very few people really care what the answer is, and few admit to feeling anything other than 'fine'. I think that, in your culture, despite the rhetoric, egocentricity is the primary religion."

"I must remember to get that programmed in somewhere," Shanning retorted with bored distain.

Samakab continued. "The second thing we say is '*tol maa tahay?*', which literally means, 'what is your lineage?' You see, for a Somali, our genealogy—our ancestry—is much more important than our address. *Whom* we are from is much more important than *where* we are from, and if we own a flashy big house, we don't think of ourselves as being better than a beggar. What we own and what we do don't define who we are."

"I'm sure you didn't come here today to discuss the vagaries of our different cultures."

"No, of course not. But I think you may have missed something when you built your weapon."

Shanning sat up. "And what do you think the greatest minds on earth might have missed that you, in your superior wisdom, have spotted, Mr Samakab?"

"You have missed the 'why', Mr Shanning."

"I don't follow you." Shanning was beginning to find this conversation amusing.

"You and your experts have spent years researching the 'hows' and the 'whats' of human nature, in an effort to understand the 'now' and be in a position to manipulate and exclude certain people in order to benefit a fortunate few in the future. What you have done is undoubtedly impressive; a colossus of human knowledge has been amassed. But it is nothing without the missing piece—the 'why'—and that comes from the past; it is the essential piece that you and your team didn't concern themselves with." He waited for Shanning to respond, but he sat motionless.

Then, Shanning shrugged his shoulders, "Why?"

"Surely it's obvious. It's the 'why' that drives the 'hows' and the 'whats'. The 'why' is the very thing that must have brought this project into being." Samakab reflected on his realization for a moment, with a growing satisfaction. "You didn't conceive of this project, did you, Mr Shanning? It must have taken a great mind to do that. And I do believe, Mr Shanning, that great minds have integrity and would have an honorable 'why'—an honorable reason to put this whole thing together. Such a mind would not plan a project of this complexity and magnitude purely for domination. But it only takes a small mind to destroy its integrity. Unfortunately, in this world, the weak are many and the strong are few. Weakness brings betrayal, betrayal brings fear and fear brings death. One single betrayal, born of a weak, greedy and fearful mind, Mr Shanning. Is that the way it happened? Is that the way of the strong?" Shanning had lost his smile.

"How dare you lecture me," Shanning fumed, his mouth tight, his clenched fist shaking beneath the table. "I seem to remember that you have profited handsomely from my generosity. You and your pirate mafia have nothing to complain about!"

"I am not complaining, and I never said I was any better than you. As I have just explained, that is not in my culture. But I am stronger, and I believe that my culture has given me a better understanding of human nature than all your fancy technologies and clever minds have given you."

"Well, in that case, maybe *you* should be running this project! Is that what you think?" Shanning scoffed.

"Yes, it is. In fact, I am running it." Samakab fixed Shanning with a steady stare. Shanning picked up his phone and started to dial. "They won't come." Shanning's finger froze above the keypad. "They work for me now—most of them, anyway. The rest will follow."

"What do you mean?"

"You weren't listening, Mr Shanning." Samakab took a small bottle from his jacket pocket. He unscrewed the top, which had a built-in pipette. Squeezing the rubber end, he drew some clear liquid up into the glass tube and, leaning toward Shanning, he released it into Shanning's glass of water as he spoke. "It's a cultural thing. Westerners who have never experienced any real suffering are less concerned about the peace of mankind beyond their borders, and more concerned about their own health. Thanks to my culture and the natural interest I have in genealogy, I know where they are from."

"I hope you know what you're doing." Shanning was so shocked at the scale and rapidity of his own demise that he could think of nothing else to say.

"Have no doubt that I do, Mr Shanning." He stood up and turned to leave. "Enjoy my parting gift to you," he said, turning back toward him from the door. "It may be a little uncomfortable for a while but it will save you from having to face the consequences of your ineptitude—not to mention some kind of unfortunate accident. But this…" he gestured towards the glass of water, "is nothing dramatic. A slow dissolution. Time enough to tie up loose ends, make your peace with the world. You'll be around long enough to watch the fruits of your labor unfold from the safety of a hospital bed. I have no doubt you will at last get the recognition you've always craved, although I doubt you will enjoy it.

It's your ideal way out, since it requires very little courage." He smiled thinly at Shanning, and added, "I'll just let everyone know that you're not feeling too well," before closing the door behind him.

Shanning could hear him calmly talking to the staff outside his office. The glass stood in front of him on the table. The liquid inside was clear and colorless. Small bubbles adhered to the sides. Concentric ripples played on the surface, generated by the hum of the computer stack in the main work area. He looked out at the sky. *Well, I've never seen that before!* He smiled as he looked far up into the atmosphere. *Altocumulus standing lenticularis.* He recalled its definition: *a stationary lens-shaped cloud that forms at high altitudes, normally aligned at right-angles to the wind direction. How appropriate!* There was a rushing in his ears, a spring tide of memories, snatches of a life unlived, the petty grasping for acceptance. Recognition? He doubted it; he knew the limp legacy of his failings. A bullet in the head when his back was turned was more likely. He looked out at the labyrinth of computers and wiring, and his employees—absorbed in futile busyness. And he felt his whole face sag, as if gravity had finally claimed it and it was no longer his. He grabbed the glass of water and gulped it down so fast it sputtered down his nose. Gasping for breath, he flung the glass at the trash can in the corner but it bounced off the wall and rolled slowly to a standstill, empty and aimless.

It was a while before the burning started. He'd had one sleepless, nightmarish night, without the pain that was now his constant companion, to reflect on the disastrous course his decisions had charted for his life. When he'd walked through the main work area that morning, his staff had watched him silently as he made his way to the office, apart from one girl who'd said, as he passed her, that she hoped he felt better soon. He felt small and frightened, weak and insignificant. Images of his childhood flashed through his mind. Flying a kite on a breezy day. The fascination he had, even then, with the unseen, ever-changing forces that shaped lives and over which we have no control. *We have no control. But maybe control is not what we should be seeking.*

@spearuler 359 am sending the cavalry - home.

CHAPTER 35

"What? That's horseshit!" Eric studied the message on his computer screen. He got up from his desk and ran through to office four, where one of the programmers was staring intently at his screen. "What's going on, Andy?"

"Damned if I know." Andy was busy checking across an array of monitors, making notes. "It came through this afternoon. It's from the Weatherman but the format is different, and this additional information here... is completely bizarre."

"You know I can't read this stuff. Explain."

"Sir, what we have here is the usual encrypted start that checks out fine and verifies this as an official and trustworthy instruction. Then there's this part here that relates to an initialization code for HAPISAD," he pointed at a string of indecipherable text on one of the screens, "and then there's this." He showed Eric a small window that appeared to be blank apart from a tiny rectangle in the top, left-hand corner.

"So, what's that?"

"I wish I knew, sir." Andy pushed his glasses up his nose and wiped some sweat from his forehead with his sleeve. "This should be a series of codes, but I can't see them. When I asked New York what they were, they just said it was a new format they were using. But that didn't make any sense to me. How am I supposed to check the codes before we upload them to the pod? That's our last positive checking procedure. It's the only way we can rectify anything that's incorrect."

"Well, tell them you need them in a format you *can* check."

"I already did that, sir."

"And what did they say?"

"Not possible. And before you ask, they said that they have a new security protocol in place now. Instructions came down from the top, apparently, after the Afghan incident."

"What the—are they blaming *us* for that, now? That's bullshit! We know and they know that was a fault in the original programming. We can only check what they send us, and they know that full well. We checked—"

"Yes, I know sir, and I re-sent the log of that event, as a precaution, just in case they turn nasty on us. I don't know what's going on, sir, but it sure looks like there's someone in New York who wants us to carry the can for that incident."

"It sure does." Eric gave him a comforting pat on the shoulder. "But let's not jump to conclusions. I'll get on to the Weatherman and see if there's been some mistake. We can't work blind, and there's no way I'm going to send that aircraft on a mission without knowing exactly what it's going to do."

"I'd appreciate that, sir, 'cause these codes are to be activated any day now, and I need a little time…" Eric went back to his office, but no sooner had he sat down than another message came through from Andy.

'Eric: before you contact WM, you should see this.'

"What now!?" He ran back to Andy's office where Andy had taken his glasses off and was rubbing his eyes.

"You may not be able to read the code, but I think you'll understand this." He limply waved in the direction of one of his monitors.

Watch Charlise Kenny, Hearts on Hold, *CTV, 10.30pm yr local time*

Eric peered at the words in disbelief. "You've got to be kidding me. What the hell is going on here?" He turned to Andy, who was diligently cleaning his glasses with a tissue. "ANDY!" Andy jumped, and put his glasses back on.

"Sir, if I knew what was going on, I would have done something about it. All I can think is that someone who doesn't know what he's doing is screwing around with the equipment in New York."

"And what do you think the chances of that are, given the kind of protocols they have in place?"

"About a zillion to one, at a rough guess."

"I concur. Don't do anything." Eric stormed out of the office. He sat at his desk, thinking. If his people at the base were being set up by someone in New York to take the rap for the Afghan incident, why would that be? And why now? Why would they have waited so long? As Andy had said, the fault clearly lay in New York, and they didn't seem to be denying that—not officially, anyway. He knew they just configured code combinations and refined the data in the New York office, and that system was linked to a much larger computer that held all the programming. No one seemed to know where the main computer was located, but he suspected that it was not in the Pentagon or at a military location, as the military were being kept in the dark about the Weatherman Project, for now. Maybe the problem had originated in the main computer and had somehow bypassed New York. Whatever the technical details, the problem for Eric was that the message Andy had shown him was genuine and verified. There was nothing unusual or suspicious about the coding instructions, other than that the crucial part was hidden from them. He was not allowed to communicate by voice, and neither was anyone else on the base. In fact, for most of the occupants of the base, no external communications were allowed at all, for fear of giving away their position. Both he and Andy could only send messages through the Project's secure satellite system that was also used to transfer data. The only other person on the base who could communicate externally was Raage, and although he had voice, his phone had been locked to sending to, and receiving from, the Weatherman Project only. But even if Raage was up to something, it wouldn't account for these strange communications, and he couldn't figure out why Raage would want to cause difficulties at the base by putting out a story that blamed Eric's people for a problem that happened weeks previously. Raage's role was to keep the base secret, as far as Eric understood, and it didn't extend to any technical details regarding AVTOL.

He referred to his manual, found the number for 'malfunction' and typed a message.

Program 485?

Within seconds the reply came back.

Negative OK Proceed

He was confused. *Damn it!* He typed another message.

Getting strange instructions. Please clarify

"Let's see if this gets a reaction."

Not recognized. Use P7945 procedure

"Okay, so you don't want to play ball. Let's try this."

Imperative 888

"If that doesn't get a response, I don't know what will."

No 888 acknowledge no 888 acknowledge

"Okay, I hear you. So, you don't want me to abort the next mission. But I need some answers here." He typed again.

Clarify 002

He didn't want to acknowledge their previous message until he'd got his answers, but he knew that if it looked as if he was challenging his superiors, he was playing a dangerous game. The next message sent him back to his manual.

No 888 acknowledge ‡ proceed M24 ‡ Ω WM640 acknowledge Δ

"Yes, well, I got the first bit, thanks guys. Wow, that's a double cross affirmative instruction on mission 24, but what does the rest mean?" The manual was comprehensive. It needed to be, to cover all situations that might arise at this remote location. He flicked through the pages. "Omega, omega... ah, there it is." He made a note: "All, everything." He continued. "I know the triangle is 'affirmative and agreed AOK', but WM640—I haven't come across that one before." He froze when he got to the page and found it. "Jesus H Christ, what the fuck?" Throwing the manual onto the floor, he ran out of the office and burst into Raage's room. Raage was sitting at his table, reading a novel. He looked up at Eric, who was gripping the door handle, shaking with anger.

"Eric, how can I help you?" Raage casually inquired.

"Ever since you arrived on this base, things have been happening that I'm finding difficult to explain. Last night, we had that incident when absolutely no evidence of an intrusion could be found, suggesting to me that whatever happened, it was something caused by someone on the base. This afternoon I get two strange communications from New York, one of which doesn't follow the strict formatting guidelines that we are required to use, and the other hiding essential mission-related information from my programmer. When I make inquiries of New York, they tell me that I should talk to my superior—the Weatherman Project representative. Obviously there's a mistake in the wording or the number code is inadequate for the communication, but I would really appreciate it if you would tell me what the hell is going on."

Raage carefully folded the top corner of the page he was reading, closed the book, and laid it on the table before answering.

"There has been no misunderstanding, and the messages you received have been clear and precise. At least one of them followed the protocol, didn't it?"

"Yes, it did, but—"

"Sir."

"I beg your pardon?"

"Yes, it did, *sir*. That's the correct way to address your superior in the military, isn't it?"

Eric lurched forward and barely managed to stop himself from flying at Raage. *This is crazy!* But crazy as it seemed to Eric, his hands were tied, and he knew it. He had no logical reason to challenge the orders from New York, and he knew that it was his intense dislike and suspicion of Raage that was interfering with his military discipline. As distasteful as it was for him to hand over control of the base to a Somali about whom he knew nothing and who had been delivered to him in the desert, accompanied by a truckload of armed thugs, he didn't know what else he could do.

"Fuck you," Eric turned to go back to his office, "and you can forget the 'sir'. I mean to find out what's going on here." He marched out of the room, leaving the door open. Raage walked to the door and watched. "Charlie!" Eric called to one of the drivers who was heading toward the washroom. "Charlie, get over here!" Charlie met him near Eric's office, but in Raage's earshot. "Charlie, I want you to get down to Berbera and see Captain Baptiste on the ship. Here's what I want…" Eric looked over and saw Raage watching. He walked away with Charlie, talking quietly so Raage couldn't hear. Raage watched as Eric spoke and Charlie nodded and made the occasional gesture. Eric finished off with an audible "on the double, Charlie" as Charlie waved and got into the driving seat of one of the Prowlers.

Raage walked over to where Eric was standing, deep in thought. "He won't get far," he said, quietly, as they watched the Prowler's plume of dust disappear into the desert. Something in Eric snapped. He grabbed Raage round the neck with his arm, and pulled his handgun out of its holster, digging it painfully into Raage's ribs.

"Give me one good reason why I shouldn't just shoot you right here, right now."

"Mandy."

Eric backed off in horror. *What the hell does he know about my Mandy?*

"The other message," Raage said, as he pulled free and rearranged his shirt, "has all the reasons. I think everyone will want to watch that show." Eric did a double-take. *What about Charlie?*

"Did you just watch while I sent him to his—?"

"Don't worry. He'll be fine..." Raage started walking to the canteen, "as long as he stops when he's asked to." Once inside the canteen, he banged on the hatch. "Walt, are you there?" The hatch opened. "Walt, hi, we're going to need to keep the canteen open late this evening—till about 11.30."

"Who says?" Walt eyed him suspiciously, wiping his hands on his dirty apron.

"I do, and Eric." He leaned out of the doorway and called to Eric, who was pacing slowly around, distracted, making patterns in the dust with his boots as he thought to himself. "That's right, isn't it Eric? We'll need the canteen open late this evening." Eric looked up and, having given it some thought, nodded. *Good*, he thought to himself. *That's progress.* "I'll have a coffee, if I may. Sumatran dark roast with a hint of Arabica?"

"Instant FUBAR roast is the best I can do," Walt snarled, and walked to the cooker mumbling "fuckin' hadji Jawa." Raage smiled to himself, enjoying some light relief before the trials of the evening began. He sat at a table and switched on the TV news. Israel was getting some bad press over Gaza, ISAF troops were getting killed in Afghanistan, there was an earthquake in Guatemala, and mounting international concern over Somali piracy. *Nothing changes*, Raage thought to himself. But the piracy debate caught his attention. The EU was in conflict with NATO over how to deal with the issue. Should cargo ships be encouraged to carry infantry units? Should there be more action focused closer to Somali ports? What was being done to recover the vast amounts being paid to Somali warlords? There was a vote coming up soon, on 'decisive and far-reaching action' within Somalia itself, proposed by the UK Government. Europe was split 50/50 for and against invading and occupying key areas. Some countries were insistent that invasion was the wrong decision. They cited the repeated experience of the USA. Supposedly quick invasions and wars had always turned into protracted occupations that were both costly to maintain and difficult to bring to a satisfactory conclusion. That was also one of the reasons the US was staying out of the debate—and the Americans no doubt had the memory of their unsuccessful efforts in Somalia during Clinton's presidency on their minds as well. The fact that their failure had come to be epitomized by a widely-viewed Hollywood film not only increased their desire to remain separated from the debate, but the film itself had clearly shown what a hell-hole soldiers would be entering if an invasion took place. Many governments were reluctant to set foot in such a violent and unstable country, or risk the lives of their citizens for what was clearly an economic war that couldn't be presented as an idealistic one. On the other hand, the economic cost of allowing the piracy to continue was becoming prohibitive. It was widely accepted that piracy would continue to escalate as the pirates were bolstered by successes and able to invest in better and better equipment. Economies were already stretched to breaking point, and governments were less and less able to hide that fact or work around it. Many governments felt that taking decisive action would 'send the right signal' to their citizens and help stem the price increases that the problem was creating. There were many more arguments that were swinging public opinion one way and then the other. Everything hinged on the outcome of a debate in the House of Commons the following week. But whatever happened in Europe, it wouldn't affect Raage. He knew he would be looked after. He would retire as a young, successful man, find a wife and start a family in his luxurious villa in western Kenya.

Eric returned to his office and typed another message. He had to be sure.

Raage?

The reply came immediately.

No 888 acknowledge ‡ proceed M24 ‡ Ω WM640 acknowledge Δ

Damn! He hadn't replied to the previous message according to the correct protocol, so this message automatically repeated, and the lack of an answer would have been flagged in New York. At least now he knew he had their full attention. But what was he to do? Should he agree to proceed with mission 24? He didn't want to, but he knew he had to tell them it would go ahead. He could always cancel later, he told himself. He could think up a technical reason for that, if necessary. So he sent the message they wanted to hear.

Δ M24 proceed

The system sent another reply back immediately.

Ω WM640 acknowledge Δ

It wanted the rest of the answer. He hesitated. Standing up, he walked around his office. He couldn't think straight any more. *But I must!* He stood in the doorway and let his gaze wander over to the AVTOL. He looked back at his computer screen.

Ω WM640 acknowledge Δ

The message had repeated again. He scrolled up and checked the other message that Raage had reminded him of a few minutes before.

Watch Charlise Kenny, Hearts on Hold, *CTV, 10.30pm yr local time*

It looked like a prank. It would have been hard to take seriously at any other time. He wondered if it could possibly have some other meaning. He searched the manual again, but it was no help at all. He'd never watched the show but, from what he could remember, *Hearts on Hold* was just a stupid afternoon TV show for bored housewives—a mixture of recipes and reunions, songs and chat. Candy floss for empty minds.

All the same, he decided to wait before acknowledging the message from New York.

✳✳✳

During the evening meal, Eric announced that there was to be a special meeting in the canteen that evening at 10.30pm, because he'd received an unusual request from New York that everyone watch a popular TV show. He was almost drowned out by laughter and wise cracks. Some of the men thought he must be up to something—a surprise treat, some sort of reward for hard work or just some relief from the monotony of life in the desert. They tried hard to get him to reveal his secret, but they couldn't even get him to smile. So they'd left the canteen in a jovial mood, nudging each other, smiling and winking at Eric as he picked at his half-eaten meal, trying to hide his anger.

By 10.15, they were drifting back in. Raage had already taken his place next to the serving hatch at the opposite end of the room to where the TV was mounted on the wall. Eric came in and also sat near the back, but on the opposite side of the room to Raage. The room filled up, the men joked with each other, in happy anticipation. The title sequence for *Hearts on Hold* started and the room went quiet. The camera flew around the primed audience who clapped and cheered and whooped and whistled, before swinging around to the stage:

"*...and here is your host, please give a warm welcome to... Chaaaar-lise!* A cheer went up in the canteen. Charlise Kenny's ample form appeared, tightly trussed up in a red jacket and black skirt, flashing a wide smile and perfect teeth, tottering slightly on heels as she waved to her fans. She walked to center stage and took a bow, before seating herself on a bright red sofa, where she paused while the warm-up guys cooled the audience down to silence.

"*Wow, thank you! I wish I got that kind of reception from my husband when I get home every night.*" Canned laughter. "*Only kiddin'. He's a gem and I wouldn't have him any other way.*" Kenny referred briefly to her notes on the low table in front of her. "*Boy, have I got a show for you today! I tell you, if you've got other plans, just ditch 'em, cause you're not gonna want to miss this. Go on, do that right now! Ditch 'em. You done it? I didn't hear anything.*" She cocked an ear playfully toward the camera. "*Okay. We all set?*" She looked around the studio, as if to check that everyone was listening. "*Right, let's not keep our hearts on hold—let's fast-forward. I don't want to keep you all waiting any longer than I have to.*" The studio lights dimmed, leaving Kenny spot-lit as the camera glided toward her for a head and shoulders view. Soft music played as she introduced the show. Her mood switched from the exuberance of the star entry to a soft, warm, sincere persona.

"*You are very welcome to* Hearts on Hold—*the show that helps you bridge the storms of passion and the heartache of separation, that can help you heal, and help you steal, the heart of someone new.*" A trademark wink and a smile. "*Who are we?*" She raised her arms to the audience.

'*We're cupid's lil' helpers!*' the audience replied in unison. Charlise laughed, regained her 'sincere' composure, and continued.

"*Thank you for joining us. Today, we are going to look at the pain of separation from loved ones, and how some folks strive to thrive in spite of it. But today we're not just talking about any folks—not that we aren't all special, special people. Today, we're talking with the families of service men and women who daily risk their lives so that we—yes, that's you and you and you and you,*" she nodded her head to different sections of the audience, "*and me,*" another brief smile as she returned eye contact to camera, "*can enjoy our safety and security without the fear of terrorism visiting us at our door.*" Some of the men in the canteen cheered and threw their fists in the air. "*So, who are these people, and how do they deal with the uncertainty, the not knowing if their loved ones are safe? How would they cope, for instance, should that terrible day arrive when they learn that their loved one—a lover, a friend, a husband, father or mother—won't be coming home again? What would they like to say to their loved ones, right now, that would let them know how much they miss them? Well, we've been able to find some very special guests who we'll be talking to, and who will be able to give you an insight into their lives, their love stories and the pain they're going through every day. And, of course, our lines are open for your calls. Here's the number, so if you have something you'd like to share, or something you'd like to offer as words of comfort, please call. We'd love to hear from you. You're watching* Hearts on Hold, *helping your love to be bold. We'll be right back after this.*" The show's logo spun out and gave way to a commercial break. The men laughed.

"Hey, Eric," Ben shouted, "don't tell me you're goin' soft on us!" Eric waved him down with a smile. He was beginning to enjoy the light-hearted banter—until he glanced over at Raage, who calmly took a swig of Coke.

"Eric… Eric," Antonio, one of the marines, tried to catch Eric's attention, "didya put one up the pipe last time you was home or somethin'? You wanna check to see if your old lady's got somethin' she wants to tell you?" Eric looked embarrassed. He had no idea where this was going. He looked over at Raage again, but Raage just smiled back at him.

"Okay, here we go, quiet down guys! Eyes front," Ben said, as the show's signature tune signaled the end of the break. A brightly-lit head-and-shoulders shot of Kenny appeared.

"*Hello and welcome back. I'm Charlise Kenny, and you're watching* Hearts on Hold, *the show for young and old, that lets your stories unfold, stories that should be told—but so often we just bottle them up, and keep them to ourselves. But we know how healing it can be to just talk, to share our concerns. As I mentioned before the break, today we are talking to the loved ones of men and women out there who are doing a great job protecting our lives and our liberties. And remember, we want to hear from you, so keep those calls coming, and as always, at the end of the show, we'll be checkin' our Cupidometer to see who's gonna win a gorgeous two-week romantic break in St Lucia with their loved one!"* Wild applause erupted as music played over a short clip showing a sun-soaked hotel pool followed by a candle-lit dinner scene. The music faded and Kenny continued. *"Boy, I bet you know someone who could use some of that! Moving on! Today, I have with me a young mother, Shannon, and her two gorgeous young boys, Nathan and Todd."* The camera panned out to reveal a young mother sitting next to her, holding two small children on her lap.

"Shannon? Hey, that's my Shannon!" Antonio leaped from his seat to get closer to the TV screen.

"Hey, sit down, I can't see," Ben shouted. Antonio ignored him.

"And my two beautiful boys! Hey," he turned to the crowded room, "they look just like me, don't they?"

"They look more like your staff sergeant, if you ask me," someone called out. Shannon was beaming. The boys were looking everywhere and Nathan was trying to get off his mother's lap.

"So, Shannon, you're from Oregon, and you have a husband…" she checked her notes, *"Antonio, who is also the loving father of these two gorgeous kids. Boy, you must be proud! And you're having to bring these little gentlemen up all by yourself while your husband is on tour. Well, I think that's very brave, Shannon, and I bet if Antonio could see you now, he'd be real proud. Give her a hand, ladies and gentlemen!"* Shannon blushed deeply as the applause rang out. Todd sucked two of his fingers and squirmed on her lap.

"My baby! My boys!" Antonio gushed proudly at the screen.

Kenny turned to Shannon with a seriously concerned expression and asked the obvious leading question. *"Shannon, is that the most difficult job you've ever had—bringing up these two boys on your own without a man around to help?"*

"Well, I guess so," Shannon replied meekly as she struggled to keep the boys on her lap, *"but it's okay, I guess. I mean loads of mothers are doin' the same as me, so I guess I'm no worse off 'n them."*

"Shannon, I think that's very brave of you, and it sounds as if you are so strong that you don't need a lil' help from Cupid. Am I right?"

"Oh, I wouldn't say that. Everyone needs a bit a help sometimes." Antonio was transfixed with watery eyes. There was silence in the canteen.

"Tell me, Shannon, do you ever pray to God for a little bit of help, just to get you through the day?"

"I sure do, all the time."

HOMININE

"And can you tell me where Antonio is stationed right now? Maybe we can work a little bit of magic here for you." Shannon's face started to crease up. Tears welled up in her eyes. The camera closed in on her face.

"I… I don't know, Charlise. I don't know where they sent him." She wiped a tear from her eye as she tried to regain her composure. Someone put a comforting arm on Antonio's shoulder as he gazed speechlessly up at the screen with a soft smile. *"I think they sent him on one of them special ops or somethin', and they won't tell me where he is."*

"That must be real hard for you, Shannon…" Kenny glanced at the camera to make sure they were framed tight on Shannon's face, *"and how does that make you feel?"* Shannon started sobbing. The producer cut to the audience where some were silently wiping tears from their faces, then back to Shannon, a wider shot with Kenny's hand on her knee. *"It's okay, Shannon. It's okay. You are one brave girl."* Then, speaking to Shannon as if confidentially, like a close friend, she said, *"Shannon, how would you feel if you knew that Antonio was safe, and that he thinks he'll be able to come home real soon?"*

"But how can I? If he's on a secret mission, he's not allowed to write me. I don't wanna raise any false hopes or nothin', and I can't tell the boys that sorta thing if it ain't true."

"Well, Shannon, maybe you can, because we received this from Antonio just a few days ago." She handed Shannon a piece of paper. She read it and her face lit up. She put her hand over her mouth and tears of joy rolled down her flushed face.

"I don't get it…" Antonio looked confused.

"Shannon," Kenny continued, *"when you are ready…"* Shannon tried to pull herself together. She kissed the boys on their heads and nodded to Kenny, *"would you like to read what it says?"*

"Sure." Shannon took a deep breath and slowly read the text. *"Dear Shannon,"* she stumbled on, trying to keep her emotions in check as Kenny kept a hand resting on her knee. *"My lovely girl. I got special permission to write you this e-mail from here in Afghanistan. I can't tell you where I am specifically, but enough to say I am safe and well, and they say that so long as the weather holds up, I should be home soon. I love you. Tell Nathan and Todd I love them too, and you are always in my heart, all of you. Oh, and tell Jack at the bar that next time I'm in Murray's the drinks are on me! Love ya! Antonio."*

"Thank you, Shannon. That's beautiful. And just one more thing. Can you show the audience what Antonio attached to the e-mail?" Shannon triumphantly held up the message to reveal a studio photo of Antonio and his family. The audience went wild.

"Thank you so much!" Shannon was crying again, hugging her children as the camera focused in on Kenny.

"We're going to take a break now. Up next, we have a call from Mandy in Iowa, who also has a message from a special man on a mission. We'll see you again, right after this!"

The excitement in the canteen disappeared as quickly as it had erupted when Shannon had displayed the photo in the e-mail. Antonio was lying in a crumpled heap on the floor, sobbing. Eric quickly went over to him and crouched down beside him.

"Antonio." He waited for Antonio to take a deep breath and stop the sobbing. "What do you know about this?" he quietly asked him.

"Nothing! Nothing, I swear it. I can't e-mail from here. You know that!"

"Why did they say you were in Afghanistan? Who did you talk to before you came over here?"

"Eric, I swear I told nothin' to no one. I didn't even know where I was going!" Eric's mind was racing, but he already knew the answer to what was happening. He just didn't want to admit it. He certainly couldn't bear the thought that Mandy from Iowa was his Mandy, but in his heart he knew it was. "Eric," Antonio wiped his face, and with a stronger voice he said, "whoever did this knows where I live. They have been in my fucking house because that's where that photo is. It's in our bedroom. They know who my friends are, where I drink and who my kids are."

"Yes, I see that. I'm sorry…"

"Eric, you've got to get me out of here. I have to get home, like *now*!"

"It's not that simple. But… I'll work something out."

"It is simple, Eric. Nobody threatens my family. I have to go."

Eric stood up. There was confusion on the faces of everyone in the canteen, except Raage, who sat calmly at the back of the room.

"How many more!?" Eric shouted. The others turned to face Raage.

"We've only seen a small part of the show, and then there are the phone calls…"

"You fuck! How many? Who?"

"I don't know how many Charlise was able to accommodate, but she may include anyone who has a loved one here."

Eric slammed his fist into the power switch on the TV. "We've had enough of this shit!"

"What's going on, Eric?" Ben asked. "What the fuck is going on?"

"Ask him. He knows a hell of a lot more about this than I do." Eric glared at Raage, waiting for him to respond.

Raage slowly got to his feet. "Nothing's going on that need concern you, and nothing will happen to anyone, as long as the weather holds up—just like it said in the e-mail," he said. "Right now, I just want to have a word with Brian, Frank and Ben—outside." The pilots looked to Eric, who shook his head and waved them toward the door. "The rest of you will please carry on and do your jobs. And here's a piece of advice: don't upset the Weatherman. When you enlisted, you signed up to protect American lives. Well, now you have a good opportunity to do just that." Raage followed the two pilots and the driver out the door.

Chapter 36

"Griff, I forgot to ask you something before you left." Griffin felt Sheryl's presence as her voice came over the loudspeaker in the Prius. He instinctively looked toward the passenger seat, but his black briefcase was sitting on it, not her.

"What is it, honey?" He'd only left their house five minutes ago. He was just coming to the end of the lake and she was calling already! But then, this was post-Bali. They'd marked the watershed. They'd moved from the dark and seemingly distant pre-Bali realm to a bright new era. Griffin now spent a lot more time at their home on the lush shores of Lake Carasaljo, just outside Lakewood, flying back from Washington to Trenton whenever he could get away from the office. It was a long journey but, to Griffin, well worth it. When they'd returned from Bali, they sold the Aston Martin quickly, for a knock-down price, and bought a small Dodge truck and a Toyota Prius with the proceeds. Griffin wanted to landscape the garden. He'd even thought of digging up part of their vast lawn and planting vegetables, so the truck was going to be useful. Sheryl wanted to downsize, so she sold her SUV and now they had some spare cash to put into their home. Once Griffin had gone through the pain of losing his beautiful, throaty Aston Martin, he'd come to love the total silence of the Prius, which he found amusing and thought of as a toy car. "It's only a Toyota, when are they going to make one for grown-ups?" he'd joked when they'd driven it away from the showroom.

"It's Fernando. I wanted to offer to help him out," said Sheryl.

"Oh." Griffin smiled. "Do I detect some pre-Bali guilt that needs assuaging here?"

"Well, maybe…" Griffin imagined Sheryl coiling the telephone cord around her finger as she spoke. They were rather attached to the old phone in the kitchen. He pictured her lodging it between her shoulder and head, trailing the coiled wire over furniture, around the blender and over work surfaces, knocking notepads, cutlery and the odd vase of flowers out of the way as she spoke.

"So, what great favor is about to be bestowed on him?" Griffin had never seen much of Fernando, Sheryl's interior designer. Pre-Bali, Griffin had preferred to spend most of his time living in Washington, in relative peace and without the complications of his relationship with Sheryl. On the few occasions he'd seen Fernando in Lakewood, the poor man had been the butt of Sheryl's vicious tempers. Being sensitive and, in Griffin's opinion, more than a little camp, he was an easy target. He was also extremely talented and very particular, precise and diligent in his work, which he loved with a passion. Griffin could remember the day that everything went wrong. The curtains had been delivered for the main living room, which had three sets of French windows opening onto a large patio, plus another four windows looking onto the lawn. It was a beautiful, airy room. Unfortunately for Fernando, Sheryl was also extremely fussy about detail and specific about colors. As Fernando was hanging the last set of curtains, Sheryl thought she saw an uneven texture in the fabric. There was a slight fault that was barely detectable until the curtain was hung in the light of the window. Sheryl had shown it to Griffin, who couldn't really see it, but she was insistent. Further investigation led to Sheryl deciding that the entire batch of very expensive fabric was a fractional shade lighter than the sample that she'd seen when she commissioned the work. Fernando's bank account plummeted as Sheryl rejected the whole job and he got caught in the middle of a raging argument. The fabric supplier thought Fernando was being ridiculous, making such a fuss. Didn't he know that they never guaranteed exact matches on shade? Sheryl refused to pay for anything and threatened to sue Fernando for the replacement curtains, lost time, stress and anything else she could think of. All this sent Fernando into a deep depression that resulted in him losing other work and eventually going bust. Griffin couldn't understand why the man was even still *speaking* to Sheryl.

"I'd really like him to have the use of the Washington apartment for a while, to help him get back on his feet." Griffin wasn't expecting her to ask for such a *big* favor. He reckoned that, by now, the telephone cord must be coiled up to Sheryl's elbow.

"What? Sheryl, I still live there… well, some of the time."

"I know, Griff, but not as much as you did. I sort of thought you could… well… share it with him, when you're there. It has two bedrooms—"

"Yes, I know. Hang on. Let me think about this for a second. I need to get my head around the idea."

"Be careful, Griff. Do you need to stop for a minute?"

Griffin laughed. "No, I don't think it's life-threatening. I can still think and drive." All the same, he slowed a little. "Is he…?"

"Is he what?"

"Look, I've never lived with a…" he couldn't say it.

"Gay? Is that what you're trying to say? Griff! What are you—homophobic or something?"

"No, no. I just…"

"What, Griff?" Griffin could feel the smile in her voice.

"It's just that, in all our time together, I've never once woken up with another man in my home—on my own, if you know what I mean."

"But you won't be on your own, Griff, he'll be there!" Sheryl giggled.

"Damn, Sheryl. I mean, what about the laundry and stuff? I mean…"

Griffin was projecting himself into a nightmare world—coming back from the office, wrecked from a hard day's work and dying for a beer, but being served Lapsang Souchong tea with cup cakes by Fernando in a pink housecoat and fluffy slippers. And what about the bathroom? God almighty!

"Griff... Griff!"

"What?"

"He's not gay."

"Are you sure? How do you know?"

"What are you suggesting?"

"No, I didn't mean *that!*"

"Griff."

"What?"

"Calm down. He's a perfectly normal, very nice man. He's just... creative. That's all. Actually, if you had to have any company in that macho male apartment of yours, he's probably the best kind of person to have. He's totally trustworthy, neat, clean and he'll look after the place really well." Sheryl paused for a reaction, but Griffin just sighed. "So, what d'you say?"

"I guess it will mean I'll want to spend even more time with you in Lakewood, so yes, let's do it!" He felt a warm surge in his heart. That was happening more and more these days. He felt loved, now, and that had changed everything.

"Yesss!!" Sheryl shouted, and Griffin heard a saucepan crash onto the floor. "Oh, shit..."

"Call you later, after I've been to Little Ferry. Enjoy dinner—or do you need to order in?" He laughed as the phone went dead.

Griffin relaxed to Bach's concerto in A minor as he cruised up Highway Nine. Once he joined the Garden State Parkway and stopped to pay the toll at Raritan, he switched the radio off and started to think about the meeting with Shanning.

Ever since he'd come back from Bali, he'd been aware of a kind of 'other-worldliness'. Somehow he was here, but at the same time he was now an observer of his own life and everything going on around him. He was involved, but on a different level. Although he felt slightly removed from people and events, he somehow connected on a very different level, although the difference was so subtle that he couldn't quite grasp what it was. Sometimes he had a laser-like clarity with a universal, all-seeing quality to it, but when he tried to capture it, keep it and file it away in his mind, it was gone. It evaporated as if it had never been there, yet it had felt as real as the ground beneath his feet.

But it was during those fleeting, unfathomable and instantly forgettable periods of extreme lucidity that he had made great, effortless strides. He'd re-organized his working life. Somehow, he was doing a lot less yet achieving a great deal more. His assistant, Judy, had done a marvelous job handling press and government inquiries and had seamlessly managed his affairs so that when he and Sheryl had returned, there was no drama to face, no angry faces and no political fall-out. He had rewarded her with an increase in salary and a much greater degree of trust. Once he could see that she was perfectly capable of making important decisions on his behalf, he had extended a greater level of autonomy to all his staff. Now, instead of the nervous glances that used to greet him every morning, he was enthusiastically received by everyone. It made him realize that he hadn't been quite as popular as he'd thought, back then. Pre-Bali, he'd wielded his authority like a weapon, trying to cover all the potential failings of his staff with a mixture of bullying and systems that they adhered to in fear of being fired should they ever slip up. Now, any uncertainty in his office was usually due to his own concern that he might let his staff down should *he* slip up. It was a complete turnabout for Griffin. It hadn't been easy for him, because trust is trust, after all, and it meant letting go of control. But, inch by inch and day by day, he was discovering that what he was gaining far outweighed what he'd let go.

Even so, he was new to all this, and sometimes he fell back into the old ways—the reliable, tried and tested, logical, sensible, safe ways of doing things. When that happened, his pre-Bali patterns of control, judgment and reactive behaviors came charging back in all their pompous self-importance. That's when things usually backfired, and Sheryl would coax him gently back onto the new track that was still being built through the rollercoaster roadways of his mind.

What was important? Just on this short journey, he'd spent five minutes talking to his wife about Fernando and his own paranoia around protecting his space, and he'd listened to some wonderful soothing music. Yet he was en route to a meeting with a man whose actions had possibly resulted in a chaotic and life-threatening situation that could have devastating consequences for the world. How could he keep a healthy perspective? He was a US Senator. He was an air-guitarist who wanted nothing more than to feel his wife's arms around him and the soft warmth of her breasts on his face. People all over the world looked to him to solve some of the most intransigent problems and bring an end to suffering, hatred and long-standing disputes. He couldn't even cook a decent scrambled egg. How did someone like him, with all the conflicts and uncertainties in his mind that any normal person had, make the right decision? Was there a right decision? Was the outcome somehow preordained? Was it all already written in the stars, the planets, in the book? Was there even a decision to be made? He would be talking with a man who had his finger on the pulse of all human characteristics. *He probably knows more about me than anyone else, including me! Surely he can wrap me round his little finger with his vastly superior intellect and manipulative ways and flick me off like a speck of dust.*

Stop! Stop this. It's ridiculous. The Prius rolled effortlessly on. The only sounds were the *tha-thump, tha-thump, tha-thump* as it bumped over concrete sections, and the constant prattling of his mind.

After the Driscoll Bridge, he turned onto the New Jersey Turnpike and headed up past Newark International Airport. A 737 lifted its nose and roared heavily upwards. To his right, he looked over the thousands of containers, stacked and waiting at Elizabeth Terminal, to the cloud-capped skyscrapers of New York, way off in the distance. *So much humanity! So much going on!* After the peace of Bali, he was hyper-aware of the vast concrete landscapes of cities, and the sheer numbers of people moving around, living their lives, each with their own important reality—and utter insignificance.

He turned on the radio and tuned in to WCBS to catch the news and any traffic delays he might encounter. He didn't want to be late. There weren't any hold-ups ahead of him, so he checked the news. Oil spills, environmental concerns, soldiers killed, bank bailouts, rising healthcare costs, celebrity banality were all being delivered as entertainment in repeating cycles between ads. He switched it off again and called Sheryl.

"Hi, this is a surprise." Sheryl's voice brought him back. That's all it took, these days, to anchor him again.

"I just wondered how you were, that's all." He moved over to the inside lane and eased off on the accelerator.

"I'm fine, thanks. Well, I was after I'd cleaned up my lunch off the floor. Remind me again why we don't throw that old phone out? That cord drags through everything. I nearly lost it in a pan of pasta the other day. You nearly got ringertoni for dinner instead of rigatoni."

"Aw, Sheryl, that's terrible!" Griffin laughed.

"So, why are you really calling? You don't want to just hear about problems with our phone system, do you?"

"No, but I could do with some solutions—or at least some suggestions."

"Just trust yourself, Griff. You'll be fine. Larry trusts you."

"I know, and I'm very flattered, but…"

"No 'buts'. Look, you've been through a lot these past few weeks. It's going to take a while for you to get comfortable with your new self, but it'll all be worth it. It *will* work. Just look at how your staff have been transformed by your change. That's powerful stuff, Griff. They trust you completely as well—and so do I. It seems the only person who has a problem with that is you."

"I guess you're right. Thanks. I love you." As he blew Sheryl a kiss in the direction of the speaker, a car passed him and a woman in the passenger seat laughed and blew one back.

He thought of the Hominine Balance Regeneration Project and how close Larry and his team had got to some deep truths about the nature of mankind, before the Weatherman changed everything. And he thought about how he was changing—the insights and sensitivities that were developing in him and upsetting his status quo as they obstinately established themselves in his psyche.

When Larry had emailed Griffin the previous day, something inside had jumped to attention and said 'this is urgent, this is something you must do, nothing else is this important'. Had that been a thought? No. It had been a deep knowing, way beyond thought. His mind had agreed with that knowing and he'd used his mind to kick-start his actions. Nothing about that knowing was calculated, conceived of or contrived by his conscious mind. Nothing spoke to him of right and wrong, of good and bad, of justification or rationality. It just was. The confusion started when he second-guessed it. That's when doubts crept in and questions started to raise their heads. But he couldn't argue with that knowing, and none of the mind chat helped, so he switched the radio on again and tuned back into the classical music station. Was that escapism or was it constructive and helpful? He didn't know and really didn't care. All he knew was that it worked. He kept his focus as he passed the crude industrial landscape with its gantry cranes, rusty containers and dull grey buildings. He drummed his fingers on the steering wheel to a light Viennese polka as he drove over the Passaic River and the road took him past untidy wetlands and reeded lakes, and he conducted with his right hand as the New York Philharmonic pounded out some robust Wagner. By the time he reached Little Ferry, he was feeling energized and able to face anything the Weatherman could throw at him.

His sat nav led him to Mehrhof Road, at the southern end of Little Ferry. Shanning's house was a characterless grey clapboard-covered construction on a corner plot. A patchy lawn was enclosed by a wire fence. Shanning's twelve-year-old grey Mercury standing in the driveway completed the picture of domestic indifference. Further down the road, Griffin could see a complex of industrial buildings and a warehouse, where trucks were maneuvering around loading bays. Behind the house, the murky Hackensack River drifted past. Over the road in front of the house, a man-made lake—all that remained of the Mehrhof brickworks that provided millions of bricks for the construction of New York in the early twentieth century—was surrounded by tall grasses. A dirt footpath led to a wooded area on the opposite shore. Under the low clouds, the air smelled of diesel fumes and damp steel machinery. *For a man who craved recognition*, thought Griffin, *this is surely the last place on earth to choose to live.*

"Senator Kirkland, I'm flattered and honored that you have come to see me." The man who stood at the front door took Griffin by surprise. He remembered that he'd met him once before, but now he seemed much older, smaller, alarmingly thin and he had a deathly grey-white complexion. He was also sweating and was very frail, holding on to the door pillar to support himself as he invited Griffin to enter. Griffin didn't respond, but followed him into the living room. It was dark and stuffy. The walls were covered with shelves that bent under the weight of hundreds of books piled in irregular stacks, their brown-edged dog-eared pages gaping at the corners. A framed image of a weather chart hung over the mantelpiece of a fireplace where an old gas heater stood. A computer desk stood in the corner. The computer looked new, unlike the furniture. A shabby 1960s three-piece suite with flock-patterned fabric stood around a cheap plywood coffee table. The room felt stale. Griffin wanted to open a window.

"Please, be seated."

They sat opposite each other. Griffin took a minute to take in the room while Shanning studied Griffin's face.

"You look well," Shanning remarked.

"You don't. How long have you been like this?" He really did look like death.

"Not long." His voice was weak. He seemed to have difficulty breathing.

"What's the problem?"

"Food poisoning, I think."

"What did you eat?"

"You know, I'm usually so careful to check the menu, but this time I didn't. Silly of me. I suppose I should know better, especially at my age."

"I'll call a doctor." Griffin started to take his cell phone from his pocket.

"Why?"

"What do you mean, 'why'? I need you alive. I need you to tell me things."

"I have a day or so before I drop into a coma from which I won't recover. Is that long enough?"

"How do you know?"

"I've been looking up my symptoms on the Internet, trying to figure out what was in the cocktail I swallowed." He coughed and wiped his mouth with a tissue. "It's been a very interesting 24 hours for me, medically speaking. I've discovered words like amatoxin and compound 1080, and conditions like centrolobular necrosis, hepatic steatosis, tubulointerstitial nephropathy and hepatorenal syndrome. All sorts of fascinating ways to destroy the body from the inside." He took a labored breath. "Have you ever heard of SADS? It's an acronym for sudden arrhythmic death syndrome. That's probably what will get me in the end, although I doubt that I will know it. It's actually quite a common way to go. About 300,000 people die from it every year in the US, and many of its victims exhibit no symptoms before dying suddenly, so no one will think anything of it, considering my age."

"I'm definitely calling a doctor—"

"No, don't." He raised an unsteady hand toward Griffin. "If you do, I will make sure that I am dead before they get here. I do not want a doctor. That's my choice, and I have every right to exercise it. Now, if you want some information, I think we should start talking, don't you?" Griffin pushed his phone back into his pocket as a surge of anger burst through him.

"Your choice? *Your* choice? *Your* rights? You're a fucking goddamn coward as well as a bastard!" He looked away, immediately regretting his loss of control.

"You are quite right but, really, Senator, sticks and stones… surely you haven't come here to vent your anger at my betrayal of our good friend?"

"No…" Griffin couldn't bring himself to apologize to this despicable creature.

"Where is he now?"

"Do you think I'd ever tell *you* that?" Griffin was seething now.

"Oh, come, come. What difference does it make now?"

"I don't know, but that's not a chance I'm going to take." He stood up and went to the window. "It's too stuffy in here." A truck went past as he swung it open, blasting a cloud of diesel fumes into the room.

"That's why I never open it, these days." Griffin left it open and sat down again. Given the choice, he preferred to have an opening to the outside air—even if it meant letting in diesel fumes—to a room of undiluted Shanning.

"Why didn't you go straight to the military," Griffin asked, "rather than getting in touch with Larry?"

"I had no choice. Only a very few people know about this project, as you know. At this stage, failure's not an option. If the Russians and the Chinese knew the US had lost control of the most important covert project the world has ever seen, do you think they would forgive and forget? The consequences would be unthinkable. If the wider military had got wind of it, it couldn't have been kept secret any more, and they would only have screwed things up, shut us down and, in the process, most likely inadvertently exposed the US for the hypocrite that it is."

"So, the easy thing was to hand the poison chalice back to your old friend?"

Shanning shrugged. "Maybe it was vanity. Maybe it was just a last-minute attempt at redemption. Maybe, having realized what an appalling mess I'd made of things, I wanted to take a step back and have Larry come to the rescue of the project before anyone else found out. I would hate to see it fall into the wrong hands. It's a brilliant project, you know. I—"

"Fall into the wrong hands?" Griffin was astonished at this delusionary comment, though he could see that Shanning had meant it quite innocently.

"But something was wrong with it, wasn't it? Maybe not with the Hominine Project, but certainly with the weapon—HAPISAD."

"No, Hominine is fine. That's intact and there's nothing wrong with it. It was the applications we were developing to use it with HAPISAD that caused the problems. We were under a lot of pressure, you know, to get a result. By the time we switched over to my project, we'd already spent far too much and they were baying for blood or results—well, blood *and* results, but we just wanted to make sure it wasn't our blood."

"What went wrong?"

"When we did the first operational tests, HAPISAD wasn't quite ready. You must understand that the sheer volume of information we had to process was phenomenal. Bigger than anything the world has ever known. The main facility was running three Jaguars at full tilt at one point, and even they couldn't keep up."

"Jaguars?"

"They are reputed to be the fastest computers in the world. They process at 1.76 petaflops or quadrillions of calculations per second. The only other one that the world does know about is at the National Laboratory in Knoxville, where they are using it to try to solve climate-change problems."

"When you say they couldn't keep up, what do you mean?"

"Could I ask you a small favor?" Shanning gestured toward the kitchen. "A glass of water?" Griffin found a glass in a cupboard and filled it from the tap, keeping an eye on Shanning all the time. He didn't want him popping anything into the water while he wasn't looking, so he stood by him as he drank, placing the glass out of his reach when he'd finished. Shanning cleared his throat. "Thank you. I'm not sure where it goes any more. I think my tubes have got a little mixed up..." He coughed, wiped his mouth and continued. "We first tested HAPISAD in Afghanistan. It was an ideal opportunity to put it to covert use. At the time, the area around Mazar-e-Sharif was under increased surveillance by the Taliban, who suspected, quite correctly, that we were about to move a lot more of our supplies through that region. Without even knowing who or where they were, we were able to program a series of HAPISAD missiles to identify a Taliban unit by a range of emotional qualities and thought patterns. The overriding qualities that we chose were anger and aggression, but we also included a vast number of other factors that I won't bore you with now. It would take too long." He coughed weakly, as if to emphasize the point. "I tell you, this weapon is absolutely brilliant, when it—"

"What happened?" Griffin cut in. He didn't want to hear Shanning waxing lyrical about his terrifying weapon, although he was relieved to see that talking about it seemed to give him a bit more energy, animating his words.

"There was a problem with timing and geo-positioning that we have since fixed and tested successfully on a small group in the Congo. We did that so we could be sure that when we demonstrated it again in China, on a much larger target, it wouldn't let us down. It was important to impress the Chinese."

"I bet it was. Please, get to the point. Afghanistan." Griffin was getting tired of this man's rambling.

"HAPISAD homed in correctly on the characteristics we had set it for—I use the word 'characteristics' loosely as the specific terminology to describe the range of attributes is just too cumbersome—but unfortunately there were other factors that came into play. Since we were not able to verify specifics by going there and surveying the results, we can only surmise that what happened was this. The Taliban unit arrived at some settlement or other in the hills. I don't know what they were doing there, but that doesn't matter. They argued with the locals, whoever they were, and exhibited all the characteristics that we had programmed in. Unfortunately, they left and their readings reverted to a different level and type of activity, presumably because they were satisfied that they had won their argument, or something—I don't know. Having left the settlement, the occupants of the settlement had a meeting in the exact same location, and started to exhibit the characteristics that had been set for the kill. They must have been very angry about what happened in their meeting with our target. By that time, HAPISAD was already in free-fall from the AVTOL, the pod read the same location and the HAPISAD missiles hit the people in the settlement. The Taliban had already left and probably knew nothing about it. It was very unfortunate, but just one of those things. If we'd had time to do the proper—"

"Shut up, for God's sake." Griffin couldn't believe the matter-of-fact way that Shanning had described the massacre of a small, defenseless and completely innocent community. He needed to gather his thoughts, and his emotions were getting in the way. He stood up and walked around the room. He'd never before come across such a pathetic, dangerous creature as Shanning. His ability to completely detach from the consequences of what he had done was incredible to him. Was it total denial or were humans capable of such detachment? Of course they were. Shanning wasn't the first or only person capable of calculated mass murder, but to actually be in the presence of someone who had done it, and seemed to be proud of it, made him feel physically sick. He had to get out of here as soon as he could. Forcing himself to control his emotions, he returned to his questions. "So how come that mistake made the whole thing fall apart?"

"Under normal circumstances, the deaths of our test targets wouldn't be reported, simply because they were always people who were... disposable—the unwanted and the unknown. In this case, the targets didn't fit that profile and people got upset. Someone took a video of the collateral damage and it found its way onto the Internet. That started a chain of events that compromised the security of the project. First, one of the NSA's contracted intelligence tracking facilities got wind of it and, by a strange quirk of fate, caused our AVTOL host in Somalia to get twitchy."

"Your AVTOL host in Somalia? Larry mentioned that you had lost control to someone else. Is this the guy you're talking about?"

"The very same, and he's not someone you can negotiate with, believe me."

"He did this to you?"

"No, I did. He just very kindly facilitated it, as the most attractive option."

Griffin looked at the old man sitting hunched over in his chair. Cold eyes staring from sunken sockets. His face deeply wrinkled, his hands shaking and saliva frothing at the edges of his mouth. If only he had a gun, Griffin could have killed him right there and then, and felt no guilt, no emotion. It flashed through Griffin's mind, as he thought these thoughts, that maybe he was guilty of the same qualities he found so repulsive in Shanning. He quickly pushed them from his mind. Shanning would be gone soon enough, that was clear. There was no more damage he could do now.

"This intelligence tracking agency…"

"Arlington Online Data Systems. The contact is a man called Troy King. He's a complete idiot, though. He doesn't know what he's doing."

"I guess it takes one to know one."

Shanning coughed and reached for a fresh tissue, dropping the used, bloody one on his lap. Griffin stood up and, without a word, left the house. As he got back into his car, a torrent of emotion crashed in on him, and he sat, bent over the steering wheel, sobbing. *Where did that come from!?* He sat up, wiped his eyes and headed home.

CHAPTER 37

The distinctive hiss of airbrakes engaging, close to the hull of the *Norfolk Defender,* woke Captain Baptiste from a fitful sleep. His head was pounding with a dull headache, brought on by the bottle of wine he'd polished off earlier that evening. *Focus.* Vehicles often passed during the day, but rarely at night, and nothing ever stopped close to the ship. Checking his watch, he got out of his bunk and peered down through his window to the dimly lit quay below. The port's mobile crane was parked directly beneath him. Someone climbed down from the cab and lit a cigarette. It was 2.30am. This didn't make any sense. He looked in the direction of the port administration office, but all the lights were out. As he watched, a HiLux 4x4 drove onto the quay and parked behind the crane, next to where the steps leading up to the deck of the ship were suspended on a pulley system.

"Permission to come aboard?" a man shouted from the quay. Baptiste could hardly make him out, as he appeared to be dark skinned and wearing dark-colored clothing. Baptiste put on his pants and walked out onto the companionway for a better view.

"Who are you?" he shouted down to the man. "What do you want?"

"The Weatherman sent me. Didn't you get the message?"

"No." *Why would the Weatherman be sending me messages at this time of night?* "Wait. I'll go and check." He went up one floor to the bridge.

"I was just going to wake you, Captain, but you beat me to it." The voice startled him. It was the crewman on watch, standing in the eerie glow of the instrument panel. Baptiste turned to acknowledge him, noticing a bottle of beer sitting on the table next to him, and the spidery white wires of an iPod hastily dropped beside it. He turned his attention to the printer.

Kaahin arr. 0230 hours. Ω WM640 acknowledge Δ

Very odd, he thought, cursing the thudding in his head. He punched in the reply without checking his manual.

Δ acknowledge Ω WM640

I'd better see what this guy wants. Rubbing his eyes, he started the motor to lower the steps onto the quay. As soon as it hit the concrete, footsteps clanged up the metal rungs. Baptiste made his way down to the deck to meet his visitor. They met at the top of the steps.

"Your name?" The man stopped and looked up.

"Kaahin. You are Captain Baptiste?" Baptiste beckoned to him to continue up to the deck. He was a young man, a Somali, probably in his thirties, who moved with the ease of an athlete. He was smartly dressed in black leather shoes, black pants and a black shirt under a lightweight brown jacket.

"If this is about fixing the crane, wouldn't it be better to wait till morning?" It was the only reason Baptiste could imagine this man had arrived at the ship.

"No, it's not that. Mission 24 has been changed. Is there somewhere we can talk? Maybe the galley? I would love a coffee." Kaahin smiled. He seemed amiable enough, and a coffee seemed like a good idea.

"Sure. Follow me." Baptiste led the way down into the galley. Two of the programmers were sitting, talking technical over bottles of mineral water.

"Hi, Cap'n," one of them called out cheerfully as they entered, as if embarrassed to have been discovered.

"Don't you guys ever sleep?" Baptiste checked the water heater.

"Most of the time, yeah. But that gets kinda boring. How many more days are we gonna hang out here with nothin' to do?"

"Well, I hope I'm going to find out right now." He turned to Kaahin. "How do you like it?"

"As it comes, thanks." Kaahin sat at a table as Baptiste poured two instant coffees and sat opposite him.

"So, tell me." Baptiste leaned his elbows on the table, cradling the cup in his hands.

"It's like this, Captain." Kaahin leaned toward Baptiste, talking in a low voice. "You're the captain of this ship, but I'm in charge of the mission now. As such, I instruct you as to what you do with the ship, and you carry out my orders to the letter, without question. I want you to be very clear about that right from the start." Baptiste tensed, and put his coffee down carefully on the table in front of him. *I should have checked that message a bit more thoroughly.* He looked Kaahin in the eye.

"Who do you think you are talking to? I got an instruction to allow you on board. That's as far as it goes, and until I get some clarification—"

"You have clarification, Captain. You got a WM640, I believe." Kaahin drank some of his coffee.

"I'm going to need further clarification. Until I get it, you will remove yourself from this vessel." He'd barely got up from the table to head toward an intercom mounted on the wall, when the shot rang out and someone screamed. The two programmers were shaking, terrified. One was bent over in agony.

"He fuckin' shot me!" There was blood dripping from his left leg.

"How much clarification do you want?" Kaahin said, as he laid the gun on the table in front of him. Baptiste ran over to the boy. Pulling his shirt off, he wrapped it tightly around the leg, above the wound.

"Get him out of here!" he shouted at the other boy, who sat transfixed, motionless. Baptiste slapped him hard across the face. "Get him out of here!" The boy leaped to his feet, watching Kaahin as he helped his friend to hobble out of the galley. Baptiste turned his attention back to Kaahin, who stood up, lifted the gun again, and pointed it at his head.

"What did you do that for? He was just a kid! I was just going to get clarification. What is this? What's going on?"

"We don't have time for formalities. You must fully open the forward hatch and raise the platform... now." Kaahin kept the gun trained on Baptiste's head. Baptiste struggled to clarify his thoughts. Days of boredom and lack of a proper routine had dulled his mind. He'd been continuously snacking on junk food and drinking too much wine. He'd told himself that with all the stresses and responsibility he carried when he was working, it was okay to let things slide, loosen up a little, when he had some time off. At 2.30am, he was not the sharp and disciplined captain that CTV reporter John Pollard had interviewed just a few days previously. He was slow. His head was thumping. He had to *do* something!

"You should know that I am the only one on board who can run this ship." The words came out as he scrambled through his thoughts for the killer argument that would enable him to take back control. "You cannot make me do anything. If you shoot me, this ship stays right where it is, so you'd be wasting your time."

"Quite right. Just do it." Kaahin lowered the gun. Baptiste backed out of the door. He wasn't in the least bit convinced that he had won the argument, but took the opportunity to get away from this madman. As soon as he was out of the galley, he slammed the door shut and locked it. As he did so, he detected a feint odor. Someone else was there, in the dimly-lit corridor behind him. He turned to find two more black faces staring at him. He recognized them. He'd seem them walking around the streets of Berbera just days before. They were local fishermen. But they weren't fisherman now. Each man wielded an AK47. *Damn, I forgot to raise the steps after Kaahin came on board!*

They didn't say anything or threaten him. They stood aside as he pushed past them and ran up to the bridge. When he arrived at the bridge, the crewman who had been on watch was sitting nervously between two large, menacing men. One had a machete, the other a handgun tucked into his belt. He was swaying to a rhythm playing on the iPod he'd sequestered. Baptiste could hear the *tsch, tsch, tsch* of the music over the hum of the electrical equipment on the bridge. Both men were chewing qat leaves—a popular stimulant the locals used that reduced appetites and induced an excited, often euphoric state. Baptiste was especially wary of these two characters; qat could induce unstable, hyperactive behavior, as well as depression and aggression when it was unavailable to a user.

"Hi!" they greeted him over-cheerfully as he scanned the room to see if anything had been tampered with—or worse. Everything seemed to be in order. He looked out over the main deck and was horrified to see several more men wandering around, across the hatches and even as far as the bow. There had to be about thirty of them. They flinched as he floodlit the entire ship so he could see more clearly the extent of the problem he faced. None of his crew appeared to be there, so he guessed they were still below-decks, probably unaware of the crisis unfolding above them. The intercom buzzed. It was Kaahin, still in the galley.

"The forward hatch, Captain. And the platform. By the time I finish my coffee. Then come back here for another chat. Do you need more clarification?"

"No, I don't. It will be three minutes before I can be there." Baptiste flicked the switch to start the hatch opening. It announced the start of its travel with a loud, hollow bang. The men who had been standing on it ran quickly to the sides of the deck, off the moving surface. A minute later, he started the hydraulic rams to lift the platform automatically to deck level, then made his way back to the galley. The two men were still there, standing guard outside the door. They smiled at him as he went past. The door was still locked, just as he'd left it.

Kaahin was sitting at the same table. As he walked into the galley he could hear more voices. The crew had been woken by the sound of the hatch opening and were moving around the accommodation quarters. He hesitated at the door.

"Don't worry; we're not interested in harming your people. Anyway, they are much more valuable to us alive. But before I leave you, there are some things you should know. Come in and sit down," Kaahin said.

"You just showed me how far your concern for my people goes." Baptiste pointed toward the pool of blood on the floor. He remained standing.

"He'll be fine. He's already on his way to hospital and he'll be back on board in no time."

"You're leaving? Why have I opened the hatch?" Baptiste was becoming disoriented by everything that was happening. It was too fast, too confusing.

"A good friend of mine will be taking over shortly. You will treat him well, and do as he says."

"If you are planning to hijack this vessel and use it as one of your mother ships, you'd better think again. The US Navy will be down on you like you wouldn't believe. They won't take kindly to having one of their vessels used for your criminal activities."

"Captain Baptiste, sit down… please." Kaahin spoke softly, gesturing to the chair on the opposite side of the table. Baptiste sat. He couldn't see the gun. He guessed that Kaahin had put it back in his jacket pocket.

Kaahin continued. "Captain Baptiste, I doubt the US military will be too concerned about this ship, since it's under the command of the Weatherman project, which is still intact and on track. You received a perfectly normal instruction from New York just now. Am I right?" Baptiste said nothing. "As we know, the Weatherman Project is a covert project that the wider military machine has no knowledge of. Anything to do with the project is strictly off-limits, off the map and simply doesn't exist, as far as all but a favored few are concerned. You are on your own, Captain Baptiste. Can we at least agree on that?" Kaahin was turning out to be an intelligent, well-informed adversary. An angry knot was building in Baptiste's stomach. None of his training had prepared him for this. He was more than prepared to fend off any pirate attack from *outside* the hull of the *Norfolk Defender* on the high seas, but to be infiltrated while the ship was in port, seemingly with assistance from New York, was beyond his comprehension. He was also berating himself for effectively assisting them in the takeover of his ship. Lulled by his own feelings of invincibility, the covert nature of the project and a bored familiarity with the routine of life in Berbera, he'd let his guard down. Sloppy discipline on his part had laid the ship wide open to attack, and he'd underestimated the sophistication and capabilities of the pirate network. *But how did the message get sent from New York? I must check those codes. I don't know what they mean.*

Kaahin helped himself to another coffee. Baptiste refused the offer of one.

"I enjoyed your interview on CTV," said Kaahin, grinning as he sat down again. "Quite the TV star, Mr Baptiste. Quite the Navy hero! And it was kind of the reporter to intimate that you were heading for the Persian Gulf with military equipment—and to let us know your name. Once we knew that, we could identify your crew. I have a list, somewhere, from our people who have been collecting information at Norfolk and cross-checking around the US…" Kaahin fumbled in his pocket and pulled out a wad of folded paper. He pressed it open on the table. It was a printout with names and addresses. Baptiste didn't need to read it. "It's for you, if you want it. Here." He pushed it toward Baptiste. *"My responsibility is first the safety of my crew, and then the ship. If there is any fighting to be done, we call in the experts."* Kaahin was quoting Baptiste's own words back to him. He let Baptiste reflect on his words as he drank his coffee. As he did so, the whole room started to vibrate. The vibrations got more and more pronounced. The pile of paper jumped, shuffled its way to the edge of the table and then fell onto the floor. Kaahin remained still, watching Baptiste, who jumped up and ran for the door as the juddering increased to a point where his feet were bouncing on the floor as he moved, and the room buzzed out of focus before his eyes. A roar was building up to a deafening pitch by the time he got to the door. He could barely grip the handle. It was locked. He turned to Kaahin.

"What the fuck is going on?" he yelled, but his words were drowned out by the thunderous sound and the wild clattering and clanging of pots and pans. Kaahin was standing, holding onto a pillar. The chairs had fallen on their sides and were dancing their way across the floor in a manic, clattering jig.

Gradually the noise subsided, the vibrations eased off and finally stopped. A minute later, the door clicked and Baptiste ran to the bridge as fast as he could. The alarm panel was aglow with flashing lights and klaxons sounding. The crew were now fully in place and dealing with them all in sequence. The chief mate was standing at the ship's control panel overlooking the main deck, a gunman at his side, apparently giving him instructions. The two men who had been guarding the watchman were standing with them, chatting excitedly and giving each other high fives. Baptiste looked out over the main deck. The forward hatch was being closed. It had traveled about halfway. Wisps of steam and smoke were escaping before the hatch as it advanced. He ran over to the chief mate.

"What the hell was that? What's going on?"

"I don't know, sir. I was only allowed up here after all that noise stopped." The chief mate turned to him. "Captain, in your absence, here on the bridge, I took it upon myself to do what they ordered—"

"It's okay. You did the right thing." Baptiste searched around to find anyone who was in charge. "*Somebody* tell me what is going on here! What the hell has been loaded onto my ship?" The forward hatch came to the end of its travel, a green light confirming that it was locked. The gunman immediately dug the chief mate in the ribs with his AK47.

"He wants me to open the aft hatch, Captain. Do I—"

"Do it." Baptiste wanted to see what was going on in the hold, but he was in a stronger position to regain control if he remained on the bridge. At this point, he didn't know where the rest of his crew were and couldn't risk using the intercom in case it was being monitored by the pirates. He'd have to wait and figure something out later. *First things first*, he thought, as he checked the computerized ballast control panel. He was desperate to know what was in the hold. Who would have been stupid enough to load something into a hold without proper supervision? What the hell caused all that noise and vibration? It had felt as if the whole ship was breaking apart. Although its revolutionary design more than compensated for weaknesses in normal cargo ship design, he had to make sure that whatever had been loaded wasn't going to snap the ship in two. Checking the panel, it was evident that there was something heavy in the forward hold. Fortunately, the computer had automatically compensated for it, and was now making its final adjustments to re-balance the ship.

"Has anyone reported any damage?" he asked around the control room. Heads shook. He switched on the ship-wide loudspeaker. "Attention. This is the Captain speaking. We appear to have an extraordinary situation. I need urgent damage checks on the hatchway corners, upper deck plating, hatch coamings and cross-deck strips topside... and if anyone is in the hold, check for fractures, buckling and broken welds. Main areas to investigate are bulkhead boundaries, side stringers and bilge hopper plating around the knuckle line. Report back any damage to the bridge."

As the aft hatch slid open, Baptiste surveyed a scene of frenzied activity on the quay. The two HEMMT trucks were parked beside the ship with people unlocking the containers from their chassis. The mobile crane was positioning itself to load the containers into the aft hold. There was a lot of shouting. Through the open door of the control room, he could hear crew arguing with their captors on the decks below. Some of the pirates were calling to people on the quay and through the aft hatch as it opened. Another truck arrived on the quay, filled with sacks and boxes strapped onto pallets, followed by a pickup truck. The young programmer who'd been shot climbed down from the passenger seat, complete with crutches and a heavily bandaged leg. Someone went to help him limp back onto the ship.

Baptiste continued to run through an exhaustive checklist—generators, engines, electrical systems, computers, auxiliary power units, pumps, structural integrity and monitoring systems. But without being able to contact his chief engineer, he couldn't be 100% certain that everything was in order.

He was so absorbed in making sure the ship was intact that he didn't notice Kaahin step into the room, with another man.

"Captain, this is my friend, Raage. I mentioned him when we were in the galley just now. He will be traveling with you."

"Traveling? Where?"

"When we are under way, Captain, we will discuss that," the man called Raage interjected. "In the meantime, Captain, make sure that all radio communication is shut down, and the ship is configured in stealth mode."

"I don't know what you mean." Baptiste was stunned. *How do they know about that?* If he put the ship into stealth mode, they would be even harder to track and it would be virtually impossible to attract attention in the hope of getting some assistance.

"I think you do, Captain. Please don't try my patience, for the sake of everyone on board."

"Very well. I'll take the ship wherever you want, but I will not compromise the safety of my crew or engage in any illegal activities."

"It's a bit late to be talking about compromising the safety of your crew, Captain. And I am not sure what you mean by 'illegal'. Whose law are you talking about? Yours, mine, international law, natural law?" Raage chuckled.

Kaahin took Raage aside and said, "I think I am finished here. Everything is in place. God is great. *Ilko wada jir bey wax ku gooyaan!*" Unity is power. They gave each other a clenched-fist salute. Baptiste winced as they embraced and kissed each other. Kaahin left the bridge and disappeared down the stairway. As Baptiste watched Kaahin leave, a thought occurred to him that gave him a small ray of hope. While the materials of the outer skin of the ship played a big part in making it difficult to spot on radar, the highest level of stealth was achieved by implementing a very precise combination of factors that included heat signature, noise, radio silence—and *shape*. Because of the many functional requirements that had to be taken into account in its development, the ship was never able to achieve a level of total stealth, but now, Baptiste believed, its capabilities had been further reduced. The shape of the *Norfolk Defender* had been compromised by the failure of the crane when they had unloaded the aircraft refueler. There was a possibility that the exposure of irregular shapes and mechanical parts that weren't treated with stealth materials could make the ship detectable at reasonably close range.

"Okay, let's get going," Raage said, as the last of the cargo was lowered into the aft hold and the hatch started to close.

"Not without a full engineer's report. Whatever you loaded into the hold could cause us to sink as soon as we leave port. I must make my own inspection as well. As Captain, I am responsible—"

"Get this ship *moving!*" Raage nodded toward one of the thugs guarding the night watchman, who immediately punched the crewman hard in the stomach, buckling him over. Then, in a low whisper, he said to Baptiste, "He is fortunate that we need a full complement of crew for this journey. But you should let your crew know that we are not so interested in the health of their families." Baptiste's heart sank. He glanced around him at the men on the bridge, all of whom were staring nervously back at him.

"What's our heading?" Baptiste asked.

"322.6 degrees, Captain." Raage surprised him with an exact bearing. *These people are thorough!* But surely that was incorrect...

"That's not the Gulf! Aren't we heading toward your rich hunting grounds around Minicoy?"

Raage looked at Baptiste and repeated, "322.6 degrees."

The Red Sea. "Okay. 322.6 degrees it is."

As Baptiste gave the orders to start the engines and cast off, his heart lifted a little. Surely this was the most foolish thing the pirates could possibly do? Even with the speed and sophistication of the *Norfolk Defender*, the Red Sea was the easiest place to trap the ship once it was discovered.

CHAPTER 38

Troy King felt out of place again. He hadn't had time to brush his shoes and, anyway, they were old, rubber-soled bargain-basement shoes he'd bought years ago and wore continuously, because they were the only comfortable pair he had. Nor had he ironed his shirt, but at least it was clean. He usually got away with taking them out of the dryer and hanging them on the back of the kitchen door before they cooled down. But today he felt he should have made the extra effort to iron it properly. He adjusted his cuffs and straightened his tie. The edges of the collar of his beige raincoat were worn and dark-rimmed, but it would have to do.

He'd suggested Bobby Van's Steakhouse for lunch but the man he was meeting wasn't comfortable with that. Being a public figure, he didn't want to be on view when he was talking privately about sensitive matters. King thought that was a little over-sensitive, considering he just wanted a signature on a document, and he couldn't imagine why it was so important to go for lunch to do it. He'd have been perfectly happy to drop by his office and get his secretary to put the document under his nose while he waited. But then Troy King wasn't a public figure, so he accepted that maybe this was the way big noises normally did things. Samakab had been the same, with his sharp suit, crazy watch and fancy bits of food arranged like they were on the Martha Stewart Show.

The taxi dropped him near the entrance of the Jefferson Hotel. A stretch limo had pride of place opposite the gold front doors, so King had to walk a few extra painful feet past it. He gathered his files under his arm, made his way into the sumptuous lobby and, having mentioned to the concierge who his meeting was with, was quickly shown to the Plume Restaurant. Despite his self-consciousness, King was beginning to appreciate the peaceful opulence that the rich seemed to enjoy. He was struck by the classy muted grey-blue-and-cream tones of the restaurant and the magnificent chandelier—a sparkling jewel in the center of the ceiling. Griffin Kirkland was seated next to the fireplace with its impressive surround of fine marble, set into a hand-painted silk mural depicting Thomas Jefferson's South Vineyard.

"Mr King. So glad to meet you. Thanks for coming." Griffin Kirkland stood to meet his guest. He walked around the table as King approached, startled by his lumbering gait. "Are you okay? Here, let me help you."

"No, I'm fine, thanks." King was momentarily thrown by Kirkland's concern. He sat down at the table—a work of art with beautiful cutlery and fine napkins arranged with flamboyant precision. He placed his files on the floor, out of sight. Griffin returned to his seat and extended his hand to King.

"Griffin Kirkland." They shook hands. Griffin watched as King took in the décor. "They call it 'White House North', you know."

"Oh?"

"Being just a few blocks away, it gets a lot of high-profile traffic, if you know what I mean."

"Well, they don't get much higher-profile than you, sir."

Griffin smiled. "It was only recently re-vamped. I like it, both in spite of and because of the clientele. Personally, I would love to have taken you up on your suggestion of a good steak at Bobby Van's. I would have enjoyed that, but at least we can rely on a discrete service here, and a quiet environment for our discussion."

"I guess so…" King replied, absent-mindedly. "That's some fancy chandelier."

"Yes, that's one from our late president's fine collection. Have you ever visited Monticello?"

"Where?"

"Monticello. It's the estate that Jefferson had built outside Charlottesville. It's quite something. You should go there someday—it's a great day out. Take the family."

"Yeah, sure. I'll do that."

"That scene, behind you, that's a view of one of the vineyards." King tried to twist around to look at the silk painting around the fireplace, but his tortured spine wanted none of it. "I'm sorry, Mr King," Griffin registered King's discomfort, "it's not important. Between you and me, I find it all a bit crazy."

"Why is that, sir?"

"He wrote our Declaration of Independence, but from what I see in this country, independence is an expensive luxury. It's very much the prerogative of the rich and powerful. I see little evidence that the spirit of the Declaration is embraced by our systems of government and business on behalf of ordinary people. Would you agree?"

"I don't know much about politics, sir." King was surprised to hear a Senator expressing such candid, personal feelings so openly and wondered where all this was leading. He picked up his file from the floor and started leafing through it. "Sir, I have the papers here, and I just need your signature in a couple of places."

"What is this about, Mr King?"

"It's…" King was confused by Griffin's question. "It's the draft statement we had drawn up for the insurance claim, sir—the one I been callin' your office about for the past two weeks."

"I'm sorry, Mr King, I know nothing about this. Here, let me see that." King handed him the file and Griffin flicked through the pages.

"Maybe you been busy sir. It was a collision that your driver had with the wife of one of my employees down on the Columbia Pike a while back. Your driver gave some cock-'n-bull story about how it happened, and I been tryin' to get to the bottom of it ever since, on behalf of my employee, y'understand." Griffin was still looking puzzled as he thumbed through the papers, frowning.

King continued with his explanation. "Now, your garage told me that your driver's been fired, so I can't get a hold of him, and your office told me you was away. Anyways, I was mighty pleased when you took the trouble to call me about it yesterday, and I appreciate you puttin' in your personal time to sort this out properly. That's real honorable of you, sir. I'm sure you have plenty more important things to deal with…"

Griffin's expression lifted as King ran out of helpful explanations. "Oh, now I understand. Yes, I was in the car."

"You *was* in the car?" A flash of relief. King was surprised to have an admission directly from Griffin Kirkland.

"Sure I was. You say the driver got fired?"

"He sure did. I spoke to a guy called Williams at the garage. He told me they didn't tolerate that kinda mistake when they're carrying such valuable cargo—sorry, important people. The driver's name was Lindemann. I reckon his report was his attempt at keepin' his job, but it didn't work. I saw right through it." King sat back, happy to be getting on top of the situation.

"No, he wasn't trying to save his job." Griffin took out his pen.

"He wasn't? What was he doin', then?"

"I'm ashamed to say, Mr King, that he was protecting me." Griffin sighed. "The poor guy lost his job, did he?"

"Yes, he did," King repeated.

"I'll have to do something about that." Griffin signed the document in the appropriate place. "And the young lady in the other car—you say she was the wife of one of your employees?"

"Yes, sir. And she had her baby boy in the back as well." King's heart sank as memories of his recent meeting with Barbara, and seeing David, crashed into his mind.

"Oh my God. Were they hurt? Were they okay?"

"No, they weren't hurt. They're… fine." *Shit, shit, shit!* If only he could relive the last month and do things differently. If only…

"I hope this clears it up for you," Griffin said, handing the papers back to King.

"That's fine, thank you, sir." King immediately felt uncomfortable, realizing that they had concluded their business within minutes of having met. What was he supposed to do now? Stay and make small-talk with the Senator or make his polite excuses and leave? The latter seemed to be more appropriate and, anyway, he could probably still get a table at Bobby Van's and have a guilty, diet-breaking lunch with his excuse of a meeting still intact. He started to lift himself from his chair.

"Did you want the washroom?" Griffin asked.

"No, I'm fine, thanks. I'll just see if they can organize a taxi for me."

"You're leaving?"

"I think so. Aren't we done here?"

"By no means. Is that all you think you were here for—the insurance claim?"

"Sure. What else could we possibly be talking about?"

"Oh, Mr King, I must apologize if I misled you. There's obviously been a misunderstanding. I'd forgotten about the insurance claim until you presented me with the papers. My assistant, Judy, had mentioned it, but I thought she was handling it. Please, take a seat and let's order some lunch. We have plenty more to talk about, believe me. Please..." Griffin smiled at King, who slowly sat down again. "Would you like to take your coat off while you eat?"

King had forgotten that he was still wearing his raincoat. "Yes, but..." The thought of maneuvering himself to remove it was as difficult to do as it was to explain why it was a challenge. Griffin seemed to understand intuitively, and called a waiter over to help him.

"Thank you. Thank you," King said to the waiter and to Griffin. He was beginning to like this man's easy charm and careful consideration.

The waiter arrived to take their order. Mindful of the way that King appeared to be uneasily scanning the menu, Griffin said, "I can recommend the roasted fillet of halibut, if you like fish. That's what I'm having."

"That looks good. I'll have the same." King was relieved to have that decision made for him. Griffin ordered a bottle of Pinot Blanc. When it came, he offered it to King to taste.

"That's a mighty fine wine, sir," said King, and he meant it.

The sommelier poured and Griffin offered a toast. "To true independence."

"Life, liberty and the pursuit of happiness," King added with a flourish.

"Wine ... the true old man's milk and restorative cordial. That's what Jefferson called it."

"Can't argue with that." King smiled. "I sure could do with some restoration and none of us are gettin' any younger, sir."

"Call me Griffin, please."

"Troy." King raised his glass to Griffin. "So, tell me, Griffin, are we celebratin' somethin' here? I am fascinated to know what else you and me have to talk about today. To my way of thinkin', your world is a long ways away from my world and, as of this moment, I can't figure out where they meet."

Griffin thought for a moment and then, choosing his words carefully, began: "I think there's something that you are in a unique position to help me with, Troy."

"Well, I hope I can, Griffin. I sure hope I can." King took another fulsome gulp of wine.

"What I have to discuss with you concerns some work you were doing recently…" Griffin watched King closely. King tore a chunk off a bread roll and stuffed it in his mouth. "…and a certain video—"

King froze. *Damn! Here we go again. How the hell does he know about that!? I'm not going there. I'm outta here!* He swallowed the lump of dough and took another swig of wine to wash it down.

"I'm sorry, Senator, I can't help you. I think I'd best be leaving now. Thank you for your—"

"I understand. But please, hear me out." Griffin held King's arm firmly. King remained seated, guarded, suspicious. "It's important, really important that I talk to you about it."

"Sir, I got took off that case and if I go anywhere near it again, I'm dead. And I mean dead, sir. I'll lose everythin'—my job, my pension, my home—everythin'. Do you understand that? I'm just a simple guy, sir. I did what I did 'cause I thought it was the right thing to do. It turned out to be just one big clusterfuck and things happened that…" King stopped short of going into detail. He didn't yet know who he was dealing with, or if he could trust him, "…I ain't got no backup plan now, and they know that."

Griffin nodded and leaned forward on his elbows. In a low voice, he said, "Would it help you to know that you and I are actually in a similar situation, in some ways?"

"You're shittin' me—sorry. How come?"

"We've both been laboring under false illusions. The jobs we've been doing are not the jobs we thought they were. Am I right, in your case?"

"Come to think of it, yeah, I guess so. Just lately, I been gettin' very confused about why I even bother to go to work, and what I get my team to do. They seem to be aksing me to do one thing, but if I ever think beyond the brief, even a tiny bit, they kinda clam up on me and get real heavy and negative."

"Is that what happened when you started to investigate that video?"

"No, not really. That was more like outright war. They was real aggressive on that one. I even got a visit from two CIA goons—you know, dark suits, shades, earpieces, serious sense o' humor failure. They ordered me to shut my investigation down, like immediately. I mean, these guys jumped on me even before we really got goin' on it. I ain't never seen them act that quick before."

"And that's when you gave it up?"

"No," King lowered his head, "that's when I got started."

"So you carried out the investigation in contravention of the direct orders of the CIA?" Griffin let out a low whistle.

King sighed. "That's just about how it was, sir."

"But why? There must have been a really strong reason for you to do that."

"I thought so, at the time—a real good reason. But it looks like I was mistaken."

"Maybe you weren't mistaken. What was your really good reason?"

Well, I guess it makes no difference now, thought King. *I'm off the case and, who knows, he may already be aware of my situation.* "I thought the Taliban had some real weird and nasty new weapon that could be puttin' our boys in danger in Afghanistan, and for some reason our people were keepin' it a secret from them. And before you aks me, no, I have no idea why they would do that. But after forty years in the military, if there's one thing I have learned, it's that I don't know nothin' about what goes on in the heads of the people who run military campaigns, or the politics of why we enter into them in the first place."

Griffin could see why King could think that fellow soldiers might have been in danger, and he admired his guts in going against a direct order for the sake of what he saw as the safety of other colleagues. He decided to take King a little further into his confidence.

"Troy, I can tell you that you're right and you're wrong. First, I would like to put your mind at rest and let you know that it is a new weapon, but our boys are not in danger from it."

"They're not?" Emotion welled up in King. "Oh, God." He could barely contain it. He turned his eyes away from Kirkland. David, Gulnaz, David's family and all the horrors they had been through. For what?

"You're not pleased?" Griffin asked. King put his head in his hands. He shook his head. He couldn't tell him. Not yet. Maybe never. He looked back at Griffin.

"What else? What was I right about?"

"Your gut feeling. Your feeling that there was something going on that needed to be fixed."

"Why?" A familiar knot had returned to his stomach. This short conversation had brought the huge weight of guilt back onto his shoulders, just when he thought he'd begun to sweep it under the acceptable veneer that he spread thinly over his broken life. The affair that he'd never had with Gulnaz before he sacrificed her to his obsession with atonement for a failed military career. Barbara's near-hysteria and David's empty-eyed rejection of him at the Alcova Heights house. The betrayal of decent human values, the entrapment of an abusive employment regime. The corruption and scheming at the top in the land of freedom and democracy.

"It's our weapon, Troy. Ours."

King's eyes were a red-veined fire of anger and sadness as they drilled into Griffin's gaze. He breathed deeply, trying to control his pounding fury, his deep, deep shame at what his ignorant, impulsive decisions had wrought—crying out inside for the pain that he had unwittingly inflicted.

"What?" King forced the word out, desperate for some chink in the madness of what he was hearing—something that would bring some semblance of rationale. Something had to take this poison out of his guts.

The meal arrived. It was a surreal moment. How crazy was it to let the discipline of composure override the desire to scream and shout the place down? *People are being killed, mutilated, their heads screwed up, their lives destroyed, but right now we must sit back quietly as starched napkins are placed nicely on our laps, and we must use the right knife and fork, and try not to drop crumbs. Talk in whispers, smile and compliment the chef.*

Once the waiters had left the table, Griffin answered.

"It's a secret weapon, developed by us in association with Russia and China."

"In association with—? What the hell is going on here, Griffin? Aren't we meant to be protecting the US from people like that?"

"I can explain, but first, tell me why you are so upset. I sense that you are devastated by what I just told you. I can feel it. It's almost tangible."

"You tell me something first, if you don't mind," King ventured. "You said that we're both kinda' in the same boat, job-wise. What did you mean by that?"

"Yes, I said we were both laboring under false illusions, didn't I? The fact is, Troy, that we are both outsiders and I doubt very much that we're the only ones. I just think we are two of the few who know it because of things that have happened to us." Griffin took a bite of the halibut. "This is good. How do you like it?"

"Real good, thanks."

"You probably know of me as being a peace negotiator for the past few years."

"That's right, yes. I seen you on CNN an' such."

"Well, that's not entirely true."

"So, what are you?"

"I found out recently that my job is to simply create the illusion of progress toward peace, but not to achieve it. When I do break some ground... Well, you might have seen what happened to the Israeli negotiator after I brokered that much-publicized deal?"

"I saw that, yeah… I don't get it."

"As they say in all the good movies, it's a long story, and it is connected to that video. But we must save it for another time. Right now, I need you to tell me why you were upset by the news that this weapon is not creating a danger for our troops."

King carefully put his fork down. He paused, then spoke thoughtfully, slowly. His eyes down-cast. "Because I didn't just investigate it in the US."

"What do you mean?"

"I sent some people over to Afghanistan to take a look and bring back some information on the incident in the video." He paused. "You seen the video, yes?"

"Not yet. I only heard about it very recently."

"Who told you about it?"

"Gerald Shanning."

"Oh. He's a strange one. But he seems to have a lot of power. I spent some time with him. Real odd. How d'you know him?"

"That's another long story, and I will tell you at the appropriate time. In the meantime, can you let me have a copy of the video?"

"Sure. Give me your email address."

"Can you give it to me on a disk?"

"No problem." King seemed to be preoccupied, staring blankly at his plate.

"So, what information did your team recover?"

"What?"

"The team who went to Afghanistan—what did they get?"

"It wasn't exactly a team." There was no longer any point in trying to hide the truth. "I set up an unofficial covert op. Two of my staff went out there—an Afghan researcher and a young English computer techno-wizard."

"That was brave—or crazy, I'm not sure which. And what did they get?"

"The Afghan girl got shot and killed and the guy lost his mind."

"Oh, my God! I'm really sorry to hear that."

"And I'm fuckin' angry!" King said, rather too loudly for comfort. Lowering his voice again, he continued, "And now you're tellin' me that all this mess happened just because our intelligence service didn't want to tell one of its own contractors what was goin' on? What? Are they afraid we can't keep a secret or somethin'? That's rich. I mean, that's really rich."

"Come on, Troy. It's nothing personal. You know how it works. There aren't even many people in NSA who know about it. The weapon's not exactly common knowledge, and they have a pretty specific agenda running here that they don't want to upset."

"Yeah, yeah. National security. That great cover-all explanation for any damned illegal, corrupt and nasty practices that they wanna keep tightly tucked away—outta sight, outta mind." King downed the remainder of his wine. The waiter immediately filled his glass again. "Look, Griffin, I really appreciate you tellin' me all this, and I really appreciate this lunch an' all. To be honest, I don't know that I want to hear any more or take this any further." He wiped his mouth on his napkin. "You know, I'm just kinda tired. I'm tired of livin' and tired of workin' and all I want to do is quietly see out the rest of my days at Arlington, pick up my pension and take some time to relax before I go and see my maker. Look, I made some terrible mistakes. I used to just make mistakes that hurt me, and I pay for those every day. I can live with that—just about. It was real hard when my injuries screwed up my marriage and turned it into a sorta distant friendship, but my most recent mistakes have involved the lives of others to an extent that I can't live with. In my misguided efforts and bull-headed determination to do *something* useful with my life, my mistakes have become way more costly. The latest ones cost a wonderful, intelligent and brave woman her life. They also cost a young man the chance of a bright future and they cost his young family a loving father and husband. I just don't want to do that anymore. I gotta give up makin' bigger and bigger mistakes. My boss was right. I'm a liability when I start thinking for myself, acting on my own initiative. So, if you want some kinda help with what's goin' on with this weapon, maybe you'd be better off getting some young, fit, intelligent college graduate or somethin', 'cause I sure ain't your man."

They finished their meals in silence. As the waiter took their plates, Griffin turned to King and said, "You're quite right, of course. I shouldn't expect anything from you. In fact, I don't. Well, maybe that's not entirely true. Maybe it's just a hope that I have, somewhere in the back of my mind, but I wouldn't want you to do anything that you're not comfortable with." King looked at him, confused. *Just leave now*, he told himself, *while you still have some dignity left.* But there was still this part of him that just wouldn't lie down, wouldn't absent itself to some distant corner of his mind and let things be, so he could live his life in peace. There was still so much he didn't understand that rampaged chaotically through his being without explanation, permission or comfort. And there was still that insistent yearning in him to break out, above and beyond the mess that consumed him in his head, and find something right and clear and strong and good …and pain-free.

"What do you mean?"

"All in good time." Griffin smiled broadly. "First, though, I want to know if you would come and work for me."

King was completely thrown. "Work for you? I thought this was a lunch for information, not a job interview! Are you some sort of masochist or somethin'? Man, you're full of surprises, ain't you?"

This was the last thing King had expected. To be offered a job by such a high-profile figure as he was inching toward his own retirement seemed ludicrous. Hadn't Kirkland heard a word he'd said about him being a magnet for mistakes and failure?

"I'm perfectly serious. I'll pay you more than what you're getting now—and don't worry, I can get your full pension transferred."

"But you don't know what I'm being paid, so how can you—?"

"I can hazard a guess, or get my office to ask your boss… or you could tell me."

King sat back in his chair, trying to take in this new turn in their conversation.

"What kind of job are you talking about?"

"I think I can give you the job you've always wanted and it would be a privilege to have you on the team."

"Well, that's mighty generous… How many on the team?"

"Just you, me, my wife Sheryl, and a good friend of mine, at the moment. Others might follow."

"I don't know what to say. I'm…"

"A little surprised? Well, you shouldn't be. I'm confident that you will be a huge asset to the team, and I want to make sure you are rewarded properly for the qualities that you bring to your work and the results you can deliver, given the opportunity." Griffin called the waiter over. "Coffee?"

"Mr Kirkland—Griffin—are you sure you got the right man here? I mean, weren't you expecting Morgan Freeman or Tom Cruise or that English guy, Clive Owen, or someone? I mean, I ain't the fittest of guys, I'm just about ready for retirement, as I mentioned—"

"I know all that, Troy. And I know a hell of a lot more about you, as well. You think I'd have lunch with someone I hadn't checked out? I know you have the mysterious Beast to dig up all sorts of information, but I have something much more sophisticated. It's called the Grapevine and it has a much bigger processing capacity." King chuckled at the comparison. "I also appreciate, and you have just confirmed, why you are so keen to get yourself back to the orchard and while away the rest of your life on a rocking chair. It's not what you really want. It's all you think you can have."

"Well, I may want a lot of things, but I guess you can't have everything, can you? I mean, life's full of compromises, right?"

"Okay, so, tell me. What is the thing you want most in life? And I mean really want." King couldn't speak. This was just too difficult. Kirkland sensed his reticence in answering. "May I make a suggestion?" King nodded. "I think that the thing you want most in the whole world is the loving care and respect of a woman who longs to be with you every minute of every day."

"Would you excuse me, please? I need the washroom." King struggled to his feet. Kirkland waved away the waiter who was hovering, ready to assist as King forced himself up from the table. King walked as fast as he could to the washroom, went straight to a cubicle, slammed the door behind him, sat down and allowed the emotion that was welling up inside him to release. It quickly reached the surface and broke through, like a dam bursting. He bawled his eyes out.

He sat there for at least ten minutes, until he felt the tears subside and the warm flush had dissipated from his face. He slowly emerged from the cubicle and washed his face. *Why me? Why can't it all just stop?*

He made his way back to the restaurant and sat down again.

"Boy, that hit the spot, Griffin. You sure don't pull any punches, do you?"

"I'm sorry. That must have been a bit of a surprise. Tell me, when did you last see Dolores?"

"New Year, I guess." King remembered the half-hearted New Year celebrations, the distance between them even when they had lain in bed together, the disappointment he felt in himself, the gnawing concerns over money and his performance as a husband and guardian, the empty orchard, unwanted fruit. "But I can't see us ever getting back to what we had... once."

"But maybe you could go forward to something new, Troy. I know it's not my business but this life you're leading—cutting her out, staying away—it's wasting valuable time."

"I know, I know... I just..."

"What?"

"I kinda made a promise to myself that I would get back to Dolores when I'd done what I gotta do, when I can look after her properly, be a real husband, you know?"

"And what about the promise you made to her? To love and to cherish, to have and to hold... You remember all that?"

"Yeah, but why would she want me now? Nah, it's better I stay outta her way till at least I can offer her some sort of life."

"She doesn't think so."

King looked up. "What do you mean?"

"I spoke to her yesterday, and you know what she said?" He continued before King had a chance to object. "She said she just wants to be with you, Troy, no matter what your circumstances. She said she wanted you and her to be a team again, and that she's fed up living alone in a washed-up orchard that you're not going to want to get going again when you retire. She wants to sell up and come and live with you here in Washington. But, of course, you wouldn't know any of that, would you?"

King was feeling extremely uncomfortable. Who was this guy? What was he doing poking his nose into his affairs, offering him a job, confiding in him, counseling him? People don't do that sort of thing. Certainly high-profile politicians didn't do it, talking on first-name terms at a first meeting over a business lunch.

"I appreciate your concern, Griffin, but I have to say I'm surprised that in sizin' me up for a job, you should personally get into such fine detail."

"It's a very special job, and I need a very special kind of person for it. You mentioned some actors; well, actors can only emulate great people and they need a script to do it. I need someone who can write his own."

"And a clumsy old fart like me fits the bill?" King was almost laughing at the suggestion.

"I need a man who knows what it's like to be knocked down and who had the courage to get back up time after time. You fit that bill. I need a man who has such high moral values that he's prepared to risk losing everything simply because something in his gut tells him that something is wrong, and despite all the resistance he'll meet along the way, he'll strive to put that wrong right. You fit that bill. I need a man who works truly from the heart and not just for money. I need a man who doesn't respect rules that make no sense. I need a man who understands his abilities and his limitations and I need a man who is full of compassion for humanity. I need a passionate, loving and real man who takes responsibility for his actions and who, when he works with me, will be fully equipped to do so without having to hide his actions, make excuses or carry the weight of guilt when something goes wrong. I need someone who is deeply honest and who I can trust with my life. You fit all of those bills. The rest is just detail."

King felt as if his chest was going to burst open. He saw himself as a seven-year-old, sitting on his grandfather's knee—the last time he could remember receiving such loving encouragement.

"I... um... I don't suppose your expense account would run to a small brandy, would it?"

Griffin ordered, and held his hand out to King. "We have a deal?" he asked, with smiling eyes.

I've always gone with my gut, thought King, *and it's been wrong more than it's been right, but this time, I kinda feel...* With cautious determination, he took Griffin's hand and shook it warmly. "We have a deal," King replied, "but more than that. I feel I might be getting my life back as well."

"Let's hope so."

"Sir, would you like your brandy in the lounge?" Griffin looked around the restaurant. Most of the lunchtime clientele had left.

"No, this is perfect here, thank you."

King waited for the waiter to go before he broached the subject of the job that he had just landed.

"Griffin, what does the job entail? What have I just agreed to do?"

"If you're looking for a job description, I don't have one for you. If I did, it would probably sound so ridiculous you wouldn't believe me."

"Try me." King grinned.

"Okay, let me think… how about 'help me to save humanity'? Is that grand enough for you?"

"You're right. I don't believe you, but if all those things you said about me just now are true, then I'm your man!" He lifted his glass toward Griffin, who lifted his.

"To humanity."

Griffin reached down and retrieved a folder from under his chair.

"This is everything I know about the project we're going to be working on together."

"Everything?" *There can't be more than ten sheets of paper in there*, thought King.

"I know, it doesn't amount to much, just yet. That's why I need you."

"Are you sure you want me to have this? I mean, we're talking some heavy-duty high-security shit here, aren't we?"

"We're a team now. I simply cannot afford for you not to know everything that I know. If there's anything you're unclear about, please ask. It's essential that you be well-informed. Needless to say, it's for your eyes only, and once you have read it, I want you to shred it. I have a secure digital version that I can give you access to in your new office." He handed King the thin plastic folder. "Take it and read it at home this evening. I'll get in touch with your boss and explain the situation, so you will be able to clear your desk tomorrow. Here's my office address. It's not my government office at the Dirksen. It's one I've rented for the sole purpose of running this project, but you'll still be on government payroll." He handed King a slip of paper with an address hand-written on it. "If I may, I would also suggest that someone would be more than happy to find a better apartment for you… both… to live in. I'm afraid it's all a bit of a rush, but you'll see why when you read what's in there. There's just one thing I would ask you to start working on right away."

"Sure, what's that?"

"There's this character—Samakab. I believe you met him."

"That's right. We'd had our eye on him at Arlington Online for a while. I wanted to check him out because The Beast was short of some vital info on him. Trouble was, every time I suggested chasing him up, I got blocked higher up, so for me, it was kinda fortuitous to bump into him like I did."

"It certainly was. You didn't know it at the time, but he's pivotal to what we have to do. As you said, information on him is hard to find. My guess is that he was being protected by the people at the top of NSA, or even higher up. I need you to start working on getting a line of communication through to him."

"Hmm, could be tough."

"I know, but if you need any resources to do it, just let me know. He doesn't stay at the Four Seasons any more. He seems to have gone to ground."

"What kinda line of communication are you hopin' for?

"A cell phone, address—anything so I can talk to him."

King took out his wallet and fished around inside. He dropped a card on the table. "How's this for starters?"

Lying on the table was the card that Samakab had given him in New York, with the Somali telephone number crossed out, but with his cell phone number clearly visible. "I reckon it will be easy enough to find someone who can dig out the rest of the information under the ball point scribbles—just as long as I can still get a bit of cooperation from the guys at Arlington Online after I've left. Let's just hope he's still got that cell phone as well."

"That's incredible! Perfect. I'll see what I can do ensure Arlington Online's cooperation." He grinned at King who was basking in the satisfaction of having pulled a rabbit out of the hat. "You see? I chose the right man."

CHAPTER 39

While most of them had opulent lifestyles, not many had ever stayed in a hotel like this. The Burj Al-Fateh was a remarkable piece of architecture. A fat, glistening bud of steel and glass perched on the shore where the Blue and White Niles met, it was designer opulence for the business traveler more used to the stuffy similitude of the Hyatts and Sheratons of the world. With six state-of-the-art restaurants, panoramic views of the Nile, Tuti Island and Khartoum from its luxurious suites, a fitness spa and a world-class commercial center, it was Vegas madness transported to the Sudanese capital. For the group arriving in dribs and drabs from Khartoum airport five miles away, however, 'business traveler' was probably not an accurate description. Most of the 52 representatives attending this special meeting mixed their business dealings with large doses of politics and criminal activity; some also included military activities—either on behalf of, or against, their national governments. Many of them were more Mafiosi than politicians or businessmen, wielding power and fear in equal measure, although they reigned in communities where they were regarded as keepers of the peace and facilitators of wealth, rather than criminals. Some were sophisticated and educated, others brutish, loud and distinctly uncouth. But all of them had several things in common: unquestioned influence in their community, a desire to succeed and the facilities to ensure that they did. They were also angry—each for their own reasons. The message they had each received, along with the hotel reservation and a plane ticket, had been designed to draw them here in the belief that their anger could at last be satisfied.

The delegates greeted each other with bows and nods and the occasional handshake as they made their way to the Syndicate Room. The atmosphere bristled with suspicion and caution, as if they were entering an assassin's convention where each felt he might be the next target. Smiles were in short supply as they took their seats around the tables set in a 'U' formation, its open end facing a large screen on the wall. A small camera peered back at the tables from above the screen, which were laid out with notepads, pens, jugs of iced water and glasses. Delicate flower features were placed—somewhat incongruously for a gathering of such indelicate-looking men—at intervals along the tables. Nervous, gangly young stewards, smartly dressed in white suits, fussed around the attendees as they sat, offering drinks and snacks, usually being dismissed with a curt flash of the eyes or an impatient wave. More staff cruised around the inside of the 'U', explaining how to work the microphones positioned in front of each delegate.

"You press this button, here, when you want to talk, and release it when you have finished, okay?" The simple instructions were met variously with bored and derisive looks, or intense concentrated appreciation. "No, no, this button here." There was only one bright red button on the microphone stand, but some of them insisted on trying to find it on the mike.

The quiet tension in the room was only broken by the occasional clink of ice cubes dropping into glasses, quickly suppressed ringing of cell phones and coughs and wheezes. Heads turned lazily to each new noise to fill the time. One or two snoozed after a long flight, others wiped handkerchiefs across their sweating brows as they acclimatized to the air-conditioned room. Then the hotel manager gave a short welcome and house-keeping information, before announcing that the link would be live in approximately ten minutes, so if anyone wanted to use the washroom, they still had time. As he finished talking, the screen behind him flickered to life and displayed a title: *Welcome to the inaugural 5T summit*.

Gradually the room came to order as a few late arrivals took their seats and the hotel staff drifted out, pulling the doors closed behind them, sealing its inhabitants in air-conditioned stillness, thick with anticipation.

"Good morning, everyone." Samakab appeared on the screen. He looked presidential in a dark-blue suit and a plain green silk tie. Behind him, a digitally applied scene of blue sky with the occasional cloud drifting across it revealed nothing of his whereabouts, but gave Samakab an uncannily God-like appearance. "Thank you for coming. I know that many of you have come a long way on the strength of a short message from someone you may not even have heard of. I am confident that, by the time you leave the hotel, you will feel your trust has been well-placed and your journey worthwhile. I hope you are all comfortable in your accommodation and that, before you leave, you will have an opportunity to acquaint yourselves with each other. You have my assurance that this is a secure connection and the room has been swept for listening devices. Should you feel uncomfortable about security, it is better that you leave now. The only consequences of leaving the meeting will be that you forego the substantial benefits that it will bring. I can see you all, thanks to the camera mounted above the screen that you are looking at, and I can identify anyone who presses the red button to talk. This meeting is not being recorded. Before I start, forgive me for speaking in English. Since there is one representative from every African nation in the room, save one, English is more practical and expedient, and I know that you all speak it. One day, perhaps, we will return to using our own languages as our main means of communication. I would like that, as I know you would. By the way, I am the 53rd delegate, representing Somalia." Samakab took a sip from a glass of water before continuing.

"Gentlemen, Africa is at a crucial point in its history, and in a unique position to take advantage of a situation that was not of its own making. This is why I have called this meeting and why I have very carefully chosen each of you to take part in it. Over the last two years, I have identified that you each hold a pivotal position of power in your country. That may come as a surprise to some of you but, believe me, you are the hidden gems inside each of your countries—the power behind the throne." Heads turned, the occasional smile cracked surly features, one or two scoffed.

"You may or may not be part of the government. You may or may not even be known by your people—most of you are not. But without you, your countries either cannot operate as successfully, cannot prosper as they do, or cannot move forward effectively. You would all like to be more effective, for a number of reasons—be they wealth, power, the desire for social change, even simply self-aggrandizement. And you are all practical people. You don't care for the cumbersome mechanisms of politics, you don't concern yourselves with established methods or routines, you are not the type of people who get embroiled in bureaucracy. You get the job done whether or not your actions or methods gain the approval of the establishment. You also have a sixth sense that instinctively recognizes a great opportunity, and you can quickly actualize the resources to take advantage of it. That's why you are here. Any questions so far?"

"I have a question." A middle-aged man in a white flowing robe raised his hand.

"Press the button or he can't hear you," somebody else volunteered.

He pressed the button and repeated, "I have a question."

"Moussa, welcome." Samakab checked his computer and reported back to the room. "Moussa is from Naimey, in Niger. He is very influential in Niger's uranium production and in transport—an essential service for his land-locked nation. Go ahead, Moussa. What is your question?"

"Why are you not talking to the African Union? Why us? Surely if, as you say, we are at a crucial point in our history and there is some advantage to be gained, they are very well-placed to realize that advantage."

"Thank you, Moussa. I can understand why you would think that. The fact is, opportunities like the one I will describe come and go very quickly. An organization like the AU cannot act quickly enough. It's too big and cumbersome, and while it is trying to improve Africa's lot, the task it has set itself is just too great and there are too many conflicting interests impeding its progress. What I'm about to propose will short-cut their processes and get the results we're looking for much more quickly. Look, we have seen the Organization of African Unity come and go. It was a disaster. Now we have the AU. It's been in existence since 2002. Nearly a decade later, do we have unity in Africa? Of course we don't. Your own country has been suspended from the AU, as have three others, and Morocco has left it. We are supposed to be moving toward a United States of Africa, but with all the divisions between and within the member countries, the self-interest, greed and clumsy diplomacy of some of our national leaders and governments, progress is painfully slow. The theory sounds good but, in practice, nations, governments and people find it hard to agree and commit, as we have seen at the endless summits in Addis Ababa and Egypt. What we need now is decisive action, not talk."

"Then I am looking forward to hearing your proposal," Moussa concluded, and sat back in his chair. No more questions were asked.

"Let me draw your attention to the emblem that the AU adopted." A graphic of the emblem filled the screen. A gold ribbon bore small interlocking red rings, from which palm leaves shot up around a gold circle that itself enclosed an inner green circle, within which there was a gold representation of Africa. "I'd like to explain what the symbolism means. The red interlinked rings stand for African solidarity and the blood that has been shed for the liberation of Africa. The palm leaves represent peace. The gold is a symbol of Africa's wealth and bright future and the green represents African hopes and aspirations. The graphic shape of Africa has no internal borders, symbolizing African unity. Gentlemen, after the formation of the AU, it took nearly a decade to come up with this emblem. That's nearly a decade before the AU even started to define the job in hand and integrate it into a symbol that communicates it. As of today, the only part of the symbolism that you see before you that has been achieved and holds true is the color of the interlocking rings—the blood that has been shed. But that blood has not achieved liberation or unity."

Samakab reappeared on the screen.

"But the AU is the best we have at the moment," protested another delegate. "They've set up a good structure for moving forward, and we have the Pan African Parliament, regional economic communities and our own financial institutions like the central bank, investment bank and the monetary fund."

"Thank you, Omar," Samakab replied. "Omar is from Egypt and deals in tourism there. He is also an influential politician with particular interest in the Suez Canal. Is that right, Omar?"

"Generally, yes."

"Generally, you are correct in your statement. Unfortunately, the reality is that those institutions are not helping the overall situation to the extent that is needed. As a continent, we are—how can I say it—'economically reactive', rather than proactive. You, Omar, will understand this as it is particularly affecting your country right now. While Egypt, like many of the other countries along our northern coastline, has not suffered many of the disadvantages that sub-Saharan Africa has experienced, you have a big problem right now. Many say that there is an economic crisis looming in Egypt because of falling tourism revenues as a result of the economic crisis in Europe, a sharp drop in foreign remittances, a halving of foreign reserves and falling revenues from the Suez Canal due to disruption in shipping—"

"Brought about by your pirates hijacking our customers!" Omar clenched his microphone in a tight fist.

"I agree and I apologize. But, believe me, that will be resolved shortly, and it is a minor nuisance when compared to the demographic time-bomb Egypt is sitting on right now, that it is powerless to do anything about."

"Apologies are not enough, Samakab. If you were here right now, I'd—"

"Please, Omar. This is not the way forward. It never has been, but it has always been the way we have dealt with our problems, and that is what has kept us weak. In our country, we have a phrase that we use a lot. *Ilko wada jir bey wax ku gooyaan.* Unity is power. As we have just seen, that sentiment is also enshrined in the AU emblem. But we never embrace what it says for long enough to achieve that power. That is why Africa has been so easy to exploit. You all know that. You don't need me to lecture you. The very reasons that you have been successful have been because you have recognized the need for unity, have built your own networks and organizations and have become strong in your own communities. You may have spent ten years or so doing that, but you have achieved results far beyond the talking shops and the committees of governmental organizations."

"I think we know what we have achieved, thank you, Samakab. And, for my part at least, I don't want a lecture in the failings of African unity and I'm not here just to get a pat on the back from you. Just get to the point." A large man with a fearsome face and dressed in a smart black suit, Arcel was a guerilla commander from Côte d'Ivoire who had been instrumental in maintaining a fragile peace since the signing of a deal between the government and rebel forces in 2007. Following his country's troubled period of drought, civil war and the economic shockwaves that had resulted, he was seen as a key figure in the re-building of the country, and was widely respected. He didn't suffer fools and didn't like to waste time on petty details or rambling, inconclusive meetings.

"You are quite right, Arcel, and thank you for bringing us back on track." Samakab was pleased with the way the meeting was going. He had their attention, for now, but he knew he had to talk fast or he lose them.

"As I said, we have an opportunity of unprecedented proportions that I would like to present to you today. Are there any more questions before I continue?" There were none. Several of the delegates were starting to fidget. He pressed on.

"As some of you know, I have been making good headway in my business. Recent investments and funding received from my 'clients' have enabled me to substantially scale up my operations and to bring all the competition under one umbrella organization, replacing squabbling competitive small groups with an efficient and well-equipped machine. Everybody is happy, because everyone is winning. I haven't involved the Transitional Government because they're not in a position to make effective decisions. Al-Shabaab cooperate in a security capacity in exchange for funds and equipment. They control a large part of the population, and many are pleased that they are imposing some discipline because it has reduced fighting between clans. Gentlemen, there is no end to the wealth I can accumulate now. Having achieved this enviable situation for myself, it made me think beyond mere wealth. I thought of the history of our continent, how it has been ravaged and raped by others, how our people have been enslaved, how we have been subjected to disease and poverty as the world sat and watched. I thought about how our lands have been passed from one colonial power to another, and how our peoples suffer as we support the lifestyles of rich nations. I thought of how poor infrastructure, instability, corruption, AIDS, unfair trade rules and tariff barriers are all set against us, to keep us poor and 'manageable'. I thought of the vast swathe of countries—most of the African Nations—that have been classified as Heavily Indebted Poor Countries. I thought of how they are shackled to a debt management regime that will never end, and of the vulture funds that circle around the weak, ready to pick them off and strangle them. And I thought of the cynical way that the ODA has been used—not to provide real development assistance to the weak, but to cycle up and down according to the whims of governments, and even to prop up the economies of donor countries."

"But your run of luck," Arcel interjected, "is going to be short-lived if the European vote goes in favor of an occupying force in Somalia. What are you planning to do about that?"

"I agree with you, Arcel. At the moment, the countries of Europe are evenly divided on the issue. Many are keen to avoid a prolonged occupation simply on the basis of the expense of it—in terms of both lives and money. They can see that it could also extend beyond our borders if they want to gain any meaningful control, and they don't want that either. Others, particularly in Belgium, Portugal, France and the UK, are extremely reluctant to get involved in anything that smacks of colonialism. However, my activities have upped the ante, as the economic cost to Europe in particular will soon reach a point where they have no other option. You may be surprised to know that I welcome this situation."

"I certainly am. It sounds like a recipe for national suicide."

"It could be, but not if we are united. In fact, it could be the beginning of a new Africa—a strong and wealthy Africa that we'd all like to be a part of."

"And how do you work that out?"

"After a lot of thought on this subject, I realized something. We can change things. We can have a new Africa." There was silence in the room. Samakab checked the monitor. He had their full attention. *The Norfolk Defender should be entering the Red Sea right about now.*

"Look at the world situation. The US definitely doesn't want to get involved in Somalia just now, if ever again. Europe is divided and economic difficulties are threatening the very existence of the Euro. Austerity measures, which we all know a great deal about and have lived with for years, are the order of the day throughout the European Community. Populations are still growing, of course. The world still has to feed itself and it needs resources in order to operate. Much of the rest of the world is cash-poor, but in real terms it is also resource-poor. Africa is cash-poor but resource-rich. For the first time in history, Africa has more to offer the rest of the world than the rest of the world has to offer Africa. We may be suffering as a result of worldwide funding and buying power shrinkage, but we have the resources that the rest of the world needs to keep going. Money, my friends, isn't worth as much as it used to be. There's a new economic reality emerging and, together, we are well-placed to take advantage of it." Silence. Samakab felt nervous, but was determined not to show it.

"You may be wondering, gentlemen, why I called this the 5T Summit. It was an idea that I trust will amuse you. It stands for 'Time To Turn The Tables'." There was a general rearranging of bums on seats, coughing and glances around the room, as if each were waiting for another to take the initiative to either condemn or praise Samakab's monologue.

"Very enlightening, in theory," said Solomon, the Ugandan representative, after what seemed to Samakab to be an eternity. "I can see that we could possibly be in a strong position, in some ways. The problem is that however much you would like us to act in unison, or even have a semblance of unity, it just isn't going to happen. From what I have learned from the colleagues I have met here, we are in very disparate trades, government departments, military organizations and industries, in countries that are, in many cases, thousands of miles apart, physically, ideologically and economically. 'Time To Turn The Tables' sounds very laudable, but I can't see how we can do anything to make that come about, either collectively or individually. We're already locked in to our own systems of whatever it is we are currently doing, and if those are working, why would we want to disturb them? Also, you haven't told us yet what your proposed plan is. Lastly, as Arcel said, if you're pushing the international community so hard that they invade Somalia and occupy it, all these fancy ideas get thrown out of the window."

"Yes, true. But is that what you want? Is that what any of us want? To just keep going down the same road? We know where that leads. You know it's only going to get worse, for the reasons I just mentioned. You are from Uganda, Solomon. Are you happy with the situation there? You have a leadership that is bordering on immovable monarchy, supported by a cabinet of over-paid, under-performing fat cats living in huge mansions surrounded by security guards, while mothers are dying in childbirth and malnutrition is rife among children. And that is just the tip of the iceberg in just one country. I'm sure all of you can tell tales of injustice in your own countries, suffering and poverty and all the environmental problems brought upon this continent by the so-called developed world's insensitive and reckless consumption. But the world is at a tipping point, Solomon. Right now. Don't you think it's worth taking some decisive action if there is a chance that things could tip in Africa's favor, for a change?"

"Of course I do. But I need evidence to assure me that I should even be sitting here listening to you before I can start to discuss 'decisive action', let alone act on it. And I am sure the others feel the same." Solomon scanned the table. Several of the delegates nodded.

I'm going to have to show them, Samakab thought.

"I can understand your reticence, of course. You ask for evidence. I will give you evidence, but first I need to know if everyone here is with me in principle. If you are not, we are all wasting our time. In just a few days, I will show you something that will convince you that we can take decisive action. In order to show you, I will need some very simple cooperation from you, Omar and you, Tarek. I will call you both after this meeting closes, if I may." Omar and Tarek both nodded.

"Thank you," Samakab continued. "Now, would anyone who does not agree with the broad sentiments that I have expressed and does not want to cooperate and be a part of the 5T group gathered here today, please press their microphone button. But be warned: you have everything to lose if you do press it and Africa continues on its present course in this world recession. On the other hand, you have the possibility of gaining everything you want, if you don't press the button."

Samakab waited as the group fidgeted. Each delegate looked around the table. Some talked quietly to the person sitting next to them. Hands occasionally drifted toward buttons, hovered for a second or two, and then withdrew. He continued to wait until all the discussions had stopped, and all of the delegates were sitting back in their chairs, watching the screen.

"Very well, gentlemen, this is what I propose."

CHAPTER 40

If the hull had sustained any damage in Berbera while the *Norfolk Defender* was being loaded, it hadn't become apparent during the time she'd been under way. Nevertheless, Captain Baptiste had only allowed himself short periods of restless sleep as they sailed up the Red Sea. A prisoner on his own ship, he was not allowed to leave the bridge and had to make do with a blanket on the floor as a bed. Meals were delivered on a trolley by one of their captors, who took pleasure in sampling their food with dirty fingers before handing them their plates. Stale smells of sweat and body odor hung in the air. Tired tension pervaded the control room. Two of the Somalis guarding the crew had run out of qat and were talking incessantly to each other in increasingly urgent tones. Baptiste hoped they would crash and sleep rather than get violent as withdrawal symptoms kicked in. The other three guarding them on the bridge were sitting on their haunches, clasping AK47s, alert and watching their every move. Baptiste's eyes were tired. He needed a shower and a shave. More than that, though, he needed to be alert.

Some 24 hours after leaving Berbera, they had left Eritrea behind and had recently passed the headland that marked the end of Sudanese territory and the beginning of the disputed Hala 'Ib Triangle, administered by Egypt. No one had been allowed into the hold and the crew had only been able to make cursory inspections of the deck. They had found some minor cracks around the hatch corners, but nothing alarming. On his infrequent visits to the bridge, Raage had refused to talk about what was in the hold, and hadn't told Baptiste where they were heading, so Baptiste just had to trust that the ship would make it to the next port without any major incidents. He hoped he could make a full inspection once they docked.

Baptiste peered into the nothingness of the far horizon as the dawn started to define it in dark, colorless hues. The *Norfolk Defender* cut effortlessly though the still morning waters at a steady 35 knots, its powerful turbines churning up a broad wake. It was ironic, he thought, that after all the effort that had gone into making this ship invisible, all he wanted now was for it to be noticed. He knew that, by 10am, they would be passing close by St John's Island. It seemed like a thin chance, but he hoped that by steering as close as he dared to the island, he might disturb some of the holidaymakers who were sure to be visiting it by speedboat or yacht—enough for them to make a complaint to the Egyptian authorities and cause them to intervene. It was risky, as he was steering the ship just with GPS, without radar or depth soundings as Raage had insisted that anything other than essential equipment was switched off. To get close to St John's Island, Baptiste would have to make some sharp turns around the smaller Rocky Island, a few miles to its southeast. Those kinds of maneuvers would almost certainly attract unwanted attention from Raage, who kept himself well-informed about their progress and was regularly reporting to someone on his satellite phone.

"Coffee," Baptiste called to the group sitting in the corner, "we need coffee." They looked to one another, to see which of them would submit to taking an order. There was a stalemate of inaction that was eventually broken by one of them shouting to one of his friends standing guard outside the door, who, in turn, called to someone else. Eventually a tray was brought up to the bridge, covered with steaming mugs sitting in a pond of dirty overspill that sloshed over the rim of the tray as it was placed carelessly on top of one of the control panels. The chief mate immediately retrieved it and cleaned off the panel with his hand, accidentally flicking a switch on the SCANTER X-band navigation and surveillance radar system. A screen flickered into life. One of the guards stood up immediately, shouted and pointed his AK47 at him.

"Sorry!" He raised his hands in surrender then carefully showed the guard that he was switching it off. "Sorry... accident." He took a mug of coffee over to Baptiste and whispered, "Dead ahead, about nine miles, we have company on our same heading." Baptiste didn't respond, but scanned the emerging horizon. This was excellent news. It gave him a glimmer of hope that they might be discovered. If there was a large vessel ahead, chances were that they would overtake it. It was highly unlikely that there was anything in the region that could travel as fast as the *Norfolk Defender*.

Within half an hour, it was bright enough to make out the occasional glint of sunlight bouncing off a dot in the far distance. Baptiste strained his eyes trying to figure out what kind of ship it was but a light sea mist made identification difficult. He prayed that the guards would remain seated on the floor as the *Norfolk Defender* gained on the ship. He didn't want anyone alerting Raage, who would surely force him to change course to avoid it. He stared at the chief mate as he drank his coffee, trying to wordlessly communicate to him to keep his eyes fixed on the ship, and pointedly rolling his eyes toward the helm so he would understand to keep following it should Baptiste have to leave the bridge at any time.

Baptiste felt wrecked but, as he drank his coffee, he took some comfort in the fact that Raage's visits to the bridge were becoming less frequent. He guessed he was taking a nap. As there was nothing Baptiste could do right now, he decided to do the same. There was a slim chance that someone might be visiting the uninhabited island at 10am that morning, so he wanted to be wide awake by the time they approached it. Once they had passed St John's Island, there would be nothing more he could do to attract attention before they reached the Gulf of Suez.

But as he lay down on his blanket on the steel floor, every part of his body ached and his mind was racing. Nearby, the machete was leaning up against the wall, vibrating with the hum of the engines, its owner snoring and twitching in drug-deficient sleep. On the other side of the room, surly black faces peered at him, resting on hands clasping the barrels of weapons. No way was he going to be able to sleep. Then there was that distant ship they had glimpsed. How could he signal to them that they'd been hijacked? There was nothing in the way they were traveling that would alarm any passing ships if they saw the *Norfolk Defender*. He had to think of something.

However, apprehension and a crushing guilt blocked all constructive thought. He'd been sloppy. He hadn't followed the proper security procedures when someone had approached the ship. How stupid he'd been to even talk to anyone arriving on the quay at that time of the morning. All it had taken was a few glasses of wine and the boredom of a few days in Berbera to put the entire crew in grave danger, lose control of the vessel and become captive on his own ship. He didn't even know what had been loaded onto it. He shuddered at the thought of the fall-out once they'd been liberated, which they surely would be, before they reached the Suez Canal. And he thought of his wife, Cathy, who so admired her shining star of a husband. He forced his mind back to the matter in hand. How to attract attention? When he'd first realized that they were heading into the Red Sea, he'd been confident that, with all the increased security that had been put in place to deal with the piracy problem, they would be easily trapped and the pirates would be dealt with quickly and efficiently. They had now traveled over halfway up the Red Sea, and there had been no communications from any of the Egyptian naval vessels that regularly patrolled it. Normally, any naval vessel that spotted them but did not get a response to a radio communication would have used other means to communicate, and eventually would have approached them.

His attention was brought sharply back to the bridge as the machete slid down the wall onto the floor and rolled next to him, its handle coming to rest just inches away from his hand. As it did, the thug it belonged to woke up and lurched quickly to his feet, shouting incomprehensibly at Baptiste as he brought one foot heavily down on Baptiste's hand and retrieved the machete. Baptiste screamed as the bones in two of his fingers snapped. Alarmed and not yet fully awake, the man raised the machete as Baptiste raised his free arm across his head in an effort to protect himself from the heavy blade. Two shots blasted through the bridge and blood rained down on Baptiste. The bullets ricocheted off the steel walls and embedded themselves in a control panel, having first traveled clean through the thug's skull. Pandemonium broke out as several of the other crewmen started shouting at the guards who, having killed one of their own, were wildly pointing their weapons around the room—

sometimes at each other—and shouting hysterically in Somali. Baptiste climbed up from the floor, nursing his throbbing right hand, and ordered his crew back to their stations. The guards continued arguing among themselves and pointed accusatory fingers at Baptiste. Raage came racing up the stairway to the bridge and joined in the fracas, eventually managing to calm them down. The air remained highly charged, as if just one wrong look could set off a massacre.

"What's all the shouting about?" Baptiste eventually managed to ask.

"You have to pay a *diya* to this man's family," Raage pointed at the disgusting, bloody mess on the floor, attached to the large, machete-wielding body, where the thug's head used to be.

"Like hell I do! That idiot tried to kill me with a machete while I was trying to get some sleep!"

"They say you upset him. They say it was your fault that he died, so you must pay the *diya*. And, anyway, they cannot because they have no money."

"*I* upset *him*? What are they talking about? And what the hell is a *diya*?" Baptiste glared at the guards, who avoided eye contact and muttered among themselves. "Look what this brute did to my hand!"

"Look what you did to his head. That's hardly a reasonable response, is it?" A wide pool of black-red blood was spreading across the floor of the bridge.

"But I—" Logic clearly wasn't going to work in this situation. "Look, okay, what's a *diya*? What do they want?"

"In our country, if a man kills someone, he must pay compensation to the victim's family, so the family is supported and can survive without the victim's income."

"What? This man tried to kill me! Don't you get that? The only reason the other guards shot him was presumably because they wanted to keep me alive to captain the ship so they can get safely back to land."

"Between you and me, Captain," Raage took Baptiste to one side, "my guess is that the motivation was more about financial survival than physical survival. These are simple fishermen. Anyone who can afford a big ship like this—"

"Don't be ridiculous, I don't own—"

"They don't know that… As I was saying, anyone who can afford a ship like this can surely afford the *diya* to keep this man's family in comfort for the rest of their life."

"For the rest of their life? You've got to be kidding me. Well, they can demand all they like, they won't get a cent out of me." He turned to face the guards. "Fucking savages!" The guards looked at each other, obviously not pleased. Raage took Baptiste's arm and spoke quietly in his ear,

"Can I tell them that when we dock you'll get some money out of the bank and give it to them for the family?"

"Do you seriously expect me to believe that they will give the family—if that pig even has a family—rather than piss it away on qat and booze?"

"No, but I don't fancy your chances—once we dock—if you don't make some sort of gesture. I'm sure it won't put too much strain on your bank account."

"Well, I guess I don't have much of a choice, do I."

"None. I'll tell them. Then we must go below and get your hand bandaged up. I will also arrange for someone to clean up this mess."

"I'm touched by your concern."

"Don't be. I am only interested in you doing your job."

As Raage explained the situation to the guards, who smiled broadly once they knew they had a deal, Baptiste glanced at the horizon. They were gaining on the ship. He checked his watch and guessed that they would probably catch up with it in approximately two hours—just as they approached St John's Island. The chief mate glanced in the same direction and gave Baptiste a nod as Baptiste and Raage left the bridge together.

When Baptiste returned to the bridge half an hour later, his hand heavily bandaged, he was accompanied by another guard to replace the dead man. The door to the bridge was wide open. The reason became clear as they approached it. The body had still not been removed. Lacking the normal control functions of a living organism, the bowels had released, their contents mixing with the bloody pool that now surrounded it. The air conditioning wasn't strong enough to mask it and, in the relatively confined space of the bridge, the smell was becoming unbearable. Turning to the new guard, Baptiste said, "Get this lot cleaned up, or this ship stops right here and now." The guard, who didn't speak much English, got the point, and disappeared back down the stairs. Baptiste pulled a handkerchief from his pocket and held it against his nose and mouth before venturing any further. Inside, everyone was trying to hold their breath for as long as they could. Much to the annoyance of the increasingly frazzled guards, the crew members braved restraining arms and gun barrels digging into their ribs, desperate to hang their heads out of the doorway and gulp large quantities of warm, fresh morning air.

The one good thing about the foul atmosphere was that it created a distraction that kept the guards' attention on the doorway. None of them were watching what was happening up ahead. The ship ahead was now clearly in view and Baptiste was relieved to see that it was a naval vessel—not just another merchant ship.

"It's a Knox class frigate. Must be Egyptian…" the chief mate murmured as he and Baptiste stood at the helm.

"It looks like the *Rasheed* to me. Can you tell?"

"No, but it's either the *Rasheed* or the *Damyat*. They're the only two the Egyptians bought from us in the 1990s. Whatever it is, it's about 40 years old and a lot slower than us."

"Keep right on its tail, until we're virtually on top of it, if it doesn't move over." Baptiste planned to break every rule in the book, if necessary. When a vessel overtakes another, it has a responsibility to keep out of the way of the vessel being overtaken. The *Norfolk Defender*, which was twice the beam and more than twice the length of the slower frigate, would present a frightening spectacle from the stern of the frigate as it approached at full speed. Since the *Norfolk Defender* was also maintaining radio silence, the frigate would have no option but to respond to a very real threat. Not only that, in planning to sail close by St John's Island, Baptiste would be deviating from the shipping lanes. He knew these waters well, so he had no fears that he might run aground, but such a large vessel traveling at speed could put other mariners in smaller craft at considerable risk. He just hoped he could raise the alarm without ramming one.

A commotion at the doorway drew his attention back to the foul-smelling bridge. One of the guards threw a stretcher on the floor beside the dead man. Ralph and Bobby—two of the young programmers—followed, carrying buckets of soapy water and mops. Raage was the last one to arrive. He stood in the doorway, grimacing in disgust and waving his hand in front of his face. Ralph gasped, dropped his bucket on the floor, spilling its contents everywhere. Bobby looked as if he was about to have a seizure. He just stood in the doorway, shaking, covering his mouth, his eyes fearfully darting around the scene.

"Why did you bring these two up here, for God's sake? They don't need to be involved in all this!" Baptiste was furious. All order seemed to have broken down on his ship. The programmers were never allowed on the bridge. He had strict orders to keep them in their quarters or working in the hold. To present them with this graphic display of the mayhem on board was not only unnecessary, it was cruel. Ralph tried to make a break for the door and was easily stopped by one of the guards who pushed him back into the room, sending him slipping and sliding across the blood and guts, unable to keep his balance.

"They needed a little clarification as to the new situation," said Raage. "They seemed to think that this is some sort of holiday camp where they can order anything they like, when they like. I asked them to do some programming earlier and they refused." He shrugged his shoulders and smiled. "So I thought they might feel more motivated if I asked them to help tidy up this mess. What do you think, Captain?"

By now, Baptiste was confident that in less than ninety minutes the *Norfolk Defender* would be under the control of the Egyptian Navy, and Raage and the rest of his gang would have other, more pressing problems on their minds. All he had to do was keep everyone distracted long enough for the *Norfolk Defender* to get dangerously close to the frigate and be seen to be flagrantly breaking basic maritime rules.

"Well, if want my opinion, you're going about it the wrong way. If you think these young men can do their work properly in a traumatized state, you're wrong. Their work is highly specialized and requires great concentration. I'd say you've just put your schedule back by a few hours. The longer they stay here, the longer the delay in getting the work finished."

"I'll take my chances on that." Raage turned to Ralph. "You two get that body onto the stretcher and tip it over the side over there." He pointed to the stairway.

"No way!" Ralph shouted at Raage, which earned him a sharp jab in the stomach with a rifle butt from the nearest guard. He fell to the floor, winded, in agony. Baptiste was appalled by this macabre game. A wet stain was spreading over Bobby's shorts.

"Don't be ridiculous!" Baptiste shouted. "They can't possibly lift that dead weight on their own, let alone lift it high enough to tip it over the railing. Some of your men will have to help." He pointed to two of the guards and gestured toward the body. They didn't budge.

"I believe," Raage said, looking at Baptiste's bandaged hand, "it's the responsibility of the chief mate to make sure that everything on board is in order. Isn't that right?" The chief mate walked forward and, with the help of one of the seamen, struggled on the slippery floor as they heaved the soggy, stinking mass onto the stretcher. Their efforts sent them gasping for air at the doorway, which had now been open for so long that the mid-morning heat was rapidly raising the temperature inside. Returning to the bridge, they each washed their hands and arms as thoroughly as they could in the one remaining bucket of water.

"This is impossible," the chief mate protested to Raage. "If we're going to tip him over the side, we have to do it from the stairway. That means the stretcher will be on an angle and he can slide off before we can tip him over."

"Well, in that case, tie him to the stretcher," Raage suggested.

"What with? We have no rope or straps up here."

"Someone will have to go to the hold," Baptiste told Raage.

"That's not an option."

"We can't move the body without straps or rope."

"You'll manage, I'm sure."

"There's another problem." The chief mate was beginning to catch on to the delaying tactic.

"What's that?" asked Baptiste.

"If we tie him to the stretcher, he won't sink. We can't just dump him in the sea where he could he a hazard to small craft."

"Quite right, but what choice do we have? Given the situation, we'd better do as the man says," Baptiste kept the conversation going, "but we'll need some straps from the hold." Out of the corner of his eye, Baptiste could see that Raage was getting twitchy.

"Very well," Raage said, "one of my men will accompany one of your seamen to the hold to get the equipment you need." Baptiste gave the order and two men left. "In the meantime, you get this floor cleaned up." Raage pointed to Bobby, who was cowering in the corner, holding onto the floor mop.

"No, don't," Baptiste said to Bobby, who looked nervously from Raage to Baptiste and back again. Who should he listen to? "When the body has been tipped over the side, my men will need to wash in that before they can continue with their duties... unless Ralph here can go and fill another one." Baptiste felt that he was making some progress at last. He now had one of his crew in the hold, so he could find out what was down there. One of the guards was with him and therefore out of the way, and now there was the possibility of sending another one to the galley with Ralph for a bucket of water.

But Raage was having none of it. "Just get on with it," he snapped, pointing at Bobby, who crept out of his corner and started to mop up the foul-smelling liquids around the stretcher, which was now saturated and had started to drip onto the floor. The seaman returned, carrying two load straps with ratchets that they used to tie vehicle wheels to the lifting frames. He headed straight toward Baptiste.

"You'll never believe what's down there—" he started to tell Baptiste.

"No talking," Raage cut in, "just secure this body and let's get it out of here." The seaman and the chief mate crouched down and slung the straps around the body and the stretcher, pulling them tight with the ratchets.

"Perhaps," Baptiste ventured as they finished their handiwork, "one of your men—who are obviously so close to the deceased and concerned for his family, despite the fact that they murdered him in cold blood—would like to say a few words? Is there some sort of ceremony we should be performing—a proper Islamic funeral or... something?" One of the guards spat on the floor. "I guess not..."

Raage waved toward the doorway. "Get him out." He followed, to keep an eye on them as they carried the stretcher from the bridge, and started to manhandle it over the sloping rail. As he did so, Baptiste checked the frigate out of the corner of his eye. He willed it to get closer. It was still too far away and he was running out of diversions.

The two men struggled with the stretcher on the stairway. They'd arranged it so that the remains of the head were at the upper end. If they dropped it, neither man wanted to be holding onto the broken skull as the body slid down the stairway. It took a herculean effort to get the legs of the stretcher over the rail. The seaman at the lower end was sweating under the strain and spitting blood away from his mouth as it dripped down onto his eyes and face. They eventually stopped for a breather, balancing the stretcher on the railing. When Raage shouted at them to continue, they inched it over, little by little, until the legs on the other side of the stretcher caught on the railing. It was a macabre performance that they played very well, playing for time, faking a struggle to push the legs over the railing while also preventing the whole thing from sliding. Eventually, they couldn't delay any longer, and the stretcher fell, banging on the hull as it tumbled into the wash.

"They need to wash and change." Baptiste was standing in the doorway of the bridge, blocking Raage's way back as he turned around. "And we need to get some sterilized wipes, more detergent and cleaning equipment up here."

"Later. Get back to your job."

Still blocking the doorway, Baptiste said, "I'll show you why." He led Raage to the rear of the bridge and indicated a blood-spattered control panel. "This cover must be removed and the electronics behind it checked. You can see that blood and flesh and possibly bone fractures have got through the joins in the panels. They're not water-proof as they're not designed to be splattered with blood, surprising as that may be to you. If these panels are not thoroughly checked and cleaned, the potential resulting damage could compromise the operation of the ship."

"How seriously?"

"The ship may stop or, at the very least, short circuits could knock out this panel as well as this one and this one." *I just hope he believes that!*

"We need some duct tape," Raage said.

"Don't be ridiculous! That won't fix anything."

"Not for that." Raage walked over to the door and told one of his guards to take the blood-spattered seaman to find some duct tape. Returning to the control panels, he said to Baptiste, "If you think you can spread my men a little thin with all these distractions, just think again, Captain. I am getting tired of your games."

"Not games, I assure you."

Raage scoffed. The seaman returned with a roll of duct tape. Snatching it from him, Raage grabbed one of the guard's AK47s. He wrapped the tape around the barrel for several turns, then grabbed hold of the seaman and started winding the tape around his head with the end of the barrel pressed into his ear. The tape covered his eyes and mouth before Raage finished off with some more turns around the barrel. He pushed the seaman down onto his knees and handed the weapon back to the guard, who wrapped his finger around the trigger, a mischievous twinkle in his eye as he watched the assembled company look on, horrified.

"You're going to push me just a little bit too far," Baptiste shouted at Raage. He needed to know what the seaman had seen in the hold, and now he couldn't talk, probably couldn't hear, and any false move would result in his brains being spattered across the bridge. "You know damned well I need all my crew to operate this ship, and I'm already operating blind. If any of my crew get hurt—"

"You'll what, Captain?"

Baptiste seethed. He turned to the crew. "Get those covers off, and let's get the electronics cleaned up." To Raage, he said, "You seem to have everything under control now, so I'm sending someone to get what we need to clean up the rest of the mess and get this place back to operational standard."

"No problem. You," Raage pointed to one of the crew, and then gestured to one of the guards, "go with him."

Baptiste glanced down at the immobilized seaman. His mind blanked. He couldn't remember the man's name. He kept visualizing the man's staring back at him in terror while Raage covered his head with duct tape. Baptiste prayed that the sight of him standing and watching as the tape closed over his eyelids would not be the last thing he saw.

As he busied himself removing one of the panel covers with Raage watching his every move, Baptiste noticed the stern of the frigate clearly reflected in the glass of one of the dials. *It's worked!* Within seconds, everyone's attention was drawn to the bow of the ship by five short blasts from the frigate's horn—the maritime signal to warn of impending danger.

"I need all hands at their stations *right now!*" Baptiste pointed toward the seaman sitting on the floor. "This is an emergency and it cannot be dealt with if I don't have all my technicians in place." Raage looked toward the bow, which was partially obscuring the much smaller frigate below it. They were very close!

"Release him!" Raage shouted at the guard, who ripped the duct tape from the seaman's head, pulling hair, eyebrows and skin from his lips. *Thank God,* thought Baptiste. On the port bow, Baptiste could see Rocky Island, a small but deadly craggy rock to the southeast of St John's Island.

"We'll take evasive action," he told Raage, and responded to the frigate's signal with two long blasts and one short one. He prayed that Raage wouldn't know that this signal told the frigate that Baptiste intended to pass him on his starboard side.

Five short bursts on the horn—signaling imminent danger—came back from the frigate as Baptiste turned the Norfolk Defender just a few degrees to starboard, maintaining full speed. *Sure, you're heading into danger. What are you going to do about it?* Baptiste knew that the frigate couldn't safely turn to port; even with its greater maneuverability, it surely wouldn't be able to avoid Rocky Island.

"What are you doing?" Raage peered over the side of the ship as the frigate's stern came level with the bow of the *Norfolk Defender*, on their port side.

"I'm passing him. I can't change course easily at this speed, so it's the best I can do. I hope you've learned your lesson. Distracting me and my crew from running the ship can cost lives, and I doubt the Egyptian Navy will be very happy about that. You'd better start figuring out how you and your men can peacefully surrender, because by the time we get to the Gulf of Suez, you can be sure we'll get a welcoming reception."

Three short blasts from the frigate, as they were starting to move alongside her, surprised Baptiste. *They're operating reverse thrust? Why would they be doing that?* He ran to the port side where Raage was looking down at the frigate rolling in their wash and churning up white clouds of froth as its engines slowed her down, and they appeared to be accelerating past her. Baptiste realized that he had given them no choice but to stop. It was the most outrageous and dangerous thing he had ever done. It was such a blatantly aggressive move it could even have been interpreted as a deliberate attempt to ram the frigate.

But what was that? Surely that wasn't the captain of the frigate waving as they passed them? Baptiste looked back, half expecting to see its MK-42 54 caliber gun being leveled at them. But the old ASROC missile system with its MK-112 'Matchbox' launcher was stationary, not swiveling around in their direction. He looked at the surface of the sea, but there were no torpedoes flashing under the waves to sink them. All was quiet. The frigate had come to a halt and done nothing.

The rest of the journey to the Suez Canal was uneventful. No aircraft flew overhead, no naval ships came to meet them. Nothing. What did Baptiste have to do to get some attention? He was completely at a loss.

Chapter 41

Manuela scuttled up the sidewalk, head down, busily searching in her shoulder bag for the keys. They were in there somewhere. She went through this ritual every morning at 7am. Every evening, she was so glad to get out of the office that once she'd locked up, she chucked them into her bag where they worked their way to the bottom through assorted make-up, tissues, tampons and sanitary pads, shopping lists, her cellphone—she constantly missed calls for the same reason—her driver's license, protein bars, crisps and even the odd small vegetable. It was a finely timed ritual she'd honed to a fine art. Once she got off the bus, she had about a minute to find them before she reached the office door. This morning, they were being particularly elusive, avoiding her fingers, running unseen to and fro, into the farthest crevices of her bag. She almost tripped over a dirty, white rubber hose that lay across her path—*¿Qué idiota puso eso allí?*—*what idiot put that there?*—and then her hand closed over the elusive keys. *Ah, bueno.* Carefully selecting the correct one between finger and thumb, she raised her head in preparation to rendezvous with the keyhole.

"*¡Oh, no! ¿Qué pasó?*" Manuela's jaw dropped. The door was open. The hose was trailing through it, and water was gushing from the doorway. Then she noticed the smell. In fact, she almost gagged on it, it was so strong. It was a pungent mixture of burning plastic and kerosene. She felt something land gently on her nose. She blew at it and brushed it away. The air was full of it. Little flakes of black snow, swaying and dancing down to the ground.

"Ma'am?" There was a man behind her. She stiffened and looked for an escape route as her hand automatically shot back into her bag to hide the keys and search for her emergency pepper spray. She'd bought it for $12.95 at a friend's house party soon after she'd arrived from Mexico City. Her friend, Isabel, had warned her about living and working in this area. It wasn't safe, she'd told her, and you need some protection. And this one was clever because it looked like a lipstick, so it wouldn't alarm the potential assailant. Manuela couldn't imagine what signals an assailant might get if she pulled out something that looked like a lipstick when he made a lewd suggestion, but she'd bought it all the same. And now, of course, she couldn't find it. "Ma'am? You can't go in there." She had nowhere to run so, clasping her bag to her bosom with both arms, she turned and faced him.

"What you want? I no have money!" Then she felt really stupid. She had just walked past three fire trucks with lights flashing. A police cruiser, another car with a blue light stuck on the roof, and a van, also with lights flashing, parked diagonally across the road, preventing traffic from driving over the fire hoses that were trailed across it. Above her head, an extending ladder reached over the top of the building from one of the fire trucks. At its far end, a fireman was spraying powder onto the roof.

"Ma'am. I'm sorry if I alarmed you." The man was tall, as most men were to Manuela, and he was smiling in a way that gave her reason to believe he wasn't after her somewhat rotund body, although she was half confident that given the chance… well, actually, he was rather cute. He was about 35, slim and… married. She clocked a gold ring on the telltale finger. She felt a familiar, mild disappointment, as she always did in such situations. A chance meeting with a nice-looking man happened all too rarely. *Go to New York; stay with Isabel and find a nice man with a good job,* her mother had said. "Ma'am, do you work here?" *Típico de mi suerte—just my luck,* she thought, *this is official business.*

"Jes, I work here. What is problema?"

"Well, ma'am, you won't be working here for a while. The top floor got burned up last night. It's all gone."

"*Ai no! No es posible!*" She covered her mouth with her hand as she looked back at the building and the full impact of what had happened finally registered. "I sorry. What happen? *Oh dios… Santa madre. Qué es un desastre!*"

"We don't know yet. I'd like to ask you a few questions, ma'am." Detective Chapple took his wallet from his inside pocket and showed Manuela his ID. Manuela bit her lip. *Don't ever talk to the police,* Isabel had told her, *you know you're legal and I know you're legal but you can't trust them. Look what's happening in Arizona right now—they're rounding up Mexicans like animals. Puta madre!*

"I know nothing. Please, sir, I go now?" A fire fighter, his face covered with a mask, came out of the front door, pulling heavy gloves off as he splashed through the stream of water. Chapple turned to him as he passed.

"Anything intact?"

The man shook his head, "Nah, all cooked to a crisp," and walked by them.

"This won't take long." Chapple took Manuela's arm. "Come and sit in the patrol car, please, ma'am."

"Oh, no…." *Not the patrol car, please!* Manuela searched around her for someone—anyone—who might save her from this terrible ordeal. It wasn't as if she knew anything anyway. Why did this man want to get her into his car? Where was he going to take her? At 7am, there were just empty parking lots and locked-up buildings. No traffic could pass. She was well and truly trapped. He put his arm out, gesturing in the direction of the car. She frowned at it in the low morning sun. As she waddled beside him, her hand searched through her bag for the spray. Running her fingers around the smooth shape of a lipstick container, she examined its size, shape and the crack in the plastic where the two halves joined, and enclosed it in her palm as he opened the door for her to sit in the back seat. Sensing her nervousness, he left the door open and stood away from it as he spoke to her.

"Ma'am, can I have your name please?"

"Manuela Hernandez Vargas, señor." He made a note in his pad.

"Ms Vargas, thank you for helping me out here." Chapple stroked his chin thoughtfully. "We're trying to get in touch with the landlord of this building, but I think he's away on vacation, and we can't find the directors of the company that's renting the top floor. Can you tell me the name of the company, so we can inform the directors about the fire?" Manuela flinched. She'd never actually thought to ask the name of the company. After spending several days walking around factory estates in Hackensack and Jersey City, she was just glad to have stumbled across some people who paid her cash to be their receptionist.

"I no know, sir."

"You don't know? Excuse me, but you are a keyholder for the company, aren't you?"

"Keyholder? Sorry, I no understan."

"You have a key to the office. You were just about to unlock the door. Yes?"

"*Si, señor*. I open office, but they open upstairs. I no go there."

"I see. And you don't know the name of the company?"

"No, sir." Manuela was beginning to feel very dejected. She was getting worried that she would be driven away and locked up. *If you do ever have to talk to the police,* Isabel had told her, *say as little as possible. Don't be helpful, but don't be rude either. They get very angry if you are rude to them and they will lock you up.* "I go now? I have to work—" She looked back at the building. Bad choice of excuse. *What am I going to do?*

Detective Chapple followed her gaze, with raised eyebrows and a half-smile.

"I think the chances of that happening are kinda slim, if you don't mind me saying so, ma'am." He flicked some black flakes off his shoulders, trying to avoid rubbing them into the fabric. "So, maybe you can tell me who your boss is and we can give him a call?"

"Oh, is Mr Shanning. But he no well now. He sick. I think maybe he dying."

"Who's in charge while he's away?"

"A tall black man. Very nice, very smart. He speak very nice—"

"And his name is?"

Manuela looked suddenly contrite. "I no know, sir. He no tell me."

"Being a keyholder, I suppose you have his contact details, in case of an emergency?" He looked back at the building. Wisps of smoke were still leaking into the sky. Windows were blackened or blown out with long black streaks of soot rising from their corners to the roof. Manuela looked puzzled.

"No, sir, he no give me his phone number."

"You are the receptionist, aren't you? Not the cleaner?"

"Jes, sir. I am very good receptionist." There was a hint of indignation in her voice.

Chapple sighed. "So, who else works here? Do you know *any* names?"

"Oh, jes, sir. There's Brian and Matt, and Kurt and—"

"Ah, good. Progress. Any phone numbers?"

"No, sir. Maybe they no like to tell me their private business," she regretfully volunteered. *Don't try to be helpful!*

Chapple stepped nearer to the car and leaned with one hand on the door, and one on the roof. Manuela felt even more nervous.

"Then what, exactly, was your job?"

Manuela tightened her grip on the container in her hand. "I answer phone, sir, and put calls to people in office."

"Do you have any names, phone numbers, addresses—anything at all that can help me identify who worked here, so I can inform them that their business has just gone up in smoke?" Chapple was rapidly losing his patience. "Ms Vargas, I want you to think very carefully about this." He lowered his head toward her for one last try. As he did so, he was confronted with the bizarre sight of Manuela pulling her lipstick from her bag, opening it and jabbing her finger into the waxy red lump as she thrust it toward his face. He pulled back from her hand.

"Not my color," he said with a smile, realizing her mistake.

Manuela gasped and started sobbing quietly.

"I sorry, sir. I thought—"

"It's okay, Ms Vargas. Look, would you like me to get you a coffee or something? I can get a female officer look after you, if you'd prefer."

She wiped her eyes and gave a coy smile. "No, is okay." She laughed through her tears and digging a tissue out of the bottomless bag, wiped the lipstick from her fingers and blew her nose. She breathed a long sigh and looked back at the building as she got out of the car. "What I do now?"

"Will you be alright? You got somewhere to stay?" Chapple asked as she started walking away. Without turning back, she waved limply back at him in acknowledgement, just as two black Suburbans swung round the corner behind them and came screeching to a halt beside the patrol car.

"Thank you, Detective, we'll take this from here. Any witnesses?"

"And what do we have here? MIB?" Chapple watched in bemusement as eight smart-suited men, some carrying briefcases, rushed toward the building.

"CIA, smartass. Agent MacIntyre. Who's that woman?" The man gestured toward Manuela's receding back as he flashed his ID at Chapple. "Jerry!" He pointed toward Manuela and one of the men stopped in his tracks and ran to apprehend her. Jerry grabbed Manuela's arm as she was accelerating to a fast waddle, and brought her back to the patrol car. He roughly pushed her into the back seat and closed the door before racing off to the building. Manuela banged on the window, but everyone was already ignoring her.

"When did *they* get here?" MacIntyre pointed at the fire trucks.

"About an hour ago. They didn't have far to come." Chapple turned to look away from the burning building. A few hundred yards up State Street they could see the open red doors of the Fire Department's building.

"What did they use?"

"Looks to me like about half of the Hackensack River, CO_2, plus some powder for decoration."

"Shit. What a mess."

"And how come you guys are here?" MacIntyre ignored the question and headed for the building, trying to avoid wetting his smart leather shoes. Chapple quickly checked on Manuela through the car window before following him. She sat hunched over on the seat, the dejected 'immigrant in the cruiser' he'd seen so many times recently.

The reception area was still intact, apart from the river that ran through it now. MacIntyre rummaged through cupboards and files in the reception area. He ran his fingers around the underside of the desk, checked behind the picture on the wall, lifted the cushions on the easy chairs in reception and checked in the boxes stacked around the water cooler. Chapple stood by, watching. *What on earth can he be looking for? Why the hell would these guys even be interested in an electrical fire in a second-rate office suite like this?* As they picked their way through the debris that had fallen from the collapsed roof onto the stairs, MacIntyre, who was getting impatient with Chapple's impotent curiosity, looked back to him and said, "It's okay, detective. We can take it from here."

"You got something to hide?"

MacIntyre rolled his eyes and continued up to the sodden remains of the office, Chapple following a few steps behind. "What have we got?" he barked as he entered the main office.

"One good thing—no bodies." Jerry was sitting on his haunches, probing a mass of powder-covered mangled metal with a screwdriver, in the center of the room. The other men were scouring the rubble and carefully placing small fragments and charred paper into plastic bags. "The reason for that, though, is that this was a pro setup. Whoever did this really knew what he was doing and he—or she—was thorough."

"We're in the process of identifying the people using this office. I should know later today," Chapple said, although he had no idea how he would obtain that information unless another employee turned up as the business day began, and no one had approached the building yet, apart from Ms Vargas.

"Thank you, Detective." MacIntyre wasn't interested in anything Chapple had to say. Jerry, poised with screwdriver holding up a piece of charred wiring, was ready to continue.

"Tell me."

"From what I can see," Jerry said, "this was set up some time yesterday evening." He poked a torch through into a dark hole. "See how all the wiring is blistered and broken? That's what set the whole thing off, and it's been made to look like a normal overheating situation. But it wasn't. This *was* a fairly heavyweight computer. It had its own cooling system. When I got one of the guys to check it, it was still relatively intact but the supply pipes for the refrigerant liquid on both the main and the backup condenser units had been crimped. Within an hour of that being done, this whole computer would be cooking, and a short while after that, certain parts of the wiring would have ignited. So this entire unit would have been pretty much useless before the main fire even started. Even if the Fire Department had been sitting right outside the building, they wouldn't have known anything about it till it was too late." He gestured to MacIntyre to come closer as he shone the torch into the hole. "If you look in there, you can see the remains of what really got the blaze going. From the smell of it and from what I can see from here, someone set up a self-igniting thermite device to trash the innards of this computer once the burning wires reached it. I don't know if you know, but this stuff burns at extremely high temperatures."

"Am I right in thinking they don't sell thermite at WalMart?" Chapple pitched in, leaning over MacIntyre's shoulder. MacIntyre and Jerry exchanged tired looks.

Jerry continued. "For our arsonist, thermite also has the advantage of not being explosive, so most of the destruction of this computer would not have been visible outside the building. It's only when the blaze in the computer was well under way that the rest of the office, which had been soaked in kerosene, would have caught fire. So he—or she—made sure to meet the objective before the fire alarm was set off."

"So, why even bother trashing the building?"

"To cover fingerprints, footprints—that kind of thing. Belt and braces, you know. Maybe he—or she—just liked the idea of the blaze. Some arsonists like to hang around and watch their plans come to fruition. People are weird…"

MacIntyre winced. "What the hell is this 'he or she' in every other sentence, Jerry?"

"Training, sir. Sorry. In my experience, 'she' usually only does this sort of thing in domestics, and they tend to use household stuff like barbeque bricks and gasoline rather than thermite. But you just don't know, these days…"

"So, if it was only the computer he—or she—was interested in, do you think there's any point…?" MacIntyre scanned the dripping mess of blackened wood, concrete, wiring and shattered terminals drooping like Salvador Dali's liquid clocks on buckled metal desks.

"I'm guessing we won't find anything useful here, and this machine certainly won't be giving up its secrets to anyone."

"You certain of that?"

"About as certain as anyone can be."

"Okay, guys," MacIntyre announced to the room, "let's wrap this up. Take what you've got and let's haul ass. No point wasting any more of my valuable time here."

"But what about—?" This was all happening a bit too quickly for Chapple.

"Your patch, Detective. Back to you."

Chapter 42

Troy King nestled the phone under his chin as he lay on the bed in his bachelor apartment. He'd just finished eating dinner—a valiant effort of a healthy meal he'd made for himself. He felt bloated. A girl with dyed red hair and rings in her nose at the deli seemed to know a lot about all these strange foods that were supposed to be good for him. For this evening's meal, she'd convinced him that Spaghetti Bolognese would contain fewer calories if he used brown rice pasta instead of wheat. When he cooked it, though, it ended up as a congealed starchy lump, nothing like the slithery strings he normally twirled around his fork. But he was open to new ideas and grateful for some useful pointers. The folder that Griffin had given him the day before lay beside him. It was empty. He'd read it and shredded its contents, as Griffin had requested. But for King, the folder still contained so much—everything he dreamed of—his hopes and aspirations, his future happiness and, most of all, his dignity. It was something he wanted to keep as a memento of the day his life turned around—if that's what it proved to be.

"Dolores?"

"Hi, Troy. How's it goin'?" Dolores always asked him that question. This evening, her voice was softer than usual.

"Real good, honey. Real good." There was silence at the other end of the line. It was his standard reply. The one he always hid behind. It hadn't worked for some time now, but Dolores never challenged him on it, so their conversations started and ended without an authentic feeling being expressed. Each feared the other admitting that they knew the lie in that first answer. They'd spent their time apart waving to each other across an ever-widening chasm, which truth found it harder and harder to bridge with every passing year. "Actually, honey, would you do me a favor?"

"Sure, Troy. What do you want me to do?"

"Just put the phone down and, when I call you back, aks me that same queshion again. Would you do that for me?"

"Sure. But I don't understand…"

"Just do it, honey. Please? I'll call you right back. Okay?" The phone went dead. Troy dialed the number. It rang once and Dolores picked up. "Hi, Dolores!" he said, much more upbeat and warmer this time.

"Hi, Troy. How's it goin'?"

"Real good honey, but real bad as well."

"Hey, things must be improving! What's up?"

"Well, I been thinkin', Dolores."

"Oh, no. Please don't tell me that, Troy. You know what happens when you do that!" King smiled at the mischief in her voice.

"I think you know what I been thinkin'."

"Oh, yeah? What do you think you know that I been thinkin'?"

"Hell, Dolores, stop playin' with me." King was grinning now. "I been thinkin' that the real bad thing in my life is that you ain't here with me, so just get your sweet ass over here and let's get our show on the road again!" He heard the squeak of suppressed excitement at the other end of the line.

"I already did, Troy. I hope you don't mind."

"You did what?"

"There's a big 'For Sale' sign on the road by the gate, and I've been packing stuff ever since I got the call."

"Boy, you didn't waste any time, did you, honey?"

"Figured I'd wasted too much already."

"Funny, I was about to say the same thing."

"So, are you takin' that job?"

"You know about the job? Was I the last one to hear about it?"

"When that guy, Griffin—was that his name?—called, he seemed real keen on you. And he was a real smooth operator too. He really likes you, Troy—thinks you're the man!"

"Sure seems that way."

"And he was real nice and understanding. And when he told me how much you missed me, I just about cried—right there and then, on the phone. Troy, why you never told me that?" Dolores didn't wait for an answer. "Anyways, that's all I needed to hear, so I just figured I'd get things moving right away. Is that okay, Troy? Did I do the right thing?"

"Course you did, honey—"

"Tomorrow!"

"What?"

"Tomorrow!"

"What's happening tomorrow?"

"That's when I fly to Washington. I'm all packed and ready. The agent is going to deal with the sale of the orchard and the house, and Albert down the road is going to sell my Honda 'cause I guess I won't be needing it no more and anyway we can buy a nice new car when we find our new home, and I've settled the utility bills up to date and canceled the newspapers, and that nice couple, Stanley and Jennifer, in the farm down the road are going to keep a check on the orchard and make sure it stays tidy till the sale goes through, and they'll also keep an eye on the house, and I won't forget to set the alarm and leave a key and the code with them, and Avril is going to pick me up at 2.30 and drive me to the airport, and I'm exhausted but I can't wait to see you."

Silence.

"Troy?"

"I'm still here." King had been searching for a tissue. He was having difficulty keeping up. It wasn't just the onslaught of excited chat from Dolores. It was the new and intense feelings that he'd been having since that lunch with Griffin. Unfamiliar feelings, intensities he thought he'd left behind long ago in the turmoil of adolescence. But even they didn't compare with this.

"So, who is this guy Griffin? Is he some sorta big shot over there in Washington or somethin'?" The innocent question floated from the phone like summer. Dolores had no idea how her voice was affecting him. He'd forgotten how it stirred him, but now it was all coming back. So immersed was he in the world of intelligence, in argument and counter-argument, justification and reason, suspicion and intrigue, deviousness and innuendo, that he'd forgotten about light-hearted, simple, innocent conversations with the woman he loved.

"You don't know?"

"No, he just said his name was Griffin… Oh, my God, I hope I didn't say anything that I shouldn't have. I mean, he could have been anyone! Troy, honey, tell me!"

"Griffin Kirkland." *This is funny. She has absolutely no idea who he is!*

"Who?"

"Senator Griffin Kirkland."

"You mean, *the* Senator Griffin Kirkland?"

"The very same." King's smirk was getting wider by the minute.

"*Oh, my God!* Oh — My – God! Troy, I am *so* proud of you! But you know I always have been. I always tell Avril how proud I am of you, Troy. I gotta tell her this tomorrow. She'll be so impressed! My Troy is gonna be working for *Senator Griffin Kirkland*! Wow!" She paused briefly, for breath, then quickly added, "You did say you're gonna take the job, didn't you?"

"I sure did. We shook hands on the deal."

"You shook hands with the Senator! Wow. I gotta tell Avril. I'm gonna call her tonight. Troy, this is the best thing ever! I'm never gonna sleep tonight. Hey, look, it's late. I gotta call Avril right now! Bye, honey. See ya tomorrow! Yeah!"

"Bye, honey. Hey, look, take it easy and let me know which flight—" click.

King looked at the empty folder lying on the bed beside him. It was a simple, semi-transparent, plastic red wallet with two elastic bands to keep its contents secure. Two worlds collided within it: his new world, along with real hope for a brighter future and another, much darker world that he was just beginning to discover—the underworld of the real politics that governed everything. The unseen self-preserving politics of the select few that was threatening to extinguish all freedom, dignity and any hope of man's evolution to a higher state.

Time to sell the orchard, find true love again, and confront the serpent. King amused himself with the metaphor.

***

"Good morning, Griffin." King cheerfully breezed into the office at 8am the following morning. Griffin was already well-established in his second office and was feverishly working at his computer. Papers were scattered everywhere on his desk, a half-finished coffee-to-go perched precariously at the edge next to his keyboard.

"I wish it was. I'm afraid it's anything but good, Troy," he remarked gravely. His expression of deep concern took Troy by surprise. Griffin had thus far been a model of composure and control. Troy pulled up a chair.

"What's happened?" He instinctively took a notepad from his inside jacket pocket and clicked his ballpoint in readiness.

"The shit has well and truly hit the fan. I got a call from Gerald Shanning this morning. He was barely coherent. I told you he was dying, didn't I?" King nodded. "Apparently, he had a visit from some of the NSA overseers of the Weatherman Project. Somebody torched the project building in Hackensack last night."

"They did what? …Why?"

"That's what they're trying to find out, and that's what we need to know. They took Shanning to the local hospital, hoping to keep him going long enough to get more information out of him. Luckily, Shanning had his cell phone in his pocket when they did that, and he was able to call me before the battery died. I doubt they'll let him talk to anyone else from here on in, so we can't rely on him to tell us any more—even if he's physically able to." Griffin was searching through some papers as he spoke. "And it means we really have our work cut out here. I'm going to get Sheryl in here to help. We're going to be spread really thin…" He tapped more keys. King could see that his head was spinning with a thousand thoughts.

"What needs to happen?"

Griffin looked up, almost surprised by the question. "Troy, could any of your guys at Arlington Online get access to the central criminal database?"

"Hell, I dunno… I can make some inquiries. What d'you need?"

"I just need some stuff taken off it, so my friend, Larry Davidson, can get back into the country. We don't have time to build him a false identity, so that would be the quickest way to stop him getting arrested at the airport."

"Lemme make some calls. So, what's the main problem?"

"It has many dimensions to it. First of all, I don't know if the NSA know about Samakab, and the fact that Shanning has lost control of the entire project to him. Shanning was fading fast on the phone. I couldn't keep him on the line long enough to find out. If they don't already know about Samakab, the first thing they'll do is go after Larry. According to their logic, he's the prime suspect for destroying the Weatherman Project, or finding someone to do it on his behalf. They know that those two really fell out over the change of direction the Hominine Project took, and they'll take him out once they've extracted from him the codes they need to take control of the main computers."

"But surely if we get Larry back into the country, he's dead at the border?"

"He'd be dead wherever he was in the world—you know that. But he won't be if we let them know about Samakab."

"You'd do that? From what I read in your report, Shanning was trying to keep the NSA from findin' out about Samakab so that Larry would have a chance to put things right."

"They're going to find out anyway and it's better they find out sooner rather than later. At least that way we have some degree of control over what happens, and we can 'sell' Larry to them as being the only person who really understands Hominine—which is true." Troy looked doubtful. "The other possibility is that if they do know about Samakab already, they'll see the Hominine computer as being the brains behind anything that Samakab may want to do with HAPISAD, and they'll destroy it immediately. We can't let that happen. All the years of good work that Larry and his team did would be lost, and we'd be back to square one in terms of finding a way to solve the global crisis. What we need to do is find Samakab and stop him from using HAPISAD—if, in fact, he even has the capacity to use it, now that the Weatherman computer has been destroyed."

"Have we even got time to do that? I mean, with what's at stake here, the guys at the NSA are goin' to be onto this already."

"That's exactly the problem. We've got to move fast. I'll talk to the NSA. You find someone who can deal with Larry's safe return."

"Well, if you're already planning to tell them about Samakab, wouldn't the NSA be the people to do that?"

"Too risky. I don't want them snatching him as he enters the country. Better they don't know anything about him being back here, so if it can be done without any red flags being waved, all the better."

"What about trying to contact Samakab?"

"We'll do that as soon as we've made these two calls—and I've contacted Sheryl. Let's just hope the cell phone number you have for him is still live." Griffin picked up his phone. Pausing for a moment, he added, "I don't know what he meant, but Shanning mentioned a name when he called me. It sounded like Karl or Kurt or something like that."

"And…?"

"Oh, nothing. I just thought I'd mention it in case the name comes up at any point." Looking up at Troy, he added, "This is going to be a real baptism of fire, Troy. I hope you don't have any other plans for a while, because they just got blown out." King smiled and gave him a thumbs up. *Damn, I forgot. Dolores at the airport… I can text her.*

Troy decided not to call his old boss at Arlington Online. They had never got on and the man clearly had no respect for King. Right now, so soon after Troy's mysterious and sudden departure for a glossy job with a high-profile senator, he'd most likely be fuming with jealousy. Also, King figured there were two ways to go about solving this particular problem: the high route or the low route. Each had its pitfalls. If he took the high route—through department heads and upwards, he'd be treading in dangerous territory. While that route would have taken him through the 'proper channels' and the decisions made would be official and incontestable, he didn't have time to battle the inertia of bureaucracy. Nor could he divulge the reason for his request. The Hominine Project was such a high-security project that he doubted anyone would have even heard about it, so his arguments would have been impotent. He also figured that the high route was Griffin's territory, and Griffin had hired him to deal with this kind of problem the other way. The low route was dangerous for different reasons. Bored operatives and impassioned idealists were easier to manipulate, once their gripes or ambitions were known, but hacking into the system carried the risk of explosive fallout and less permanent outcomes. However, in this case, speed was what mattered most.

He called Ken Fellows. Ken had been there a long time and got on with everyone. He never ruffled feathers; he just did his job and kept a low profile. By being a great networker, he also made his own life easier. He had a beige neutrality about him that was completely non-threatening and allowed him to extract information from the most guarded and cynical agents and operatives around the intelligence system, with an air of smooth innocence. Having been there for a while, he'd also seen many people come and go, and he didn't ask awkward questions. He'd come to his own conclusions about what happened to David and Gulnaz, and never once asked King—whom he'd tolerated as a boss and liked in a guarded sort of way—about their sudden disappearance.

Once the connection with Ken was made, he could move quicker. A series of calls followed, some by Ken, some by King, both trading fractional pieces of information, asking, offering or calling in favors, never completing the picture with any one of them. This led, eventually, to a middle manager with responsibility for the specific, relevant part of the huge mass of information held on the central criminal registry. They decided that Ken would make the final call. Troy's breathing stalled and stuttered as he waited for Ken to call him back, his fists clenched as he watched Griffin through the glass partition that separated their offices, wrestle with similar frustrations.

"He won't do it." Ken reported flatly.

"*Dammit!* He will do it, Ken. He's gotta. Ain't no queshion about it. Root around him a bit and find another way. There ain't no way I'm goin' back to the senator with a 'no'—understand?"

"You mean start another investigation on this guy to find a lever? Hey, this is taking favors a bit far, Mr King. If I did that, I might as well resign right now because no one in any of the agencies would ever talk to me again and, anyway, it would take some time to find anyone who's gonna rat on this guy. He's straight as they come."

"If you knew what was at stake… No, you're right. I shouldn't be aksing you to do that. Lemme think o' somethin' else. How do I get hold of this guy?" Ken gave him the contact details. King sat and thought for a few minutes, then made a call.

Griffin was making progress, of sorts, in the other office. He held the earpiece away from his head as an NSA director spat pure venom down the phone after it had dawned on him that the most closely-guarded, contentious and controversial weapons project in the history of the world was now probably under the control of a Somali pirate. Another tirade followed as the director learned that Shanning was at death's door and could hardly speak—vital information that his agents, for some reason, had omitted to include in their report about the Weatherman computer going up in smoke. Nor had he been aware that the only other person who had access to the codes that would unlock the most expensive computing project the world had ever known—along with the means to control HAPISAD—was now classified as a dangerous criminal and had left the country. More vitriol blasted down the phone, as the director realized he now had some difficult explaining to do, to the President.

"No, I wouldn't do that. If I may suggest, that's the worst thing you could do." Griffin was trying to calm the man down, and help him to see the logic of the situation. "We need to keep a lid on this and deal with it quietly."

"What the hell are you talking about? Of course we need to tell the President!"

"I repeat, no. First, the President is accountable to the people. He would have to act in the Nation's best interests, and he's not in a position to do that."

"Of course he is, God damn it. He's the President!"

"You'd embarrass him and risk the Presidency if you tell him."

"He's the Commander-in-Chief, for Chrissakes!"

"He's a security risk."

"A what? What's the matter with you, Kirkland? How can he be a security risk? He's the President. He's everything that America stands for."

"Exactly. And that's why he's a security risk. Well, to be precise, his office—the Presidency—is a security risk. Let's be clear about what we're dealing with here. The Hominine Balance Regeneration Project is the property of three nations—Russia, China and the USA. It's a peaceable project that has massive potential for the whole world and its peoples, in ways the world has never seen before and has no knowledge of, as yet. Completely separate from that is the Weatherman Project—a weapons project. Now, I'm not going to discuss my feelings about the rights and wrongs of that project in this conversation. We don't have time to pontificate on its morality or benefits for the select few. Suffice it to say that the people who own the Weatherman Project are not accountable to anyone, and they don't have to act in the best interests of their people, or ours. The day just a few highly-placed, unelected and unaccountable people in the USA decided to partner up with these people and go to war on the world with this project, with the deluded notion that they were somehow protecting our interests—that's the day this country lost everything it supposedly stood for. Now, I know our slate hasn't exactly been clean in terms of upholding justice and the rule of law, or even ensuring a reasonable level of humanity in our various dealings around the world. However, we have entered a whole new level of corruption and deviousness with this project, and the few people who are responsible for it know that all too well. Because they know it, they've had to build a lie that cannot be sustained. In keeping the project secret and by-passing tried and tested security protocols, they entered the realm of the criminal and the ruthless in such a way that the whole thing was certain to backfire. The problem for us, now, is that should news of this fuckup start doing the rounds of the Capitol, the position of the President will become untenable, and the shit storm that the nation will face from its partners in this project will be unprecedented. Once that happens and the whole thing explodes into public view, the American people will feel completely betrayed and, if you think Iraq was a pariah under Saddam Hussein with his *fictional* WMDs—"

"Okay, okay, I get the picture."

"I believe that you have access to the bastards who set this up?"

"Yes, I do."

"Well, those are the people you need to talk to. I believe I can get the Hominine computer shut down, so at least it cannot be used to program any HAPISAD attacks. You just need to make sure the Russians and the Chinese sit on their hands while we handle it."

"I doubt they'll do that. The first thing they'll do is eliminate the Hominine computer."

"They can't do that. It would mean launching an attack on American soil."

"No, it wouldn't."

"What do you mean?"

"I don't believe the Hominine computer is on American soil." Griffin felt a rush of panic.

"Where the hell is it, then?"

"I don't know."

"You don't know? But you're the head of—"

"As you said, this is an international project and, doing the job I do, I'm surely another security risk, as far as they're concerned. I also doubt that, given our track record as a warmonger, they would trust us with their very expensive baby, which was originally designed for peaceful purposes. And it looks like their distrust was justified, doesn't it? My guess is that it's sitting in some neutral territory that they have easy access to."

"Well, God help us all." Griffin slammed the phone down. He looked out of the window. Rain was running down the outside of the glass. Fractured images of cars, trucks and taxis passing in the street below jerked between the drops. People. What a miserable—

"Griffin?" King put his head cautiously around the door and Griffin wearily turned to look at him. "I got it. Larry Davidson is now a good American citizen again. Squeaky clean."

"Well done, Troy. How the hell did you do that?" He gave a faint smile of encouragement.

"Oh, you don't really want to know…"

"Why's that?"

"Well, I ain't particularly proud of this kinda way of workin' these days, but in this business there's always a trade to be done, if you dig deep enough…"

"Will it stick?"

"Yeah, it'll stick." Troy rubbed his eyes and sighed a tired sigh. "But it never ceases to amaze me that with all the intelligence, computers, rules and stuff we got, people can still be fooled real easy into breakin' the simplest of security protocols—just in case somethin' gets out…"

"Tell me about it."

"I was just thinkin'," Troy said as he stood at the door, "would your guy at the NSA give us names of the people who were workin' at Hackensack?"

"No. He's not in the mood to tell anyone anything—especially after the conversation I just had with him. What do you want them for?"

"I was just thinkin' of what Shanning said. You said he mentioned Karl or Kurt. I wondered if it might have been someone in his office who might be able to help us out."

"Very possibly, but I think that door is shut now. Look, I'm just going to call Sheryl and get a message to Larry. Can you think of anyone else who could help out here? Just sitting on the phone... that kind of thing. I don't want to involve NSA or Arlington Online..."

"Dolores? I mean, she's—"

"Family. Perfect. But she's in Walla Walla—"

"She's on her way to Washington, thanks to you—and I really do thank you, Griffin."

Griffin smiled, a little wider this time.

"Check the flight number. I'll arrange a car for you to pick her up."

"That's real nice, but I can get her to hitch a ride in a taxi—"

Griffin shook his head. "If she's going to be working here, she's a really important person. And I think she's a really important person in your life as well, right? Let's agree that people are important, otherwise we're all wasting our time here."

"Got it." Troy King still couldn't believe his luck.

The phone rang on Griffin's desk.

"Yes?" Griffin said, "Oh, hi, Judy... You got who on the line? Oh good, put him on." He covered the phone with his hand. "A lucky break. This is Kurt coming on the line. He got through to my office. She says he sounds desperate and will only talk to the 'peacemaker Senator guy'. I guess that's me. Sit down, I want you to hear this." He put the phone on speaker.

"Hello, Kurt, this is Senator Griffin Kirkland. You're on speakerphone. I have Troy King in the room. He works with me. You can speak freely."

"Hi, Kurt, this is Troy." There was the sound of white noise on the line.

"What's this about, Kurt?" The signal fluctuated, as if the caller was underground.

A voice came through, patchily. "If I mention... ...Weatherman, would that mean... to you?"

"Sure, Kurt." Griffin said loudly into the phone. "What about it?"

"I need..." the signal kept fading as he spoke, "verification... you... say you are."

"Okay. If I say State Street, Hackensack—"

"Can't... say again."

"State Street, Hackensack."

"Got that."

"Okay, what is your involvement?" Griffin leaned toward the speaker.

"... was a..."

"A what?"

"Programmer."

Griffin glanced at Troy.

"Damn it. Can you go somewhere to get a better signal? We keep losing you."

"No way man. ...after me." Kurt was getting agitated. "... need more verifica..."

"Shanning, HAPISAD. Will that do? Look, we can pick you up. You're not safe. Where are you?"

"No can... ...up and listen."

"Okay, go ahead."

"That black... got me... ... ... laptop... ... up...."

"Again!"

"... ... guy got me... program hap... ... laptop... backup."

"Oh, Jeez...," King rolled his eyes heavenward. "Samakab's gone mobile with HAPISAD!" He leaned toward the speaker. "Is that right, Kurt? Samakab can operate HAPISAD from the laptop with backup drives?"

"Affirmat..."

"Damn, damn, damn!" Griffin pounded his fist on the desk. "Kurt. Can you still hear me?"

"... about."

"Do you have a copy of what you gave him?"

"A copy? You kidding? He had ... to my head. I ... lucky... ... pull the trigger!"

"Kurt! Let us help you."

"No can... ... I'd be dead."

"Griffin, there's no way we can help this guy right now," Troy said, quietly. "He's too scared to break cover, and he's probably safer wherever he is now than if we tried to hide him without the resources we'd need to do it properly." Griffin turned back to the speaker.

"Good luck, Kurt. And thanks. You are one brave guy."

"... my wife, I love..." The line went dead.

Griffin and Troy sat in silence. How on earth could this have come about? It was just too crazy to contemplate. It made no sense, given all the security, backups, safety checks... But there was no point in thinking about all that any more. Now they had to get hold of Samakab and find a way to deal with him. Whatever his plans were, he had to be stopped—immediately.

Griffin's phone rang again. It was Judy. Her voice was shaky.

"Griffin? Have you got a TV in your office?"

"No, that's one thing we didn't think we'd be needing here."

"You'd better find one. Something's happened."

CHAPTER 43

Frank Boyle was late. He didn't like being late for a major debate, but this had been unavoidable. He'd enjoyed a good lunch, though, at his favorite Knightsbridge restaurant. And he was confident that he'd not only given the journalist his money's worth, but also assured himself of a full-page feature in tomorrow's *Independent*. He'd steal the limelight from the government whichever way the vote went. Boyle was an old campaigner for peace with a reputation for gritty realism and an uncanny ability to turn a debate with a skillfully-placed argument plucked out of left field. The press and the public loved him. However, he also knew that the article could be slanted either way if he wasn't seen to be particularly aggressive in his opposition to the government's stance on sending in the troops. Everything hung in the balance. Europe was evenly split on the issue, so it was up to the British to make the decision for them. *Typical—Brussels soup served up by a gaggle of gutless career politicians.* The entire course of European military policy over the next ten years could come down to a few recently-elected, wet-behind-the-ears British politicians tipping the vote one way or the other.

He was glad of a cool breeze as he pushed his way undiplomatically through a group of foreign students blocking the sidewalk. *What, am I invisible? Damned Eurobrats.* Healthy, happy and olive-skinned, each with the obligatory backpack, they were taking photos of the peace protesters encamped on the green or idly fingering their phones, consumed by desperately important messaging. All were being ignored by a disgruntled Winston Churchill, who kept his eye on the Clock Tower from his lofty pedestal.

Fortunately, Westminster Hall was almost empty. He walked quickly, purposeful and focused, hoping not to attract unwanted attention. However, by the time he reached the Central Lobby, he knew he wouldn't make it through the afternoon without a speedy diversion via the washrooms. Having relieved the pressure on his bladder, he could better enjoy the familiar swell of gladiatorial energy that met him as he finally arrived at the packed Chamber. Red-faced and out of breath, he wiped his glistening forehead with his handkerchief as he entered the fray. The proceedings were already in full swing. Having bowed to the Speaker, who was otherwise engaged—monitoring behavior during what was already a very lively debate—he made his way up to his favorite hunting ground—the opposition back benches. He singled out George Harrington to sit next to. Making his excuses, he edged his way past the obstinate knees of MPs waving order papers and pointing fingers, eventually wedging his backside between George and an impatient young female who didn't appreciate the sudden and intimate introduction to his pinstriped buttocks.

"Frank, good to see you," Harrington mocked. "You're positively glowing." Boyle sat for a minute, breathing heavily as he took his glasses from their case, put them on, sniffed and surveyed the scene, assessing his targets.

"Anything happened yet?" Boyle asked, as he rearranged his jacket and the woman next to him freed hers from under him.

"Well, if you'd been here at the beginning rather than schmoozing with—"

"Fuck off, George." Boyle turned and gave Harrington a paternal, warning look. He liked George Harrington. He was relatively new to the game and played a good Robin to Boyle's Batman. They'd developed a convenient trade-off between Boyle's experience, advice and tips, and Harrington's unwavering support and advocacy for Boyle's agenda. Boyle really didn't need to know if anything had happened before he arrived. He just wanted to see if Harrington was paying attention to the debate or simply looking for an opportunity to joust with a government front-bencher and establish his name on the political map.

"Who's that?" Boyle whispered in Harrington's ear, pointing surreptitiously to the woman he'd almost just sat on.

"Carol Bartlett. She just took over from John Crabtree when he died. Did a good job keeping the seat. It had looked like a dead cert for the Tories."

"I really should pay more attention…" Boyle tried and failed to stifle a belch. An MP sitting in front of him turned round with a snarl on his lips, but thought better of complaining when he saw whose gut it came from. Boyle's attention was drawn to the Dispatch Box. The Foreign Secretary was speaking.

"… I'd like to thank my Honorable friend for his constructive comments. He is absolutely right. In addition, I am happy to report that the EUTRA Somalia mission has been hailed a success by all parties involved. As my Right Honorable friend, the Minister for Europe, said that it would, in his explanatory memorandum, it has contributed to strengthening the Somali security forces through the provision of military training and continues to do so in collaboration with, and to the enhancement of, the ongoing Ugandan training mission. It is training a total of 2,000 Transitional Federal Government troops, with EU Member States providing instructors for specialist training, an operational headquarters in Uganda, a liaison office in Nairobi and a support cell in Brussels. The mission has requested partners—including the US—to assist the EU by providing equipment and salaries.

"Further to our efforts in supporting the Transitional Federal Government, we are also pleased to announce that ATALANTA, the EU naval force in Somalia, has been extremely successful—" groans on the opposition benches threatened to drown out the rest of his sentence.

"Order," the Speaker intervened. "Let the Secretary of State finish his point."

"...extremely successful in substantially reducing piracy in the Gulf of Aden."

"We all know where this is going," Boyle nudged Harrington, "let's help him get to the point." He stood up.

"I'm happy to give way to the gentleman opposite." The Foreign Secretary gathered his folder from the Dispatch Box and sat down. At this early stage, he was happy to let Boyle rant, in the expectation that the House would tire of him by the time he himself raised the crucial points of his proposed actions in Somalia.

"Mr Speaker," Boyle began, "how much longer does the Foreign Secretary think he can pull the wool over the eyes of the public with the kind of drivel he has just expressed? Anyone who knows anything about the situation in Somalia and the seas that surround it can work out the folly in what he has just said. Training 2,000 troops for the Transitional Government—an impotent government under siege that doesn't even have control of its own nation's capital city, let alone the rest of the country—is like training a fly to piss on an elephant's ear and hoping it will roll over and die. The ATALANTA operation has just been a bit of fancy footwork—a PR job that has simply had the effect of pushing piracy out of the Gulf of Aden and further afield. I said in this House just a short while ago that piracy has quadrupled. It has not been reduced in any way, shape or form but merely pushed—as a member opposite once said—'like toothpaste from a tube'—to the areas around the Seychelles and Minicoy Islands. I have not seen a single new initiative from this government that will seriously address the problems within this broken country that is now regularly referred to as a failed State, and that have caused this situation to arise. My fear, Mr Speaker, is that today the Foreign Secretary will announce that he intends to join with the hawks in NATO and the European Community in committing vast military resources that this country can ill-afford, in order to put a decisive, brutish face on years of exploitation, invasions, fumbling and indecision that have resulted in this appalling situation. Mr Speaker, Members of the House, I put it to you that Somalia is already on its knees and it needs—deserves—a better solution than a sound beating. I would have hoped that, as a supposedly civilized country, we could, and should, come up with a more civilized and constructive way to re-build this shattered nation." Boyle pulled a printout from his jacket pocket. "Is it not obvious that something is very, very wrong when the *Prime Minister* of a country is moved to say, and I quote, 'after 20 years without government, the situation in Somalia would appear to be beyond repair. Piracy and the growth of Islamic extremism are not the natural state of being. Regional stability is increasingly at stake as Islamic extremism and the piracy problems grow. We need effective government and the training of forces'. He then went on to say, and again, I quote, 'Somalia has its vast potential wealth in fish, oil and gas to fund its own future. Our fishermen currently watch as other countries plunder our waters. While we condemn it outright, it is no wonder these angry and desperate people resort to 'fishing' for ships instead.' Mr Speaker, if our government proposes to deal with such desperate people by exacting lethal punishment on top of their suffering, then they are not fit to govern anyone."

Shouts of approval from the opposition benches were met by jeers from the government benches. The Foreign Secretary rose to the Dispatch Box again. He smiled.

"I would like to thank the Honorable gentleman for his elucidative talk on the situation in Somalia and the seas surrounding it. It is always good to know that we can rely on the member opposite for an entertaining and colorful—if wholly inaccurate—assessment of our intentions, which I have yet to enunciate. If I may suggest, it would behoove the Honorable gentleman to remain seated until he is acquainted with the substance of the proposals that the government will present here today."

"Well, get on with it then!" someone shouted from the opposition benches.

"*Order!*" the Speaker barked impatiently, "the electorate does not appreciate schoolyard behavior in this place." The Foreign Secretary straightened his tie and leaned forward, head lowered, his hands resting on the edges of the Dispatch Box as he referred to his notes before speaking.

"Mr Speaker," he continued, "Somalia has many long-term problems that are well known. It has many displaced people, many have little to eat and many more are considered to be at risk from war, famine or disease. As such, it is a breeding ground for instability, criminality and radicalization. The piracy we have seen is a glaring symptom of these problems. It is true that the route to finding a solution to all of these problems has been long, winding and arduous, and I don't think I need to remind the House of the many factors that have stood in the way of us playing a decisive and committed part in helping to solve them. The worldwide recession, our own fiscal problems and our existing military commitments in Afghanistan and elsewhere, to name just three, have all occupied us in other directions. And I don't say that by way of an excuse for inaction. Of course, the situation in Somalia must be resolved.

"The challenges have been many-fold and the machinery available to resolve them has, in many cases, been woefully inadequate. This inadequacy has been evident, for example, in the procedural maze that has had to be navigated to arrive at a strong decision. The number of bodies in which the matter appears: the European Scrutiny Committee, the Defence Committee, the Foreign Affairs Committee and the European Committee B all failed to get to the bottom of it. There are also many players involved in addition to all the countries of Europe. Most notably India and China are playing a very active part in helping to resolve many of the maritime difficulties. There are potential concerns as well, that trading blocs such as Europe, China and India will act purely in their own economic interests in ways that may be detrimental to the best interests of all parties.

"What is needed is a coordinated, holistic, sustainable and workable plan, which I am pleased to say we have now arrived at, in conjunction with the UN and our partners in the European Community. We believe that the system that is being committed to embraces these qualities. We believe that because it sits alongside a series of other measures in which the United Nations and other countries are actively engaged to ensure that there is security, stability and economic possibility for the people of Somalia. It also includes a commitment for active engagement to ensure that food is provided to those who need it, to enable security across the whole country and to ensure that the long-term problems that led to radicalization are addressed. Mr Speaker, in order to play our part in the plan, we propose to commit 20,000 troops to—" A roar went up in the Chamber that completely drowned out the Foreign Secretary's voice. He sat down and waited for the Speaker to bring the House back to order.

"Bastard!" Boyle shouted at the top of his voice. He turned to Harrington amid the commotion. "That's more than twice the number we've got in Afghanistan, and if that's just our contribution, we're talking about a full-scale occupation. There's a hidden agenda here, and I don't like how it smells." The commotion lasted for a full minute before the Foreign Secretary could return to the Dispatch Box and continue.

"Thank you, Mr Speaker." He continued to plow through the outline of the UK's contribution to the plan. "We propose to commit 20,000 troops, over a five-year fixed period, to a coordinated joint European force that will bring stability to the region and provide robust support to the Transitional Government in its efforts to return the country to being, once again, a peaceful and profitable nation. The decision to make such a sizable commitment has only been taken following exhaustive research and discussion. The gravity of the decision, the government believes, matches the gravity of the situation and, unlike the party opposite, we do not shy away from making the correct decisions in the face of difficult problems, and I am confident that the people of Britain will concur." The Foreign Secretary sat down again, maintaining a neutral expression as he steeled himself for an onslaught. Boyle shot out of his seat, as did several other opposition MPs. An opposition front-bencher caught the Speaker's eye. He began to speak as everyone got settled again.

"Mr Speaker, I think I speak on behalf of many of my colleagues on this side of the House when I say that I am utterly appalled at this government's decision to embroil this nation in another endless occupation of a foreign land, with all the associated costs—mainly in terms of the lives of our armed forces, some of whom will be signing up for certain death." A murmur of approval swelled up from the opposition benches. "I am aware, Mr Speaker, that the Secretary of State mentioned a fixed term for this operation. Unfortunately, the government has a track record of not being wholly candid about such commitments. I have a very real concern that this operation will be subject to what is known as 'mission creep'. Although he is proposing that we commit 20,000 British forces at this juncture, we all know that, in the future, this could well expand to 30,000 or 40,000. It happened in Sierra Leone, it happened in Afghanistan. While many of us on this side of the House were not initially opposed to making deployment commitments, those who made the decisions did not do so openly and honestly. They were not candid with Parliament. Members need to watch out to ensure that there is no mission creep. Deploying resources and armed forces personnel is a grave matter, and it should be done with the full knowledge and consent of Parliament. However, that has not always happened, and I am not confident that it will happen now."

The Foreign Secretary stood, and said, "We have no plans to extend our commitment in the region beyond the stated 20,000 troops."

Boyle stood again and, this time, caught the Speaker's eye.

"Does the Foreign Secretary really expect us to believe that old cherry—'we have no plans to extend our commitment'? Can he tell the House—" Shouts of derision emanated from the government benches. "Can he tell the House what safeguards are built into this plan to ensure that he can stick to the promise he's making to the British people? Does he even want to stick to his promise or is this just the thin end of the wedge of another, more sinister agenda?"

"Perhaps," the Foreign Secretary responded, "the Honorable Member would like to expand on the question and let the House know what kind of cock-eyed conspiracy theory he is cooking up now?"

"Certainly, but I think the only cock-eyed conspiracy that—"

"Order, *order!*" The Speaker interjected, impatiently. "Can the Honorable Member please stick to answering the question?"

"I apologize, Mr Speaker." The device had worked. Now there was quiet in the Chamber and Boyle had their full attention. "I have two points that I would like to raise. Mr Speaker, it is common knowledge, and recent military interventions by various countries have demonstrated, that substantial foreign occupation leads to an increase in resistance, a hardening of attitudes and the risk of a long-term escalation of violence and occupation. My first point, then, is that this 'plan' is simply a reflection of a government that is bankrupt of ideas, that has dithered for far too long—thus allowing a manageable situation to turn into a disaster of epic proportions—and that has no real vision of an outcome that will truly benefit the Somali people. This grossly misconceived plan will simply subjugate them, extend their misery and have the exact opposite to the desired outcome by increasing radicalization and piracy." Loud cheers filled the Chamber. Boyle waited for the noise to subside before carrying on. "It is also common military knowledge, Mr Speaker, that dealing with Somalia in isolation in this way will not solve its problems. Somalia has many thousands of miles of borders. It borders Ethiopia, Djibouti and Kenya to the south. Many of these borders were created to form administrative boundaries, but the peoples that inhabit the area relate more to their tribal backgrounds than administrative boundaries. We have seen how the borders of Somalia have been changed and manipulated throughout history to include and exclude such territories as Puntland, 'British' Somaliland, even the Ogaden. We cannot ignore the rich tribal history of the region that has no regard for artificial borders, whether defined by foreign powers or even their own governments. This brings me to my second point, the *region*. In introducing his 'plan', the Foreign Secretary said, and I quote, 'a coordinated joint European force that will bring stability to the *region*'." Boyle undid his jacket and wedged his thumbs into his waistband as he scanned the benches opposite. "Now, I don't know if that was a slip of the tongue, and the word 'region' can mean a whole host of different things, but I was under the impression that we were talking about Somalia, the *country*, and not the *region*. But, having heard the word 'region' mentioned, and having just been told of the planned British contribution—which we can reasonably assume will scale up to in excess of 300,000 troops once the contributions from other EU countries are factored in—I am compelled to conclude that the planned European operation is designed to bring not only Somalia under control, but also several of its neighbors. We are already seeing troop build-ups and military cooperation in Uganda—which makes no logical sense at all, given our existing presence in Kenya—while the mineral resources of the Democratic Republic of Congo are falling from our grasp as their government takes a stronger nationalistic stance. It would seem that, far from learning our lessons from history, and far from supporting the African Union in their efforts to at last build a strong continent, this is the beginning of a European free-for-all with an extremely sinister agenda. I put it to the House that the only creep that we should be concerning ourselves with here is the Foreign Secretary himself." He leaned forward, jabbing his pointed finger in the direction of the Foreign Secretary. "I believe that the Foreign Secretary is not only *expecting* mission creep but is actually *planning* it. Will the Foreign Secretary come clean and tell us what the ultimate plan actually is, and how much of Africa Europe plans to annex, if that is their intention?"

Amid the angry shouts, catcalls and drumming of fists, above the shouts of the Speaker and the cackles of laughter, nobody heard the shattering of glass in the rows of small skylights, high above their heads.

"Well, that's men, innit?" Jackie Stevens appealed to the studio audience, *"I mean, when they come in, they just dump their jacket on the sofa or sommit like that. That's what my hubby does, anyway. They just don't care, do they? Men! They're messy, aren't they? I mean, it's not just me, is it?"* Loud cheers from the predominantly female crowd. *"No, well, there you go, you see. I mean, when I come in, I put my coat on the hanger, I mean, that's what it's there for, innit?"*

"Time to take him in hand, perhaps?" Carol, her co-presenter, offered.

"Again?" Raucous laughter from the studio audience. *"Oooh, I can't believe I just said that!"* Jackie gave a wide-eyed smile as she cowered in mock embarrassment.

"And is he messy?" Jane, their celebrity guest, chipped in. More hilarity.

"Well, I tell you—" The screen went black.

David shifted Josh onto his other knee as he reached for the remote and flicked through the channels. They were all the same. What was going on?

"Mum!" he shouted to his mother who was reading the paper in the kitchen.

"What is it, David?" she called back.

"What's wrong with the TV?" Margaret replaced her cup on its saucer, folded the newspaper and walked into the living room. David was furiously pressing buttons on the remote. All the channels were blank. "What the f… Nothing works in this damned house. What's the matter with it?"

"Here, darling, let me try." Margaret felt panic gripping her again. How to get Josh away from David before he lost it completely? She lived in fear of that day.

"What? Now I can't even press buttons on a remote properly? Is that what you're saying? Fucking hell, Mum." Josh began to cry. David put him on the sofa beside him, much to Margaret's relief, and went to investigate the back of the TV. Margaret took Josh in her arms and watched as he pulled the aerial lead out and then replaced it. He did the same with the DVD player and the satellite box. That brought up a setup screen. He cursed again, found the manual and went through the setup procedure to bring the channels back to life again. Nothing happened.

"How old is this TV, Mum? It looks like something from the dark ages."

"It's only a few years old, darling. It's been fine till now."

"Well, it isn't now, is it? Fuck."

"I'll call the repair people and see if there's something they can do. Why don't you…" Margaret frantically tried to think of something David could do—something she could suggest that wouldn't send him into a blind fury. All David seemed capable of, at the moment, was watching banal afternoon TV programs and endless repeats of 1980s sitcoms. "Why don't you call Barbara and see when she's coming home this evening?"

"Where are you taking him?" David shouted as she walked toward the kitchen, carrying Josh.

"I said I'm just going to phone to see if I can get the TV repaired. Why don't you use your cell phone to call Barbara?" His mother's patronizing niceness was really getting on his nerves, but somehow he controlled his urge to walk over to her and slap her across the face.

"Okay, okay." David stomped out of the room and thumped his way up the stairs to get his cell phone.

"David!" Margaret called after him. "It's back on. The TV." There was an image of a newscaster, Jonathan Gately. He wasn't saying anything to camera. Instead, he appeared to be arranging papers and talking to people out of view, in the studio. Occasionally he glanced at the camera, only to be distracted again by a girl with a clipboard talking in his ear. David sat down again on the sofa.

"I don't want the news." David flicked through the channels. The same image came up on all of them. "Damn. It's still not working."

"Wait a minute, dear. Look…" A message was scrolling across the bottom of the screen. '*Normal TV transmissions have been suspended. Do not adjust your set. All channels are broadcasting this message.*'

"Look, I don't want to watch the news, Mum."

"Well, I'm sorry David, but it looks as if we can't do anything about it. I'm sure we'll get the normal channels back again soon. Don't worry."

"*We are interrupting all UK broadcasts.*" Their attention was drawn back to the screen where the announcer was now in news-reading mode. "*It appears that there has been an attack on the House of Commons. Details are patchy at the moment, but from what we understand, an explosive device has been detonated in the Chamber during the final debate on the Joint European Intervention in Somalia. We don't yet know if there have been any injuries. Rebecca Ford is at the Palace of Westminster and we are going there now to find out the latest. Rebecca?*" The scene changed to a view of a windswept Rebecca Ford standing in front of the railings outside the Palace of Westminster. She was being jostled by news crews, police and photographers crowding round her. There was a lot of shouting, sirens wailing and the *thwap-thwap-thwap* of helicopters hovering overhead. She glanced over her shoulder to see if anything was happening behind her in New Palace Yard. It appeared to be deserted. Past the trees and the fountain that partially obscured the view, it was just possible to see that the doors of Westminster Hall were shut. Rebecca pressed her earpiece harder into her ear in an effort to hear her cue over the commotion around her.

"*Yes. Can you hear… Okay…*" She lifted her head and looked at the camera. "*As you say, Jonathan, details are patchy, and the entire Palace of Westminster has* been sealed off. Since the incident, no one has come out and no one is being allowed in. Well, that's not entirely correct—" She looked down at her notes. "The only people who have been allowed out were a party of schoolchildren from Barnsley and their teacher. We understand that they have been taken somewhere and are being debriefed right now."

"Is there anything you can tell us about the reports of an explosion?"

"Nothing yet. There's been a complete lockdown on information. Since no one is allowed to take their mobile phones into the House, and all telephone communications appear to have been cut, the only way we even found out about this was through SO17—the Palace of Westminster Division of the Metropolitan Police—when they came to shut the entire Palace down. They moved extremely fast. Jonathan?"

"Is there any chance that this is an unannounced routine exercise that they're rehearsing? There's been a lot of talk recently about the security of the Palace…"

"That's always a possibility, but I don't think so. If they were going to do that, SO17 would, at the very least, have informed the police on the gates. From the little I've been able to find out, they were just as surprised about this as everyone else. Also, the complete communications blackout is unprecedented. There are hundreds of people inside that building, including members of the public who must be very frightened at this time."

"Rebecca, I'm sure you are finding out all you can, and I can see that there's a lot of activity around you, but can you tell us when you expect to get a briefing on the situation? As you say, all lines of communication with Westminster have been cut and we've not been notified of anything at the BBC. Is there someone on the ground explaining what is happening?" Rebecca Ford looked around her, and signaled to one of the outside broadcast crew.

"No, nothing as yet, but of course I'll let you know as soon as we have something. For now, it would appear that all traffic has been prevented from entering this area… oh, my goodness—" The camera swung round to show Westminster Bridge. A wall of soldiers in full battle dress, carrying machine guns, was heading toward them at a fast jog.

"That's enough, thank you, no more filming. We're clearing the area. Thank you. Turn the camera off, sir… NOW!" The camera jerked from side to side. Partial images of police helmets, yellow reflective vests, metal badges and automatic weapons flashed across the screen. "Okay, okay, get your hands off—"

"We appear to have lost Rebecca for now," Jonathan Gately said, his eyes flashing around the studio. He paused, listening to instructions from his producer in his earpiece. Looking back to the camera, he said, "We have just received a statement from Downing Street that they have requested we read over the air." He put his hand out and a sheet of paper was placed in it. He quickly scanned the sheet before reading it out. He took a deep breath and read: "The

Office of the Prime Minister can confirm that there has been a terrorist attack on the Chamber of the House of Commons. No other part of the Palace of Westminster has been affected by the attack. All communication with the Palace of Westminster has been suspended pending the outcome of an investigation, which is on-going. An area around the Palace of Westminster has been sealed off. No attempt should be made to enter this area, which is now under military control. Any attempt to do so will be treated as a terrorist threat and dealt with as may be appropriate. Further bulletins will be issued as and when information becomes available. In the meantime, we advise all citizens to go about their business in the normal way."

As soon as Gately had finished the announcement, his sound was cut and an announcement on the screen read, '*We apologize for the break in transmission, and we are now returning to the scheduled program.*'

"What was *that* all about?" David stared open-mouthed at the screen, as the banal afternoon chat show continued. He immediately switched it off. *What do I do now*, Margaret thought.

"It looks very serious," she said.

David stared at the screen with empty eyes. Without the soporific distraction of the TV, he could be a loose cannon. Margaret sat down on the sofa beside him and offered him Josh to hold. She hated herself for using Josh in this way, but she wanted David to be able to hold Josh if he wanted to. She knew that he would never intentionally harm him and was always calmer when Josh was close by.

"Too right it does. Is Dad in town? Where's Barbara?"

"Barbara's in Tunbridge. No need to worry about her. She's at work. Dad's in town. Do you want to call him?"

"No, you call him. I need to Tweet."

"To what?"

"Tweet... Never mind, Mum." He smiled at his mother. She nearly fell of the sofa with shock. Despite her confusion, she managed to force a smile back at him. "Can you look after Josh for a while? I'll be in my room. Oh, and can I take the TV from your bedroom? I want to keep an eye on this."

"Em... yes, of course, David. Take the TV..." *Never mind the bizarre events on the TV, what was* this *all about?* David's periods of lucidity did seem to be more frequent these days, but this was something special. A smile! Margaret felt like breaking out the champagne. It was his first smile since he'd returned from the US. But her excitement was tempered by the realization that this breakthrough probably wouldn't last. David always went back into his black hole, sucked in by an irresistible force. This is how she lived, these days, trapped between despair and excitement that could never be really celebrated, living each lighter moment in gratitude and fear.

She listened from the bottom of the stairs as David moved the TV into his room. She heard the chimes of his laptop booting up. The bedroom door closed. All was quiet. She set Josh to play with his toys on the kitchen floor and called Roger.

"Roger, something incredible just happened!"

"You're telling me! Did you see it on the news?"

"What? Oh that, yes. No, I mean David. Something incredible happened with David."

"What do you mean?" Roger was taken aback.

"He smiled, Roger. He smiled at me!" She could barely hold it together.

"I'm so glad to hear it, Margaret. What on earth brought that on?"

"Well, it's really strange. It was that newsflash about an attack on the House of Commons."

"So you did hear about it. What do you make of it?"

"I was hoping you'd be able to tell me." Margaret felt as if she wasn't getting her point over. She wanted Roger to celebrate with her, but already she felt the moment was passing. "He smiled at me, Roger. The first time."

"That's wonderful, darling, but this attack—"

"Yes, I know. And then, do you know what he did?"

"Um, no."

"He went upstairs to his room, and he's *switched his computer on*! Isn't that amazing?"

Roger couldn't quite see why this was so amazing, but he tried to show some enthusiasm. "Yes, excellent, darling. What's he doing on the computer?"

"Oh, he said he had to tweet or something—but that's not the point." She rolled her eyes in impatient frustration at Roger's insensitivity. "Roger. First smile. First time he's switched the computer on. That's major. Don't you get it? He's come back to us, even if it's just for a few moments. He's come back." She could feel her lip quivering as she finished the sentence.

"That's fantastic, Margaret. Really, it's wonderful." Roger had got it at last. "I hope he's still there for when I get home. I'd really like to be with David again."

"Yes, I know." Margaret couldn't prevent a soft sob.

"Margaret," Roger said, softly, "I may not be able to get home this evening. If David is still… there… can you explain that to him?"

"Why can't you come home?"

"It's all gone crazy around here. They've shut the railway stations—well, Waterloo, Victoria and Charing Cross, at least—so you can imagine the mayhem. Emergency measures. I don't even know if there are any buses running. I'll see if I can get a taxi, but really…"

"Oh, darling, there must be some way…"

"Well, I could walk and it may come to that. I tell you, I've never seen anything like this before. Here in the City, we're not as affected as they are in Westminster, but people say there are soldiers all over the place in fatigues, brandishing automatic weapons—even pointing them at people, pushing them around. They've set up roadblocks and people are being herded out of an 'exclusion zone', as they're calling it. Someone said it looked like something out of a World War II film—like the Nazis herding Jews out of the ghetto." He paused. "Can you hear that?" He held the phone nearer to his open office window. The chorus of alarms and sirens was deafening.

"My goodness, Roger, it sounds just like a war!"

"Yes, and some shots have been fired, but I think they were just to get people's attention. You know that peace camp on Parliament Square? They rounded all of them up and locked them in the back of a cattle truck while they trashed their tents. Sounded pretty desperate."

"Roger, just get home, please. Maybe if you can get across one of the bridges, you can find transport of some kind, or I can come and meet you in the car—"

"No. No, you mustn't come anywhere near this place. Anyway, it's completely jammed. Look, I'll see if I can make it to Elephant and Castle on foot. I should be able to get something from there. I'll call you later if I need to be picked up once I'm out of London. Okay?"

"Okay, Roger. Take care, love. Keep your mobile handy."

"Bye, Margaret. And love to David and Josh and Barbara—and a particularly large dollop of it to you."

"Roger and out." Their standard telephone goodbye. Margaret crawled on the floor next to Josh and helped him laugh a little. It seemed to be the best way to handle all the mixed emotions she was feeling.

CHAPTER 44

The world was holding its breath. More than 18 hours after the attack, with the world's media clamouring for an explanation, nothing had come out of the exclusion zone around the Houses of Parliament. A raw stillness hung heavily in the deserted streets. Soldiers paced to and fro at barriers, talked on radios and pointed their weapons at anyone who dared to approach. All vantage points overlooking the Houses of Parliament had been evacuated. The London Eye was closed for business, as were the railway stations and all businesses and offices within a third of a mile radius. The occasional car moved quietly and quickly, between Downing Street, Whitehall and the entrance of the Houses of Parliament. Armored troop carriers occasionally backed up to entrances. Catering vans, buses, military vehicles and ambulances were parked around Parliament Square. Every now and then, a helicopter landed on the grass and men, their heads bowed low, hugged briefcases and held onto jackets as they ran through its whirlwind downdraught—before it it took off again and was gone. And all the time, soldiers on rooftops, sitting in office windows or atop armored vehicles, machine guns at the ready, peered through binoculars at distant movements and unknown threats.

Some foreign news crews had tried and failed to set up cameras pointed at the desolate scene. None of them had managed more than a minute or so of transmission before the camera had been roughly removed, along with the entire crew. The only images being transmitted around the world were news reporters keeping a safe distance from the barriers that could be seen behind them as they filed monotonously empty reports. This left the news channels filling their airtime with endless discussions, where just about every hypothesis imaginable was explored in minute detail. In the absence of any statement from anyone in authority within the British Government, it was all they could do.

It also seemed as if every political group in the world that had some sort of gripe with the UK or its government were using the opportunity of official silence to advertise their complaints or to take credit for the attack. Organizations that claimed to be acting on behalf of those affected by a range of conflicts, suppressed peoples, impoverished nations, religious groups, imprisoned activists, injustices and abuses—even whales, dolphins and the environment—were all jostling for airtime and column inches. So many thousands of people looking for a voice, a platform to right a wrong, and finding an opportunity in the perpetration of this high-profile act.

Griffin Kirkland had arranged to have several televisions installed in the Washington office, each one permanently tuned to a different news channel.

The only channel that didn't seem to be broadcasting endless interviews with political commentators and experts was the BBC World Service, which simply displayed a bald caption on its silent screen: 'Normal service has been suspended on the instructions of HM Government.'

Troy King put his tenth cup of coffee back down on his cluttered desk. He gently squeezed Dolores's arm as she passed by to remove the remains of his last takeaway meal. He checked his iPhone and plugged his cell phone in to re-charge again.

"I still can't get him to answer. Sometimes it rings and sometimes it don't. I guess he's on the move." Remarkably, he had discovered that Samakab's cell was still connected. He'd first called it when he and Griffin had raced down to the nearest coffee bar, following Judy's call, to find a TV and catch the news as it broke. He'd let it ring until it cut off. Since then, he'd tried several times every hour, but it had never once been answered. He and Griffin knew there was only a slim chance of the phone still being in Samakab's possession. He could have given it to anyone—even a bum on the street—but it was the only possibility they had to talk to him directly.

The official word from the White House was that Britain had suffered 'a strike at the very heart of democracy' of 'unprecedented ferocity and audaciousness', and they were 'working speedily to establish the source of the attack.' The British Government had requested that 'in the interests of national security, they conduct a full investigation in private without outside interference'. It was of crucial importance at this 'time of national crisis' that the efforts of all those involved in the investigation be concentrated 100% on the job in hand without distraction of any kind. The US President had requested that everyone respect their wishes. He'd also stressed that time was of the essence in such a serious investigation and he was confident that the British Government would bring the investigation to a satisfactory and comprehensive resolution. And he expressed his heartfelt sympathy for everyone who had suffered in the attack. He was praying for them and their families.

"Where's Larry?" Griffin sighed as yet another repeat of soundbites from the President's speech was broadcast. *I wonder if they've told the President about Samakab yet.*

"In the air," Sheryl replied. She'd booked flights for him as soon as Griffin had called with the news that his fictitious criminal record had been cleaned off the central registry. "He should touch down in LA in about an hour. Then he's got an hour before his connection to Dulles."

"Damn." Griffin felt impotent, and the lack of direct flights just when they needed them added to his growing frustration.

But he was glad that he'd followed his intuition and set up this office. Following his conversation with their top director, the NSA had already visited his official office at the Dirsken Senate Office Building. He'd gained some time, but he knew it wouldn't be long before they walked through the door of this office. He needed time to think, and he needed Larry. When Larry had told him in Bali that he was the only person he knew who could deal with Shanning and save the Hominine project, Samakab hadn't even been in the picture. This escalation of the problem had taken him way outside his realm of experience, courage and ability, as far as he was concerned. He glanced at Troy and had to immediately suppress a very nasty thought. It wasn't his fault. It wasn't his fault at all.

He tried Shanning's cell phone again. He wondered if Shanning had watched the news. It was dead. Maybe Shanning was dead as well, by now.

He willed the NSA to keep away. *I need time. Just let me think. There's nothing you can do to help now, you'll only complicate and confuse the situation with your ferreting and manic control ethos. This is delicate. It's about people and feelings—things you don't understand.*

Sheryl kept an eye on him from across the office, determined to maintain his space for him, should anyone encroach. Griffin tried to rein in his thoughts. Samakab must have torched the Weatherman computer at Hackensack because development of HAPISAD was complete. He didn't need it any more. He had the means to program the missiles, from a laptop with additional space on separate hard drives. The only other thing he needed was access to the Hominine computer, which he apparently had. That computer wasn't in the US. Where the hell was it? The overseers of the project would know, but he doubted that he would ever discover their identities, and certainly not quickly. So, who else? There must also have been a large team of people who built the computer and supplied the parts, but he'd already seen how tightly security was controlled around that. Anyone involved at any level would have known only partial information, and not the nature or even the name of the project. Added to that, there were so many private and government computing projects on the go at any time that it would be near-impossible to find the people who'd worked on this particular one. A swift decommissioning of the AVTOL wasn't a viable option, given that no one was even sure where the attack came from—or they weren't admitting to knowing. And the only person who had the knowledge to shut down the Hominine computer and prevent Samakab from accessing it was Larry Davidson.

Safe flight, Larry.

But as he sat there, with the sensationalist ramblings of the world's press flashing across multiple TV screens, his frenzied thoughts became increasingly black. The news had to break, at some point. Those people locked in the House of Commons would have to come out. They couldn't keep them in there forever. They would tell their stories, and it would quickly become obvious that this was not an attack that any terrorist group could carry out. Its sophistication, its stealth and the undoubtedly specific nature of the targets would be obvious. The way they died would be questioned. What weapon was used to kill them? How could it be that there were no injured people—only dead ones, each with identical wounds in identical positions? Why was there no evidence, other than those empty black holes? How could this have happened without Northwood picking it up or anything being seen until the moment the missiles hit their targets? Who would have the capability to deliver such a deadly accurate, high-tech attack? All thoughts would lead to one obvious conclusion: the United States. Briefly, they would ask, 'why?' Then… He shuddered at the thought as his mind moved quickly on to the next scenario.

Maybe there was another reason for the long delay in making any official announcements about the attack. Griffin thought back to the Kennedy assassination, Nicaragua, 9/11, Iraq, Afghanistan and so many more. The US Government was well-versed in managing popular opinion—pushing the carefully crafted official version of events on people everywhere, however unlikely. With a tight grip on the media, they forced the hand of the historians—marginalizing the nay-sayers as unpatriotic, wacky conspiracy theorists. The politics behind the politics always ruled the day. The real questions were consigned to a disorganized and powerless few who dared to challenge, in the face of overwhelming odds. Sometimes they were proved right, sometimes the unpalatable taste of murky half-truths and hidden, deadly lies lingered for years, downgraded and trivialized by time. Maybe this is what the delay was all about. In a way, he hoped it was. Damage limitation. But then who will they blame? What unfortunate group or whole nation would be blamed for Samakab's apocalyptic act? There were plenty of candidates. Yes, maybe that was what was going on. And what of the 'special relationship' that the UK and the US appeared to hold so dear? What devious deals were being done at this very moment, what favors were being called in, what pressures were being brought to bear, whose heads were being singled out for sacrifice? He imagined the spin doctors feverishly working on an announcement—the right form of words to disguise the madness with some semblance of rationale that would prevent the world diving into a tailspin of violent conflict. Those spin doctors would know that each additional minute of silence increased the pressure to get things not necessarily right, but workable. They had to find a way to extinguish the fuse lit by this deadly silence.

Troy King's cell phone jolted everyone's nerves and got their immediate attention. Troy ripped the recharging cord from the socket and looked at the cell phone's screen. 'Unknown'. "Hello?"

"Mr King. This is Samakab. You remember me?"

"Sure I do. What the hell have you done?" Troy couldn't help himself shouting at the phone.

"Ouch! Not so loud, Mr King."

"Look, I'll pass you over to—" Troy leaned forward, ready to pass the phone to Griffin, who already had his hand out, ready to receive the phone.

"No, don't do that. I only want to talk to you. After all, we know each other, don't we?" Troy waved Griffin away and sat down again.

"Mr Samakab, this is no time to play your fancy games."

"I assure you, this is no game. I think you know I am perfectly serious."

"What do you want, and why are you calling me?" As Troy spoke, Griffin was signaling to him to keep the conversation going, trying to indicate to him to talk more calmly. He shoved a quickly written note in front of his eyes: 'BE REASONABLE!!!' Troy nodded. "Apologies, Mr Samakab. I was feeling kinda emotional as a result o' seein' the news an' all."

"I understand. Look, Mr King, I need you to give them a message."

"Who?"

"The American people."

"Well, I don't know if I can do that…"

Griffin scribbled another note and showed it to Troy: 'MEET HIM'.

"Look, is there somewhere we can meet an' talk about this? Maybe one o' your favorite fancy hotels or somethin'?"

"Ha, ha. I don't think so. Now, just listen. You can switch it onto speaker if you want the others with you to hear this. I just don't want to talk to anyone else, and I won't respond to anyone else. Is that clear?"

"Sure, Mr Samakab. I'm switchin' it on now."

"Very good. I will be making an announcement shortly and I want you to make sure that everyone hears it. I will put it on a video disc that will be delivered to you soon." The line went dead. Troy immediately punched in Samakab's number and pressed 'call'.

"He's switched it off." Troy looked at his cell phone. "Well, I'll be… He's using me as his damn' delivery boy."

"I'm sure it's not personal," Sheryl offered.

"I think it's all personal. It's just kinda multiplied to include everyone," Troy replied.

"Who knows that you know Samakab?" Griffin asked Troy.

"Hell, I guess it's just everyone here and… Ken Fellows at Arlington Online. I don't know for certain, but a coupla' the guys at NSA may know that I met him, but Shanning may not have been that specific with them. He was so damn' devious an' secretive on that flight back to Washington that he may have been the same way with them. All I know is that Shanning got 'em to stop me interfering with the Weatherman Project—which I didn't even know I was doin', at the time."

"Well, we must make sure no one else knows that you know him. And keep that cell phone on you all the time, 24 hours a day."

"Of course I will."

"Have a word with Ken Fellows as well. But be careful. Can you trust him?"

"I reckon, yeah. He won't talk. He's good." He turned toward the door as four men burst in.

"Senator Kirkland?"

"That's me." Griffin stood to meet them.

"What do you know about this?" The man came to a halt directly in front of Griffin. The other three fanned out, checking out the office, the TV screens, the desks. One of them thumbed through the papers on Troy's desk. Griffin, Troy, Sheryl and Dolores all froze.

"About as much as you obviously do."

"This is no time for smart answers, Senator."

"You'll have my full cooperation, should I find out anything of use."

"And who's this?" He turned his attention to Troy. "Aren't you from Arlington Online?" He turned to one of his associates. "Hey, John, isn't this the guy you went to see recently? You know, the one that was snoopin' around in New York?"

"Yeah, that's him."

"So you're the one who briefed the Senator on all this, are you?"

"No, actually, *I* briefed *him*," Griffin interjected. Troy was glad to be momentarily off the hook.

"So, you *do* know all about it."

"I don't know anything about this attack, and I don't know who you are either. You're the ones who'd better explain yourselves. I don't appreciate goons like you bursting in on my meeting."

"Agent Perry." He flashed his NSA identity card at Griffin, and picked up the phone on Griffin's desk, offering it to him. "This looks more like a family get-together than a meeting, to me. You want to call my boss? Be my guest. You spoke to him yesterday, and he asked me to come over here. He wants us to work together."

"Forget it, and get out of my office. I'll talk to your boss and you'll get instructions from him."

"We already have our first instruction." With his free hand Perry pulled a slip of paper from his jacket pocket and handed it to Griffin. Griffin breathed in sharply. It was signed by the director. They wanted Troy.

Hiding his concern, he glanced at Troy. He didn't trust the NSA and their methods. There was no way he was going to release Troy into the hands of these jumped-up happy sadists. He'd suffered enough and, anyway, he was the only person that Samakab would talk to, as far as he knew.

"I'll take it in my office," Griffin said, calmly. Perry lowered the phone back

into its cradle as Griffin turned and closed the door behind him. As he sat down at his desk, he shot a glance at Sheryl, who took the look as a prompt. Griffin needed more time.

"Maybe this is the guy you're looking for," she said, cheerfully. Her computer monitor was displaying a press report from the *Independent*. Perry wandered over, leaning down to peer at the screen. There was a grainy picture of a man stepping out of a silver Jaguar in Parliament Square. The headline read, 'What did he know?' The article was about an opposition politician, Frank Boyle, based on the transcript of an audio recording of the previous day's incomplete debate, which had been transmitted live before the attack. The article suggested that Boyle may have been trading inside knowledge of a secretly planned European invasion of the Horn of Africa, because of the depth of information he expressed, which the newspaper suggested went beyond mere conjecture. It carefully insinuated that Boyle may have leaked official secrets that ultimately lead to the attack. It stopped short of calling him a traitor or a spy, but did enough to ensure his credibility would be shot to pieces once he was let out of the House of Commons. It was a vicious character assassination, based entirely on conjecture. "What do you make of that, Agent Perry?"

"Journos having fun," Perry scoffed, turning his attention back to Griffin's office. Through the glass, he could see Griffin talking on the phone. He looked intense, animated. He saw Perry smirking at him, turned his head away to the window and continued talking. He put the phone down and walked over to the fax. He stood watching it as a sheet of paper inched its way into his hands. He picked up the fax and opened the office door.

"Perry. A moment…" He gestured to Perry to enter his office, and closed the door behind him. The others watched as they talked briefly. Griffin handed him the faxed sheet, which Perry snatched, immediately exiting the office, his jaw set in suppressed fury.

"Okay, guys, let's go." The four of them left. Griffin came to the door of his office and watched them leave.

"What was that all about?" Sheryl asked.

"They wanted Troy." He turned to Troy. "We'd better find somewhere safe for you and Dolores for a while. When they find out what I just did, they'll be back with fresh enthusiasm." He paused, rubbing his forehead. "I have an idea." Troy looked perplexed. Griffin sensed what he was thinking. He took Dolores by the hand and said, "While you are away, can you get it into this guy's head that he is not the problem, he hasn't precipitated this situation, he is totally innocent and he's a great guy?" She nodded, smiling. "It's a good thing you didn't unpack."

"Where are you thinking?" Sheryl was already at her computer terminal ready to make arrangements.

"Payson."

"Really?" Sheryl looked at him in disbelief. "But that place has been mothballed for years."

"Sure, but... why not? The phone's disconnected but our old neighbor, Alfred, has been keeping an eye on the place. I have absolutely no doubt that he'll have kept the lawn neat and tidy and there'll be a new flag flying on the pole. You know Alfred. He was like family when I was growing up."

"Where's Payson?" Troy had no idea what they were talking about.

"South of Salt Lake City. In Utah. It's where I grew up. The house is probably a little old-fashioned and musty—and don't worry, my parents are long gone—but no one will bother you there. Hell, they probably haven't even discovered the Internet there yet. It sure isn't the most inspiring town on the planet, but I hear things are starting to improve, and the scenery around it is stunning. While you're there, you could rent a car and check out the old gold mines around Eureka. It's just up the road. And then there's Utah Lake, Saratoga Springs, of course. You'll love it. It'll be like a second honeymoon."

"I'm onto it." Sheryl was already checking flights.

"Sheryl," Griffin said, "rent a car, in your name, to take them to the airport. Get it delivered here. We can't use an official car or a taxi. Troy, go to an ATM and pay for the flight with cash. We've got to keep our footprint light. Chances are they'll find out soon enough exactly what you're up to, but we just need to buy some time for a while, and keep you and your cell phone in circulation. Troy, I want you to have some quality time with Dolores, but keep your eyes open. Keep moving. Be a tourist and use cash whenever you can. I don't know how long you'll have, but you might as well use it as catch-up time. If and when they get you, cooperate. Definitely. Do whatever they ask you to do, tell them whatever they want to know. Don't lie. That's an order."

"Got it," Troy said, "but what about the video disc? We don't know where he's—"

"Right. Surely the only address he has for you is Arlington Online? "

"If he's done his homework, he'll most likely have Walla Walla as well."

"But he'll know you're not there. Call Ken Fellows."

Troy rushed back to his office and made the call. Emerging a few minutes later. "He'll look out for it and grab it before it gets to the office—and bring it here personally."

"Good."

"Car should be here in ten," Sheryl called from her desk.

"Get them to pick up from the coffee bar on the next block. Not Starbucks... That nice little independent one."

"Pepito's?"

"That's the one. It's easier for the driver to stop there anyway." Griffin grabbed Troy's arm. "You two. Go! Keep that phone charged. Call me on my cell." Dolores grabbed her suitcase and started wheeling it toward the door. Troy followed at a fast lope. "Good luck!"

After the flurry of activity, Griffin sat down wearily next to Sheryl by her computer. The TVs flickered their muted messages from across the room. It was strangely quiet.

"What did you do?" Sheryl asked him.

"Oh, nothing much. I just called in a favor. I wasn't proud of it, but I wasn't going to let them get hold of Troy that easily."

"A favor?" Sheryl was concerned that Griffin might have done something in the heat of the moment that could backfire. He took in her stern expression. *No secrets.*

"You remember Dan Zielinski who did some organizing for me last year?"

"Vaguely. Was he that really hyper over-keen geek with glasses?"

"That's the one. I got him a job in the White House after that."

"And…?" Sheryl didn't like the sound of this.

"Well, it was just a scan of the President's signature on a note, with the White House seal…"

"Griffin!"

"I know, I know. It was a dumb-ass thing to do. I just…" He slumped in his chair and shook his head. He didn't 'just' anything. The truth was he simply couldn't think of anything else quickly enough to get those bullies out of his office and keep Troy—and his cell phone—safe. His main hope was that the President would be too busy right now, and no one would want to bother him with questions about the validity of a faxed document about someone he'd never heard of. "Okay. I know it was stupid, and I could end up getting fired, maybe worse, but…" he glanced up at the screens. "What's happening?" There was activity in London. "Turn up Al Jazeera… and CNN."

Both channels were showing footage of busloads of people being driven from the exclusion zone, through the barriers. There was chaos as cars, motorbikes with cameramen perched on the back, and outside broadcast vehicles de-camped and tried to follow them. They needn't have bothered. The first bus stopped a few yards after crossing the barrier and opened its door to let passengers off. The press swarmed around the door as people were seen through the windows, inching their way between the seats and down the steps. Some held bags to hide their faces, others waved and smiled triumphantly as they descended the steps to the road, still more were studying their mobile phones, messaging or talking into them. Some were angry, some were plainly relieved, some were scared.

"Can you tell us what the scene is inside the House of Commons?"

"No, I was in the House of Lords public gallery."

"Excuse me, sir, were you in the House of Commons?"

"I can't say."

"Surely you know where you were?"

"I can't talk to you. I must go and find my wife."

"Was anyone here in the House of Commons?" All faces turned away. These people had been briefed, probably threatened. The female reporter targeted a middle-aged woman and tried another tack.

"Were you treated well?"

"As well as could be expected, under the circumstances, yes."

"And what was it like?"

"Well, it was very uncomfortable sleeping on the benches. I didn't sleep much."

"Were you fed and could you contact your family?"

"Yes and no."

"What happened?"

"I have to go now."

The reporter singled out another likely target, a man in a suit, walking at a brisk pace, away from the activity around the bus. *"Sir, excuse me, sir... Sir!"* She had to run to catch up with him. The cameraman followed as quickly as he could. She held the man's arm as the camera was maneuvered into position. The man frowned at her hand. She released him, smiling apologetically. *"What can you tell us about what happened in the House of Commons, sir?"*

"Precious little!" the man shouted impatiently, above the din around them.

"Why is that, sir?"

"Why do you think? We've been gagged, that's why! Gagged, I tell you. It's outrageous. This is Britain, for God's sake. What's this country coming to?"

"Is there anything at all that you can tell us about the incident?"

"Incident? This was no 'incident'. This was an act of bloody war, that's what this was!"

"Let me get this straight, sir, you're telling me that this was an act of war, is that correct?"

Another news crew heard the man shouting and zoomed in on him. Both cameramen moved in closer, each applying discreet pressure on the shoulder of the other to get the best position. Both microphones were held close to his mouth.

"I have nothing more to say," the man said, regretting his outburst. *"I'm going to see my solicitor."* He walked off. The news crews didn't follow.

"There's your next headline," Griffin murmured as he scanned the screens. Another screen showed Trafalgar Square, where members of the Nationalist Party were holding an impromptu rally. A manic-looking speaker with a bullhorn was complaining about immigration and calling for tighter controls. An anti-war rally blocked Regent Street. Griffin flicked through the channels. Around the world, there were scenes of huge crowds gathered outside embassies or in the main squares of their capital cities, waiting for news. Seas of flickering candles, silent vigils or people marching, shouting. Everywhere there were talk shows discussing war, terrorism, aggression, religion. Picking over the history, motivations, politics, reasons, psychology, weaponry. Questions, opinions, no answers.

Come on, Larry! But he knew it would be well into the evening before Larry arrived.

Movement on another screen drew his attention to the BBC World News. The caption that had remained statically displayed there for nearly a whole day had disappeared. A new caption read: 'An announcement concerning the situation at the House of Commons will follow shortly.'

The phone rang on Griffin's desk. He answered it and then returned to watching the TV screens.

"Who was that?" Sheryl asked him.

"Oh, nothing important—not now, anyway. It was the hospital in Jersey City. Apparently Shanning came round after they boosted his medication. He was sitting up, watching TV for a while. Then he pulled the connection to his own life support. He's gone."

"So, it's all up to Larry?"

"It's all up to Larry." Griffin squeezed Sheryl's hand. "Thank you," he whispered in her ear.

"For what?"

"Oh… just, everything."

As he kissed her gently on the forehead, he was distracted by the TVs. One by one, all the screens switched their transmissions to the BBC World News image.

"Here it comes," Griffin said. They sat on a desk in front of them as the last one switched over. The world fell silent, in readiness for the news that was to be revealed. *I can't hear any traffic,* Griffin suddenly realized.

A head-and-shoulders image of a man in a dark-grey suit appeared, wearing a white shirt and plain black tie. He appeared to be in his late 60s. His thinning silver hair was combed straight back from his forehead. His expression was somber and his eyes were bloodshot with pronounced bags drooping onto his cheekbones. He was set against a digital blue background that was plain but for a slightly lighter blue image of the familiar portcullis logo—the official symbol of the British Parliament—in the top right-hand corner of the screen.

"Who's that?" Griffin didn't recognize the man. It surprised him, given the importance of the announcement, that it wasn't the familiar face of the Prime Minister.

"I don't know," Sheryl replied. A caption appeared at the bottom of the screen.

'The Rt Hon. Lord Blakey of Coulside, Leader of the House of Lords.'

"Who?" Griffin had never heard of him, but then he wasn't that conversant with the members of the House of Lords.

"I have been asked by Her Majesty the Queen, on behalf of the British people, to make this solemn and grave announcement." He was having difficulty maintaining his composure. He lifted a glass of water to his lips and took a shaky sip. His hand was trembling almost uncontrollably. *"Yesterday, the House of Commons was attacked by a person or persons unknown. No prior warning was given. The attack was sudden and deadly. The consequences of this attack for the British people are devastating. The implications for people worldwide and the very existence of representational government, human rights and the freedoms that we take for granted are frightening. Indeed, this unprecedented attack marks an entirely new level in terrorist activity that, if left unchecked, threatens all civilized society."*

He carefully placed a sheet of paper over to one side, and continued reading from the next one. *"It grieves me to inform you that many Members of Parliament are now deceased. The majority of those killed were government ministers and back-benchers. Some Members of the opposition were also targeted and are now deceased. The Prime Minister and the Deputy Prime Minister are among the dead."* He paused, overcome. *"In total, 200 ministers lost their lives and the government no longer has a majority. Indeed, it cannot function at all, having lost all but four of its Cabinet members who are thankfully still with us—the Secretary of State for Foreign and Commonwealth Affairs, the Secretary of State for Education, the Secretary of State for Communities and Local Government and the Secretary of State for Culture, Olympics, Media and Sport. As of midnight, Parliament is dissolved."*

Lord Blakey paused to compose himself again. Griffin's mind went numb. Lord Blakey continued to announce the emergency measures for governing the country and listed every victim by name and constituency, his voice quivering, his staunch resolve carrying him through a litany of details, names and procedures. The words were spoken, but they slid past Griffin's mind in a faraway mist.

Griffin walked back to his office and stood at the window. Washington was at a standstill. He thought back to his time in Bali, when he'd struggled to come to terms with a concept that seemed so outlandish, so crazy, so impossible. At the time, he'd thought Larry had lost it. Now he knew that Larry was the only person who hadn't and, remarkably, Larry had put his faith in Griffin to clean up the mess. Griffin had no idea how to do that, and there wasn't a person in the world who could tell him.

A pigeon startled the hell out of him, crashing into the window directly in front of his face. He ducked instinctively, then watched as it tumbled down the side of the building to the street below. *Wake up, Griffin. For God's sake, wake up!*

CHAPTER 45

"What's this bullshit note I've just been handed?" the NSA Director barked down the phone. Griffin had been expecting the call and, despite the Director's attitude, he was glad to see that the line of communication was still open, especially after sending his agents away empty-handed.

"What was that bullshit visit I got earlier?" Griffin was filled with a new resolve. He'd already blown this guy off once, and now it was time to take control of the situation—at least until Larry arrived. "If you want to resolve this situation, there's one person you have to cooperate with, and that person is me. Understood?" There was silence at the other end of the line. "What the hell did you want with Troy King anyway? Were you going to strap him to a chair and feed him a few thousand volts of encouragement to tell you how to fix this mess?"

"Whatever he knows, I have to know. You know that. What kind of a mess do you think this *whole world* will be in if I don't get a result—and fast?"

"Well, thank God I didn't let you get hold of him then. Look, in our previous conversation, I think it was clear that you, your methods and the people you deal with are a major part of the problem. I wouldn't be surprised to find out that you were the one who found that location for AVTOL in Somalia in the first place."

"As it happens, it wasn't, but—"

"Never mind the details. We don't have time. But understand this: if you want to keep your head from parting company with your body—courtesy of either myself or your President—you'll keep your sadistic hands off Troy King and anyone else on my team." Griffin's heart was leaping against his ribcage. He just hoped that the ferocity of his delivery would convey enough confidence to make the Director think twice about interfering with whatever Griffin had to do. He was flying blind, without a parachute.

"Is that why you packed him off to join the Mormons? He's so vital to your strategy that a trip to Salt Lake City with his wife is in the best national interest? Is that part of your strategy for resolving this evolution? What actually is your strategy, Kirkland?"

"Just leave him alone. We're all looking for solutions and he is part of that process." Griffin just managed to stop himself from saying that Troy could be a *key* part of the solution. That would have got him picked up as soon as they touched down at Salt Lake City. "Dammit, we're supposed to be on the same side, or is that concept anathema to you? As I said to Agent Perry, the NSA has my full cooperation. Should anything come up that would be useful for you to know, of course I will inform you. Did you talk to the people who are running the show, like I suggested?"

"Yes, I did, through an intermediary. They're pulling back, as you'd expect. The message they gave us was that if there's another attack like London, they'll shut the Hominine computer down."

"Shut it down?"

"Yes, shut it down."

"You're sure they said 'shut it down'?"

"Yes. Why? Is that significant?"

"It could be. Thanks. That's all for now." Griffin wanted to get off the line and have a few moments to think this through but, at the same time, he knew he needed to keep this communication going, however unpleasant it was. He had to give the Director something that would keep the NSA away, something at least half-plausible that would prevent him blundering in with more ham-fisted actions, piling disaster on disaster. "I will get a communication soon, as long as Troy King isn't disturbed. Understood?"

"This is something we're better equipped to deal with." The inference was clear. The Director was going to pull them *all* in.

"It won't happen if you make a move."

"We'll see about that."

"Do you think this guy is bluffing? Do you want to take that risk, knowing what's at stake and how you are complicit in what has happened already?"

"Stay in touch." The line went dead. Griffin breathed again. *Shut it down, they'd said.* As far as he could work out, given the little information he had, that could mean one of two things. The first possibility was they wanted to keep the Hominine computer intact so they could use it in the future once this crisis had all been explained away. The other possibility was that they couldn't risk destroying it because it was on another country's sovereign territory, and such an act would cause the crisis to escalate into a conflict of biblical proportions. Either way, the words they'd used, if that's what they really meant, suggested that the Hominine computer was relatively safe as long as Larry could shut it down before Samakab had a chance to use it again—if that's what he planned to do.

"They're going the Al-Qaeda route," Sheryl said, peering through the open door of his office. Griffin turned and acknowledged her. Behind her, the screens were variously showing familiar old footage of the training camps, Bin Laden and other terrorist leaders, interspersed with spokesmen making grave announcements at podiums, flanked by flags. The international PR machine was grinding into action with all its assurances of government protection, revenge and justice, laced with warnings and calls for diligence. Governments of grown-up children with no idea what was really happening, putting on a confident face, projecting the illusion of competence and control.

Griffin focused his eyes back onto Sheryl, standing in the doorway. In that moment, she shone. She still held all the promise and excitement that he'd seen in her in that instant of recognition, so long ago at Woodstock.

"What are the chances, do you think, of lightning striking twice in the same place?" he asked her.

"Not too good," she answered, with a warm curiosity in her eyes. "Why do you ask?"

"Oh, I was just thinking about something Larry said back in Bali. We were talking about our search for answers to explain the state of the world, our place in it, and how to find solutions to its problems. He said 'it's a bit like looking for a diamond in a mudslide'. That gave me the tiniest ray of hope that I could do something about all this."

"I don't get it. That doesn't sound like much cause for celebration."

"Oh, yes it is. You see, I've already done it once, haven't I?" Griffin replied. A smile spread across Sheryl's face as she realized what he was saying.

"And I have every faith you'll do it again." She grinned back at him. They held each other's gaze for a moment, then Sheryl's expression changed as she thought of something. She checked her watch. "I'd better get to the airport to pick up Larry. Are you going to be okay here, on your own, for a while?"

"Sure. You get going. I've got plenty to be getting on with." She picked up her purse, blew him a kiss and left the office.

To suddenly find himself alone as the TV monitors shouted their silent rage at the unknown enemy was actually the last thing he wanted. He stood for a moment, watching their faces. The whole charade suddenly seemed ludicrous, impossible, beyond crazy. The complexity of humanity in a glowing wall of faces—desperate, angry, confused, some even conceited—reflected back at him. It was like an animated version of the famous painting by Hieronymus Bosch—the part that illustrated his concept of hell. At that moment, Griffin couldn't even clearly define what he felt. Was he angry at the madness of man that could create such a weapon and take him from one precipice of his own making to an even higher one? Was he sorry for all those confused people who had played no part in it? People felt so powerless that they didn't even bother to say 'no' to whatever was foisted upon them! Children were going through the age-old process of soaking up the fears, beliefs and limitations of their parents, teachers and religious leaders and would, in turn, perpetuate the cycle. Did he sympathize with the fears and concerns of ordinary people who passively took part in the whole process while living a life of self-serving consumerism? Was he angry at the mullahs, clerics, priests and evangelists—some of whom even seemed to take some warped pleasure in this awful manifestation of man's deviation from whichever doctrine they preached? *We told you so!* Did he respect the leaders, whom everyone was looking to for advice and guidance, knowing they were just ordinary people, compromised by their very positions of power? Did he care—really care—about any of it?

What was the point? Why do anything? The only person he truly cared about had just walked out of the door to go to the airport and pick up the only other person he truly respected. Did he feel guilty thinking such thoughts? Wasn't he being ultra-cynical? There were arguments both ways. He turned his back to the screens. He desperately needed some clarity. He needed to find something deeper and stronger than the thoughts that were ransacking his mind like rabid dogs on mescaline.

Somewhere, a buzzer sounded. Griffin shook his head and rubbed his eyes. The gossamer membrane he had momentarily crossed through was now back in place. The buzzer sounded again. This time he heard it in the room. He jabbed the button on the intercom.

"Yes?"

"Ken Fellows for Senator Kirkland."

"Come on up." Griffin poured himself a glass of water and stood next to the dispenser as he drank it. He held the paper cup limply in his hand, dropping it into the bin when the door opened and Ken Fellows walked in. He had a package in his hand.

"Hello, sir. This came for Mr King," he said, handing the padded envelope to Griffin.

"Who delivered it?"

"I don't know. It came on a bike. The guy had a helmet on, apparently, with a tinted visor. We couldn't identify him." Griffin looked at the envelope. No delivery company sticker, no plastic wallet enclosing a delivery note.

"Thanks. Have you looked at it?" Griffin asked.

"No, no." Ken shook his head vigorously, as if taken aback at the suggestion that he would snoop around someone else's mail. "I brought it straight over. It sounded like it was really important when Mr King called. Is he here?"

"No, he had to step out for a while. Coffee?" Griffin asked casually as he started to carefully peel the sticky seal of the envelope, half expecting his fingers to get blown off.

"Thanks. Anything to keep out of the office for a while. It's not been the same since Mr King left. A new regime, you know?"

"Sure... Coffee's over there. Help yourself." Griffin gestured to the percolator in the corner of the room. Since Ken Fellows was here, he wanted to take the opportunity to ask him a few things.

"What's the package—or shouldn't I ask?"

"Best not." Griffin had opened one end of the envelope. Pulling the two sides apart a little, he looked inside. There was a plastic DVD case. He pulled it out. It still had the manufacturer's paper sleeve inside. Griffin opened the case.

The DVD had no markings or title. Unclipping it from the case, he turned it over. The slight discoloration of the recording spread to about half of the width of the disc. "You knew David Arbuthnot, didn't you?" he asked Ken as he walked over to one of the computers and popped open a disc drive.

"Yeah. Nice guy. Pity he left. Why do you ask?"

"Oh, Mr King mentioned him. He said he was really good at social media and other things to do with computing."

"Yeah," Ken smiled, "I think that's why they had to give him the Dear John letter. He was doing stuff a bit beyond his station, if you know what I mean." Ken sat on one of the desks and sipped his coffee.

"They fired him?"

"Looks that way to me. He and Mr King didn't exactly see eye to eye. It was a real pity, though. He'd just recently moved his family over from England and they were setting up home, here in Washington."

"Well, that happens, I guess, when you start acting beyond the call of duty... Do you ever hear from him?" Griffin snapped the disc into the drive, but left the drawer open.

"It's funny you mention that, but I hadn't heard from him since he left, and then all of a sudden yesterday he sent me two DMs on Twitter."

"DMs on Twitter?" Griffin had never used it himself.

"Direct messages."

"I see. How is he doing?"

"To be honest, I couldn't tell you. The message didn't make much sense to me."

"Oh? What did he say?" Then, embarrassed by his intrusive questioning, he added, "I'm sorry. It's none of my business."

"No, no, it's okay." Ken felt flattered to even be in a conversation with the Senator. "The first one was weird. All it said was 'star falling whisper'. I mean, go figure."

"That is strange. What did the second one say? Did it give any sort of explanation?"

"No, just as weird. It said, 'Time for Vaspan'." Ken shrugged. "I mean, look, we're used to getting strange messages and deciphering stuff, and I happen to know that the first one relates to something we'd been working on before he got fired, but that's hardly how you say 'hi' to a friend when you've been gone a while, is it?"

"I guess not." Griffin sat down and turned to Ken, looking at him expectantly.

"You gonna play that thing, sir?" Ken waved his coffee cup at the computer.

"Soon, yes."

"Oh, I get it. Sorry, Senator." He slurped the last of his coffee and stood up. "I guess I'd better be going."

"Before you go," Griffin said, "can you keep Mr King and me in the loop on any more communications you get from Mr Arbuthnot?"

"Why?" Ken asked. Griffin looked at him, expressionless and silent. "Okay, sure." Ken thought better than to pursue the question. "Thanks for the coffee." He dumped the cup in a bin and left.

Griffin locked the door after him and, returning to the computer, pushed the drawer of the drive in and waiting as it loaded. There were three files on the disc, a notepad document simply named 'ReadMeFirst', and two video files named '1' and '2'. He opened the notepad document.

The New Africa 5T Movement

By the time you receive this information, you will know that the UK is in the throes of forming its own Transitional Government. It was important that they understand the true significance of what they were deciding to do. The action that was taken against them will also give them a clearer understanding of what it is like when your country is in turmoil, no citizen is safe and the foreign governments that played a large part in creating that turmoil sit by and do nothing, except for taking actions that serve their interests alone.

Here are your instructions.

Show video one to your Head of State within 24 hours. I will allow two full days for your Head of State to give a public response. Immediately after that, this video will be made public.

Show video two to your Head of State within 24 hours.

A cool, stark and calculating message. There was no mention of what would happen after the second video had been viewed. Griffin guessed that the wording was very deliberate in not mentioning the President of the United States, but rather saying 'your Head of State'. How many Heads of State had this gone to? Whoever had received this had basically been put on notice that if they wanted to prevent their populations from seeing the video, their government would have to shut down the Internet in their country. That would be easier to do in some countries than others, but with the convergence that was taking place in new media technologies, it would be virtually impossible to close off all possible means of communicating its contents.

Griffin clicked on the first video. It was an amateur production, with a simple yellow-on-blue title that read, 'New Africa 5T Movement'. A second title, with each 'T' highlighted in red, spelt out the words, 'Time To Tell The Truth'. At any other time, Griffin would have dismissed the video, at this point, convinced he was dealing with some low-grade amateur nutter, and passed it on to the NSA. Not this time.

The first scene showed a close-up of a metal table. A single item, a missile—

it looked like a large bullet. Its casing, which had narrow fins, small holes and other details in its sides, stood on the table. A voice with an accent that Griffin took to be Somali started speaking in a steady, flat tone.

"This missile tells the truth. If it has your name on it, it will kill you. It knows what you are thinking, what you intend to do. Wherever you are in the world, if you even think a bad thought about those who control it, you are dead, if that's what they want. This is the latest secret weapon developed by those that have, to wage covert wars on those that don't have, to ensure their supply lines are protected and to maintain their rich lifestyle. It has been developed and built by a small group of powerful men in the USA, Russia and China.

It is the ultimate weapon for the greedy and the inhumane in a world that is running short of resources.

Unfortunately for them, their secret was discovered and they no longer control this fearsome weapon, or its delivery system. Doubly unfortunate for them, their dark secret will now be revealed to the world.

Have no doubt that this is not a hoax. Watch and learn.

The image switched to a close-up of an aircraft. The shot initially showed the nose and the windows above it. Then it moved under the wide wing, past huge jet vents on their underside. The camera wobbled in the hands of its operator, but the images were clear. Open bomb doors revealed a large metal container located just inside the aircraft's underbelly. The camera was then walked to the rear of the aircraft where the distinctive jagged edges and the jet exhaust outlets on top of the wings identified it as a stealth bomber.

The next image was a view looking up into the sky. Excited voices could be heard shouting in a language that Griffin didn't recognize. The camera swung across the clouds, lurching to a halt when the cameraman found the aircraft, hovering, dark and heavy in the sky, its wings wobbling slightly as if it was struggling to keep its balance as its vertical thrusters pushed it steadily, slowly upwards. It moved forward and, as it did so, the rear thrusters started to take over and the monstrous black dart of a machine raised its head and soared vertically up, quickly disappearing through the clouds.

Griffin felt sick to his stomach as the next scene, which started as a black screen, suddenly flashing to light. He could only guess at what was happening, but from how Larry had described it, it made sense. It appeared that they had mounted a forward-facing camera in the HAPISAD pod. As the pod split open to release the missiles, Griffin could make out the roof of the House of Commons coming rapidly into view, with the pod homing in on it at an alarming rate. It suddenly lurched as the 200 missiles released and shot forward from around the camera. Erratically-weaving plumes of white exhaust gas identified the missiles' positions as they got closer to the roof and curved around to locate the windows. Then they were gone, and the image disappeared as the pod self-destructed. The whole scene had taken mere seconds.

Finally, the screen returned to blue, with a caption that read, 'Time To Turn The Tables'. Griffin sat back on his chair, numb with shock. His cell phone rang in his pocket. He lifted himself out of his stupor and scrambled to dig it out. *Sheryl.*

"What's up?"

"It's Larry…"

"Oh, thank God. Get him over here as fast as you can, will you? This thing has taken on a whole new dimension, and I haven't a clue how to—"

"GRIFFIN!" Sheryl shouted down the phone.

"What?"

"Larry wasn't on the flight."

"What do you mean, he wasn't on the flight?"

"Just that. He wasn't on the flight."

"But he must have been! Did you check—?"

"Of course I did. He didn't board at LAX either, and when I got them to put out an announcement for him, they got no response."

"Here or in LA?"

"Both."

"Shit! What's happened? He's got to be here! Tell me this isn't happening!" Griffin leaned forward, his head in his hands.

"I'm sure he'll call," Sheryl said, trying to offer some comfort, trying to be reasonable.

"If he can…"

"What do you mean?"

"Oh, I don't know." He bit his lip. "Just come back, Sheryl. There's nothing more you can do there." His head was swimming.

"Griff?" Sheryl sensed his desperation.

"Yes, honey?" he said, weakly.

"Whatever is going on, whatever the challenge, Larry made it clear that you are the man to make things right. I know that too. I also know that although it may seem like things are impossible right now, there's no one else in the world I would rather be with, and I *know* you'll find the perfect answer to all of this."

"Just get back here and tell me that to my face. That's exactly what I need right now. And thank you, Sheryl."

There was time for him to watch the second video before Sheryl got back to the office. He pressed 'play'.

CHAPTER 46

It was about a four-foot swell, Tarek estimated. That was manageable. There was a cool, light breeze, and a blanket of cloud overhead. The rendezvous had been timed to perfection, 100 nautical miles due south of Malta. The *Norfolk Defender* had slowed to ten knots, as agreed. It dwarfed the oil tanker he was aboard, so he was glad that the conditions were being kind to him.

This was going to be a particularly dangerous operation. As far as he knew, it had never been attempted before. He'd taken some convincing to do it at all, given the potential for fatal accidents—even in perfect conditions. When Samakab had called and explained what he wanted him to do, he'd thought it would be impossible. But when Samakab had also explained the importance of achieving this key part of his plan, he'd pulled out all the stops and exerted his considerable influence in Tripoli to make it happen. Under normal circumstances, he would have left it to others to carry out the task, but these circumstances were anything but normal and he wanted to personally oversee the operation.

"The key to the success of this operation," Samakab had told him, "is extreme diligence, attention to every detail, absolute attention to safety, thorough cleaning of the tank and the pumping mechanism, and a very skilful captain and crew. Oh, and you will need some special equipment. Find an MD-1 pressure fueling nozzle and a quick-disconnect coupling. The hoses must be API 1529, BS 3158 or MIL-H-6521 rated. I'll e-mail you the specs. Keep the number of sections to a minimum. It's preferable to use just one continuous piece, but if you have to couple hoses, only use screw couplings. Don't let the hose kink. Keep it out of sunlight. Protect exposed ends with dust covers. Just before you start the operation, do 'clear and bright' and 'particulate contamination' tests."

Tarek's men had spent hours in port, cleaning marine diesel out of the tank. It was a disgusting job. They had to work in rotation, wearing breathing apparatus in the dark, echoing enclosure. Finding the specialist equipment and preparing the ship hadn't been easy, either. He'd found the hoses at Tripoli's airport, but had to fly in the pressure nozzle and other fitments from Iran, as their own equipment was of an older specification.

On the signal from the *Norfolk Defender*, the captain brought the tanker alongside and the crew positioned themselves to begin. Before they'd left Tripoli, Tarek had checked to make sure that none of the crew were carrying matches, lighters or even cell phones. All of them were wearing proper deck shoes with rubber soles. All unnecessary electrical equipment was to be switched off during the operation. But none of the precautions would protect them should they break the essential, major rule of refueling: that the aircraft, fueling vehicle and equipment should be grounded together to dissipate static electricity collected during the operation. That's where the skill of the captain came in. He would have to concentrate hard, making tiny course changes of one or two degrees, and infinitesimally small speed adjustments, to maintain his exact position relative to the *Norfolk Defender*, to make sure he didn't risk snapping the grounding wire—or breaking the hose. Even dropping a piece of metal equipment or a tool could spark an explosion. The thousands of gallons of JP-8 military-grade jet fuel beneath their feet would take no prisoners.

The two ships were less than 100 feet apart, the smaller tanker level with the bow of the *Norfolk Defender*, as close as it could get to the forward hatch without being disturbed by the larger vessel's wash. A thumbs-up from the tanker captain was followed by a loud report from the *Norfolk Defender* as a projectile carrying a 'gun line' was fired. It crashed alarmingly onto the deck and was immediately grabbed by a sailor who attached a heavier line and a telephone wire, then signaled for it to be hauled back onto the *Norfolk Defender*. The heavy line was followed by a steel cable attached to an auto-tensioning winch on the tanker. Once attached to the *Norfolk Defender*, the taut cable was used to carry the fuel hose and the grounding wire, suspended beneath it in loops running on pulley blocks. The two ships held steady on their courses as the men on the deck of the *Norfolk Defender* fed the hose and grounding wire down into the hold and one of them plugged the telephone wire from the tanker into a portable phone unit.

Baptiste was standing at the helm, unshaven, grey with worry, his broken fingers still throbbing. The open forward hatch was surrounded by black scorch marks created by the AVTOL when it blasted off two days previously, returning from its mission a few hours later. He was more concerned than ever, following that third bone-shaking episode, that the integrity of the hull may have been compromised. Wide cracks had appeared at the corners of the forward hatch and although the ship was very strong, it was not designed for the stresses that were being brought to bear on it by the AVTOL. Despite his angry protests, he had not been allowed to inspect the damage. It seemed that these thugs would keep going with whatever their crazy mission was, even if they risked sinking the ship. And now they were committing another act of lunacy—attempting to refuel an aircraft at sea, from a tanker alongside.

Under the watchful eye of six machine-gun-brandishing men, the two pilots, Brian and Frank, supervised the connection of the pressure fueling nozzle to one of the wing tank valves. Raage looked on. He'd insisted on taking the third seat in the cockpit on the London mission. Neither pilot knew the nature of the mission or the target. They knew the coordinates of the drop zone, which they could have worked out as being an area over London, and they knew that the lives of their families and communities back home were at risk if they didn't cooperate. Additionally, they were under strict instructions to keep the aircraft secret at all costs, and since the orders for the mission appeared to have come through official channels, they were not entirely sure where they stood.

They had other much more immediate and very grave concerns, as well. While taking off from the *Norfolk Defender* had been relatively easy, landing on a moving ship was a maneuver they had neither training for, nor special software to support. From the cockpit located on top of the wide fuselage, they couldn't see anything directly below them, so all the delicate, computer-assisted handling on the vertical thrusters had to be performed blind, using instruments alone. There was no room for error; the landing area was only fractionally larger than the dimensions of the aircraft itself. If they drifted to one side or the other, one of the thrusters could suddenly be pushing down over the side of the ship and the aircraft would simply barrel-roll into the sea. The only way they had been able to land safely had been to approach the ship from ahead of the bow, calculate when they were directly above it, then hover with a slight reverse thrust to match the speed of the ship, gently lowering the aircraft until they could see the superstructure. Once that was in sight and they were just a few feet above the deck, they rotated the aircraft anti-clockwise 66 degrees. They were then able to touch down in a position that allowed the aircraft to be lowered into the hold on the hydraulic platform without snagging the wings on the sides of the hatch. As soon as they switched off the vertical thrusters, six sailors had the unenviable task of racing across the burning-hot deck to chock the wheels in the fierce heat under the wings, just in case a freak wave moved the aircraft before it could be safely stowed belowdecks.

The man on the phone called the pump operator on the tanker to begin fueling. For its next trip, the AVTOL had to be filled to capacity. Each of the two tanks took just over 15,000 gallons of JP-8 fuel.

"Did they do the last-minute tests?" Raage shouted from the hold to the phone operator, who checked and came back with a thumbs-up.

"Even if they have, we can't take off again without running through the proper maintenance routine first!" Brian shouted, as he felt the hose stiffen with the pressure of the fuel flowing into the tank. Raage didn't reply. It was a risk they were going to have to take and, anyway, they'd left all the equipment and maintenance crew at the base in Somalia. Brian ducked down and looked toward Raage. "It'd be suicide. You know that, don't you? If anything needs adjusting and we can't fix it, anything can happen. It takes all 140 on-board computers to keep this baby operational, and we can't fly it—"

"Have faith, Brian, in your wonderful American technology," Raage said, with a forced smile. "I'm sure this will be your last mission in this aircraft, so you might as well both enjoy it. I know I certainly will." Raage looked around the aircraft. "Where's Frank?"

"Monitoring delivery in the cockpit."

"He doesn't need to do that. We're monitoring it from the tanker. I want him where I can see him."

"You have a death wish or what? If that clown on the telephone doesn't get the pump shut off at exactly the right time, you will definitely be flying nowhere—apart from out of this hold, when it catches as the fuel tank bursts. Your dinosaur of a pump on the tanker thinks it's delivering fuel into a massive ventilated ship's fuel tank, not an enclosed aircraft tank with airflow restricted through a small valve."

"Okay, well how's the acid situation? Has that been replenished?" An essential addition to AVTOL's stealth qualities, chloro-fluorosulphonic acid was injected into the exhaust gases of the AVTOL to inhibit the formation of giveaway contrails at high altitude.

"Not yet, but I'm not moving from here till both fuelings have been completed. If that tanker moves…" As he said the words, the hose jerked suddenly upwards. In a flash, Brian snapped open the quick release coupling just as all of the slack was taken up, just in time to watch it whip through the air, narrowly missing one of the guards, who dived to avoid it, dropping his gun as he fell. The coupling banged against the wall of the hold and continued to slide noisily upwards to the hatch opening. The man at the hatch opening was shouting into the phone, standing back in case the hose shot up and hit him. It stopped before it reached the hatch and slid lazily back down, clattering onto the steel floor.

"That's just priceless!" Brian shouted over the din. He sniffed the air for any sign of fuel vapors and checked the connector at the wing, before walking over to where the hose lay and picking up the metal coupling mechanism. "One of the handles is bent." He showed it to Raage, who was shouting at the phone operator in Somali. "HEY!" Brian finally got his attention. "If this doesn't create a proper seal, you can forget about fueling that aircraft! Okay?"

Raage looked up. "Give me that!" he shouted at the phone operator, in English this time. The man shrugged and indicated that the wire for the phone wouldn't extend down to Raage in the hold. "You're in charge!" he shouted to one of the guards, as he headed for the lift.

"They've got to put their guns down!" Brian shouted furiously after him.

"What?" Raage stopped in his tracks.

"We were very lucky that time. We had a loose hose full of volatile fuel waving around the hold and one of your idiots dropped his gun. This is fuckin' insane. I'm not re-connecting this—even if it will connect properly now—unless all those weapons are secure. The slightest leak will fill this hold with vapor in less than a minute. Your call." Raage was getting more and more frustrated. He wanted to stay with the pilots and the aircraft to make sure the fueling went properly, but he also needed to take control of the process from the deck. Brian was pushing him to the limit, doing everything he could to delay matters or get him to abort the whole thing. But no way was Raage going to tell the guards to give up their weapons.

"Make it work!" Raage shouted back at him as he entered the lift.

"Well, maybe I'll have a chance to, if your drunk idiot of a captain can keep his ship headed in the same direction for another hour or so. Jeez, if your guys are planning to take over the world, they're going to have to figure things out a bit better than this bunch of rank amateurs."

"And is your bunch of rank amateurs doing a better job?" The lift doors closed. When Raage arrived on deck, he saw what the problem was. The wind had picked up and the sea was much choppier. The auto-tensioning winch on the tanker working furiously to keep the cable taut and prevent the fuel hose from getting crushed between the two ships. While the increasing swell didn't affect the *Norfolk Defender* too much, the tanker had developed a pronounced roll. Each time the rig holding the cable swung away from the *Norfolk Defender*, the fuel hose went tight. Raage snatched the phone.

"Give it more slack!" he shouted. The wind was buffeting his ear, making it hard to hear the reply.

"We're using the full length."

"Can you add another section?"

"Can do. But it will take half an hour."

"Wait." He stood and concentrated for a moment. He hadn't figured on bad weather at this time of year, although he knew the Mediterranean could be unpredictable. He considered running up to the bridge, getting the equipment switched on and running a weather report to see if the squall would pass quickly, but he didn't want to risk giving away their position. Anyway, it would probably take longer to do that than it would to add the extra hose. "Do it." He resigned himself to a nail-biting half-hour with the *Norfolk Defender* attached by the cable to the tanker, hoping that the auto-tensioning winch would hold out, and not knowing if the wind would get worse or die down.

Up on the bridge, Captain Baptiste looked down with some satisfaction as he leaned casually on the control for the tunnel thrusters at the bow. Normally, they were only used to help move the ship sideways when docking, but he'd been moving the control to and fro to magnify the effect of the tanker's rolling action.

***

"This is highly irregular and mighty peculiar, if you ask me," General James

Carlson, Commander of AFRICOM, the US Africa Command responsible for US military operations and relations with all of Africa except Egypt, scowled as Griffin handed him a coffee. He'd arrived hotfoot from the White House, having been dispatched by the President to see Griffin. Griffin had made sure the President saw the videos, as specified, within 24 hours of their delivery to him. The President had shown them to Carlson and General Bernard Hall, who had also just arrived and was draping his coat over a chair. Hall was in charge of SOCOM, the Special Operations Command that had a string of successful high-profile operations under its belt. Both men had arrived alone, without assistants, secretaries or other staff they would normally have brought to a high-level meeting, under the specific instructions of the President. He wanted them to appraise the situation for themselves before involving others. If there was any chance that this was a hoax, he didn't want to have egg on his face, even if the smirks of ridicule were tightly confined to their immediate subordinates.

It was immediately apparent to Griffin that Hall was the man he wanted to deal with. Even physically, the difference between them made that obvious. Hall was tall, relaxed and looked fit. He must have been in his early 60s. His eyes were sharp and he exuded confidence in every move and look. He was a powerful and positive presence, dressed in a camouflage shirt bearing four stars on the collar and his name simply stated on his breast pocket. Carlson, on the other hand, exuded negativity, Griffin thought. He was busily dressed in a stiff military uniform that chafed around his bulging neck and was buttoned tightly round a lazy politician's stomach that had seen far too many long lunches. He felt overbearing and self-satisfied, yet at the same time appeared to lack the basic confidence that he would have needed to be effective in carrying out his office. As head of AFRICOM, Carlson had a more frustrating political situation on his hands than did Hall, who was master of all he surveyed and right in on the action. Carlson's job involved knocking on a lot of closed doors, hoping to find a way in to the territory he was supposed to be managing. He was tasked with building a network of facilities—so-called 'cooperative security locations'—across a continent that was highly resistant to any US military presence. In fact, only one country—Liberia—had ever indicated that they would welcome an American headquarters for AFRICOM in their country. The US weren't impressed by the offer, so they kept their African headquarters in Stuttgart, Germany, with an 'African' navy presence in Vicenza and Naples in Italy. As far as most African leaders were concerned, US interests in Africa were mainly limited to oil, minerals they could possibly acquire, and anti-terrorism. Many African leaders still had emotional memories of recent fights for their country's independence from occupying powers, so anything that remotely smacked of foreign military interference was given short shrift. Carlson had risen to the top of a heap of frustration, and this errand didn't make him feel any better.

Griffin had had a brief conversation with the President. Much as he expected, the reaction was: "No contact. We don't deal with terrorists. Deal with it by other means." There would be no public announcement relating to the video, under any circumstances. That would only endorse its credibility. But he had taken it seriously enough to send his two top commanders to see him, probably on the strength of Griffin's other work in the Middle East, and because he had no information from anyone else that explained what had happened in London. Griffin also figured that the President—if he had now been briefed on it—must have been under pressure to keep AVTOL and HAPISAD firmly under wraps. This would probably have been the first time he'd actually seen images of the aircraft or heard any details of HAPISAD, just as it may have been for one or both of the two men in Griffin's office now. However, there was no time for conjecture as to who knew what and when they found out. The only thing that mattered now was stopping Samakab.

Fortunately for Griffin, the NSA Director had been tasked with the preparation and dissemination of disinformation, should the videos become public. It was a classic move that Samakab had unwittingly facilitated by offering a reasonable deadline. Suppression of information wasn't really an option these days. It had limited effect and a tendency to backfire. Discreditation was the preferred weapon of authority. By the time the video was received by other world leaders or by the press—or even if it was uploaded to all the Internet video-hosting sites in the world— the story it contained would be easy to discredit as crazy fanaticism and a fabrication. Many would even ban it as a distasteful and sick effort to exploit a terrible situation in a pathetic attempt to serve some wacky political agenda. Those in authority would distance themselves from it and all but the most marginal press would avoid it, preferring to defer to 'experts' and credible political commentators as worthy sources of information. 'Freedom of information', Griffin wearily acknowledged, was also freedom of manipulation of information. Those who reported it created a new 'reality', its new 'truth' being the last in line to be born from the spin, weaving its way through media and through 'serious' discussion into the belief systems of communities around the world until it was solid and immovable.

"Let's get started," Hall said as he sat down with Griffin and Carlson. He pulled out a notepad and scribbled a few words before looking up at the other two. "We have less than 48 hours to sort this out. First thing: where is it?"

"Where's what?" Griffin asked, having first registered the puzzled look on Carlson's face.

"AVTOL."

"You mean you don't know?" Carlson's jaw dropped.

"Senator? You seem to know more about this than most people around here and you are the one this guy..." Hall flicked through the pages of his notepad, "Samakab contacted."

Griffin felt sick. *You're the Commander of SOCOM, and you don't know where your most-expensive-ever secret weapon is located?* They also didn't know that it was Troy who was the primary contact. Better to leave it that way for now. Although that might mean he was free to come back, Griffin decided to leave him where he was. At long last, Troy had a chance to re-build his relationship with Dolores, and all he had to do was to keep his cell phone close by in case Samakab called again. Other than that, there was little he could contribute here. For once, he could contribute to his own situation.

"I don't know," Griffin shrugged his shoulders. "The last I heard, it was based in Somalia—somewhere in the north. Haven't you located the base yet?"

"Of course we have. It's been hijacked. They haven't seen AVTOL since before the London incident. It must have landed somewhere else." Although he spoke calmly, his steely grey eyes could have pierced armor with their intensity.

"Fuck." Carlson stared into space.

"That's very helpful, Jim. It must have moved further into your territory. There was nowhere else it could go. What's the intel?"

"What makes you think that?" Carlson was fishing for time.

"Simple. AVTOL could not have hit London from the base in Somalia. It's out of range. What's the intel, Jim? Come on, we don't have time—"

"There is none, Bernie." Carlson wiped his mouth with a handkerchief.

"Come on, Jim. There has to be. What the hell are your guys doing in Africa?"

"I called, on the way over. There's nothin'. In fact, the word I've been getting is that there's a hell of a lot less comin' out of Africa than there was. Even the guys at the DIA are saying the same. It's like the place is shuttin' up shop. I tell you, it's kinda weird."

"Jim," Hall leaned forward, clenching his fists on the table, "we have less than 48 hours to take this weapon out. You heard what the President said. I can put a team together right now and mobilize them, but I need a destination."

"Well, if you hadn't lost it—" Carlson spat a knee-jerk response.

"*I* didn't lose it!" Hall threw back at him.

"Whoa!" Griffin interjected, holding out his hands—a referee at the fight. "Let me get this straight. General Hall, you said that you didn't lose it. How can that be?"

"I..." Hall averted his eyes, his confidence momentarily gone. Pulling himself back up, he continued. "I wasn't in on it."

"You weren't in—"

"The Weatherman Project. I'd heard rumors about a weapon, and I knew they were developing a substantial upgrade of the B-2 Spirit, but they wanted to finish developing and testing the weapon before they released details to us."

He looked at the other two. "There was some guy called Shanning who was running—"

"He's dead," Griffin said. "Samakab made sure of that. And then he destroyed the development computer for HAPISAD." There was silence in the room as they each processed this.

"So, what was so secret," Carlson said, slowly and pensively, "that the top US military weren't involved?" He looked around the table. Who the hell was organizing this and spending billions on it?

"That's a long story," Griffin offered, "but not for now." The other two stared at him. What did he know that had so obviously been kept from them? Why? Under his outward display of composure, Griffin sensed that Hall was devastated by what appeared to be the President's lack of confidence in him, and the impossible situation he had now been placed in. "If it's any consolation," Griffin continued, "I think the videos you just saw were the first the President knew of any of this as well."

"That's impossible!" Hall flared up. Of course it was impossible. The President was the Commander in Chief. He *had* to know.

"Unfortunately, it isn't. I can tell you that other governments are also involved, but beyond that, I'm not at liberty to tell you anything. It has to come from the President, and it will only come from him once this mess is cleared up. At least, that's how I'm guessing this will pan out." He watched each of them as they took in this fresh information—a shock for both and an insult to their offices.

"We need a solution," Griffin said. "How can we locate AVTOL?"

Hall looked at Carlson, who looked back at him. Neither spoke.

"How can we locate AVTOL?" Griffin asked again, with more urgency.

"From what I understand… we can't," Hall said, looking at his notepad, clicking his ballpoint.

"Can't?" Griffin tried to catch Hall's eye. Hall looked up at him.

"From what I was told on the phone on the way over here, it has the highest level of stealth known to man. Higher than the old B-2. Unless it wants to be found, we can't see it."

"What about satellites or an eye in the sky?" Griffin was scrambling for clues. He wasn't sure of the technology, let alone the terminology. Hollywood drama was his only point of reference for the snooping technology that might be available. *Why am I driving this conversation?*

"The area we have to search is just too big. It could extend to the whole of northern Africa," Carlson mumbled.

"But surely it would have to be near a source of fuel?" Griffin asked.

"It depends how organized they are. They could transport fuel to most places, and hide both AVTOL and all the ancillaries. We've already set the wheels in motion for a visual from space, and we can overfly the area but... 48 hours isn't long enough. Anyway, we may turn up nothing."

"What about the guys at the base in Somalia? Surely they can help? They must know something."

"We flew some marines from Camp Arifjan—that's in Kuwait, our nearest base to the location," Hall said, "but the guys at the AVTOL base said they knew nothing and the recent mission instructions came through encrypted so they couldn't figure them out. Also, they had been compromised."

"How so?"

"Threats to their families and friends—their entire local communities, in some cases."

"This is crazy!" If these two men couldn't offer anything, who could? "What about the videos? Were there any clues on those? Let's look at them again."

"Forget it," Hall replied. "The videos say nothing useful, and there's nothing in them that identifies location. In the first one, we just have a table and a cloudy sky. In the second one, there's just that dreary monologue with old footage and captions about Africa's history of invasions, exploitation and abuse by western countries, and how they intend to 'turn the tables'."

"But it also contains an ultimatum to cut off supplies of all mineral resources, oil and just about everything else."

"We'll see if that happens," Carlson chipped in. "In our experience, African countries can't organize jack squat without it breakin' into a fight, and the day they all start cooperatin' with each other on an organized basis, pigs will fly. But," he continued with a renewed aggression in his voice, "I'm gonna nail that son of a bitch who gave it that title—Educatin' the Gothic Serpent, my ass."

"What was that about?" Griffin hadn't understood the significance.

"Operation Gothic Serpent. That was the 'Black Hawk Down' operation in '93..." His voice trailed off as he remembered the disaster that had cost the US military so dearly.

"So... Let me get this clear." Griffin loosened his tie and undid the top button of his shirt. "We have less than 48 hours to locate and destroy a weapon that cannot be found by any means at our disposal. At the same time, the NSA is weaving a story for the world's media that will discredit the video and trump it as a hoax and a bad joke. What happens if Samakab has the ability and the will to use AVTOL again to deliver HAPISAD somewhere else?"

CHAPTER 47

Sheryl arrived back at the office as the two generals were about to leave.

No Larry.

In an effort to fulfill their appointed roles, both generals had devised plans, although their plans seemed more like aimless, random acts of desperation. *When you are lost in the forest, stop running,* was the phrase that came to Griffin's mind, but the generals were men of action, with heavy responsibilities, and stopping was not an option for them. They had to do *something*, and they were experts at defining lists of possibilities, tactics, research and strategies. But, as they left the office, Griffin had no doubt that these two men, working with the best of the Defense Intelligence Agency and the considerable military might at their disposal, would be wreaking unjustified and deadly havoc in all the wrong places. A show was required, and they would deliver it with gusto. The stage had already been set with the usual suspects as the main characters. No doubt the first act would be a quick and decisive thrust of a sword into the heart of a well-known villain: Al-Qaeda.

And what of the British? They were, after all, the ones who had been hit. But to the US military, it was almost as if that incident were just a side show—a taste of what could be coming. As the evening wore on, Griffin kept in close contact with both generals and the White House. It appeared that the disc had not been delivered anywhere else, as no other countries were admitting to having received one. The British would surely have reacted strongly if they had seen it.

So, what was really going on? Griffin was working in a vacuum yet, ironically, fate had placed him firmly at the center of this problem. He was the one the President and the military were focusing on as he was the only person with any information at all. Or, as with the Middle East peace deal he brokered, was he just being set up as the fall guy again? He couldn't afford to think such thoughts now. Anyway, this conundrum hadn't come about as a result of the usual international political bickering. It was due to the greed and inhumanity of powerful people. It was high-level corruption run amok.

And who was Samakab, anyway? As Troy had mentioned, the intelligence services had little or nothing on him, probably because he was being protected—but by whom? Griffin's uncertainty around Samakab's intentions left him in a tortuous limbo, as they appeared to be doing with the governments of all countries. It appeared to him that everyone in the corridors of power worldwide was playing a waiting game—waiting for someone else to play their hand and set the world's collective reaction in motion. Griffin was certain that the Americans would be falling over themselves, at the top level, to cooperate with the British investigation and assist them in any way they could. They needed to be fully conversant with every detail, every thought, every nuance. The only way they could control the story that finally emerged was to lead it, and the Americans were far better equipped than the British to do that. Keeping the lid firmly on the ugly truth of the matter would be their top priority. The fact that the ugly truth was such a fantastic scenario worked in their favor, in that respect. Who would believe it?

"You look wrecked." Sheryl's voice pulled him from his vortex of thoughts.

"I think I am." He looked up at her with tired eyes, blood-shot and grey with heavy shadows. "Shipwrecked in space, on a distant planet. I don't feel I'm a part of this place any more. I feel alienated—as if I don't belong here." He squeezed Sheryl's hand. "You're my only anchor. The only person I can truly trust and the only one who's keeping me here. What's the point of all this, Sheryl? Look at us. We're spending our lives trying to 'do the right thing' within a system that's rotten to the core. We're working without the full cooperation of those who stand to gain most from what we're trying to do. We're tip-toeing around protocols and niceties so we don't offend the egos of people who've messed up. We're afraid of being locked away by people who are looking for scapegoats. We try to protect people from their own lies and dreadful acts. Why? Why don't we just step out of it all and let them get on with it? If people want to kill each other, why should we stop them? They hate each other anyway." He let go of her hand and gave a hopeless wave. "Oh, I don't know. I don't know what I'm talking about any more. I don't know what to think. Am I going nuts?"

"No, I think you're just tired and hungry." It was a coward's answer, and she knew it. She could no more answer those questions than Griffin could. All she wanted to do right now was rescue her husband and leave the other questions for later—when there was time, when they had the luxury of headspace to muse over life's meaning. "I hope you don't mind, but I've asked Fernando to join us."

"Why on earth did you do that?"

"Because he's a great cook. I figured that we wouldn't be going back to the apartment for a while, so I called him on the way back from the airport, and he offered to make us something to eat. He'll be bringing it in a few minutes."

"I'm not sure I have time to eat. I have to keep up with what's going on—"

"And what is going on?"

Griffin stopped. *When you are lost in the forest, stop running.* "You're right—as always—thank you." He put his feet on his desk, leaned back and cradled his head in his hands, smiling. "Okay, bring it on! Let's eat."

His cell phone buzzed and started edging its way over the desk toward him.

"Troy?"

"Hi, Griffin."

"Any word from Samakab?"

"No, but I'm gettin' Twitters on my iPhone from David Arbuthnot in the UK. You remember, the guy who went to Afghanistan?"

"I remember. What is he saying?"

"I'm not sure. The messages are kinda garbled and strange."

"Yes?"

"Well, bear in mind that this guy's mind is a bit outta balance since his trip, but…"

"Never mind that, what's he saying, Troy?"

"I don't know, but I just kinda got a hunch…"

"What kind of hunch?"

"It's a long shot, but I think he can help us sort this mess out."

"Troy. I need a little more than that. Give me some reasons."

"Truth is, Griffin, I don't have any more than this hunch. Look, I feel kinda outta my depth here. It's just a feelin', you know?"

"Just a feeling?" Griffin thought back to the meeting he'd just finished with the two generals—people who were meant to know how to deal with these things, and yet were at a complete loss. Maybe it was time to explore some new ways—*weirdo ways?*—to discover new solutions, even if it meant working with a computer geek in his 20s whose mind didn't seem to be quite in balance, by 'normal' standards. *But then,* Griffin thought, *it was supposedly normal minds that had created the mess they were in.* The more he thought about it, the more it made sense—on an intuitive level. "At this point, feelings are all we have, so maybe we should act on them." He paused to reflect. "Should we get him over here, do you think?"

"I'd hate to send y'on a wild goose chase…"

"Troy, remember our deal. I'll support you. We're all out of our depth here, and we need to investigate everything that could give us any idea as to how to deal with this."

"Okay, but he won't wanna come, you know. And his wife, Barbara, will protect him like a Rottweiler. She hates us and everything we stand for—and for good reason. By the way, she has no idea that he went to Afghanistan. We fed her a cover story. I don't know if David's told her…"

"Sure. I understand. I think we can handle all that. Just send me his contact details. And send me those Twitters… tweets or whatever you call them, so I can take a look at them."

"Will do."

"Oh, and Troy… I think you're in the clear, for now. The guys at the NSA have other things on their mind."

"That's good. I'll get on a plane—"

"Do you like it there?"

"Sure. Dolores loves Saratoga Springs and we've been shopping in—" Troy caught himself. "Hey, we got more important things to talk about—"

"No, that sounds pretty important to me. Stay there. Enjoy. I'll call you when it's time to come back."

Fernando arrived, bearing food and wine in two large paper bags. The contrast that Fernando cut with the generals who had recently left couldn't have been more marked. His skinny, effeminate frame was clad in tightly-fitting black leather pants and a silky red long-sleeved T-shirt with a multi-colored Chinese dragon graphic wrapped around it. His hair was colored pitch-black and cut with a long asymmetric fringe that he was continually brushing out of his left eye. It annoyed the hell out of Griffin, who just wanted to get a pair of scissors and cut the damned thing off, although he didn't really want to get that close. They unpacked plastic boxes and plates, and Griffin uncorked the wine while Fernando served up a delicious-looking meal.

"We have a starter of leek tagliatelle and micro chives, followed by Paella Royale, with braised saffron rice, shrimp and clams. And for dessert, we have a choice of cheese or caramelized peach," Fernando enunciated the words so they oozed with delicious promise.

"I'm stunned! Fernando, thank you, from the bottom of my—our—hearts. I had no idea…" Griffin gazed in wonder at the feast laid out before them. Fernando had even brought freshly-starched white napkins and their best silverware.

"I'm not just a pretty face, you know." Fernando pursed his lips, cocked his head to one side and smiled cheekily at Griffin. Griffin still didn't feel quite comfortable with that, but he was slowly getting used to Fernando's effeminate mannerisms.

"You're joining us, of course," Griffin said, not sure if it was an offer or a question, as Fernando had laid three plates on the table already.

"Oh, thank you, sir," Fernando answered, coyly. He suddenly stiffened and looked around the room like a startled gazelle. "What a lot of TVs!" he said, as he sat down. "I didn't realize you were a closet couch potato, Griffin. And all this time I thought you were working late at the office. Shame on you!" He flicked a camp hand at Griffin. Sheryl smiled at Griffin's obvious embarrassment. Fernando glanced at the screens that were still displaying news items and discussions on the mayhem following the attack in London. The hunger for an explanation was turning to anger. The anger was turning to Al-Qaeda. "I suppose you've heard all about this simply awful attack on the British

Parliamentary Houses of Commons?" He rolled his eyes dramatically. "Well, I don't know. All those poor British people in London, England!" He leaned across and touched Griffin's wrist. Dipping his head to Griffin, with a deep intensity he asked, "What do you feel about all this, Griffin?"

"Well, it doesn't matter what I feel, it's my job to—" Griffin stopped short. He carefully scooped up some tagliatelle with his fork—as much to remove Fernando's hand from his wrist as to feed the intense hunger he'd become aware of since the food arrived. He started again. "What I feel..." He was struggling to find the words. He'd been focused on trying to work it all out, look for clues, reasons, answers. He'd seen all the misery and confusion on the TVs and had neatly filed it all away, each morbid detail tidily packaged with its own explanation. But had he stopped to feel anything? He wasn't sure. He'd been carried along by the momentum of *things that needed to be done.* Yet, when he was talking to Troy just a few moments before, he'd acknowledged feelings as the driving force of all actions. But he wasn't aware of his own feelings. Sure, he'd been horrified by the event. A torrent of emotion had swept over him. Ever since Bali, and his emotional reunion with Sheryl, his feelings had been growing and playing a much bigger part in his life. But what did he feel now? What was the feeling he needed to be in touch with to take responsibility, to take the right action? Was it compassion, aggression or something else? What part did cool, calculating reason play in a mad situation like this? How much ego would he need to exhibit to draw attention to what he had to say, so that he could deliver a solution—should he find one—and get people to listen and act on his words? Maybe there would be no answers if he wasn't able to get in touch with his own feelings. What did that mean, anyway—to be 'in touch with one's feelings'? *Am I being ridiculous?* He chewed his tagliatelle slowly as he thought it over.

"What I feel," he said, once he'd swallowed that first delicious mouthful, "is fear, uncertainty and an overwhelming desire to make things right." *Where did that come from?*

"Well, that's a relief," said Fernando, gently tapping Griffin's wrist.

"How so?"

"I'd always had this idea that you were some sort of doyen of government superheroes that live in Capitol Palace way up in the stars, but I guess you're just like the rest of us, really."

"Of course I am. Maybe I thought I was a superhero, in the past. But it's good to know that I'm actually completely ordinary."

"Not ordinary. Human. That's really super-incredible in itself. Well, I think so, anyway." Fernando turned his attention back to his meal, delicately picking up his fork.

"I think you're right." Griffin turned to Sheryl, who was concentrating hard on twisting tagliatelle onto her fork while, with her free hand, she covered her mouth, suppressing a giggle. He felt a bit silly. But he found the conversation quietly amusing. Here he was, struggling to understand himself and his feelings while talking to someone who seemed to be such a naïve innocent, totally immersed in his emotions and oblivious to what was really going on.

The phone rang on Griffin's desk.

"Excuse me." He went into the office and closed the door behind him.

"*What* is Griffin up to?" Fernando thrust his skinny shoulders forward, his head following like a gannet snapping at a fish. He was all conspiracy and gossip, reveling in being on the inside track. Sheryl flashed a glance at him, then took a deep breath and swallowed a mouthful of pasta. She took a sip of wine as she considered what to say to Fernando.

"Fernando, what's important to you—I mean, really, really important? Personally, what's the most important thing in the world for you?"

"Wow, that's a biggy! Well, let me think…" he leaned his elbows on the table and cupped his face in his bejeweled hands. "I suppose it would have to be peace and happiness for me and my family. Yes, a happy home. How's that?"

"Yes, I think I see that. And I know the lengths you go to make sure that others have a happy home as well. You certainly made ours more beautiful than I could ever have imagined a home could be—when I finally came to my senses." *Is he actually blushing?*

"Why do you ask?"

"That's what Griffin's up to. That's what's important to him as well."

The door of the office opened and Griffin came back in and sat down to continue his meal.

"Anything?" Sheryl asked. Griffin glanced at both of them. He didn't really want to have to start explaining everything to Fernando.

"Oh, it was just someone looking for Larry. I told him I don't know where he is." Sheryl looked up, concerned. Griffin sighed and decided to talk anyway. "I'm worried about him, Sheryl. That was someone at the CIA."

"Then surely we have the comfort of knowing they haven't got him."

"Yes, but we don't know if he's free, on the run, or in the hands of the Weatherman people, whoever they are."

"We have to believe he's still free, Griff."

"I'd like to believe that too, but I don't know." He slammed his fist on the table. The plates jumped. "I don't know, I don't know, I don't *know*! I'd just like to actually know something—anything! All this conjecture, the guessing games, uncertainties… How are we ever supposed to work anything out at all? Everybody has a different agenda! All these little pockets of self-interest, all these stupid, guarded half-conversations! Does anyone actually want to resolve this— even now, after all that's happened? How on earth can man survive if, when he's on the verge of annihilating everything he holds as important, essential, right, he's still playing these stupid fucking games?"

"Should I go? I should go." Fernando pushed his chair back as he stood up. Griffin waved him back down.

"Damn it, you're here now, so you might as well stay. I'm tired of secrets and lies. This involves all of us—the whole damn world, actually. What right have you got to butt out?" Griffin was as shocked by his outburst as Sheryl and Fernando. "I'm sorry." He put his fork down and rubbed his forehead. Fernando sat transfixed, staring at his plate. This time it was Griffin's turn to put a comforting hand on Fernando's arm.

"Well, I don't think—" Fernando started, faintly.

"No, you're quite right," Griffin jumped in. "I'm so sorry. I should know better."

"No," Fernando continued, "*you're* quite right. It's so silly to have to try to guess at how to help people. The problem is that people know how they want to feel about their home, but they just don't know how to do it themselves. That makes them angry and frustrated, because it's very, very important to them—to have a nice feeling in their home. I see it all the time. Some women aren't happy so they substitute their home for their heart, and pamper it and fuss with it to a ridiculous extent. The husbands usually get fed up and try to find that feeling elsewhere, in an affair or playing golf or something. It's desperate sometimes, and I get really, really upset seeing how important my work is for people."

There was a simple wisdom in Fernando's innocence that impressed and humbled Griffin. Surely, the achievement of a better feeling was the reason behind doing anything at all. Whether it was the simple action of taking a sip of wine, helping someone, even getting out of bed in the morning—everything was done to make a situation better or avoid it getting worse, to raise feelings to a better place. Fernando's ability to see things in terms of the ultimate aim of all actions, without the clouds of intellectualism and deviancy getting in the way, was something he was learning to appreciate. It was the kind of simplicity that attracted millions to great spiritual leaders throughout the centuries. They appealed directly to the heart. There was no place, or need, for rationalization and justification. It was the universal common understanding. And he was reminded of Larry again, and his work on the Hominine Balance Regeneration Project. It was all the same.

Griffin's cell phone rang. It was General Hall at the Pentagon.

"Griffin, we don't have time to pussyfoot around, so I want to come clean with you. This is just between you and me, understand?"

"Whatever we talk about will be shared with my team, General. We're clutching at straws here, so I'm not too concerned any more about political niceties. If you can live with that, then I think we can get somewhere." Griffin could hear Hall sighing at the other end of the line.

"I guess I'm going to have to. Actually, thinking about that, it will be a pleasure working with you on that basis. Kind of refreshing."

"Good. I'm relieved to hear that. What's on your mind?"

"First, I don't think we're going to get anything useful from Carlson. The intel coming out of Africa is patchy and it takes time to verify …so, bearing in mind the tight deadline we're working to, we can't rely on that. I think you could also guess from our meeting that we don't know how to defend ourselves against our own weapon. We built it too well."

"Right. So what are you suggesting?"

"We have to find a way to neutralize HAPISAD."

"I know that. That's why we're trying to get the Hominine computer shut down. The problem is that the only person who knows how to do that has either gone AWOL or has been compromised, and we don't know where either the computer or the weapon is."

"We need to concentrate minds. Have you got room for one more there?"

"Be my guest, but surely you're better off where you are? I mean, you have all the considerable resources of the State there. I have an office suite, some TVs and computers, my wife, Sheryl and our interior designer—and now chef…"

"I'm on my way."

Griffin stared quizzically at the phone, before gently returning it to its cradle.

"Is there enough of that paella for four?" He shook his head and chuckled.

A few minutes later, a wail of sirens in the street below announced the arrival of General Hall. Fernando prepared another place at the table, and was dishing up by the time Hall arrived.

"Welcome back," Griffin shook his hand. He introduced Hall to Sheryl and Fernando. "Hungry?"

"My stomach could eat a horse, but I have a feeling that my brain and mouth will be otherwise engaged. Thanks, all the same." He sat. "As you know, we have been seriously caught out by this situation. It would seem that you're the only person I can talk to about this weapon, so I hope you know a hell of a lot more than you told us at our previous meeting."

"You're talking about the original Hominine Project as well as HAPISAD, I guess."

"That's right. Who's running it?"

"I don't know, and I don't think we'll ever find out. Whoever they are, they have the US, Chinese and Russian governments in their pocket. They're smart, ruthless and pretty much untraceable. And I don't know about the whereabouts of the computer but I suspect that it's not on US soil."

"Okay, so we have to find a weak spot. What do we know about HAPISAD as of this moment? I understand that it's programmed to match moods, intentions, emotions and so on. Apart from the attack on London, how has it performed so far?"

Fernando placed a plate of steaming paella in front of Hall.

"Apart from the first mission, when it hit the wrong targets because the software was still in development, it's been faultless."

"What about London, though? It was surely meant to be taking out all the government members who were going to vote to send the troops into Somalia." Hall couldn't resist any longer. He let his hunger get the better of him and took a stab at some paella, raising his eyebrows and nodding his approval as he chewed.

"Yes… So, what are you saying?"

"Well, it missed some of its main targets, didn't it?"

"Who?"

"The Foreign Secretary. It hit everyone around him—the Prime Minister, the Deputy Prime Minister, the Chancellor of the Exchequer and just about everyone else on the front bench, but it missed him." He took the opportunity to have another mouthful as he waited for Griffin's reply. "This is great paella, by the way."

Fernando shifted in his chair, a smile breaking on his lips as he brushed his fringe out of his eyes.

"I wouldn't assume that it misfired," Griffin replied.

"Why not? This guy was the biggest advocate of the Somalia mission in the whole of the British Government. It must have misfired." Hall wagged his fork in Griffin's direction. "This is something we can work with, I'm certain of it."

"Party politics."

"What?"

"Party politics. That's all it was. I can guarantee it. The Foreign Secretary had a duty to follow the party line on Somalia. The reason he didn't get hit was most likely that he didn't believe in the mission, that he privately disagreed with it. He couldn't say that in the House, though. He's a professional. He knows how to lie convincingly."

"What about that other guy, Boyle? He was showing plenty of aggression. Why didn't it get him?"

"Because he was passionate about the people of Somalia. His anger was supporting them, not aimed against them. The way this weapon works is just as the voice said on that video. It knows the truth of what is going on inside you. It's a phenomenal piece of programming."

"If it knows that kind of truth, we have to find it and destroy it." Hall continued eating. Griffin did a double take.

"Did you hear that?" Griffin asked. Everyone stopped moving and listened.

"What?" Sheryl asked.

"What the General just said."

"What about it?" Hall looked up from his paella.

"You said, 'If it knows that kind of truth, we have to find it and destroy it'."

"Well, of course we do. If something knows the truth better than us... I mean, if we... Shit. Look, all I know is that we've got to protect our democracy..." He gave up trying to explain and looked around the table. All eyes were on him. Everyone was speechless. He carried on eating. Having set him up for the fall, Griffin came to the rescue.

"Of course, the General is right. We need to destroy the weapon and preserve truth. Is that what you were saying, General?"

Hall nodded.

Chapter 48

@troydolores In yr opinion, was London attack same as Afghanistan?
@rbuttnot Yes. Good to hear from you. Are you feeling better?
@troydolores Yes
@rbuttnot Good
@troydolores It is time for Vaspan
@rbuttnot What do you mean? What is Vaspan?
@troydolores Assalaam alaikum
@rbuttnot What is that?
@troydolores Language of peace
@rbuttnot We all need some of that
@troydolores Bacha Baazi – your betrayal. G. danced your dance
@rbuttnot Don't understand. We miss G. very much
@troydolores Dead men don't walk
@rbuttnot Too many dead in London
@troydolores I don't buy Taliban. idea. Hardly possible for them. Who did it?
@rbuttnot Rogue militant. Have to stop him. Trying to find solution
@troydolores You have it. Everybody has it
@rbuttnot Pls explain
@troydolores Look at the bodies
@rbuttnot No time for mysteries. Pls explain
@troydolores Nobody wants the answer. Everyone searching. No one listening.
@rbuttnot Of course they want the answer. If you know something, pls explain
@troydolores lol
@rbuttnot can we talk?

'…and that was the last I heard from him. I didn't get a reply to my last question.

Regards, Troy.'

Griffin couldn't figure out the Twitter conversation. But although it was jumbled, he could see why Troy had a hunch that David Arbuthnot might know more. And the David who'd returned from Afghanistan didn't seem to be the kind of person to make things up or play practical jokes. On the other hand, David hadn't known anything of HAPISAD, even after the London attack, so what could he possibly know now? Presumably, all he knew about that attack was what he had seen in the press, and that wasn't exactly enlightening.

The press hadn't been briefed on the true nature of the injuries. Additionally, those who had been in the Chamber but had not been targeted, were either mute on the subject or locked away to keep them from talking. But whatever hidden meanings this Twitter conversation contained, Griffin didn't feel that General Hall would know how to use it constructively, so he decided to keep it between him and Sheryl, for now, and work on ways to find out more from David directly. He closed the e-mail window and walked through to the main office where Sheryl was at her computer. Fernando was clearing away the dinner plates and carefully arranging grapes and cheese on a platter. Hall was sitting at a desk in the corner of the main office, talking on his cell phone, getting updated on the military defense plan his people were working on, should there be a similar attack on US soil. However, based on AVTOL's range, its relatively low cruising speed and the assumption that it was somewhere in northern Africa, he regarded a defense plan as something of a routine precaution.

"Any luck?" Griffin asked Sheryl.

Hall finished one conversation and his cell phone immediately rang again.

"Some progress, I think," Sheryl replied. "I'm now following his @rbuttnot identity as @sherylbcool. Let's see if he'll follow me back so we can start sending direct messages and we won't have to be so obscure in our conversations."

"That's great. I just hope he doesn't suspect he's being watched. He may be keeping this identity for conversations with specific people."

"If he is, he simply won't follow back."

"I'm impressed. I still find Twitter a complete mystery. How on earth did it get so popular?"

"Well, I'm no expert," said Sheryl, "but it's the programs around Twitter that seem to make it useful, so you can search subjects, conversations, places— all sorts of things. Hey!" She looked at her second screen as it alerted her to the arrival of an e-mail. "He's following me back! Great. Now we can figure out a real conversation. What shall I talk about with him, Griff?"

"Wow, that's good news!" Hall suddenly closed his cell phone, stood up and walked back to the table, his eyes fixed on the cheese platter. "I think we have a lead on that aircraft."

"Hallelujah! What's the story?" Griffin joined him at the table as Sheryl sat thinking about how to strike up a conversation with David in the UK.

"Apparently, some truck driver in Djibouti was on a stop-over in Berbera— that's the sea port in northern Somalia—the same night that the AVTOL was hijacked. He said there was something going on in the port. From the window of his hotel nearby, although he didn't have a clear line of sight, he said he thought he saw an aircraft landing on the dock—but coming straight down, unlike a normal aircraft. When he went down to the port in the morning, to pick up his load for the trip back to Djibouti, there was no aircraft there. He couldn't figure it out. He said there was no way it could have taken off again. He'd have heard it."

"Why did it take him so long to say anything about it?"

"It took him a few days to get back to Djibouti, and he didn't see any reason to mention it to anyone. Anyway, he said he thought that people would think he'd been chewing too much wacky weed and he'd lose his job. Whoever heard of a plane landing on the dock in Berbera?"

"So why did he eventually say something?"

"It was when they told him to go back to Berbera for another load from the dock. He didn't want to, because there'd been a lot of guys with guns hanging around. That's when he told his story, and it started doing the rounds in Djibouti as tea house gossip." Hall popped a handful of grapes into his mouth.

"But if he said the aircraft wasn't there in the morning, how do we know he's reliable, and how does that help us?"

"Because I am now told the Weatherman Project was using our latest cargo ship, the *Norfolk Defender*, for supplies. It also left Berbera that night, according to what we could ascertain from another contact." He cut a large slice of Emmental.

"So, you're saying…?" *Doesn't this guy ever get a square meal?*

"Exactly. The AVTOL landed on the *Norfolk Defender*."

"That's incredible!"

"It's insane. That's what it is. And very worrying from another point of view."

"And that is?"

"If they've also hijacked the *Norfolk Defender*, and they're somehow launching the AVTOL from its deck—which, in my opinion, is about the stupidest, most irresponsible and dangerous thing they could do—it means they must have sailed up the Red Sea, through the Suez and into the Med. That would explain how they could have hit London. *And* it would also explain the lack of intel Carlson was getting from Africa. They're closing ranks and cooperating with each other. Those bastards are really looking for a fight and, believe me, they're gonna get one!" He rammed the Emmental between his teeth as he hastily picked up his jacket and put it on. "Mmmm… mmmm…" He removed the cheese from his mouth. "We've got the Sixth Fleet in the Med, Command and Control on the Mount Whitney. I think we have a carrier in Naples and we've got Task Force 66/69 submarines underneath. These amateurs have bitten off more than they can chew. Gotta go." He shoved the cheese so forcefully into his mouth it made him cough as he fast-marched to the door, slamming it hard behind him.

"My, oh my! There's a man on a mission!" Fernando brushed his fringe out of his eyes, as if regaining his composure in the wake of Hall's energetic turbulence. "He should try some of that wacky weed before he gives himself a hernia."

Griffin was in a more somber mood. All the private reasons why Hall had chosen to work with them rather than immerse himself in Pentagon politics had evaporated with that phone call. Something fresh in Hall's mind had been snuffed out and he had reverted to his familiar role and methodology. It was all the more worrying as Griffin instinctively felt that this was no time for kneejerk military reactions. He wasn't sure what the appropriate response should be to this new intelligence, but Hall's reaction felt dangerous to him—just like the reaction to 9/11 had felt wrong. It felt as if everything Hall represented was designed to bring about a bigger conflict. The same old reactive cycle fed by fear and national ego would be repeated. Nothing learned and everything lost. Again. Even now, with the future of the world balanced so finely, the old ways of doing things still held sway. There had to be another way—one that worked. Wasn't that exactly why the visionary Hominine Balance Regeneration Project had been put in place? If the old ways caused an escalation in violence around the world, which they surely would, Griffin feared that the Hominine Project might never be used and would probably be destroyed. If that happened, he could see no end to the destruction.

"Griffin?" Sheryl had turned away from her monitor and seen the look on his face. "Is there anything more we can do here, right now?"

"Yes. We have everything to do. We have to find a real answer." Griffin forced his attention away from Hall and his war games and tried to re-focus. The 48 hours they had were diminishing so much faster than he could find a workable solution. "Any luck with David in the UK?" He felt desperate asking such a question. It was such an unlikely possibility that talking to David would lead anywhere at all, but it was, alarmingly, the only option Griffin had, right now.

"Not yet. We need to figure out what we say to him, first," Sheryl replied, her eyes fixed on her monitor.

"Of course. I'm distracted… Look, never mind Twitter. We have to call him. Get his number in the UK."

Sheryl started searching the UK telephone directory. "Damn," she said, "I don't know what to look for. Troy said he's staying with his parents somewhere. He probably doesn't have a phone account."

"Well, there can't be many Arbuthnots in the directory, surely?"

"Can I suggest something?"

"Anything."

"Skype. I'll probably find him easily on Skype and, if he will talk, we can use video. It'll be more private for him, and I think we could put his mind at rest more easily if he could see us."

"That's a great idea. Let's do it!"

Sheryl pulled up Skype and discovered 11 David Arbuthnots, but only one in the UK. She put in a contact request.

"I'm using the same ID as on my Twitter account, so hopefully he'll recognize me as the person who just connected with him there."

"What time is it with him?" Griffin asked.

"It's early evening. I just hope he's coherent. Those Twitter messages were fairly confusing."

"Can you talk to him, Sheryl?"

"Why me?"

"I don't know… I just feel he'd be more at ease with you."

"Hmm… he doesn't want to talk. He's just blocked me on Skype. He must think I'm after his body or something…" Sheryl fired off a message on Twitter.

@rbuttnot Hi David. Can we talk on Skype?

The reply came back in an instant.

@sherylbcool too busy. What you want?

"Griff," Sheryl looked pleadingly at him, "give me a hint, a clue… something!"

"What makes you think *I* know what to say?" Griffin scratched his head. "Hold on. Let me think." He paced the room then came back to Sheryl's desk. "Be his mother... No, be a concerned friend. Damn it—just be you. I can't think of any better tactic here. If we want some help, we've just got to tell him."

"He could freak out." Sheryl was feeling the pressure of this one-hit chance.

"He could be grateful." Griffin leaned on the back of her chair. "Yes, he could be grateful for a chance to say something. Let's put that out there, and see if he comes back to us in a positive vein."

"Okay, here goes."

@rbuttnot V. important. Need to talk with you about London attack

@sherylbcool As does rest of world. All waste of time

"Shit." Griffin shook his head. Sheryl tapped a quick reply.

@rbuttnot and Afghanistan

@sherylbcool What you know about that?

@rbuttnot Your pain. No need to be a Tower of Silence any more

"That's a bit risky," Griffin murmured.

"Nothing ventured, nothing gained."

Nothing came back.

"Plan 'B'? E-mail?" Sheryl looked up at Griffin. He shook his head.

"Let's give him a few minutes." In his mind, Griffin was starting to berate himself for having no fresh ideas. It seemed ridiculous to be struggling with this kind of touch-and-go communication when so much was at stake. His cell phone rang. "Yes? Troy. Hi. What's up?" Griffin rubbed his eyes as Troy spoke. "Yes, just do that, and stay by the phone in case we need to talk more." He slipped his cell phone back into his pocket. "David just sent Troy a tweet. It simply said 'traitor'. I guess he figured that Troy must have set this up as he was the only person who knew about Afghanistan. But at least it confirms that David has made a clear link in his mind between the two attacks—for all the good that does us at this moment."

"Maybe I shouldn't have—"

"No, it's okay, honey. It was always going to be delicate, and we don't really know his state of mind yet. Let's keep trying. Troy is replying and is going to try and put his mind at rest about you."

"Coffee?" Fernando asked from the other side of the office. "I have a nice Fair Trade, Rainforest-friendly 100% Arabica…"

"Thanks. Come on, Sheryl. Leave it for now. Even if Troy can convince him you're okay, he'll need a few minutes to think this over."

Fifteen long minutes passed. They all drank their coffees in silence. In front of them, the muted images on the TV screens continued to show the now familiar mix of discussion with scrolling headlines and quotes from world leaders. There was footage of terrorist camps, men with faces obscured by black cloths waving guns in the air, scenes and animated graphics of the House of Commons overlaid with commentators offering their opinions. All of these images were interspersed by the regular advertising slots with their incongruous smiling faces, clean washing, neat lawns, elaborately-designed razors, flashy cars and computer graphics. Griffin felt dog-tired. He walked over to a window to get some fresh air, only to find that they were all sealed. He had to make do with the dry, soporific air conditioning. His cell phone pinged. It was an SMS from Troy.

'Sweet-talked DA. Told him u + S r good guys. Saved my life. Filled him in on H***S*D. Shud b OK now'

"Good work, Troy." He showed Sheryl the message. She went straight back to her computer.

"Nothing yet. Oh, hang on, I'll just refresh…"

"Anything?"

"*Yes!* He's unblocked us."

Griffin pulled up a chair beside Sheryl. She opened Skype and located David in the list of contacts. He'd personalized his account with a picture of Popeye guzzling a can of spinach.

"Has he got video? I'd like to see him while we're talking."

"Yes, see?" Sheryl pointed at the blue video icon on his page. "But it's up to him whether or not he switches it on. I'll switch ours on as soon as we connect."

"Okay, go!"

"Are you sure? I mean, shouldn't we talk about strategy or something first?"

"No. Better to wing it. This guy will know if we're being authentic. We need to talk with him on a very human level. I don't want to come over all official and that after what he's been through on our behalf, I think he deserves our respect."

"That's all very well, Griff, but if he's got PTSD, we need to be aware of—"

"No. We're talking to the man, not the condition. It's up to us to be real with him."

"Right. I like it." Sheryl smiled at him. "Wherever did I find a wonderful man like you?"

"Don't you remember? I was in the mud. Just like everyone else."

Sheryl pressed the button to connect the call.

CHAPTER 49

Griffin was taken aback by the young man who appeared on the screen. He knew David's age but, somehow, with everything that was going on, it hadn't occurred to him that he and Sheryl would be talking to someone who was young enough to be their grandchild. He hardly even looked as if he shaved. He felt a wave of guilt and remorse about what he'd suffered.

"Hi, David. I'm Griff and this is my wife, Sheryl."

"Hi. Nice to meet you." David's voice was a little flat, his eyes vacant. They flicked from side to side as he spoke.

"Thank you for agreeing to talk to us this evening, David."

"So much information. Nothing understood. Nothing." David looked to the side of the screen. "Oh, sorry. I have three monitors. Look." His hand covered the lens for a second as he reached out and unclipped the camera from over the monitor and moved it around to show Griffin and Sheryl two other monitors. He replaced the camera in its original position and gave them a weak smile.

"What are you watching?" Sheryl asked.

"Oh, it's Twitterfall, Tweetbeep, Twitturly and a few others. I've never seen so much activity going nowhere."

"You're following the fallout of the London attack? That looks like an impressive setup you have there."

"It's what I do. What I *used* to do. It isn't very healthy..."

"Yes, I guess you need to make sure you get some exercise. Do you have a gym near you?" Sheryl smiled into the camera. Griffin put his arm around her shoulder. David watched.

"I can't go out. I have to look after Josh—keep him safe while Ba—Barbara, my wife— is out working."

"Sure. Well, I guess that's a full-time job in itself."

"Yes, it is. Do you want to talk about the wounds?" The directness of the question took them aback.

"Yes, if you feel up to it. That would be great," Griffin said.

"That's why we're talking, isn't it? I don't want to waste your time or mine. I have a lot to do."

"You're right. We're all very busy. Let's talk about the wounds."

"If Ba comes in, I will have to shut the call off."

"Sure, whatever. Let's get started."

"I lied to her, you see." David looked round, checking to see the door was closed. "I haven't told her about... my trip."

"Okay. We understand, but if you do have to shut the call off, will you promise to get back to us as soon as the coast is clear?"

"Yes, I can do that… Sheryl?"

"Yes, David." Sheryl leaned into the monitor a little.

"Can you come over?"

"Well, I, er…"

"I'd really like you to."

"One day, sure. But with all this going on right now, it's a bit difficult."

"Promise me. I just promised you, now you promise me."

"Okay. I promise. I just don't know when I can—"

"Soon. Please. Troy just told me about you. I want you to do something for me."

"What's that, David?"

"I want you to tell Ba about my trip. She wouldn't believe me because my head is all screwed up, I think. Please? I can ask her to forgive me. Yes, I can do that, but I need you to tell her about the trip." Sheryl looked at Griffin, who gave her the slightest of nods.

"Sure I will, David. Just as soon as I can. Let me have your address and phone number and I'll let you know the minute I can arrange it."

David put his hand to his mouth to suppress a cry. He breathed heavily and then said, "Thank you." There was a long pause. Griffin and Sheryl waited while David blew his nose and checked his other screens. He seemed to have lost track of the conversation and forgotten about them.

"David?" Griffin cautiously leaned toward the monitor.

"Yes? Oh, sorry. I forgot. Look, I don't have long. Josh has to be put to bed soon. Let's get on with it."

"Yes, let's." Sheryl pressed 'record' on a voice recording program, and they both sat back as a torrent of words, accompanied occasionally by gestures and David leaning into the camera whenever he wanted to emphasize something, flooded from him through the video screen.

"Do you know about chakras? They're the energy centers along the spine located at major branches of the human nervous system. That's made up of three systems: the sympathetic, parasympathetic and central nervous systems, right? They start at the base of the spinal column and finish at the top of the skull. Each chakra is a nexus of the body's biophysical energy. It's the most basic component of your *subtle body*, your energy field, and it's the key to life and the source of all energy in the universe. There are three groups of chakras. The first are the lower or animal chakras. They go from the toes to the pelvis and relate to our evolutionary origins in the animal kingdom."

Sheryl looked at Griffin and raised her eyebrows. He nodded again and turned back to David. *Let's hear him out.*

"Next, the human chakras run along the spinal column. Lastly, the higher or divine chakras are located from the top of the spine to the crown of the head. So, anyway, a chakra receives, assimilates and expresses life force energy. Each chakra in your spinal column governs bodily functions near its region of the spine. There are seven of them, which reflect how the unified consciousness—some people call it the soul—is divided to manage different aspects of earthly life like the body, our instincts, emotions, communication, our view of life and even our connection to God—if you believe in that stuff. The chakras are placed at different spiritual levels. Sahasrara, that's the crown chakra, is the one at the crown—as you'd expect—and it's concerned with pure consciousness. Muladhara, the base chakra, is at the bottom and is concerned with matter... Was that Ba?" He turned around again and then returned to the camera. "No, it's okay. So, anyway, where was I? Oh, yes. Well, it's obvious, isn't it?"

Griffin and Sheryl were knocked out of their dazed state by the question.

"Obvious?" Sheryl said.

"Yes, of course it is!"

"I'm sorry, you'll have to help me out a bit here, David. I'm not really up on my chakras." Griffin was really beginning to wonder if they were wasting precious time on wacky New Age stuff. But his conversation with Larry about 'weirdos' was in the back of his mind, so he thought he'd better not cut the conversation just yet.

"Those wounds! They were all at specific chakras!"

"Go on." Sheryl felt Griffin flinch beside her, but she was determined to hear David out.

"The wounds in the top of the head were at the crown chakra. The crown chakra is to do with meditation, mental action, emotions, universal consciousness and unity. But its role is tied to the pituitary gland, which secretes hormones to communicate to the rest of the endocrine system and also connects to the central nervous system via the hypothalamus. The thalamus has a key role in the physical basis of consciousness. The wounds at the throat were at the throat chakra, which is all about communication and self-expression. Emotionally, it governs independence; mentally, it governs fluent thought; and spiritually, it governs a sense of security. The wounds in the torsos were at the solar plexus chakra. This one governs issues of power, fear, anxiety, opinion-formation and introversion. Physically, it governs digestion; mentally, it governs personal power; emotionally, it governs expansiveness; and spiritually, all matters of growth. Do you get it now?"

"That's fascinating, David," Sheryl took over, sensing that Griffin was getting impatient, "but how does that help us?"

"It doesn't, actually," David replied. Griffin couldn't stifle a tense sigh. "Well, not as such, anyway."

"So…?" Sheryl prayed he'd come up with *something*.

"Well, what's interesting is the chakras that didn't get hit."

Griffin perked up at this. "How so?" he asked.

"Think about it." David sounded more upbeat now, and his eyes were brighter. "Whatever killed those people didn't hit the heart chakra. That's the interesting one. The heart chakra is all about complex emotions: compassion, tenderness, equilibrium and well-being. Physically, it governs circulation; emotionally, it governs unconditional love for the self and others; mentally, it governs passion; and, spiritually, it governs devotion. There's your answer."

"Er, where's the answer?" Griffin couldn't see any relevance whatsoever.

"Think about the video. You know, the one that was uploaded to YouTube."

"What about it?"

"Who didn't get hit?"

"As far as I could see, everyone in the village got hit."

"No, they didn't. The four priests didn't get hit."

"Why not, do you suppose?"

"Because they were meditating. They were in a higher state."

"I'm sorry, David, but you're going to have to explain."

"Whatever this weapon is, it's damn clever. But it has a weakness. It's not a flaw, but it's definitely a weakness."

"Please, just tell me."

"It can identify and target those parts of people that govern negative emotions, bad or angry thoughts, fear, anxiety. In other words, it targets all those qualities that those three specific chakras where the wounds are always located represent and that would have been active at the time those people were hit. But it can't target the highest, most powerful and best human quality of all—love."

"My God." Griffin and Sheryl sat back in stunned amazement.

CHAPTER 50

It was getting very late. They were all exhausted after a long and intense day. Fernando had gone back to the apartment to get some rest, promising to return first thing with fresh coffee and breakfast. Griffin and Sheryl felt obliged to stay in the office, just in case there was some communication from Troy, or anyone who could shed some light on the likely course of events, or even offer some tangible solution. They weren't hopeful.

The call with David had been a revelation. Both of them were euphoric to have found a possible weakness in HAPISAD, but that quickly turned to exhausted depression since they were at a complete loss as to how to exploit it. The military machine would now be in full swing in the Mediterranean, in an attempt to somehow prepare a reaction to Samakab's non-specific threat. Griffin could imagine the tense alertness in the pitch black of the Mediterranean night sky, as they searched for the *Norfolk Defender*, determined to neutralize it before dawn, if possible.

Following the call with David Arbuthnot, Griffin had had a short conversation with General Hall to brief him on the new information David had given them. Hall had brushed the information aside, preoccupied as he was with overseeing urgent military maneuvers.

"Senator, I'm surprised at you," Hall had said. "I don't have time for this hippy crap right now. I enjoyed our meal but I think we can take it from here. Why don't you get some sleep and check the news in the morning?" He was all bravado and confidence, thankful to be back in the saddle again, among friends, and enjoying a favorite military pastime of dissing a politician. Griffin couldn't think of a convincing argument, so he and Sheryl slipped off their shoes, cleared a desk and lay down for a brutally uncomfortable rest.

They didn't have to wait till morning for some news. From where Griffin was lying, he could see the TV screens. In his heavy, sleepless stupor, he slowly became aware of a change in the rhythm of the images. He opened his eyes and tilted his head up. 'Breaking News' was coming up on three of the screens. He looked over at Sheryl who was shifting around, trying to find a comfortable position where the desk didn't dig painfully into her bones. Griffin rolled over, away from the screens, determined to try and relax. He closed his eyes. A few seconds later, they were open again. What was he doing? They'd stayed because they wanted to keep informed. They wanted to be in a position to act. Otherwise, they might just as well have made themselves comfortable at the apartment. But he didn't want to get up. Nor did he want to lie here. It was just too painful. Maybe a chair would be more comfortable. His mouth felt dry. His saliva tasted stale and sticky on his lips. His shoulder hurt. So did his hips. He sat up. The screens were reflected in the window. 'Breaking News'. *Get a coffee.* He tip-toed over to the coffee machine and looked at it. The bag of freshly ground coffee was there, and a jug of water next to the machine. The machine had dials and buttons with little icons on them. Griffin couldn't figure out what they meant. Too complicated. He wondered past the TV screens to the water dispenser. What he would give for a shower! The cool water was refreshing as it slipped down his throat.

The telephone rang and brought his attention fully into the room. *Damn!*

"Judy? Hell, what time is it?" He looked at his watch. "It's 3.30 in the morning, for God's sake. What's up?"

"Sorry to call so early, but we need you back here, Griffin."

"Judy. What the hell are you doing in the office at this unearthly hour?"

"I got a call. Someone at the White House was asked to find you. Have you seen the news?"

"Well, no, actually, I was trying to get some shut-eye..." He looked toward the screens. This time he was awake and it registered. 'Breaking News'. "Hold on, Judy." He walked through to the main office, found a remote and turned up the sound on one of the screens. Sheryl shifted and turned her head toward him. She scowled.

"Sorry, honey."

"*... actually is unclear, but it appears that a Turkish cargo ship operating under radio silence as it attempted to break the Israeli blockade of Gaza, was hit by a torpedo and is now listing heavily to port. All crew and personnel have been safely rescued from the ship, which they say was carrying food, medical supplies and equipment, schoolbooks and other educational supplies.*"

The images were night-vision camera shots from a helicopter hovering above the stricken ship. Lifeboats were being lowered from the deck and a winch operator in the helicopter was lowering a cradle for an injured member of the crew.

"*No one has yet claimed responsibility, although naturally all eyes are on Israel as being the only nation in the area with the motive and the capability to launch such an attack...*"

"Judy. What the hell is going on?"

"It's another mess, Griffin, but you'd better resume your Middle East peacemaker role. The White House is in negotiations with the Israelis to see if they will take responsibility for the attack. I think we have a good chance, and it would seem to be the most expedient way to deal with this. They'll take a lot of flack, but they're well able to deal with it, with all the experience they've had—"

"Judy! Stop right there. What are you talking about—'negotiations to see if they'll take responsibility', 'the most expedient way to deal with this'? Are you not telling me something?"

"Oh, darn. Griffin... you're not going to like this..."

"Hit me with it."

"It was the Sixth Fleet."

"*What?*"

"You'd better talk to General Hall. He can brief you on what to do now."

"Like hell he will!" Griffin slammed the phone down so hard its plastic casing cracked. Just like the world, events were spinning on an axis. Old mistakes were buried in propaganda and the inertia of time, lessons left unlearned. New mistakes spun into view—each more catastrophic than the last. And with each new mistake, the stakes got higher. Griffin could act out the entire play in his mind. Act 1: the public shocked reaction and sympathetic statements; the secret deals to apportion blame and decide on how to cut the cake. Act 2: the publicly declared resolve to get to the bottom of the problem; the secret creation of a new script, while replacing the ugly truth with officially sanctioned 'evidence'. Act 3: wow the invited audience of political leaders and media with decisive action. Arrange some heads on plates and hope that the audience has been so well-entertained that, by the final curtain, the problem has been 'finessed' enough that they can continue partying. Unfortunately, it wasn't usually that neat and tidy, and the people that suffered were so often innocent. Griffin felt like screaming. How many more times would he be asked to play this game?

Griffin called Hall's number.

"Hall?"

"No, General Hall is busy right now—"

"Get him. This is Senator Kirkland." Griffin could hear raised voices as the person who answered the phone called out to Hall.

"What?" Hall barked down the phone. He was seething.

"That's what I want to know. If you're asking me to explain this away..." Hall changed his tone immediately as it registered who he was talking to.

"Oh, lordy, lordy. Have we got a shit storm going here! Look, Senator, I was out of line earlier, when I made those comments to you, and I apologize. And now look at me—egg all over my face and an international crisis on my hands into the bargain."

"Never mind all that—but thank you anyway. What happened?"

"Our guys were under extreme pressure—from me—to find the *Norfolk Defender*. Some trigger-happy submarine captain who wanted to be a hero didn't do all the checks..."

"You mean he couldn't tell the difference between an old Turkish diesel cargo ship and the latest American nuclear-powered vessel—?"

"There were some doubts, a lot of pressure, and the *Norfolk Defender* is known to disguise itself pretty well… but no, he didn't check it out…"

"General Hall, my office just told me that we're actually in negotiations with the Israelis to see if we can get them to take the rap for this. Is that correct?"

"That's kinda the way we were thinking of going—"

"Don't you think that's just a little immoral, politically suicidal and downright stupid?"

"Senator, diplomacy is your bag, not mine. I just do my job—"

"If only!"

"Senator. We're playing a dangerous game here—"

"Correction: *you're* playing a—"

"We have to find a solution that will create the least impact. Look, Israel needs us a hell of a lot more than we need them, and they would feel mighty isolated should we withdraw our support."

"A friend in need…"

"Sure they are. And I think they'll see reason. If they take the rap for this, they'll be assured of extra support from us to help them over this immediate crisis and into the future. If they don't…"

"As you say, General, diplomacy is not your bag. Unfortunately, it is mine, and I have a feeling that you'll be passing this bag of worms back to me once the deal is done. You'll want me to build some trust around your lies. Unfortunately, your brand of pragmatism isn't one that I can support."

"Then I am sure the President will find someone who can. We don't have the luxury of time or resources to pussyfoot around on this one, Senator. Are you in or are you out?"

"General Hall, when you first came over to my office, I thought I could work with you. I had a lot of respect for the way to chose to look for new answers in unlikely places. Right now, I'm really disappointed. I don't think I judged you wrong, but you've let yourself sink back into the political mire. You started slipping as soon as you thought an easy solution had turned up, with the discovery that AVTOL was on the *Norfolk Defender*. Now you're actively embracing the charade, because you think it will protect you from your mistakes. Can't you do better than that? Don't you think it's time for us to start finding fresh solutions?"

"Thanks for the character assessment, Senator. Let me know what you decide." Griffin put the phone down and slumped in his chair. Stark choices. Sheryl shuffled into his office, rubbing her eyes and yawning under a haystack hairdo. She plonked herself on his lap.

"What's happening?" She breathed warm air in his ear.

"Same shit, different day," he said, nuzzling her neck. He longed for some soft comfort, oblivion.

"Different day? Already? I haven't finished the last one yet…" Dawn was breaking. They'd been up for hours in Lebanon, Iran, Iraq and Gaza. The TVs showed them shouting on the streets, waving banners and burning Israeli flags. But for Griffin and Sheryl, in their sleep-deprived stupor, it was all a blur. Within seconds, they'd finally surrendered to blissful sleep.

Ten minutes later, they were jolted awake by the phone on Griffin's desk.

"Don't move." Griffin reached past Sheryl and picked it up.

"Senator. Apologies for the early call. This is Jim Carlson, AFRICOM."

"How can I help, Jim?" Griffin leaned back in his chair, letting the phone slide off the desk and hang, suspended just above the floor.

"Well, sad to say, it looks like Bernie Hall fucked up in the Med. Can't say it surprised me. He was always an arrogant—"

"I've spoken to General Hall already."

"Good, good. Well, anyways, we got a few more problems now, in addition to the London thing, and well, how shall I put it, we've got ourselves a bit of firefighting to do here."

"That's an understatement, if ever I heard one."

"Yes, well. Here's what we're gonna do. I'm lettin' you in on it first so you can start makin' preparations, you know?"

"I don't know yet. It would help if you told me what I have to prepare for." Griffin rubbed his eyes, willing himself to pay attention, concentrate.

"We think the Israeli situation can be brought under control in just a few days, but we need to show some action on the terrorist threat, to kinda divert attention from it and distract the Brits from lookin' too deeply into how their Houses of Parliament came under attack. At the same time, we gotta protect our supply routes and our raw material resources. So, we've come up with a plan to do both—kill two birds with one stone, so to speak."

"Unfortunate metaphor, but what's the plan?" Griffin couldn't stop himself yawning. He wished Carlson would get to the point.

"Well, I think it's kinda neat, 'cause it'll also create some great PR opportunities for you guys into the bargain."

"This doesn't sound good, Jim." Griffin sat up. Sheryl stirred and leaned over onto the desk, resting her head in her arms, trying to edge back into sleep.

"Hey, Griffin, you're a real cynic… but you're an okay guy as well." Carlson gave a tense laugh. "Seriously, Griffin, I've always admired your work." He paused to allow Griffin to acknowledge his ingratiating comment. Griffin said nothing, so he continued. "It's like this. Iraq is just about finished, as we know. The President has committed to no more combat activities. We done that one and we already had a plan to pull the troops out but, as you know, that got kinda complicated and it hasn't happened yet. So, we're gonna speed that up, and transfer some units from Iraq to Suez for the time bein', to secure the canal.

It seems the Egyptians have a lot on their hands and can't be trusted with that right now, and we don't expect a whole lot of aggression from them 'cause they need to get more revenues outta the canal. They've been fallin' *precisely because* the canal and the Red Sea haven't been secure."

Carlson paused so Griffin could react, but Griffin remained silent. Carlson continued. "Then I—that's AFRICOM, you understand—am going to offer logistical support to the Europeans who are itching to get stuck into Somalia. Between you and me, I think they will spread out beyond Somalia once they get in, but we can't be seen to be gettin' in the way of the Chinese by getting' too involved in the scrap. With all the money they're plowin' into the region and the resources at stake, it's best we leave them to get on with organizin' things on everyone's behalf. As you may know, we're kinda workin' with them—on Africa... Anyways, for now, a bit of logistical support is real cheap for us, as we already have units in the area, the navy is already working the Gulf of Aden and we figure that an early withdrawal from Iraq will save us a shitload o' money even after we've got set up in Egypt. They're gonna make a decision about that on the Hill, maybe tomorrow or the next day."

"And how does all this help in terms of finding AVTOL and stopping Samakab?"

"Oh, yeah. The other neat thing is that we're blockading the Straits of Gibraltar. We have three destroyers heading there right now. In a few hours time, the *Norfolk Defender* won't have a hope in hell of getting outta the Med."

"And what if it isn't trying to get out of the Med? What if it's already docked and AVTOL is unloaded?"

"If that's the scenario, that's fine too. Then there's no threat."

"No threat?"

"No threat, that's correct."

"No threat to whom?"

"To us, of course. The good ol' US of A."

"And that's meant to make the Europeans feel better?"

"That's up to them. Look, I can only be concerned with our national interests and security. All I know is, if there's no immediate threat to the US, and if the Europeans are clearly focused on Africa, should—God forbid—there be another attack, then the situation is contained, so far as we are concerned."

"Contained." Griffin was lost for words. This was pure farce. Worse than that, it was amateur farce being played with very dangerous big boys' toys. Griffin just wanted to go to sleep and wake up in Bali.

As Griffin scooped up the phone and replaced it on his desk, 3,800 miles away, the *Norfolk Defender* sailed west-southwest, hugging the coastline past Tangier, into the Atlantic Ocean.

Chapter 51

Raage checked his watch: 36 hours had passed. It was time. He made his way through the *Norfolk Defender*'s deserted hold, between the metal tables decked out with humming computer equipment and screens playing a variety of what looked like drug-induced screensaver animations, to the container where he'd hidden the case he'd transferred from his SUV at the base in Somalia. He unlatched the locking bars and swung the doors open. Pulling the key from the cord around his neck, he unlocked the case. The booby trap device he'd switched on in Somalia was still showing that the case had not been tampered with. From among the contents of the case, he removed one of two satellite phones, a rugged laptop and a cable to connect the two. He locked the case again and replaced the cord around his neck, then headed for the lift to the main deck. He set the computer and phone down on the aft hatch, booted up the computer and attached the phone via the cable and pressed its power button. He checked he had a signal and dialed a number. Once the connection was made, he punched in a code. A single tone on the handset indicated a successful connection and the screen displayed a message: 'Begin download 1?' He pressed 'yes' and sat himself down on the hatch, watching the blackening clouds drifting slowly across the yellow-tinged horizon as the download bar on the laptop's screen inched its way across its window. The download completed in half an hour. It was followed by three more downloads. One was a small one entitled 'Messages'.

"So, this is it." Raage took a deep breath and looked up again at the evening sky before opening the message.

‡ proceed M25 ‡

Route 3

Ilko wada jir bey wax ku gooyaan

"Double-cross, proceed with mission 25. Fantastic! But what's this? Route 3? No!" His heart sank. Everything had been going so well, apart from a few minor setbacks with the crew on the ship. He quickly fired of a question.

Why Route 3?

The answer came back in an instant.

Katla

"What on earth…?"

Katla?

Volcano-Iceland-eruption anticipated

Damn! There had been warnings of a second eruption in Iceland—from Katla, a volcano with ten times the explosive power of the one that had disrupted flights all across the northern hemisphere in April 2010. Now he knew he was on his own. He wouldn't be coming back. He reluctantly sent a confirmation message.

Δ acknowledge Route 3

His sacrifice, though, was an honor. He knew that, but it still scared the hell out of him. He had to do it. He would do it. He owed it to Samakab and to their shared family to exact a long-overdue act of revenge. And his act of martyrdom would also lift their troubled nation to new heights. He had always known that, one day, the call would come. He'd prepared all his life for this moment of glory. He was to become immortal.

"Route 3 it is, then. *Ilko wada jir bey wax ku gooyaan.*" Unity is power.

Raage closed the laptop and returned to the hold. AVTOL stood silently in the gloom at the far end on the hydraulic platform below the forward hatch. A huge dark leviathan in surgery, with cables and hoses dropping from its body and wings, snaking across the platform, some attached to the computer banks on the tables. It was almost ready to launch, as far as Raage was concerned. None of the multitude of essential checks had been done, of course. Blemishes on the wing surfaces and their carbon-reinforced plastic leading edges had not been patched. Some ragged tapes around the few access panels had not been replaced. None of the 140 on-board computers had been run through their extensive checking procedures. But it was fueled up, and it *would* fly. He sat down at a computer at one of the desks, connected a network cable to the laptop and set to work. During the voyage from Somalia, Raage hadn't been idle. He'd worked with the programmers to understand all he needed to know about programming HAPISAD. Ralph's cooperation had been won after he'd helped mop up the remains of the Somali guard who'd been shot early in the voyage. Raage had spent hours with the pilots who, in unguarded moments, had given away vital pieces of information about AVTOL's operation. And, of course, he'd accompanied them on the London mission, so he had seen, from the seat behind them in the cockpit, how certain operations were carried out. He didn't know how to launch or land the aircraft, but Samakab had made provisions to deal with that as well, in a way that wouldn't require their cooperation—which was just as well, as they were among the most difficult of his captors to deal with, and yet essential for success.

Four hours later, he'd finished working on the computer. He had to be ready to take off in eight hours. He disconnected the network cable, slipped the satellite phone into his pocket and returned the laptop to its case in the container, where he connected it to the second satellite phone and launched a procedure. He closed the lid of the laptop having first switched off 'sleep' mode. He powered up the phone, placed it carefully back in the case, removed a small package that he slipped into his jacket pocket, and locked the case again. Hiding the case behind other equipment, the last thing he did was to open several of the metal cases that were stacked in its floor-to-ceiling racking system. As he exited the container, he swung both doors wide open, then made his way back to the lift, setting his watch alarm as he walked. He had a long day ahead of him, and he wanted to be sure to get some rest.

His alarm jerked him awake. For a second, his mind told him to forget. Just keep sailing. Go to the Canaries—they are straight ahead. Find a nice hotel on a beach. Even as he dragged himself off Baptiste's bunk and glanced at the photo of Baptiste's girlfriend on the nightstand, his mind was imagining a different life— a happy one that continued into old age. He washed and opened the door.

"Get the pilots," he told the guard. "Bring them to the galley for breakfast."

Raage worked fast but in a daze, preferring not to be quite conscious of where his carefully conceived actions would take him. Going through the procedure mechanically, he fought to keep his emotions under control. Like a pack of hungry hyenas circling his fear, they threatened to devour his resolve. He tried to blank them out, force them down, by focussing obsessively on the details of the job in hand. Fortunately, there was a lot to occupy his mind. He organized the guards, briefed the pilots on what he referred to as 'a short trip southwest, over the Canaries'. Then he paid a final visit to Baptiste who, after so many days in captivity on the bridge, out of contact with a world that appeared to have deserted him, was a pale reflection of the man Raage had first met in Berbera.

"Soon, you will have your ship back, Captain," Raage told him, crouching down next to him where he lay on the floor of the bridge, trying to rouse himself after yet another dreadful night. "Why don't you go home, and marry that nice girl?" Baptiste looked at him but said nothing—his eyes vacant, his mind switched off. Raage ordered the chief mate to open the forward hatch and prepare to raise the platform. Turning to the guards, he said, "Once we have gone, lower the platform and close the hatch. Your job here will be done and you will no longer have to guard the crew. All you will need to do is to gather all the men in the hold where I have made preparations for your departure." The guards let out a cheer and waved their guns in the air. This was good news.

Back in the hold, Brian and Frank were doing their final checks as the hatch above them slid open. It had been an extremely delicate task for Raage to maintain their cooperation. Raage was constantly vigilant, just in case they were tempted to risk the lives of their families and friends by doing something to disrupt the mission. Fortunately, the family values they held dear were among the many reasons they were chosen to pilot such an aircraft. As long as they were unaware of the nature of the mission, Raage felt he could manage their priorities. Additionally, Raage could see how, as the only people with access to AVTOL, they actually seemed to have developed a deep affection for it. They knew they had a huge responsibility to protect the aircraft, and this was something that came naturally to them as a result of their intense training. At this moment, as they walked around under the wings, making sure everything was in order, they felt challenged—working outside the rulebook, unable to fully meet their responsibilities yet committed to doing a professional job.

"Let's get on board," Raage said, as he signaled to one of the guards to start raising the platform. Brian opened the crew access hatch in the aircraft's underbelly and the three of them climbed up inside. The cockpit was cramped, with every inch of wallspace bristling with controls and equipment. Brian, as mission commander in charge of navigation and weapons delivery, sat in the left-hand ACES ll 'zero speed, zero altitude' ejection seat, and Frank, as pilot, sat in the right-hand one. In front of each of them was a 'glass cockpit' with four color CRT multifunction displays and a fighter-style control stick to control the aircraft. The third seat, where Raage took up position, was behind them and to the right, separated from the pilots by a large bulkhead with more controls built into it. To Raage's left were a fridge, a microwave oven and a chemical toilet.

Raage had spent many hours, both on his own and during the flight to and from London, observing and learning. Having trained as a pilot, he could recognize and work many of the features but, of course, this aircraft was unlike anything he'd experienced before and he had to learn them from scratch. He was now familiar with the AN/APQ-181 radar—a Ku band, high-microwave radar, with an electronically steered antenna in the lower leading edge of each wing that provided high-resolution images for navigation and targeting. It also had modes that would allow the aircraft to follow the terrain when flying at low altitudes, look at weather patterns, follow moving targets and refuel in flight. It operated under 'low probability of intercept', with the radar constantly switching frequencies and changing pulse patterns so that its signals couldn't be picked out of background noise until it was too late. Another feature was a countermeasures suite—the Defensive Management System—that would protect the aircraft should it come under attack. All the avionics were controlled by 15 radiation-hardened Avionics Control Units, run by sophisticated software that provided a detailed cockpit data display to enhance the crew's 'situational awareness'. Raage had also grown fond of this cockpit, with its large windows and multicolored interior.

"It's a bit like flying a dumpster," Frank had said in one of his rare friendly moments, when the excitement of piloting this huge flying wing had momentarily melted the ice between them. AVTOL was easy and pleasant to fly, being so aerodynamically 'clean'. Also, although technically it was aerodynamically unstable, its fly-by-wire system and flight-control computer kept it in the air, demanding little of its pilot, other than a natural aptitude for computer games backed up by solid training.

It was easy to forget, sitting among the array of flashing lights and animated displays, that this Disneyland leviathan was actually the gatekeeper to Hell.

Frank fired up the auxiliary power unit on the forward end of the left engine assembly as the platform neared deck level, ready to start the engines. The platform stopped moving. The morning sunlight shone on a calm sea. The *Norfolk Defender* was gliding effortlessly, without a hint of vibration. Raage punched some numbers into his satellite phone and waited for a signal before shutting off its power and closing the access hatch to seal the three of them into the aircraft. He signaled to the bridge to hold the ship steady as Frank started the engines. Then Frank and Brian ran through the take-off procedure. As the pitch of the engines increased from a whine to a roar, Frank slid back the jet direction control to divert the power through the vertical thrusters. Brian kept a wary eye on the ship's crane, stored near the superstructure toward the stern, as Frank increased the thrust and the aircraft vibrated with the reflected buffeting from the blackened platform. Slowly, it lifted and rotated to face the superstructure. Frank applied a touch of reverse thrust to match the forward speed of the *Norfolk Defender* until they were clear of the crane and the superstructure. That done, he carefully applied forward thrust until the forward momentum carried them onto a cushion of air and he lifted the nose, firing the black dart upwards with gut-wrenching acceleration into the dark blue of the upper levels of the stratosphere. They roared up to 60,000 feet, floating off their seats momentarily as the aircraft leveled out.

"You know, Raage, this is just about the only place I feel at peace," Brian said, twisting round in his seat as the gently-curved horizon came back into view and the engines quietened down, leaving them suspended in a perfect dome of dark, cloudless blue. "Where do you find peace?"

"In my devotion."

"Devotion to what?"

"To doing what is honorable in the sight of God."

Brian scoffed. "Is stealing and killing honorable? That seems to be your main occupation."

"You tell me. Your country is much better at both than I could ever hope to be." Raage laughed at Brian's feeble attempt to take the high moral ground, and looked out at the blue that surrounded them—a vast, protective enclosure. Brian and Frank just saw a despot, a terrorist, a man without humanity or morality. But Raage knew he was a lover and a freedom fighter, and a man of honor. They were all riding in the same leviathan, and the only difference between them was who was in control. For the pilots, that was what would ultimately determine how history would remember them. For Raage, only God's judgment mattered. His was no sacrifice. "No more talking," he said, and settled into his memories for a while.

After half an hour, Raage's watch alarm beeped. He looked down at it briefly, smiled and then returned his gaze to the blue canopy. They were gone. Justice had been done. His and Samakab's family had been avenged with the blood of the children of their oppressors—the fishermen from Berbera who Kaahin had recruited for the journey.

Far below him, Baptiste was opening the door of the lift. The smell of burning flesh was like a kick in the gut, insufferable in the enclosed space of the hold, where all the guards lay lifeless, guns still in their hands. The open container was still smoking from the heat from the rocket-propelled HAPISAD missiles that had burst from it on the unsuspecting group. The twisted, burnt-out remains of a metal case lay on the floor of the container. Other than that, there was no damage in the hold. But the damage to Baptiste was complete. He stood, ragged and empty, surveying the wreckage of his life and career and the devastating consequences of a few unguarded moments brought on by simple boredom.

Raage kept an eye on the navigation radar display. They had been in the air for approximately one hour. He could see images of Tenerife and Gomera below them. In a few more minutes, they would pass over the smallest of them all—the tiny island of Hierro. He waited another five minutes, then reached into his pocket and pulled out the small package he'd taken from the case the previous evening. He removed the paper packing to reveal a small, zipped pouch. Inside, there were two hypodermic syringes and two glass vials containing a white liquid. Each syringe had been marked on the sleeve with three red lines numbered 1, 2 and 3. These correlated to the route numbers for the mission, with each number representing a specific amount of the drug that would be required for the time it would take to travel each route. Raage attached the needles to the syringes, and filled them both to the line marked '3'. Taking a syringe in each fist and locating his thumbs carefully on the plungers, he leaned forward and knelt on the bulkhead just behind Frank and Brian. Before they registered what he was doing, Raage aimed the syringes into the only bare flesh he could see—their necks. He connected with Brian's neck first time, but Frank suddenly leaned forward to alter a control, and the syringe went into his shoulder, puncturing his anti-G suit, before Raage quickly retrieved it and found his neck. He pushed hard on both plungers, emptying the syringes into their bodies.

Both men shouted in shock. Pain burned as they clutched their necks but, being fully strapped in, neither man could fight Raage off. Within seconds, they were succumbing to the drug.

"Enjoy a bit of moon walking, my friends," Raage murmured as their heads slumped forwards, relieved that the drug seemed to be working exactly as planned.

A doctor friend at the recently-opened hospital in Burco had supplied it. "It's 'milk of amnesia'," the doctor had told him. "It should do the trick, but you'll have to make sure you administer the right amount for the time you need them to be out of action. Too little, and they'll wake up too early; too much, and they could end up like Michael Jackson did when his physician prescribed some for him just before he died. Its proper name is propofol. It's used all over the world and it induces a little euphoria, hallucinations, and disinhibition— like a date rape drug. Just keep an eye on their breathing while they're out. It's a respiratory depressant; without proper monitoring and mechanical ventilation, they could get lazy about their breathing. You might have to force-ventilate them a bit—you know, kiss of life. You like the idea of a bit of mouth-to-mouth with an American pilot?" The doctor grinned at Raage's grimace. "The good thing is that, when they wake up, they won't remember anything and should be well enough to land the plane safely within a short while. When they first wake up, they may have a little trouble integrating information and focusing. Don't be alarmed by that. They'll get over it quickly."

As soon as the pilots were unconscious, Raage pushed himself forward on the bulkhead, taking care not to disturb the controls as he climbed over them. First, he changed the AVTOL's course to 285 degrees, which would take him just south of Bermuda, checked that the aircraft was traveling at its ceiling of 60,000 feet, and set the autopilot. Then he found the mission information on the weapons system computer and logged into the HAPISAD pod in the bomb bay, to run the final programming he'd uploaded the previous evening. Having nothing else to do for a few hours, he sat back in his seat and tried to stay calm. It was far too long to be alone at a time like this. His main fear was that he, Raage, would do something stupid. But what could he do? He could fly the aircraft anywhere he wanted but he didn't know how to land it. He searched his jacket pockets with his hands, hoping to find a few grains of sand to rub between his thumb and fingers.

CHAPTER 52

The rumblings were growing louder by the minute. The TV screens in Griffin's office now showed a sea of angry faces demanding recriminations, occasionally interspersed with other news—the imminently expected eruption of Katla in Iceland being the most aired. Sheryl was there on her own, most of the time—waiting for any news of Larry and any word from Samakab. Griffin's time was split between his two offices, juggling crises.

The sinking of the Turkish supply ship had effectively trashed Griffin's Middle East peace efforts. Worldwide, intolerance of Israel's policies was at an all-time high, based on the assumption that Israel had done it. Much of Griffin's time was taken up with trying to cajole the Israeli Government into accepting the blame for it. For their part, the Israelis were delaying the process in the hope of striking a better bargain with the US, in the form of military equipment. This, of course, was familiar territory for Griffin, who took it all in his stride but, this time around, hated every minute of it. It felt like a huge betrayal of the person he had now become. The only reason he continued doing it was to maintain his political status so that he would be in a stronger position to deal with Samakab and HAPISAD—although that particular challenge was proving greater than anything he'd ever faced before.

What government mechanism could he use to bring this daunting problem to the urgent attention of Congress? It was already straining under a vast and complex workload caused by crippling national debt, a broken healthcare system, rising unemployment, shrinking export markets, an energy crisis, the wars they were involved in—the list was endless. Added to that, the secrecy around the Hominine Balance Regeneration and Weatherman Projects made discussion of it virtually impossible. Time was running out. It would not be possible to arrange a closed session of the Senate, and there were no House Committees that enveloped all the cross-cutting issues and factors involved. A Committee of the Whole wasn't a practical option either. The available government mechanisms were simply not responsive or flexible enough to deal with an immediate crisis, especially at a time of paralyzing partisan gridlock and obstructivism. As with the mechanisms, so with the people involved—when a problem as far-reaching and unusual as this one landed on their doorstep, the systems and rules simply didn't work and the people who relied on them were lost. The harder Griffin tried to fight the fires, the more the blaze spread. The more the blaze spread, the more new fires it started. Like floating embers landing on new kindling, news was emerging of fresh crises being triggered by the existing ones—a nightmare expanding with unstoppable momentum.

One of the biggest raging fires was China. Since the big financial crisis of 2008, the Chinese had been voicing their concerns over loan repayments by America. The assumption in the US had been that such crises were cyclical, and that after the low there would be a recovery, just as it had always been in the past. However, this simply wasn't happening, and it was clear to economists worldwide that, while the Chinese had a strategy and a plan, the US didn't and confidence in it was waning. Even so, the US had assumed that it would not be in China's best interests to call in the loans, since it would be a sure way to lose some of its best markets. However, the US market itself was now shrinking and, in China, there was deep unrest. There was a growing resentment at grassroots level—a sturdy belief that hard-earned money had been squandered on investments in the US rather than being spent on building infrastructure to support their own hyper-expansion, which was now becoming unstable. According to intel, there were riots on the streets in many Chinese cities that were not being covered in the press because newspapers were being censored. Their first priority was to manage and control their own people, but now China also wanted their money back, and to hell with the consequences for the US market. Griffin also suspected that, with America's failure to keep the Weatherman Project under control, the Chinese were going to cut their losses, ditch the partnership and continue working on protecting their own sources of supply without US help. They had already made successful inroads into Africa, using checkbook diplomacy, a disregard for internationally-accepted market principles and a willingness to build relationships with African leaders considered by many world governments to be unsavory despots.

In Africa, attitudes toward the US were hardening sharply. Griffin couldn't be sure about it but he suspected that Samakab had shown copies of the videos to influential people in many African countries in the wake of the London attack. Even if he hadn't, the prospects for the US as a business or military supplier were being seriously eroded. Influential fundamentalist Islamic insurgents operating in many countries could depend on China for their military equipment at very competitive rates. They were putting increasing pressure on governments both militarily and in terms of turning populations away from Western influence— by coercion or conversion, it didn't matter to them. Everywhere it appeared, whether in commercial ventures or in military presence, the word 'America' seemed more like a call to arms than the promise of easy wealth that it once had been. Even relatively stable countries such as Kenya, Morocco and Egypt were realigning their allegiances as African unity began to establish itself as a viable concept. The tables were turning.

And now there were rumblings in Britain that threatened to ripple out to the rest of the European Community. It had become very clear, very quickly to the intelligence community at Northwood as well as the military services that the attack on the Houses of Parliament had been an extremely high-tech operation. In their frenetic search for a likely culprit, they had discounted a range of countries, one after the other, that might conceivably have had the capability to launch such an attack. The more they investigated, the less likely it appeared that any country, other than the USA, could have a weapon as sophisticated as the one that had been used. Even the lack of evidence in the aftermath of the attack pointed to a super-sophisticated weapon-delivery mechanism. So the British were asking some serious questions of the US, and they weren't getting convincing answers. As a few more upper-level people in the US military were being briefed on AVTOL and HAPISAD on a 'need to know' basis, it was only a matter of time before the system sprang a leak. Whether it was someone who found the whole idea of the Weatherman Project to be immoral, unacceptable and distastefully un-American, or whether it was simply a blunder, the truth would come out sooner or later. Griffin wondered who they would choose as peacemaker to sort that one out.

He was watching a whole new dimension developing in international relations. They had always been maintained through a fine balancing act of give and take, carried out variously in public and in private. But now it was different. Griffin cast his mind back to the death-defying high-wire act performed by Phillippe Petit between the Twin Towers in New York in 1974— a triumph of skill driven by a deep passion for perfection. Now they were trying to walk the tightrope of international relations without the towers of principles and humanity that the public might have rightly assumed supported them. A transformation was taking place in governments and societies around the world. An animal that was outwardly quite docile was now cornered and fighting for its life.

And it was all happening at lightning speed. The brushfire of communications technologies that had swept the globe facilitated and accelerated a process that would, just a few years previously, have taken months or years to establish itself. Now it was taking mere hours. Thoughts and ideas that had been lurking in the collective subconscious of entire nations, waiting for a chance to be expressed, could now burst out of the pressure cooker of tension, frustration and dissatisfaction. What would have been kept under wraps, hidden and suppressed to maintain balance in the interests of both sides of a dispute, was now freely flowing in the public domain. The result was a frighteningly frank expression of the dark side of humanity, and the shady shenanigans of its elected representatives. And it was all spurred on by the media and the Internet in their appetite for drama, giving voice to the basest of instincts, demanding answers—and never offering solutions.

"We're going back to the apartment," Sheryl said as soon as Griffin dragged himself through the door for another session of phone calls with Hall and Carlson. Sheryl had already switched off the TVs. "There's nothing we can do here, and you're in no fit state to decide anything. Come on." Placing her hands on his shoulders, she turned Griffin round and pointed him back toward the door. He offered no resistance. He was spent.

Fernando had already prepared something for them to eat by the time they arrived. They ate in silence. Griffin was preoccupied with a stream of problems that circulated endlessly through his mind. Sheryl was preoccupied with concern for Griffin's and her own fatigue. He wasn't getting any younger and she'd seen this kind of stress kill some of his colleagues in the past. Griffin was fearful of sleeping. He thought he would never wake up again, and there was far too much to think about, far too much to do…

Sheryl gently guided him to their bed, sat him down and removed his shoes. The relief! It took little more to convince him to undress and lie down. Just the softness of the mattress and the sensation of fresh, clean sheets against his skin was heavenly. He felt safe, and he entrusted himself to sleep.

Fernando watched the news.

"Katla has a caldera six miles in diameter. It was covered with ice up to 2,300 feet deep in places. Recent measurements that show that this ice cap is rapidly melting are of grave concern to scientists. To give you an idea of its potential for causing damage, you can compare the discharge at the peak of an eruption to the combined average discharge of the Amazon, Mississippi, Nile, and Yangtze rivers— about 9.4 million cubic ft per sec. Ash from the volcano has been found as far away as Norway and Scotland. There have been 16 documented minor eruptions since 1930. The last major eruption in 1918 resulted in Iceland's southern coastline being extended by 5km. Volcanologists who have been recording an unprecedented number of earthquakes in the area close to Katla say that an eruption is now imminent. Following the eruption of a neighboring volcano in 2010, the Icelandic President warned that 'The time for Katla to erupt is coming close. We have prepared. It is high time for European governments and airline authorities all over Europe and the world to start planning for the eventual Katla eruption'.

CHAPTER 53

'Go Vaspan!' The message from David Arbuthnot arrived on Griffin's cell phone while he was breaking a piece off his second croissant, the morning after a deep, deep sleep.

"What is this?" He pushed the phone across the table to Sheryl and took another sip of coffee. It was a fine, bright morning and the curtains waved lazily in the breeze. Griffin, fresh from the shower, wearing a clean, crisp, striped shirt, felt human once more.

"No idea, but it's a word I've seen before. He used it in the messages he sent to Troy. I'll look it up." Sheryl took her coffee through to the office and switched on the computer.

Still no word from Samakab. Heading back. Arr DCA 10.30. This one was from Troy. He must have figured out that there was little point in hiding out in Utah any longer, since Samakab's deadline was so close.

Griffin blanked and drank some more coffee. He felt neither happy nor sad, neither determined to act nor relaxed and content to do nothing. It was a strange limbo-land—a kind of sensory switch-off where nothing worked any more. None of the ways he'd done things in the past seemed relevant to the current situation or how to handle it. He'd personally gone through profound changes in a very short time, and the world had undergone its own shifts, taking it to a place where the rules that governed society's existence had changed. It was all unfamiliar to Griffin, as it was to the world as a whole. But everything that was happening—Samakab, Israel, London, Africa, China, Katla—seemed to be pushing him toward some pivotal point. And he had no markers, no framework—nothing he could use to define it. He could only guess that, because this was new, he couldn't possibly know the nature of it until it happened. He just hoped he would somehow find a meaning, have an epiphany, discover a reason and formulate a solution. *Damn!* He needed more than hopes and dreams right now. He needed something grounded and solid. His mind kept grasping for comprehension, order and logic so he could neatly package and communicate it all. Yet something inside him—deep, deep inside him—knew… something. *What?* Something in him knew that there were answers and solutions. He knew how incredibly resourceful and creative human beings could be—and that was, ironically, both the problem and the solution. From the little he'd grasped about the Hominine Project, he knew that Larry and his team had glimpsed the realm beyond conscious thought. The electric enthusiasm Larry emanated when he'd described the 'crude connection with the soul' that he and his team had achieved after years of research, had convinced Griffin that humans were so much better, more intricate and so much *bigger* than the sum of all their achievements. After all, what they'd achieved with the Hominine Project represented a connection with something that's a natural part of every single human being—the unique human consciousness, the true identity. Somewhere, in all that infinite subtlety, in all that unparalleled perfection residing in everyone, there must be answers. Griffin leaned back in his chair and caught a glimpse of Sheryl in the office, curved intently toward the computer screen. He called out to her.

"What?" she said, not looking at him.

He didn't reply and she eventually turned toward him, her nose crinkled in concentration.

"Nothing," he said, smiling. "I just wanted to look at you." How could he have neglected this beauty beside him during all his years of political pandering? Had he been out of his mind? Maybe the conscious mind was not the place to look for answers at all. He knew that the conscious part of the brain only represented a fraction of its total capability—only accounted for 5% of its mass—so it was hardly surprising that humans were unaware of their total brain power. Most brain functions were subconscious, and the subconscious processed a million times more information per second than the conscious. If the answers were in the subconscious—the more powerful part of the brain— was he wasting his time even trying to consciously conjure them up?

"I've found that name," Sheryl said, returning to her breakfast. "Vaspan. It means 'he who reaches the entire creation', or 'embracing all creation'. *Go Vaspan*. What did David mean by that, I wonder."

"I remember now." Griffin sat up straight. "David told Troy that was the name of the monk in Afghanistan—the one who made the original cell phone recording for the video about the HAPISAD attack that went wrong. My God…"

"What is it, Griff?"

"I was just thinking of everything that video set in motion. Just one video shot by a man on a mountain in the middle of nowhere who probably knew very little about the world situation. 'He who reaches the entire creation'."

"Yes. Talk about the butterfly effect… Do you think David's passing the torch on to you?"

"Ha! I don't think I have anything of great value to share with the entire creation."

"I wouldn't be so sure."

"What do you mean?"

"Griff, you of all people know that this situation isn't sustainable. Someone has to step outside the craziness and say *something*. I think you're just slightly better equipped to do that than that poor man standing on a rock in Afghanistan.

And look what an effect he had!"

Griffin slowly took a sip of coffee as he mulled this over.

"It gives me hope," he mused, glancing at the newspaper on the table.

"What do you mean?"

"Well, of course you're right. If he can get a message out to the whole world, we sure as hell should be able to do it as well."

"But we do nothing but that, every day, and nothing changes. Nothing improves. Nothing gets fixed. Nothing! That newspaper, those TVs in the office—"

"Yes, I know. But think about it, Sheryl. All those messages are about the problem—just as that video was about a problem. That's what gets our attention. Sometimes they trumpet some solution or other, but none of the 'solutions' are truly creative or free of an agenda. They're not really there for the good of mankind. They're generally Band-Aids, compromises, deals and PR. The problems are temporarily addressed to serve certain interests, until something else comes along and upsets things again. We never get to the *real* root of problems because we never truly deal with the human dynamics that create them in the first place. That's what Larry was talking about in Bali, and that's why the Hominine Project is so important. It was a first step toward redressing the balance in humanity that we've been eroding and destroying for centuries."

"But Larry isn't here, and he's the only one who can really understand the Hominine computer. Anyway, from what Carlson said, there isn't any immediate threat—"

"Of course there's an immediate threat! We've got a lunatic with access to the computer who knows enough about the program to feed information to HAPISAD. Just because we don't know what Samakab plans to do with HAPISAD, and Carlson thinks it's 'contained' in Africa, doesn't mean there isn't an immediate threat. And, by the way, I'd trust Carlson about as much as I'd trust you with my last bar of chocolate. He's just making an assumption—" Griffin was interrupted by his cell phone ringing.

"Yes?" His face dropped as he listened. He put the phone down. "That was Hall. An F-15 pilot flying over the Atlantic, reported a UFO above him, about 350 miles southeast of Virginia Beach. He reckoned that, whatever it was, it was heading toward Norfolk. They couldn't find it on the radar, so they've sent up another three F-15s to track it visually and to engage if it gets anywhere near the coast. Luckily, the F-15 can fly higher and nearly three times faster than AVTOL. The problem is that—if it is AVTOL— it's most likely seen the F-15, and could already be taking evasive or defensive measures."

Griffin's cell phone rang again. "Judy, hi. What's happening?"

"The President wants you for a press call on the lawn. It's about the Israeli situation. He needs to talk to you about it first. They're arranging it for 11am."

"I thought Carlson was dealing with that. It's a military matter."

"Carlson's AFRICOM, as you know. And as far as talking to the media is concerned, this is a mediation job, and the President needs someone who knows the territory. It's your patch, Griffin, and the President has every confidence that you'll deal with it far better than he could."

Griffin snorted. "And what about Samakab and the video? The deadline's almost up."

"From what I hear, the President isn't giving that one much credence. He's going to tough it out. And with everything that's going on, he can't be seen to be caving in to the demands of a terrorist. The military have it in hand, anyway…"

"Judy, have Hall's people been in touch with him—about a UFO?"

"I don't know."

"Make sure you talk to them."

"I'll try, but lines of communication are pretty well jammed up, right now."

"Do your best. It's important. In the meantime, I'll get down there and find out what the President wants me to do."

Griffin sighed heavily as he put the phone down.

"You're not going to do it, are you?" Sheryl was staring intently at him.

"What?" Griffin turned to her.

"Commit political suicide to protect the image of the President… again."

"Sheryl, it's my job. Come on, give me a break. We have a major crisis on our hands—probably the biggest one we've ever had."

"I thought your job was to work for peace. Last I heard, that was your special responsibility."

"That's what I intend—"

"The last time you did this, you didn't know you were being set up. This time, you do."

"The last time I did this, we didn't have a lunatic flying around God knows where, with our deadliest weapon in our own stealth bomber. I didn't even know about AVTOL or HAPISAD. Now I do, and I have a duty to help—"

"A duty? What is your duty, Griff? And you're right—now you do know. You *know!* So are you going out there to perform the same old charade that you played when you didn't know—when *they* were playing *you?*"

"Sheryl, you don't understand. People are dying—"

"Don't patronize me, Griff! I know people are dying. They always have died and they always will die—precisely because of the lies that we so efficiently spread through all our wonderful technology. Who, exactly, are the lies meant to protect? What lofty ideals do they support? How do they ultimately serve humanity? Wasn't it you who told me that we're at a tipping point? Didn't you tell me only two minutes ago that we're not offering any real solutions and that's exactly why this madness continues? 'Band-Aids, compromises, deals and PR'—that's what you said, isn't it? We're right on the edge and yet we're so blinkered, so conditioned and idiotic that we're still, even now, blindly following the broken, stupid, inhumane, selfish, destructive... Shit! Shit, shit, shit!" She marched over to the counter and slammed her plate down so hard that it shattered, leaving her holding a small ceramic crescent, which she threw on the floor.

Griffin got up and put his arms around her, squeezing her tightly. "I'm sorry, Sheryl. Of course you're right. It's a stupid game, and it's led us nowhere good."

He turned and leaned heavily against the countertop. "Fucknutsville. That's what they call it, you know—the people in the White House. The whole damned White House machine is grinding to a halt under the inhuman pressure of bureaucracy, congressional paralysis, systemic corruption and an irresponsible caffeine-powered media gagging for soundbites. How to break out of it?" He wearily shook his head. "I know it doesn't work. I know it's crazy. I know it's not going to produce any answers. It if did, we wouldn't be where we are right now. We'd be somewhere much, much better, if we..." he lost his train of thought, drifting back into the space he'd been in before the discussion with Sheryl and the phone calls that had brought him down to earth again. *If we... what?*

"Goddamn it! This stuff is so elusive, so slippery. Every time I think I have some clarity, it's there for an instant and then it's gone, as if it never existed. Why is it so damn difficult to hold onto it long enough to formulate some real thoughts so I can act on them? Sometimes, I feel that if I could just keep them there for a second, I could change the world."

"Griff," Sheryl put her hand over his, "what you're grappling with is huge. You not only have to navigate these complex international negotiations, which they're probably going to sabotage again anyway, but you're also working with a completely new frame of reference, *and* you're trying to formulate creative new solutions." She turned her head to face him. "Give yourself a break. Just take it one step at a time, but make sure that when you talk to the President, and to the press afterwards, you maintain your integrity and your authenticity. Nothing is worth compromising your values for—not now. You'll find that the right words come naturally, when you keep your real values front and center."

"I guess that's all I can do," Griffin said, shoulders slumping at the prospect. "The trouble is, I don't think the President or the press will be impressed with intuitive ramblings. They need structure and strong decisions to build confidence again. I don't think I've ever in my entire career felt so ill-prepared for a top-level meeting, and if I don't come up with some solid arguments and good sound bites, the press will eat me alive."

"You know what I think?" Sheryl slipped a hand around his waist. "I think you have to try something new. In fact, I don't think you have a choice. But that's good. If you can allow yourself to let go of the clever rationale you've been so good at in the past, and speak from the heart, you just might break through the slippery stuff in your mind to a place of real communication. People would appreciate that much more than a veneer of spin and empty reassurances. We're all tired of the gloss. Give us something real. I think that's what Larry was hinting at."

"But I don't know—"

"You will."

✷✷✷

Samakab checked his watch: 9am. CTV had just announced the upcoming press call. He looked out the window of his suite at the Willard, past the Treasury Department building to the White House gardens beyond. It was particularly satisfying to be staying at this historic hotel as he prepared himself for the moment that would change everything. It felt fitting to be standing at a window in the 'residence of presidents', where Woodrow Wilson once drew up plans to create the League of Nations, and Martin Luther King wrote 'I have a dream'.

The stage was set. Raage had done an excellent job and, by his calculations, he would be in position within the next two hours, and the videos had obviously had the desired effect: the President was going to address the nation.

Route 3 had always been the route he had intended for AVTOL. He just hadn't told Raage—in case he got cold feet at the last minute. Once this job was done, he had no further use for AVTOL. The fallout for the world was going to be so immense that AVTOL would become irrelevant anyway. The members of the 5T Movement had been hugely impressed by Samakab's display of power in London. It had given them renewed confidence and a solid unity that had only been politically-inspired wishful thinking until then. Once they saw this final, glorious act, they would spring into action—taking control of the African economies and striking new and much better deals with other nations. Africa would be reinstated as the powerful continent it once was, recognized and valued by a world in disarray—a world that still depended heavily on everything Africa had to offer. With insufficient resources to sustain its way of life and only worthless paper money propping up its economies, the developed world would collapse and the balance of power would reverse. Africa, the ancient seat of civilization, would also become its savior.

He had anticipated AVTOL being spotted on its approach to the South Carolina coast but, by now, Raage would already be heading for Chesapeake Bay with AVTOL's Defensive Management System activated to deflect any attack. The Air Force couldn't risk attacking it over American homes anyway, and AVTOL's final maneuver would make any attack all but impossible. Samakab relished the thought of AVTOL turning inland, making the wide swing to pass over Andrews Air Force Base while dropping steeply down from 60,000 feet to 2,000 feet and lining up for the final approach. He was especially looking forward to the moment when it swooped in from the Potomac, above the Washington Monument and onwards, over the White House.

Today, Samakab was posing as a network correspondent. He wore a checked shirt, khaki pants, a light jacket and deck shoes. In his wallet, he carried a forged White House press pass to get through security at the Pennsylvania Avenue gate. Once inside, he would mingle with the network and affiliate TV correspondents on 'pebble beach'—the gravel-covered area close to the West Wing lobby where they camped out and made 'stand-up' reports. He packed a shoulder bag containing a handheld TV, video camera, notepad and cell phone. Placing it on the table by the door of his suite, he checked his watch and settled down to read the newspaper.

Chapter 54

"Ready?" The President stood in front of Griffin, looking him square in the eyes. There was just the two of them in the Oval Office.

"You don't have to do this," Griffin replied. They'd only had 30 minutes for their meeting before the news conference. Half an hour to tell the President all he knew. It wasn't enough—nowhere near enough. He wasn't even sure that the President had actually heard him, preoccupied as he was with the immediate matter in hand: the statement on the sinking of the Turkish ship, and Israel's supposed part in it.

"Yes, I do, and I'd really appreciate your support." He offered Griffin his hand. Had he taken his warning about Samakab seriously? Had he dismissed the idea that the UFO sighting could possibly be AVTOL?

"You see, in this job, there are few people you can rely on. I can rely on my family—totally. I can rely on my team, to the extent that they are capable of doing what I ask them to do. Beyond that, I rely on rules, contracts, the law, agreements and good will. They're not so consistently reliable."

Griffin took his hand and shook it. He tried to read the President's eyes. Was he feeding Griffin to the lions? He couldn't tell. Griffin had performed magnificent tricks in the past—for him and his predecessor. Was this what the President was expecting of him now? There hadn't been time to draft a complete statement, so they had agreed that, once the President had spoken, Griffin would brief the press in more detail. But given the speed of their conversation and the topics they'd been under pressure to cover, although they'd scripted an outline statement that the President would deliver, Griffin wasn't exactly sure what was expected of him. He'd been so focused on Samakab that he hadn't had time to focus on his role in this event, which, serious though it undoubtedly was, was a sideshow to a much more threatening situation that was unfolding at lightning speed. He needed some reassurance. He needed Sheryl or Larry to walk in the door and clarify his options for him, to tell him what he should say and make him feel good about it. He'd changed, and he knew it. He knew he couldn't play the old game anymore, but it was so, so hard to find the courage to say it, let alone do it. Everything in his gut said, *walk away*.

"What do you want of me?" He even surprised himself as he asked the question.

"What do you mean?" There was a hint of impatience in the President's response. This was not the time to show insecurity, and this was the last thing he expected from a Senator of Griffin's long experience.

"Mr President, the last time I—" The President raised a hand to stop him.

"I know. We've both learned a lot since then."

"So what do I—"

"Just follow my lead." He turned and beckoned to Griffin to follow as he marched quickly to the door. It was time.

"We're doing the news conference in the Rose Garden."

"The Rose Garden?"

"Yes. You have a problem with that?"

"Not at all. I'm just a little surprised."

The Rose Garden had a special place in the history of the White House. The tradition of previous administrations had been to reserve it for peaceful and unifying measures. In 1994, for instance, Israel and Jordan had signed their historic peace agreement there. The garden had first been established by Ellen Wilson—the wife of Woodrow Wilson—in the early 1900s. It was a haven of peace and color, and a fitting backdrop to events that celebrated national achievements, heroes, peace and accord. Only once had that tradition been broken when President Bush made a speech there, advocating a ban on same-sex marriage. Conflict, disputes and the ugly details of war were discussed in the adjacent Press Room. So, to Griffin, it seemed like an odd choice for today's news conference.

However, as he and the President made their way through the colonnades to the podium, followed by the President's entourage, Griffin began to realize that this was no ordinary news conference. His car had dropped him at the West Wing lobby, so he'd not been aware of the activity taking place in the Rose Garden until this moment. The press were there, but not directly in front of the podium as he'd expected. Instead, they were arranged in two groups— one on each side of the lawn, just close enough to the podium for cameras to get a three-quarter view of it. Directly in front of the podium, and covering the entire lawn, were rows of seats, all occupied. *What's going on? We don't have time for this!*

Before he stepped out to the podium, the President stopped and, turning to the Homeland Security Secretary, said quietly, "Peter, I need you to do something for me."

"Sure, Mr President. What do you need?"

"I want you to send the security detail home."

"Mr President?" Peter drew a sharp breath of disbelief. "You want me to swap them over? Is there something wrong with—?"

"No, they're fine, and I really appreciate their diligence and professionalism."

"Hell, sir, I can't leave you unprotected. No way! I can't allow that to happen. What is this?" Peter was bristling. This was like a body blow to *his* diligence and professionalism. Then he remembered who he was talking to.

"Excuse me sir, for being direct, but really…"

The President held his gaze but said nothing.

"Okay, sir. I'll have them all go back to the office. But this is madness. It goes against everything we've ever done, Mr President, and after that security breach back in January, I thought—"

"I understand. But this is different and I have good reason. Don't worry. Nothing will happen and you're covered. Look, all these people are witness to me making this direct request." He made a broad sweep with one hand and placed his other on Peter's shoulder. Peter glanced around at the others, confused. Griffin noticed Dan Zielinski nearby. He managed to catch his eye and raised a questioning eyebrow. Dan shrugged. This was completely out of order.

"And by the way," the President continued, "I said 'home', not 'office'. I want them to go home to their families—spend some quality time. They can come back in again tomorrow." He signaled to Griffin as Peter walked away, trying to maintain his composure.

"A word, Senator." Griffin moved closer to him. The President looked over his shoulder at the others in the group as he placed a hand on Griffin's arm. They moved back to allow them some privacy. He spoke to Griffin in hushed tones. "We can't have any anger or fear here today." Griffin looked at him, astonished.

"What do you mean, sir?"

"I've been doing my own research, and I've been following your activities. Primarily thanks to you, but also thanks to the reluctant cooperation of certain other people in the wake of the mistake that we both know about, I now understand a lot more about a certain secret project that was initiated before I assumed office here. Also thanks to you and the young English friend you just told me about, I understand much more about the danger we now face. Andrews Air Force Base has confirmed a visual sighting of AVTOL. Because of its comprehensive defense systems, the Air Force cannot shoot it down. It will arrive shortly. My security detail would have been the first to be hit, should they have been on duty when it arrives. As I understand it, there's only one way to defend ourselves against this weapon. Whether or not we go out onto that podium, we are not safe, nor are all the people you see sitting out there. HAPISAD will seek out its targets wherever they may be, and we cannot operate the country from a concrete bunker, while leaving our citizens exposed."

He looked out onto the lawn. Expectant faces looked back. "There are many of your fellow senators sitting out there, as well as congressmen and women from the House. All of us were elected on promises we made and all of us recite the pledge of allegiance, with our hand on our heart, every day. What's happening right now may seem like a disaster, but what it's really doing is requiring that we genuinely step up to the plate, and live up to our responsibilities, whole-heartedly. And I mean 'whole-heartedly'. That's the only thing that can save us from AVTOL—our own product of our own fears. And even if AVTOL wasn't focusing our attention on what's really needed, strictly between you and me, it's the only thing that can save us anyway."

The President buttoned his jacket and straightened his tie. "You asked me back there what I wanted of you. I think you already know where the answer to that resides." He paused. "Shall we?"

✳✳✳

"Look, we have company," Raage said to the two comatose pilots in front of him. "We'll lose them soon, no problem." Three F-15s now accompanied AVTOL, keeping a safe distance, but occasionally swooping closer. Their pilots waved and signaled for AVTOL to land, but otherwise there was little they could do. Raage unclipped the pilots' oxygen masks and, pulling them away from their faces, held a small mirror in front of each pilot's mouth to confirm that they were breathing. Brian's breath was strong, but Frank's breath hardly fogged the mirror at all. Perhaps Raage had administered the wrong amount of sedative for him, or puncturing his anti-G suit had affected his lungs. The suit had sent a fine spray of fluid over the cockpit at their previous scheduled turn, when it automatically compensated for pressure as they pulled a few Gs. Either way, he wasn't too concerned. Brian could also pilot AVTOL …and land it, if necessary. Raage knew enough to make the final maneuver down to 2,000 feet, open the vertical thrust vents and slow the aircraft down to 100 knots by the time they arrived at the target. The F-15s couldn't follow him at that speed. They would stall if they slowed to 130 knots, so they'd just have to fly on by. Opening the bomb doors and releasing HAPISAD was simply a matter of flicking two switches, and the downdraught from the thrusters would accelerate HAPISAD's delivery. Nothing could stop it.

✳✳✳

"Good morning, ladies and gentlemen. Thank you all for coming. Today, I am going to make a statement concerning the recent sinking of a Turkish vessel in the Mediterranean, and I will, with the assistance of my Special Negotiator for Middle East Affairs, Senator Griffin Kirkland, be discussing wider security issues and peace initiatives." The President glanced alternately at the teleprompts on either side of the podium and scanned the audience as he spoke. Griffin stood beside him, in nervous anticipation. The rattle of press cameras punctuated the otherwise hushed gathering. Griffin faced the audience and waited for the President to continue. But he didn't. Instead, he turned to someone behind them, in the shadow of the colonnades.

443

"Charlie," he called. One of the technicians stepped forward out of the shadow.

"Yes, Mr President?"

"Charlie," he pointed to the teleprompts, "can you switch these things off? They're kind of distracting."

Charlie looked uncertain. "Yes, sir, if that's what you want." This came as a complete surprise to Charlie. He was thinking of the few times that the teleprompt had broken down and left the President embarrassed—thrown off by the unexpected disappearance of his prepared words, he had faltered and lost his way. He'd always made light of it and regained his composure, humorously citing a lack of sleep or some other reason for his stumble, but Charlie lived in fear of it happening again at an important moment. And now he was actually being asked to switch it off!

"Yes, that's what I want, Charlie," the President confirmed. Stiff sideways glances and hushed comments were exchanged among the entourage while Charlie fiddled with the controls on the teleprompt. The screens went blank.

"Thank you, Charlie." The President glanced briefly at Griffin. In that moment, Griffin saw a different man—a more vulnerable, less self-assured, warmer man. This was a complete departure from the format they had agreed, and Griffin had no idea what to say if the President deliberately changed the course of the whole news conference now. He felt a sharp tightening in his chest as panic crept through him. Was this the ultimate set-up? He couldn't afford to think that now. He could not allow his fears and insecurities to trigger automatic defenses and knee-jerk reactions. He had to be clear and present. He forced himself to relax. He breathed deeply and thought about what Sheryl had said to him before he left the apartment. *They need something new, from the heart.* And he reminded himself of what the President had just said to him. AVTOL was heading their way; *we can't have any anger or fear here today.*

The President laid both hands on the lectern and continued speaking. "The sinking of the Turkish cargo ship that was making its approach to Gaza yesterday was not carried out by Israel or anyone acting on Israel's behalf. I regret to inform you that the sinking of this ship was caused by a torpedo launched in error by a ship of the US Navy's Sixth Fleet."

Absolute silence fell over the Rose Garden.

The President continued. "However, as violent and appalling as that mistake was, it was not an act of aggression prompted by hatred. It was an act of human error. Thankfully, no lives were lost. What was lost was the essential humanitarian supplies and educational tools for the children of a small, besieged nation—supplies that were being sent to help them build a future out of the rubble of Gaza and its broken economy. As Commander-in-Chief of the US Forces, I apologize for this failure to protect the basic humanitarian rights of these people, and I will make full compensation for our mistake. I will replace what was lost, and also replace the Turkish cargo ship with one from our own merchant fleet."

The President scanned the stunned faces in front of him. To the sides of the podium, messages were frantically being punched out on PDAs and phones. Notes were being furiously scribbled on pads. Just one journalist—a tall black man carrying a shoulder bag—stood motionless, staring blankly at him. The President brought his focus quickly back to his speech, allowing the press a little time to re-engage with him before he continued.

"You may be wondering why I asked for the teleprompt to be switched off. Well, I'll tell you." He glanced again at Griffin before continuing. "It's an experiment, and one that I intend to repeat every day from now on. You see, I've grown to rely on that machine, with all the words that I and others prepare and perfect before I speak, to give the appearance that I'm a great performer, and to give you confidence that I'm fully in command. Fortunately, I'm a human being, which means that I'm not always fully in command—just like anybody else. Sanitized statements and prepared performances are not the mark of authenticity. They merely represent an effort to take away fear and provide reassurance. Sometimes they succeed and sometimes they fail. Their primary purpose is management—of opinion and circumstances. Truth, on the other hand, comes in the moment, from the heart. It's not necessarily tidy, sanitized or even welcome, sometimes, but we all recognize it when we hear it, because there's something inside each and every one of us that knows it, intuitively. It's not an intellectual process. We don't have to learn it."

Griffin stood stiffly beside the President as he spoke, locked in his own internal battle—fearful of the nightmare that would surely fall from the sky at any moment, trying to somehow keep his cool, relax.

"Just as the sinking of that Turkish ship was not a premeditated act for political gain, so the response to it cannot be a premeditated act for political gain. It cannot be couched in terms that make it seem righteous and just, or even in ways designed to save face for the perpetrators. Nor can deals be done behind the scenes to minimize its impact, curry favors and dampen down the fires of recrimination. It was an unforgivable mistake, and we must face up to it with dignity and respect for all involved."

Trying not to make it look too obvious, Griffin quickly cast his eyes across the sky. *Where is it? How close? Will we even hear it?*

"And this brings me to the main point of what I want to express to you today. I made a speech at my inauguration. Some of you may remember it. I talked passionately about this country, our ancestors, the crises we have to overcome and more. I meant what I said. But the answers to our problems are not in the words we speak. They are in our actions. As this administration has continued to work, it has become clear that, while some actions have succeeded in solving some problems, a lot more can be done, and a lot more needs to be done. While the words that got me elected were filled with passion and good intent, some of the actions so far have succeeded, some have been left wanting or have fallen short, and some have simply failed. That's human, and we continue to strive to do better. Naturally, diligence and attention to improvement is always needed, but it's the inner work that we must now focus on. Peace and harmony between people start with peace residing inside each individual. It spreads from there. We cannot look to our leaders for peace, just as we cannot look outside ourselves for strength. Living in fear generates more fear, which ultimately leads to our destruction, one way or another."

Griffin suppressed a cough. He glanced sideways just as the tall black reporter lifted a video camera and pointed it at the two of them.

"Conversely, living in clarity promotes more clarity. Living in authenticity generates more authenticity. Living in truth promotes more truth. These are attractive qualities that grow and spread if they are nurtured. And it is these positive qualities that will ultimately bring us success in every way. So I ask you this: even if there is the smallest possibility that we can achieve peace in our world, simply by nurturing these qualities and making them the focus of our attention, isn't it worth making the effort?"

Just as the President finished this sentence, Griffin felt his cell phone vibrate in his pocket. *Damn, I forgot to switch it off!* He didn't want to move. The press would surely have a field day if they saw him picking it up. However, this must surely be important. Few people had this number. He decided to risk it. Slipping the phone out of his jacket pocket, he held it down by his side, behind the lectern. He surreptitiously glanced down at it and had to stifle a gasp. *Access codes changed. Larry.* He couldn't believe it. Larry—wherever he was—had done it! Larry had changed the codes and Samakab could no longer access the Hominine computer. But his exuberance was immediately extinguished by the sober realization that if AVTOL was approaching as they spoke, the HAPISAD pod it carried would already be programmed. There was no escape. And, right now, there was no room for fear. He tried to push the thought out of his mind, returning his focus to what the President was saying.

"All too often, we see our country as the center of our universe. It is not. It's part of the world as a whole—and just a small part of it, at that. It's a great country, but only if it lives by the good values it purports to hold. Otherwise, it is nothing. The world is changing and we are playing a big part in that change. We cannot hide behind the notion of national boundaries when we are part of, and dependent on, the whole world for our existence. Nor can we continually face inwards and only experience our own cultural ghetto. Doing so only creates narrow stereotypes and prejudices about those outside our borders. We would do well to embrace and celebrate the diversity of mankind, learn from our neighbors around the world, recognize that we are just another part of that diversity, and make them feel welcome."

This is going on far too long! What's he doing? Samakab's deadline must surely have passed.

"The consequences of the decisions we make and the actions we take around the globe are all being reflected back to us more rapidly and with greater exposure than ever before. Increasingly, we're being called upon to be accountable and transparent in all our dealings throughout the world. Whenever we fail to do so, the consequences are harder and harder to bear. Many say that we are at a climactic, political and humanitarian tipping point, where just a few wrong or ill-intentioned actions will set off a chain of events that will destroy our world as we know it, setting us back generations or even destroying us entirely. But I'm an optimist. I believe in the human spirit—its resilience, adaptability, incredible strength and love. Let's face it, the very fact that we're still here as a race, and that we are alive today, is a miracle in itself. We are born through an act of love, and all we ever really want to experience is kindness, joy, gratitude and understanding. That's where every religious institution in the world started—with a longing to experience peace and unity. And here in the United States of America, above and beyond our political system, we recognize God as the higher ideal."

The longer the President spoke, the less Griffin was able to control the panic that was growing inside him. *Maybe I'm missing the point. Listen to the words!* He unclenched his fists, determined more than ever to relax his neck, shoulder and stomach muscles.

"So, let us not simply repeat empty words by rote. Empty words and misguided actions have led us to where we are right now. And what is the point of going through a crisis if you don't learn from it and change, as a result? I'm talking to everyone who may be listening or watching this, wherever you might be, when I say: let's start making that change. Let's start taking responsibility for ourselves, living authentically and living in truth. Let's each commit to taking actions to make that a reality in our own lives. We don't have to try and do it for anyone else, because if we each do it for ourselves, I guarantee that we will lift this whole country up, to a much, much better place. And that will inspire the rest of the world to do the same. That's when we will become a great nation."

Gradually, as the words washed over him, Griffin found himself becoming more focused, present and peaceful.

"I can't do it for you; your government, your religious leaders, your community leaders, your spouse, your lawyer can't do it for you. You can, and you are the very best person to do it. For my part, I will continue to work tirelessly to manifest in reality the words that come from my heart. I will strive to keep the promises I made and keep to the spirit of my inaugural speech. I ask that you all welcome in a new era in our country, where all the wonderful qualities that I know we have in our people are celebrated."

Loud applause reverberated through the Rose Garden—an enthusiastic acknowledgment of shared values and ideals that the President had articulated so eloquently. He scanned the sea of faces in front of him—attentive, intrigued, some of them beaming. To his right and left, the press were busy filming, writing and punching keypads as cameras rattled. Still, the black journalist with the shoulder bag stood motionless, staring. *This man has a deadly intensity.* At any other time, he would have reached inside his pocket and sent the signal to his security detail.

"Lastly, I want to say something about this man standing next to me."

Griffin flinched. He wasn't expecting this. He'd been lulled into a dream state by the President's impromptu speech and had completely forgotten that he would be talking on the subject of peace.

"As you all know, Senator Griffin Kirkland has been a staunch supporter of the current and previous administrations, and a fine ambassador for this country in searching for ways to establish peace in the Middle East. Just recently," he turned to face Griffin, "you will remember that he brokered a historic agreement that, as a result of the insincere motives and criminal actions of others, was sabotaged. I would like to take this opportunity to apologize on behalf of the nation, for the way in which our part in the follow-up to that agreement was handled."

Griffin stared, open-mouthed, at the President, until the cameras started clicking and he clamped his jaw shut.

"What you may not know, ladies and gentlemen, is that Senator Kirkland has also not only been working, against impossible odds, to protect us from our own folly, but he has, at considerable personal risk, protected a valuable asset that we share with Russia and China. We will be sharing details of this asset with you shortly but, for now, I would like to ask Senator Kirkland to say a few words about his vision for peace. Senator?"

Griffin was reeling. Not only had he been put on the spot in the most public way possible, but the President had hinted at the existence of the Hominine Project for all of the world's media to hear. Once he got over the initial shock, he realized it was a smart move, on two levels. First, in departing from the agreed agenda at the last minute, he was asking Griffin to speak completely without preparation—from the heart. Secondly, he was announcing to the entire world the shared ownership of the world's most valuable peace-enabling project. It could no longer be hidden, and those behind it would have no choice but to bring it back on track with its original intentions.

The President stood to one side and Griffin stepped up to the podium. Turning toward the President, he saw that he was facing forward, looking out at the audience. He didn't return his gaze. This time, Griffin didn't feel the pain of rejection but understood that he was giving him the floor—to say whatever he wanted. A surge of excitement was immediately followed by a swelling fear that raced like a bowling ball through his gut. His knees threatened to buckle and his head wanted to abscond to a safe hiding place. His hands shook as he placed them on the lectern, as much to support himself on trembling legs as to give the appearance of resolve as he began to speak. He looked up at the sky—a sky without boundaries—infinite, free space without the weight of attachment to everything it contained. A silent observer, a lover's light caress.

"Thank you, Mr President." He brought his attention back to the assembled group. He felt alive, hyper-aware, floating. In his peripheral vision, he could sense the the networks and the press waiting and watching. His mind was simultaneously racing and perfectly still—a strange and impossible paradoxical state of extreme peace and utter panic. He felt as if he'd lost the connection between his brain and his mouth. Words weren't there. What was happening? He'd spoken to groups like this all his political life. After the first few news conferences, he could perform like a veteran actor. But now, when so much depended on it, he couldn't summon the mental resources to even shape his lips and form the first word. He knew he had to say something. Perhaps if he could kick-start the process somehow, the words would start to flow. Perhaps *not* thinking was the way to do it. Maybe this was what people meant when they talked about being 'in the flow', talking 'from the heart'. *Is that prayer? I don't know. Talking 'from my feelings' seems so alien in this political, intellectual, media environment. They have entirely different expectations of me. Yet our feelings govern everything about us. God, I'm such an amateur human!*

"Mr President, ladies and gentlemen. In my professional capacity, I am not prepared. You know me now as the President's Special Negotiator for Middle East Affairs and, previously, for the various roles I have played in trying to serve my country the best I could and, frankly, in trying to carve out a successful career for myself. In the past five years, you've seen my efforts to build peace in the Middle East, and you have seen that there is still no peace there. I have come to realize that peace is not something that can be applied externally, like a soothing cream. It has to grow from the inside and be nurtured on the outside. And we all play a part in that process, every day of our lives. Why? Because we are all connected—now more than ever before. We are all responsible. And that responsibility is not a weight—a mantle to be suffered and borne with anguish and guilt—but a light and natural part of our abiding spirit of humanity, to celebrate and carry before us."

Griffin turned to the President, who'd been checking his watch before returning his attention to Griffin.

"Mr President, you asked me to say a few words about my vision for peace. I can do that, but as a human being, not as a negotiator, because I don't believe that peace is a subject for negotiation. Peace is a fundamental human right. Peace is the destination of all of our lives. And the miracle of it is that we are all endowed with the hearts to achieve it. Peace is a choice, not a negotiation.

"There is an active volcano, some 3,000 miles northeast of here in Iceland, that erupts every hundred years or so. If you saw it today, you'd think it was dormant, because it's covered with more than 1,000 feet of ice. However, right now, it's rumbling up a storm that could change our lives forever. We're not prepared for it. We prefer not to think about it. But it will come. Inside me, as I believe exists inside many people throughout the world, another volcano is building up pressure—one that could change our lives in positive ways, but I keep a lid on that too. Why? Because of my upbringing, conditioning, beliefs, programming—whatever you want to call it. Ideas. That's all they are, handed down from generation to generation, with all their shortcomings, problems and untruths. We all buy into them—different versions according to our circumstances, location and other accidents of birth. We maintain the status quo that's leading the world to the very edge of its own existence, without question. And all the time, we deny serious conscious airtime to the truly powerful part of us that can fix it all. We're inspired by the creative dreamers among us who risk expressing it, but then we shove the feelings aside, rather than integrate them into our lives—only occasionally peeking at them when we need a dose of hope or a pick-me-up."

Griffin was momentarily distracted as the President cleared his throat. Glancing in his direction, he saw that he was looking out over the South Lawn, at a patch of sky that was visible through the trees. Griffin returned his focus to the audience in front of him, resisting the temptation to follow the President's gaze.

"So, for what they are worth, here are a few of my own personal feelings that, in my professional capacity, I have, like that volcano, kept locked beneath the ice." Griffin paused, but held his space. He looked neither left nor right. He knew he was in a different kind of flow to what he was accustomed to, but it felt good. He didn't want to disturb it. A move of the head, a change of focus from the blurry middle distance, even thinking about how he felt—anything could tip him back into thinking and rationalizing, excitement or fear.

"Let's start at the beginning," he continued. "In my vision of the ideal peaceful world, I see children whose parents understand that they are their guardians, not their owners, and that they're there to guide them with love to help them grow. They help them to play, to open doors and to unlock their own mysteries. They don't indoctrinate them and tell them about their concept of

God. God is a personal discovery that they will make when they are ready—when their minds have traveled beyond the formative years of play and have absorbed the things they need to learn to live their lives fully.

"I see education as a means of personal discovery, expansion, creativity and empowerment, not a training ground to serve narrow political ideals or the short-term economic goals of those in power. I see economics serving humanity, rather than the other way around. I see the achievement of rank, commercial success or high office as an acknowledgement of service and responsibility, and not for pomposity, pretention or merely to wield power. I see our international relations and trade being fair and of benefit to all parties—not exploiting the poor and weak to provide for the rich and powerful, or to control their territory and resources. I see a country where everyone is truly equal under the law, where the law is genuinely about justice and everyone has equal access to it, and it's not merely a tool for the wealthy and the devious. I see a place where health services are about healing and not a playground for a self-serving pharmaceutical industry to make huge profits from the suffering of others. I see a planet where all its peoples can enjoy the abundance of truly healthy food that nature provides without the need to artificially distort it or claim ownership of any part of it. I see a world where we take pride in, and love, our beautiful planet, and where we shape our lifestyles to work in harmony with it. I see us celebrating our differences as much as our commonalities. I see pure spirituality flourishing and prayer not drawn from any book, but directly from the core, the spirit, the center of each individual. I see a population in touch with reality and fully appreciative of creation, with no need for symbols or totems, texts, icons, flags or other substitutes because they have the real experience that those things so poorly represent. I could go on, but I think you understand what I'm saying.

"Mankind is capable of incredible things. Using the vast creative power of our conscious minds, we have made huge advances in many ways. Now we are being called upon to engage the subconscious, the intuitive, the heart in equal measure. I truly believe that the pledge we need to make first is a pledge to ourselves—each and every one of us—to be the best we can be, in love and peace. We'll have to work at it. There's a lot of dead wood that we carry in our minds that we'll need to throw out. But we can do it, and I know that because we will simply be returning to what we truly are, which is pretty incredible. Only then will we have a country that we can be truly proud of."

As he spoke, he became aware of a distant rumble, a roar approaching. But his audience was focused on him, spellbound by his passionate image of peace.

"So, Mr President, ladies and gentlemen, let's try something different, right here and now, just for a few minutes. All of us—including the press."

He turned toward the President and caught his eye. The President nodded then faced forward again. Griffin quickly searched his mind for words that would sustain the sense of peace that pervaded the Rose Garden. He was grateful for the support of the President in maintaining the integrity of the group, simply by his focused presence and his assent. Out of the corner of his eye, he saw the black reporter walking away from the press group. Everyone else remained where they were.

"I invite each of you, right now, to simply close your eyes, relax your muscles and breathe. Pray, meditate, whatever you want to call it, but see if you can clear your mind and let go of any anxiety, concerns or fear. Simply feel what you feel right here in this beautiful garden. Just for a few minutes, see if you can release yourself from the chatter of your mind, from the affairs of State, the demands of your job—whatever it is that holds your mind hostage for most of your waking hours."

He glanced to his side again. The President was standing there, eyes closed, breathing deeply. There were the sounds of shuffling and muffled murmurs from the audience. The press were surprisingly quiet and, eventually, the Rose Garden fell into a peaceful silence. Griffin closed his eyes. He was, for the first time that day, aware of the sounds of birds and insects buzzing nearby. Gradually the sounds of nature were drowned out by approaching jet engines. Three F-15s flew quickly overhead, their engines moaning sadly as they passed. Then they were gone. Without opening his eyes, Griffin sensed the approach of AVTOL, its dark presence slowly making its way high above them from the Potomac and over the Washington Memorial. He felt naked in the presence of the approaching all-powerful executioner. He felt free.

Within seconds, the insides of his eyelids were ablaze with white light as a quiet hissing sound swept across the Rose Garden. He opened his eyes to the spectacle of hundreds of trails of white smoke darting wildly across the sky above them, this way and that, zipping and spluttering in a wild, erratic dance. The audience on the lawn sat transfixed by the unexpected display. One by one, the missiles ignited in mid-air in a glittering, incandescent flash of blue-white light, and then vanished. It was all over in seconds. The only evidence that it had happened at all was a blue mist that hung over the Rose Garden, and a distinctive aroma that Griffin couldn't identify. Cameras clicked, network commentators hurriedly arranged stand-ups. Griffin turned to the President, who was still standing there, smiling, his right hand placed on his heart. Griffin looked up over the roof of the press room and glimpsed the dark shape of AVTOL as it flew north, into the distance. He looked back into the Rose Garden. A sea of smiling faces looked back at him. Somebody clapped and, gradually, more joined it, until the applause erupted into cheers. *They thought it was a show!*

But that was fine by Griffin. Just fine.

Griffin gripped the lectern tightly for support. His legs shook and his heart was pounding as though it might explode. He and the President stood in silence as the commotion played out around them and the applause gradually subsided. Griffin offered up a silent prayer of thanks to the sky.

***

When the press had packed up their gear and filed their reports, there was just one sad piece of news that marred the occasion. One of the 'fireworks' had struck an African reporter in the top of his head, killing him instantly. No one knew who he was. Police appealed for anyone with information to come forward.

CHAPTER 55

High up in the mountains, Larry felt an unfamiliar sense of peace. As he emerged, squinting, from the cool womb of the bunker, the sparkling mountain sunshine seemed to wash him clean of the past few months in exile. He breathed deeply as he tapped out a text message to Griffin. The world—for now, at least—was safe from another HAPISAD attack. As he hit 'send', a large Mövenpick truck swished by, its colorful logo making him smile: ice cream—Evelyn's favorite. Momentarily distracted, he dropped his phone. As he bent to pick it up, he thought of the conversation he'd had with Evelyn last night, and that made him smile again. It was time to go home.

✳✳✳

Alexei Sidorov was still fuming. *Road works!* After all his meticulous planning—of all the things he had allowed for—he hadn't expected to be held up by road works. Not in Switzerland. Not on the autoroute at Montreux, of all places. He ordered a second bottle of his favorite mineral water as he waited for Luis to arrive at the Club Nautique. Since his trip to the mountains, life had returned to its reassuring predictability. Even the man in the Land Cruiser was loading his boat onto the trailer again. Same time, same place—but something was different... *Ah, no wife, this time.*

"Alexei! Hey, why you look so sad, my friend? You look like you could kill someone!" Luis de Granja's cheerful greeting startled him.

"Funny you should say that." Alexei called the waiter over. Luis sat down and ordered the same wine as last time. "I had a bad day at the office. How is it going for you?"

"Much the same. I did small one for Italian—"

"A small one? Not the usual fat cat, then?"

"Sorry, I mean 'not much money'. But keep me going for while. And you?"

"Mmm... not so great. I think I'm losing my grip."

"No way. You're the best. What happen?" Luis was itching to find out if the great man had finally messed up. It was a competitive business they were in, and even though they had a friendship, of sorts, Luis would give anything to land the kind of contracts that Alexei had won in the past, and would have stolen them from him if he thought he could get away with it.

Alexei shrugged, slumped back in his chair and pushed his sunglasses back up his nose. He checked the tables nearby. It was more of a habit than a necessity, as the waiters only ever filled the tables next to Alexei as a last resort.

He had sometimes been known to pay for entire meals that no one ate, just to keep adjacent tables empty when he had company.

"I got this contract. It looked like a real beauty. It came from Russia, but the great thing about it was that it was local. Amazing, I thought, no bloody Aeroflot flights, no messing around with officialdom and having to pick up crappy tools for the job."

"Local? That's nice…"

"Yes, in Ticino, just up the road from Locarno."

"Sound like dream."

"It was—theoretically. I was looking forward to using the Accuracy International. My favorite. And the drive is fantastic along the lake here— absolutely beautiful—especially once you get near Vevey. Then you head up between the mountains, into Sion and through the Simplon Pass. Absolutely gorgeous, especially in my Merc."

"I'm already envious! So, what was problem?"

The waiter arrived to take their lunch order. Alexei looked at the menu and dropped it back on the table.

"I'm not hungry. You go ahead." He was too preoccupied with the memory of that job to eat.

"Same as last time," Luis said, hoping the waiter would remember, because he couldn't. He couldn't be bothered trying to figure out the French and, anyway, he really wanted to hear Alexei's story.

"The roast veal with thyme and grilled vegetables?" The waiter, thankfully, had remembered.

"Yes, please."

"Unfortunately, that isn't on the menu today sir. May I suggest—"

"Yes, anything." He dismissed the waiter with a cursory wave and returned his focus to Alexei. "What was problem?"

"Bloody road works on the autoroute." He looked round to check on the Toyota, but it had already gone. *Damn. Missed it.* "They were digging up a section near Montreux, so there were cones, barriers and huge traffic jams… Damn it! They *never* have road works here. Not on the autoroute, anyway. They build the damned things far too well in the first place."

"Must be wearing out…" Luis offered.

"Nah." Alexei shook his head in disgust. "Anyway, it cost me half an hour. *Half a bloody hour!* It threw off my schedule completely." Even in the relative security of a Swiss restaurant by Lac Léman, Alexei's anger made Luis feel somewhat nervous.

"So… what was job?"

"Oh, some American guy… I just got a photo. Here, take a look." He fished a color photo out of his pocket and slapped it onto the table. It showed a man in a Hawaiian shirt driving a Suzuki jeep with pink trim. He looked slim, fit and had grey hair. "No name—just a location and time, of course... It was interesting, though."

Much to Luis's relief, Alexei perked up a little.

"You'd have laughed. It was almost a James-Bond-cliché job, if you know what I mean."

"James Bond? You screw girl in leather jumpsuit as well?"

"No, it wasn't *that* good," he chuckled. "I checked the place out beforehand, of course. It was way up in the mountains. Apparently, in the 70s, the Swiss Government, in their eternal diligence and desire for security, had blasted their way into the side of a mountain and put a vast network of mainframe computers in there, in a cavern they created deep in the rock. They'd intended to store all the tax details of everyone in the country. Don't you just love the Swiss and their obsession with keeping things safe? Unfortunately, by the time they'd finished it, the mainframes were out-dated and what they originally wanted to store on huge tape drives could now be more efficiently stored on much smaller media. So it was never used—until recently, when someone filled it up with more computers and stuck a kind of decoy building on the entrance. Now it just looks like an ordinary house against the cliff on a mountain road."

"*Opa!* So you arrive late at scene—shaken, not stirred, I hope..."

"You can imagine that I was not happy, and that is the worst way to start a job. I was supposed to take out the target on his way into the building, but he was already inside by the time I arrived."

"What you do?"

"I had to wait for him to come out and it was difficult to find a good vantage point, because of the mountains and lack of access to good places. I had to set up on another road on the opposite side of a valley."

"On the road?" Luis couldn't believe what he was hearing.

"I know. And it was getting busy. But I had no choice. I was able to work from a ditch where the traffic wouldn't see me, but I felt uncomfortable about the whole thing."

"You could not do it another time? I would not even attempt that."

"No, it had to be done that day."

"*Meu Deus!* I no like this. Did you get clear shot?"

"Yes. It should have been easy. It was less than 700 meters, a nice clear day, no wind... But that's the other thing. Yes, I had line of sight to the head, but the target's car was parked directly in front of the doorway. I only had one chance. I don't mind that, of course, but after getting stuck in that traffic jam, the job felt jinxed."

"Alexei, you did not miss—?"

"Of course not!" Alexei shot Luis a fearsome look, causing him to edge backwards in his seat. "No, it's just that…" he paused as Luis's meal was placed on the table, before leaning forward and continuing in a low voice. "He came out of the door—he looked as if he was sending a text message as he walked. He was in a hurry, but he was walking directly toward me, so it was easy. Even so, I only had a window of about three seconds. As I took the shot, a truck was passing him. Based on the velocity of the bullet, the distance across the valley and his position, it should have reached him before the truck passed in front. Normally, I am certain, so I don't have to check. You know how it is—take the shot, pack up and go." He snapped his fingers. "But this time, because of the truck, I decided to take another look—to make sure." He dropped his head and shook it. He was angry and *so* disappointed with himself. "As soon as I'd done it, though, someone stopped their car behind mine, and I didn't get a chance to take another look through the sights…"

***

MORE ON LEWIS EVANS

A prolific artist, writer and inventor, Lewis Evans currently lives in Vancouver, Canada with his wife (author and empowerment coach Olga Sheean) and rather a lot of paintings. In 2009, as the result of a dream, he was inspired to write Hominine, a novel that emerged as a new genre—a geo-political thriller with heart and a social conscience.

In fictionalizing tough, real-life issues, political dilemmas and global crises, Evans depicts frighteningly plausible scenarios, while providing refreshingly sane solutions. His second novel is due to be published in 2013.

To keep up with developments with *Hominine,* and to be notified when his new novel is published, go to www.hominine.info.

If you would like to comment on this novel, join a discussion, write a review, or post information or links to news articles relevant to the book, go to the Hominine Facebook Page. To see his artworks, visit www.lewisevans.net.